# THE OVERSTORY

Richard Powers is the author of twelve novels, including *Orfeo* (which was longlisted for the Man Booker Prize), *The Echo Maker*, *The Time of Our Singing*, *Galatea 2.2* and *Plowing the Dark*. He is the recipient of a MacArthur grant and the National Book Award, and has been a Pulitzer Prize and four-time NBCC finalist. He lives in the foothills of the Great Smoky Mountains.

ALSO BY

RICHARD POWERS

•

*Three Farmers on Their Way to a Dance*

*Prisoner's Dilemma*

*The Gold Bug Variations*

*Operation Wandering Soul*

*Galatea 2.2*

*Gain*

*Plowing the Dark*

*The Time of Our Singing*

*The Echo Maker*

*Generosity: An Enhancement*

*Orfeo*

# THE
# OVERSTORY

## RICHARD POWERS

WILLIAM HEINEMANN: LONDON

1 3 5 7 9 10 8 6 4 2

William Heinemann
20 Vauxhall Bridge Road
London SW1V 2SA

William Heinemann is part of the Penguin Random House group of companies
whose addresses can be found at global.penguinrandomhouse.com.

Penguin
Random House
UK

First published in Great Britain by William Heinemann in 2018
First published in the United States by W. W. Norton & Company in 2018

www.penguin.co.uk

A CIP catalogue record for this book is available from the British Library.

ISBN 9781785151637 (Hardback)
ISBN 9781785151644 (Trade paperback)

*Book design by Marysarah Quinn*

Printed and bound by Clays Ltd, St Ives plc

Penguin Random House is committed to a sustainable future
for our business, our readers and our planet. This book is made
from Forest Stewardship Council® certified paper.

*For Aida.*

# CONTENTS

ROOTS • 1

NICHOLAS HOEL • 5

MIMI MA • 24

ADAM APPICH • 47

RAY BRINKMAN AND DOROTHY CAZALY • 64

DOUGLAS PAVLICEK • 73

NEELAY MEHTA • 91

PATRICIA WESTERFORD • 112

OLIVIA VANDERGRIFF • 145

TRUNK • 153

CROWN • 353

SEEDS • 473

*The greatest delight which the fields and woods minister, is the suggestion of an occult relation between man and the vegetable. I am not alone and unacknowledged. They nod to me, and I to them. The waving of the boughs in the storm, is new to me and old. It takes me by surprise, and yet is not unknown. Its effect is like that of a higher thought or a better emotion coming over me, when I deemed I was thinking justly or doing right.*

—RALPH WALDO EMERSON

*Earth may be alive: not as the ancients saw her—a sentient Goddess with a purpose and foresight—but alive like a tree. A tree that quietly exists, never moving except to sway in the wind, yet endlessly conversing with the sunlight and the soil. Using sunlight and water and nutrient minerals to grow and change. But all done so imperceptibly, that to me the old oak tree on the green is the same as it was when I was a child.*

—JAMES LOVELOCK

*Tree . . . he watching you. You look at tree, he listen to you. He got no finger, he can't speak. But that leaf . . . he pumping, growing, growing in the night. While you sleeping you dream something. Tree and grass same thing.*

—BILL NEIDJIE

ROOTS

*First there was nothing. Then there was everything.*

*Then, in a park above a western city after dusk, the air is raining messages.*

*A woman sits on the ground, leaning against a pine. Its bark presses hard against her back, as hard as life. Its needles scent the air and a force hums in the heart of the wood. Her ears tune down to the lowest frequencies. The tree is saying things, in words before words.*

*It says*: Sun and water are questions endlessly worth answering.

*It says*: A good answer must be reinvented many times, from scratch.

*It says*: Every piece of earth needs a new way to grip it. There are more ways to branch than any cedar pencil will ever find. A thing can travel everywhere, just by holding still.

*The woman does exactly that. Signals rain down around her like seeds.*

*Talk runs far afield tonight. The bends in the alders speak of long-ago disasters. Spikes of pale chinquapin flowers shake down their pollen; soon they will turn into spiny fruits. Poplars repeat the wind's gossip. Persimmons and walnuts set out their bribes and rowans their blood-red clusters. Ancient oaks wave prophecies of future weather. The several hundred kinds of hawthorn laugh at the single name they're forced to share. Laurels insist that even death is nothing to lose sleep over.*

*Something in the air's scent commands the woman*: Close your eyes and think of willow. The weeping you see will be wrong. Picture an acacia thorn. Nothing in your thought will be sharp enough. What hovers right above you? What floats over your head right now—*now*?

*Trees even farther away join in*: All the ways you imagine us—bewitched mangroves up on stilts, a nutmeg's inverted spade, gnarled baja elephant trunks, the straight-up missile of a sal—are always amputations. Your kind never sees us whole. You miss the half of it, and more. There's always as much belowground as above.

*That's the trouble with people, their root problem. Life runs alongside them, unseen. Right here, right* next. *Creating the soil. Cycling water. Trading in nutrients. Making weather. Building atmosphere. Feeding and curing and sheltering more kinds of creatures than people know how to count.*

*A chorus of living wood sings to the woman*: If your mind were only a slightly greener thing, we'd drown you in meaning.

*The pine she leans against says*: Listen. There's something you need to hear.

# NICHOLAS HOEL

 Now is the time of chestnuts.

People are hurling stones at the giant trunks. The nuts fall all around them in a divine hail. It happens in countless places this Sunday, from Georgia to Maine. Up in Concord, Thoreau takes part. He feels he is casting rocks at a sentient being, with a duller sense than his own, yet still a blood relation. *Old trees are our parents, and our parents' parents, perchance. If you would learn the secrets of Nature, you must practice more humanity. . . .*

In Brooklyn, on Prospect Hill, the new arrival, Jørgen Hoel, laughs at the hard rain his throws bring down. Each time his stone hits, food shakes down by the shovelful. Men dash about like thieves, stuffing caps, sacks, and trouser cuffs with nuts freed from their enclosing burrs. Here it is, the fabled free banquet of America—yet one more windfall in a country that takes even its scraps right from God's table.

The Norwegian and his friends from the Brooklyn Navy Yard eat their bounty roasted over great bonfires in a clearing in the woods. The charred nuts are comforting beyond words: sweet and savory, rich as a honeyed potato, earthy and mysterious all at once. The burred husks prickle, but their *No* is more of a tease than any real barrier. The nuts *want* to slip free of their spiny protection. Each one volunteers to be eaten, so others might be spread far afield.

That night, drunk on roasted chestnuts, Hoel proposes to Vi Powys, an Irish girl from the pine-framed row houses two blocks from his tenement, on the edge of Finn Town. No one within three thousand miles has the right to object. They marry before Christmas. By February, they are Americans. In the spring, the chestnuts bloom again, long, shaggy catkins waving in the wind like whitecaps on the glaucous Hudson.

Citizenship comes with a hunger for the uncut world. The couple assemble their movable goods and make the overland trip through the great tracts of eastern white pine, into the dark beech forests of Ohio, across the midwestern oak breaks, and out to the settlement near Fort Des Moines in the new state of Iowa, where the authorities give away land platted yesterday to anyone who will farm it. Their nearest neighbors are two miles away. They plow and plant four dozen acres that first year. Corn, potatoes, and beans. The work is brutal, but theirs. Better than building ships for any country's navy.

Then comes the prairie winter. The cold tests their will to live. Nights in the gap-riddled cabin zero their blood. They must crack the ice in the water basin every morning just to splash their faces. But they are young, free, and driven—the sole backers of their own existence. Winter doesn't kill them. Not yet. The blackest despair at the heart of them gets pressed to diamond.

When it's time to plant again, Vi is pregnant. Hoel puts his ear to her belly. She laughs at his awe-slapped face. "What is it saying?"

He answers in his blunt, thumping English. "Feed me!"

That May, Hoel discovers six chestnuts stuffed in the pocket of the smock he wore on the day he proposed to his wife. He presses them into the earth of western Iowa, on the treeless prairie around the cabin. The farm is hundreds of miles from the chestnut's native range, a thousand from the chestnut feasts of Prospect Hill. Each month, those green forests of the East grow harder for Hoel to remember.

But this is America, where men and trees take the most surprising outings. Hoel plants, waters, and thinks: *One day, my children will shake the trunks and eat for free.*

. . .

THEIR FIRSTBORN DIES in infancy, killed by a thing that doesn't yet have a name. There are no microbes, yet. God is the lone taker of children, snatching even placeholder souls from one world to the other, according to obscure timetables.

One of the six chestnuts fails to sprout. But Jørgen Hoel keeps the surviving seedlings alive. Life is a battle between the Maker and His creation. Hoel grows expert at the fight. Keeping his trees going is trivial, compared to the other wars he must wage each day. At the end of the first season, his fields are full and the best of his seedlings stands over two feet tall.

In four more years, the Hoels have three children and the hint of a chestnut grove. The sprigs come up spindly, their brown stems lined with lenticels. The lush, scalloped, saw-toothed, spiny leaves dwarf the twigs they bud from. Aside from these starts and a few scattered bur oaks in the bottomlands, the homestead is an island in a grassy sea.

Even the skinny starts already have their uses:

> Tea from infant trees for heart trouble,
> leaves from young sprouts to cure sores,
> cold bark brew to stop bleeding after birth,
> warmed galls to pare back an infant's navel,
> leaves boiled with brown sugar for coughs,
> poultices for burns, leaves to stuff a talking mattress,
> an extract for despair, when anguish is too much. . . .

The years unfold both fat and lean. Though their average tends toward runty, Jørgen detects an upward trend. Every year that he plows, he breaks more land. And the future Hoel labor pool keeps growing. Vi sees to that.

The trees thicken like enchanted things. Chestnut is quick: *By the time an ash has made a baseball bat, a chestnut has made a dresser.* Bend over to look at a sapling, and it'll put your eye out. Fissures in their bark swirl like barber poles as the trunks twist upward. In the wind the branches flicker between dark and paler green. The globes of leaves sweep out, seeking ever more sun. They wave in the humid August, the way Hoel's wife will still sometimes shake free her once-amber hair. By the time war comes again to the infant country, the five trunks have surpassed the one who planted them.

The pitiless winter of '62 tries to take another baby. It settles for one of the trees. The oldest child, John, destroys another, the summer after. It never occurs to the boy that stripping half the tree's leaves to use as play money might kill it.

Hoel yanks his son's hair. "How do you like it? Hm?" He cracks the boy with his open palm. Vi must throw her body in between them to stop the beating.

The draft arrives in '63. The young and single men go first. Jørgen Hoel, at thirty-three, with a wife, small children, and a few hundred acres, gets deferred. He never does help preserve America. He has a smaller country to save.

Back in Brooklyn, a poet-nurse to the Union dying writes: *A leaf of grass is no less than the journey-work of the stars*. Jørgen never reads these words. Words strikes him as a ruse. His maize and beans and squash—all growing things alone disclose the wordless mind of God.

One more spring, and the three remaining trees burst out in cream-colored flowers. The blooms smell acrid, gamy, sour, like old shoes or rank undergarments. Then comes a thimbleful of sweet nuts. Even that small harvest reminds the man and his exhausted wife of the falling manna that brought them together, one night in the woods east of Brooklyn.

"There will be bushels," Jørgen says. His mind is already making bread, coffee, soups, cakes, gravies—all the delicacies that the natives knew this tree could give. "We can sell the extra, in town."

"Christmas presents for the neighbors," Vi decides. But it's the neighbors who must keep the Hoels alive, in that year's brutal drought. One more chestnut dies of thirst in a season when not even the future can be spared a drop of water.

Years pass. The brown trunks start to gray. Lightning in a parched fall, with so few prairie targets tall enough to bother with, hits one of the remain-

ing chestnut pair. Wood that might have been good for everything from cradles to coffins goes up in flames. Not enough survives to make so much as a
three-legged stool.

The sole remaining chestnut goes on flowering. But its blooms have no
more blooms to answer them. No mates exist for countless miles around,
and a chestnut, though both male and female, will not serve itself. Yet still
this tree has a secret tucked into the thin, living cylinder beneath its bark. Its
cells obey an ancient formula: *Keep still. Wait.* Something in the lone survivor knows that even the ironclad law of Now can be outlasted. There's work
to do. Star-work, but earthbound all the same. Or as the nurse to the Union
dead writes: *Stand cool and composed before a million universes.* As cool and
composed as wood.

THE FARM SURVIVES the chaos of God's will. Two years after Appomat-
tox, between tilling, plowing, planting, roguing, weeding, and harvesting,
Jørgen finishes the new house. Crops come in and are carried off. Hoel sons
step into the traces alongside their ox-like father. Daughters disperse in marriage to nearby farms. Villages sprout up. The dirt track past the farm turns
into a real road.

The youngest son works in the Polk County Assessor's Office. The
middle boy becomes a banker in Ames. The eldest son, John, stays on the
farm with his family and works it as his parents decline. John Hoel throws in
with speed, progress, and machines. He buys a steam tractor that both plows
and threshes, reaps and binds. It bellows as it works, like something set free
from hell.

For the last remaining chestnut, all this happens in a couple of new fissures, an inch of added rings. The tree bulks out. Its bark spirals upward like
Trajan's Column. Its scalloped leaves carry on turning sunlight into tissue. It
more than abides; it flourishes, a globe of green health and vigor.

And in the second June of the new century, here is Jørgen Hoel, in bed
in an oak-trimmed upstairs room of the house he built, a bedroom he can no
longer leave, looking out the dormer window onto a school of leaves, swim-

ming and shining in the sky. His son's steam tractor hammers down in the north forty, but Jørgen Hoel mistakes the sounds for weather. The branches dapple him. Something about those green and toothy leaves, a dream he once had, a vision of increase and flourishing, causes a feast to fall all around his head again.

He wonders: What makes the bark twist and swirl so, in a tree so straight and wide? Could it be the spinning of the Earth? Is it trying to get the attention of men? Seven hundred years before, a chestnut in Sicily two hundred feet around sheltered a Spanish queen and her hundred mounted knights from a raging storm. That tree will outlive, by a hundred years and more, the man who has never heard of it.

"Do you remember?" Jørgen asks the woman who holds his hand. "Prospect Hill? How we ate that night!" He nods toward the leafy limbs, the land beyond. "I gave you that. And you gave me—all of this! This country. My life. My freedom."

But the woman who holds his hand is not his wife. Vi has died five years ago, of infected lungs.

"Sleep now," his granddaughter tells him, and lays his hand back on his spent chest. "We'll all be just downstairs."


JOHN HOEL BURIES HIS FATHER beneath the chestnut the man planted. A three-foot cast-iron fence now surrounds the scattering of graves. The tree above casts its shade with equal generosity on the living and the dead. The trunk has grown too thick for John to embrace. The lowest skirt of surviving branches lifts out of reach.

The Hoel Chestnut becomes a landmark, what farmers call a *sentinel tree.* Families navigate by it on Sunday outings. Locals use it to direct travelers, the lone lighthouse in a grain-filled sea. The farm prospers. There's seed money now to breed and propagate. With his father gone and his brothers off on their own, John Hoel is free to chase after the latest machines. His equipment shed fills with reapers and winnowers and twine-binders. He travels out to Charles City to see the first two-cylinder gas-powered tractors. When phone lines come through, he subscribes, although it costs a fortune and no one in the family can think what the thing might be good for.

The immigrant's son yields to the disease of improvement years before there's an effective cure for it. He buys himself a Kodak No. 2 Brownie. *You push the button, we do the rest.* He must send the film to Des Moines for developing and printing, a process that soon costs many times more than the two-dollar camera. He photographs his wife in calico and a crumpled smile, poised over the new mechanical clothes mangle. He photographs his children running the combine and riding swaybacked draft horses along the fields' headers. He photographs his family in their Easter finest, bound with bonnets and garroted by bow ties. When nothing else of his little postage stamp of Iowa is left to photograph, John turns his camera on the Hoel Chestnut, his exact coeval.

A few years before, he bought his youngest girl a zoopraxiscope for her birthday, though he alone kept playing with it, after she grew bored. Now those squadrons of flapping geese and parades of bucking broncos that come alive when the glass drum spins animate his brain. A grand plan occurs to him, as if he invented it. He decides, for whatever years are left to him, to capture the tree and see what the thing looks like, sped up to the rate of human desire.

He builds a tripod in the equipment shop. Then he sets a broken grinding stone on a rise near the house. And on the first day of spring, 1903, John Hoel positions the No. 2 Brownie and takes a full-length portrait of the sentinel chestnut leafing out. One month later to the day, from the same spot and the same hour, he takes another. The twenty-first of every month finds him up on his rise. It becomes a ritual devotion, even in rain and snow and killing heat, his own private liturgy of the Church of the Spreading Vegetative God. His wife teases him without mercy, as do his children. "He's waiting for it to do something interesting."

When he assembles the first year's twelve black-and-white prints and riffles them with his thumb, they show precious little for his enterprise. In one instant, the tree makes leaves from nothing. In the next, it offers up everything to the thickening light. Otherwise, the branches merely endure. But farmers are patient men tried by brutal seasons, and if they weren't plagued by dreams of generation, few would keep plowing, spring after spring. John Hoel is out on his rise again on March 21, 1904, as if he, too, might have another hundred years or two to document what time hides forever in plain sight.

TWELVE HUNDRED MILES EAST, in the city where John Hoel's mother sewed dresses and his father built ships, disaster hits before anyone knows it. The killer slips into the country from Asia, in the wood of Chinese chestnuts destined for fancy gardens. A tree in the Bronx Zoological Park turns October colors in July. Leaves curl and scorch to the hue of cinnamon. Rings of orange spots spread across the swollen bark. At the slightest press, the wood caves in.

Within a year, orange spots fleck chestnuts throughout the Bronx—the fruiting bodies of a parasite that has already killed its host. Every infection releases a horde of spores on the rain and wind. City gardeners mobilize a counterattack. They lop off infected branches and burn them. They spray trees with a lime and copper sulfate from horse-drawn wagons. All they do is spread the spores on the axes they use to cut the victims down. A researcher at the New York Botanical Garden identifies the killer as a fungus new to man. He publishes the results and leaves town to beat the summer heat. When he returns a few weeks later, not a chestnut in the city is worth saving.

Death races across Connecticut and Massachusetts, jumping dozens of miles a year. Trees succumb by the hundreds of thousands. A country watches dumbstruck as New England's priceless chestnuts melt away. The tree of the tanning industry, of railroad ties, train cars, telegraph poles, fuel, fences, houses, barns, fine desks, tables, pianos, crates, paper pulp, and endless free shade and food—the most harvested tree in the country—is vanishing.

Pennsylvania tries to cut a buffer hundreds of miles wide across the state. In Virginia, on the northern edge of the country's richest chestnut forests, people call for a religious revival to purge the sin behind the plague. America's perfect tree, backbone of entire rural economies, the limber, durable redwood of the East with three dozen industrial uses—every fourth tree of a forest stretching two hundred million acres from Maine down to the Gulf—is doomed.

NEWS OF THE BLIGHT doesn't reach western Iowa. John Hoel returns to his rise on the twenty-first of each month, in all weather. The Hoel Chestnut keeps lifting the high-water mark of its leaves. *It's after something*, the farmer thinks, his lone venture into philosophy. *It has a plan.*

On the night before his fifty-sixth birthday, John wakes up at two a.m. and feels around on the bed as if looking for something. His wife asks what's wrong. Through clenched teeth he answers, "It'll pass." Eight minutes later, he's dead.

The farm descends upon his first two sons. The elder, Carl, wants to write off the sunk costs of the photo ritual. Frank, the younger, needs to redeem his father's decade of obscure research by carrying it forward as stubbornly as the tree spreads its crown. More than a hundred frames along, the oldest, shortest, slowest, most ambitious silent movie ever shot in Iowa begins to reveal the tree's goal. A flip through the shots shows the subject stretching and patting about for something in the sky. A mate, perhaps. More light. Chestnut vindication.

When America at last joins the world conflagration, Frank Hoel is sent to France with the Second Cavalry Regiment. He makes his nine-year-old son Frank Jr. promise to keep taking pictures until his return. It's a year for long promises. What the boy lacks in imagination he makes up for in obedience.

Pure, dumb fate leads Frank Sr. out of the cauldron of Saint-Mihiel only to liquefy him with a mortar shell in the Argonne, near Montfaucon. There isn't enough left to put in a pine box and bury. The family makes a time capsule of his caps, pipes, and watches and sinks it in the family plot, under the tree that he photographed every month for a too-short while.

. . .

IF GOD HAD A BROWNIE, He might shoot another animated short subject: blight hovering a moment before plunging down the Appalachians into the heart of chestnut country. The chestnuts up North were majestic. But the southern trees are gods. They form near-pure stands for miles on end. In the Carolinas, boles older than America grow ten feet wide and a hundred and twenty feet tall. Whole forests of them flower in rolling clouds of white. Scores of mountain communities are built from the beautiful, straight-grained wood. A single tree might yield as many as fourteen thousand planks. The stocks of food that fall shin-deep feed entire counties, every year a mast year.

Now the gods are dying, all of them. The full force of human ingenuity can't stop the disaster breaking over the continent. The blight runs along ridgelines, killing off peak after peak. A person perched on an overlook above the southern mountains can watch the trunks change to gray-white skeletons in a rippling wave. Loggers race through a dozen states to cut down whatever the fungus hasn't reached. The nascent Forest Service encourages them. *Use the wood, at least, before it's ruined.* And in that salvage mission, men kill any tree that might contain the secret of resistance.

A five-year-old in Tennessee who sees the first orange spots appear in her magic woods will have nothing left to show her own children except pictures. They'll never see the ripe, full habit of the tree, never know the sight and sound and smell of their mother's childhood. Millions of dead stumps sprout suckers that struggle on, year after year, before dying of an infection that, preserved in these stubborn shoots, will never disappear. By 1940, the fungus takes everything, all the way out to the farthest stands in southern Illinois. Four billion trees in the native range vanish into myth. Aside from a few secret pockets of resistance, the only chestnuts left are those that pioneers took far away, to states beyond the reach of the drifting spores.

FRANK HOEL JR. keeps his promise to his father, long after his father fades into blurry, black-and-white, overexposed memories. Each month the boy lays another photo in the balsam box. Soon he's an adolescent. Then a young man. He goes through the motions the way the extended Hoel family keeps celebrating St. Olaf's Day without remembering what it is.

Frank Jr. suffers nothing from imagination. He can't even hear himself think: *It's very possible that I hate this tree. It's very possible that I love it more than I loved my father.* The thoughts can mean nothing to a man with no real independent desire, born under the thing he is chained to and fated to die under it, too. He thinks: *This thing has no business here. It's no good to anyone unless we chop it down.* Then there are months when, through the viewfinder, the spreading crown seems to his surprised eye like the template for meaning itself.

In summer, water rises through the xylem and disperses out of the million tiny mouths on the undersides of leaves, a hundred gallons a day evaporating from the tree's airy crown into the humid Iowa air. In fall, the yellowing leaves fill Frank Jr. with nostalgia. In winter, bare branches click and hum above the drifts, their blunt resting buds almost sinister with waiting. But for a moment each spring, the pale green catkins and cream-colored flowers put thoughts into Frank Jr.'s head, thoughts he doesn't know how to have.

The third Hoel photographer keeps on taking pictures, just as he keeps going to church long after deciding that the entire faithful world has been duped by fairy tales. His pointless photographic ritual gives Frank Jr.'s life a blind purpose that even farming cannot give. It's a monthly exercise in noticing a thing worth no notice at all, a creature as steadfast and reticent as life.

The stack of photos hits the five-hundred mark during World War II. Frank Jr. stops one afternoon to flip through the pictures. He himself feels like the same boy who made an ill-advised promise to his father at the age of nine. But the time-lapse tree has changed beyond all recognition.

When all the mature trees in the chestnut's native range are gone, the Hoel tree becomes a curiosity. A dendrologist in Iowa City comes out to confirm the rumor: a chestnut that escaped the holocaust. A journalist from the *Register* does a feature on one of the last of America's perfect trees. *More than twelve hundred places east of the Mississippi have the word "Chestnut" in them. But you have to come to a rural county in western Iowa to lay eyes on one.* Ordinary people, driving between New York and San Francisco on the new interstate that cuts a channel alongside the Hoel farm, see only a fountain of shade in the lone and level expanses of corn and soy.

In the bitter cold of February 1965, the No. 2 Brownie cracks. Frank Jr. replaces it with an Instamatic. The stack grows thicker than any book he has ever tried to read. But each photo in the sheaf shows only that lone tree, shrugging off the staggering emptiness that the man knows so well. The farm is to Frank Jr.'s back, each time he opens the lens. The photos hide everything: the twenties that do not roar for the Hoels. The Depression that costs them two hundred acres and sends half the family to Chicago. The radio shows that ruin two of Frank Jr.'s sons for farming. The Hoel death in the South Pacific and the two Hoel guilty survivals. The Deeres and Caterpillars parading through the tractor shed. The barn that burns to the ground one night to the screams of helpless animals. The dozens of joyous weddings, christenings, and graduations. The half dozen adulteries. The two divorces sad enough to silence songbirds. One son's unsuccessful campaign for the state legislature. The lawsuit between cousins. The three surprise pregnancies. The protracted Hoel guerrilla war against the local pastor and half the Lutheran parish. The handiwork of heroin and Agent Orange that comes home with nephews from 'Nam. The hushed-up incest, the lingering alcoholism, a daughter's elopement with the high school English teacher. The cancers (breast, colon, lung), the heart disease, the degloving of a worker's fist in a grain auger, the car death of a cousin's child on prom night. The countless tons of chemicals with names like Rage, Roundup, and Firestorm, the patented seeds engineered to produce sterile plants. The fiftieth wedding anniversary in Hawaii and its disastrous aftermath. The dispersal of retirees to Arizona and Texas. The generations of grudge, courage, forbearance, and surprise generosity: everything a human being might call the *story* happens outside his photos' frame. Inside the frame, through hundreds of revolving seasons, there is only that solo tree, its fissured bark spiraling upward into early middle age, growing at the speed of wood.

THE OVERSTORY · 17

Extinction sneaks up on the Hoel farm—on all the family farms in western Iowa. The tractors grow too monstrous, the railroad cars full of nitrogen fertilizer too expensive, the competition too large and efficient, the margins too marginal, and the soil too worn by repeated row-cropping to make a profit. Each year, another neighbor is swallowed up into the massive, managed, relentlessly productive monocrop factories. Like humans everywhere in the face of catastrophe, Frank Hoel Jr. goes blinking into his fate. He takes on debt. He sells off acreage and rights. He signs deals with the seed companies he shouldn't. Next year, he's sure—*next year*, something will come along and save them, as it always has.

All told, Frank Jr. adds seven hundred and fifty-five photos of the solitary giant to the hundred and sixty that his father and grandfather shot. On the twenty-first day of the last April of his life, with Frank Jr. confined to bed, his son Eric travels out to the farm from his home forty minutes away and sets up on the rise to snap yet one more black-and-white, now filled to the frame with exuberant branches. Eric shows the print to the old man. It's easier than trying to tell his father he loves him.

Frank Jr. grimaces at a taste like bitter almonds. "Listen. I made a promise, and I kept it. You don't owe nobody. Leave that damn thing be."

He might as well command the giant chestnut itself to stop spreading.


THREE-QUARTERS OF A CENTURY dances by in a five-second flip. Nicholas Hoel thumbs through the stack of a thousand photos, watching for those decades' secret meaning. At twenty-five, he's back for a moment on the farm where he has spent every Christmas of his life. He's lucky to be there, given the cancellations. Snowstorms sweep in from the west, grounding planes all over the country.

He and his folks have driven out to be with his grandmother. Tomorrow, more family will arrive from all over the state. With a flip through the photos, the farm memories come back to him: the holidays of his childhood, the entire clan gathering for turkey or carols, midsummer flags and fireworks. It's all encoded somehow in that animated tree, the gatherings in each season, joining his cousins for days of exploration and corn-bound boredom. Flipping backward through the photos, Nicholas feels the years peel off like steamed wallpaper.

Always the animals. First the dogs—especially the three-legged one, half wild with affection every time Nick's family pulled into the long gravel drive. Then the horses' hot breath and the stiff shock of cows' bristles. Snakes threading the harvested stalks. A stumbled-on rabbits' nest down by the mailbox. One July, half-feral cats emerging from under the front porch, smelling of mystery and curdled milk. The small gifts of dead mice on the farm's back doorstep.

The five-second film triggers primal scenes. Prowling the machine shed, with its engines and arcane tools. Sitting in the Hoel-crowded kitchen, breathing in the moldy, cracked linoleum while squirrels thumped in their hidden nests between the wall studs. Digging for hours with two younger cousins, their antique pear-handle shovels cutting a trench down into what Nick promised would soon be magma.

He sits upstairs at the rolltop desk in his dead grandfather's study sampling a project that outlasted four generations of its makers. Of all the cargo packed into the Hoel farmhouse—the hundred cookie jars and glass snow globes, the attic box containing his father's old report cards, the foot-pumped bellows organ rescued from the church where his great-grandfather was baptized, his father's and uncles' archaic toys, polished pine skittle bowling pins, and an incredible city run by magnets underneath the streets—this stack of photos has always been the one farm treasure he could never get enough of. Each picture on its own shows nothing but the tree he climbed so often he could do it blind. But flipped through, a Corinthian column of wood swells under his thumb, rousing itself and shaking free. Three-quarters of a century runs by in the time it takes to say grace. Once, as a nine-year-old, at the farm for Easter dinner, Nick riffled through the stack so many times that his grandfather cuffed him and hid the pictures away on the highest shelf of the mothballed closet. Nick was up on a chair and into the stack again as soon as the adults were safely downstairs.

It's his birthright, the Hoel emblem. No other family in the county had a tree like the Hoel tree. And no other family in Iowa could match the multi-generation photo project for pure weirdness. And yet the adults seemed sworn never to say where the project was going. Neither his grandparents nor his father could explain to him the point of the thick flip-book. His grandfather said, "I promised my father and he promised his." But another time, from the same man: "Makes you think different about things, don't it?" It did.

The farm was where Nick first started sketching. The penciled dreams of boys—rockets, outlandish cars, massed armies, imaginary cities, more baroque with detail each year. Then wilder textures, directly observed—the forest of hairs on a caterpillar's back and the stormy weather maps in the grain of floorboards. It was at the farm, drunk on the flip-book, that he first started to sketch branches. He lay on his back on the Fourth of July, looking up into the spreading tree while everyone else pitched horseshoes. There was a geometry to this constant splitting, a balance to the various thicknesses and lengths that lay beyond his powers as an artist to reveal. Sketching, he wondered what his brain would have to be like to distinguish each of the hundreds of lancet leaves on a given branch and recognize them as easily as he did the faces of his cousins.

One more flip through the magic movie, and faster than it takes for the black-and-white broccoli to turn again into a sky-probing giant, the nine-year-old cuffed by his grandfather turns into a teen, falls in love with God, prays to God nightly but rarely successfully to keep from masturbating to visions of Shelly Harper, grows away from God and toward the guitar, gets busted for half a joint of pot, is sentenced to six months in a juvie scared-straight facility near Cedar Rapids, and there—sketching for hours at a shot everything he can see through his steel-webbed dorm room windows—realizes that he needs to spend his life making strange things.

He was sure the idea would be a hard sell. Hoels were farmers, feed store owners, and farm equipment salesmen like his father, violently practical people grounded in the logic of land and driven to work long, relentless days, year after year, without ever asking why. Nick prepared himself for a showdown, something out of the D. H. Lawrence novels that helped him survive high school. He practiced for weeks, choking on the absurdity of the request:

*Dad, I would very much like to plunge off the edge of commonsense existence, at your expense, and become certifiably unemployable.*

He chose an early spring night. His father lay on a divan on the screened-in porch, as he did most nights, reading a biography of Douglas MacArthur. Nicholas sat in the recliner next to him. Sweet breezes blew in through the screen and uncombed his hair. "Dad? I need to go to art school."

His father looked out over the top of his book, like he was gazing out on the ruins of his lineage. "I figured it would be something like that." And Nick was gone, reeled out on a leash long enough to reach the Chicago Loop, with the freedom to test all the flaws inherent in his own desire.

At school in Chicago, he learned many things:

1. Human history was the story of increasingly disoriented hunger.
2. Art was nothing he thought it was.
3. People would make just about anything you can think to make. Intricate scrimshawed portraits on the tips of pencil leads. Polyurethane-coated dog shit. Earthworks that could pass for small nations.
4. Makes you think different about things, don't it?

His cohort laughed at his little pencil sketches and hyperreal, trompe-l'oeil paintings. But he kept making them, season after season. And by his third year, he became notorious. Even cattily admired.

Winter night of senior year, in his rented broom closet in Rogers Park, he had a dream. A woman student he loved asked him, *What is it that you really want to make?* He bared his hands to the sky, shrugging. Tiny wells of blood pooled in the center of his palms. Up from those pools grew two branching spines. He thrashed in a panic, back up to consciousness. Half an hour passed before his heart slowed enough for him to realize where those spines came from: the time-lapse pictures of the chestnut his gypsy-Norwegian great-great-great-grandfather planted, one hundred and twenty years before, while self-enrolled in that correspondence school of primitive art, the plains of western Iowa.

Nick sits at the rolltop, flipping once more through the book. Last year he won the Stern Prize for Sculpture from the School of the Art Institute. This year, he's a stock boy for a famous Chicago department store that has been dying a slow death for a quarter of a century. Granted, he has earned a degree that licenses him to make peculiar artifacts capable of embarrassing his friends and angering strangers. There's a U-Stor-It in Oak Park crammed with papier-mâché costumes for street masques and surreal sets for a show that ran in a little theater near Andersonville and closed three nights later. But at twenty-five, the scion of a long line of farmers wants to believe that his best work might still be ahead of him.

It's the day before Christmas Eve. Hoels will descend en masse tomorrow, but his grandmother is already in hog heaven. She lives for these days when the old, drafty house fills up with descendants. There's no farm anymore, just the house on its island rise. All the Hoel land is long-term leased to outfits run from offices hundreds of miles away. The Iowa earth has been brought to its rationalized end. But for a while, for this holiday, the place will be all miracle births and saviors in mangers, as it was at Hoel Christmases for a hundred and twenty years running.

Nick heads downstairs. It's midmorning, and his grandmother, father, and mother huddle around the kitchen table where the pecan rolls flow and the dominoes are already getting worn down to little Chiclets. Outside, the cold dips well below bitter. To counter the polar north winds pouring through the cedar-sided walls, Eric Hoel has cranked up the old propane space heater. There's a fire blazing in the fireplace, food enough to feed the five thousand, and a new TV as big as Wyoming tuned to a football game no one cares about.

Nicholas says, "Who's up for Omaha?" There's an American Landscapes exhibit at the Joslyn Museum, only an hour away. When he pitched the idea the night before, the old folks seemed interested. Now they look away.

His mother smiles, embarrassed for him. "I'm feeling a little fluish, honey."

Hs father adds, "We're all pretty cozy, Nick." His grandmother nods in woozy agreement.

"'Kay," Nicholas says. "Heck with you all! I'll be back for dinner."

Snow blows across the interstate, while more is falling. But he's a midwesterner, and his father wouldn't be his father without putting virgin snow tires on the car. The American Landscapes show is spectacular. The Sheelers alone send Nick into fits of jealous gratitude. He stays until the museum kicks him out. When he leaves, it's dark and the drifts swirl up above his boots.

He finds his way back onto the interstate and creeps east. The road is whited out. All the drivers foolish enough to attempt travel cling to one another's taillights in slow procession through the white. The rut Nick plows has only the most abstract relation to the lane beneath. The shoulder's rumble strip is so muffled by snow he can't hear it.

Under a viaduct, he hits a sheet of frictionless ice. The car slaloms sideways. He surrenders to the freestyle slide, coaxing the car like a kite until it straightens. He flips his high beams on and off, trying to decide which is less blinding against the snowy curtain. After an hour, he has gone almost twenty miles.

A scene unfolds in the snow-black tunnel like a night-vision clip from a cop documentary. An oncoming eighteen-wheeler jackknifes into the median and swings around like a wounded animal, popping up on Nick's side a hundred yards in front of him. He swerves past the wreck and slides off onto the right shoulder. The right rear of the car bounces off the guardrail. His front left bumper kisses the truck's rear tire. He skids to a stop and starts shaking, so hard he can't steer. The car edges itself into a rest area crawling with stranded motorists.

There's a pay phone in front of the toilets. He calls the house, but the call won't go through. Night before Christmas Eve, and phone lines are down all over the state. He's sure his parents must be worried sick. But the only sane thing to do is curl up in the car and sleep for a couple of hours until everything blows over and the plows catch up with God's shit fit.

He's back on the road a little before dawn. The snow has mostly stopped, and cars creep by in both directions. He crawls home. The hardest part of the drive is climbing the little rise at the end of the interstate exit. He fishtails up the ramp and turns onto the road back to the farm. The way is drifted over. The Hoel Chestnut appears from a long way off, piled up in white, the only spire all the way to the horizon. Two small lights shine from the house's upstairs windows. He can't imagine what anyone is doing up so early. Someone has waited up all night for word of him.

The road to the house is piled high in snow. His grandfather's old truck-plow is still in the shed. His father should have run it down and back at least a couple of times by now. Nick fights the drifts, but they're too much. He leaves the car halfway up the drive and walks the last stretch to the house. Pushing through the front door, he bursts out singing. "Oh, the weather outside is frightful!" But there's no one downstairs to laugh.

Later, he'll wonder whether he knew already, there in the front doorway. But no: He must walk around to the foot of the stairs where his father is lying, head downward and arms bent at impossible angles, praising the floor. Nick shouts and drops to help his father, but there's nothing left to help. He stands and takes the stairs, two at a time. But by now everything is as clear as Christmas, everything anyone needs to know. Upstairs, the two women curl up in their bedrooms and can't be wakened—a late-morning sleep-in on Christmas Eve.

Blur rises up his legs and torso. He's drowning in pitch. He runs back downstairs, where the old propane heater still cranks away, venting gas that rises and pools invisibly underneath the ceiling that Nick's father has so recently snugged up with extra insulation. Nick blunders through the front door, trips down the porch steps, and falls into the snow. He rolls over in the freezing white, gasping and reviving. When he looks up, it's into the branches of the sentinel tree, lone, huge, fractal, and bare against the drifts, lifting its lower limbs and shrugging its ample globe. All its profligate twigs click in the breeze as if this moment, too, so insignificant, so transitory, will be written into its rings and prayed over by branches that wave their sema-phores against the bluest of midwestern winter skies.

# MIMI MA

THE DAY IN 1948 when Ma Sih Hsuin gets his third-class ticket for a crossing to San Francisco, his father starts addressing him in English. Forced practice, for his own good. His father's magisterial British colonial speech runs rings around Sih Hsuin's own electrical engineer's functional approximations. "My son. Listen to me. We're doomed."

They sit in the upstairs office of the Shanghai complex, half company trading house, half family compound. The enterprise of Nanjing Road percolates up to the window, and doom is nowhere to be seen. But then, Ma Sih Hsuin is not political, and his eyesight is that of a man who has worked too many math problems by candlelight. His father—scholar of art, master calligrapher, patriarch with one major and two minor wives—can't help lapsing into metaphor. Metaphor embarrasses Sih Hsuin.

"This family has come so far. From Persia to the Athens of China, you might say."

Sih Hsuin nods, although he would never say any such thing.

"We Hui Moslems have taken everything this country threw at us, and packaged it for resale. This building, our mansion in Hangzhou . . . Think of what we have outlasted. Ma resilience!"

Ma Shouying gazes out into the August sky, staring at all the calamities the Ma Trading Company has survived. Colonial exploitation. The Taiping uprising. The destruction of the family's silk plantations by typhoon. The 1911 revolution and the '27 massacre. His face turns toward the room's dark corner. Ghosts are everywhere, victims of violations that not even the philosopher magnate who hired a pilgrim to go to Mecca for him dares to name out loud. He spreads one palm on the paper-stacked desk. "Even the Japanese couldn't break us."

HISTORY GIVES SIH HSUIN a rash, the random ebb and flow. He'll travel to the States in four days, one of a handful of Chinese students in all of 1948 to be granted visas. For weeks he has studied the maps, gone over the letters of acceptance, practiced all the inscrutable names: *USS* General Meigs. *Greyhound Supercoach. Carnegie Institute of Technology.* For a year and a half, he's attended matinees of movies with Gable Clark and Astaire Fred, practicing his new tongue.

He plows on in English, out of pride. "If you want, I stay here."

"Want you to *stay?* You have no idea what I'm saying."

His father's stare is like a poem:

> *Why do you linger*
> *at this fork in the road*
> *rubbing your eyes?*
> *You don't get me,*
> *do you, boy?*

Shouying pushes up from the chair and crosses to the window. He looks down the Nanjing Road, a place as eager as ever to profit from that bedlam, the future. "You're this family's salvation. The Communists will be here in six months. Then all of us . . . Son, face facts. You're not cut out for business. You should go to engineer's school forever. But your sisters and brothers? Your cousins and aunts and uncles? Hui traders with lots of money. We won't last three weeks, once the end comes."

"But the Americans. They promise."

Ma Shouying crosses back to the desk and takes his boy's chin in his fingers. "My son. My naïve son with his pet crickets and homing pigeons and shortwave radio. The Gold Mountain is going to eat you alive."

He releases his son's face and leads the way down the hall into the bookkeeper's cage, where he unlocks the grate and shoves aside a filing cabinet to reveal a wall safe whose existence Sih Hsuin never suspected. Shouying extracts three wooden flats wrapped in satin rags. Even Sih Hsuin can tell what they contain: generations of Ma family profit, from the Silk Road to the Bund, sunk into movable form.

Ma Shouying rakes through handfuls of sparkling things, considering each for a moment, then chucking them back into their trays. At last he hits on what he's after: three rings, like small birds' eggs. Three jade landscapes that he lifts to the light.

Sih Hsuin gasps. "Look the color!" The color of greed, envy, freshness, growth, innocence. Green, green, green, green, and green. From a pouch around his neck, Shouying produces a jeweler's loupe. He sets the jade rings in the light and peers at them for what will be his last look. He hands the first ring to Sih Hsuin, who stares at it as at a rock from Mars. It's a sinuous mass of jade trunk and branches several layers deep.

"You live between three trees. One is behind you. The Lote—the tree of life for your Persian ancestors. The tree at the boundary of the seventh heaven, that none may pass. Ah, but engineers have no use for the past, do they?"

The words confuse Sih Hsuin. He can't read his father's sarcasm. He tries to hand the first ring back, but his father is busy with the second.

"Another tree stands in front of you—Fusang. A magical mulberry tree far to the east, where they keep the elixir of life." He palms the loupe and looks up. "Well, you're off to Fusang now."

He hands the jade over. It's detailed beyond belief. A bird flies above the topmost tangle of foliage. From the crooked branches hangs a row of silkworm cocoons. The carver must have used a diamond-tipped microscopic needle.

Shouying presses his magnified eye up close to the last ring. "The third tree is all around you: Now. And like *Now* itself, it will follow wherever you go."

He gives the third ring to his son, who asks, "What kind of tree?"

The father unwraps another box. Dark lacquered wood unfolds on two sets of hinges to reveal a scroll. He undoes the scroll's ribbon, which hasn't been loosened for a long time. The scroll unrolls into a series of portraits, wizened men whose skin droops more than the folds in their robes. One leans on a staff in a forest opening. One peers through the narrow window in a wall. Another sits underneath a twisted pine. Sih Hsuin's father taps the air above it. "This kind."

"Who these men are? What they do?"

His father regards the script, so old Sih Hsuin can't read it. "*Luóhàn.* Arhats. Adepts who have passed through the four stages of Enlightenment and now live in pure, knowing joy."

Sih Hsuin doesn't dare touch the radiant thing. His family is rich, of course—so rich that many of them do nothing anymore. But rich enough to own *this?* It angers him that his father has kept these treasures secret, and Sih Hsuin isn't a man who knows how to get angry. "Why I don't know about this?"

"You know *now.*"

"What you want I do?"

"My word, your grammar is atrocious. I assume your instructors in electricity and magnetism were more competent than your English teachers?"

"How old, this? One thousand years? More?"

One cupped palm calms the young man. "Son: listen. You can only store a family fortune so many ways. This was my way. I thought we would gather these things and protect them. When the world returned to sanity, we'd find them a home—a museum somewhere, where every visitor would connect our name with . . ." He nods at the *Luóhàns* playing on the threshold of Nirvana. "Do what you like with them. They're yours. Perhaps you'll discover what they want from you. The main thing is to keep them out of the hands of the Communists. The Communists will wipe their asses with them."

"I take these to *America*?"

His father rolls up the scroll again, wrapping the frayed ribbon around the cylinder with great care. "A Moslem from the land of Confucius, going to the Christian stronghold of Pittsburgh with a handful of priceless Buddhist paintings. Who are we missing?"

He places the scroll back into its box, then hands it to his son. Taking the box, Sih Hsuin drops one of the rings. His father sighs and stoops to retrieve the treasure from the dusty floor. He takes the other two rings from Sih Hsuin's hands.

"These we can bake into moon cakes. The scroll . . . We'll have to think."

They put the trays of jewels into the safe and push the file cabinet back in front of it. Then they lock up the bookkeeper's cage, seal the office, and go downstairs. They pause outside in the Nanjing Road, thronged with people doing business, despite the looming end of the world.

"I bring them back," Sih Hsuin says, "when my school is done, and everything safe here again."

His father gazes down the road and shakes his head. In Chinese, as if to himself, he says, "You can't come back to something that is gone."

WITH TWO STEAMER TRUNKS and a cardboard suitcase, Ma Sih Hsuin takes the train from Shanghai to Hong Kong. There he learns that his health certificate, acquired at the American consulate in Shanghai, isn't good enough for the ship's medical officer, who must be paid another fifty dollars to examine Sih Hsuin again.

The *General Meigs* has just been decommissioned and transferred to the American President Lines for use as a Pacific passenger liner. It's a little world fifteen hundred people wide. Sih Hsuin bunks on one of the Asian decks, three stories beneath daylight. The Europeans are above, in the sun, with their deck chairs and liveried waiters serving cold drinks. Sih Hsuin must shower with dozens of other men, under buckets, bare naked. The food is vile and hard to keep down—waterlogged sausages, pasty potato, and salted ground cow. Sih Hsuin doesn't care. He's going to America, to the great Carnegie Institute, to get a graduate degree in electrical engineering. Even the squalid Asian quarters are a luxury—no falling bombs, no rape or torture. He sits in his berth for hours, sucking on mango stones, feeling like the king of creation.

They dock in Manila, then Guam, then Hawaii. After twenty-one days, they reach San Francisco, port of entry for the lucky land of Fusang. Sih Hsuin stands in the Immigration line with his two trunks and flimsy suitcase, each stenciled with his English name. He's Sih Hsuin Ma now—his old self turned inside out, like a jaunty, reversible jacket. Colorful patches cover the suitcase—stickers from the ship, a pink University of Nanking pennant, an orange one from the Carnegie Institute. He feels carefree, American, filled with affection for people of all nations except the Japanese.

The customs official is a woman. She looks over his papers. "Is Ma your Christian or family name?"

"No Christian name. Only Moslem name. Hui."

"Is that some kind of cult?"

He smiles and nods many times. She narrows her eyes. For a panicked moment, he thinks he's been caught. He lied about his date of birth, putting down November 7, 1925. In fact, he was born on the seventh day of the eleventh month—the lunar calendar. The conversion is beyond him.

She asks him the length, purpose, and location of stay, all detailed in his paperwork. The whole conversation, Sih Hsuin decides, is a crude test of his ability to remember what he's written down. She points at his steamer trunks. "Could you open that, please? No—the other one."

She inspects the contents of the food box: three moon cakes surrounded by thousand-year eggs. She gags as the tomb is opened. "Jesus. Close it."

She picks through the clothes and engineering texts, stopping to examine the soles of a pair of shoes he has repaired himself. She lights upon the scroll box, which Sih Hsuin and his father decided to leave hidden in the open. "What's in here?"

"Souvenir. Chinese painting."

"Open, please."

Sih Hsuin blanks his mind. He thinks about his homing pigeons, about

Planck's constant, anything except this suspect masterpiece that will, at very least, bring down customs duty far in excess of his stipend for the next four years, or, at worst, get him arrested for smuggling.

The agent's face wrinkles at the sight of the arhats. "Who are they?"

"Holy people."

"What's wrong with them?"

"Happiness. They see the True Thing."

"And what is that?"

Sih Hsuin knows nothing about Chinese Buddhism. He has only a rough estimate of English. Now he's supposed to explain Enlightenment to this American woman official.

"The True Thing mean: human beings, so small. And life, so very big."

The agent snorts. "They've just worked this out?"

Sih Hsuin nods.

"And this makes them happy?" She shakes her head and waves him through. "Lotsa luck in Pittsburgh."

SIH HSUIN BECOMES WINSTON MA: a simple engineering fix. In myths, people turn into all kinds of things. Birds, animals, trees, flowers, rivers. Why not an American named Winston? And Fusang—his father's mythic land to the east—turns, over the years after Pittsburgh, into Wheaton, Illinois. Winston Ma and his new wife plant a substantial mulberry in their bare backyard. It's a single tree with two sexes, older than the separation of yin and yang, the Tree of Renewal, the tree at the universe's center, the hollow tree housing the sacred Tao. It's the silk tree on which the Ma family fortune was made, a tree to honor his father, who'll never be allowed to see it.

He stands near the planting, its black ring of soil like a promise at his feet. He won't wipe his muddy hands even on his dungarees. His wife Charlotte, scion of a fallen southern planting family that once sent missionaries to China, tells him, "There's a Chinese saying. 'When is the best time to plant a tree? Twenty years ago.'"

The Chinese engineer smiles. "Good one."

" 'When is the next best time? Now.' "

"Ah! Okay!" The smile turns real. Until today, he has never planted any-thing. But Now, that next best of times, is long, and rewrites everything.

COUNTLESS NOWS PASS. In yet one more, three little girls eat corn flakes underneath their breakfast tree. It's summer. The mulberry puts forth its messy clusters of achenes. Mimi, the firstborn, nine years old, sits among the fruit spatters with her little sisters, her clothes stained red, bemoaning their family's fate. "It's all Mao's fault." A Sunday morning, midsummer, 1967, with Verdi blasting out of their parents' locked bedroom, as it has every Sunday of Mimi's childhood. "That pig Mao. We'd be millionaires if it wasn't for him."

Amelia, the youngest, stops stirring her cereal into a paste. "Who's Mao?"

"World's biggest crook. He stole everything Grandpa owned."

"Somebody stole Grandpa's stuff?"

"Not Grandpa Tarleton. Grandpa Ma."

"Who's Grandpa Ma?"

"Chinese Grandpa," middle Carmen says.

"I've never seen him."

"*Nobody's* ever seen him. Not even Mom."

"Dad never saw him?"

"He's in a work camp. Where they put rich people."

Carmen says, "How come he won't ever talk Chinese? It's suspicious." One of the many mysteries their father is so generous with.

"Dad stole *my* poker chips, when I was beating him." Amelia pours milk from her bowl to feed the tree.

"Stop talking," Mimi orders. "Wipe your chin. Don't do that. You'll poison the roots."

"What does Dad even do?"

"Engineer. Dope."

"I know *that*. 'I drive the train. Toot, toot!' He wants me to laugh, every time."

Mimi tolerates no stupidity. "You know what he does." Their father is inventing a phone no bigger than a briefcase that runs off a car battery and can travel anywhere. The whole family helps test it. They must go out to the garage and sit in the Chevy—*phone booth*, he calls it—every time they make a long-distance call.

"Don't you think the labs are creepy?" Carmen asks. "How you have to sign in, like it's a big prison?"

Mimi holds still and listens. Verdi pours out of her parents' upstairs window. They're allowed to eat under their breakfast tree, but only on Sunday. On a Sunday morning they could walk to Chicago, and no one would even know.

Carmen follows Mimi's gaze. "What do you think they *do* in there, all morning?"

Mimi shudders. "Will you get off my wavelength? I *hate* when you do that!"

"Do you think they touch each other, naked?"

"Don't be gross." Mimi sets down her bowl. She needs clarity and a place to think, and that means getting altitude. She steps up into the low vee of the mulberry, heart pumping. *My silk farm*, her father always says. *Only no silkworm.*

Carmen shouts, "No climbing. Nobody in the tree. I'll tell!"

"I'll squash you like a bug."

This makes Amelia laugh. Mimi pauses in the stirrup. The fruits dangle down around her. She eats one. It's sweet, like a raisin, but she's sick of them, she's had so many already in her short life. The branches zigzag. It bothers her, so many different shapes of leaves. Hearts, mittens, crazy Boy Scout hands. Some are furry underneath, which creeps her out. Why would a tree need hair? All the leaves are notched, with three main veins, like the three of them. She reaches up and snaps one off, knowing the horror that will follow. Thick, milky tree blood oozes from the wound. This, she thinks, is what the worms must somehow turn into silk.

Amelia starts to cry. "Stop! You're hurting it. I can hear it scream!"

Carmen looks up at the window that Mimi is trying to reach. "Is he even Christian? Whenever he goes to church with us, he never says the Jesus stuff."

Their father, Mimi knows, is some other, distant thing. He's a small, cute, smiling, warm, Muslim Chinese guy who loves math, American cars, elections, and camping. A long-term planner who stocks up sale items in the basement, works late every night, and falls asleep in the recliner to the ten o'clock news. Everyone loves him, especially kids. But he never speaks Chinese, not even in Chinatown. Now and then he'll say something about life before America, after butterscotch ice cream or on a cool night around the campfire in a national park. How he kept pet crickets and pigeons in Shanghai. How he once shaved a peach and put the fuzz down the blouse of a servant to make her itch. *Don't laugh. I still feel bad, one thousand year later.*

But Mimi knew nothing much about the man until yesterday, an awful Saturday, when she came home from the playground in tears.

"What happen? What you do?"

She squared off in front of the man. "Are Chinese all Communists who eat rats and love Mao?"

At last he talked to her, a story from another world. Much was lost on Mimi. But as he spoke, her father turned into a character from a late-night black-and-white thriller full of dark corners, eerie music, and a cast of thousands. He told her of the Stranded Scholars, changed into Americans by the Displaced Persons Act. He described other Chinese who'd come with him, including one who went on to win the greatest prize in science. It stunned Mimi: the U.S. and the Communists were fighting over her father's brain.

"This man Mao. He owe me lot of money. He pay me back, I take this family to very fancy dinner. Best rat you ever eat!"

She cried again, until he assured her that he'd never even seen a rat up close until Murray Hill, New Jersey. He hushed and cooed. "Chinese eat many strange thing. But rat not so popular."

He took her into his study. There, he showed her things she still couldn't grasp, a day later. He unlocked the filing cabinet and removed a wooden box. Inside it were three green rings. "Mao, he never know about this. Three magic ring. Three tree—past, present, future. Lucky, I have three magic daughter." He tapped his finger on his temple. "Your father, always thinking."

He took the ring he called *the past* and tried it on Mimi's finger. The twisting green foliage mesmerized her. The carving was deep—branches beyond branches. Impossible that anyone could carve a thing so small.

"This all *jade*."

She jerked her hand, and the ring flipped to the floor. Her father knelt down and swept it back into the box. "Too big. We wait for later." The box went back into the file cabinet, which he locked again. Then he crouched in his closet and removed a lacquered case. He placed the case on his drafting table and undid the ritual of latches and ribbons. Two flicks of the scroll rollers, and there, spread in front of her, was China, the half of her no more real than a fable. Chinese words tumbled down in columns, swirling like tiny flames. Each ink stroke shone as if she had just made it herself. It didn't seem possible that anyone could write like that. But her father could, if he wanted.

After the flowing words came a parade of men, each a chubby skeleton. Their faces laughed but their skin sagged. They seemed to have lived for hundreds of years. Their eyes smiled at the best joke in creation, while their shoulders bowed under the weight of a thing too heavy to bear.

"Who are they?"

Her father studied the figures. "These men?" His lips tightened like the smiling figures. "*Luóhàn*. Arhat. Little Buddha. They solve life. They pass the final exam." He turned her chin toward him. When he smiled, the thin gold edge of his front tooth flashed. "Chinese superhero!"

She wriggled free from his hand and studied the holy men. One sat in a small cave. One had a red sash and earrings. Another paused on the edge of a high cliff, with crags and fog trailing off behind him. One leaned against a tree, as Mimi would lean against her mulberry the next day, telling her sisters.

Her father pointed at the dream landscape. "This China. Very old." Mimi touched the man under the tree. Her father lifted her hand and kissed her fingertips. "Too old for touch."

She stared at the man, whose eyes knew everything. "Superheroes?"

"They see every answer. Nothing hurt them anymore. Emperor come and go. Qing, Ming, Yuan. Communism, too. Little insect on a giant dog. But these guy?" He clicked his tongue and held up his thumb, as if these little Buddhas were the ones to put money on, in the run of time.

At that click, a teenage Mimi lifted from her own nine-year-old shoulders to gaze at the arhats from high up and years away. Out of the gazing teen rose another, even older woman. Time was not a line unrolling in front of her. It was a column of concentric circles with herself at the core and the present floating outward along the outermost rim. Future selves stacked up above and behind her, all returning to this room for another look at the handful of men who had solved life.

"Look the color," Winston said, and all her later selves collapsed around Mimi. "China surely a funny place." He rolled up the scroll and put it, in its case, back on the closet floor.

In the mulberry, Mimi thinks that if she could ascend another few feet above the Earth, she might look into her parents' window and see what Verdi is doing to them. But down on Earth, revolution erupts. "No climbing!" Amelia yells. "Get down!"

"Shut your trap," Mimi suggests.

"*Dad!* Mimi's in the silk farm!"

Mimi drops to the ground, a foot from crushing her little sister. She grabs the kid's mouth and gags her. "Shut up, and I'll show you something."

With the perfect hearing of childhood, both sisters know: the *something* is worth seeing. In another moment, under cover of the swelling Verdi chorus, they creep together, commando-style, into their father's office. The filing cabinet is locked, but Mimi opens the lacquered box. The scroll unrolls on Winston's drafting table to the image of a figure seated underneath a gnarled, patient tree.

"Don't touch! They're our ancestors. And they're *gods*."

AS MUCH AS HE LOVES ANYTHING in life, the Chinese electrical engineer who brings his family into the garage to make long-distance calls to their Virginia grandparents on a car phone bigger than a yule log loves his national parks. Winston Ma spends half a year planning the annual June ritual, marking up maps, underlining guidebooks, taking neat notes into scores of pocket notebooks, and tying strange trout flies that look like tiny Chinese New Year dragons. By November the dining room table is so full of preparation that the family must eat their Thanksgiving meal—clams and rice—in the breakfast nook. Then vacation comes and they're off again, the five of them crammed into the sky-blue Chevy Biscayne with roof rack and back seat as wide as a continental shelf, no air-conditioning and a cooler full of juice on ice, logging thousands of miles on trips to Yosemite, Zion, Olympic, and beyond.

This year they return to his beloved Yellowstone. Every campground along the way gets an entry in Winston's notebooks. He writes down the campsite number and evaluates it according to a dozen different criteria. He'll use the data over the winter to perfect next year's route. He makes the girls practice their musical instruments in the back seat. This is easier for Mimi, on trumpet, and Carmen, on clarinet, than for little Amelia and her violin. They forget to pack books. Two thousand miles with nothing to read. The two older girls stare at their little sister for dozens of Nebraska miles until Amelia breaks down and cries. It passes the time.

Charlotte gives up trying to control them. No one suspects yet, but she has already begun to slip into the long private place that each passing year will deepen. She sits in the front seat, navigating maps for her husband and humming Chopin nocturnes under her breath. Dementia starts here, in these days of quiet, automotive sainthood.

They camp near Slough Creek for three days. The younger girls spend hours playing Old Maid. Mimi joins her father in the stream. The shared lassitude of casting, the C of the line as it lengthens in the air, that four-stroke swelling rhythm with the stiff hand stopping at ten and two, the ripple of the dry fly as it alights on the water, her small dread that something might actually strike, the startle of the fish's mouth when it breaks the surface: these are charmed to her and will stay so forever.

Knee-deep in the cold current, her father is free. He maps the sandbars, measures the speed of the water, reads the bottom, watches for hatch—those simultaneous equations in multiple unknowns that one must solve to think like a fish—all the while conscious of nothing but the sheer luck of being on the water. "Why these fish hiding?" he asks his daughter. "What they do?"

This is how she'll remember him, wading in his heaven. Fishing, he has solved life. Fishing, he passes the final exam, the next arhat, joining the ones in the mysterious scroll at the bottom of his closet that Mimi has continued to visit in secret, over the years. She's old enough now to know that the men in the scroll are not her ancestors. But seeing her father like this, on the river, complete and at peace, she cannot help but think: *He's their descendant*.

Charlotte sits in a camping chair by the side of the river. Her only job is to unsnag the lines of the two fishermen, untying Byzantine, microscopic knots, hour after hour. Winston watches the sun set over the river, the reeds going from gold to dun. "Look the color!" And again, a few minutes later, a whisper to himself under the sky's collapsing cobalt: *Look the color!* There are colors in his spectrum that no one else can see.

They picnic on the shores of a small lake not far off the road toward Tower Junction. Mimi and Carmen look for stones to make into jewelry. Charlotte and Amelia begin their seventeenth consecutive game of Chinese checkers. Winston sits in a foldable camping chair, updating his notebooks. There's a funny motion near the table. Amelia shouts, "Bear!"

Charlotte leaps up, sending the game board flying. She lifts her youngest daughter into the air and dashes into the lake. The bear ambles toward the jewelry gatherers. Mimi checks for high shoulders or a sloping face. She must do one thing for grizzlies, the opposite for black bears. One climbs trees, the other doesn't. She can't remember which. "Climb," she shouts to Carmen, and they each scramble up their own lodgepole.

The bear, which could reach either of them in two easy scooches, loses interest. It stands on the lakeshore, wondering if today might be a good day for a swim. It regards the chest-deep woman in the water holding her tiny daughter on high like she's about to baptize the girl. It waits to see what the always insane species will do next. It wanders over to Winston, who has been sitting stock-still at the camping table, taking pictures with the Nikon.

The camera—the only Japanese item the man allows himself to own—goes click, snick, whir.

Winston rises to his feet as the animal approaches. Then he starts to chatter to the bear. In Chinese. A primitive toilet stands near the site, door open. Winston talks to the bear, cajoling it while edging toward the door. This baffles the bear, who reconsiders his whole approach to the situation. Sadness percolates up in him. He sits and claws at the air.

Winston keeps talking. It astounds Mimi, this alien language coming from her father's mouth. Winston draws a handful of pistachios from his pocket and tosses them into the latrine. The bear ambles after them, grateful for the diversion. "Get in car," Winston shout-whispers. "Fast!" They do, and the bear doesn't even lift its head. But Winston stops to retrieve the camping table and stools. He's paid good money for them, and he's not about to leave them behind.

That night, at the campsite near Norris, Mimi asks him, awed. Her father has changed before her eyes. "Weren't you afraid?"

He laughs, embarrassed. "Not my time yet. Not my story."

The words chill her. How can he know his story, ahead of time? But she doesn't ask him that. Instead, she says, "What did you say to it?"

His brow crumples. He shrugs. What else is there to say, to a bear? "Apologize! I tell him, people very stupid. They forget everything—where they come from, where they go. I say: Don't worry. Human being leaving this world, very soon. Then the bear get top bunk to himself again."


AT HOLYOKE, Mimi is a LUG: lesbian until graduation. It's the same at half of the other Seven Sisters colleges, rounded up. Scissors and paste, they call it. Fun, sinning, healthy, shameful, sweet—great practice for something. Life, say. Whatever happens after school.

She reads nineteenth-century American poetry and drinks afternoon tea in South Hadley for three semesters. It beats Wheaton. But one April day she's reading Abbott's *Flatland* for a sophomore survey called Transcendence, when she reaches the part where the narrator, A. Square, gets lifted out of his plane into the expanses of Spaceland. Truth comes over her like a revelation: The only thing worth believing in is measurement. She must become an engineer, like her daddy before her. It's not even a choice. She's an engineer already, and always has been. And as with Abbott's Square, the minute she comes back to Flatland, her Holyoke friends want to lock her up.

She transfers to Berkeley. Best place for ceramic engineering she can find. The place is a staggering time warp. Future masters of the universe study alongside unrepentant revolutionaries who believe the Golden Age of Human Potential peaked ten years before.

She thrives, reborn Mimi, looking like a diminutive Kazakh carrying a programmable calculator, and, in the estimation of many, the cutest thing ever to mouth the Hall-Petch equation. She savors the eerie *Stepford Wives* climate. She sits in the eucalyptus grove, the trees that explode in the dry heat, solving problem sets and watching the protesters with their placards full of all-caps slogans. The better the weather, the more irate the demands.

The month before graduation, she dons a killer interview suit—sleek, gray, professional, inexorable as a NoCal earthquake. She interviews with eight campus reps and gets three offers. She takes a job as a casting process supervisor for a molding outfit in Portland, because it offers the most chance to travel. They send her to Korea. She falls in love with the country. In four months, she learns more Korean than she knows Chinese.

Her sisters, too, wander across the map. Carmen winds up at Yale, studying economics. Amelia gets a job nursing wounded wildlife in a discovery center in Colorado. Back in Wheaton, the Ma mulberry is assailed on all fronts. Mealybugs cover it in cottony wisps. Scale insects mass on its branches, invulnerable to all her father's pesticides. Bacteria blacken the leaves. Her parents are helpless to save the thing. Charlotte, in her thickening fog, murmurs about bringing in a priest to pray over it. Winston pores through horticulture bibles and fills his notebooks with impeccably printed speculations. But each season brings the tree closer to capitulation.

Winston calls Mimi when she's back in Portland from another Korea trip.

He reaches her from the family phone booth, the Ma garage. His invention has shrunken down to the size of a hiking boot, so reliable and power-thrifty that Bell Labs starts licensing it to other outfits. But Winston takes no pleasure in telling his daughter that his life's work has at last come to fruition. All he can talk about is his failed mulberry.

"That tree. What he do?"

"What's wrong with it, Dad?"

"Bad color. All his leaves, falling."

"Have you tested the soil?"

"My silk farm. Finish. It never make one thread."

"Maybe you should plant another."

"Best time to plant a tree? Twenty years ago."

"Yep. And you always said the next best time was now."

"Wrong. Next best time, nineteen years ago."

Mimi has never heard this cheerful, endlessly resourceful man sound so low. "Take a trip, Dad. Take Mom camping." But they've just come back from a ten-thousand-miler up to the salmon streams in Alaska, and the notebooks are filled with meticulous notes that will take years to go over.

"Put Mom on."

There's a sound—the car door opening and closing, then the door to the garage. After a while, a voice says, "*Salve filia mea.*"

"Mom? What the hell?"

"*Ego Latinam discunt.*"

"Don't do this to me, Mom."

"*Vita est supplicium.*"

"Put Dad back on. Dad? Is everything okay out there?"

"Mimi. My time coming."

"What's that supposed to mean?"

"My work all done. My silk farm, finish. Fishing going down, little bit every year. What I do now?"

"What are you talking about? Do what you've always done." Make charts and graphs of next year's campsites. Fill up the basement with stacks of soap and soup and cereal and any other items that happen to go on sale. Fall asleep every night to the ten o'clock news. Freedom.

"Yes," he says. But she knows the voice that formed her. Whatever he pretends that *yes* to mean, it's a lie. She makes a note to call her sisters and discuss the Wheaton collapse. Parents on the fritz. What to do? But long-distance to the East Coast is two dollars a minute, if you don't have a magic shoe phone. She decides to write them both that weekend. But that weekend is her ceramic sintering conference in Rotterdam, and the letters slip her mind.

IN THE FALL, with his wife in the basement studying Latin, Winston Ma, once Ma Sih Hsuin to everyone who knew him, sits under the crumbling mulberry and, with Verdi's *Macbeth* blasting out the bedroom window, puts a Smith & Wesson 686 with hardwood grips up to his temple and spreads the workings of his infinite being across the flagstones of the backyard. He leaves no note except a calligraphic copy of Wang Wei's twelve-hundred-year-old poem left unfurled on parchment across the desk in his study:

> An old man, I want
> only peace.
> The things of this world
> mean nothing.
> I know no good way
> to live and I can't
> stop getting lost in my
> thoughts, my ancient forests.
> The wind that waves the pines
> loosens my belt.
> The mountain moon lights me
> as I play my lute.
>
> You ask: how does a man rise or fall in this life?
> The fisherman's song flows deep under the river.

Mimi is in SFO, on her way to Seattle for a site inspection. She's mock-shopping the concourse when out of the cacophony of gate calls and public service announcements her name blares out. Something cold grabs at her scalp. Before the people at the customer service desk even hand her the phone, she knows. And all the way home to Illinois she thinks: *How do I recognize this already? Why does this all feel so much like* remembering?

HER MOTHER IS HELPLESS. "Your father doesn't want to hurt us. He has some ideas. I don't understand all of them. That's just how he is." Her words come from a place where the blast she heard from the basement is only one of several possibilities that branching time might try. She looks so gentled, so at peace in her confusion, so utterly under the surface of the flowing river that Mimi can do nothing but share her unreal calm. The job her father leaves is Mimi's to finish. No one has touched the scene except to remove the body and the gun. Pieces of brain dot the stones and tree trunk, like new species of garden slug. She turns into a cleaning machine. Bucket, sponge, soapy water, for the spattered deck. She failed to alert her sisters or stop what she saw happening. But she can do this—clean up the backyard carnage forever. Cleaning, she becomes another thing. The wind loosens her hair. She looks at the bloodied paving stones, the bits of soft tissue that housed his ideas. She sees him by her side, amazed by the flecks of his own brain lying in the grass. *Look the color!* You ask how people rise or fall in this life? Like this.

She sits under the diseased mulberry. Wind slaps at the coarse-toothed leaves. Wrinkles score the bark, like the folds in the arhats' faces. Her eyes sour with animal confusion. Even now, every square foot of ground is stained with fruit, fruit stained, the myths say, with the blood of a suicide for love. Words come out of her, crumpled and tinny. "Dad. *Daddy!* What you do?"

Then the silent howls.

CARMEN AND AMELIA ARRIVE. United, the trio sit together one last time. They have no explanation. There never will be one. The least likely person in the world has gone on an impossible tour without them. In place of explanation, memory. They put their hands on each other's shoulders and tell each other stories of how things were. Sunday opera. The epic car journeys. Trips to the lab, where the tiny man floated down the halls, celebrated by all his giant white colleagues, the happy maker of the cellular future. They remember the day the family scattered from the bear. Their mother holding Amelia above her head, in the water. Their father talking to the animal in Chinese—two creatures, not quite of the same order, sharing the same woods.

They hold a silent liturgy of memory and shock. But they hold it indoors. Mimi's sisters don't go near the yard. They can't even look at the old breakfast tree, their father's silk farm. Mimi tells them what she knows. The call. *My time coming.*

Amelia holds her. "It's not your fault. You couldn't know."

Carmen says, "He told you that, and you didn't tell us?"

Charlotte sits nearby, smiling a little. It's like the family is still on a camping trip somewhere, and she is at lakeside, unsnagging the smallest knots in her husband's fishing line. "He hates it when you three fight."

"Mom." Mimi shouts at the woman. "Mom. Enough. Clear your head. He's gone."

"Gone?" Charlotte frowns at her daughter's foolishness. "What are you talking about? I'll see your father again."


THE THREE GIRLS attack the mountain of paperwork and reporting. It has never before occurred to Mimi: The law doesn't stop with death. It reaches far beyond the grave, for years, entangling the survivors in bureaucratic hurdles that make the challenges of pre-death seem like a cakewalk. Mimi tells the others, "We have to divvy up his stuff."

"Divvy?" Carmen says. "You mean, like *take?*"

Amelia says, "Shouldn't we let Mom . . . ?"

"You see how she is. She's not even here."

Carmen rears up. "Can you stop solving problems for a minute? What's the hurry?"

"I'd like to get things done. For Mom."

"By throwing out his stuff?"

"Distribute. Each thing to the right person."

"Like solving a big quadratic equation."

"Carmen. We have to take care of it."

"Why? You want to sell the house out from under Mom?"

"Like she's going to be able to take care of it by herself, in her state?"

Amelia puts her arms around them both. "Maybe those things can wait for now? We only have a little while to be with each other."

"We're all here now," Mimi says. "It could be a long time before that happens again. Let's just get it done."

Carmen shakes free of the hug. "So you're not coming home for Christmas?" But something in her tone is as good as a signed confession. *Home* has gone wherever their father went.

CHARLOTTE CLINGS to a few token things. "This is his favorite sweater. Oh, don't take the waders. And these are the slacks he wears when we go hiking."

"She's fine," Carmen says, when the three of them are alone. "She's managing. She's just a little weird."

"I can come back in a few weeks," Amelia offers. "Check in. Make sure she's okay."

Carmen faces Mimi, pre-enraged. "Don't even dream of putting her in a home."

"I'm not dreaming anything. I'm just trying to take care of things."

"Take care? Here. You're the compulsive one. Knock yourself out. Eleven notebooks filled with report cards on every campsite we've ever stayed in. All yours."

THE THREE OPERA HEROINES hover above a silver plate. On the plate are three jade rings. On each ring is a carved tree, and each tree branches in one of time's three disguises. The first is the Lote, the tree at the boundary of the past that none may pass back over. The second is that thin, straight pine of the present. The third is Fusang, the future, a magical mulberry far to the east, where the elixir of life is hidden.

Amelia stares. "Who's supposed to get which one?"

"There's a right way to do this," Mimi says. "And a dozen wrong ones."

Carmen sighs. "Which one is this?"

"Shut up. Close your eyes. On the count of three, take one."

On three, there's some light grazing of arms, and each woman finds her fate. When they open their eyes, the platter is empty. Amelia has her eternal present, Carmen her doomed past. And Mimi is left holding the thin trunk of things to come. She puts it on her finger. It's a little big—gift from a homeland she will never see. She spins the endless loop of inheritance around on her finger like an open sesame. "Now the Buddhas."

They don't understand her. But then, Amelia and Carmen haven't been thinking about the scroll for the last seventeen years.

"The *Luóhàn*," Mimi says, butchering the pronunciation. "The arhats." She rolls the scroll out on the table where their father used to tie his trout flies. It's older, stranger than any of them remembers. Like someone has been reworking it with colors and ink, from the world beyond this one. "We could take it to an auction house. Split the money."

"Meem," Amelia says. "Didn't he leave us enough money?"

"Or Mimi could just take it for herself. That would be enlightened."

"We could give it to a museum. In memory of Sih Hsuin Ma." The name sounds hopelessly American in Mimi's mouth.

Amelia says, "That would be beautiful."

"And we'd have tax write-offs for life."

"Those of us who are making money." Carmen sneers.

Amelia rolls up the scroll in her small hands. "So how do we do that?"

"I don't know. We should get it appraised first."

"You do that, Mimi," Carmen says. "You're good at getting things done."

. . .

THE POLICE give them back the gun. They own it, technically, by virtue of inheritance. But none of their names is on the permit. No one knows what to do with it. It sits on the buffet, huge and humming through the wooden crate. It has to be destroyed, like the ring that must be thrown into the volcano's caldera. But how?

Mimi steels herself and takes the crate. She bungees it to the back carrier of her high school bicycle, which her parents have kept in the basement for years. Then she pedals down Pennsylvania toward the gun shop in Glen Ellyn, where the firearm came from. She doesn't know if they'll buy it back. She doesn't care. She'll donate it to charity. The box is ungodly heavy on her rear carrier, and she wants it gone. Cars pass her, the drivers annoyed. The neighborhood is too affluent for adults on bicycles. The crate looks like a tiny coffin.

Then a police car. She tries to act normal, that thing the Ma family always pretended to be. The squad car crawls behind her, flashing lights invisible at noon. It pops the siren for a quarter second, a hiccup of ultimate authority. Mimi wobbles to a stop and almost tips over. Mandatory jail sentence for handguns you aren't licensed to carry. Gun recently wiped clean of so much human tissue. Her heart hits so hard she can taste the blood up under her tongue. The cop comes out and over to where she cowers on the bike. "You didn't signal back there."

Her head is quivering on its stalk. She can only let it bob.

"Always use your hand signals. It's the law."


THEN MIMI IS AT O'HARE, waiting for a flight back to Portland. She hears herself being paged over the airport speakers again and again. Each time she bolts upright, and each time the syllables turn back into other words. The flight is delayed. Then delayed again. She sits twisting the jade tree around her finger, tens of thousands of times. The things of this world mean nothing, except for this ring and the priceless ancient scroll in her carry-on. She wants only peace. But this is where she must live now: In the shadow of the bent mulberry. The inexplicable poem. The fisherman's song.

# ADAM APPICH

A FIVE-YEAR-OLD in 1968 paints a picture. What's in it? First, a mother, giver of paper and paints, saying, *Make me something beautiful.* Then a house with a door floating in the air, and a chimney with curls of spiraling smoke. Then four Appich children in descending order like measuring cups, down to the smallest, Adam. Off to the side, because Adam can't figure out how to put them behind the house, are four trees: Leigh's elm, Jean's ash, Emmett's ironwood, and Adam's maple, each made from identical green puffballs.

"Where's Daddy?" his mother asks.

Adam sulks, but inserts the man. He paints his father holding this very drawing in his stick hands, laughing and saying, *What are these—trees? Look outside! Is that what a tree looks like?*

The artist, born scrupulous, adds the cat. Then the horned toad Emmett keeps in the basement, where the climate is better for reptiles. Then the snails under the flowerpot and the moth hatched from a cocoon spun by another creature altogether. Then helicopter seeds from Adam's maple and the strange rock from the alley that might be a meteorite even if Leigh calls it a cinder. And dozens of other things, living or nearly so, until nothing more will fit on the newsprint page.

He gives his mother the finished picture. She hugs Adam to her, even in front of the Grahams from across the street, who are over for drinks. The painting doesn't show this, but his mother only ever hugs him when her whistle is wet. Adam fights her embrace to save the painting from getting crushed. Even as an infant, he hated being held. Every hug is a small, soft jail.

The Grahams laugh as the boy speeds off. From the landing, halfway up the stairs, Adam hears his mother whisper, "He's a little socially retarded. The school nurse says to keep an eye."

The word, he thinks, means special, possibly superpowered. Something other people must be careful around. Safe in the boys' room at the top of the house, he asks Emmett, who's eight—almost grown—"What's retarded?"

"It means you're a retard."

"What's that?"

"Not regular people."

And that's okay, to Adam. There's something wrong with regular people. They're far from being the best creatures in the world.

The painting still clings to the fridge months later, when his father huddles up the four kids after dinner. They pile into the shag-carpeted den filled with T-ball trophies, handmade ashtrays, and mounds of macaroni sculpture. They spread on the floor around their father, who hunches over *The Pocket Guide to Trees*. "We need to find you all a little sibling."

"What's a sibling?" Adam whispers to Emmett.

"It's a small tree. Kind of reddish."

Leigh snorts. "That's a sapling, pinhead. A sibling's a baby."

"Butt sniff," Emmett replies. The image is so richly animalistic that Adam will carry it with him into the corridors of middle age. That moment of bickering will make up a good share of everything he'll recall of his sister Leigh.

Their father hushes the brawl and puts forward the candidates. There is tulip tree, fast-growing and long-lived, with showy flowers. There's small, thin river birch, with peeling bark that you can use to make canoes. Hemlock forms big spires and fills up with small cones. Plus, it stays green, even under snow.

"Hemlock," Leigh declares.

Jean asks, "Why?"

"Do I have to give my reasons?"

"Canoes," Emmett says. "Why are we even voting?"

Adam's face reddens until his freckles almost vanish. Near tears, in the press of impossible responsibility, trying to save others from terrible mistakes, he cries out, "What if we're wrong?"

Their father keeps flipping through the book. "What do you mean?"

Jean answers. She has interpreted for her little brother since before he could speak. "He means, what if it's not the right kind of tree for the sibling?"

Their father swats at the nuisance idea. "We just have to pick a nice one."

Teary Adam isn't buying. "No, Dad. Leigh is droopy, like her elm. Jean is straight and good. Emmett's ironwood—look at him! And my maple turns red, like me."

"You're only saying that because you already know which tree is whose."

Adam will preach the point to undergrad psych majors, when he's even older than his father is on the night they pick a tree for unborn Charles. He'll build a career on that theme: cuing, priming, framing, confirmation bias, and the conflation of correlation with causality—all these faults, built into the brain of the most problematic of large mammals.

"No, Daddy. We have to pick right. We can't just choose."

Jean pets his hair. "Don't worry, Dammie." Ash is a noble shade tree, full of cures and tonics. Its branches swoop like a candelabra. But its wood burns when still green.

"Canoes, already," Emmett shouts. Ironwood will break your ax before you bring it down.

As usual, their father has rigged the election. "There's a sale on black walnut," he says, and democracy is over. By chance, nothing in the American arboretum could better suit what baby Charles will grow into: a towering, straight-grained thing whose nuts are so hard you have to smash them with a hammer. A tree that poisons the ground beneath itself so nothing else can grow. But wood so fine that thieves poach it.

The tree arrives before the baby. Adam's father, cursing and blaming, wrestles the burlap-wrapped root ball toward a hole torn out of the lawn's perfect green. Adam, lined up with his siblings on the edge of the hole, sees something terribly wrong. He can't believe no one intervenes.

"Dad, stop! That cloth. The tree is choking. Its roots can't breathe."

His father grunts and wrestles on. Adam pitches himself into the hole to prevent the murder. The full weight of the root ball comes down on his stick legs and he screams. His father yells the deadliest word of all. He yanks Adam by one arm out of his live burial and hauls the boy across the lawn, depositing him on the front porch. There the boy lies facedown on the concrete, howling, not for his pain, but for the unforgivable crime inflicted on his brother-to-be's tree.

Charles comes home from the hospital, a heavy helplessness wrapped in a blanket. Adam waits, month by month, for the choked black walnut to die and take his baby brother with it, smothered in his own clown-covered coverlet. But both live, which only proves to Adam that life is trying to say something no one hears.

FOUR SPRINGS LATER, with the leaves' first flush, the Appich kids fight over whose tree is the most beautiful. They fight again when the seeds come out, and later the nuts, and finally the autumn rush of color. Health and power, size and beauty: they fight over everything. Each child's tree has its own excellence: the ash's diamond-shaped bark, the walnut's long compound leaves, the maple's shower of helicopters, the vase-like spread of the elm, the ironwood's fluted muscle.

Nine now, Adam decides to hold an election. He cuts a slit in the top of an egg carton to make a secret-ballot box. Five ballots, five trees. Each child votes for their own. They have a runoff. Emmett buys four-year-old Charles's vote for half a Butterfinger, and Jean changes her vote to Adam's maple out of what can only be called love. It comes down to ironwood versus maple. Campaigning is ruthless. Jean helps Adam make pamphlets. Leigh takes over as Emmett's manager. For a slogan, Leigh and Emmett doctor a poem they find scribbled in their father's old high school yearbook:

Don't worry if your job is small
and your rewards are few.
Even the mighty Ironwood
was once a nut, like you.

To counter, Adam has Jean make a poster reading:

Come on, Sugar, Vote for Maple.
Up in Canada it's a staple.

"I don't know, Dammie." Jean, three years older, has her finger more squarely on the pulse of the electorate. "They might not get it."

"It's funny. People like funny."

They lose the election, three to two. Adam sulks for the next two months.

BY TEN, Adam travels mostly alone. Kids have it out for him. His brother takes him on a hike, then gives him a canteen full of urine on ice to drink. In the park, his friends tell him his scalp is turning green from eating too many potato chips. He rushes home to a mother who chides him for being so gullible. He can't figure out why people do what they do. His cluelessness only makes others keener to dupe him.

He keeps to himself, but even the subdivision's barest lot is home to millions of creatures. *The Golden Guide to Insects* and a jar with a punched lid turns the loneliest Sunday afternoon into a collector's dream. Armed with *The Golden Guide to Fossils*, he concludes that the bumps and nubs in the front flagstones are the teeth of ichthyosaurs who went extinct long before mammals were anything but a sideshow on the forest floor. *The Golden Guide to Pond Life*, *The Golden Guide to Stars*, *to Rocks and Minerals*, *to Reptiles and Amphibians*: humans are almost beside the point.

Months pass in amassing specimens. Owl pellets and oriole nests. The shed skin of a corn snake, complete with tail tip and eye caps. Fool's gold, smoky quartz, silver-gray mica that flakes like sheets of paper, and a shard of flint he's sure is a Paleolithic arrowhead. He dates each find and tags it with a location. The collection takes over the boys' room and spills down the hallway into the den. Even the sacred living room breaks out in exhibits.

He comes home from school late one winter afternoon to find the entire museum in the incinerator. He flies through the rooms, wailing.

"Honey," his mother explains, "it was all junk. Moldy, bug-infested junk."

He slaps her. She stumbles back from the sting, hands to her face, staring at the boy. She can't believe the evidence of her pain. She doesn't understand what has happened to her son, the one who, at age six, once took a damp dish towel from her hands and told her he'd take over from here.

Adam's father learns of the slap that evening. He teaches the boy a lesson that involves twisting his wrist until it fractures. No one realizes the wrist is broken until late that night, when it swells up weird and blue like something out of *The Golden Guide to Crustaceans*.

The Saturday in late spring when the cast comes off, Adam climbs up into his maple as high as he can and doesn't come down until dinner. Sun passes through the foliage, turning the air the color of a not-quite-ripe lime. It gives him bitter comfort to gaze over the neighborhood's roofs and know how much better life is above ground level. The palmate leaves wave in the gentle breeze, a crowd of five-fingered hands. There's a sound like light rain, the shower of thousands of tiny bud scales. High above his head squirrels gnaw at the massed flowers, sucking out their liquid sap, then scattering the spent reddish yellow bouquets across the ground below. Adam counts fifteen different crawling things, from mealy worms to flattened flecks with legs almost too small to see, circling his dimpled limb in search of sweet wellsprings. Brown- and black-hooded birds dart through, feeding on the rafts of eggs that bugs and butterflies leave all over the branchlets. A woodpecker ducks in and out of a hole it made while grub-fishing the year before. It's a stunning secret that no one in his family will ever know: there are more lives up here, in his one single maple, than there are people in all of Belleville.

Adam will remember the vigil many years later, from two hundred feet up in a redwood, when he'll look down on a knot of people no bigger than bugs, a democratic majority of whom want him dead.

WHEN HE'S THIRTEEN, the leaves of his sister Leigh's elm turn yellow long before autumn. Adam sees the withering first. The other kids have stopped looking. One by one, they've drifted out of the neighborhood of green things into the louder, flashier party of other people.

The disease that gets Leigh's tree has been coming their way for decades. Back when Leonard Appich planted his first child's tree in a fit of fifties optimism, Dutch elm had already ravaged Boston, New York, Philly, and *Elm City*, New Haven. But those places were so far away. Science, the man figured, would soon come up with a cure.

The fungus gutted Detroit while the kids were still small. Then Chicago, soon after. The country's most popular street tree, vases that turned boulevards into great tunnels, was leaving this world. Now the disease comes to the outskirts of Belleville, and Leigh's tree, too, succumbs. Fourteen-year-old Adam is the only one who mourns. His father curses the expense of taking the thing down. Leigh herself hardly notices. She's on her way to college—tech theater, at Illinois State.

"Of course you'd pick an elm, Dad. You've had it out for me since before I was born."

Adam salvages a bit of wood from the men who come to grind out the stump. He takes it into the basement, planes it down, and engraves it with his woodburning kit. He finds the words in a book: *A tree is a passage between earth and sky.* He messes up *passage. Earth* and *sky* both come out retarded. But he gives it to Leigh anyway, as a going-away present. She laughs at the gift and hugs him. He finds it after she moves out, in the crates she leaves behind for the Salvation Army.

THAT'S THE AUTUMN—1976—when Adam falls for ants. One September Saturday, he watches them flow across the neighbors' sidewalk, carrying a spilled Popsicle back to their base. The rust-colored shag carpet stretches for several yards. Ants wind through obstacles, piling over themselves. Their massed deployment matches any human genius. Adam pitches camp in the grass alongside the living foam. Ants on the edge of the saturnalia seethe across his socks and up his skinny shins. They mount at his elbows into the sleeves of his tee. They scout his shorts and tickle his nuts. He doesn't care. Patterns reveal themselves as he watches, and they're *wild*. Nobody's in charge of the mass mobilization, that much seems clear. Yet they port the sticky food back to the nest in the most coordinated way. Plans in the absence of any planner. Paths in the absence of a surveyor.

He goes home to get his notebook and camera. There, he has a brainstorm. He begs some nail polish off of Jean. His sister has gone foolish with age, lost in the swirl of fashion. But she'll still do anything for her little brother Dammie. She, too, once loved the Golden Guides. But the humans have her in their grip, and she'll never get free again.

She gives him five colors, a rainbow running from scarlet to cyan. Back at the site, he begins daubing. A tiny globe of Smokin' Rose sticks to the abdomen of one of the scavengers. One by one, he brands dozens more ants with the same hue. Several minutes later, he starts in again with Neat Peach. By midmorning, the whole spectrum of polish is in play. Soon, colored daubs reveal a tangled conga line of unreal beauty. The colony possesses something; Adam doesn't know what to call it. Purpose. Will. A kind of awareness—something so different from human intelligence that intelligence thinks it's nothing.

Emmett, passing by with rod and bait, finds him lying in the grass, snapping pictures and sketching in his notebook. "The fuck you doin'?"

Adam hedgehogs and keeps working.

"This is your idea of a Saturday? No wonder people don't get you."

Adam doesn't *get* people. They say things to hide what they mean. They run after pointless trinkets. He keeps his head down and keeps counting.

"Hey! Bug boy! Bug boy—*I'm talking to you!* Why're you playing in the dirt?"

It startles Adam to hear the evidence in Emmett's voice: he frightens his brother. He whispers to his notebook, "Why do you torture fish?"

A foot flicks out and catches Adam's ribs. "The fuck you talking about? Fish can't *feel things*, Shit-for-Brains."

"You don't *know* that. You can't prove it."

"You want proof?" Emmett reaches down, tears a handful of grass, and stuffs it in his brother's mouth. Adam, impassive, spits it out. Emmett walks away, shaking his head in pity, victor in yet another one-sided debate.

Adam studies his living map. After a while, the time-lapse flow of color-coded ants begins to suggest how signals might get passed along without any central signaler calling the shots. He moves the food a little. He scatters the ants. He makes barriers and times the ants' recovery. When the Popsicle is gone, he puts bits of his lunch in different spots and measures how long it takes for those bits, too, to disappear. The colony is swift and cunning—as cunning at getting what they need as anything human.

The bells of the Episcopal carillon peal their foursquare hymn. Six o'clock—time for all delinquent Appiches to head home for dinner. The day's yield is twelve scribbled pages, thirty-six time-keyed photos, and half a theory, none of which would earn him a broken yo-yo on the open exchange.

All autumn long, whenever he isn't in school, mowing lawns, or working at the soft-serve, he studies ants. He plots graphs and draws charts. His respect for the cleverness of ants grows without limit. Flexible behavior in the face of changing conditions: What else can you call it but wicked smart?

At year's end, he enters the district science fair. *Some Observations of Ant Colony Behavior and Intelligence.* There are better-looking efforts throughout the hall, and ones where the student's dad has clearly done all the science. But none of the other entrants has looked at a thing the way he has.

The judges ask, "Who helped you with this?"

"No one," he says, with maybe too much pride.

"Your parents? Your science teacher? An older brother or sister?"

"My sister gave me the nail polish."

"Did you get the idea from somebody? Did you copy an experiment that you aren't citing?"

The thought that such an experiment might already have been carried out crushes him.

"You made all those measurements yourself? And you started four months ago? During *vacation*?"

His eyes fill with tears. He shrugs.

The judges award him no medal—not even a bronze. They say it's because he has no bibliography. A bibliography is a required part of the formal report. Adam knows the real reason. They think he stole. They can't believe a kid worked for months on an original idea, for no reason at all except the pleasure of looking until you see something.


IN SPRING, his sister Leigh goes down to Lauderdale with several girl-friends for spring break. On the second night of vacation, outside a beach-front clam shack, she gets into a red convertible Ford Mustang with a guy she met three hours earlier. No one ever sees her again.

His parents are frantic. They fly down to Florida twice. They scream at law officials and spend lots of money. Months pass. There are no leads. Adam realizes there never will be any. Whoever has taken his sister is shrewd, meticulous, human. Intelligent.

Leonard Appich won't give up. "You all know Leigh. You know how she is. She's run away again. We're not holding any service until we know for sure what happened to her."

*Know for sure*. They know. Adam's mother throws Leigh's words from the previous spring back in the man's face. *You've had it out for me since before I was born*. Patterns rise up, and she grabs at them. "You planted an elm for her, when they'd been dying everywhere for years? What were you *think-ing*? You never did like her, did you? And now she's raped and lying dead in a landfill, and we'll never know where!"

Lenny breaks her elbow, by accident. In self-defense, he keeps telling anyone who'll listen. That's when Adam realizes: Humankind is deeply ill. The species won't last long. It was an aberrant experiment. Soon the world will be returned to the healthy intelligences, the collective ones. Colonies and hives.

. . .

JEAN TAKES HER BROTHERS into the forest preserve. There, the three of them hold the service their father won't allow. They build a bonfire and tell stories. Twelve-year-old Leigh, running away from home after Dad slapped her for whispering *asshole* under her breath. Fourteen-year-old Leigh, punishing them all for hating her by refusing to speak to anyone except in her sophomore Spanish. Eighteen-year-old Leigh, playing Emily Webb, coming back to Earth to relive her twelfth birthday. A brilliant ghost who had the whole high school in tears.

Adam takes the elm plaque he inscribed for his sister and throws it on the fire. *A tree is a passage between earth and sky.* Elm isn't a great firewood, but it burns without too much persuasion. All his botched words turn perfect and vanish into the general black—first *tree*, then *passage*, then *earth*, then *sky*.

The science fair judges cure Adam Appich of any desire to keep a field notebook on anything at all. He outgrows ants. He puts the Golden Guides by the curb. The secret museum treasures hidden from his mother's vacuum cleaner he now gladly trashes. Childish things.

High school is four dark years in the bunker. He's not without friends or fun. In fact, there's a surplus of both. Nights getting smashed and skinny-dipping in the reservoir above town. Entire weekends in basements pitching dice and arguing over esoteric role-playing rules with obese, anemic boy-men who tote suitcases full of collectible trading cards. The game's monsters are like natural history gone wrong. Giant bugs. Killer trees. The point of the game is to extinguish them all.

"Testosterone," his father explains. He's now afraid of the hulking boy, and Adam knows it. "Storms of hormones, and no port in sight."

Though Adam wants to hurt the man, his father is not wrong. There are girls, but they baffle him. They pretend to be stupid, by way of protective coloration. Passive, still, and cryptic. They say the opposite of what they mean, to test if you can see through them. Which they want. Then resent when you do.

He organizes raids on the neighboring high school, intricate nighttime operations involving miles of toilet paper tossed up in the branches of lindens. The strips dangle for months like giant white flowers. He passes under them on his mountain bike, feeling like a genius guerrilla artist.

He and a friend map the school, the supermarket, the branch bank. They plan what kind of hardware they'd need to make a heist. The plans get elaborate. They price weapons, just for grins. It's a game for Adam: logistics, planning, resource management. For his friend, it's one step away from religion. Adam watches the precarious boy, fascinated. A seed that lands upside down in the ground will wheel—root and stem—in great U-turns until it rights itself. But a human child can know it's pointed wrong and still consider the direction well worth a try.

HE GROWS GOOD at figuring the absolute minimum work required to pass any class. No adult gets anything from him but what he's required to give. The plummeting report cards baffle his mother. "What's going on, Adam? You're better than that!" But her voice is flat and defeated. Jean sees him going down. She scolds, jokes, and pleads. But then she heads to college, in Colorado. There's no one left to make him answer for himself.

Leigh never comes back. Adam's father's search tapers off to nothing. His mother starts nursing quantities of codeine. Soon enough, she's on a circuit of drugstores across many towns. She stops cooking and cleaning house. Adam's lifestyle isn't impacted. He adapts and evolves. Survival of those who survive.

A JOKE OFFER from a friend—*Three bucks if you do my algebra*—and he finds himself with easy pocket money. So easy, in fact, that he starts to advertise. Assignments completed in any subject except foreign languages, at any desired quality, as fast as you need them. It takes a while to find the right price point, but when he does, the clients fall in line. He experiments with volume discounts and pay-ahead plans. Soon he's the proprietor of a successful small business. His parents are relieved to see him doing home-work again, for hours each night. They love that he stops bugging them for cash. It's like win-win-win. Morning in America, with the free market doing its thing, and Adam goes to bed each night thankful to have been born into an entrepreneurial culture.

He's quick and conscientious. Every assignment is ready by deadline. Soon he has built the most reliable and respected cheating franchise at Hard-ing High. The business makes him almost popular. He socks away most of the cash. There's nothing he can spend it on that gives him more pleasure than looking at the balance accumulating in his passbook savings account and calculating dollars per duped educator.

Demanding work does requires sacrifice, however. He's forced to learn all kinds of interesting things that shouldn't interest him.

EARLY IN THE FALL of senior year, Adam's in the public library crank-ing out a psychology paper for a classmate who understands the bipedal beast even less than he does. *Cite at least two books.* Whatever. He rises from his carrel and wanders to the proper spot in the library shelves. Hours of work leave him cross-eyed. In the low library light, the books look like town houses for pipe-cleaner people.

One spine jumps out at him. Its electric lime letters scream out against a black field: *The Ape Inside Us,* by Rubin M. Rabinowski. Adam pulls down the hefty volume and plops into a nearby armchair. The book falls open to an image of four cards:

Beneath, a caption reads:
> *Each of these cards has a letter on one side and a number on the*

*other. Suppose someone tells you that if a card has a vowel on one side, then it has an even number on the other. Which card or cards would you need to turn over to see if the person is right?*

He perks up. Things with clean, concise, right answers are antidotes to human existence. He solves the puzzle fast, with total confidence. But when he checks his solution, it's wrong. At first he thinks the printed answer is in error. Then he sees what should have been obvious. He tells himself he's just wiped out from hours of working on other kids' assignments. He wasn't focusing. He would have gotten it, if he'd been paying attention.

He reads on. The book claims that only four percent of typical adults get the problem right.

What's more, almost three quarters of people who miss the problem, when shown the simple answer, make excuses about why they failed.

He sits in the armchair, explaining to himself why he has just done what almost every other human being also does. Below the first row of cards, there's another:

Now the caption says:

*Each one of these cards stands for a person in a bar. One side shows their age and the other shows their drink. If the legal drinking age is 21, which card or cards do you need to turn over to see if everyone is legal?*

The answer is so obvious Adam doesn't even need to find it. He gets it right this time, along with three-quarters of typical adults. Then he reads the punch line. The two problems are the same. He laughs out loud, drawing looks from the gray-haired, late-night public library crowd. People are an idiot. There's a big old OUT OF ORDER sign hanging from his species' pride-and-joy organ.

Adam can't stop reading. Again and again, the book shows how so-called *Homo sapiens* fail at even the simplest logic problems. But they're fast and fantastic at figuring out who's in and who's out, who's up and who's down, who should be heaped with praise and who must be punished without mercy. Ability to execute simple acts of reason? Feeble. Skill at herding each other? Utterly, endlessly brilliant. Whole new rooms open up in Adam's brain, ready to be furnished. He looks up from the book to see a library closing down and throwing him out.

At home, he reads on into the night. He picks up again, through breakfast the next morning. He almost misses the bus. He fails to deliver the day's homework to his clients. It's the first blow to his good name since he set up the cheating business. He holds *The Ape Inside Us* under his desk during the first three periods, educating himself on the sly. He finishes before lunch, then starts it all over again.

The book is so elegant that Adam kicks himself for not having seen the truth long before. Humans carry around legacy behaviors and biases, jerry-rigged holdovers from earlier stages of evolution that follow their own obsolete rules. What seem like erratic, irrational choices are, in fact, strategies created long ago for solving other kinds of problems. We're all trapped in the bodies of sly, social-climbing opportunists shaped to survive the savanna by policing each other.

For days, the book carries him along in a happy stupor. Armed with the patterns the book reveals, he imagines himself running experiments on every girl in school, a dollop of nail polish on their shoe-heels to keep track of their comings and goings. The best part is Chapter 12, "Influence." Had he read it as a freshman, he'd be school president-for-life. The mere idea that human behavior—his lifelong nemesis—possesses hidden but knowable patterns as beautiful as anything he once witnessed in insects makes his insides sing. He feels lighter and righter than he has since his sister disappeared.

. . .

WHEN THE TIME COMES to take the college entrance exams, he nails them. His analytical skills top out in the ninety-second percentile. In grade-point ranking, however, he barely manages to sneak into slot 212 in a graduating class of 269. No self-respecting college will even consider him.

His father waves him off. "Go to JC for two years. Wipe the slate clean and start again."

But Adam doesn't need to wipe the slate. He just needs to show it to someone who can read between the chalky lines. He sits down at the dining room table one Saturday morning before winter break and composes a letter. It feels like entering observations into his boyhood field notebooks. Outside the window are what remain of the children's trees. He remembers how he once believed in some magic link between the trees and the children they were planted for. How he made himself into a maple—familiar, frank, easy to identify, always ready to bleed sugar, flowering top-down in the first sunny days of spring. He loved that tree, its simplicity. Then people made him into something else. He takes his pen to the top of the page and writes:

> Professor R. M. Rabinowski
> Department of Psychology
> Fortuna College, Fortuna, California
>
> Dear Professor Rabinowski,
>     Your book changed my life.

He tells a full-fledged conversion narrative: wayward boy saved by a chance encounter with brilliance. He describes how *The Ape Inside Us* awakened something in him, although the awakening has come, perhaps, too late. He says how he failed to take school seriously until the book fell into his lap, and how he may now have to spend years clearing his record at community college until he gets the chance to study psychology at a serious institution. No matter, he writes. He is in the professor's debt, and as Rabinowski himself says, on page 231: "Kindness may look for something in return, but that doesn't make it any less kind." Perhaps unlooked-for kindness along the way might yet shorten the path ahead.

Outside the window, his maple catches a breeze. Its branches scold him. He'd turn scarlet for shame, if he wasn't desperate. He forges on, larding the letter with half a dozen techniques picked up from Chapter 12, "Influence." His words of thanks contain four of the top six releasers for producing action patterns in someone else: reciprocity, scarcity, validation, and appeal to commitment. He hides the evidence of his begging under another trick gleaned from Chapter 12:

> If you want a person to help you, convince them that they've already helped you beyond saying. People will work hard to protect their legacy.

It stuns his parents but doesn't entirely shock Adam when a return letter shows up at the house from the author of *The Ape Inside Us*. Professor Rabinowski writes that Fortuna College is a small, alternative school for unconventional students seeking an intense, questioning approach to education. The admission process places no great store on high school transcripts but looks for other evidence of special motivation. And while he makes no guarantees, Professor Rabinowski promises that Adam's application will be given serious consideration. Adam need only write the strongest entrance essay that he can.

Clipped to the formal letter is an unsigned index card. In wild and spooky blue-inked scrawl, someone has printed, "Don't ever blow smoke up my ass again."

# RAY BRINKMAN AND
# DOROTHY CAZALY

THEY'RE NOT HARD TO FIND: two people for whom trees mean almost nothing. Two people who, even in the spring of their lives, can't tell an oak from a linden. Two people who have never given woods a second thought until an entire forest marches for miles across the stage of a tiny black-box theater in downtown St. Paul, 1974.

Ray Brinkman, junior intellectual property lawyer. Dorothy Cazaly, stenographer for a company that does work for his firm. He can't stop watching her as she takes depositions. The silent, fluid beauty of her manual ballet boggles him. Appassionata Sonata, slewing out of her miming fingers.

She catches him gazing, and dares him, with a glance, to own up. He does. It's easier than dying from acute distant admiration. She agrees to go out with him, if she can pick the venue. He signs off on the deal, never imagining the hidden clauses. She picks an audition for an amateur production of *Macbeth*.

Why? She says *no reason*. A lark. A whim. Freedom. But there is, of course, no freedom. There are only ancient prophecies that scry the seeds of time and say which will grow and which will not.

For *amateur* production, read *terrifying*. The audition is like monster-hunting without a flashlight. Neither has been in a play since high school. But they screw their courage to the sticking-place, and both end up squeezing a blackly masochistic, white-knuckle fun out of the evening.

"Whoa," he says, walking her from the hall. "What in the world was *that*?"

"I've always wanted to pretend I could act. I just needed an accomplice."

"So what do we do for an encore?"

"You pick."

"How about something a little less nerve-crushing, next time?"

"Ever gone cliff diving?"


HERE'S THE THING: they both get cast. *Of course* they get cast. They were cast already, before they tried out. That's how myths work. Macduff, and Lady Macbeth.

Ray calls up Dorothy in a total panic. Like he's been playing with his father's shotgun and it just went off. "We don't actually have to take the parts, right?"

"It's *community* theater. I think they're counting on you."

She knows already the precise worst button she can press in him, right there in their first week together. Criminally responsible, this man. Pathologically accountable to the hopes and expectations of his kind. And the lady, reckless enough for ten of him. She pretty much tells him: no *Macbeth*, no more dates. They take the parts.

Dorothy is a natural. But Ray: even the casting director, the night of the first read-through, thinks she may have made a terrible mistake. Dorothy watches the man, awed. He's the best worst actor she has ever seen. He just speaks his lines, with a lanky gall and astonishing naïveté, as if he's putting forward the case for his own existence in front of the End of Time Debate Club.

She raids the public library for books on method acting and getting into character. He falls back on stoicism. "I'll be lucky to memorize all the lines."

After two weeks, he's almost competent. After three, something more starts to happen.

"No fair," she says. "Have you been practicing?"

He has been, in ways he just now discovers. He never realized it before, but the law itself is theater, long before you take anyone to court. Ray has one gift: to play himself with a fearsome intensity. This will make him, over the coming years, a highly successful litigator of copyright and patent. Now that simple gift turns his Macduff weirdly hypnotic. By standing still in deadpan earnestness, he seems to tap into the planetary will.

Dorothy's main superpower, in place since girlhood, is being able to read every muscle around a person's mouth and eyes and tell with perfect accuracy whether he's lying. This does nothing for her stenography or her Lady Macbeth. But it does make her want to test the outer limits of this man's innocence. Three nights a week of rehearsals for five weeks, and she's convinced: Ray Brinkman would indeed leave his wife and kids alone and unprotected, out in a castle in the sticks, just to save his godforsaken country.

The staging is very seventies. Very Watergate. Admission is free, and the community gets its money's worth. For three nights running, Lady Macbeth goes down in spectacular flames. For three nights running, Macduff and his men, kitted out as trees, help the forest migrate from Birnam Wood all the way to Dunsinane. Trees actually journey across the stage. Oak, hearts of oak, armies and navies of oak, post and lintel of the house of history. The men hold great branches, and while unwitting Macbeth declares his prophecy-ensured safety, his attackers dance so slowly across the boards they seem not to move at all. And each night, Ray has almost forever to think: *Something is happening to me. Something heavy, huge, and slow, coming from far outside, that I do not understand.*

He has no idea. The thing that comes for him is a genus more than six hundred species strong. Familiar, protean, setting up camp from the tropics all the way up through the temperate north: the generalist emblem of all trees. Thick, clotted, craggy, but solid on the earth, and covered in other living things. Three hundred years growing, three hundred years holding, three hundred years dying. Oak.

The oaks swear him in as temporary deputy in their fight against the human monster. Good Macduff hides behind their cut branches (*Many living things were harmed in the making of this production*), hoping he'll remember his next lines, praying he'll defeat the usurper again tonight, and marveling at the strange, irregular, lobed shapes fleshing out his camouflage like the letters of an alphabet from outer space, each glyph shaped by something that looks for all the world like deliberation. He can't read the text on his banner. It's written by a thing with five hundred million root tips. It says, Oak *and* door *come from the same ancient word.*

After the closing night party, Ray and Dorothy end up in bed. Theater and Dorothy's whim have held them in suspended thrall for that long. Then, a cliff dive for him, after all. It's dark enough to hush the worst of their many inner sirens and alarms. But six inches from his candlelit face, she can still make out the smallest muscles around his eyes.

"How do you feel about your parents? Have you ever had racist thoughts? Did you ever shoplift?"

"Am I on trial? Why are you torturing me?"

"No reason." Her whole face twitches like a Mexican jumping bean.

He rolls onto his back and looks up to the ceiling. "I've never been onstage like that before. It makes you feel like you're talking to the gods."

"Doesn't it, just?"

And then: "Do you think we're going somewhere?"

She scrambles up on her elbow to find his face. "We? You mean, like, humanity?"

"Sure. But you and me, first. Then everybody."

"I don't know. How the hell should I know?"

He hears her anger, and thinks he understands. His hand pats about on the sheets, feeling for hers. "I feel like this was supposed to happen."

"*This?*" Merciless Lady M. Mocking. "Destiny, you mean?"

It's like he's frozen-floating across the stage in time-lapse again, disguised as Birnham Wood. "I earn a good salary. I'll be all paid up on my loans in five more years. They'll make me a partner before you know it."

Her eyes squeeze shut. In a few years, the bombs will be falling, the Earth will be spent, and the only humans left will be fleeing the planet in rockets to nowhere.

"You wouldn't have to work, if you didn't want to."

She sits up. Her hand presses down on his sternum, pinning him. "Hang on. Oh, god. Are you *proposing?*"

He cocks his head and dares her. Heart of oak.

"Because we slept together? *Once?*" She doesn't need her special gift to see how badly the mockery stings him. "Wait. Am I your *first?*"

He holds still, frozen, halfway across the stage. "Maybe you should've asked me that two hours ago."

"Look. I mean . . . marriage?" The mere word in her mouth turns baroque and alien. "I can't get married. I'm supposed to . . . I don't know! Go backpacking in South America for two years. Move to the Village and take drugs. Get involved with a light plane pilot who moonlights for the CIA."

"I have a backpack. They have patent lawyers in New York. I'm not sure about the pilot part."

She's ambushed and laughing and shaking her head. "You're *joking.* You're *not* joking. What the hell?" She does a back dive onto the pillows. "What the hell, I say. Lead on, Macduff!"

They have each other again. This time, it's binding. In the stillness of afterward, she can feel the wet on his temple. "Is something wrong?"

"Nothing."

"I don't scare the crap out of you?"

"No."

"You're lying to me. First time."

"Perhaps."

"But you love me."

"Perhaps."

" 'Perhaps?' What the hell is that supposed to mean?"

Something huge and heavy and slow and far away and altogether unknown to him begins to say what it might mean. And then he proceeds to show her.

. . .

RAY'S PREDICTION COMES TRUE. It takes just five years to pay off all his debts. He makes partner soon after. He's brilliant at what he does: nailing intellectual property thieves and getting them to cease and desist or pay up. His earnestness is hypnotic, his commitment to fairness and stability. *You're profiting from something that belongs to someone else. The world can't work that way.* Almost always, the other side settles out of court.

Dorothy's prediction, for her part, is not exactly wrong. The bombs are indeed falling. But mid-sized bombs, all over the globe, small enough that nobody has to flee the planet, just yet. She, for one, keeps the day job, transcribing the words of people under oath as fast as they can speak. The secret is not to care what the words mean. Paying attention decimates your speed.

Half a dozen years pass as if a single season. They break up. They get re-engaged, while playing the romantic leads in an Alter Ego Community Theater production of *You Can't Take It with You.* Her feet go stone-cold again. They recommit, after walking five hundred miles of the Appalachian Trail together in twenty-eight days. Then again by hand signals, while skydiving.

Their average run is five months. The fourth time she breaks things off, it's so traumatic she quits her job and disappears for weeks. Her friends won't tell Ray anything. He begs them for news, a phone number—anything. He tasks them with long letters, which they say they can't deliver. Then a note from her, neither apologizing nor cruel. She won't say where she is. She simply lays out the deathly claustrophobia, the killing panic she feels at signing a legally binding document determining the bearing and conduct of the rest of her life.

> *I want to be with you. You know that. That's why I keep saying yes. But a legal business deal? Rights and owner- ship? Oh Ray, if only you were a discredited doctor or a bankrupt businessman. A shyster real estate agent. Any- thing but a* property *lawyer.*

He writes to the return address—a post office box in Eau Claire. He tells her that slavery is outlawed everywhere in the world. She'll never be anyone's property. He won't change his career for her; copyright and patent law is what he knows. It's necessary work, the engine of the world's wealth, and he's good at it. Maybe better than good. But if he must choose between giving up the idea of marriage or giving up the idea of acting in another amateur theatrical production with her, well, nolo contendere.

> *Just come back, and we'll live together in sin with two separate cars, two separate bank accounts, two separate houses, two separate wills.*

Shortly after he mails the letter, she shows up on the doorstep of his bungalow, late at night, with two tickets to Rome. It raises some questions at his office, but he leaves with her on a non-honeymoon two days later. On the third night in the Eternal City, with the prosecco flowing freely and all the pretty lights, and the crumbling antiquities, and the damn street music, and the lime trees with their glorious crowns and white lights strung all through their graceful boughs, she asks him—"What the hell, hey, Ray?"—if he will be her lawfully acquired chattel, contractually bound to her forever. They end up chucking coins over their left shoulders into the Trevi Fountain. Not an original idea, and they probably owe someone royalties.

They make it back to St. Paul in time for Octoberfest. They swear to each other never to tell anyone, to deny everything. But their friends guess, the moment the couple steps out smirking in public together. What happened to you two in Rome? *Nothing special.* No one needs any superpower in reading facial muscles to know they're lying through their teeth. Did you get thrown in jail or something? Did you get married? You two got married, didn't you? You're *married*!

And it makes no earthly difference in the world. Dorothy moves back in. She insists on scrupulous bookkeeping, splitting every shared expense down the exact middle. But something in the back of her brain thinks, as she drifts through his lovely library and dining room and sunroom: *When it happens, when it's time to brood, when I turn all weird and hot to propagate, then all of this will belong to* my babies*!*

On their first anniversary, he writes her a letter. He puts some time into the wording. He can't possibly speak the words, so he leaves them on the breakfast table when he goes to work.

> *You have given me a thing I could never have imagined,*
> *before I knew you. It's like I had the word "book," and*
> *you put one in my hands. I had the word "game," and you*
> *taught me how to play. I had the word "life," and then you*
> *came along and said, "Oh! You mean this."*

He says there's nothing on Earth he can give to her, for their anniversary, to thank her for what she has given him. Nothing, except for a thing that grows. *Here's what I propose we do.* He doesn't know where he gets the idea. He has forgotten the slow, heavy, outside prophecies that came over him on his first amateur theatrical outing, when he had to play a man who had to play a tree.

Dorothy reads the words while driving herself to the courthouse for an afternoon of transcribing hearings.

> *Every year, as close to this day as we can, let's go to the*
> *nursery and find something for the yard. I don't know any-*
> *thing about plants. I don't know their names or how to care*
> *for them. I don't even know how to tell one blurry green*
> *thing from another. But I can learn, as I've had to re-learn*
> *everything—myself, my likes and dislikes, the width and*
> *height and depth of where I live—again, alongside you.*
>
> *Not everything we plant will take. Not every plant will*
> *thrive. But together we can watch the ones that do fill up*
> *our garden.*

As she reads, her eyes cloud, and she drives up onto the curb and wraps the car around a parkway linden wide enough to destroy her front grille.

Now, the linden, it turns out, is a radical tree, as different from an oak as a woman is from a man. It's the bee tree, the tree of peace, whose tonics and teas can cure every kind of tension and anxiety—a tree that cannot be mistaken for any other, for alone in all the catalog of a hundred thousand earthly species, its flowers and tiny hard fruit hang down from surfboard bracts whose sole perverse purpose seems to be to state its own singularity. The lindens will come for her, starting with this ambush. But the full adoption will take years.

She requires eleven stitches to close the gash above her right eye, where the steering wheel cut her open. Ray rushes from his office to the hospital. In his panic, he crunches the rear right bumper of a doctor's BMW in the hospital parking garage. He's in tears when they lead him into surgery. She's sitting up in a chair with bandages wrapped around her head, trying to read things. Everything is double. The brand name on the gauze wrappings looks to her like *Johnson & Johnson & Johnson & Johnson*.

Her eyes light up to see him—both of him. "RayRay! Honey! What's wrong?" He rushes to her, and she recoils in confusion. Then she gets it. "Hush. It's okay. I'm not going anywhere. Let's plant something."

# DOUGLAS PAVLICEK

 THE COPS ARRIVE on the landing of Douglas Pav-
licek's tiny efficiency in East Palo Alto just before break-
fast. The actual police: a nice touch. What you might call
realism. They charge him with armed robbery and read
him his Miranda. Violations of Penal Codes 211 and 459.
He can't help smirking as they frisk and handcuff him.

"You think this is funny?"

"No. No, of course not!" Well, maybe a little.

It gets less funny when the neighbors come out on their balconies in
their pajamas as the cops perp-walk Douggie to the waiting squad car. He
smiles—*It's not what you think*—but the effect is mitigated a little, what with
his hands cuffed behind his back.

One of the officers shoehorns him into the back seat. The rear doors have
no handles. The cops call in his arrest on the radio. Everything very *Naked
City*, although this perfect Central Peninsula August and the thought that
he's getting paid fifteen dollars a day brighten the sound track. He's nineteen, two years orphaned, recently laid off from his job as supermarket stock
boy, and living on his parents' life insurance. Fifteen bucks a day for two
straight weeks is a lot of dough, for doing nothing.

At the police station—the *real* police station—he's fingerprinted, deloused, and blindfolded. They throw him back in the car and drive him around. When they remove the blindfold, he's in prison. Warden's office, superintendent's office, and several cells. Chains on his legs. All very well thought out, convincing. He has no idea where he is, in real life. Some office building. The people running the show are improvising, same as he is.

All the guards and most of the prisoners are there already. Douggie becomes Prisoner 571. The guards are just Sir, with clubs and whistles, uniforms and sunglasses. They're a little too liberal with the sticks, for hourly volunteers. Getting into their roles, pleasing the experimenters. They strip Doug down and put him in a smock. They mean to hit his pride, but Douglas preempts them by having none. There's a "count"—roll call and ritual humiliation—several times that evening. Sloppy joes for dinner. It's better than what he's been eating.

Around lights-out, Prisoner 1037 gets a little truculent at the overdone theatrics. The guards smack him down. Clear already: there are good guards, tough guards, and crazy guards. Each slides down a grade when others are present.

As soon as Douggie—571—manages to doze off, he's ripped out of bed for another gratuitous count. It's two-thirty a.m. That's when things turn weird. He gets the idea that the experiment isn't about what they claim it's about. He realizes they're really testing something much scarier. But he only needs to survive fourteen days. A body can take two weeks of anything.

On day two, a tiff over dignity in Cell One blows out of control. It starts as a shoving match and escalates. Some prisoners—8612, 5704, and a couple of others—barricade themselves in the cell by swinging their beds sideways against the door. The guards call in reinforcements from the night shift. Young males shove each other and grapple over the bedframes. Someone starts to scream: "It's a simulation, dammit. It's a fucking simulation!"

Or maybe not. The guards crush the uprising with fire extinguishers, chain up the leaders, and throw them in the hole. Solitary. No dinner for the rebels. Eating, as the guards remind their captives, is a privilege. Douggie eats. He knows what hunger is. Number 571 isn't going hungry for the sake of a little amateur theater. The others can all go nuts, if that's how they want to pass the time. But nobody's keeping him from his hot meal.

The guards set up a privilege cell. If any prisoner wants to say what he knows about the insurrection, he can relocate his bunk to plusher quarters. Cooperators can wash and brush their teeth and even enjoy a special meal. Privilege is not something Prisoner 571 needs. He'll watch out for himself, but he's no snitch. In fact, none of the prisoners takes up the privilege cell offer. At first.

The guards begin routine strip searches. Smoking becomes a special privilege. Going to the bathroom becomes a privilege. It's shit buckets or hold it, for the next two days. There are grueling, hours-long, pointless chores. There are late-night counts. There's cleaning out other people's slop buckets. Anyone caught smirking must sing "Amazing Grace" with his arms flung out. Prisoner 571 is forced to do hundreds of push-ups for every little trumped-up offense.

The guard who all the prisoners call John Wayne says, "What if I told you to fuck the floor? Five seventy-one, you're Frankenstein. You, 3401, you're the Bride of Frankenstein. Okay, kiss, motherfuckers."

Nobody—not the guards, not the prisoners—ever breaks character. It's insane. These people are dangerous; even 571 can see that. All of them, out of control. And they're laying him low along with them. He doubts that he can make it two weeks, after all. Sitting in his efficiency reading the want ads with the lights turned low starts to seem pretty luxurious.

Some small incident during a count and Prisoner 8612 loses it. "Call my parents. Let me out of here!" But that's not possible. His term must last two weeks, like everybody's. He starts to rave. "This really is a prison. We're really prisoners."

They all see what 8612 is doing: feigning craziness. The bastard wants to escape the game and leave everyone else to shovel shit for however many days are left. Then the act becomes real.

"Jesus Christ, I'm burning up! I'm *fucked up* inside. I want out! Now!"

Doug has seen a guy go crazy once before, back in high school in Twin Falls. This one is number two. Just watching scrambles his own brain.

They take 8612 away. The warden won't say where. The experiment must stay intact. The experiment must extend itself. There's nothing 571 wants more than to get out himself. But he can't do that to the others. His fellow inmates would hate him forever, as he now hates 8612. It's sick—symptom of a little pride he didn't think he had—but he wants to keep 571's reputation intact. He doesn't want any university psychologist, peering through the two-way mirror and videotaping, saying, *Ah, that one—we got that one to crack, too.*

A priest comes to visit, a Catholic prison chaplain. A real one, from the outside. All the prisoners must go see him in the consultation cell. "What's your name?"

"Five seventy-one."

"Why are you here?"

"They say I committed armed robbery."

"What are you doing to secure your release?"

The question sinks down 571's spine and settles into his bowels. He's supposed to be doing something? And if he doesn't—if he fails to figure it out? Could they keep him in this hellhole beyond the agreed-on term?

The next day is shaky for all the prisoners. The guards play on their distress. They make the prisoners write letters home, but they dictate the words. *Dear Mom. I fucked up. I was evil.* One of them tears into 819 for being hapless, and the guy breaks down. The authorities have had it out for him since the barricade, and now they throw him in the hole. His sobs carry throughout the prison. The rest of the inmates are called out into the hallway for a count. The guards make them chant, *Prisoner 819 did a bad thing. Because of what he did, my shit bucket won't be emptied tonight. Prisoner 819 did a bad thing. Because of what he did . . .*

A new prisoner, 416—8612's replacement—organizes a hunger strike. He gets a couple prisoners to join him, but others slam him for stirring shit. When there's trouble, everybody suffers. Five seventy-one refuses to choose sides. He's not a joiner, but he's no Kapo, either. Everything's falling apart. The prisoners are turning on each other. He can't afford to get involved. He tells everyone he's nonaligned. But there is no nonaligned.

John Wayne threatens 416. "Eat the damn sausage, boy, or you are going to regret it." Four-sixteen throws the sausage on the floor, where it rolls around in the filth. Before anyone knows what's happening, he's shoved into the hole, the dirty sausage in his hand. "And you'll stay there until it's eaten."

There's a general announcement: If any prisoner wants to give up his blanket for tonight, 416 will be released. If no one does, 416 will spend the night in solitary confinement. Five seventy-one lies in bed, under his blanket, thinking: *This isn't life. It's just a fucking simulation.* Maybe he should fight back against the experimenters, screw with their expectations, turn into a holy Superman. But damn it: no one else does. Everyone's waiting for *him* to sleep cold tonight. He hates to disappoint them all, but he's not the one who told 416 to pull his dumbfuck stunt. They could all have bored each other to death for two weeks and everything would've been fine.

He lies there warm all night, but he doesn't sleep. He can't turn off the thoughts. He wonders: And if this were all real? If he were put away for two years, or ten, or two hundred? Locked up for eighteen years for manslaughter, like the drunken junior high teacher back in Townsend who smashed into his parents' Gremlin while they were coming back from line dancing? Put away behind bars, like the invisible millions across this country who he's never thought twice about? He'd be nothing. He wouldn't even be 571. The real authorities could turn him into anything at all.

Next morning brings a hasty meeting. The warden and superintendent are summoned by the higher powers. Some big-brained scientist in a position of authority at last wakes up and realizes people can't do this. The whole experiment is fucking criminal. All the prisoners are to go free, pardoned early, sprung from a nightmare that has lasted only six days. *Six days.* It doesn't seem possible. Five seventy-one barely remembers what he was, a week ago.

The experimenters debrief everyone before turning them out into the world. But the victims are way too keyed up for reflection. The guards defend themselves while the prisoners go apeshit with anger. Douggie, too—*Douglas Pavlicek*—jabs his finger in the air. "The people who ran this—the so-called psychologists—should all be locked up for ethics violations." But he didn't give up his blanket. He will now, forever, be the guy who wouldn't take sides and didn't surrender his blanket, even in a tame little two-week playact experiment.

He comes up out of the dungeon into the brilliant, beautiful Central Peninsula air. A sweet little breeze smelling of jasmine and Italian stone pine goes down his shirt and ruffles his hair. He knows where he is now: the Psych Building, on the robber baron's campus. Stanford. Land of knowledge, cash, and power, with its endless tunnel of palms and the intimidating stone arcades. That fat-cat monastery where he has always been afraid to walk, or even run an errand, for fear that somebody will arrest him as an imposter.

They give him his check for ninety bucks and drive him back to his efficiency in East Palo Alto. He holes up in his private bunker, eating Fritos stewed in Pabst and watching television on a tiny black-and-white with crumpled tinfoil horns for antennae. It's there, three weeks later, that he sees a broadcast about the hundred-some U.S. helicopters lost in a bungled operation in Laos. He didn't even know the U.S. was *in* Laos. He sets his can of beer on the spool table and has the distinct impression that he's leaving a water-ring stain on someone's pine coffin.

He stands up light-headed, feeling like he did the night 416 spent in the hole. He runs his fingers through the lush curls that will decamp from his skull early and en masse. Something is distinctly fucked up in the status quo, and that includes him. He doesn't want to live in a world where some twenty-year-olds die so that other twenty-year-olds can study psychology and write about fucked-up experiments. He's perfectly aware that the war is lost. But that changes nothing. The next morning, he's out in front of the recruiting center on Broadway when they open. Steady work, and honest at last.

TECHNICAL SERGEANT DOUGLAS PAVLICEK flies two hundred–plus trash hauler missions in the years following his enlistment. Loadmaster on a C-130, he balances up planes with tons of barrier material and Class A explosives. He puts ordnance on the turf under mortar fire so thick it froths the air. He fills outbound flights with deuce-and-a-half trucks, APCs, and pallets full of C-rations, loading up return flights with body bags. Anyone paying attention knows that the cause tanked long ago. But in Douglas Pavlicek's psychic economy, paying attention is nowhere near as important as staying busy. As long as he has work to fill his hours and his crewmates keep the radio on R&B, he doesn't care how late or soon they lose this pointless war.

His habit of blacking out from dehydration earns him the nickname Faint. He often forgets to drink—in the daytime, anyway. After sundown, in quadruped crawls down Jomsurang Road in Khorat or the sex mazes of Patpong and Petchburi in Bangkok, City of Angels, the rivers of Mekhong and vats full of Singha flow freely enough. The hooch makes him funnier, more honest, less of an asshole, more capable of holding expansive philosophical conversations with samlor drivers about the destiny of life.

"You go home now?"

"Not yet, my man. War's not over!"

"War over."

"Not for me it isn't. Last guy out still has to turn off the lights."

"Everyone say war over. Nixon. Kissinger."

"Fuckin' Kissinger, man. Peace Prize, my flaming ass!"

"Yes. Fuck Le Duc Tho. Everyone go home now."

Douggie no longer quite knows where that might be.

When not working, he gets high on Thai stick and sits for hours playing bass riffs along with Rare Earth and Three Dog Night. Or he'll prowl around the ruined temples—Ayutthaya, Phimai. There's something about the blasted chedis that reassures him. The toppled towers swallowed up by teak and ruined galleries left to crumble into scree. Jungle will get Bangkok, before too long. L.A., one day. And it's okay. Not his fault. Simple history.

The monster bases with their fleets of carpet bombers are closing down, and the thousand piggyback cottage industries of an addicted economy turn violent. All Thailand knows what's coming. They've been forced into this pact with the White Devil, and now it seems they've backed the wrong side. Yet the Thais Douglas meets show nothing but kindness to their destroyer. He's thinking of staying on when his tour and the endless war are over. He's been here for the good times, he should stick around and pay back, in the coming bad. He already knows a hundred words of Thai. *Dâai. Nít nói. Dee mâak!* For now, though, he's the shortest of short-timers, crewing the most reliable transport ever built. It's job security, for a few more months, anyway.

He and his crewmates prep the Herky Bird for yet another daily commute to Cambodia. They've been running resupply into Pochentong for weeks. Now resupply is turning into evacuation. Another month, maybe two—surely no longer. Cong are overrunning everything, like the summer rains.

He buckles himself into the jump seat and they're up, routine, above the still lush and verdant world, the patchwork rice terraces and encircling jungle. Four years ago, the route was still green all the way across the rivers to the South China Sea. Then came the shitstorms of rainbow herbicides, the twelve million gallons of that modified plant hormone, Agent Orange.

A few minutes into Rouge Land they're hit. Impossible; all their instruments had them clear the whole way into Phnom Penh. Flak rips into the cabin and cargo compartment. Forman, the flight engineer, catches shrapnel in the eye. A shell fragment slashes open the flank of the navigator, Neilson, and something warm, moist, and wrong comes spilling out of him.

The whole crew stays eerie-calm. They've queued up this particular horror one-reeler in their dreams for a long time, and here it is at last. Disbelief keeps them efficient. They fall in, attending to the wounded and inspecting the damage. Thin twin greasy black smoke trickles out of two engines, both starboard, which isn't good. In a minute, the trickles thicken into plumes. Straub swings the plane into a wicked bank, back toward Thailand and salvation. It's only a couple hundred clicks. A Hercules can fly on a single engine.

Then they start to drop, like a duck homing in on a lake. Smoke licks out from the back of the cargo bay. The word evacuates Pavlicek's mouth before he knows what it means: *Fire!* On a plane packed to the hull with fuel and ordnance. He fights his way back toward the spreading flames. He must get the pallets out of the bay before they ignite. He, Levine, and Bragg struggle with the tie-downs and the releases. A bleeding air duct, ruptured in the blast, pisses molten steam on him. The heat scalds the left side of his face. He doesn't even feel it. Yet.

They manage to jettison all the cargo. One of the pallets explodes on the way out of the plane. Shit detonates as it falls through the air. Then Pavlicek, too, is floating down to earth like a winged seed.

MILES BELOW and three centuries earlier, a pollen-coated wasp crawled down the hole at the tip of a certain green fig and laid eggs all over the involute garden of flowers hidden inside. Each of the world's seven hundred and fifty species of *Ficus* has its own unique wasp tailored to fertilize it. And this one wasp somehow found the precise fig species of her destiny. The foundress laid her eggs and died. The fruit that she fertilized became her tomb.

Hatched, the parasite larvae fed on the insides of this inflorescence. But they stopped short of laying waste to the thing that fed them. The males mated with their sisters, then died inside their plush fruit prison. The females emerged from the fig and flew off, coated in pollen, to take the endless game elsewhere. The fig they left behind produced a red bean smaller than the freckle on the tip of Douglas Pavlicek's nose. That fig was eaten by a bulbul. The bean passed through the bird's gut and dropped from the sky in a dollop of rich shit that landed in the crook of another tree, where sun and rain nursed the resulting seedling past the million ways of death. It grew; its roots slipped down and encased its host. Decades passed. Centuries. War on the backs of elephants gave way to televised moon landings and hydrogen bombs.

The bole of the fig put forth branches, and branches built their drip-tipped leaves. Elbows bent from the larger limbs, which lowered themselves to earth and thickened into new trunks. In time, the single central stem became a stand. The fig spread outward into an oval grove of three hundred main trunks and two thousand minor ones. And yet it was all still a single fig. One banyan.

· · ·

LOADMASTER PAVLICEK belly-flops through the blue, faultless air. The whoosh perplexes him. Disaster floats high above him in the cloud, no longer needing to be solved. He wants only to forgive the world, forget, and fall. The wind takes him where it will, halfway across Nakhon Ratchasima Province. As the earth rushes up to meet Douglas, he revives. He tries to steer the chute toward a rice terrace, topped with water and stippled in green bundles. But the toggles tangle, he overshoots, and in the mad collapse of the last hundred feet a sidearm strapped to his thigh discharges. The bullet enters below his kneecap, shatters his tibia, and tears out through the heel of his Leather Personnel Carriers. His scream pierces the air, and his body tumbles into the branches of the banyan, that one-tree forest that has grown up over the course of three hundred years just in time to break his fall.

Branches slash through his flight suit. His silks tangle him in a shroud. Between lacerations and burns, the gunshot wound and his pulverized leg, the airman passes out. He hangs twenty feet above the Earth in friendly territory, facedown and spread-eagled in the arms of a sacred tree bigger than some villages.

A baht bus full of pilgrims comes to pay devotion to the divine tree. They walk through the colonnade of aerial prop roots toward the central trunk, the trunk that crept down around a foster parent it choked to death ages ago. Set into that meandering bole is a shrine covered in flowers, beads, bells, prayer-covered papers, root-cracked statues, and sacred threads. The visitors parade toward the altar through the mazy pergola of spreading limbs, chanting in Pali. Their arms are full of joss sticks, stackable lunch tins filled with *gang gai*, and garlands of lotus blossom and jasmine. Three little children run ahead, singing a *lûk thûng* song as fast as their lips can move.

They draw near the shrine. They add their garlands to the rainbow of offerings already spidering across the branches. Then the sky falls and a missile crashes into the foliage above. Joss sticks, garlands, and lunch tins scatter at the impact. The shock knocks two pilgrims to the ground.

Chaos clears. The pilgrims look up. A giant *farang* hangs above their head, threatening to crash through the branches and fall the last short stretch to the ground. They call up to the foreigner. He doesn't respond. A debate begins on how to reach the man and cut him loose from the stranglehold of fig and parachute. Technical Sergeant Pavlicek wakes to several Thais standing on benches and prodding him. He thinks he's lying on his back, bobbing in a pool of atmosphere, while inverted people lean down and snatch at him from under the mirror surface. The pain from his leg and face crushes him. He coughs up a trickle of red spittle. He thinks: *I'm dead*.

*No*, a voice near his face corrects. *Tree saved your life*.

The three most useful syllables from his four years in Thailand bubble out of Douggie's mouth. *"Mâi kâo chai."* I don't understand. With that, he blacks out again and resumes the long, cyclic task of falling. This time, he keeps on tumbling as the Earth beneath him opens wide and takes him in. He falls deep underground, a long, luxurious drop into the kingdom of roots. He plunges beneath the water table, downward toward the beginning of time, into the lair of a fantastic creature whose existence he never imagined.

THE LOCAL CLINIC won't touch the leg of an American soldier. A staffer drives him to Khorat in a coral-colored Mazda with a Buddhist Wheel flag flying from its antenna. The car sounds like a choking khlong boat and trails a similar cloud of oily fumes in its wake. Pavlicek, drugged to the gills in the back seat, watches the green kilometers slide past. The low, lush landscape, the rolling hills. *In the waters there are fish; in the fields, there is rice*. The entire region will sink like a banana-leaf boat in a typhoon. Charlie will be sunning himself at the Siam Intercontinental, this time next year. A tree saved his life. It makes no sense.

When the injection from the clinic begins to wear off, Pavlicek begs the driver to kill him. The driver waves fingers around his mouth. "No *Angrit*."

Douglas's shinbone is cored. A doctor at the base in Khorat patches him up and ships him to Fifth Field, Bangkok. All his crewmates have survived—thanks in large part, the after-battle report says, to him. And he—he owes his own life to a tree.

.   .   .

THE AIR FORCE has no use for gimps. They give him crutches, an Air Force Cross—second highest medal for valor they hand out—and a free ticket back to SFO. He gets thirty-five bucks for the medal at Friendly's Pawn on Mission. He's not sure whether Friendly is helping a wounded vet or ripping him off blind. Nor does he much need to know. So ends loadmaster Douglas Pavlicek's efforts to help preserve the free world.

The universe is a banyan, its roots above and branches below. Now and then words come trickling up the trunk for Douglas, like he's still hanging upside down in the air: *Tree saved your life*. They neglect to tell him why.

LIFE COUNTS DOWN. Nine years, six jobs, two aborted love affairs, three state license plates, two and a half tons of adequate beer, and one recurring nightmare. With another fall ending and winter coming on, Douglas Pavlicek fetches the ball-peen hammer and smashes a row of potholes into the somewhat surfaced road that runs past the horse ranch and down toward Blackfoot. The goal is to slow people down so he can stand by the fence and see their faces a little. Come November, it may be some time before he'll have that pleasure again.

Douglas makes a Saturday of it, after the horses have been fed and read to. The scheme works. If the car slows down enough, he and the dog jog alongside until the driver either opens the window to say hello or pulls a gun. Couple of nice conversations that way, real give-and-take. One guy even stops for a minute. Douggie is aware that the behavior could appear somewhat eccentric, from the outside. But it's Idaho, and when you spend all your hours with horses, your soul expands a bit until the ways of men reveal themselves to be no more than a costume party you'd be well advised not to take at face value.

In fact, it's Douggie's growing conviction that the greatest flaw of the species is its overwhelming tendency to mistake agreement for truth. Single biggest influence on what a body will or won't believe is what nearby bodies broadcast over the public band. Get three people in the room and they'll decide that the law of gravity is evil and should be rescinded because one of their uncles got shit-faced and fell off the roof.

He has tried this idea out on others, without much success. But a bit of steel floating near his L4 vertebra, a small war chest of kiss-off pension, an Air Force Cross (pawned), a belated Purple Heart the back of which reminds him of a toilet seat, and the ability to make things with his hands all entitle him to strong opinions.

He still limps a bit, as he swings the hammer. His face has grown long and horsey, in unconscious imitation of the animals he tends. He lives by himself for seven months out of the year while the ranch's elderly owners make the circuit of their other hobbies and houses. Mountains hem him in on three sides. The only TV reception he can get is the ant races. And still a part of him wants to know if his few and private thoughts might in fact be ratified by someone, somewhere. The confirmation of others: a sickness the entire race will die of. And still he spends the second Saturday of October working the road in front of the house, hoping a good-sized pothole will slow folks down.

He's about to bag the checkpoint for the day and head back to the barn to talk Nietzsche with Chief Plenty Coups, the Belgian draft horse, when a red Dodge Dart crests the rise at somewhere near the speed of sound. Seeing the stretch of craters, the car slams into an admirably controlled skid. Douggie and the dog start their lope. The window is down by the time they come up alongside. A substantially redheaded woman leans out. They have much to talk about, Douglas sees. Destined to become friends. "Why is the road so messed up, just here?"

"Insurgents," Douglas explains.

She rolls up her window and speeds off, axles be damned. Not even a look. Game over. It takes something out of Douglas. Yet another last straw. Not even enough élan vital left over to read the next bit of *Zarathustra* to the horse.

That night the temperature drops into the teens, with sandpapery snow-flakes scouring his face like the whole great outdoors has turned into a California exfoliation parlor. He heads to Blackfoot, where he lays in a month's

worth of fruit cocktail, in case the drifts come early. He ends up at the bil-
liards bar, dispensing silver dollars like they're aluminum extrusion slugs.

"You must be ready to burn yourself in your own flame," he tells a fair
chunk of the clientele. Thus speaks former prisoner 571, who will forever
have to say that he didn't give his blanket to a fellow inmate when he should
have. He comes home after eighteen rounds of eight ball with more money
than he left with. Buries the cash in the north pasture, alongside the rest of
the nest egg, before the ground gets too cold to dig.

Winter here is longer than civilization's running tab. He whittles. He
builds things out of his pile of antlers: a lamp, a coat rack, a chair. He thinks
about the redhead and her glorious, unattainable kind. He listens to the
animals doing calisthenics in the attic. He makes it through *The Portable
Nietzsche* and continues with *The Complete Nostradamus*, burning it page by
page in the woodstove as he finishes each one. He grooms the hell out of the
horses, rides them daily by rotation in the indoor ring, and reads them *Paradise Lost*, since Nostradamus is too upsetting.

In the spring, he takes a .22 out into the brush. But he can't pull the trig-
ger, even on a lame hare. There's something wrong with him, he is aware.
When his employers return in early summer, he thanks them and quits. He's
not sure where he's going. Since his last flight as a loadmaster, such knowledge has been an impossible luxury.

He wants to keep heading west. Trouble is, the only strip still west of
him feels like going east again. And yet he's got his used but solid F100, new
tires, a fair amount of coin, his veteran's disability, and a friend in Eugene.
Beautiful back roads lead through the mountains all the way to Boise and
beyond. Life is as good as it has been since he fell out of the sky and into
the banyan. The truck radio drifts in and out through the canyons, like the
songs are coming from the moon. High lonesome blending into techno. He's
not listening anyway. He's trancing out on the miles-long walls of Engel-
mann spruce and subalpine fir. He pulls off onto the shoulder to relieve himself. Out here on these ridges, he could pee on the highway's center line and
humanity would be none the wiser. But savagery is a slippery slope, as he has
often read to the horses. He steps off the road and into the woods.

And there, flag at half mast, eyes toward the wilderness, waiting for his bladder to lift the lockdown, Douglas Pavlicek sees slabs of light through the trunks where there should be shadow all the way to the forest's heart. He zips and investigates. Walks deeper into the undergrowth, only deeper in turns out to be farther out. The shortest of hikes, and he pops out again into . . . you can't even call it a clearing. Call it the moon. A stumpy desolation spreads in front of him. The ground bleeds reddish slag mixed with sawdust and slash. Every direction for as far as he can see resembles a gigantic plucked fowl. It's like the alien death rays have hit, and the world is asking permission to end. Only one thing in his experience comes even close: the patches of jungle that he, Dow, and Monsanto helped to clear. But this clearing is much more efficient.

He stumbles back through the curtain of concealing trees, crosses the road, and peers through the woods on the other side. More moonscape stretches down the mountainside. He starts up the truck and drives. The route looks like forest, mile after emerald mile. But Douggie sees through the illusion now. He's driving through the thinnest artery of pretend life, a scrim hiding a bomb crater as big as a sovereign state. The forest is pure prop, a piece of clever artistry. The trees are like a few dozen movie extras hired to fill a tight shot and pretend to be New York.

He stops at a gas station to tank up. He asks the cashier, "Have they been *clear-cutting*, up the valley?"

The man takes Douggie's silver dollars. "Shit, yeah."

"And hiding it behind a little voter's curtain?"

"They're called beauty strips. Vista corridors."

"But . . . isn't that all national forest?"

The cashier just stares, like maybe there's some trick to the question's sheer stupidity.

"I thought national forest was protected land."

The cashier blows a raspberry big as a pineapple. "You're thinking national *parks*. National *forest's* job is to get the cut out, cheap. To whoever's buying."

Well—education run amok. Douglas makes it a practice to learn something new every day. This little datum will last him for some days to come. Anger starts to boil over, somewhere before Bend. It's not just the hundreds of thousands of acres that have vanished on him from one morning to its adjacent afternoon. He can accommodate the fact that Smoky Bear and Ranger Rick are socking away pensions paid by Weyerhaeuser. But the deliberate, simpleminded, and sickeningly *effective* trick of that highway-lining curtain of trees makes him want to smack someone. Every mile of it dupes his heart, just like they planned. It all looks so real, so virgin, so unspoiled. He feels like he's on the Cedar Mountain, from that *Gilgamesh*, which he found back in the ranch library and read to the horses last year. The forest from the first day of creation. But it turns out Gilgamesh and his punk friend Enkidu have already been through and trashed the place. Oldest story in the world. You could drive across the state and never know. That's the fury of the thing.

In Eugene, Douglas converts a hefty tower of silver dollars into a ride in a small prop plane. "Just take me in the biggest circle you can make for the money. I want to see what down here looks like from up there."

It looks like the shaved flank of a sick beast being readied for surgery. Everywhere, in all directions. If the view were televised, cutting would stop tomorrow. Back on the planet's concealing surface, Douglas spends three days on his buddy's couch, mute. He has no capital. No political savvy. No golden tongue. No economic sophistication or social wherewithal. All he has is a clear-cut in front of him, whether his eyes are open or closed, haunting him all the way to the horizon.

He makes some inquiries. Then he hires out his one and a half good legs to a contractor, planting seedlings back into the stripped lands. They kit him out with a shovel and a Johnny Appleseed bag filled with seedlings for which they charge him a few pennies each. And for each planted tree that's still alive in a month, they promise to pay him twenty cents.

Douglas-fir: America's most valuable timber tree, so, sure—why not grow a tree farm full of nothing but? Five new houses per acre. He knows he's slinging trees for middlemen to the same fuckers who cut down the primordial gods to begin with. But he doesn't have to vanquish the lumber industry or even get nature's revenge. He just needs to earn a living and undo the look of those cuts, a look that tunnels into him like a beetle into sapwood.

He spends his days traversing the silent, slop-filled, sloping dead zones. He drags himself across the scattered crap on all fours, losing his footing in the impenetrable slash, hauling himself forward by his claws over the chaos of roots, sticks, branches, limbs, stumps, and trunks, fibrous and shredded, left to rot in a tangled graveyard. He masters the art of a hundred different ways to topple. He stoops, makes a little wedge in the ground, stuffs in a seedling, and closes the hole with a loving nuzzle from his boot tip. Then he does that again. And again. In starbursts and scattered nets. Up hillsides and down denuded gullies. Dozens of times an hour. Hundreds of times a day. Thousands by thousands every week until his whole throbbing thirty-four-year-old body puffs out like it's filled with viper venom. Some days, he'd saw off his gimpy leg with a file if he had one handy.

He sleeps in tree-planter camps filled with hippies and illegals, tough, lovable people too tired at day's end to bother much with talk. A saying comes to him as he lies down at night, stiffened with pain—words he once read to his charges in his prior life as a ranch hand. *If you're holding a sapling in your hand when the Messiah arrives, first plant the sapling and then go out and greet the Messiah*. Neither he nor the horses could make much of it. Until now.

The smell of the cuts overwhelms him. Damp spice drawer. Dank wool. Rusty nails. Pickled peppers. Scents that return him to childhood. Aromas that inject him with inexplicable happiness. Smells that plunge him down to the bottom of the deepest well and hold him there for hours. Then there's the sound, like his ears are wadded up with pillow. The snarl of saws and feller bunchers, somewhere in the distance. A great truth comes over him: Trees fall with spectacular crashes. But planting is silent and growth is invisible.

Some days, dawn breaks in Arthurian mists. There are mornings when the chill threatens to kill him, noons when the heat knocks him on his semi-numbed butt. Afternoons so profligate with blue he lies on his back and stares upward until his eyes water. There come mocking and merciless rains. Rain the weight and color of lead. Shy rain, auditioning with stage fright.

Rain that leaves his feet sprouting moss and lichen. There were huge, spiked skeins of interwoven wood here once. They will come again.

Sometimes he works alongside other tree slingers, some of whom speak no language he recognizes. He meets hikers who want to know where the forests of their youth have gone. The seasonal *pineros* come and go, and the hard cores, like him, keep on. Mostly, it's him and the brute, blank, stripped-down rhythm of the work. Wedge, squat, insert, stand, and boot-tip seal.

They look so pitiful, his tiny Douglas-firs. Like pipe cleaners. Like props for a train set. From a distance, spread across these man-made meadows, they're a crew cut on a balding man. But each weedy stem he puts into the dirt is a magic trick eons in the making. He rolls them out by the thousands, and he loves and trusts them as he would dearly love to trust his fellow men.

Left alone—and there's the catch—left alone to the air and light and rain, each one might put on tens of thousands of pounds. Any one of his starts could grow for the next six hundred years and dwarf the largest factory chimney. It could play host to generations of voles that never go to ground and several dozen species of insects whose only desire is to strip their host bare. Could rain down ten million needles a year on its own lower branches, building up mats of soil that grow their own gardens high in the air.

Any one of these gangly seedlings could push out millions of cones over the course of its life, the small yellow males with their pollen that floats across entire states, the drooping females with their mouse tails sticking out from the coil of scales, a look he finds dearer than his own life. And the forest they might remake he can almost smell—resinous, fresh, thick with yearning, sap of a fruit that is no fruit, the scent of Christmases endlessly older than Christ.

Douglas Pavlicek works a clear-cut as big as downtown Eugene, saying goodbye to his plants as he tucks each one in. *Hang on. Only ten or twenty decades. Child's play, for you guys. You just have to outlast us. Then no one will be left to fuck you over.*

# NEELAY MEHTA

THE BOY WHO'LL HELP CHANGE humans into other creatures is in his family's apartment above a Mexican bakery in San Jose watching tapes of *The Electric Company*. In the kitchen, his Rajasthani mother chokes on clouds of ground black cardamom that clash with the cinnamon of *pan fino* and *conchas* trickling up from the bakery below. Outside, in the Valley of Heart's Delight, the ghosts of almond, cherry, pear, walnut, plum, and apricot trees spread for miles in every direction, trees only recently sacrificed to silicon. *The Golden State*, the boy's parents still call it.

The boy's Gujarati father comes up the stairs balancing a massive box on his broomstick body. Eight years before, he arrived in this country with two hundred dollars, a degree in solid-state physics, and a willingness to work for two-thirds of his white colleagues' salaries. Now he's employee number 276 at a firm rewriting the world. He stumbles up two flights underneath his load, humming his son's favorite song, the one they sing together at bedtime: *Joy to the fishes in the deep blue sea, joy to you and me.*

The child hears his steps and rushes to the landing. "Pita! What is it? A present for me?" He's a seven-year-old little Rajput who knows that most of the world is a present for him.

"Let me come in first, Neelay, please-thank-you. A present, yes. For both of us."

"I *knew* it!" The boy goose-steps around the coffee table hard enough to clack the steel balls on the pendulum toy. "A present for my birthday, eleven days early."

"But you have to help me build it." The father nurses the box onto the table, pushing the clutter to the floor.

"I'm a good helper." The boy counts on his father's forgetfulness.

"And that will take patience, which you are working on, remember?"

"I remember," the boy assures him, tearing at the box.

"Patience is the maker of all good things."

The father steers his son by the shoulders into the kitchen. Mother barricades the door. "Don't come in here. Very busy!"

"Yes, hello, too, *moti*. I got the computer kit."

"He tells me he got the computer kit."

"It's a *computer kit*!" the boy shrieks.

"Of course you got the computer kit! Now you two boys go play."

"It's not exactly playing, *moti*."

"No? Go work, then. Like me." The boy yips and tugs at his father's paw, pulling him back to the mystery. Behind them, the mother calls out, "One thousand words memory or four?"

The father blossoms. "Four!"

"Four thousand, of course. Now go away and make something good."

THE BOY POUTS when the green fiberglass backplane comes out of the box. "That's a computer kit? What use is *that*?"

His father grins the most foolish grin. The day is coming when *use* will be rewritten by this thing. He reaches into the box and turns up the heart of the matter. "Here it is, my Neelay. Look!" He holds up a chip three inches long. His head wags with pleasure. A look dangerously like pride spreads across his ascetic face. "Your father helped make this one."

"That's *it*, Pita? That's a *microprocessor*? It's like a bug with square legs."

"Oh, but think what we managed to put inside."

The boy looks. He remembers his father's bedtime stories from the last two years—tales of heroic project managers and adventuring engineers who suffer more mishaps than the white monkey Hanuman and his entire monkey army. His seven-year-old brain fires and rewires, building arborized axons, *dendrites*, those tiny spreading trees. He grins, cagey but uncertain. "Thousands and thousands of transistors!"

"Ach, my smart little man."

"Let me hold it."

"*Chh, chh, chh.* Careful. Static. We could kill this fellow before he even comes to life."

The boy blooms with luscious horror. "It's coming to *life?*"

"If . . . !" The paternal finger wags. "*If* we get all our solders right."

"Then what will it do, Dad?"

"What do you *want* it to do, Neelay?"

In front of the boy's widening eyes, the component turns into a jinn. "It does whatever we want?"

"We just have to figure out how to get our plans into its memory."

"We're putting our plans in *there?* How many plans will fit?"

The question stops the man, as simple ones sometimes do. He stands lost in the universe's weeds, hunched a little from the stronger gravity of the world he visits. "Someday, it may hold all the plans we have."

His son scoffs. "*This little thing?*"

The man scrambles up to the bookshelf, takes down the family scrapbook. A few flips, and he calls out in triumph. "Hee! Neelay. Come see."

The photo is small, green, and mysterious. A tangle of giant boa constrictors pour out of broken stone.

"See, *na?* A tiny seed fell on this temple roof. After centuries, the temple collapsed under the seed's weight. But this seed just keeps going and going."

Dozens of braided trunks and roots feed on the ruined walls. Tentacles drip down to fill the chinks and split stones open. A root thicker than Neelay's father's body creeps across a lintel and seeps like a stalactite into the doorway beneath. This vegetable probing horrifies the boy, but he can't look away. There's something so animal in the way the trunks find and follow the openings in the masonry. Like those other kinds of trunks—the trunks of elephants. They seem to know, want, find their way. The boy thinks: *Something slow and purposeful wants to turn every human building into soil*. But his father holds the photo in front of Neelay as if it proves the happiest destiny.

"You see? If Vishnu can put one of these giant figs into a seed *this big* . . ." The man leans down to pinch the tip of his son's pinkie. "Just think what we might fit into our machine."

THEY BUILD THE BOX over the next several days. All their solders are good. "Now, Neelay-*ji*. What might this little creature do?"

The boy sits frozen by possibility. They can release any process they want into the world, any kind of willful thing. The only impossible thing is how to choose.

His mother calls from the kitchen. "Teach it to cook the bhindi, please."

They make it say, "Hello World," in flashing coded lights. They make it say, "Happy Birthday, Neelay Dear." The words that father and son write arise and start *doing*. The boy has just turned eight, but in this moment, he comes home. He has found a way to turn his innermost hopes and dreams into active processes.

Right away, the creatures they make begin to evolve. A simple, five-command loop expands into a beautiful segmented structure of fifty lines. Little portions of program detach into reusable parts. Neelay's father hooks up a cassette tape player, for easy reloading of their hours of work in mere minutes. But the volume button must be set just right, or everything explodes with a read error.

Over the course of a few months, they graduate from four thousand bytes of memory to sixteen. Soon they leap again, to sixty-four. "Pita! More power than any human has ever had to himself in all of history!"

The boy loses himself in the logic of his will. He housebreaks the machine, trains it for hours like it's a little puppy. It only wants to play. Lob a cannon-ball over the mountain onto your enemy. Keep the rats out of your corn harvest. Spin the wheel of fortune. Seek and destroy every alien in the quadrant. Spell the word before the poor stick man hangs.

His father sits watching what he has unleashed. His mother bunches up her blouse-tails in her fist and berates all males within earshot. "Look at the boy! He just sits and types. He's like a sadhu, stoned on something. He's hooked, worse than paan-chewing." His mother's hectoring will go on for years, until her son's checks start rolling in. The boy never stops to answer. He's busy making worlds. Small ones, at first, but his.

There's a thing in programming called *branching*. And that's what Neelay Mehta does. He will reincarnate himself, live again as people of all races, genders, colors, and creeds. He'll raise decaying corpses and eat the souls of the young. He'll tent high up in the canopies of lush forests, lie in broken heaps at the bottom of impossibly high cliffs, and swim in the seas of planets with many suns. He'll spend his life in the service of an immense conspiracy, launched from the Valley of Heart's Delight, to take over the human brain and change it more than anything since writing.

There are trees that spread like fireworks and trees that rise like cones. Trees that shoot without a ripple, three hundred feet straight skyward. Broad, pyramidal, rounded, columnar, conical, crooked: the only thing they do in common is branch, like Vishnu waving his many arms. Among those spreaders, the wildest are the figs. Strangler trees that slip their sheaths around the bodies of others and swallow them, forming an empty cast around their decomposed hosts. *Peepal*, *Ficus religiosa*, the Buddha's Bo, their leaves tapering into exotic drip tips. Banyans that plump out like whole forests, with a hundred separate trunks fighting for a share of the sun. That temple-eating fig in his father's photo inhabits the boy. It will keep on growing faster with each new chunk of reusable code. It will keep on spreading, searching the cracks, probing all the possible means of escape, looking for new buildings to swallow. It will grow under Neelay's hands for the next twenty years.

Then it will flower to become the boy's belated thanks for an early birthday present. His homage to skinny little Pita, lugging that massive shipping box up the apartment stairs. His praise to Vishnu, known only through cheap newsprint Hindi comic books he could never read. His farewell to a species turning from animal into data. His effort to raise the dead and make them love him again. So many trunks growing downward from the same tree. The seed his father plants in him will eat the world.


THEY MOVE INTO A HOUSE down the valley along El Camino, in Mountain View. Three bedrooms: Such luxury confuses Babul Mehta. He still drives a twenty-year-old car. But every five months he upgrades the computers.

Ritu Mehta panics each time a new crate arrives. "When does it end? You're pauperizing us!"

The garage fills with so much old gear the car won't fit. But every component, however outdated, is a marvel of mind-boggling complexity created by a team of heroic engineers. Neither father nor son can throw even these obsolete miracles away.

The snail's pace of Moore's law tortures Neelay. He's starved for more RAM, more MIPS, more pixels. Waiting for the next barrier-breaking upgrade takes a tenth of his young life. Something inside these tiny, mutable components is waiting to get out. Or rather: there's something that these reticent things might be made to do, something humans haven't even imagined yet. And Neelay is on the verge of finding and naming them, if he can only find the next new magic words.

He skitters through the schoolyard like a traitor to childhood. He learns the shibboleths—the famous refrains from countless sitcoms, the hooks of pernicious little radio tunes, the bios of fifteen-year-old sexpot starlets he's supposed to be slayed by. But at night, his dreams fill not with playground battles or the day's take-down gossip but with visions of tight, lovely code doing more with less—bits of data passing from memory to register to accumulator and back in a dance so beautiful he can't begin to tell his friends. They wouldn't know how to see what he put in front of their eyes.

Every program tunnels into possibility. A frog tries to cross a busy street. An ape defends himself with barrel bombs. Under those ridiculous, blocky skins, creatures from another dimension pour into Neelay's world. And there's only the narrowest window of time in which to really *see* them, before these things that never were turn into things that have always been. In a few years, a kid like him will be given cognitive behavioral therapy for his Asperger's and SSRIs to smooth out his awkward human interactions. But he knows something certain, before almost anyone else: People are in for it. Once, the fate of the human race might have been in the hands of the well-adjusted, the social ones, the masters of emotion. Now all that is getting upgraded.

He still binges on old-school reading. At night, he pores over mind-bending epics that reveal the true scandals of time and matter. Sweeping tales of generational spaceship arks. Domed cities like giant terrariums. Histories that split and bifurcate into countless parallel quantum worlds. There's a story he's waiting for, long before he comes across it. When he finds it at last, it stays with him forever, although he'll never be able to find it again, in any database. Aliens land on Earth. They're little runts, as alien races go. But they metabolize like there's no tomorrow. They zip around like swarms of gnats, too fast to see—so fast that Earth seconds seem to them like years. To them, humans are nothing but sculptures of immobile meat. The foreigners try to communicate, but there's no reply. Finding no signs of intelligent life, they tuck into the frozen statues and start curing them like so much jerky, for the long ride home.

HIS FATHER IS THE ONLY PERSON Neelay will ever care for more than he cares for his creations. They understand each other, with no words spoken. Neither of them is happy unless they're sitting at a keyboard together. Cuffs of the neck and pokes in the ribs. Teasing and giggles. And always that gentle, head-tilted, singsong lilt: "Watch out, Neelay-*ji*. Be careful! Don't abuse your powers!"

The whole wide universe waits to be animated. Together, they must create possibilities out of the smallest atoms. The boy wants scales and songs, but his machines are mute. So Neelay and his father create their own sawtooth waves, clicking the little piezo speaker on and off so fast it starts to sing.

His father asks, "How is it that you have turned into a creature of such concentration?"

The boy doesn't answer. They both know. Vishnu has put all of living possibility into their little eight-bit microprocessor, and Neelay will sit in front of the screen until he sets creation free.

In middle age, the boy will be able to drag a cute icon and drop it into a tree diagram, producing in one flick of the wrist things that took him and his father six weeks of evenings in the basement together to create. But never again, this sense of the inconceivable, waiting to be conceived. In the redwood-trimmed lobby of the multimillion-dollar office complex paid for by a galaxy right next to this one, he'll hang, for many years, a plaque inscribed with the words from his favorite author:

*Every man should be capable of all ideas,*
*and I believe in the future he shall be.*

ELEVEN-YEAR-OLD NEELAY makes his Pita a kite for Uttarayan, the great kite festival. Not a real kite: something better. Something the two of them can fly together without anyone in Mountain View thinking they're ignorant cow-worshippers. He tries out a new technique for animating sprites he read about in a mimeographed hobby magazine called *Love at First Byte*. The idea is clever and beautiful. You rough out the kite in different sprites, then poke them directly into video memory. Then you shuffle them onto the screen like a flip-book. The first little flutter makes him feel like God.

His brainstorm is to write the program so that it can *itself* be programmed. Let the user key in the melody of his choice, with simple letters and numbers, then make the kite dance to that rhythm. The grandeur of the plan spins Neelay's head. His Pita will set his own kite dancing to a real Gujarati tune.

Neelay fills a loose-leaf binder for the project with notes, diagrams, and printouts of the latest version. His father picks up the binder, curious. "What is this, Mr. Neelay?"

"You don't touch that one!"

His father grins and bobs. Secrets and gifts. "Yes, Neelay, my master."

The boy works on the project when his father's not around. He takes it to school, that maze of halls full of organized torture that will inspire many a dungeon crawl of his later making. The black notebook binder looks official. He pretends to take notes in it, while working on his code. His teachers are too flattered to suspect.

His plan works like clockwork until fifth period—American literature, with Ms. Gilpin. The class is reading Steinbeck's *The Pearl*. Neelay kind of likes the story, especially the part where the baby gets stung by the scorpion. Scorpions are outstanding creatures, especially giant ones.

Ms. Gilpin drones on about what the pearl symbolizes. To Neelay, it's a pearl. He's beating his head against a *real* problem: how to synchronize the dancing kite with the music. He flips through pages of printout when the solution jumps out at him: two nested loops. It's like the gods draw it in bright chalk on his mind's blackboard. He burbles to himself, "*Oh, yeah!*"

The class bursts out laughing. Ms. Gilpin has just asked, "No one wants to see the baby die, do they?"

Ms. Gilpin daggers everybody silent. "Neelay. What are you doing?" He knows not to say a word. "What's in the notebook?"

"Computer homework." Everyone laughs again at the insane idea.

"Are you taking a *computer course*?" He shakes his head. "Bring it here."

Halfway through the journey up to her desk, he considers tripping and spraining his ankle. He hands over the notebook. She flips through it. Drawings, flowcharts, code. She frowns. "Sit down."

He does. Ms. Gilpin returns to Steinbeck while he soaks in a pool of injustice and shame. After the bell, when the room clears, he returns to Ms. Gilpin's desk. He knows why she hates him. His kind will drive hers extinct.

She opens the notebook to grids filled with images of blocky kites. "What is this?"

She has no idea of Uttarayan, or what it's like to have a father like his. She's blond, from Vallejo. Machines are her enemy. She thinks logic kills everything fine in the human soul. "Computer stuff."

"You're a smart boy, Neelay. What don't you like about English? You're so good at diagramming sentences." She waits, but can't outlast him. She taps the notebook. "Is this a game of some kind?"

"No." Not the way she means it.

"Don't you like to read?"

He feels sorry for her. If she only knew what reading could be. The Galactic Empire and its enemies are sweeping across the entire spiral of the Milky Way, waging wars that last for hundreds of thousands of years, and she's worried about those three poor Mexicans.

"I thought you liked *A Separate Peace*."

He liked it enough. It even punched him in the lungs, a little. But he can't see what that has to do with getting his private property back.

"Doesn't *The Pearl* interest you? It's about *racism*, Neelay."

He stands blinking, as at his first contact with alien intelligence. "Could I just get my notebook back, a little? I won't bring it to class anymore."

Her face crumples. Even he can see how he's betrayed her. She thought he was in her camp, but he has slipped away from her over the weeks and turned enemy. She touches his notebook and frowns again. "I'm going to hold on to it for now. Until you and I are back on track."

In a few years, students will shoot their teachers over less. He goes to her office at the end of the day. He fills his mind with sincere reform. "I'm very sorry about working in my notebook when you were teaching."

"*Working*, Neelay? Is that what you were doing?"

She wants a confession. She wants him to thank her for saving him from the perils of playing games while all the rest of the class was hard at work extracting fiction's pearls. Fifty hours of effort on his father's kite lies four feet away, unreachable. She wants to humiliate him. Outrage boils over. "May I have my damn notebook back? Please?"

The word slaps her. Her eyes set and she goes to war. "That is a demerit. You swore at a *teacher*. What will your parents say?"

He freezes. His mother will fell him with one great blow, like so much *jhatka* meat.

Ms. Gilpin checks her watch. Too late to send him to the principal. Her boyfriend is picking her up in ten minutes. They'll laugh together over the pigheadedness of this Indian boy with his notebook full of hieroglyphs. How he insisted that it wasn't play. She turns into a pillar of authority. "I want you back at this desk tomorrow morning, before the first bell. Then we'll talk about what you have coming to you."

The boy's blood hammers and his eyes burn.

"You may go." Her eyebrows do a little push-up of command. "Until tomorrow. Seven a.m. sharp."

HE NEEDS TO THINK. He skips the bus and heads home on foot. The day is one of those eerie Central Peninsula imitations of heaven—seventy degrees and clear, the air thick with bay laurel and eucalyptus. He drags along the familiar route at half his usual pace, past the modest middle-class bungalows that people will soon pay a million and a half for, just to tear down and rebuild. He has to make a plan. He swore at a teacher, and his old, golden life shatters in the single, terrible syllable. This disrespect of white people will cripple his father. *Patience, Neelay. Reserve. Remember? Remember?* Word will spread through the community of Indian expats. His mother will die of disgrace.

He walks along the fingerprint-whorl of tree-lined streets, that neighborhood hemmed in by three highways. Four blocks from home, he cuts through the park, the place he goes whenever his parents force him outdoors. The path snakes through a gauntlet of low-slung *encinas* with phantasmagoric branches growing since California was Spain's remotest outpost. If he's ever noticed the species at all, it was only in the movies: the trees of Sherwood and Bagworthy, stand-in forests to frighten Pilgrims and challenge castaways. When Hollywood needs trees, it turns to the only nearby broadleaf that will do.

They beckon, bizarre, dreamlike, contorted. One huge beam of branch swoops toward the ground like it's lying down to rest. A single swing, and from that low branch Neelay shimmies up into the roost, where he sits like he's seven again. There, he takes stock of his ruined life. From high up in this crazy cantilevered oak, looking down on the sidewalk where two kids swing a stick at pebbles and a humpbacked white-haired woman walks her dachshund, he can see this whole mess from Ms. Gilpin's eyes. She wasn't wrong to reprimand him. And yet, she stole his *property*. The whole disaster, from up in this crow's nest, has what Ms. Gilpin might call moral ambiguity.

He makes room on the oak's sinuous branch for the two boys from *A Separate Peace*. He watches them play their white-guy, prep school games of love and war in their tree above their river. Way below, the brown-green California ground bounces each time a breeze pitches the branches. He knows almost nothing of his parents' world, but one thing is as certain as math. Shame, for Indians, is worse than death. Ms. Gilpin may already have called them with details of his crime. His head throbs at the thought and his tongue tastes metal. He hears his mother howl: *You let that rat-haired woman humiliate your whole family?* Soon a distant country filled with aunts, uncles, and cousins will know what he has done.

And his poor father, who has made himself invisible for years, just for the right to live and work in this Golden State: he stares at Neelay in horror, wondering how a child might be so arrogant as to think that he could talk back to an American authority and live.

Neelay peers down from this oak aerie onto the path below, his mind a mass of tangled code. An idea flashes through him, a glimpse of easy peace. If he could get dusted up a little bit, it might win him the sympathy vote. You can't beat up on a wounded boy. Delicious terror strokes his neck, like it does when he watches old *Twilight Zones*. The idea is nuts. He must suck things up, go home, and take his punishment. He leans out for a good look at the big picture, his last for a while. His parents will ground him for months.

He sighs. Steps down onto the branch below him to descend. And slips.

There will be years to wonder whether the branches jerked. Whether the tree had it in for him. Limbs slam him on the way down. They bat him back and forth like a pinball. Earth rushes up. He lands on the concrete path and bounces on his coccyx, which cracks the base of his spine.

Time stops. He lies on his shattered back, looking upward. The dome above him hovers, a cracked shell about to fall in shards all around him. A thousand—a thousand thousand—green-tipped, splitting fingerlings fold over him, praying and threatening. Bark disintegrates; wood clarifies. The trunk turns into stacks of spreading metropolis, networks of conjoined cells pulsing with energy and liquid sun, water rising through long thin reeds, rings of them banded together into pipes that draw dissolved minerals up through the narrowing tunnels of transparent twig and out through their waving tips while sun-made sustenance drops down in tubes just inside them. A colossal, rising, reaching, stretching space elevator of a billion independent parts, shuttling the air into the sky and storing the sky deep underground, sorting possibility from out of nothing: the most perfect piece of self-writing code that his eyes could hope to see. Then his eyes close in shock and Neelay shuts down.

HE WAKES DAYS LATER in the hospital, strapped down and vised. Tubes restrain his arms and legs. Two wedges press against each ear, arresting his head. He can see nothing but ceiling, and it isn't blue. He hears his mother shout, "His eyes are open." He can't understand why she keeps sobbing those words, like they're a bad thing.

He lies in a cloud of narcotic unknowing. Sometimes he's a string of stored code in a microprocessor bigger than a city. Sometimes he's a traveler in that country of surprise that he'll come to build, when machines are at last fast enough to keep up with his imagination. Sometimes monstrous, splitting tendrils come after him.

The itching is insane. Every spot above his waist is unreachable fire. When he drops back down to earth again, his mother is there, curled up in the chair next to his bed. A change in his breathing wakes her from her sleep. His father is there, too, somehow. Neelay worries; what will his employers say when they discover he's not at work?

His mother says, "You came down out of a tree."

He can't connect the dots. "Fell?"

"Yes," she argues. "That's what you did."

"Why are my legs in tubes? Is that to keep me from breaking things?"

Her finger wags in the air, then touches her lips. "Everything will be fine."

His mother doesn't say such things.

The nurses ease him by degrees off the pain drip. Anguish sets in as the drugs dry up. People come to see him. His father's boss. His mother's card-playing friends. They smile like they're doing calisthenics. Their comfort scares the crap out of him.

"You've been through a lot," the doctor says. But Neelay has been through nothing. His body, perhaps. His avatar. But he? Nothing important in the code has changed.

The doctor is kind, with a tremor when his hand drops to his side, and eyes that fix on a blank spot high up on the walls. Neelay asks, "Can you take the vise-things off my legs?"

The doctor nods, but not in agreement. "You have some mending to do."

"It's bugging me, not to be able to move them."

"You concentrate on healing. Then we'll talk about what happens next."

"Can you at least take off the boots? I can't even wriggle my toes."

Then he understands. He's not yet twelve. He has lived for years in a place of his own devising. The thought of countless good things passing out of his life doesn't quite occur to him. He still has that other place, the heaven in embryo.

But his mother and father: *they* fall apart. Awful hours set in, days of disbelief and desperate bargaining that he won't remember. There will be years of supernatural solutions, alternative practices, and miracle cures. For a long time, his parents' love will make his sentence worse, until they finally put their faith in moksha and accept that their son is a cripple.

HE'S STILL LYING in the traction bed, days on. His mother has stepped away on an errand. Maybe not by chance. His teacher comes through the doorway, all warmth and energy, prettier than he remembers.

"Ms. Gilpin. Whoa!"

Something goes wrong with her face. But then, people's faces always look wrong, from his new vantage place, underneath them. She comes near and touches his shoulder. It freaks him.

"Neelay. I'm glad to see you."

"I'm glad to see you, too."

Her whole torso trembles. He thinks: *She knows about my legs. The whole school knows.* He wants to tell her: *It's not the end of the world.* No crucial world, anyway. She talks about the class and what they're reading now. *Flowers for Algernon.* He promises to read it by himself.

"Everyone misses you, Neelay."

"Look." He points to the wall, where his mother has taped the giant fold-out card signed by the entire ninth grade. She breaks down. He's helpless to do anything. "It's okay," he tells her.

Her head jerks up, crazy with hope. "Neelay. You know I never meant . . . I never thought . . ."

"I know," he says, and wants her gone.

She pushes her face back with two splayed palms. Then she reaches into her satchel and retrieves his notebook. The kite program for his father. "This belongs to you. I should never . . ."

He's so happy he doesn't even hear the words she keeps on mouthing. He thought the notebook was gone forever, another thing he'd never get back from his life before the tree dropped him.

"Thank you. Oh, thank you so much!"

A moan comes out of her. When he looks up, she turns and runs. Distress lasts only until he opens the notebook. Then he lies flipping through the recovered pages, remembering everything. So much work, so many good ideas—*saved*.

Six years pass. Puberty transforms Neelay Mehta. The boy shoots up into a fantastic creature: Seventeen years old, six-foot-six, 150 pounds, and fused to his wheelchair. His torso stretches out. Even his legs, shriveled to thick twigs, grow stupidly long. His cheeks shift like continental plates and his face spawns shoals of pimples. Black wires sprout from his once-pristine privates. He drops from soprano to high tenor. His hair grows as long as a Kesh-practicing Sikh's, though he doesn't tie it up into a rishi knot. He lets it flow in thick vines that fall all around his elongated face and down his bony shoulders.

He lives in his rolling metal rig—captain's chair on a starship forever voyaging through strange regions of thought. Some people who can no longer walk grow fat. But those people eat. He gets through the day on fifty cents of sunflower seeds and two caffeinated sodas. Of course, he rarely spends a pointless calorie. Once he rolls up to his custom desk in the morning, his CPU tower and CRT need more power than he does. His fingers graze the keyboard and his eyes scan the screen, but his brain burns considerable glucose as he fashions his prototype creations, in eighteen-hour increments, command by careful command.

Stanford accepts him, two years early. The campus is just up El Camino. Its CS department flourishes, fertilized by extravagant gifts from the founders of his father's company. Neelay has haunted the campus since the age of twelve. Long before he starts school as an official freshman, he's a de facto mascot of the computer science set. *You know: the ectomorph Indian kid, in the fancy chair.*

Something is being born in the bowels of half a dozen different buildings across the Farm. Magic beanstalks erupt everywhere, overnight. It comes up in conversation with friends, in the basement computer lab where Neelay hangs out and codes. They can be a taciturn bunch, but on Sunday nights, the coders lift their heads from their do-loops long enough to dole out the liter soda bottles and break pizza crusts together, while shooting a little philosophical shit.

Someone says, "We're evolution's third act." Sauce dribbles from his gaping mouth.

It's like they all have the idea together. Biology was phase one, unfolding over epochs. Then culture throttled up the rate of transformation to mere centuries. Now there's another digital generation every twenty weeks, each subroutine speeding up the next.

"Chips doubling their transistor count every eighteen months...? I mean, take Moore's law *seriously*, man."

"Say it holds for the rest of our lives. We could live another sixty years."

A giggle passes through them at the insane math. Forty doubling periods. Stratosphere-high piles of rice on the fabled chessboard.

"A trillionfold increase. Programs a million *million* times deeper and richer than the best thing anybody's yet written."

They pause for sober marveling. Neelay hangs his head over his untouched pizza, staring at the wedge as if it's a problem in analytic geometry. "Living things," he says, almost to himself. "Self-learning. Self-creating." The whole room laughs, but he doubles down. "So fast, they'll think we're not even here."

AT FIRST, the point of coding is to give everything away. Pure philanthropy. He'll find a marvelous seed program in the public domain. Then he'll flesh it out, add new features, switch on his 1,200-baud modem, dial in to a local bulletin board, and upload the source for anyone who wants to grow it some more. Soon his creatures propagate on hosts across the planet. Every day people around the globe add new species to the repositories. It's the Cambrian Explosion all over again, only a billion times faster.

Neelay gives away his first masterpiece, a turn-based romp where you play a Japanese movie monster eating its way across the world's metropolises. Hundreds of people in a dozen countries grab it, even at forty-five minutes per download. So what if playing it does to your free time what the monsters do to Tokyo? His second game—conquistadores ravaging the virgin Americas—is another freeware hit. A Usenet group forms just to trade game strategies. The program generates a new, geologically realistic New World each time you play. It turns any grocery store bag boy into stout Cortez.

His games spawn imitations. The more people steal from him, the better Neelay feels about his chair-bound life. The more he gives away, the more he has. From his vantage, stranded in his wheelchair in a basement lab, whole new continents swing into view. The gift economy—free duplication of well-shaped commands—promises to solve scarcity at last and cure the hunger at the heart's core. The name *Neelay Mehta* grows mini-legendary among the pioneers. People thank him on dial-up boards and in game news groups. College kids talk about him in chat rooms as if he's some Tolkien character. On the Internet, nobody knows you're a beached, elongated freak, unable to move without machines.

But by his eighteenth birthday, paradise is sprouting fences. Former philanthropists of free code start taking out copyrights and making actual coin. They even have the nerve to form private companies. Granted, they're still just peddling floppy discs in baggies, but it's clear how things will go. The commons are getting enclosed. The gift culture will be throttled in the cradle.

Neelay blasts the betrayal at each week's meeting of the Home-Rolled Club. He spends his free time re-creating one of the most famous commercial offerings, improving on it, then releasing the clone into the public domain. Infringement? Maybe. But every one of the so-called copyrighted properties relies on decades of prior unpaid art. For a year, Neelay plays Robin Hood, camped out in the anarchic forest with his merry men, under a massive oak older than the deed to the land it grows on.

HE WORKS FOR MONTHS on a role-playing space opera slated to be his greatest giveaway yet. The graphics are sixteen-bit high-res sprites, come to life in sixty-four glorious colors. He heads out on a hunt for surreal bestiaries to populate his planets. Late one spring evening he winds up in the Stanford main library, poring over the covers of golden age pulp sci-fi magazines and flipping through the pages of Dr. Seuss. The pictures resemble the mad vegetation in those cheap Vishnu and Krishna comics from his childhood.

Needing a break, he rolls across campus down Serra Mall to see what's cooking in the labs. It's near dusk, in that soft perfection that flavors this place for nine months of the year. He heads toward his cubicle in the networked lab, navigating as through a first-person adventure. The Oval's grandiose palm arcade snakes away to his right. To his left, the Santa Cruz Mountains peek out from behind the fake Spanish Romanesque cloisters. Once, in another life, he walked the trails up near Skyline under the redwoods with his father and mother. Behind the mountains, half an hour away by wheelchair-ready van, lies the sea. The beaches and bays are not for-bidden him. He visited them only three months ago. Several friends had to carry him down near the shore and set him in the sand. He sat and stared at the waves and watched the diving shorebirds and listened to their spectral complaints. Hours later, when his friends were done swimming and throw-ing Frisbees and chasing each other up and down the sand, he was the only one who hadn't had enough.

He turns up the ramp to Memorial Court into the main quad, past Rodin's life-sized *Burghers of Calais*. The night will be long, and he needs to stock up on snacks to power him through. He motors straight into the inner court, toward the back exit to the Union and all the best vending machines. Lost in his intergalactic plans, he almost mows down a group of Japanese tourists photographing the chapel. Backing away, apologizing, he runs over the toes of an elderly woman on her first trip abroad. She bows, mortified. Neelay extricates himself, slams the chair into a hard left, and looks up. There, in a car-sized planter, just to the side of the chapel entrance, bulbous and ele-phantine, is the most mind-boggling organism he has ever seen. It's the thing he has been searching for, for his intergalactic opera. A living hallucina-tion from a nearby star system at the other end of a wormhole in space. The groundskeepers must have snuck it in last night under cover of dark. Either that, or he has rolled past it every evening for months, without once seeing.

He wheels up to the tree and laughs. The trunk looks like a giant upside-down turkey baster. The branches skew and spike out at foolish angles. He reaches out to touch the bark. It's perfect. Absurd. Up to something. A tiny placard reads: BRACHYCHITON RUPESTRIS. QUEENSLAND BOTTLE TREE. The name excuses nothing and explains even less. It's an alien invader, as surely as Neelay.

He can't decide which is more incredible: the tree, or the fact that he's never noticed it. Shapes flicker on the edge of his vision. Something is hap-pening behind his back. He has the overwhelming feeling of being watched. A silent chorus in his head sings: *Turn and look. Turn around and see!* He spins the chair in place. Nothing is right. The whole cloister courtyard has changed. One hyper-jump, and he has landed in an intergalactic arboretum.

On all sides, furious green speculations wave at him. Creatures built for otherworldly climates. Crazies of every habit and profile. Things from epochs so old they make dinosaurs look like upstarts. All these signaling, sentient beings knock him back in his seat. He has never done drugs, but this must be what it's like. Plumes of cream and yellow; a purple waterfall that evaporates before it touches the ground. Trees like freak experiments beckon from out of eight large planters, each one a miniature starship ark on its way to some other system.

Neelay sweeps the chair around the courtyard. His paraplegic body tenses as the council shimmers in their standing circle, watching him make the circuit. He rolls past another Seussian monster as alien as the first. He reads the tag: a silk floss tree, from Brazilian forests even now shrinking by a hundred thousand acres a day. Sharp-tipped warty cones cover the trunk, spines that evolved to fend off grazing beasts that went extinct tens of millions of years ago.

He rolls from planter to planter, touching the beings, smelling them, listening to their rustles. They have come from hot islands and desiccated outback, from remote valleys in Central Asia breached only recently. Dove tree, jacaranda, desert spoon, camphor tree, flame tree, empress tree, kurrajong, red mulberry: unearthly life, waiting to waylay him in this courtyard while he was searching for them on distant planets. He touches their bark and feels, just beneath their skins, the teeming assemblies of cells, like whole planetary civilizations, pulse and hum.

The Japanese tourists disappear back to their bus on Galvez. Neelay holds still in the emptied space, like a rabbit evading a raptor. He's alone for no more than a few seconds. But in that interval, the alien invaders insert a thought directly into his limbic system. There will be a game, a billion times richer than anything yet made, to be played by countless people around the world at the same time. And Neelay must bring it into being. He'll unfold the creation in gradual, evolutionary stages, over the course of decades. The game will put its players smack in the middle of a living, breathing, seething, animist world filled with millions of different species, a world desperately in need of the players' help. And the goal of the game will be to figure out what the new and desperate world wants from you.

The vision ends, depositing him again in Stanford's inner quad. The vision, religious and dark green, fades back into its Platonic shadow, wood. Neelay holds still, clinging to what he has just seen, the thing his brain has somehow apprehended, lurking out at the end of the curve of Moore's law. He'll have to drop out of school. No time for more classes now. He must pace himself for the long run. He'll finish the quaint little role-playing space opera he's working on, then put it up for sale. Real money, earth dollars. His fans will howl. They'll smear him on the country's dial-up bulletin boards as the worst traitor. But at fifteen bucks for thirty parsecs, the game will be a steal. The profits from his first foray into alien life will pay for the sequel, a game to surpass the original in ambition many times over. And by such small steps, he'll get to the place he has just seen.

He rolls out of the cloister just as the light vanishes behind the mountains. The hills cast a shadow on themselves, bruise-blue turning to forgetful black. High up, beyond his sight, rocky outcrops crawl with manzanita, shedding their curling, crimson barks. Bay laurels rim the logger-made meadows. Canyons thicken with orange madrone peeling to creamy, clammy green. Coast live oaks like the one that crippled him gather on the crags. And down in cool riparian corridors smelling of silt and decaying needles, redwoods work a plan that will take a thousand years to realize—the plan that now uses him, although he thinks it's his.

# PATRICIA WESTERFORD

 IT'S 1950, and like the boy Cyparissus, whom she'll soon discover, little Patty Westerford falls in love with her pet deer. Hers is made of twigs, though it's every bit alive. Also: squirrels from pairs of glued walnut shells, bears made of sweetgum balls, dragons from the pods of Kentucky coffee trees, fairies donning acorn caps, and an angel whose pine-cone body needs only two holly leaves for wings.

She builds these creatures elaborate homes with pebbled front walks and mushroom furniture. She sleeps them in beds fitted with magnolia-petal comforters. She watches over them, the guiding spirit of a kingdom whose towns nestle behind closed doors in the burls of trees. Knotholes turn into louvered windows, through which, squinting, she can see the inviting parlors of woody citizens, the lost kin of humans. She lives there with her creatures in the minuscule architecture of imagination, so much richer than the offerings of full-sized life. When her tiny wooden doll's head twists off, she plants it in the garden, certain it will grow another body.

All her twig creatures can talk, though most, like Patty, have no need of words. She herself said nothing until past the age of three. Her two older brothers interpreted her secret language for their frightened parents, who began to think she must be mentally deficient. They brought Patty into the clinic in Chillicothe for tests that revealed a deformation of the inner ear. The clinic fitted her with fist-sized hearing aids, which she hated. When her own speech started to flow at last, it hid her thoughts behind a slurry hard for the uninitiated to comprehend. It didn't help that her face was sloped and ursine. The neighbors' kids ran from her, this thing only borderline human. Acorn people are so much more forgiving.

Her father alone understands her woodlands world, as he always understands her every thickened word. She has a pride of place with him that the two boys accept. With them, Dad may throw softballs and tell bubble-gum wrapper jokes and play tag. But he reserves his best gifts for his little plant-girl, Patty.

Their closeness bothers her mother. "I ask you. Has there ever been such a little nation of two?"

Bill Westerford takes Patricia with him when he visits southwestern Ohio farms on his tours as an ag extension agent. She rides copilot in the beaten-up Packard with the pine side paneling. The war is over, the world is on the mend, the country is drunk on science, key to better living, and Bill Westerford takes his daughter out to see the world.

Patty's mother objects to the trips. The girl should be in school. But her father's soft authority prevails. "She won't learn more anywhere than she will with me."

Mile after plowed mile, they hold their roving tutorial. He faces her so she can read his moving lips. She laughs at his stories —thick, slow booms—and stabs enthusiastic answers to each of his questions. Which is more numerous: the stars in the Milky Way or the chloroplasts on a single leaf of corn? Which trees flower before they leaf, and which flower after? Why are the leaves at the top of trees often smaller than those at the bottom? If you carved your name four feet high in the bark of a beech tree, how high would it be after half a century?

She loves the answer to that last one: *Four feet*. Still four feet. Always four feet, however high the beech tree grows. She'll love that answer still, half a century later.

In this way, acorn animism turns bit by bit into its offspring, botany. She becomes her father's star and only pupil for the simple reason that she alone, of all the family, sees what he knows: plants are willful and crafty and after something, just like people. He tells her, on their drives, about all the oblique miracles that green can devise. People have no corner on curious behavior. Other creatures—bigger, slower, older, more durable—call the shots, make the weather, feed creation, and create the very air.

"It's a great idea, trees. So great that evolution keeps inventing it, again and again."

He teaches her to tell a shellbark from a shagbark hickory. No one else at her school can even tell a hickory from a hop hornbeam. The fact strikes her as bizarre. "Kids in my class think a black walnut looks just like a white ash. Are they *blind*?"

"Plant-blind. Adam's curse. We only see things that look like us. Sad story, ain't it, kiddo?"

Her father has a little trouble with *Homo sapiens* himself. He's caught between fine folks whose family farms are failing to subdue the Earth and companies that want to sell them the arsenal to bring about total domin-ion. When the frustrations of the day grow too much for him, he sighs and says, for Patty's impaired ears alone, "Ah, buy me a hillside that slopes away from town."

They drive through a land once covered in dark beech forest. "Best tree you could ever want to see." Strong and wide but full of grace, flar-ing out nobly at the base, into its own plinth. Generous with nuts that feed all comers. Its smooth, white-gray trunk more like stone than wood. The parchment-colored leaves riding out the winter—*marcescent*, he tells her—shining out against the neighboring bare hardwoods. Elegant with sturdy boughs so much like human arms, lifting upward at the tips like hands prof-fering. Hazy and pale in spring, but in autumn its flat, wide sprays bathe the air in gold.

"What happened to them?" The girl's words thicken when sadness weighs them down.

"We did." She thinks she hears her father sigh, though he never takes his eyes off the road. "The beech told the farmer where to plow. Limestone underneath, covered in the best, darkest loam a field could want."

They drive from farm to farm, between last year's blights and next year's vanishing topsoil. He shows her extraordinary things: the spreading cambium of a sycamore that swallowed up the crossbar of an old Schwinn someone left leaning against it decades ago. Two elms that draped their arms around each other and became one tree.

"We know so little about how trees grow. Almost nothing about how they bloom and branch and shed and heal themselves. We've learned a little about a few of them, in isolation. But nothing is less isolated or more social than a tree."

Her father is her water, air, earth, and sun. He teaches her how to see a tree, the living sheath of cells underneath every square inch of bark doing things no man has yet figured out. He drives them to a copse of spared hardwoods in the bottoms of a slow stream. "Here! Look at this. Look at *this*!" A patch of narrow stalks, each with big, drooping leaves. A sheepdog of trees. He makes her sniff the giant spoonlike foliage, crushed. It smells acrid, like blacktop. He picks up a thick yellow pickle from the ground and holds it to her. She has rarely seen him so excited. He takes his army knife and cuts the fruit in half, exposing the buttery pulp and shiny black seeds. The flesh makes her want to scream with pleasure. But her mouth is full of butterscotch pudding.

"Pawpaw! The only tropical fruit ever to escape the tropics. Biggest, best, weirdest, wildest native fruit this continent ever made. Growing native, right here in Ohio. And nobody knows!"

*They* know. The girl and her father. She'll never tell anyone the location of this patch. It will be theirs alone, fall after prairie-banana fall.

Watching the man, hard-of-hearing, hard-of-speech Patty learns that real joy consists of knowing that human wisdom counts less than the shimmer of beeches in a breeze. As certain as weather coming from the west, the things people know for sure will change. There is no knowing *for a fact*. The only dependable things are humility and looking.

He finds her out in the backyard making birds from the twinned wings of maple samaras. An odd look comes over his face. He holds up one of the seeds and points it toward the giant that shed it. "Have you noticed how it releases more seeds in updrafts than when the wind is blowing downward? Why is that?"

These questions are her favorite thing in the world. She thinks. "Travels farther?"

He puts his finger to his nose. "Bingo!" He looks at the tree and frowns, working through old puzzlements all over again. "Where do you think all the wood comes from, to get from this little thing to *that?*"

Wild guess. "The dirt?"

"How could we find out?"

They design the experiment together. They put two hundred pounds of soil in a wooden tub by the south face of the barn. Then they extract a three-angled beechnut from its cupule, weigh it, and push it into the loam.

"If you see a trunk carved full of letters, it's a beech. People can't help writing all over that smooth gray surface. God love 'em. They want to watch their lettered hearts growing bigger, year after year. *Fond lovers, cruel as their flame, cut in these trees their mistress' name. Little, alas, they know or heed how far these beauties hers exceed!*"

He tells her how the word *beech* becomes the word *book*, in language after language. How *book* branched up out of beech roots, way back in the parent tongue. How beech bark played host to the earliest Sanskrit letters. Patty pictures their tiny seed growing up to be covered with words. But where will the mass of such a massive book come from?

"We'll keep the tub moist and free of weeds for the next six years. When you turn sweet sixteen, we'll weigh the tree and the soil again."

She hears him, and understands. This is science, and worth a million times more than anything any person might ever swear to you.

IN TIME, she gets almost as good as her father at telling what's wilting or gnawing on a farmer's crops. He stops quizzing her and starts consulting, not in front of the farmers, of course, but later, back in the car, when they have the luxury of thinking through the infestations as a team.

On her fourteenth birthday, he gives her a bowdlerized translation of Ovid's *Metamorphosis*. It's inscribed: *For my dear daughter, who knows how big and wide the family tree really is.* Patricia opens the book to the first sentence and reads:

*Let me sing to you now, about how people turn into other things.*

At those words, she's back where acorns are a step away from faces and pine cones compose the bodies of angels. She reads the book. The stories are odd and fluid, as old as humankind. They're somehow familiar, as if she were born knowing them. The fables seem to be less about people turning into other living things than about other living things somehow reabsorbing, at the moment of greatest danger, the wildness inside people that never really went away. By now Patricia's body is well along its own tortured metamorphosis into something she in no way wants. The new flare to her chest and hips, the start of a patch between her legs turns her, too, halfway into a more ancient beast.

She loves best the stories where people change into trees. Daphne, transformed into a bay laurel just before Apollo can catch and harm her. The women killers of Orpheus, held fast by the earth, watching their toes turn into roots and their legs into woody trunks. She reads of the boy Cyparissus, whom Apollo converts into a cypress so that he might grieve forever for his slain pet deer. The girl turns beet-, cherry-, apple-red at the story of Myrrha, changed into a myrtle after creeping into her father's bed. And she cries at that steadfast couple, Baucis and Philemon, spending the centuries together as oak and linden, their reward for taking in strangers who turned out to be gods.

Her fifteenth autumn comes. The days shorten. Night falls early, signaling the trees to drop their sugar-making project, shed all vulnerable parts, and harden up. Sap falls. Cells become permeable. Water flows out of the trunks and concentrates into anti-freeze. The dormant life just below the bark is lined with water so pure that nothing is left to help it crystallize.

Her father explains how the trick is done. "Think about it! They've figured out how to live trapped in place, with no other protection, whipped by winds at thirty below zero."

Later that winter, Bill Westerford is coming home from a field trip after sundown when the Packard hits a patch of black ice. He's thrown from the car as it flips off the road into a ditch. His body flies for twenty-five feet before crashing into a row of Osage orange that farmers planted for a hedge a century and a half earlier.

At the funeral, Patty reads from Ovid. The promotion of Baucis and Philemon to trees. Her brothers think she has lost her mind with grief.

She won't let her mother throw anything out. She keeps his walking stick and porkpie hat in a kind of shrine. She preserves his precious library—Aldo Leopold, John Muir, his botany texts, the Ag Extension pamphlets he helped to write. She finds his copy of adult Ovid, marked all over, as people mark beeches. The underscores start, triple, on the very first line: *Let me sing to you now, about how people turn into other things.*

HIGH SCHOOL tries to kill her. Viola in the orchestra, the maple howling with old hillside memories, under her chin. Photography and volleyball. She has two almost-friends who understand the reality of animals, at least, if not quite plants. She shuns all jewelry, dresses in flannel and denim, carries a Swiss Army knife, and wears her long hair wrapped around her skull in braids.

A stepfather arrives, one who's smart enough not to try to reform her. There's a trauma involving a quiet boy who dreams for two years of taking her to the senior prom, a boy whose dream must die from a white-oak stake through the heart.

In the summer of her eighteenth year, preparing to head to Eastern Kentucky to study botany, she remembers the beech growing in its tub of soil, out by the barn. Shame rushes through her: How could she have forgotten the experiment? She has missed her promise to her father by two years. Skipped sweet sixteen altogether.

She spends an entire July afternoon freeing the tree from the soil and crumbling every thimble of dirt from its roots. Then she weighs both the plant and the earth it fed on. The fraction of an ounce of beechnut now weighs more than she does. But the soil weighs just what it did, minus an ounce or two. There's no other explanation: almost all the tree's mass has come from the very air. Her father knew this. Now she does, too.

She replants their experiment in a spot behind the house where she and her father liked to sit on summer nights and listen to what other people called silence. She remembers what he told her about the species. People, God love 'em, must write all over beeches. But some people—some fathers—are written all over by trees.

Before she goes away to school, she puts the tiniest notch in the smooth gray booklike bark of the trunk with her army knife, four feet above the ground.


EASTERN KENTUCKY UNIVERSITY turns her into someone else. Patricia blooms like something southern-facing. The air of the sixties crackles as she crosses campus, a change in the weather, the smell of days lengthening, the scent of possibility breaking the cast of outdated thought, a clear wind rolling down from the hills.

Her dorm room overflows with potted plants. She's not the only one on her floor to fit a botanical garden between the student desk and bunk bed. But her plants are the only ones with strips of data taped to their terra-cotta pots. Where her friends grow baby's breath and blue-eyed violets, she grows tickseed and partridge pea and other experiments. And yet, she also cares for a bonsai juniper that looks to be a thousand years old, a spiky haiku of a creature with no scientific purpose whatsoever.

The girls from upstairs come down some nights to check on her. They've made her into a pet project. *Let's get Plant-Patty drunk. Let's fix Plant-Patty up with that beatnik econ guy.* They mock her studiousness and laugh at her calling. They force her to listen to Elvis. They slip her into sleeveless sheaths and pile up her hair in a bouffant. They call her the Queen of Chlorophyll. She's not of the herd. She doesn't always hear them well, and when she does, their words don't always make sense. And yet her frantic fellow mammals do make her smile: miracles on all sides, and still they need compliments to keep them happy.

Sophomore year, Patty gets a job in the campus greenhouses—two hours stolen every morning before classes. Genetics, plant physiology, and organic chemistry take her through evening. She studies every night at her carrel until the library closes. Then she reads for pleasure until she falls asleep. She does try the books her friends are reading: *Siddhartha*, *Naked Lunch*, *On the Road*. But nothing else moves her more than Peattie's *Natural Histories*, books from her father's shelves. Now they're her endless refreshment. Their phrases branch and turn to catch the sun:

> *Thrones have crumbled and new empires arisen; great ideas have been born and great pictures painted, and the world revolution-ized by science and invention; and still no man can say how many centuries this Oak will endure or what nations and creeds it may outlive. . . .*

> *Where the deer bound, where the trout rise, where your horse stops to slather a drink from icy water while the sun is warm on the back of your neck, where every breath you draw is exhilaration — that is where the Aspens grow. . . .*

And of her father's beloved tree:

> *Let other trees do the work of the world. Let the Beech stand, where still it holds its ground . . .*

She never exactly becomes a swan. Yet the senior who emerges out of freshman ugly ducklinghood knows what she loves and how she intends to spend her life, and that's a novelty among the youth of any year. Those she doesn't scare away come sniff her out, this keen, homely, forthright girl who has escaped the stoop of constant social compliance. To her astonishment, she even has suitors. Something about her perks boys up. Not her looks, of course, but an ever-so-slightly head-turning quality to her walk that they can't quite place. Independent thought—a power of attraction all its own.

When boys come calling, she makes them take her for a picnic lunch in Richmond Cemetery—serving the needs of dead people since 1848. Sometimes they flee, and that's that. If they stick around and mention the trees, she'll see them again. Desire, she scribbles into her field notebooks, turns out to be infinitely varied, the sweetest of evolution's tricks. And in the pollen storms of spring, even she turns out to be a more than adequate flower.

One boy sticks around, month after month. Andy, the English major. He plays in the orchestra with her and loves Hart Crane and O'Neill and *Moby-Dick*, although he can't say why. He can get birds to land on his shoulder. He's waiting for something to come and redeem his aimless life. One night, over cribbage, he says he thinks it might be her. She takes him by the hand and leads him to her narrow bed. Clumsy and green, they peel back the shields of clothing. Ten minutes later, she's turned into a tree just a little too late to be spared.

REAL LIFE STARTS in graduate school. There are mornings in West Lafayette when Patricia Westerford's luck scares her. *Forestry* school. She feels unworthy. Purdue pays her to take classes that she has craved for years. She gets food and lodging for teaching undergraduate botany, something she'd gladly pay to do. And her research demands long days in the Indiana woods. It's an animist's heaven.

But by her second year, the catch becomes clear. In a seminar on forest management, the professor declares that snags and windthrow should be cleaned up from the forest floor and pulped, to improve forest health. That doesn't seem right. A healthy forest must need dead trees. They've been around since the beginning. Birds turn them to use, and small mammals, and more forms of insects lodge and dine on them than science has ever counted. She wants to raise her hand and say, like Ovid, how all life is turning into other things. But she doesn't have the data. All she has is the intuition of a girl who grew up playing in the forest litter.

Soon, she sees. Something is wrong with the entire field, not just at Purdue, but nationwide. The men in charge of American forestry dream of turning out straight clean uniform grains at maximum speed. They speak of *thrifty* young forests and *decadent* old ones, of *mean annual increment* and *economic maturity*. She's sure these men who run the field will have to fall, next year or the year after. And up from the downed trunks of their beliefs will spring rich new undergrowth. That's where she'll thrive.

She preaches this covert revolution to her undergrads. "You'll look back in twenty years, amazed at what every smart person in forestry took to be self-evident truth. It's the refrain of all good science: '*How could we not have seen?*'"

She works well with her fellow grads. She goes to the barbecues and hoo-tenannies and manages to take part in departmental gossip while remaining her own little sovereign state. One night there's a dizzy, warm, wild misunderstanding with a woman in plant genetics. Patricia puts the embarrassed fumble away in a drawer of her heart and never takes it out again, even to look at.

A secret suspicion sets her apart from the others. She's sure, on no evidence whatsoever, that trees are social creatures. It's obvious to her: motionless things that grow in mass mixed communities must have evolved ways to synchronize with one another. Nature knows few loner trees. But the belief leaves her marooned. Bitter irony: here she is, with her people, at last, and even they can't see the obvious.

Purdue gets hold of one of the first prototype quadrupole gas chromatography-mass spectrometers. Some pagan god brings the machine right to Patricia, as a reward for her constancy. With such a device, she can measure which volatile organic compounds the grand old eastern trees put into the air and what these gases do to the neighbors. She pitches the idea to her advisor. People know nothing about the stuff trees make. It's a whole new green world, ripe for discovery.

"How will that produce anything useful?"

"It might not."

"Why do you need to do this in a forest? Why not the campus test plots?"

"You wouldn't study wild animals by going to the zoo."

"You think cultivated trees behave differently than trees in a forest?"

She's sure of it. But his sigh is as clear as a public service announcement: Girls doing science are like bears riding bikes. Possible, but freakish. "I'll reserve some trees in the wood lot. It'll make things easier and save you lots of time."

"There's no hurry."

"Your dissertation. Your time to waste."

She wastes it with the most intense pleasure. The work isn't glamorous. It consists of taping numbered plastic bags over the ends of branches, then collecting them at measured intervals. She does this over and over, dumbly and mutely, hour by hour, while the world around her rages with assassination, race riot, and jungle warfare. She works all day in the woods, her back crawling with chiggers, her scalp with ticks, her mouth filled with leaf duff, her eyes with pollen, cobwebs like scarves around her face, bracelets of poison ivy, her knees gouged by cinders, her nose lined with spores, the backs of her thighs bitten Braille by wasps, and her heart as happy as the day is generous.

She brings the collected samples back into the lab and spends hour after tedious hour puzzling out the concentrations and molecular weights, determining which gases each of her trees breathed out. There must be thousands of compounds. Tens of thousands. The tedium makes her ecstatic. She calls it the science paradox. It's the most brain-crushing work a person can do, yet it can spring the mind enough to see what else but the mind is really out there. And she gets to work in the dappling sun and rain, the stink of humus filling up her nose with relentlessly musky life. Out in the woods, her father is with her again, all day long. She asks him things, and the mere act of asking out loud helps her see. What starts a shelf fungus growing at just a certain height up a trunk? How many square meters of solar panel does a given tree put out? Why should there be such tremendous difference in size between the leaf of a serviceberry and that of a sycamore?

It's a miracle, she tells her students, photosynthesis: a feat of chemical engineering underpinning creation's entire cathedral. All the razzmatazz of life on Earth is a free-rider on that mind-boggling magic act. The secret of life: plants eat light and air and water, and the stored energy goes on to make and do all things. She leads her charges into the inner sanctum of the mystery: Hundreds of chlorophyll molecules assemble into antennae complexes. Countless such antennae arrays form up into thylakoid discs. Stacks of these discs align in a single chloroplast. Up to a hundred such solar power factories power a single plant cell. Millions of cells may shape a single leaf. A million leaves rustle in a single glorious ginkgo.

Too many zeros: their eyes glaze over. She must shepherd them back over that ultrafine line between numbness and awe. "Billions of years ago, a single, fluke, self-copying cell learned how to turn a barren ball of poison gas and volcanic slag into this peopled garden. And everything you hope, fear, and love became possible." They think she's nuts, and that's fine with her. She's content to post a memory forward to their distant futures, futures that will depend on the inscrutable generosity of green things.

Late at night, too tired from teaching and research to work more, she reads her beloved Muir. *A Thousand-Mile Walk to the Gulf* and *My First Summer in the Sierra* float her soul up to her room's ceiling and spin it like a Sufi. She writes her favorite lines in the inside covers of her field notebooks and peeks at them when department politics and the cruelty of frightened humans get her down. The words withstand the full brutality of day.

*We all travel the Milky Way together, trees and men. . . . In every walk with nature one receives far more than he seeks. The clearest way into the universe is through a forest wilderness.*

PLANT-PATTY becomes Dr. Pat Westerford, a way to disguise her gender in professional correspondence. Her work on tulip trees earns her a doctorate. It turns out that those thick, long lengths of culvert pipe stood on end are factories richer than anyone suspects. *Liriodendron* has a repertoire of scents. It breathes out volatile organic compounds that do all kinds of things. She doesn't yet know how the system works. She just knows it's rich and beautiful.

She lands a postdoc at Wisconsin. She searches Madison for relics of Aldo Leopold. She looks for the towering black locust, with its fragrant racemes and pea-pod seeds, the tree that stunned Muir into becoming a naturalist. But the world-changing locust was cut down twelve years before.

The postdoc turns into an adjunct position. She makes almost nothing, but life requires little. Her budget is blessedly free of those two core expenses, entertainment and status. And the woods teem with free food.

She starts to examine sugar maples, in a forest east of town. Her breakthrough comes as breakthroughs often do: by long and prepared accident. Patricia arrives in her copse on a balmy day in June to find one of her bagged trees under full-scale insect invasion. At first it seems that the last several days of data are ruined. Improvising, she keeps the samples from the damaged tree, as well as several nearby maples. Back in the lab, she widens the list of compounds she looks at. Over the next few weeks, she finds something that even she isn't ready to believe.

Another nearby tree gets infested. She measures again. Again, she doubts the evidence. Fall begins, and the leaves of her complex chemical factories shutter and drop to the forest floor. She battens down for the winter, teaching, double-checking her results, trying to accept their crazy implications. She wanders the woods, wondering if she should publish or run the experiment for another year. The oaks in her forest shine scarlet still, the beeches a stunning bronze. It seems wise to wait.

Confirmation comes the following spring. Three more trials, and she's convinced. The trees under attack pump out insecticides to save their lives. That much is uncontroversial. But something else in the data makes her flesh pucker: trees a little way off, untouched by the invading swarms, ramp up their own defenses when their neighbor is attacked. Something *alerts* them. They get wind of the disaster, and they prepare. She controls for everything she can, and the results are always the same. Only one conclusion makes any sense: The wounded trees send out alarms that other trees smell. Her maples are *signaling*. They're linked together in an airborne network, sharing an immune system across acres of woodland. These brainless, stationary trunks are protecting each other.

She can't quite let herself believe. But the data keep confirming. And on that evening when Patricia finally accepts what the measurements say, her limbs heat up and tears run down her face. For all she knows, she's the first creature in the expanding adventure of life who has ever glimpsed this small but certain thing that evolution is up to. Life is talking to itself, and she has listened in.

She writes up the results as soberly as she can. Her report is all chemistry, concentrations, and rates—nothing but what the gas chromatography equipment records. But in her paper's conclusion, she can't resist suggesting what the results spell out:

> *The biochemical behavior of individual trees may make sense only when we see them as members of a community.*

Dr. Pat Westerford's paper gets accepted by a reputable journal. The peer reviewers raise their eyebrows, but her data are sound and no one can find any problems except common sense. On the day the article appears, Patricia feels she has discharged her debt to the world. If she dies tomorrow, she'll still have added this one small thing to what life has come to know about itself.

The press picks up on her findings. She does an interview for a popular science magazine. She struggles to hear the questions over the phone and stumbles with her answers. But the piece runs, and other newspapers pick it up. "Trees Talk to One Another." She gets a few letters from researchers across the country, asking for details. She's invited to speak at the midwestern branch meeting of the professional forestry society.

Four months later, the journal that ran the piece prints a letter signed by three leading dendrologists. The men say her methods are flawed and her statistics problematic. The defenses of the intact trees could have been activated by other mechanisms. Or these trees might already have been compromised by insects in ways she didn't notice. The letter mocks the idea that trees send each other chemical warnings:

> *Patricia Westerford displays an almost embarrassing misunder-*
> *standing of the units of natural selection. . . . Even if a message is*
> *in some way "received," it would in no way imply that any such*
> *message has been "sent."*

The short letter contains four uses of the word *Patricia* and no mention of *Doctor*, until their own signatures. Two Yale professors and a name chair at Northwestern, versus an unknown adjunct girl at Madison: No one in the profession bothers trying to replicate Patricia Westerford's findings. Those researchers who wrote her for more information stop responding to her letters. The newspapers that ran the wide-eyed articles follow up with accounts of her brutal debunking.

Patricia goes through with her scheduled talk at the midwestern forestry conference, in Columbus. The room is small and hot. Her hearing aids howl with feedback. Her slides jam in the carousel. The questions are hostile. Fielding them from behind the podium, Patricia feels her old childhood speech defect returning to punish her for her hubris. For the three agonizing days of the conference, people nudge each other as she passes them in the halls of the hotel: *There's the woman who thinks that trees are intelligent.*

Madison doesn't renew her lectureship. She scrambles to line up a job elsewhere, but it's too late in the season. She can't even get work washing glassware for some other researcher. No other animal closes ranks faster than *Homo sapiens.* Without a lab to use, she can't vindicate herself. At thirty-two, she starts substitute teaching in high schools. Friends in the field murmur in sympathy, but none goes public to defend her. Meaning drains from her like green from a maple in fall. After long weeks in solitude replaying what happened, she decides it's time to shed.

She's too cowardly to give in to the scenarios that play in her head most nights as she tries to fall asleep. The pain prevents her. Not hers: the pain she'd inflict on her mother and brothers and remaining friends. Only the woods protect her from undying shame. She tramps the winter trails, feeling the thick, sticky horse chestnut buds with her frozen fingers. The understory fills up with tracks like longhand accusations scribbled on the snow. She listens to the forest, to the chatter that has always sustained her. But all she can hear is the deafening wisdom of crowds.

Half a year passes at the bottom of a well. One bright blue crisp Sunday morning in high summer, Patricia finds several unexpanded caps of *Amanita bisporigera* under a stand of oak in the bottomlands of Token Creek. The fungi are beautiful, but take forms that would make the old Doctrine of Signatures blush. She gathers them in her mushroom bag and brings them home. There, she cooks up a Sunday feast for one: chicken tenderloins in butter, olive oil, garlic, shallots, and white wine, all seasoned with just enough Destroying Angel to shut down both her kidneys and her liver.

She sets the table and sits down to a meal that smells like health itself. The beauty of the plan is that no one will know. Every year, amateur mycologists mistake young *A. bisporigera* for *Agaricus silvicola* or even *Volvariella volvacea*. Neither her friends nor family nor former colleagues will think anything but this: she was wrong in her controversial research, and wrong in her choice of fungal fruiting bodies for her dinner. She brings the steaming forkful to her lips.

Something stops her. Signals flood her muscles, finer than any words. *Not this. Come with. Fear nothing.*

The fork drops back to the plate. She rouses as from sleepwalking. Fork, plate, mushroom feast: everything turns, as she watches, into a fit of madness, lifted. In another heartbeat, she can't believe what her animal fear was willing to make her do. The opinion of others left her ready to suffer the most agonizing of deaths. She runs the entire meal down the garbage disposal and goes hungry, a hunger more wonderful than any meal.

Her real life starts this night—a long, postmortem bonus round. Nothing in the years to come can do worse than she was ready to do to herself. Human estimation can no longer touch her. She's free now to experiment. To discover anything.

Then several missing years. From the outside, yes: Patricia Westerford disappears into underemployment. Sorting storeroom boxes. Cleaning floors. Odd jobs leading from the Upper Midwest through the Great Plains toward the high mountains. She has no affiliation, no access to equipment. Nor does she try for lab positions or teaching stints, even when former colleagues encourage her to apply. Pretty much all her old friends add her to the roster of science roadkill. In fact, she's busy learning a foreign language.

With few claims on her time and none on her soul, she turns back outside, into the woods, the green negation of all careers. She no longer theorizes or speculates. Just watches, notes, and sketches into a stack of notebooks, her only persistent possessions aside from clothes. Her eyes go near and narrow. She camps out many nights with Muir, under the spruce and fir, completely lost, turned wildly around by the smell of inland oceans, sleeping on beds of thick lichen, sixteen inches of brown needle pillow, the living earth beneath her bag, its fluid influence rising up into the fiber of her and all the towering trunks that surround and watch over. The particle of her private *self* rejoins everything it has been split off from—the plan of runaway green. *I only went out for a walk and finally concluded to stay out till sundown, for going out, I found, was really going in.*

She reads Thoreau over wood fires at night. *Shall I not have intelligence with the earth? Am I not partly leaves and vegetable mould myself?* And: *What is this Titan that has possession of me? Talk of mysteries!—Think of our life in nature,—daily to be shown matter, to come in contact with it,—rocks, trees, wind on our cheeks! the* solid *earth! the* actual *world! the* common sense! Contact! Contact! Who are we? where are we?

Now she drifts farther west. It's amazing how far a little war chest will go, once you learn how to forage. This country is awash in food free for the eating. You just need to know where to look. She glimpses her own face once, while splashing water on it in the bathroom of a service station near a national forest in a state where she's the merest beginner. She looks marvelously weathered, old beyond her years. She has gone to seed. Soon she'll start to scare people. Well, she has always scared people. Angry people who hated wildness took away her career. Frightened people mocked her for saying that trees send messages to each other. She forgives them all. It's nothing. What frightens people most will one day turn to wonder. And then people will do what four billion years have shaped them to do: stop and see just what it is they're seeing.

On a late fall afternoon she pulls her ancient beater over to the side of the road along a stretch of the Fishlake Scenic Byway, on the western edge of the Colorado Plateau in south-central Utah. She has followed back roads from Las Vegas, capital of clueless sinners, toward Salt Lake, capital of cunning saints. She gets out of the car and walks up into the trees on the crest west of the road. Aspens stand in the afternoon sun, spreading along the ridge out of sight. *Populus tremuloides.* Clouds of gold leaf glint on thin trunks tinted the palest green. The air is still, but the aspens shake as if in a wind. Aspens alone quake when all others stand in dead calm. Long flattened leafstalks twist at the slightest gust, and all around her, a million two-toned cadmium mirrors flicker against righteous blue.

The oracle leaves turn the wind audible. They filter the dry light and fill it with expectation. Trunks run straight and bare, roughed with age at the bottom, then smooth and whitening up to the first branches. Circles of pale green lichen palette-spatter them. She stands inside this white-gray room, a pillared foyer to the afterlife. The air shivers in gold, and the ground is littered with windfall and dead ramets. The ridge smells wide open and sere. The whole atmosphere is as good as a running mountain stream.

Patricia Westerford hugs herself, and, for no reason, begins to cry. The tree of the Navajo sun house chant. The tree Hercules turned into a wreath, the one he sacrificed, when coming back from hell. The one whose brewed leaves protected native hunters from evil. This, the most widely distributed tree in North America with close kin on three continents, all at once feels unbearably rare. She has hiked through aspens far north into Canada, the lone hardwood holdout in a latitude monotonous with conifer. Has sketched their pale summer shades throughout New England and the Upper Midwest. Has camped among them on hot, dry outcrops above gushing streams of snowmelt, in the Rockies. Has found them etched with knowledge-encoded native arborglyphs. Has lain on her back with her eyes closed, in far southwestern mountains, memorizing the tone of that restless shudder. Picking her way across these fallen branches, she hears it again. No other tree makes this sound.

The aspens wave in their undetectable breeze, and she begins to see hidden things. High up on one trunk, she reads claw-gashes above her head, the cryptic writing of bears. But these slashes are old and rimmed with blackened scars; no bears have crossed these woods in a long time. Tangled roots spill from the banks of a rivulet. She studies them, the exposed edge of a network of underground conduits conducting water and minerals across dozens of acres, up the rise to other, seemingly separate stems that line the rocky outcrops where water is hard to find.

At the height of the rise is a little clearing, slashed down with a chain saw. Someone has been out improving things. She produces her loupe from her key chain and applies it to one stump to estimate the number of rings. The oldest downed trees are about eighty years. She smiles at the number, so comical, for these fifty thousand baby trees all around her have sprouted from a rhizome mass too old to date even to the nearest hundred millennia. Underground, the eighty-year-old trunks are a hundred thousand, if they're a day. She wouldn't be surprised if this great, joined, single clonal creature that looks like a forest has been around for the better part of a million years.

That's why she has stopped: to see one of the oldest, largest living things on earth. All around her spreads one single male whose genetically identical trunks cover more than a hundred acres. The thing is outlandish, beyond her ability to wrap her head around. But then, as Dr. Westerford knows, the world's outlands are everywhere, and trees like to toy with human thought like boys toy with beetles.

Across the road from where she's parked, aspens tumble down the basin toward Fish Lake, where five years earlier a Chinese refugee engineer took his three daughters camping on the way to visiting Yellowstone. The oldest girl, named for a Puccini opera heroine, will soon be wanted by the feds for fifty million dollars of arson.

Two thousand miles to the east, a student sculptor born into an Iowa farming family, on a pilgrimage to the Met, walks past the single quaking aspen in all of Central Park and doesn't notice it. He'll live to walk past the tree again, thirty years later, but only because of swearing to the Puccini heroine that no matter how bad things get, he won't kill himself.

To the north, up the curving spine of the Rockies, on a farm near Idaho Falls, a veteran airman, that very afternoon, builds horse stalls for a friend from his old squadron. It's a pity hire, one that comes with room and board, and the vet plans to leave the gig as soon as he can. But for today, he makes the corral siding out of aspen. As poor as the wood is for lumber, it won't shatter when a horse kicks it.

In a St. Paul suburb not far from Lake Elmo, two aspens grow near the south wall of an intellectual property lawyer's house. He's only dimly aware of them, and when his free-spirit girlfriend asks, he tells her they're birches. In time, two great strokes will lay the lawyer low, reducing all aspens, birches, beeches, pines, oaks, and maples to a single word that will take him half a minute to pronounce.

On the West Coast, in the emerging Silicon Valley, a Gujarati-American boy and his father build primitive aspens out of chunky, black-and-white pixels. They're writing a game that feels to the boy like walking through the forest primeval.

These people are nothing to Plant-Patty. And yet their lives have long been connected, deep underground. Their kinship will work like an unfolding book. The past always comes clearer, in the future.

Years from now, she'll write a book of her own, *The Secret Forest*. Its opening page will read:

> You and the tree in your backyard come from a common ancestor. A billion and a half years ago, the two of you parted ways. But even now, after an immense journey in separate directions, that tree and you still share a quarter of your genes. . . .

She stands in the clearing at the top of the rise, looking out over a shallow gully. Aspens everywhere, and it boggles her mind that not one of them has grown from seed. All through this part of the West, few aspens have done so in ten thousand years. Long ago, the climate changed, and an aspen's seeds can no longer thrive here. But they propagate by root; they spread. There are aspen colonies up north where the ice sheets were, older than the sheets themselves. The motionless trees are *migrating*—immortal stands of aspen retreating before the latest two-mile-thick glaciers, then following them back north again. Life will not answer to reason. And *meaning* is too young a thing to have much power over it. All the drama of the world is gathering underground—massed symphonic choruses that Patricia means to hear before she dies.

She looks out over the draw to guess which way her male, this giant aspen clone, might be headed. He has been roving around the hills and gullies in a ten-millennium search for a female quaking giant to fertilize. Something on the next rise punches her in the chest. Carved out from the heart of the spreading clone, a housing development sits among a ribbon of new roads. Condos, a few days old, cut through several acres of the root system of one of the earth's most lavish things. Dr. Westerford closes her eyes. She has seen dieback across the West. Aspens are withering. Grazed on by everything with hooves, cut off from rejuvenating fire, whole groves are vanishing. Now she sees a forest, spreading across these mountains since before humans left Africa, giving way to second homes. She sees it in one great glimpse of flashing gold: trees and humans, at war over the land and water and atmosphere. And she can hear, louder than the quaking leaves, which side will lose by winning.

IN THE EARLY EIGHTIES, Patricia heads northwest. Giants still grow in the Lower 48, pockets of old growth scattered from Northern California on up to Washington. She means to see what uncut forest looks like, while there is any left to see. The western Cascades in a damp September: nothing in her experience prepares her. From mid-distance, with no clue for scale, the trees seem no larger than the biggest sycamores and tulip poplars out East. But up close the illusion disappears, and she's lost in reason's opposite. All she can do is look and laugh and look some more.

Hemlock, grand fir, yellow cedar, Douglas-fir: buttressed monster conifers disappear in the mist above her. Sitka spruces bulge out in burls as big
as minivans—pound for pound, a wood stronger than steel. A single trunk
could fill a large logging truck. Even runts here are big enough to domi-
nate an eastern forest, and each acre holds at least five times as much wood.
Beneath these giants, way down in the understory, her own body seems
freakishly small, like one of those acorn-people she made in childhood. A
knothole in one of these columns of solidified air could be her home.

Clicks and chatter disturb the cathedral hush. The air is so twilight-green
she feels like she's underwater. It rains particles—spore clouds, broken
webs and mammal dander, skeletonized mites, bits of insect frass and bird
feather. . . . Everything climbs over everything else, fighting for scraps of
light. If she holds still too long, vines will overrun her. She walks in silence,
crunching ten thousand invertebrates with every step, watching for tracks
in a place where at least one of the native languages uses the same word for
*footprint* and *understanding*. The earth gives beneath her like a shot mattress.

An exposed ridge takes her down into a basin. She swings her singing
stick before her, and the temperature plummets as she passes through a ther-
mal curtain. The canopy is a colander stippling the beetle-swarmed surfaces
with specks of sun. For every large trunk, a few hundred seedlings huddle in
the litter. Sword fern, liverworts, lichen, and leaves as small as sand grains
stain every inch of the dank, downed logs. The mosses are themselves as
dense as thumbnail forests.

She presses on fissures of bark and her fingers sink in knuckle-deep. A
bit of bushwhacking reveals the extent of the prodigious rot. Crumbling,
creature-riddled boles, decaying for centuries. Snags gothic and twisted,
silvery as inverted icicles. She has never inhaled such fecund putrefaction.
The sheer mass of ever-dying life packed into each single cubic foot, woven
together with fungal filaments and dew-betrayed spiderweb leaves her woozy.
Mushrooms ladder up the sides of trunks in terraced ledges. Dead salmon feed
the trees. Soaked by fog all winter long, spongy green stuff she can't name
covers every wooden pillar in thick baize reaching higher than her head.

Death is everywhere, oppressive and beautiful. She sees the source of that forestry doctrine she so resisted in school. Looking at all this glorious decay, a person might be forgiven for thinking that *old* meant decadent, that such thick mats of decomposition were cellulose cemeteries in need of the rejuvenating ax. She sees why her kind will always dread these close, choked thickets, where the beauty of solo trees gives way to something massed, scary, and crazed. When the fable turns dark, when the slasher film builds to primal horror, this is where the doomed children and wayward adolescents must wander. There are things in here worse than wolves and witches, primal fears that no amount of civilizing will ever tame.

The prodigious forest pulls her along, past the trunk of an immense western red cedar. Her hand strokes the fibrous strips that peel from a fluted trunk whose girth rivals the height of an eastern dogwood. It reeks of incense. The top has sheared off, replaced by a candelabra of boughs promoted to stand-in trunks. A grotto opens at ground level in the rotted heartwood. Whole families of mammals could live inside it. But the branches, a thousand years on, drooping with scaly sprays a dozen stories above her, are still crammed full of cones.

She addresses the cedar, using words of the forest's first humans. "Long Life Maker. I'm here. Down here." She feels foolish, at first. But each word is a little easier than the next.

"Thank you for the baskets and the boxes. Thank you for the capes and hats and skirts. Thank you for the cradles. The beds. The diapers. Canoes. Paddles, harpoons, and nets. Poles, logs, posts. The rot-proof shakes and shingles. The kindling that will always light."

Each new item is release and relief. Finding no good reason to quit now, she lets the gratitude spill out. "Thank you for the tools. The chests. The decking. The clothes closets. The paneling. I forget. . . . Thank you," she says, following the ancient formula. "For all these gifts that you have given." And still not knowing how to stop, she adds, "We're sorry. We didn't know how hard it is for you to grow back."

SHE FINDS WORK with the Bureau of Land Management. Wilderness ranger. The job description seems as miraculous as the outsized trees: Help preserve and protect for present and future generations places where man is a visitor who does not remain. The wild woman must don a uniform. But they pay her to be by herself, carry the welcome weight of a pack, read a topographic map, dig a water bar, look for smoke and fire, teach folks to leave no trace, follow the rhythms of the land, and live wholly within the arc of the year. To clean up after humankind, yes. To gather the endless twisties, baggies, six-pack rings, foil, cans, and bottle caps strewn through meadows of wildflower, on remote scenic outlooks, skewered in the boughs of noble firs, under cold running streams, behind waterfalls. She would gladly pay the government, to do that much.

Her supervisor apologizes for the state of the cabin they give her, on the edge of an ancient cedar grove. There's no running water, and the varmints outweigh the new biped in biomass, many times over. She can only laugh. "You don't understand. You don't understand. It's the Alhambra."

TOMORROW SHE'LL HIKE twenty-five miles, loosening the bolts on the signs attached to trailside trees, so their cambium can keep growing. There's a spot on the other side of the ridge where the bark of a big spruce has swallowed an old Forest Service plaque from the forties that now says only BEWARE OF.

The nightly rain starts. She goes out to the clearing and sits in the downpour, dressed only in a loose cotton shirt, listening to the wood put forth fresh cells. She comes back inside. In the kitchen, she lights the kerosene lamp with chunky strike-anywhere matches and takes the flame into the bedroom. The thump of a bushy-tailed wood rat telegraphs another raid on her worthless belongings. Last week it was a pair of barrettes. Too dark to search for the latest missing loot tonight. She sponges off over the cold-water zinc basin in the corner and gets in bed. No sooner does her ear listen in to the musty pillow than she's transported to the ancestral vacation home, where the future still radiates endless forms most beautiful.

. . .

SHE WORKS for eleven blissful months. The wildlife never once threatens her, and deranged campers do so only twice. In the constant rain, everything grows mold. Monster trees suck up the downpour and respire it back into the air as steam. Spores spread across every damp surface. Both her legs sport athlete's foot up to the knees. Sometimes, when she lies down and closes her eyes, she feels that moss will cover her lids by the time she opens them again. She labors for days to make a storage pad, hacking back the brush from a few square feet. By year's end, the little nick in the undergrowth is covered again in shrub and saplings. She loves feeling that every headway man tries to make into the relentless green blitz will be crushed.

UNKNOWN TO HER, while she rehabs backcountry fire rings and cleans up illegal campsites fouled with beer cans and toilet paper, an article appears. It's published in a reputable journal, one of the best that humankind has managed. Trees trade airborne aerosol signals, the article says. They make medicines. Their fragrances alert and awaken their neighbors. They can sense an attacking species and summon an air force to come to their aid. The authors cite her earlier, much-mocked article. They reproduce her findings and extend them into surprising places. Words of hers that she has all but forgotten have gone on drifting out on the open air, lighting up others, like a waft of pheromones.

PATRICIA IS OUT ONE DAY in an unfamiliar drainage, sawing windthrow from a remote trail. She sees a motion in the undergrowth—the most dangerous game. Drawing nearer, she spies two researchers, a couple of vagabond scientists from that loose confederation who gather every summer in the flimsy trailers full of lab gear in a clearing a handful of miles from her own cabin. She dreads these run-ins with her old tribe. She always says as little as possible. Today, she holds back and watches. Through the woods, at this distance, the two men look like upright, blundering circus bears in lumberjack costumes.

The pair bushwhack a little, closing in on a spot that interests them. One of the men hoots softly, a perfect, purring impersonation. She has heard the call at night, although she has never seen the caller. This imitation would fool her. The man calls again. Incredibly, something answers. A duet ensues: the bright, pert, human come-on, followed by the logy but obliging bird, hidden in the trees. A streak in the air, and the owl appears. Bird of wisdom and sorcerers. It's the first *Strix occidentalis* Patricia has ever seen. Spotted owl: the endangered species that scientists propose to save by locking up billions of dollars of old growth, the only place it can live. It settles down, mythic, on a branch three yards from its seducers. Bird and men regard each other. One species takes pictures. The other just spins its head and blinks its enormous eyes. Then the owl is gone, followed, after further note-taking, by the humans, leaving Patricia Westerford wondering if she wakes or sleeps.

Three weeks later, she's near the same spot, pulling invasive plants. The thick, furry twigs of ailanthus suckers leave her fingers stinking of coffee and peanut butter. She climbs a switchback at a good clip and runs into the two researchers again. They're several yards up the slope, kneeling by a downed log. Before she can flee, they see her and wave. Caught, she waves back and hikes up to them. The older man is on the ground, on his side, popping tiny creatures into specimen bottles.

"Ambrosia beetles?" The two heads turn toward her, startled. Dead logs: the topic was her passion once, and she forgets herself. "When I was a student, my teacher told us that fallen trunks were nothing but obstacles and fire hazards."

The man on the ground looks up at her. "Mine said the same thing."

"'Clear them off to improve forest health.'"

"'Burn them out for safety and cleanliness. Above all, keep them out of streams.'"

"'Lay down the law and get the stagnant place producing again!'"

All three of them chuckle. But the chuckle is like pressing on a wound. *Improve forest health*. As if forests were waiting all these four hundred million years for us newcomers to come cure them. Science in the service of willful blindness: How could so many smart people have missed the obvious? A person has only to look, to see that dead logs are far more alive than living ones. But the senses never have much chance, against the power of doctrine.

"Well," the man on the ground says, "I'm sticking it to the old bastard now!"

Patricia smiles, hope pushing through the ache like a breeze through rain. "What are you studying?"

"Fungi, arthropods, reptiles, amphibians, small mammals, frass, webs, denning, soil. . . . Everything we can catch a dead log doing."

"How long have you been at it?"

The two men trade looks. The younger man hands down another sample bottle. "We're six years in."

Six years, in a field where most studies last a few months. "Where on earth did you find funding for that long?"

"We're planning to study this particular log until it's gone."

She laughs again, a little wilder. A cedar trunk on the wet forest floor: their grad students' great-great-great-grandchildren will have to finish the project. Science, in her absence, has gone as crazy as she always thought it should be. "You'll disappear long before it does."

The man on the ground sits up. "Best thing about studying the forest. You're dead by the time the future can blame you for missing the obvious!" He looks at her as if she, too, is worth researching. "Dr. Westerford?"

She blinks, as baffled as any owl. Then she remembers her uniform badge, on her chest for anybody to read. But that *Doctor*. He could only have gotten that from her buried past. "I'm sorry," she says. "I don't remember ever meeting you."

"You haven't! I heard you talk, years ago. Forest studies conference, in Columbus. Airborne signaling. I was so impressed, I ordered offprints of your article."

*That wasn't me*, she wants to say. *That was somebody else. Someone lying dead and rotting somewhere.*

"They hit you pretty hard."

She shrugs. The younger scientist looks on like a kid on a visit to the Smithsonian.

"I knew you'd be vindicated." Her bafflement is enough to tell him everything. Why she's in the uniform of a wilderness ranger. "Patricia. I'm Henry. This is Jason. Come visit the station." His voice is soft but urgent, like there's something at stake. "You'll want to see what our group is doing. You'll want to learn what your work's been up to, while you were gone."

BY DECADE'S END, Dr. Westerford makes her most surprising discovery of all: she may just love her fellow men. Not all of them, but robustly and with enduring green gratitude, at least those three dozen regulars who take her in and make a home for her in the Dreier Research Station, Franklin Experimental Forest, the Cascades, where she spends several dozen months in a row that are happier and more productive than she imagined possible. Henry Fallows, the group's senior scientist, puts her on a grant. Two other research teams from Corvallis add her to their payrolls. Money is tight, but they give her a mildewed trailer in the Ghetto in the Meadow and access to the mobile lab—all the reagents and pipettes she needs. The latrines and the community showers are sinful indulgences, compared to her BLM cabin, with its frigid sponge baths on the porch at night. Then there's cooked food, in the shared mess hall, although some days she's so immersed in work that someone must come remind her that it's time to eat again.

Her public reputation, like Demeter's daughter, crawls back up from the underworld. A scattering of scientific papers vindicates her original work in airborne semaphores. Young researchers find supporting evidence, in species after species. Acacias alert other acacias to prowling giraffes. Willows, poplars, alders: all are caught warning each other of insect invasion across the open air. It makes no difference, her rehabilitation. She doesn't much care what happens, outside this forest. All the world she needs is here, under this canopy—the densest biomass anywhere on Earth. Steep, steely streams scour through rickles of rock where salmon spawn—water cold enough to kill all pain. Falls flash over ridges turned jade by moss and tumbled with shed branches. In the scattered openings, shot here and there through the understory, sit secret congregations of salmonberry, elderberry, huckleberry, snowberry, devil's club, ocean spray, and kinnikinnick. Great straight conifer monoliths fifteen stories high and a car-length thick hold a roof above all. The air around her resounds with the noise of life getting on with it. *Cheebee* of invisible winter wrens. Industrial pock from jackhammering woodpeckers. Warbler buzz. Thrush flutter. The scatterings of beeping grouse across the forest floor. At night, the cool hoot of owls chills her blood. And, always, the tree frogs' song of eternity.

Through this Eden, her colleagues' astonishing discoveries confirm her suspicions. Slow, long observation makes a laughingstock of what people think about trees. In a nutshell: the rich brown batter of soil—itself mostly unknown microbes and invertebrates, perhaps a million species—channels decay and builds on death in ways she only now begins to suss out. It thrills her to sit at meals and be part of the laughter and shared data, the dizzy network trading in discoveries. The whole group of them, *looking*. Birders, geologists, microbiologists, ecologists, evolutionary zoologists, soil experts, high priests of water. Each of them knows innumerable minute, local truths. Some work on projects designed to run for two hundred years or more. Some are straight out of Ovid, humans on their way to turning into greener things. Together, they form one great symbiotic association, like the ones they study.

Turns out that the temperate jungle's million invisible tangled loops need every kind of death-brokering intermediary to keep the circuits coursing. Clean up such a system, and the countless self-replenishing wells run dry. This gospel of new forestry is confirmed by the most wonderful findings: beards of lichen high in the air, that grow only on the oldest trees and inject essential nitrogen back into the living system. Subterranean voles that feed on truffles and spread the spores of angel fungi across the forest floor. Fungi that infuse into the roots of trees in partnerships so tight it's hard to say where one organism leaves off and the other begins. Hulking conifers that sprout adventitious roots high in the canopy that dip back down to feed on the mats of soil accumulating in the vees of their own branches.

Patricia gives herself to Douglas-firs. Arrow-straight, untapering, soaring up a hundred feet before the first branch. They're an ecosystem unto themselves, hosting more than a thousand species of invertebrates. Framer of cities, king of industrial trees, that tree without which America would have been a very different proposition. Her favorite individuals stand scattered near the station. She can find them by headlamp. The largest of them must be six centuries old. He's so tall, so near the upper limits imposed by gravity, that it takes a day and a half for him to lift water from his roots to the highest of his sixty-five million needles. And every branch smells of deliverance.

The things she catches Doug-firs doing, over the course of these years, fill her with joy. When the lateral roots of two Douglas-firs run into each other underground, they fuse. Through those self-grafted knots, the two trees join their vascular systems together and become one. Networked together underground by countless thousands of miles of living fungal threads, her trees feed and heal each other, keep their young and sick alive, pool their resources and metabolites into community chests. . . . It will take years for the picture to emerge. There will be findings, unbelievable truths confirmed by a spreading worldwide web of researchers in Canada, Europe, Asia, all happily swapping data through faster and better channels. Her trees are far more social than even Patricia suspected. There are no individuals. There aren't even separate species. Everything in the forest is the forest. Competition is not separable from endless flavors of cooperation. Trees fight no more than do the leaves on a single tree. It seems most of nature *isn't* red in tooth and claw, after all. For one, those species at the base of the living pyramid have neither teeth nor talons. But if trees share their storehouses, then every drop of red must float on a sea of green.

THE MEN want her to come back to Corvallis and teach.

"I'm not good enough. I don't really know anything yet."

"That doesn't stop us!"

But Henry Fallows tells her to think about it. "Let's talk when you're ready."

. . .

THE RESEARCH STATION MANAGER, Dennis Ward, drops by with little gifts, when he's on site. Wasps' nests. Insect galls. Pretty stones polished by the creeks. Their standing arrangement reminds Patricia of the one she had with the pack rat she shared her BLM cabin with. Regular visits, lightning and shy, trading in worthless trinkets. Then days of hiding. And just as Patricia once warmed to her resident pack rat, so she grows fond of this gentle, slow-moving man.

Dennis brings her dinner one night. It's an act of pure foraging. Mushroom-hazel casserole, with bread he has baked in a cloche laid in a brush burn. Tonight's conversation is not inspired. It rarely is, and she's grateful enough for that. "How're the trees?" he asks, as he always does. She tells him what she can, minus the biochemistry.

"Walk?" he asks, when they finish rinsing the dishes into a graywater catch. A favorite question, to which she always answers, "Walk!"

He must be ten years older. She knows nothing about him and doesn't ask. They talk only of work—her slow research into the roots of Douglas-firs, his impossible job of corralling scientists and getting them to abide by the minimal rules. She herself is well into autumn. Forty-six—older than her father was, when he died. All her flowers have long since faded. But here's the bee.

They don't go far; they can't. The clearing is small, and the trails are too dark to navigate. But they don't need to go far to be in the thick of all she loves. Out into the rot, the decay, the snags, the luxuriant, prolific dying all around them, where a terrible green rises, riding forth in all directions with its converting coils.

"You're a happy woman," Dennis says, somewhere in that great basin between question and claim.

"I am *now*."

"You like everyone who works here. That's remarkable."

"It's easy to like people who take plants seriously."

But she likes Dennis, too. In his spare motions and abundant silence, he blurs the line between those nearly identical molecules, chlorophyll and hemoglobin.

"You're self-reliant. Like your trees."

"But that's just it, Dennis. They aren't self-reliant. Everything out here is cutting deals with everything else."

"That's what I think, too."

She laughs at the purity of his hunch.

"But you have your routines. You have your work. It keeps you going, full time."

She says nothing, spooked now. On the threshold of a contented middle age, this ambush.

He feels her clench; for the length of several owl calls, he adds no syllable. Then: "Here's the thing. It's nice to cook for you."

She sighs long and slides down into the way things need to be. "It's good to be cooked for."

But everything is so much less spooky than she could have supposed. So much lighter. He says, "What if we kept our separate places? And just . . . came to each other from time to time?"

"That . . . could happen."

"Did our work. Saw each other for dinner. Like now!" He sounds surprised to make the connection between his wild proposal and what the present already holds.

"Yes." She can't yet believe that luck might extend so far.

"But I'd want to sign the papers." He peers out into an opening in the western firs, where the sun has undeniably started to set. "Because then, when I die, you could get the pension."

She takes his shaking hand in the dark. It feels good, like a root must feel, when it finds, after centuries, another root to pleach to underground. There are a hundred thousand species of love, separately invented, each more ingenious than the last, and every one of them keeps making things.

# OLIVIA VANDERGRIFF

 SNOW IS THIGH-HIGH and the going slow. She plunges through drifts like a pack animal, Olivia Vandergriff, back to the boardinghouse on the edge of campus. Her last session ever of Linear Regression and Time Series Models has finally ended. The carillon on the quad peals five, but this close to the solstice, blackness closes around Olivia like midnight. Breath crusts her upper lip. She sucks it back in, and ice crystals coat her pharynx. The cold drives a metal filament up her nose. She could die out here, for real, five blocks from home. The novelty thrills her.

December of senior year. The semester so close to over. She might stumble now, fall face-first, and still roll across the finish line. What's left? A short-answer exam on survival analysis. Final paper in Intermediate Macroeconomics. Hundred and ten slide IDs in Masterpieces of World Art, her blow-off elective. Ten more days plus one more semester and she's done forever.

Three years ago, she thought actuarial science was the same as accounting. When the counselor told her it dealt in the price and probability of uncertain events, the rigor combined with ghoulishness made her declare, *Yes, please.* If life demanded a slavish commitment to one pursuit, there were worse things to commit to than calculating the cash value of death. Being one of three females in the program also gave her a little frisson. A kick, to defy the odds.

But the kick has long since gone limp. She's taken the national Society of Actuaries preliminary exam three times and failed all three. Part of the problem is aptitude. Part is the sex, drugs, and all-night parties. She'll get the degree; she can still manage that. If not, she'll sample whatever opportunities disaster presents. Disaster is, as actuarial science proves and Olivia reassures her overly concerned friends, just another number.

She turns the corner onto Cedar in the half dark. Other students, stumbling under the weight of their own backpacks, have beaten trails through the snow, clumping around the first walker's mostly terrible guesses. Beneath the fresh drifts, cracked sidewalks ride up over bulging tree roots in the world's slowest seismic waves. She looks up. Although she'll miss precious little when she leaves this shit-kicking backwater, she does love the streetlamps. Their Gilded Age cream-colored globes look like stilled candles. They light a soft path through the student rentals all the way to her own rambling American Gothic, once some surgeon's mansion, now chopped up into private cubbies with five separate fire escapes and eight mailboxes.

Lit by the streetlamp in front of her house is a singular tree that once covered the earth—a living fossil, one of the oldest, strangest things that ever learned the secret of wood. A tree with sperm that must swim through droplets to fertilize the ovule. Its leaves vary as much as human faces. Its limbs, in the streetlight, have that extraordinary profile, lined with bizarre short sidespurs that make the tree unmistakable, even in winter. She has lived under the tree for a whole semester and doesn't know it's there. She passes it again tonight without seeing.

She stumbles up the snowy steps into a dark hall full of bicycles. She shuts the front door behind her, but frigid air keeps pouring through around the seams. The light switch teases her from across the foyer. Six steps into the black gauntlet, Olivia slits her ankle on a derailleur. Her curses echo up the stairs. She has raged against the bikes at house meetings all semester long. But here the bikes are, despite all the house votes, her frozen ankle gouged and smeared with bike grease, and her enraged sense of justice shouting, "Shit, shit, *shit!*"

Nothing matters. Five little months, and life will begin. Even if she's still living in rented squalor in a cold-water apartment over a breakfast dive where she waitresses, all the forthcoming crimes and misdemeanors will be gloriously hers alone.

Someone snickers at the top of the stairs. "Everything all right?" Suppressed giggles seep down from the kitchen. Her housemates, entertained by her routine rage.

"Just fine," she chirps. Home. December 12, 1989. The Berlin Wall, coming down. From the Baltic to the Balkans, millions of oppressed people take to the winter streets. Her scraped-open ankle spills blood through the foyer. So what? She bends to press a dry Kleenex to her wound, stanching the flow. It stings like mad.

HUGS AWAIT HER ABOVE: two routine, one mocking, one cold, and one filled with half a year of hangdog longing. She hates her housemates' endless cheap hugging, but she hugs them back in kind. The group converged the previous spring in an orgy of mutual enthusiasm. By the end of September, the communal lovefest spun out into daily recrimination. *Whose hairs are these in my razor? Somebody stole the thimble of hash I left in the freezer. Who the hell stuffed that leftover turkey log down the disposal?* But a girl can do anything, with the finish line in sight.

The kitchen smells like heaven, though no one invites her to share the meal. She checks the refrigerator. The prospects are abysmal. She hasn't eaten for ten hours, but she decides to hold out a little longer. If she can wait to eat until after her private party, eating will be like dancing with demigods.

"Got divorced today," she announces.

Scattered cheers and clapping. "Took you long enough," says the least favorite of her former soul mates.

"True. Been getting divorced for longer than I was married."

"Don't change your name back. This one's much better."

"What were you thinking anyway, getting married?"

"That ankle looks bad. You should at least clean off the grease." Another round of stifled giggles.

"Love you guys, too." Olivia steals a bottle of somebody's nut-brown ale—the only thing in the refrigerator not rancid—and squirrels it away into her rehabbed attic room. There, in bed, she knocks back the contents of the bottle without lifting her head. Acquired talent. Grease and blood from her ankle smear the bedspread.

SHE AND DAVY met in court one last time, that afternoon, between her Econ and Linear Analysis. Now they're done, and the final decree has no power to sadden her further. She does have her regrets. Tying her life to another's—a whim of sophomore spring—felt so all-in, so sweeping and innocent. For two years, their parents raged at the idiocy. Their friends never understood. But she and Davy were determined to prove everyone wrong.

They did love each other, in their way, even if their way consisted mostly of getting high, reading Rumi out loud, then screwing each other senseless. But marriage turned them both abusive. After the third time through the fun-house werewolf act, which ended up with her fracturing her fifth metacarpal, somebody had to sober up and pull the plug. They had no property to speak of, and no kids except the two of them. The divorce should have taken a day and a half. That it took more than ten months was mostly a function of nostalgic lust on the part of both litigants.

Olivia sets the empty beer on the radiator with the other dead recruits and fishes in the nest of crap by her bed until she finds her disc player. Divorce requires a memorial service. Marriage was her adventure, and she needs to commemorate. Davy kept the Rumi, but she still has scads of their favorite trance music and dope enough to turn the regrets into laughs sufficient for today. There's her Linear Analysis final to worry about, of course. But that's still three days off, and she always studies better when a little loose.

It should have occurred to her two years ago, even in the initial thrill, that any relationship where she lied three times in the first two hours might not be a great long-term bet. They walked under the cherry blossoms in the campus arboretum. She professed a deep love for all flowering things, which was a flavor of true, at least right then. She told him that her father was a human rights lawyer, again not entirely false, and that her mother was a writer, which was pretty much bullshit, though based on a fact-like scenario. She isn't ashamed of her parents. In fact, she once got suspended from grade school for punching a chick who called her father "flaccid." But in the world of satisfying stories—her preferred domain—both of Olivia's parents are so much less than they should have been. So she spruced them up a tad, for the man she'd already decided she would spend the rest of her life with.

Davy lied, too. He claimed he didn't need to graduate, that he'd done so well on the civil service exam the State Department had offered him a job. The fib was outrageous enough to be kind of beautiful. She did have a thing for fantasists. Later, under the cherry-blossom snow, he'd flashed her the little Victorian tin with the mustache-wax ad on the top and the six long thin bullets of weed inside. She'd never seen anything like it, except in high school anti-drug films. And soon enough, she was sold on the fine art of hang gliding above the busy earth. So began her still-unfolding romance with a gift that kept on giving, a romance that, unlike the one with Davy, was sure to last a lifetime.

She cues up the trance playlist, sits in her beloved window seat, opens the sash to the frigid night, and blows puffs of smoke onto the death-trap fire escape. The phone rings, but she doesn't pick up. It's one of three men whose beliefs about her logistics she can no longer keep straight. The phone rings on. She has no answering machine. Who would use a device that leaves you responsible for calling someone back? She counts the rings, a kind of meditation. A dozen summons, while she blows two fat puffs of hash cloud into the frozen outdoors. The crazed persistence narrows down the caller, until she knows. It can only be her ex checking in, hoping to mark the occasion with one last loving brawl.

·  ·  ·

THE PSYCHO-SOCIO-SEXUAL AWAKENING of little Olivia: so much more education than she signed on for when she came to town. She arrived on campus three years before with a teddy bear, a hair dryer, a hot-air popper, and a high school varsity letter in volleyball. She means to leave next spring with a crater-strewn transcript, two tongue studs, a florid tattoo on her scapula, and a scrapbook of mental travels she could never have imagined.

She's still a good girl, of sorts. The plan is simply to be a semi-bad girl for a few more months. Then she'll straighten up, fly right, and head westerly, where all good fuck-ups always head. Once out there—wherever *there* is— there'll be plenty of time to figure out how to salvage her bungled degree. She can be ingenious, when required. And she knows how to make herself more than cute, with a little application. Things are happening; the world is cracking open. She might check out Berlin, now that the future is headed that way. Vilnius. Warsaw. Someplace where the rules are being hammered out from scratch.

The music pelts her deltoids and takes her brain out for a lazy adult swim. Spiders set up a colony under her skin. When she places a palm on her thigh, the push of it keeps gliding all the way out to the idea horizon. Soon the beautiful brainstorms come, the ones that link up in front of her eyes and make the whole mess of human history so lovely and self-evident. The universe is big, and she's allowed to fly around through the nearby galaxies for a while, zapping things for fun, if she doesn't abuse her powers or hurt anyone. She does so love this ride.

Then the tunes start up, the inner ones. She shuts off the disc player and tries to figure out how to cross the ocean of room. When she stands, her head keeps rising, straight up, into a whole new layer of being. Her laugh propels her, helps her balance, and she sails off across the floorboards, her tits glowing like precious pearls. After a while, she gets to where she was going and holds still for a minute, trying to recall why she needed to get there. Hard to hear anything, over the magic melodies of her own devising.

She sits at her chipboard student desk and fishes out her song notebook. Real musical notation reads to her like so much secret writing, but she has devised her own system for preserving the tunes that come to her while stepping out. Line color, thickness, and location all encode a record of the gift melodies. And the next day, after her buzz wears off, she can look at these scribbles and hear the music all over again. Like copping a contact buzz, for free.

Tonight's tune pushes her back into the chair as a band of unknown instruments play the song the angels will play for God on the night He decides to bring everybody home. It's the best inner sound track she has ever managed, perhaps the best thing she's done with her entire life. She starts crying and wants to call her parents. She wants to go back down into the rooming house and embrace her housemates, this time for real. The music says: *You don't know how brilliantly you shine.* It says: *Something is waiting for you, the clean, perfect thing you've wanted since childhood.* Then that hallowed bliss turns ridiculous, and she laughs, a little wildly, at her own wasted soul.

But the tune and the bliss leave her tingling all over. The idea of a hot shower takes on religious urgency. Her rigged-up bathroom—carved out of the same attic as her bedroom—sports a skin of frost on the inside of its north wall. The secret is to run the hot water before disrobing. By the time she gets into the do-it-yourself shower, she's faint from hunger and the bathroom air is a paisley swirl of fire and ice. She looks down. The floor of the stall fills with bloody lather. She screams. Then she remembers her sliced ankle. As she soaps the oozing wound, the giggles come again. Humans are so frail. How have they survived long enough to wreak all the shit they have?

The cleaning stings like hell. The gash is jagged and ugly. If it scars, she can hide it with another tattoo—some kind of ankle-chain, perhaps. She works the soap up her legs. The slickness of her skin feels like the best divorce present a girl could ask for. Each touch is electric. Her body brightens, demanding satisfaction.

Someone knocks hard. "You okay in there?"

Her voice takes a moment to catch. "Go away, please."

"You screamed."

"Scream over. Thank you!"

She materializes back in her room. Her body, draped in towel and steam, shines with need. Even the gelid air strokes her like a sex toy. The world offers nothing better than bringing yourself over the crest of ecstasy. She drops the towel and splays into bed. The fall into the blankets lasts forever and keeps improving. She reaches up into the shade of the floor lamp to shut it off and plunge herself into delicious darkness. But as her damp hand pats for the switch on the cheap socket, all the current in the sub-code house enters her limb and pours into her body. Her muscles close around the jolt as in some science experiment, clamping her hand around the electricity that's killing her.

She lies there, naked, wet, convulsing, her hand snaked up in the air, trying to force the word *help* from the bottom of her lungs out through a mouth that the voltage locks rigid. She manages to birth up one ambiguous moan before her heart stops. Down below, her housemates hear the cry— her second of the night. The sound's raw intimacy makes them blush.

"Olivia," one says, smirking.

"Don't even ask."

The whole house dims, the moment she dies.

TRUNK

A man sits at a desk in his cell in a medium-security prison. Trees have landed him here. Trees and too much love of them. He still can't say how wrong he was, or whether he'd choose to be so wrong again. The only text that can answer that question spreads, unreadable, under his hands.

His fingers trace the grain in the desk's wooden top. He's trying to see how these wild loops in the wood could ever have come from so simple a thing as rings. Some mystery in the angle of the cut, the place of the plane inside the nested cylinders. If his brain were a slightly different thing, the problem might be easy. If he himself grew differently, he might be able to see.

The grain under his fingers swings in uneven bands—thick light, thin dark. It shocks him to realize, after a lifetime of looking at wood: He's staring at the seasons, the year's pendulum, the burst of spring and the enfolding of fall, the beat of a two-four song recorded here, in a medium that the piece itself created. The grain wanders like ridges and ravines on a topo map. Pale rush forward, darker holding back. For a moment, the rings resolve from out of the angled cut. He can map them, project their histories into the wood's plane. And still, he's illiterate. Wide in the good years—sure—and narrow in the bad. But nothing more.

If he could read, if he could translate. . . . If he were only a slightly different creature, then he might learn all about how the sun shone and the rain fell and which way the wind blew against this trunk for how hard and long. He might decode the vast projects that the soil organized, the murderous freezes, the suffering and struggle, shortfalls and surpluses, the attacks repelled, the years of luxury, the storms outlived, the sum of all the threats and chances that came from every direction, in every season this tree ever lived.

*His finger moves across the prison desk, trying to learn this alien script, transcribing it like a monk in a scriptorium. He traces the grain and thinks of all the things this antique, illegible almanac could say, all the things that the remembering wood might tell him, in this place where he is held, with no change of seasons and one fixed weather.*

SHE'S DEAD for a minute and ten seconds. No pulse, no breath. Then Olivia's body, shucked from the lamp when the fuses blow, spills over the edge of the bed and hits the floor. The impact restarts her stopped heart.

Naked and comatose on the pine floorboards: that's how Olivia's new ex-husband finds her when he comes over in hope of a major blowout followed by make-up sex. He rushes her to the university hospital, where she revives. She's still buzzed. Her ribs are bruised, her hand burned, and her ankle lacerated. The physician's assistant wants a full account, which Olivia can't give.

The feckless, distraught ex-husband leaves her in doctors' hands. The doctors want to do some neurological assessment. They want a scan. But Olivia escapes when no one's looking. It's a university hospital, and everyone's busy. She strolls out through the lobby, the picture of health. Who's to stop her? She heads back to the boardinghouse and barricades herself in her room. Her housemates ascend to the attic to check on her, but she refuses to open the door. For two full days, she hides in the room. Each time anyone knocks, the voice inside calls out, "I'm fine!" Her housemates don't know who to call. No sounds come from behind the door except for muffled shuffling.

Olivia sleeps and keeps still, holds her bruised ribs, and tries to remember what happened. She was dead. In those seconds while she had no pulse, large, powerful, but desperate shapes beckoned to her. They showed her something, pleading with her. But the moment she came back to life, everything vanished.

She finds her song notebook wedged behind the desk. Colored jottings re-create the tune in her head just before her electrocution. Through the tune, she retrieves much of the evening's disaster. She sees herself parading around the renovated attic, addicted to her body. It's like watching a zoo animal circle its cage. For the first time, she realizes that *being alone* is a contradiction in terms. Even in a body's most private moments, something else joins in. Someone spoke to her when she was dead. Used her head as a screen for disembodied thoughts. She passed through a triangular tunnel of strobing color and emerged into a clearing. There, the presences—the only thing to call them—removed her blinders and let her look *through*. Then she fell back into her prison body, and the incredible vistas blurred to nothing.

She thinks: *Maybe I have brain damage.* Several times an hour she must shut her eyes, while words move her speechless lips. *Tell me what happened. What am I supposed to do, now?* It takes a while before she realizes she's praying.

SHE SKIPS ALL HER FINALS. Calls her parents to say she won't be flying home for Christmas. Her father is baffled, then hurt. Ordinarily, she'd resort to outshouting the man. But nobody's anger can hurt a girl who has already died. She tells him everything—her solo divorce party, her electrocution. Hiding is pointless now. Something's watching—huge, living sentinels know who she is.

Her father sounds lost, the way she feels when she lies in bed at night, sure she'll never retrieve what was shown to her while she was dead. Now, postmortem, she hears her father's fear—dark undercurrents in the lawyer she never suspected. For the first time since she was a child, she wants to comfort him. "Daddy, I screwed up. I hit the wall. I need to rest."

"Come home. You can rest here. You can't be alone at the holidays."

He sounds so frail. He has always been alien to her, a man of procedures where there should be passions. Now she wonders if he might have died, once, too.

They talk for longer than they have in years. She tells him what dying feels like. She even tries to tell him about the presences in the clearing, the ones that showed her things, though she uses words that won't freak him. *Impulses. Energy.* Twice he's on the verge of hopping in the car and driving the 650 miles to bring her back home. She talks him down. Seventy seconds of death have invested her with strange power. Everything between them has altered, as if he's the child now and she the guardian.

She asks for something she has never asked for before. "Put Mom on for a minute. I want to talk to her." Even her mother's fury is Olivia's now to know and soothe. By the end of their conversation, both women are in tears, promising each other crazy things.

SHE'S ALONE in the boardinghouse from Christmas until New Year's. Every intoxicant she owns goes down the toilet. Her grades arrive: two Fs, a D-minus, and a C. The letters are a distraction from that thing she's fighting to remember. Whole days pass when she barely eats. An ice storm coats the town in a lapidary crust. It tears boughs off the oaks and maples. Olivia sits on the bed where her heart stopped, her knees to her chest and her song notebook in her lap. She stands and steps. The spot on the floor where Davy found her that night feels hot under her bare feet. She's alive, and she doesn't know why.

She lies awake at night, staring upward, remembering being right next to the only discovery that matters. Life was whispering instructions to her, and she failed to write them down. The prayer thing becomes easier. *I'm still. I'm listening. What do you want from me?* On New Year's Eve, she's asleep by ten. Two hours later, she wakens to gunfire and bolts up, screaming. Then the clock tells her: fireworks. The nineties have arrived.

Her housemates return in the new year. They treat her like she's ill. They're afraid of her, now that her bitchiness has vanished. She sits in the kitchen while people around her joke and get smashed and try to ignore the ghost at the table. It amazes her that she has never felt their sadness or noticed their distress. Incredibly, they still believe in safety. They live as if a shim and some duct tape might hold them together. They have become vulnerable in her eyes, and infinitely dear.

On the first day of the new semester, Olivia sits on the rim of an auditorium bowl while a brilliant lecturer calculates the premiums and payout needed for both the insurance company and the dead person to feel that they've won. "Insurance," the lecturer says, "is the backbone of civilization. No risk pool—no skyscrapers, no blockbuster movies, no large-scale agriculture, no organized medicine."

The empty seat next to her rustles. She turns. There, inches from her face, is the thing she's been praying for. A cone of charged air gusts into her thoughts. They've returned, beckoning. They want her to stand and leave the auditorium. She will do whatever they ask. Down the stone steps in her winter coat, she crosses the icy main quad. She skirts the classroom buildings, the library, a freshman dorm, walking without thinking, drawn along by the presences. For a moment, she imagines her destination is the Civil War cemetery south of campus. Then it's clear she's heading toward the parking lot where she keeps her car.

Inside the car, she understands that she'll be driving for a while. She stops at the boardinghouse to fetch some things. Three trips to her room suffice to salvage everything she could want. She piles the clothes on the back seat. Then she's gone.

The car finds its way to the state highway. Soon she's passing the sedge meadows and oak openings northwest of town. Last fall's stubble dots the snow-covered fields. She drives for a long time, obeying the presences. Like a radio station from another city, their signal wavers between clear and static. She makes herself an instrument of their will.

Across the Maumee, the way jogs southwest. A breakfast bar in the glove compartment passes for lunch. Her change purse holds several bills and a debit card for an account containing just under two thousand dollars. Her mind has nothing even faintly resembling a plan. But she remembers what Jesus said about the flowers, and not worrying about tomorrow. Once the nuns made every student memorize a Bible passage; she chose that one to irritate the teacher, who was big on personal responsibility. She liked the Jesus who would appall every law-abiding, property-acquiring American Christian. Jesus the Communist, the crazed shop-trasher, the friend of deadbeats. *Sufficient unto the day is the evil thereof.* A gust of remorse passes through her as she drives. *I'm missing Statistical Inference.* Fitting. To this point in life, she has missed everything. Now inference vanishes, and soon she'll *know.*

Dusk and Indiana come faster than she expects. Darkness, ridiculously early, still so close to the solstice. She's starved for real food and so tired she keeps hitting the snowdrifted rumble strip. The presences vanish for half an hour. Her confidence slips. It's hard to pray and drive at the same time. In front of her spread the vacant cornfields of the true Midwest. She has no idea why she's here. Then something occupies the passenger seat, and she's good for another hundred miles.

Davy once told her that the best place to sleep rough is outside a warehouse store. She finds one easily and pulls the car into a well-lit corner of the plowed lot, under the security camera. A quick duck inside to pee and buy snacks, and she returns to the car to set up camp in the back seat. She falls asleep under three armloads of clothes, praying, waiting, listening.

It's Indiana, 1990. Here, five years is a generation, fifty is archaeology, and anything older shades off into legend. And yet, places remember what people forget. The parking lot she sleeps in was once an orchard, its trees planted by a gentle, crazed Swedenborgian who wandered through these parts in rags and a tin pot cap, preaching the New Heaven and extinguishing campfires to keep from killing bugs. A crackpot saint who practiced abstinence while supplying four states with enough fermentable apple mash to keep every pioneer American from nine to ninety half crocked for decades.

All day long, she has followed Johnny Appleseed's path into the interior. Olivia read about the man once, in a comic her father gave her. The comic made him a superhero, with the power to make things spring up from the dirt. It said nothing about the philanthropist with a shrewd sense of property, the tramp who'd die owning twelve hundred acres of the richest land in the country. She always thought he was just myth. She must still discover that myths are basic truths twisted into mnemonics, instructions posted from the past, memories waiting to become predictions.

Here's the thing about an apple: it sticks in the throat. It's a package deal: lust and understanding. Immortality and death. Sweet pulp with cyanide seeds. It's a bang on the head that births up whole sciences. A golden delicious discord, the kind of gift chucked into a wedding feast that leads to endless war. It's the fruit that keeps the gods alive. The first, worst crime, but a fortunate windfall. *Blessed be the time that apple taken was.*

And here's the thing about an apple's seeds: they're unpredictable. Offspring might be anything. Staid parents generate a wild child. Sweet can go sour, or bitter turn buttery. The only way to preserve a variety's taste is to graft a cutting onto new rootstock. It would surprise Olivia Vandergriff to learn: every apple with a name goes back to the same tree. Jonathan, McIntosh, Empire: lucky rolls in *Malus*'s Monte Carlo game.

And a named apple is a patentable apple, as Olivia's father would tell her. She once fought with him over a case of his. He was helping a transnational company prosecute a farmer who'd saved some of last year's soybean crop and replanted, without paying royalties again. She was outraged. "You can't own the rights to a living thing!"

"You can. You should. Protecting intellectual property creates wealth."

"What about the soybean? Who's paying the soybean for its intellectual property?"

He looked at her with that judging frown: *Whose child are you?*

The man who once owned the lot she sleeps in—the wandering apple missionary in the stove-pot hat—was sure that grafting caused a tree pain. He'd pick apple seeds out of the pomace of a mill and sow an orchard with them, a little farther west. And whatever seeds he sowed ran their own willful and unpredictable experiments. Like arcane magic, the man's waving hand transformed a swath from Pennsylvania to Illinois into fruit trees. All day long, she drove that country. She sleeps now in a parking lot that was once an orchard full of unpredictable apples. The trees have vanished and the town forgets. But not the land.

She wakes early, stiff with cold, under a pile of clothing. The car is filled with beings of light. They're everywhere, unbearable beauty, the way they were the night her heart stopped. They pass into and through her body. They don't scold her for forgetting the message they gave her. They simply infuse her again. Her joy at their return spills over, and she starts to cry. They speak no words out loud. Nothing so crude as that. They aren't even *they*. They're part of her, kin in some way that isn't yet clear. Emissaries of creation—things she has seen and known in this world, experiences lost, bits of knowledge ignored, family branches lopped off that she must recover and revive. Dying has given her new eyes.

*You were worthless*, they hum. *But now you're not. You have been spared from death to do a most important thing.*

*What thing?* she wants to ask. But she must keep silent and still.

*Life's moment is here. A test that it has not yet had.*

She lives through eternity, under a pile of clothes, in the back seat of a freezing car. Disembodied entities from the far side of death make themselves known, here, now, in the parking lot of this store, calling on her for help. The sun edges up out of the earth. Two shoppers exit the store. It's only dawn, and they're pushing a cart with a carton as large as her car. Her thoughts narrow to a point. *Just tell me. Say what you want, and I'll do it.* A container truck passes, grinding its gears on its way to the loading docks. In the noise, the beings disperse. Olivia panics. They haven't finished giving her the assignment. She scrambles in her shoulder bag for something to write with. On the back of a box of cough drops, she scribbles, *spared, test*. But these words mean nothing.

It's morning in earnest now. Her bladder is bursting. A minute more, and nothing matters but peeing. She leaves the car and crosses the lot into the store. Inside, an older man greets her as if she's an old friend. The store is a drag show of well-being and mirth. Televisions line a wall at the back, ranging in size from bread box to monolith. They're all tuned to the same morning diversion. Hundreds of skydivers join for a simultaneous midair church service. She plunges fifty yards through the gauntlet of screens into the bathroom. Relief, when it comes, is heavenly. Then sad again. *Just a sign*, she pleads, drying herself. *Just say what you want of me.*

Back in the TV gauntlet, the mass aerial church service gives way to another gathering. All down the wall, on scores of different sets, people sit chained together in a trench in front of a bulldozer, in a small town that the title text identifies as Solace, California. A quick cut, and a dozen people form a human ring around a tree they barely enclose. The tree looks like a special effect. The shot, even from a distance, encompasses only the bare base. Blue paint stains the behemoth trunk. A voice-over narrates the show-down, but the tree, replicated across a wall of screens, so stuns Olivia that she misses the details. The camera cuts away, to a woman of fifty with pulled-back hair, a plaid shirt, and eyes like beacons. She says, "Some of these trees were around before Jesus was born. We've already taken ninety-seven per-cent of the old ones. Couldn't we find a way to keep the last three percent?"

Olivia freezes. The creatures of light that ambushed her out in the car swarm her again, saying, *This, this, this*. But the instant she knows she must pay strict attention, the segment ends and another begins. She stands, star-ing at a debate over whether flamethrowers are protected by the Second Amendment. The light beings vanish. Revelation collapses into consumer electronics.

She wanders, dazed, out of the monster store. She's starving, but she buys nothing. She can't even imagine eating. In the car, she knows now that she must press on west. The sun rises behind her, filling her rearview mirror. Dawn-pinked snow coats the fields. Across the western sky, pewter clouds begin to lighten, and somewhere beneath them lies life's moment.

She needs to call her parents, but she has no way to tell them what's hap-pening. She drives another fifty miles, trying to reconstruct what she just saw. Plats of harvested Indiana farmland shine yellow-brown-black, all the way to the horizon. The road is clear and cars are few, with no towns to speak of. Two days ago, down a road like this, she would have been doing eighty. Today, she drives like her life might be worth something.

Near the Illinois border, she crests a rise. Down the road, a railroad gate flashes. A long, slow, heartland freight rolls through on its way north to the superhub of Gary and Chicago. The steady *ka-thump* of the wheels through the intersection sets up a dub tune in her head. The train is endless; she settles in. Then she notices the cargo. Car after car clicks past, each loaded with pallets of dimensional lumber. A rolling river of wood cut into uniform beams streams by without end. She begins to count cars, but stops at sixty. She has never seen so much wood. A map animates her head: trains like this, this very minute, thread the country in every direction, feeding all the great metro sprawls and their satellites. She thinks: *They have arranged this for me.* Then she thinks, *No: such trains pass by all the time.* But now she's primed to see.

The last of the wood-stacked cars passes, the zebra guard lifts, and the red lights stop flashing. She doesn't move. Someone behind her honks. She holds still. The honker lays into the horn, then peels out around her, screaming in the sealed cabin and shaking a middle finger at her like he's trying to ignite it. She closes her eyes; across her lids, small people sit chained together around an enormous tree.

*The most wondrous products of four billion years of life need help.*

She laughs and opens her eyes, which fill with tears. *Confirmed. I hear you. Yes.*

She looks over her left shoulder to see a car pointed the other direction, stopped alongside her with the window down. An Asian man wearing a T-shirt that reads NOLI TIMERE is asking her, for the second time, "Are you all right?" She smiles and nods and waves apology. She starts her engine, which stalled while she was watching the endless river of lumber. Then she rolls out west again. Only now she knows where she's headed. Solace. The air all around sparks with connections. The presences light around her, singing new songs. *The world starts here. This is the merest beginning. Life can do anything. You have no idea.*

YEARS BEFORE and far to the northwest, Ray Brinkman and Dorothy Cazaly Brinkman head back home after midnight from the party following the St. Paul Players' opening night of *Who's Afraid of Virginia Woolf?*

They've just played the young couple Nick and Honey, who, over a few drinks with new friends, learn what their species can do.

Months ago, at the start of rehearsals, the four leads savored the play's viciousness. "I'm *nuts*," Dorothy announced to the rest of the cast. "I grant you that. But these people—these people are *truly gone*." By opening night, all four of them are frayed and sick of each other and ready to do real damage. It makes for great community theater. The play is the Brinkmans' best outing, by far. Ray stuns everyone with his petty conniving. Dorothy is brilliant in that two-hour free fall from innocence into knowing. It takes only the slightest Stanislavski to find their inner demons.

Next Friday is Dorothy's forty-second birthday. Over the course of several years, they've spent a hundred and fifty thousand dollars on fertility treatments that turn out to be voodoo. Three days before the play opened, they received the final blow. There's nothing left to try.

"My life, right?" Dorothy is looped and weepy in the passenger seat, coming home from her triumph. "All mine. I'm supposed to *own it*, right?"

It has become a sore spot between them, *ownership*: what Ray spends all day safeguarding. He has never quite convinced his wife that prosecuting the theft of good ideas is the best way to make everyone richer. Drink does not help the level of debate. "My own private personal property. Can I have a fucking garage sale?"

Dorothy's own job now makes her ill. People suing other people, and she must record every slanderous sentiment with her narrow, chorded keyboard stenotype, word by precise word. All she wants is to have a child. A child would give her meaningful work at last. Barring that, she wants to sue someone.

Ray makes an art of staying still under her attacks. He tells himself, not for the first time, that he has taken nothing away from her. *If anything* . . . he thinks. But he refuses to think that thought. That's his right—not to think what it's only fair to think.

He doesn't have to. She has the thought for him. He clicks the clicker and the garage opens. They pull in. "You should leave me," she says.

"Dorothy. Please stop. You're making me crazy."

"Really. Leave. Go somewhere. Find somebody where you can have a family. Men do that forever. Guys can knock chicks up when they're eighty, for fuck's sake. I wouldn't mind, Ray. Really. Only fair. You're the fairness guy, remember? Oop. He says nothing. Got nothing to say. Nothing to say in his defense."

Silence is what he has. His first and last best weapon.

They come in the front door. *What a dump*, they both think, though neither needs to say it. They drop their crap on the couch and head upstairs, where they take off their clothes, each in a separate walk-in closet. They stand at the his-and-hers sinks, brushing their teeth. The best night of acting they've ever done. A nice-sized theater full of enthusiastic applause. Calls for an encore.

Dorothy puts one foot in front of the other, exaggerated, like the police— her husband—are making her walk a straight line. She raises her toothbrush to her mouth, waves it around, then breaks into tears, biting down on one end of the plastic stick while clutching the other.

Ray, the night's designated driver, soberer than he cares to be, sets down his brush and goes to her. She leans her head on his collarbone. Toothpaste dribbles out of her mouth down his plaid bathrobe. Toothpaste and saliva everywhere. Her words are full of pebbles. "I just want to stand in the lobby before the show and tell everyone as they come in. *There's no fucking baby!*"

He gets her to spit and wipes her off with a washrag. Then he leads her to bed, a place that has felt much like a double-wide pine box, these last two months. He must lift her feet in, then nudge her to make room. "We can go to Russia." It feels good to speak in his own voice, after way too many hours as someone smarmy. He doesn't want to play in any more plays, ever again. "Or China. So many babies that need parents who'll love them."

There's a thing people in the theater call *hanging the lampshade*. Say there's a big ugly piece of pipe sticking out the backstage wall, and you can't get rid of it. Stick a shade on it and call it a fixture.

Her words blur into the damp pillow. "Wouldn't be ours."

"Of course it would."

"I want a little RayRay. Your little guy. A boy. Like how you were."

"It wouldn't be—"

"Or a little girl, like you. I don't care."

"Sweetie. Don't be like this. A child is what you raise. Not what genes you—"

"Genes are what you *get*, goddamn it." She slaps the mattress and tries to bolt upright. The speed of the ascent tumbles her over. "The only. Thing. You. Truly. Own."

"We don't own our genes," he says, neglecting to add that companies can own them for us. "Listen. We go someplace where there are too many babies. We adopt two. We love them and play with them and teach them how to tell right from wrong, and they grow up all tangled together with us. I don't care whose *genes* they have."

She pulls the pillow over her head. "Listen to him. This guy can love everybody. Let's just get him a dog. Better yet, some vegetable we can stick out in the yard and forget about." Then she remembers their anniversary custom, neglected for the past two years. She springs up to retrieve the words that fly out from her. But her shoulder clips him in the jaw just as he leans forward. His teeth mash up through the side of his tongue. He yells, then grabs his face, contorted with pain.

"Oh, Ray. Shit. *Damn me!* I didn't . . . I didn't mean . . ."

He waves his hand in the air. *I'm okay.* Or: *What's wrong with you?* Or even: *Get away from me.* She can't tell, even after a decade of marriage and other amateur theatricals, which. Out in the yard, all around the house, the things they've planted in years gone by are making significance, making meaning, as easily as they make sugar and wood from nothing, from air, and sun, and rain. But the humans hear nothing.

FIVE INTERSTATES LEAD WEST, the fingers of a glove laid down on the continent with its wrist in Illinois. Olivia takes the middle one. She has a goal now—Northern California by the fastest route, before the last trees as big as rocket ships go down. She crosses the Mississippi at the Quad Cities and stops at the World's Largest Truck Stop, on I-80, over the Iowa border. The place is a small town. She has her choice of more gas pumps than she can count before freezing. Several hundred trucks school around the spot where she pulls up, colossal sharks in a feeding frenzy.

The light is gone. Olivia rents a shower and gets herself human again. She strolls down a crowded covered avenue of restaurants that offer hundreds of ways to partake of corn, corn syrup, corn-fed chicken, and corn-fed beef. There's a dentist's office and a masseuse. An enormous two-story showroom. A museum revealing how much of the world depends on trucks. There are game rooms and entertainment alleys, exhibits, lounges, and a fireplace flanked by stuffed chairs. She curls up in one and dozes off. She wakes to a security guard kicking her ankles. "No sleeping."

"I was just sleeping."

"No sleeping."

She returns to the car and dozes under her clothes again until dawn. Back in the food tunnel, she buys a muffin, changes four dollars into quarters, finds a phone, and braces for the worst. But in her chest, a strange and new-found calm. The words will come.

An operator tells her to deposit lots of money. Her father picks up. "Olivia? It's six in the morning. What's wrong?"

"Nothing! I'm fine. I'm in Iowa."

"*Iowa?* What's going on?"

Olivia smiles. What's going on is too big to fit into the phone. "Dad, it's all right. It's something good. Very good."

"Olivia. Hello? Olivia?"

"I'm here."

"Are you in trouble?"

"No, Dad. Just the opposite."

"Olivia. *What on Earth is happening?*"

"I've made . . . some new friends. Uh, organizers. They have work for me."

"What kind of work?"

*The most wondrous products of four billion years of life need help.* It's simple enough, and self-evident, now that the light-beings have pointed it out. Every reasonable person on the planet should be able to see. "There's a project. Out West. Important volunteer work. I've been recruited."

"What do you mean, *recruited?* What about your classes?"

"I won't be finishing school this term. That's why I called. I need to take some time off."

"You *what?* Don't be ridiculous. You don't *take time off* four months before you graduate."

Generally true, although saints and soon-to-be billionaires have done exactly that.

"You're just tired, Ollie. It's only a few weeks. It'll be over before you know it."

Olivia looks out on the motorists gathering in the court for breakfast. Curious beyond saying: In one life, she dies of electrocution. In another, she's in the world's largest truck stop, explaining to her father that she's been chosen by beings of light to help preserve the most wondrous creatures on Earth. The voice on the other end of the phone turns desperate. Olivia can't help smiling: the life her father begs her to return to—the drugs, the unprotected sex, the psycho parties and life-threatening dares—is hell itself, while this trip westward is bringing her back from the dead.

"You won't be able to get your rent back. It's too late for any kind of tuition refund. Just finish up, and you can do your volunteer work in the summer. I'm sure your mother—"

In the background, Olivia's mother shouts, "I'm sure your mother *what?*"

Olivia hears her mother yell something about paying for her own education. People mill around her. She feels their anxiety—the moving goal line of hunger. Her own life had been a haze of privilege, narcissism, and impossibly extended adolescence, filled with mean, sardonic hipness and self-protection. Now she has been called.

"Look," her father whispers into the phone. "Be sensible. If you can't deal with one more semester right now, just come home."

More love courses through Olivia than she has felt since childhood. "Dad? Thank you. But I need to do this."

"Do *what?* Where? Honey? Are you still there? Sweetheart?"

"I'm here, Daddy." Bits of the girl that she was only days ago tug at her, chanting, *Fight, fight.* But the fight is real now, and elsewhere.

"Ollie, sit tight. I'll come get you. I can be out there by . . ."

Everything is so obvious, so blissfully clear. But her parents can't see it. There is great, joyous, and essential work to do. But first a person needs to graduate from endless self-love.

"Daddy, I'm good. I'll call when I have more information."

A recorded woman cuts in, asking for another seventy-five cents. Olivia has no more change. All she has is a message, spoken by the flashing-eyed woman on the wall of discount televisions and reworked by the light-beings, who dictate to her now as clearly as if they were on the other end of the phone. *The most wondrous things alive need you.*

Through the front glass doors of the truck stop, Olivia sees the dozens of gas pumps, and beyond them, the flat expanse of I-80 in the dawn, the snowcapped fields, the endless hostage swap of travelers east and west. Her father goes on talking, using all the persuasion techniques they teach you in law school. The sky does amazing things. It bruises a little in the freedom of the west, while to the east it spills open like a pomegranate. The phone clicks and goes dead. Olivia hangs up, a newly minted orphan. A thing reaching toward the sun, ready for anything.

SHE LEAVES THE TRUCK STOP, in love with aimless humanity. Back on the interstate, the sun rises again in her rearview mirror. Drumlins lift and fall. The road cuts a double trench through winter's white, all the way to the horizon. Attractions are few, but each one delights her. The Herbert Hoover Library and Museum. Sharpless Auction. Amana Colonies. The interstate exits sound like characters in a novel about wayward, fey southern aristocracy: Wilton Muscatine, Ladora Millersburg, Newton Monroe, Altuna Bondurant . . .

Something comes over her, strange and beautiful courage. She has no resources, only a name for a destination, and no real clue about what she must do once there. Outside the car, it's bleak and arctic, and all her worldly possessions are back in her rooming house. Yet she has a bank card linked to a small war chest, a sense of destiny that won't quit, and friends in what she can only assume are very high places.

Hours pass like the rolling clouds. She's a ways down that flattening surveyor's line between Des Moines and Council Bluffs, with nothing in any direction except endless frozen-over chaff, when something beckons from the side of her eye. She turns to see a phantom hitchhiker standing in the snow beyond the interstate's right shoulder. He waves more arms than Vishnu. One of them holds a banner she can't read.

She pulls her foot off the gas and taps the brake. The hitchhiker turns into a tree so big it could fill an entire car of that lumber death train back in Indiana. The fissured trunk corkscrews up for dozens of feet before fountaining into several hulking limbs. The tree stands back from the interstate, a column against the sky, the only thing taller than a farmhouse for miles around. Presences stir in the passenger seat. As she draws abreast of the tree, Olivia makes out words painted on the shingle hanging from one enormous branch: FREE TREE ART. The presences run their twigs up the back of her neck.

She pulls off at the next exit. Under the stop sign where the ramp meets a county highway, a hand-painted poster with the same vine-like lettering signals her to turn right. A second sign, half a country mile along, points her back toward the fabulous tree. Down the rolling road, Eden leaps out at her—a glade of broadleaf trees flowering as if it's May. It's like an opening in the side of this frozen, forgetting Earth onto a hidden summer. A hundred yards closer, the glade becomes the wall of an old barn, transformed by fabulous tromp l'oeil. She heads up the gravel drive into a pull-off alongside the barn and gets out. She stands staring at the mural. Even up close, the illusion knocks her out.

"You're here about the sign?"

She whirls. A man in jeans and a gray-white waffle shirt with hair like a

Bronze Age prophet regards her. His breath steams. Bare hands clasp each opposite elbow. He's a few years older than she is, sad and wild, frightened to see a customer. The door of the farmhouse twenty feet behind him hangs open. The tree stands off alongside the house. It strikes Olivia that someone planted it here a very long time ago simply to attract her attention. "Yes. I think I might be."

She stands shivering, wanting her parka from the car. He studies her as if he means to flee. His chin rises and falls twice. "Well. You're the first." He points a long finger toward the painted barn, hand of a Renaissance Crucifixion. "Would you like to see the gallery?"

He leads her up a slight rise and ducks into the building. A flick of a switch reveals a space half homeless-person's midden, half pharaonic tomb. Talismans everywhere: totems, drawings, and cargo cult, laid out on plywood planks spread across sawhorses. They look like the work of an autistic Neolithic pantheist, unearthed by archaeology.

Olivia swings her head, baffled. "You're giving these away?"

"It's not going to work, is it?"

"I don't understand." She wants to say, *This is crazy*. But since she started hearing voices, the word has become less useful. It occurs to her to worry, here in the middle of nowhere with a man who by any generous measure would count as strange. But a glance is enough to verify: the strangest thing about him is his innocence.

And the art is real. She leans in toward a painting with a weird Gothic feel. Even in the dim barn light, the image is clear enough. A man lies in a narrow bed, staring down the tip of a tree branch that grows in through his window, right up to his face. A green sticker on the panel reads *so*. She drifts to the piece next to it. It's painted on a piece of recessed door panel stood on its side. The inset panel in turn becomes a door, which opens onto a clearing through a thick tangle of branches.

She scans the table, covered in works with similar subjects. Always trees, snaking in through the windows, walls, or ceilings of seemingly safe rooms, seeking out some human target like heat-seeking probes. In some of the works, painted words float above the surreal scenes: *Family Tree. Shoe Tree.*

*Money Tree. Barking up the Wrong Tree.* On another table, four sculptures of black clay wave like the hands of the dead rising out of the ground on the Judgment Day. Every one of the pieces bears a green tag reading *$0*.

"Okay. First of all . . ."

"I'll give you two for the price of one. Since you're my first customer."

She sets down the drawing in her hands and looks at its maker. His arms cross his chest and grasp his shoulders, like he's putting himself in a straitjacket before the world does. "Why are you doing this?"

He shrugs. "Free seems to be what the market will bear."

"You should be selling these in New York. Chicago."

"Don't talk to me about Chicago. I drew anamorphic sidewalk chalk illusions down in Grant Park for two and a half years. Got stepped on a lot."

She purses her lips, listening for guidance. But, having brought her here—FREE TREE ART—the beings of light abandon her. "I'm the first person who has stopped?"

"I know! Like: Who wouldn't stop for a sign like that? The nearest town is twelve miles away, and that one has fifty people. I was thinking I'd get mainly fleeing felons. You're not a fleeing felon, by any chance?"

She must think, figure out how this fits into the mission she has just been given. She goes from one table to the next. Surreal Cornell boxes filled with intricate woody contraband. Assemblages of broken ceramic, beads, and slices of tire rubber made to look like roots and tendrils. The branches that led her here. "You made all this? And they're all . . . ?"

"My tree period. Nine years and a couple months."

She studies his face for the key it must contain. Perhaps she has a key for him. But she doesn't even know what the lock might be. She steps toward him and he lurches back, sticking out his hand. She takes it, and they trade names. Olivia Vandergriff holds Nick Hoel's hand for a moment, feeling for an explanation. Then she lets it drop and turns back toward the art. "Almost a decade? And everything . . . is trees?"

For some reason, this makes him laugh. "Another half a century, and I'll be my own grandfather."

She looks at him, puzzled. By way of explanation, he leads her to a card table on the side of the exhibit. He passes her a thick, handmade book. She opens to the first page, a fanatically detailed pen-and-ink drawing of a young tree. The next page has the same drawing.

"Flip it." He mimes the suggestion with his own thumbs.

She does. The thing spirals upward into life. "Jesus! That's the tree out front." Another fact he doesn't deny. She flips again. The simulation runs too accurately to be the product of mere imagination. "How did you make these?"

"From photographs. One a month for seventy-six years. I come from a long and distinguished line of obsessive-compulsives."

She browses some more. He watches, edgy, eager, a small business owner on the brink of bankruptcy. "If there's anything you like, I can pack it up for you."

"Is this your farm?"

"My extended family's. They just sold it, to the devil and all his subsidiaries. I have two months to vacate."

"How do you live?"

The man grins and tips his head. "You're making a big assumption."

"You have no income?"

"Life insurance policies."

"You sell them?"

"No. I get paid by them. Until now." He looks at the tables of stock like a dubious auctioneer. "I'm thirty-five years old. Not a whole lot to show for a life's work."

The man's confusion radiates from him like heat from a log fire. She feels it from two yards away. "*Why?*" The word comes out wilder than she planned.

"Why the giveaway? I don't know. It felt like another artwork. The last of the series. Trees give it all away, don't they?"

The equation electrifies her. Art and acorns: both profligate handouts that go mostly wrong.

The man casts a cold eye over the sawhorses and planks. "You could call it a fire sale. No—a fungus sale."

"What does that mean?"

"Here." He moves toward the barn door. "I'll show you."

They cut across the snow-crusted field, past the house. She stops to grab her parka; he has nothing but jeans and the waffle shirt. "Aren't you cold?"

"Always. Cold is good for you. People keep themselves way too warm."

Nick leads her across the property, and there the mammoth thing stands, spread out against the porcelain sky. Strange and beautiful math governs the subtending of the hundred branches, thousand twigs, ten thousand twiglets, a beauty that the barn full of art has just primed her to see.

"I've never seen a tree anything like that."

"Few living people have."

From the interstate, she failed to notice the thing's thick, tapering grace. The way it flows upward to the first, generous cleave. She wouldn't have noticed, except for the flip-book. "What is it?"

"Chestnut. The redwoods of the East."

The word puckers her flesh all over. Confirmation, though she hardly needs it. They pass through the drip line and under the crown.

"All gone now. Why you've never seen one."

He tells her. How his great-great-great grandfather planted the tree. How his great-great-grandfather started photographing, at the century's start. How blight crossed the map in a few years and wiped out the best tree in eastern America. How this rogue and loner specimen, so far from any contaminant, survived.

She looks up into the net of branches. Each limb is a study for another of those stricken sculptures back in the barn. Something happened to this man's family: She sees that as if reading it off a crib sheet. And he has been living in this ancestor-built house for a decade, making art from a freak titan survivor. She puts her hand on the fissured bark. "And you've . . . outgrown it? Moving on?"

He recoils, horrified. "No. Never. It's done with me." He circles to the other side of the gigantic bole. The long, Renaissance finger points again. Dry rings with orange spots spread from several places across the bark. He presses the spots. They cave in at his touch.

She touches the spongy trunk. "Oh, shit. What is this?"

"Death, unfortunately." They back away from the dying god. With slow steps, they make their way up the rise toward the house. He kicks his shoes against the back-door stoop, to clear the snow from them. He waves toward the barn, his would-be gallery. "Would you please take a piece or two with you? That would make today a very good day."

"First I have to tell you why I'm here."

HE MAKES TEA on the stove in the kitchen where his parents and grandmother sat on that morning a decade ago when he said goodbye to them and drove to the art museum in Omaha. His visitor tells her story, through grimaces and smiles. She describes the night of her transformation—the hash, the damp nakedness, the fatal lamp socket. He sits and listens, blushing and hanging on her every description.

"I don't feel crazy. That's the weird thing. I was crazy *before*. I know what crazy feels like. This all feels . . . I don't know. Like I'm finally seeing the obvious." She cups her hands over the hot teacup.

The dead chestnut agitates her in a way he doesn't fully get. She's young, free, impulsive, and full of a new cause. By every reliable measure, she's more than a little tilted. But he wants her to stay like this, talking crazy theories in his kitchen, all night. There's company in the house. Someone has come back from the dead. "You don't sound crazy," he fibs. Not crazy *dangerous*, anyway.

"Believe me, I know what I sound like. Resurrection. Bizarre coincidences. Messages from television sets in a discount warehouse store. Beings of light I can't see."

"Well, when you put it that way . . ."

"But there's an explanation. There must be. Maybe it's all my subconscious, finally paying attention to something other than me. Maybe I heard about these tree protesters weeks ago, before I electrocuted myself, and now I'm finally seeing them everywhere."

He knows what it means to take dictation from ghosts. He has been alone for so long, sketching his own dying tree, that he wouldn't dare gainsay any-one's theories. No strangeness stranger than the strangeness of living things. He chuckles, chewing on the bitter nib. "I've made magical trinkets for the last nine years. Secret signals are my idiom."

"That's what I don't get." Her eyes beg him for mercy. Her tea, the steam on her face, the wilds of snowy Iowa: a story so old and large she can't wrap her head around it. "I'm driving down the road and see your sign, hanging from a tree that looks like . . ."

"Well, you know, if you drive far enough . . ."

"*I don't* know. I don't know what to believe. It's stupid to believe anything at all. We're always, always wrong."

He sees himself painting that face in bright war paint.

"Call it whatever you want. *Something's* trying to get my attention."

Someone thinks all his studies of the Hoel Chestnut over the last decade might mean something. That's enough for him. He shrugs. "It's amazing how crazy things become, once you start looking at them."

She goes from distress to conviction in zero seconds. "That's what I'm saying! What's crazier? Believing there might be nearby presences we don't know about? Or cutting down the last few ancient redwoods on Earth for decking and shingles?"

He lifts a finger and excuses himself upstairs. He comes back down car-rying an old road atlas and three volumes from a shelf of encyclopedias his grandfather bought from a traveling salesman back in 1965. There is, indeed, a Solace, California, in the heart of the tall trees. There are, in fact, red-woods thirty stories tall and as old as Jesus. Crazy is a species under no threat at all. He looks at her; her face glows with purpose. He wants to follow wherever her vision leads. And when that vision fails, he wants to follow wherever she goes next.

"Aren't you hungry?" she asks.

"Always. Hunger's good for you. People should stay hungry."

He makes her oatmeal with melted cheese and hot peppers. He tells her, "I'll need to think about it overnight."

"You're like me."

"How so?"

"I hear myself best when I'm sleeping."

He puts her in his grandparents' room, which he hasn't entered since Christmas, 1980, except to dust. He sleeps down below, in his childhood cubby, under the stairs. And all night long he listens. His thoughts stretch in every direction, seeking the light. It comes to his attention that nothing else in his life can even generously be called a plan.

When he wakes, she's in the kitchen, wearing a change of clothes from her car, scrounging up pancakes from flour he has let get infested by weevils. He sits at the center-post table in his flannel robe. His voice catches on the words. "I need to clear out this house by the end of the month."

She nods at the pancakes. "This can be done."

"And I need to dispose of my art. Beyond that, I have a little window on my calendar for the rest of the year."

He looks out the many-paned kitchen window. Through the Hoel Chestnut, the sky is so stupid with blue that it looks like it was slathered on by a primary-schooler with finger paints.

SPRING COMES AGAIN for Mimi Ma, the first without her father. The crabs, pears, redbuds, and dogwoods explode in pink and white. Every heartless petal mocks her. The mulberries, especially, make her want to set fire to everything that blooms. The man will never see a single part of this dazzlement. And still they overflow, the cruel, indifferent colors of Now.

Another spring follows hard on that one, then a third. Work toughens her, or the flowers start to dull. Mimi's frequent flier account turns platinum by May. They send her to Korea. They send her to Brazil. She learns Portuguese. She learns that people of all races, colors, and creeds have unlimited hunger for custom ceramic molding.

She takes up running, hiking, and cycling. She takes up ballroom dancing, then jazz, then salsa, which banishes all other dance for her forever. She takes up bird-watching and soon has a life list 130 species long. The company promotes her to section leader. She takes a course in Renaissance art, night courses in modern poetry, all the Holyoke stuff she tossed to become an engineer. The goal is almost patriotic: play in every playground. Have it all. Be everything.

A colleague talks her into playing hockey in the office league. Soon she can't get enough. She plays poker with men on four continents and sleeps with men on two. She spends a week in San Diego with a girl of astonishingly varied appetites whose heart she breaks, despite their up-front agreement. She falls pretty much in love with a married guy on another hockey team who is ever so gentle when checking her into the boards. They meet once, in Helsinki, in December, for a magic three-day alternate life in the noonday dark. She never sees him again.

She almost gets married. Immediately afterward, she can't remember how it ever came so close to happening. She turns thirty. Then (dependable engineer) thirty-one and thirty-two. In her sleep, she's forever passing through epic airports, in the middle of teeming crowds, when her name is paged.

THE COMPANY MOVES HER into HQ. The nine-thousand-dollar raise does almost nothing for her but make her hungry right away, again. But she graduates from a cubicle in a production facility to a corner office with a floor-length window looking out on a stand of pines that in her head somehow becomes the destination at the end of a very long family car trip. The world's smallest, most private wilderness stand-in.

She decorates the office with things her mother doesn't know she's stolen. A suitcase covered in pennants—CARNEGIE INSTITUTE, GENERAL MEIGS, UNIVERSITY OF NANKING. A steamer trunk stenciled with an unpronounceable name. Framed on her desk is a photo of two people, reportedly her grandparents, holding a photo of their three inexplicable grandchildren. Next to that, there's a print of that same photo-within-a-photo: three little racially ambiguous girls sitting primly on a couch, pretending they're Wheaton's Own. The oldest seems ready to bully her way into belonging. Ready to punch out anyone who thinks she's lost.

Around the walls of the office, like a classical frieze, runs her father's scroll. It's wrong to expose the paintings even to the tiny amounts of Northwest sun that trickle through her floor-to-ceiling window. Wrong to apply an adhesive to the backing of art so old and rare. Wrong to leave something priceless where anyone on the night crew might roll it up and pop it into an overall pocket. Wrong to hang the thing where it reminds her of her father's suicide, every time she lifts her eyes.

People who step into her office for the first time often ask about the Junior Buddhas in the foyer of Enlightenment. She hears her father, on the day he showed her the scroll for the first time. *These men? They pass the final exam.* There are days at her desk, in her furious professional success, looking up at the scroll from the rising tide of invoices and estimates, when she sees herself getting the same final grade her father did. When the drowning feel tightens up under her breasts, she looks out through the floor-length window onto her grove, where three briefly free and wild girls collect pine cone currencies on the shores of an ancient lake. Sometimes it almost calms her. Sometimes she can almost see the man, squatting on his haunches and writing everything there is to say about this campground into his copious notebook.

Her colleagues use her office as a lunchroom, during lunches when she isn't eating thousand-year eggs. Today her menu is chicken sandwich, so the place is safe for all ethnicities. Three other managers and a punk from HR pile in for penny ante Up and Down the River. Mimi's in. She's always in for any game involving pointless risk and temporary oblivion. Her only stipulation is that she gets the Commander's Chair.

"What exactly does it *command*, Captain?"

She waves toward the window. "This view."

The other players look up from their cards. They squint and shrug. Okay: A small parkway across the shallow lot, filled with trees. Trees are what the Northwest does. Trees everywhere at every elevation, crowding each other out, creeping in, closing out the sky.

"Pines?" the VP of marketing guesses.

A QC manager who wants Mimi's job declares, "Ponderosas."

"Willamette Valley ponderosa pine," says Britannica Man, director of R&D.

Cards float across the office table. Penny piles change hands. Mimi fingers her jade ring. She wears it carving-inward, so no one's tempted to hack off her finger to steal it. She gives the ring a twist. The gnarled mulberry of Fusang—the tree she drew when the sisters divvied up her father's possessions—spins around her finger. Her palm cups toward the dealer, all business. "Come on. Give me something to work with, here."

Another bust hand. She raises her eyes again. Blue noon pours through her private woodland. The sun cuts starbursts in the needles' verdigris, a thousand sconces of astral light. The great dinosaur plates of the trunks turn shades of orange, terra-cotta, and cinnamon. The QC man, who wants her job, says, "You ever smell the bark?"

"Vanilla," the QC guy says.

"That's the Jeffrey pine," announces Britannica Man.

"Look who's an expert. Again!"

"Not vanilla. Turpentine."

"I'm telling you," says the QC guy. "Ponderosa pine. Vanilla. I took a course."

Britannica Man shakes his head. "Nope. Turpentine."

"Somebody go sniff the cracks." Snickers all around.

The QC guy smacks the table. Cards skim and pennies fall. "Ten bucks."

"Now we're talking!" says the punk from HR.

Mimi's halfway to the door before anyone knows what's happening.

"Hey! We've got a game going here."

"Data," the engineer's engineer daughter answers. And in a few steps, she's outside. The smell is on her before she reaches the trees—the scent of resin and wide western places. The clean smell of her childhood's only untouched days. The music of the trees, too, tuning the wind. She remembers. Her nose slips into one of those dark fissures between the flat terra-cotta plates. She falls into the smell, a devastating whiff of two hundred million years ago. She can't imagine what such perfume was ever meant to do. But it does something to her now. Mind control. It's neither vanilla nor turpentine, but replete with highlights of each. A shot of spiritual butterscotch. A sprig of pineapple incense. It smells like nothing but itself, pungent and sublime. She breathes in, eyes closed, the tree's real name.

She stands with her nose in the bark, perversely intimate. She doses herself for a long time, like a hospice patient self-administering the morphine. Chemicals rush down her windpipe, through the bloodstream to her body's provinces, across the blood-brain barrier and into her thoughts. The smell grips her brain stem until she and the dead man are fishing side by side again, under the pine shade where the fish hide, in the soul's innermost national park.

A woman passing by on the sidewalk sees her sniffing and wonders whether there might be an emergency. Blissed by memory and volatile organics, Mimi calms her with a look. Back in the office, her card-playing companions stand at her floor-length window, watching her like she's turned dangerous. She leans back into the tree, falling one last time into that unnamable scent. Eyes shut, she summons up the arhat under his pine, that slight amusement on his lips as he tips over the brink into full-fledged acceptance of life and death. Something comes over her. The light grows brighter; the smell deepens. Detachment floats her upward, buoyed by the tides of her childhood. She turns from the trunk with a profound sense of well-being. *Is this it? Am I there?* Taped to the trunk of the next tree over is a handmade sign:

## Town hall meeting! May 23rd!

She drifts toward the poster and reads. The city has declared the accumulation of dead needles and bark to be a fire hazard and the trees too old and expensive to clean up, year after year. They plan to replace the pines with a cleaner, safer species. Forces opposed to the removal have asked for a public hearing.

## Come make your feelings known!

They want to cut her trees. She looks back across the way to the office. Her colleagues press to the glass, laughing at her. They wave their hands. They rap on the window. One of them takes her picture with a disposable camera. Her nose fills with a sachet beyond the crudity of words. Call it remembering. Call it prediction. Vanilla, pineapple, butterscotch, turpentine.

A MAN JUST SHY OF FORTY hands out silver dollars in the Spar roadhouse, off Route 212, not far from a town aptly named Damascus. Damascus, Oregon. "Celebration, damn it. You have to spend it on a beer."

The request has its takers. "The hell we celebrating, Rockefeller?"

"My fifty thousandth tree. Nine hours a day, rain or shine, five and a half days a week, through every planting month, for almost four years."

Scattered applause and one owl hoot. Everybody in the place says he'll drink to that.

"Tough work for an old guy."

"You replace your lumbar region yet?"

"You know they're just gonna cut them right back down again, couple more years."

Gratitude of roadhouse strangers, bought a drink for nothing. Douglas Pavlicek smiles and abides. He stacks twenty more silver dollars on the corner of a pool table and waves his stick with the hard rock maple shaft in the air, inviting all comers. Soon he has two takers, Dum and Dee.

They play three-ball, in rotation. Douglas is beyond pitiful. Four years of scrambling across slash, slag, and mud, stooping and planting, has shot his nervous system, wrecked his bum leg, and left him with a motor tremor that shows up on seismometers down in the Bay Area. Dum and Dee feel almost bad, taking his money, rack after rack, inning after inning, pot after pot. But Douggie has a time of it, here in the big city, knocking back foamy dog piss and remembering the joy of anonymous company. He'll sleep in a bed tonight. Take a hot shower. Fifty thousand trees.

Dum sinks all three balls on the break. His second on-the-snap tonight. Maybe he's racking them for an instant win. Douglas Pavlicek doesn't care. Then Dee completes in four.

"So. Fifty thousand trees," Dum says, just to distract Douggie, who's struggling enough without the cognitive load of having to carry on a conversation.

"Yup. Could die now, and I'd be ahead of the game."

"What do you do for women, out there?"

"Plenty of women tree slingers. Summer vacation for a lot of them. Anything goes." Distracted by happy memories, he pockets the cue ball. Even that's worth a laugh.

"Who're you planting for?"

"Whoever pays me."

"Lotta new oxygen out there, because of you. Lotta greenhouse gases put to bed."

"People have no idea. You know they make shampoo with wood? Shatterproof glass? Toothpaste?"

"I did not know that."

"Shoe polish. Ice-cream thickener."

"Buildings, am I right? Books and such. Boats. Furniture."

"People have no idea. Still the Age of Wood. Cheapest priceless stuff that ever has been."

"Amen, buddy. Twenty bucks on another round?"

They play for hours. Douggie, who can drink without apparent consequence, battles back from the brink. Dee and Dum cycle out, replaced by newcomers, Things One and Two. Doug buys another round, explaining for the graveyard shift just what they're celebrating.

"Fifty thousand trees. Huh."

"It's a start," Douglas says.

Thing Two is in strong contention for asshole of the night. Week, even. "Hate to burst your bubble, friend. But you know that BC alone takes out two million log trucks a year? By itself! You'd have to plant for like four or five centuries just to—"

"Okay. Let's keep shooting, here."

"And those companies you plant for? You realize they get good-citizen credits for every seedling you plant? Every time you stick one in the ground, it lets them raise the annual allowable cut."

"No," Douglas says. "That can't be right."

"Oh, it's right, all right. You're putting in babies so they can kill grandfathers. And when your seedlings grow out, they'll be monocrop blights, man. Drive-through diners for happy insect pests."

"Okay. Shut the fuck up for a second, please." Douglas holds up his cue, then his head. "You win, friend. Party's over."

MIMI DROPS OUT of next noon's card game. Eats her lunch al fresco, under the pines.

"Can we use your office anyway?" the HR punk asks.

"All yours. Knock yourself out."

She sits, her back to the orange trunks. Looks up into the flares of light cutting through the sheaths of needles. Imitates the arhat, waits, breathes. This is how it was with the Indian prince Siddhartha, when life abandoned him and his pleasures went away. He sat under a magnificent peepul—a Bo, *Ficus religiosa*—and vowed not to stand up again until he understood what life wanted from him. One month passed, then another. Then he woke up from the dream of humankind. Truths blazed into his head, things so simple, hidden in broad light. At that moment, the tree above the new Buddha— cuttings from which still grow across the globe—burst into flowers, and the flowers changed into plump purple figs.

Mimi waits for nothing even a hundredth so grandiose. In fact, she waits for nothing at all—for enough nothing to lose herself in. That unnameable scent—that's all she wants. This grove. That two-hundred-million-year-old scent. Her family at its freest best, their own native nation. Fishing again, at the side of the only man who ever knew her, in the current of a river that isn't long gone.

A woman with a double-wide stroller packed with twins sits for a moment on a nearby bench. "Nice spot of shade," Mimi says. "Did you know the city wants to cut these down?"

Getting political. Agitating. She hates agitators, how they're always in your face about something that has nothing to do with you. In another minute, she's telling the frightened young mom about the town hall meeting on the twenty-third. And the ghost of her father stands not far away, under his pines, smiling at her.

DOUGLAS PAVLICEK WAKES as Mimi fills her lungs one last time and returns to climate control. He takes another brief forever to realize he's in his motel room, the one he rented after giving away two hundred dollars in beers and losing another hundred at three-ball. None of that even makes him wince. This afternoon, the waking dread is more substantial. All his anxiety is trained on the annual allowable cut, and whether, for the last four years, he's been suckered into wasting his life, or worse.

He's missed the complimentary continental breakfast by four hours. But the clerk sells him an orange, a chocolate bar, and a cup of coffee, three price-less tree treasures that get him to the public library. There he finds a librarian to help him research. The man pulls several volumes of policy and code off the shelf, and together they search. The answer isn't good. Thing Two, that loud bastard, was right. Planting seedlings has done nothing but green-light more colossal clear-cuts. It's dinnertime when Douggie accepts this fact beyond all doubt. He has eaten nothing all day since his three tree gifts. But the idea of eating again—ever—nauseates him.

He needs to walk. Walking: the only sane thing left. What he really wants is to rush out to a scalped hillside and get the future back into the ground. It's what his muscles know, especially that largest muscle in his inventory—his soul. A shovel and a shoulder bag full of green recruits. What he, until today, thought of as hope.

He walks all evening, stopping only to compromise with his body: a burger, which skips his taste buds on the way down. The night is soft and the air so light that for half a mile he forgets his free-fall dread. But he can't stop the questions: *What do I do now, for the next forty years? What work can't the efficiency of unified mankind chop into pure fertilizer?*

He walks for hours and miles, skirting downtown Portland into a peaceful mixed-use neighborhood, drawn along by a scent he can't name. He stops into a corner grocery to get a bottle of greenish juice, which he drinks while reading notices on a bulletin board by the store's exit. *Highly Intelligent Missing Cat. Qi Rebalancing. Cheap Long Distance Calling.* And then:

## Town hall meeting! May 23rd!

Some lunatic legacy inside his species' brains does not work and play well with others. He asks the kid at the cash register where the park in question is. Kid looks like a rat bit his nose. "That's too far to walk."

"Try me." Turns out Douggie passed it on the way here. He doubles back along the route he came. He smells the little pocket park before he sees it—like a slice of God's birthday cake. The condemned trees all have three needles to a bundle, large orange plates. Old friends. He sets up base camp on a bench under the pines. He lets the trees comfort him. It's dark, but the neighborhood seems safe. Safer than flying transports over Cambodia. Safer than a lot of bars he's fallen asleep in. He'd like to fall asleep here. Fuck practicality and all its binding obligations. Give a guy a night outdoors, with nothing between his bare head and a seed rain. The twenty-third, it occurs to him—town meeting—is only four days away.

His dream, when it comes, is more vivid than it has been for years. This time, the plane goes down in the Khmer jungle. Captain Straub is impaled on some malignant undergrowth Douglas can't see. Levine and Bragg land nearby, but Douglas can't reach them, and in a while they stop answering his shouts. He's alone again, in what he realizes is a Bizarro Portland, swallowed entirely by a single banyan. He wakes to the sound of helicopters scouring the canopy, shining floodlights and looking for him.

Tonight the helicopters turn into trucks. Men pile out of them, with gear. For a minute, they're still grunts, coming to immolate Douggie's village in a final firefight. Then he wakes up enough to see chain saws. He checks his watch: a little after midnight. At first he thinks he has fallen asleep for four days. He gets himself vertical and heads out on recon.

"Hey!" He draws near the gear drop. "Hello!" The hard hats recoil, as from a crazy person. "You're not setting up, are you?"

They keep working, gassing up the hardware. Running a tape corral around the perimeter. Positioning the saurian cherry picker into place and locking down its braces.

"You've made a mistake or something. The hearing's in a few days. Read the poster."

Some kind of crew head comes up to him. Not *threatening*, exactly. The word is *authorized*. "Sir, we're going to have to ask you to leave before we start cutting."

"You're cutting? It's pitch-dark." But, of course, it isn't. Not with twin banks of arc lights wheeled into place. There is no more *pitch-dark*. Then the civics-sized penny drops. "Hang on a sec."

"City orders," the foreman says. "You're going to have to move to the other side of the tape."

"City orders? What the hell does that even mean?"

"It means move out. Beyond the tape."

Douglas breaks toward the doomed trees. The move stuns everyone. It takes a second before the hard hats give chase. He's a few feet up one of the trunks before they reach him. They grab his feet. Somebody knocks him with the butt of a long pruning shaft. He smacks to the ground and lands on his bum leg.

"Don't do this. This is fucked up!"

Two cutters pin him on the ground until the police show. It's one in the morning. Just another crime against public property, executed while the city sleeps. This time the charges against him are public nuisance, obstructing official business, and resisting arrest. "You think this is funny?" demands the officer who handcuffs him.

"Believe me, you would, too."

At the station on Second Street, they ask his name. "Prisoner 571." It takes removing his wallet from his jeans by force to get his real ID. And they need to isolate him, to keep him from rabble-rousing the other criminals into an uprising.

SEVEN-THIRTY A.M. Mimi hits the office early. An Argentinian order of impellers for centrifugal pumps has gone awry. She sets down her coffee, flips on the overhead lights, powers up her machine, and waits to boot into the corporate LAN. She swivels for a glance outside, and howls. Where there should be foliage, there's only an expanse of gray-blue cumulonimbus.

In two minutes, she's standing on the bald patch, the trees she used to look out on for a moment's remembering and peace. She hasn't even changed out of her trainers into her slingbacks. The prim clearing denies that anything ever happened. Not a trunk or a branch left behind. Only sawdust and shed needles around the fresh, flat cuts flush with the ground. Yellow-orange wood exposed to the air, sap rising on the outmost edge of the rings—rings beyond rings, many more rings than she has years.

And the scent of it, the smell of anticipation and loss, of fresh-cut pine. The message, the drug that worked her brain, concentrated now, laid open in death. It starts to drizzle. She closes her eyes. Outrage floods into her, the sneakiness of man, a sense of injustice larger than her whole life, the old loss that will never, ever be answered. When her eyes open again, truths rush into her head. Like Enlightenment, but without the glow.

GERMINATION HAPPENS FAST. Neelay finishes his space opera. Some part of the elongated boy in the futuristic wheelchair still wants to give the game away for free. But there comes a moment, as there always does in the game itself, when you must turn your pretty backwater sector of the universe into a revenue stream.

Publishing the game requires a company, if only a fake one. Corporate HQ is his ground-floor efficiency with access ramp near El Camino in Redwood City. The business needs a name, even if the entire outfit is nothing but a crippled twenty-something Indian-American rolling around like a bundle of twigs in a dogcart. But naming a company turns out to be harder than coding up a planet. For three days, Neelay plays with portmanteaus and neologisms, all of which come up short or have already been taken. He's sucking on his dinner—a cinnamon toothpick—and staring at some faked-up letterhead when the word *Redwood* pops out of his return address. It's like someone whispers the obvious answer into his ear. Using a paint program, he mocks up a logo—a rip-off of Stanford's fearsome tree. And Sempervirens is born.

He calls the company's first release *The Sylvan Prophecies*. With state-of-the-art DTP software, he designs an ad. At the top of the page, he centers the words:

THERE'S A WHOLE NEW PLANET RIGHT NEXT DOOR

Then Neelay runs the ad in the back of comics and computer magazines across the country. A disc dupe outfit over in Menlo Park pumps out three thousand floppies. He hires two ex-Stanford friends to get the game into stores up and down both coasts. Within a month, *The Sylvan Prophecies* sells out. Neelay dupes more discs. They sell out again. He's stunned that so many rigs out there meet the game's minimum specs. Word of mouth keeps spreading. Revenues flow in, and soon there's too much work for him to handle alone.

He signs a five-year lease on a former dentist's suite. He hires a secretary and calls her the office manager. He hires a hacker and calls him the lead programmer. He signs a guy with an accounting degree who metamorphoses into a business manager. Assembling the team feels like building up the home planet in *The Sylvan Prophecies*. From scores of applicants, he hires the ones who flinch the least when they see his stick-figure body sprouting from the motorized chair.

Astonishingly, the new employees prefer cash up front to shares in the future. It's a total failure of imagination. They haven't a clue where their species is headed. He tries to talk them around, but they all elect for safety and cash.

Soon the business manager breaks it to Neelay: it's not enough to pretend he's a company. He has to incorporate for real. Sempervirens becomes a legal person. Neelay goes to bed at night dreaming of branching and spreading. It's a brand-new industry with an unlimited growth curve. He needs only a few market hits, each one compounding the success of the previous. Then he'll make the world over, the way it was shown to him, in a flash, by alien life-forms in the wild terrarium of Stanford's inner court.

By day, when he isn't learning how to run a company, Neelay keeps on coding. Programming still amazes him. Declare a variable. Specify a procedure. Call each well-formed routine to do its part, inside larger, cleverer, more capable structures, like organelles building up a cell. And up from simple instructions emerges an entity with autonomous behavior. Words into action: it's the planet's Next New Thing. Coding, he's still a boy of seven, with the whole world of living possibilities coming up the stairs in his father's arms.

The first game is still selling at a healthy clip when Sempervirens releases the sequel. *The New Sylvan Prophecies* employs unbelievable verisimilitude in an astonishing 256 colors. There's real packaging now, with professional artwork, though the gameplay is the same old exploration and trading set in a glorious new higher-res galaxy. The public doesn't care that it's a rehash.

The public can't get enough. They love the world's open-ended nature. There's no real way to win the game. As with running a business, the point is to keep playing for as long as possible.

*The New Sylvan Prophecies* tops the charts, even before its ancestor falls out of the top ten. Players post messages in online bulletin boards about wild creatures they find on backwater planets, odd, unpredictable combinations of animal, vegetable, and mineral. Lots of people find baiting the game's flora and fauna more entertaining than finding the treasure at the galaxy's core.

Together, the two games make more money than many Hollywood movies, on a much lower outlay. Neelay plows all profits back into the third installment, already more ambitious than the previous two games combined. When *The Sylvan Revelation* appears nine months later, it lists for an outrageous fifty bucks. But for growing numbers of people, that's a small price to pay for a transformative experience that didn't even exist two years ago.

A big publisher called Digit-Arts offers to purchase the brand. The arrangement makes all kinds of sense. Professionals would take over sales and distribution of all future products, freeing Sempervirens to devote itself to development. Neelay doesn't want to run a company; he wants to make worlds. The Digit-Arts offer would guarantee his freedom and keep him in state-of-the-art wheelchairs forever.

The night he agrees in principle to the deal, Neelay can't sleep. He lies in his adjustable bed, trimmed by his mother's runner of quilted storage pockets and arched over by a steel grab-bar wrapped in foam padding. Around midnight, his legs start spasming like an ambulatory person's. He needs to get up. That would be easier with the caregiver, but Gena doesn't come for another several hours. A button press brings the bed's head all the way upright. He wraps his arm around the right-hand vertical post and flings his left up in front of the horizontal bar. Muscle wastage has left his forearms looking like paired pieces of driftwood. His elbows flare out in swollen knots. It takes all his strength to lever himself into a seated position. His shoulders shake, and he squeezes past that moment when he always threatens to flop back onto the bed. He rocks for a while, to tilt his torso forward enough to fling both arms behind him and buttress himself upright. Step one. Of fifty-two or so, depending on how you count.

His sweatpants are down around his knees in the ready position, where he keeps them when the cath is in. He leans as far as he can, bends almost double, so that the weight of his head and shoulders stays put long enough for him to plant his hands forward near his butt. His right arm slips under his left thigh. There's precious little meat left there as well—none, really—but it testifies to the baggage of his legs that they're still anchor enough to brace against and keep his shriveled torso upright.

He grapples at the sweats and falls back onto his left elbow. Up swings the limp drawbridge of the leg. His butt lifts enough for him to fumble the seat of the pants over himself. Success is a while in coming. The leg drops, he falls back on his protruding shoulder blades, and he's prostrate all over again. Craning himself up once more with the bar-hung stirrup, he repeats the process on his right until the sweats are drawn tight squarely over his waist. Smoothing out the leggings on both sides takes time, but time, in the middle of the night, is an ample resource. Then a grab of the overhead bar, and, stabilized again, reaching out to one of the many hanging hooks filled with gear, he snags the U-shaped canvas sling and, in a hundred small increments, spreads it out on the bed around his body's upright stem. Each leg gets wrapped underneath in a strap pulled up through the middle.

He stabs out again and spears the head of the winch, drags it across its own horizontal brace beam until it's positioned directly above. All four sling loops go over the winch's latches, two per side. He pops the remote in his mouth and, holding the straps in place, bites down on the power button until the winch lifts him upright. He affixes the remote to the sling and detaches the catheter's urine sack from the side of the bed. Holding the hose in his teeth to free both hands, he attaches the bag to the satchel he has wrapped himself in. Then he presses the winch button again, holds on, and goes airborne.

There's always that moment, as he scooches sideways through the air from bed to waiting chair, when the whole precarious system wavers. He has shifted wrong before and come down hard, smacking metal struts and crashing to the floor in pain and urine. Tonight's ride, though, is error-free. The seat of the wheelchair must be adjusted, the wheels repositioned, but he sticks the landing. There, in the chair, he reverses all the steps, detaches the winch, hangs the bag, and like Houdini, slips free of the sling underneath him without ever lifting. Donning the cassock is easy. The shoes, though slip-on and big as a clown's, are less so. But he's mobile now, zipping about by joystick and throttle as easily as doing Immelmanns in a flight simulator. The whole ordeal has taken only a little over thirty minutes.

Another ten, and he's out by the van, waiting for the hydraulic floor of the lift to lower to the ground. He rolls his chair onto the steel square and rides it up. He rolls through the open hull into the emptied-out cabin. The lift retracts, the doors slide shut, and he positions his chair in front of a console where pedal and brake are levers at waist level that even wasted arms can operate.

Several dozen more commands in this algorithm of liberty, and he parks the van, exits, and rolls into the Stanford inner quad. He spins 360, surveying, surrounded again by those otherworldly life-forms the way he was six years earlier. All those creatures from another galaxy, far, far away: dove tree, jacaranda, desert spoon, camphor, flame, empress, kurrajong, red mulberry. He remembers how they whispered to him about a game he was destined to make—a game played by countless people worldwide, a game that puts the players smack in the middle of a living, breathing jungle filled with potential only dimly imaginable.

Tonight, the trees are tight-lipped, refusing to tell him anything. He drums his fingers on his shriveled thighs, waits, listening, for even longer than it took him to get here. No one's around. The moon is a blazing telephone that anyone on Earth might call him on, simply by looking up and seeing what he sees. He wills the menagerie of trees to give him a sign. The extraterrestrial beings wave their bizarre branches. The collective tapping in the air nags at him. Memory rises inside, like sap. And now it's as if the blowing, bending branches point him outward, behind the quad, out to Escondido, then down Panama Street, past Roble. . . .

He heads where the waving sends him. Off to the south, the rounded tops of the Santa Cruz Mountains rise above the campus roofs. And now he remembers: a day, half his life ago and more, walking a forest trail on that ridge with his father and coming across a spectacular, monstrous redwood, a lone Methuselah that somehow escaped the loggers. He sees, now: it's the tree he must have named his company after. And without a second thought, he knows he must consult it.

The switchbacks up Sand Hill Road, harrowing at noon, are deadly in the dark. He tacks back and forth as if in one of those flying pods you can build at tech level 29 in the *Sylvan Prophecies*. The road is empty at this hour, no one to see the emaciated Ent with the worthless legs piloting a modified van with his freakish bony fingers. At the top of the ridge, on Skyline, a road named for the cableway that stripped these hills bare to build San Francisco, he turns right. That much he remembers. If memories change the pathways of the brain, then the trail must still be there. It's just a matter of waiting for the wild things to emerge out of the understory.

He drives through the tunnel of second growth, which has returned enough in a hundred years to fool him, in this pitch-black, into thinking it's virgin forest. A pull-off on the right triggers enough recognition to make him stop. There's a flashlight in the glove compartment. He rides the van's lift down to the spongy earth and waits, unsure how to pilot the chair, however fat-tired and ruggedized, down the path in front of him. But that's what this point-and-click adventure wants.

For a hundred yards of trail, he's fine. Then his left tire hits a wet declivity and slips. He guns the joystick, trying to power through. He backs up and spins, hoping to pop out laterally. The tire kicks up mud and digs in. He waves the flashlight in front of him. Shadows rear up like lunging specters. Every snapped branch sounds like the work of extinct apex predators. A car engine crescendos up from nothing, far away down Skyline. Neelay screams at the top of his skinny lungs and waves the beam like a crazy man. But the car blasts past.

He sits in total darkness, wondering how mankind ever survived such a place. Some hiker will find him, once the sun comes up. Or the day after. Who knows how much traffic this trail gets? A screeching comes from behind. He whirls the flashlight, but can't turn far enough. His heart takes a while to return to baseline. When it does, he must empty the filled catheter bag onto the ground, as far from his wheels as he can reach.

Then he sees it, woven into the other shadows less than a dozen yards in front of him. He knows how he missed it: It's too big. Too big to make sense of. Too big to credit as a living thing. It's a triple-wide door of darkness into the side of the night. The beam goes no more than the smallest way up the endless trunk. And up the trunk runs, straight up, beyond comprehension, an immortal, collective ecosystem—Sempervirens.

Underneath the stupendous life, a tiny man and his even tinier son look up. Together, they're shorter than the buttress growing out of this thing's root system. Neelay watches, knowing what's to come. The memory is as dense as if it were just encoded in him. The father bends back and raises his hands to the sky. *Vishnu's fig, Neelay-*ji. *Come back to swallow us!*

The standing boy must have laughed then, as the sitting one wants to now. *Pita? Don't be crazy. It's a redwood!*

The father lays it out: All the world's trunks come from the same root and are rushing outward, down the spreading branches of the one tree, trying for something.

*Think of the code that made this gigantic thing, my Neelay. How many cells inside? How many programs is it running? What do they all do? Where are they trying to reach?*

Lights go on all over the inside of Neelay's cranium. And there, in the dark woods, waving his tiny beam and feeling a hum come from the towering black column, he knows the answer. The branch wants only to go on branching. The point of the game is to keep playing. He can't possibly sell the company. There's a bit of ancestral code, already present in the earliest programs he and his father wrote, that has yet to have its way with him. He sees the next project, and it's the simplest thing. Like evolution, it reuses all the old, successful parts of everything that has come before. Like *evolution*, it just means unfolding.

Now he can't afford to wait until tomorrow to be found. He has another brainstorm, much smaller, but more immediate. He lifts the cassock off his back and drops it on the ground in front of his stuck tire. A push of the joystick and he is free, up the path and into the van, where he rides, bare-chested, via a thousand steps and subroutines, back down to Redwood City and his workstation.

The next day, he calls Digit-Arts and breaks off the deal. Their property lawyers threaten and bellow. But the only thing they really wanted from the merger was him. He is Sempervirens' only capital worth acquiring. Without his goodwill, the deal means nothing.

With the merger broken off, he assembles his staff into the conference room and tells them how the next project will go. The player will start in an uninhabited corner of a freshly assembled new Earth. He'll be able to dig mines, cut down trees, plow fields, construct houses, build churches and markets and schools—anything his heart desires and his legs can reach. He'll travel down all the spreading branches of an enormous technology tree, researching everything from stone working to space stations, free to follow any ethos, to make whatever culture floats his state-of-the-art boats.

But there's a kicker: other people, real people, on the other end of modems, will each be furthering their own culture in other parts of this virgin world. And every one of those other, actual people will want the land beneath any other player's empire.

Within nine months, an alpha copy floating around the office brings Sempervirens to a standstill. Once the employees get playing, they want nothing else. They stop sleeping. They forget to eat. Relationships are a minor irritation. *One more turn. Just one more turn.*

The game is called *Mastery.*

THEY SPEND TWO WEEKS closing the Hoel house, Nick and his drive-by visitor. The Des Moines Hoels come by to buy Nick's car and take possession of the family heirlooms. They're followed by the auctioneers, who put a green sticker on any furnishings and appliances that might fetch anything. Large men with legible biceps load the movable goods and rusting farm equipment into a twenty-four-foot truck and haul it two counties away, where everything will sell on consignment. Nick sets no minimum bids. The accumulated possessions of generations disperse like wind-borne pollen. Then it's the Hoel house no longer.

"My ancestors came to this state empty-handed. I should leave the same way, don't you think?"

Olivia touches his shoulder. They've spent fourteen days and thirteen nights closing up a house together, as if, after half a century of planting crops and outlasting the whims of weather, they're retiring at last to Scottsdale to die hunched, forehead to forehead, over a checkerboard. The bottomless weirdness of the situation keeps Nick up at night. He's going to California with a woman who pulled off the interstate on impulse, seeing his absurd sign. A woman who hears silent voices. *Now, this*, thinks Nicholas Hoel, *is a real performance piece.*

People have sex with strangers. People marry strangers. People spend half a century in bed together and wind up strangers at the end. Nicholas knows all this; he has cleaned house after his dead parents and grandparents, made all the terrible discoveries that only death affords. How long does it take to know anyone? Five minutes, and done. Nothing can move you off a first impression. That person in your life's passenger seat? Always a hitch-hiker, to be dropped off just down the road.

The fact is, their obsessions interlock. Each has half of a secret message. What else can he do but try to fit the halves together? And if they spin out, wake from the dream with nothing, what has he sacrificed but solitary waiting?

Nick sits in his ancestors' empty bedroom after midnight, reading by the lantern's low glow. Ten years of squatting in this place, and he feels like he's homesteading in a remote cabin. He keeps rereading the Redwood article in the encyclopedia, the encyclopedia marked with the auctioneers' sticker. He reads of trees as tall as a football field is long. A tree whose stump made a floor where two dozen people danced a cotillion.

He reads the encyclopedia article on mental disorders. The section on diagnosing schizophrenia contains this sentence: *Beliefs should not be considered delusional if they are in keeping with societal norms.*

His housemate hums to herself as she prepares for departure. Her frown stops his breathing. She's young and guileless, stripped of fear, with a calling stronger than any medieval nun's. He could no more pass up a road trip with her than he can stop turning his dreams into drawings. He was decamping anyway. Now his life has a luxury he's never had: a destination, and someone to head there with.

Two weeks in a house together in a midwestern midwinter, and he doesn't even try to touch her. That's the only delusional part. And she knows he won't. Her body, around him, is untainted by anything so crude as nervousness. She's no warier of him than a lake's surface is wary of the wind.

They share a cold breakfast the morning after the auction truck hauls off the last of the Hoel possessions. They've spent the night in sleeping bags. Now she sits on the white pine floor, near where the oak table made by Nick's great-great-great grandfather stood for more than a century. Dimples in the floorboards will remember it forever. She's wearing an oxford shirt with fortunately long tails, and panties striped like a candy cane.

"Aren't you freezing?"

"I seem to run hot these days. Since dying."

He averts his face and flaps his hand at her bare legs. "Could you—cover up, or something? A guy could get hurt."

"Oh, please. Nothing you haven't seen before."

"Not on *you*."

"It's all the same basic inventory."

"I wouldn't know."

"Ha. Women have lived here. Recently."

"Wrong. I'm a celibate artist. I have a special gift."

"Wrinkle cream in the medicine cabinet. Nail polish." She stops and blushes. "Unless you . . ."

"No. Nothing so creative. Recent women. A woman."

"Story?"

"She took off not long after I discovered the chestnut blight. Scared away. She thought a guy should paint something other than branches now and then."

"This reminds me. We need to house the gallery."

"House?" His smile twists like he's sucking alum—memories of the U-Stor-It in Chicago that was home to the great works of his twenties, until he turned them into a large, combusting concept piece.

She gets that faraway look, like she's taking dictation from other life-forms again. "How about burying it out back?"

Ancient techniques occur to him, patinas and crazings, subterranean ceramic practices he learned about back at art school. The idea feels at least as fine as trying to give the stuff away to passing motorists. "Why not? Let them decompose down there."

"I was thinking bubble wrap."

"It's January, you know. However mild it has been. We'd have to rent a backhoe to dig any kind of hole." Then he remembers. The idea makes him laugh. "Put some clothes on. Your coat. Come on."

They stand side by side on the rise behind the machine shed, invisible from the house, gazing at a waist-sized hill of scree and the sizable hole next to it.

"My cousins and I were always digging back here, when we were kids. Heading for the Earth's molten core. Nobody ever bothered filling it back in."

She surveys the plot. "Huh. Nice. Thinking ahead."

They bury the art. The stack of photos—that flip-book of a century of chestnut growth—goes in, too. Safer there than anywhere aboveground.

That night they're in the kitchen again, prepping for a morning departure. She more modest, in sweatshirt and leggings. He pacing, filled with that stomach-flop feel that comes with leaping into the blue. Half terror, half thrill: Everything scattering on the air. We live, we get out a little, and then no more, forever. And we *know* what's coming—thanks to the fruit of the taboo tree that we were set up to eat. Why put it there, and then forbid it? Just to make sure it gets taken.

"What are they saying now? Your handlers."

"It's not like that, Nicholas."

He folds his hands together under his mouth. "What's it like, then?"

"They're saying, *Check the oil.* Okay?"

"How are we going to find them?"

"My handlers?"

"No. The protesters. The tree people."

She laughs and touches his shoulder. She has started doing that, and he wishes she wouldn't.

"They're *trying* to get into the newspapers. It should be easy. If we get close and still can't find them, we'll start our own movement."

He tries to laugh back, but she seems to be serious.

In the morning, they set off. Her car is crammed full to overflowing. Five hours west, they know each other as well as any two people can know each other, short of catastrophe. He tells her, as he drives, what he has never told anyone. About that unscheduled overnighter to Omaha, coming home to find his parents and grandmother gassed to death.

She touches his upper arm. "I knew it was that. Almost exactly that."

TEN HOURS IN, she says, "You're so comfortable with silence."

"I've had some practice."

"I like that. I have a lot of catching up."

"I wanted to ask . . . I don't know. Your posture. Your . . . aura. Like you're atoning for something."

She laughs like a ten-year-old. "Maybe I am."

"For what?"

Olivia finds the answer on the western horizon, bubbling up with distant mountains. "For the bitch I was. For the attentive person I wasn't."

"There's a whole lot of comfort in saying nothing."

She tries on the idea and seems to agree. He thinks: *If I were ever imprisoned, or trapped in a fallout shelter with someone, I'd choose this person.*

At the motel just past Salt Lake, the clerk asks, "King or two queens?"

"Two queens," Nick says, hearing that child's laugh beside him. They take awkward turns in the bathroom. Then they lie awake for another hour, chatting across the two-foot chasm between the beds. Garrulous, compared to the thousand miles they've just passed.

"I've never been part of a public protest."

He must think: surely some act of political anger, back in college. He's surprised to have to say, "Me neither."

"I can't imagine who wouldn't join this one."

"Lumberjacks. Libertarians. People who believe in human destiny. People who need decks and shingles." Soon his eyes close on their own accord, and he's swept back into sleep, that nightly place of plantlike deliverance.

NEVADA IS WIDE and bleak enough to mock all human politics. Desert in winter. He gazes in secret as she drives. She's seasick with awe. Then up into the Sierras, where they hit a snowstorm. Nick must buy chains from a roadside scalper. In the Donner Pass, he gets trapped behind a semi, both lanes thick with metal going sixty on a sheet of packed snow. He guides the car by telepathy, finds a little gap in the left lane, and pulls out to pass. Then whiteout. Gauze bandages across the windshield.

"Livia? Shit. I can't *see!*"

The car thuds onto the shoulder and veers back out. He fumbles into the lane, accelerates, blunders forward, and clears their death by snowy inches.

Miles later, he's still shaking. "Jesus God. I almost killed you."

"No," she says, like someone's telling her how things will go. "That's not happening."

They come down the western slope into Shangri-la. In less than an hour, the world outside their capsule goes from conifer forests under feet of snow to the broad green Central Valley, with perennials flowering on the highway banks.

"Cali," she says.

He does not even try to fight his smile. "I believe you may be right."

DOUGLAS has his day in court.

"You are charged with obstructing official business," the judge says. "How do you plead?"

"Your Honor. The official business stank like something steamy somebody's dog left on the parkway."

The judge removes his glasses and rubs his nose. He gazes down into the depths of jurisprudence. "Unfortunately, that has no bearing on your case."

"Why not, Your Honor, if I may respectfully ask?"

In two minutes, the judge explains to him how the law works. Property. Civil governance. Done.

"But the officials were trying to shut down democracy."

"The courts are here for any group of citizens to seek justice for any action that the city took."

"Your Honor. I'm a decorated veteran. They gave me a Purple Heart and an Air Force Cross. Over the last four years, I've planted fifty thousand trees."

He has the court's attention.

"I've walked I don't know how many thousands of miles, sticking seedlings in the ground, trying to roll back progress just a tiny bit. Then I learn that all I'm doing is giving the bastards credits to cut down more and older trees. I'm sorry, but seeing stupidity up close in that city park put me over the edge. Simple as that."

"Have you ever been to jail before?"

"Tough question. Yes and no."

The court deliberates. The defendant obstructed a job being done by a private tree-cutting company on city orders in the dead of night. He took no pokes at the crew. No destruction of property. The judge gives Douglas a seven-day suspended sentence, plus a two-hundred-dollar fine or three days of labor, planting Oregon ashes for the city arborist. Douglas chooses the planting. When he rushes from the courtroom back to the motel, his truck has already been towed. The henchmen want three hundred bucks to return it. He asks them to hold the truck until he rakes the money together. He's got some silver dollars buried here and there.

He busts his hump for the city, planting trees for a week—days longer than his obligatory service requires. "Why?" the arborist asks. "When you don't have to?"

"The ash is a noble tree." Resilient as all get-out. Stuff of tool handles and baseball bats. Douglas loves those compound, pinnate leaves, how they feather the light and make life feel softer than it is. Loves the tapered, sailboat seeds. He likes the idea of planting a few ashes, before doing that only thing that anyone really *has* to do.

The harder the man works, the guiltier the arborist feels. "Not the city's finest hour, what happened in that park." It's a small concession, but for a man on the city payroll, it's almost incendiary.

"Shit straight. Cover of darkness. Days before a town hall hearing people were planning."

"Life's a blood sport," the arborist says. "Like nature."

"Humans don't know shit about nature. Or democracy. You ever think the crazies might be right?"

"Depends. Which crazies?"

"Green crazies. Bunch of them were helping plant a cut, down in the Siuslaw. I met some others at a protest in the Umpqua. They're coming out of the woodwork all over Oregon."

"Kids and druggies. Why do they all take after Rasputin?"

"Hey!" Douggie says. "Rasputin had a look." He hopes the arborist won't turn him in for sedition.


HE DOESN'T LEAVE PORTLAND right away. He heads back to the public library, to read up on guerrilla forestry. His old librarian friend there continues to be more than helpful. The man seems to have a little thing for Douggie, despite his aroma. Or maybe because. Some people get off on loam. A news story of an action near the Salmon-Huckleberry Wilderness gets his attention—an outfit training people how to blockade logging roads. All Douglas needs to do is get his truck out of hock. First, though, he must perform a little guerrilla action of his own. He's not sure of the legality of returning to the scene of his crime. Another act of civil disobedience could very possibly land him back in jail. The part of Douglas that likes to gaze on the Earth from way up high, like he did when he was a loadmaster, almost hopes it does.

Rage builds as he nears the park. It's not quite midday. His shoulders, neck, and bum leg feel it again—thrown to the ground by thugs pulling one over on the general populace. Rage doesn't puff him up, though. Just the opposite. It stoops him over and sucker-punches his solar plexus until, by the time he's in the grove, he's shuffling.

The first of the fresh stumps still oozes resin. He drops down alongside it on the ground and pulls out a fine-line Magic Marker and his driver's license, to use as a straight edge. He holds both to the sawn wood like he's doing surgery, and counts backward. The years roll away under his fingers—their floods and droughts, their cold spells and scorched seasons all written into the varying rings. When the countdown reaches 1975, he makes a fine black X and pens in that date. Then he peels back another twenty-five years, makes another X on a ray just a little bit counterclockwise from the first, and labels it 1950.

The work goes on, in quarter-century increments, until he reaches the still center. He doesn't know how old this city is, but the tree was clearly a sturdy sapling before any white people came near this spot. When Douglas pens in the closest year he can count with accuracy, he travels back out to the rim, so recently still expanding, and writes, in block caps that run like a wheel around half the circumference, CUT DOWN WHILE YOU SLEPT.

He's still there, marking the stumps, when Mimi comes out for lunch. Anger is her new lunchtime card game, played solitaire while eating her egg and hot pepper sandwiches on a bench in the newly minimized Zen garden. Since the night raid, she has made scores of phone calls, attended an impotent public meeting, and talked to two lawyers, both of whom advised her that justice was a fantasy. Outdoor lunch is her only recourse, staring at the raw stumps and chewing her rage. She sees the man on his hands and knees annotating the damage and explodes. "What are you doing *now*?"

Douggie looks up at a woman the image of a Patpong B-girl named Lalida he once loved more than breathing. A woman worth punching any number of potholes to get next to. She advances, threatening him with a sandwich lance.

"It's not enough to murder them? You have to deface them, too?"

He bares his palms, then points at the hieroglyphics on a cut stump. She stops and sees—the labeled rings running backward to the circle's center. The year her father blew his brains all over the backyard. The year she graduated and got this godforsaken job. The year the whole Ma family scattered from the bear. The year her father showed her the scroll. The year of her birth. The year her father came to study at the great Carnegie Institute of Technology. And in the outermost ring, the caption: CUT DOWN WHILE YOU SLEPT.

She glances back down at the man on his knees. "Oh, God. I'm so sorry. I thought you were . . . I almost kicked you in the face."

"Guys who did this beat you to it."

"Wait. *You were there?*" Her eyebrows draw together as she does the yield-stress calculation. "If I'd been there, I'd have hurt someone."

"Big trees are coming down all over."

"Yeah. But this was *my* park. My daily bread."

"You know, you look at those mountains, and you think: *Civilization will fade away, but* that *will go on forever.* Only, civilization is snorting like a steer on growth hormones, and those mountains are going down."

"I talked to two lawyers. No laws were broken."

"'Course not. The wrong people have all the rights."

"What can you do?"

The crazy man's eyes dance. He looks like the twelfth arhat, amused by the folly of all human aspiration. He wavers. "Can I trust you? I mean, you're not here to steal one of my kidneys or anything?"

She laughs, and that's all he needs to believe.

"Then listen. You wouldn't happen to have three hundred bucks anywhere? Or maybe a car that works?"

THE BRINKMANS TAKE TO READING, when they're alone together.
And, together, they're alone most of the time. Community theater is over;
they haven't acted in a play since the one about the nonexistent baby. They've
never said out loud to each other that their acting days are over. No dialogue
required.

In place of children, then, books. In their reading tastes, each of them
stays true to the dreams of youth. Ray likes to glimpse the grand project
of civilization ascending to its still-obscure destiny. He wants only to read
on, late into the night, about the rising quality of life, the steady freeing of
humanity by invention, the breakout of know-how that will finally save the
race. Dorothy needs wilder reclamations, stories free of ideas and steeped in
local selves. Her salvation is close, hot, and private. It depends on a person's
ability to say *nevertheless*, to do one small thing that seems beyond them, and,
for a moment, break the grip of time.

Ray's shelves are organized by topic; Dorothy's, alphabetical by author.
He prefers state-of-the-art books with fresh copyrights. She needs to communicate with the distant dead, alien souls as different from her as possible. Once Ray starts a book, he force-marches through to its conclusion,
however hard the slog. Dorothy doesn't mind skipping the author's philoso-
phies to get to those moments when one character, often the most surprising,
reaches down inside herself and is better than her nature allows.

Life in their forties. Once any given volume enters the house, it can
never leave. For Ray, the goal is readiness: a book for every unforeseeable
need. Dorothy strives to keep local independent booksellers afloat and save
neglected gems from the cutout bin. Ray thinks: *You never know when you
might finally get around to reading that tome you picked up five years ago.* And

Dorothy: *Someday you'll need to take down a worn-out volume and flip to that passage on the lower right-hand face, ten pages from the end, that fills you with such sweet and vicious pain.*

The conversion of their house into a library happens too slowly to see. The books that won't fit she lays on their sides, on top of the existing rows. This warps the covers and makes him crazy. For a while they solve the problem with more furniture. A pair of cherry cases to set between the windows in his downstairs office. A large walnut unit in the front room, in the space traditionally reserved for the television altar. Maple in the guest room. He says, "That should hold us for a while." She laughs, knowing, from every novel she has ever read, how brief a while a *while* can be.

Dorothy's mother dies. They can't bear to part with a single volume of the dead woman's titles. So they add them to a collection that would have been the envy of kings. Dorothy finds an incredible deal on Walter Scott's *Complete Waverly Novels* in a downtown antiquarian bookstore. "Eighteen eighty-two! And look at these beautiful endpapers. Marble waterfall."

"You know what we could do?" Ray tosses off the idea on the way to the cashier. Next to the Scott, he slips in a copy of *The Age of Intelligent Machines*. "That funky wall in the small bedroom upstairs. We could have a carpenter design some built-ins."

The plans they once had for that room now seem older than anything on their shelves. She nods and tries to smile, reaching down inside herself for a word. She doesn't know the word. She doesn't even know that that's what she's doing. *Nevertheless.* The word is *nevertheless.*


THEY HAVE A STANDING JOKE, at Christmas, a joke always ready not to be one, on a moment's notice. One gift they give each other must be the annual attempted conversion. This year, he gives her *Fifty Ideas That Changed the World.*

"Honey! How thoughtful!"

"Sure changed me."

He will never change, she thinks, and kisses him near the lips. Then she comes through with her part of the ritual: a new annotated edition of *Four Great Novels by Jane Austen*.

"Dorothy, darling. You read my mind!"

"You know, you *could* try her, one of these years."

He tried her, years ago, and almost choked to death from claustrophobia.

They spend the holidays in their robes, each reading the gift they bought the other. On New Year's, they struggle to make it to midnight. They lie in bed, side by side, leg to leg, but with hands firmly on the pages in front of them. Falling asleep, he reads the same paragraph a dozen times; the words turn into twirling things, like winged seeds spinning in the air.

"Happy New Year," he says, when the ball drops at last. "Survived another one, huh?"

They pour the bubbles that have been waiting by the bedside on ice. She clinks, drinks, and says, "We should have an adventure this year."

The bookcases are full of previous resolutions, taken up and shelved. *No-Sweat Indian Cooking. A Hundred Hikes in the Greater Yellowstone. A Field Guide to Eastern Songbirds. To Eastern Wildflowers. Off the Beaten Path in Europe. Unknown Thailand.* Manuals of beer brewing and wine making. Untouched foreign language texts. All those scattered explorations theirs to sample and squander. They have lived like flighty and forgetful gods.

"Something life-threatening," she adds.

"I was *just* thinking that."

"Maybe we should run a marathon."

"I . . . could be your trainer. Or whatever."

"Something we could do together. Pilot's license?"

"Maybe," he says, comatose with fatigue. "Welp." He sets the glass down and slaps his thighs.

"Yep. One more page before lights-out?"


SHE DESCENDS into the real anguish of imaginary beings. She lies still, trying not to wake him with her sobs. *What is this, grabbing at my heart, like it means something? What gives this pretend place so much power over me?* Just this: the glimpse of someone seeing something she shouldn't be able to see. Someone who doesn't even know she's been invented, staying game in the face of the inescapable plot.

FOR SOME REASON, when their anniversary comes, the Brinkmans again forget to plant anything.

THE REDWOODS knock all words out of them. Nick drives in silence. Even the young trunks are like angels. And when, after a few miles, they pass a monster, sprouting a first upward-swooping branch forty feet in the air, as thick as most eastern trees, he knows: the word *tree* must grow up, get *real*. It's not the size that throws him, or not *just* the size. It's the grooved, Doric perfection of the red-brown columns, shooting upward from the shoulder-high ferns and moss-swarmed floor—straight up, with no taper, like a russet, leathery apotheosis. And when the columns do start to crown, it happens so high, so removed from the pillars' base, that it might as well be a second world up there, up nearer eternity.

All the agitation of the journey ebbs from Olivia. It's like she knows the place, although she has never been west of Six Flags Over Mid-America. Along a narrow road through the coastal forest she calls out, "Stop the car."

He pulls over onto a shoulder soft with needles a few feet deep. The car door opens and the air tastes sweet and savory. She wanders out from the passenger side into a grove of giants. When he joins her, her face is streaked and her eyes hot and liquid with joy. She shakes her head, incredulous. "This is it. This is *them*. We're here."

. . .

THE DEFENDERS of the forest aren't hard to find. Different groups are organizing throughout the Lost Coast. There's a report of some action almost every day in the local papers. Nick and Olivia live rough, car-camping for a few days, feeling out who's who in a ragtag cast that is makeshift and an organization that is improvised, to say the least.

They learn about a volunteer encampment in the muddy fields of a sympathetic retired fisherman, not far from Solace. The bivouac swarms with more activity than coherence. Quick young people, loud in their devotion, call across the tent-dotted meadow. Their noses, ears, and eyebrows flash with hardware. Dreadlocks tangle in the fibers of their multicolored garb. They stink of soil, sweat, idealism, patchouli oil, and the sweet sinsemilla grown all through these woods. Some stay for two days. Some, judging from their microflora, have been in this base camp for more than a few seasons.

The camp is one of many nerve centers for a chaotic movement without leaders that mostly goes under the name of Life Defense Force. Nick and Olivia scout the fields, talking to everyone. They share a dinner of eggs and beans with an older man named Moses. He, for his part, questions and vets them, too, assuring himself that they aren't spies for Weyerhaeuser or Boise Cascade or the more proximal force in these parts, Humboldt Timber.

"How do we get . . . assignments?" Nick asks.

The word makes Moses laugh out loud. "No assignments here. But no end of work."

They cook for dozens and help clean up afterward. There's a march the next day. Nick letters posters while Olivia joins the sing-along. A flame-haired, plaid-clad, hawk-silhouetted woman passes through camp wrapped in a woven shawl. Olivia grabs Nick. "It's her. The one from the television clip back in Indiana." The one the beings of light wanted her to find.

Moses nods. "That's Mother N. She can turn a megaphone into a Strad."

As the light falls, Mother N holds an orientation talk in a clearing next to Moses's tent. She scans the rings of seated bodies, acknowledging veterans and welcoming newcomers. "It's good to see so many of you still here this late in the season. In the past, a lot of you have headed home for the winter, when the rains shut down the logging shows until spring. But Humboldt Timber has started working year-round."

Boos ripple through the crowd.

"They're trying to get the cut out before the law catches up with them. But they haven't counted on all of *you*!"

A cheer breaks like a whitecap over Nicholas. He turns to Olivia and takes her hand. She squeezes back, as if this isn't the first time he has touched her in gladness. She beams, and Nick marvels again at her certainty. She has gotten them this far navigating by feel—*Warmer, this way, warmer*—whispered instructions from presences only she can hear. And here they are, like they knew where they were going all along.

"A lot of you have been out here for a while," Mother N continues. "So much useful work! Picketing. Guerrilla theater. Peaceful demonstrations."

Moses rubs his shaved head and shouts, "Now we put the fear of God in them!"

The cheer redoubles. Even Mother N smiles. "Well, maybe! But the LDF takes nonviolence seriously. For those of you who just arrived, we want you to take passive resistance training and pledge the nonviolence code before joining any direct action. We do not condone outright property destruction. . . ."

Moses shouts, "But you'd be surprised at what a little quick-drying cement around a wheelbase can do."

The edges of Mother N's lips twist. "We're part of a very long, very broad process, all over the world. If those beautiful Chipko women in India can let themselves get threatened and beaten, if Brazilian Kayapo Indians can put their lives on the line, so can we."

It's drizzling. Nick and Olivia hardly notice.

"Most of you already know all about Humboldt Timber. For those who don't, they were a family business for almost a century. They ran the last progressive company town in the state and paid incredible benefits. Their pension system was overfunded. They took care of their own and rarely hired gypos. Best of all, they cut selectively, for a yield they might have sustained forever.

"Because they cut the old stuff slowly, they still had several billion board feet of the best softwood on the planet, long after their competitors all along the coast shot their bolts. Two hundred thousand acres—forty percent of the area's remaining old growth. But HT's stock price lagged compared to those companies out there maximizing profits. Which, by the rules of capitalism, meant somebody had to come in and show the old-timers how to run a business. You remember Henry Hanson, the Junk Bond King? The guy who went to jail last year for racketeering? He set up the deal. A raider buddy of his pulled off the steal, all the way from Wall Street. Ingenious, really: you pour junk-raised cash into a hostile takeover and sell the debt to your savings and loan, which the public ultimately must bail out. Then you mortgage the company to the hilt to pay off the funny money, loot the pension fund, run through the reserves, sell off everything of value, and dispose of the remaining bankrupt husk for whatever you can get. Magic! Loot that pays you extra to plunder it.

"Right now they're in that second-to-the-last stage: cashing out every salable scrap of timber in the inventory. Which in this case means lots of seven- and eight-hundred-year-old trees. Trees wider than your dreams are going into Mill B and coming out as planks. Humboldt is cutting at four times the industry rate. And they're speeding up, before legislation can catch up with them."

Nick turns to Olivia. The girl is years younger than he is, but he has begun to look to her for explanations. Her face stiffens and her eyes close in pain. Tears roll down her cheekbones.

"Obviously, we can't wait for legislation. The new, efficient Humboldt Timber will have killed all the giants by the time the law catches up with them. So this is the question I ask each of you. What can you bring to the effort? We'll take anything you can give. Time. Effort. Cash. Cash is surprisingly helpful!"

Applause and cheers ring out after her talk, and people retreat to a meal of lentil soup made over several campfires. Olivia helps cook, she who used to steal her housemates' food from the fridge rather than boil a little water for ramen. Nick senses these forest men, some who haven't bathed in weeks, striving for blasé as she serves them, as if a dryad hasn't just dropped down into this meadow next to them.

A band under the supervision of a man named Blackbeard returns from a raid gumming up a parked Caterpillar D8 engine with corn syrup. They glow with accomplishment in the campfire's flicker. They mean to go out again, after dark, to test the company's vigil on larger gear farther up the hillside.

"I don't like property crimes," Mother N says. "I really don't."

Moses laughs her off. "No valuable property has been destroyed except these forests. We're in a war of attrition. We tie the lumber crews up for a few hours, then they repair the machines. But in the meantime, they lose time and dollars."

Blackbeard glowers at the flames. "Humboldt is nothing *but* property crimes. And we're supposed to make nice?"

Two dozen volunteers start talking over one other. After years in rural Iowa, Nick's like a kid raised on a tinny radio hearing his first live symphony. He has landed in a druid tree cult like the ones he read about on winter nights in the Hoel family encyclopedia. Oak veneration at the oracle at Dodona, the druids' groves in Britain and Gaul, Shinto sakaki worship, India's bejeweled wishing trees, Mayan kapoks, Egyptian sycamores, the Chinese sacred ginkgo—all the branches of the world's first religion. His decade of obsessive sketching has been practice for whatever art this sect requires of him.

Olivia leans in. "Are you okay?" His reply sticks in his wide, coprophagic grin.

The raid party readies to head out again. Blackbeard, Needles, Moss-Eater, and the Revelator: warriors competing for the palm, the laurel, the olive.

"Hang on," Nick tells them. "Let's try something." He sits them on a camping stool in the shadows of the fire, while he paints their faces. He dips a brush into a can of green latex that a woman named Tinkerbell uses to letter banners. He follows the contours of their skulls, the curves of their foreheads and the mounds of cheekbone, finding his way forward into whorls and spirals, surreal freehand memories of Maori *tā moko* tattoos. Tie-dyed tees and paisley faces: the effect is devastating. The night's commandos stand back and admire each other. Something enters them; they become other beings, inscribed and altered, filled with power by ancient signs.

"*Jesus H!* This'll scare the shit out of them."

Moses shakes his head at the new guy's handiwork. "It's good. We want them to think we're dangerous."

Olivia comes up behind Nick in pride. She curls her hands beneath his upper arm. She has no clue what that does to him, after days together on the cross-country car ride, nights side by side in thick sleeping bags. Or maybe she knows, and doesn't care. "Nice work," she whispers.

He shrugs. "Not especially useful."

"Urgent. I have it on good authority."

They christen themselves with forest names that night, in the soft drizzle of the redwoods, on a blanket of needles. The game seems childish, at first. But all of art is childish, all storytelling, all human hope and fear. Why shouldn't they take new names for this new work? Trees go by a dozen different labels. There's Texas and Spanish and false buckeye and Monillo, all for the same plant. Trees with names as profligate as maple seeds. There's buttonwood, aka plane tree, aka sycamore: like a man with a drawer full of fake passports. In one place there's *lime*, in another *linden*, *Tilia* at large, but *basswood* when turned into lumber or honey. Twenty-eight names for longleaf pine alone.

Olivia appraises Nick in the darkness, far from the fire. She squints for evidence of what to call him. Pushes his hair back behind his ear, tilts his chin in her cool hands. "Watchman. Does that sound right? You're my Watchman."

Observer, bystander. Would-be protector. He grins, discovered.

"Name me now!"

He reaches out and takes a fingerful of that wheaty stuff that soon will never be lighter than mud. It fans out under his fingers. "Maidenhair."

"That's a real thing?"

It is, he tells her, another name for a living fossil, earlier than flowering trees, early as the earliest conifers, a native for a while, in these headwaters, then disappeared for millions of years before returning in cultivation. A tree from back at the beginning of trees.

. . .

SHE CURLS against him in the pup tent as they fall asleep, made safe from anything more intimate than warmth by the proximity of so many other volunteers. He lies gazing at her back, the slight rise and fall of her rib cage. The T-shirt she uses for pajamas slips off her shoulder, revealing a tattoo across her scapula, in florid script: *A change is gonna come.*

He lies as still as he can, a tumescent monk. He counts the poundings of his heart high up in his ears until the surf weakens into sleep. As he drifts off, a spidery thought spins through him. People from another planet will wonder what's wrong with earthly names, that it takes so many different ones to tag a thing. But here he lies, alongside this friend he has known only weeks, joined again after so many lifetimes. Nick and Olivia, Watchman and Maidenhair—the complete quartet of them—open to the January night, under topless columns of coastal redwood, the ever-living *Sempervirens*.

PATRICIA WESTERFORD sits on her ladder-backed chair at the pine farmhouse table, pen in the air, taking dictation from the insects. Eleven o'clock nears and she has nothing—not one sentence she hasn't revised to death. The wind wafts through the window, smelling of compost and cedar. The scent triggers an old, deep longing that seems to have no purpose. The woods are calling, and she must go.

All winter she has struggled to describe the joy of her life's work and the discoveries that have solidified in a few short years: how trees talk to one another, over the air and underground. How they care and feed each other, orchestrating shared behaviors through the networked soil. How they build immune systems as wide as a forest. She spends a chapter detailing how a dead log gives life to countless other species. Remove the snag and kill the woodpecker who keeps in check the weevils that would kill the other trees. She describes the drupes and racemes, panicles and involucres that a person could walk past for a lifetime and never notice. She tells how the woody-coned alders harvest gold. How an inch-high pecan might have six feet of root. How the inner bark of birches can feed the starving. How one hop hornbeam catkin holds several million grains of pollen. How indigenous fishermen use crushed walnut leaves to stun and catch fish. How willows clean soils of dioxins, PCBs, and heavy metals.

She lays out how fungal hyphae—countless miles of filaments folded up in every spoon of soil—coax open tree roots and tap into them. How the wired-up fungi feed the tree minerals. How the tree pays for these nutrients with sugars, which the fungi can't make.

> Something marvelous is happening underground, something
> we're just learning how to see. Mats of mycorrhizal cabling
> link trees into gigantic, smart communities spread across hun-
> dreds of acres. Together, they form vast trading networks of
> goods, services, and information. . . .

> There are no individuals in a forest, no separable events. The
> bird and the branch it sits on are a joint thing. A third or more
> of the food a big tree makes may go to feed other organisms.
> Even different kinds of trees form partnerships. Cut down a
> birch, and a nearby Douglas-fir may suffer. . . .

> In the great forests of the East, oaks and hickories synchro-
> nize their nut production to baffle the animals that feed on
> them. Word goes out, and the trees of a given species—
> whether they stand in sun or shade, wet or dry—bear heavily
> or not at all, together, as a community. . . .

> Forests mend and shape themselves through subterranean
> synapses. And in shaping themselves, they shape, too, the
> tens of thousands of other, linked creatures that form it from
> within. Maybe it's useful to think of forests as enormous
> spreading, branching, underground super-trees.

She tells how an elm helped start the American Revolution. How a huge five-hundred-year-old mesquite grows in the middle of one of the planet's most arid deserts. How the glimpse of a horse chestnut through a window gave Anne Frank hope, even in hopeless hiding. How seeds brought to the moon and back sprouted all over the Earth. How the world is inhabited by magnificent creatures no one knows. How it may take centuries to learn as much about trees as people once knew.

Her husband lives fourteen miles away in town. They see each other once a day, for lunches that Dennis makes from whatever is in season. All day and all night long, her only people are the trees, and her only means of speaking for them are words, those organs of saprophytic latecomers that live off the energy green things make.

Journal articles have always been hard enough. Her years as an outcast come back to her each time she writes one, even when she's only one of a dozen coauthors. She feels even more anxiety when others are on board. She'd sooner retire again than inflict on these beloved colleagues anything like what she once suffered. Yet even journal articles are a walk in the woods compared to writing for the public. Scientific papers sit in archives, matters of indifference to almost everyone. But this millstone book: She's sure to be mocked and misunderstood in the press. And she'll never earn out what her publisher has already paid.

All winter long she has struggled with how to tell a stranger everything she knows. The months have been hell, but paradise, too. Soon enough, the hellish paradise will end. In August she'll close her field lab, pack up the gear, and remove all her meticulous samples to the coast and that university where she'll—unthinkable—begin to teach again.

The words refuse to come, tonight. She should simply sleep, and see what her dreams might say. Instead, she cranes to glimpse the kitchen clock above the antique, slope-shouldered refrigerator. Still time for a midnight wander down to the pond.

The spruces near the cabin wave spooky prophecies under the near-full moon. There's a straight line of them, the memory of a vanished fence where red crossbills once liked to sit and shit out seeds. The trees are busy tonight, fixing carbon in their dark phase. All will be in flower before long: huckle-berry and currant, showy milkweed, tall Oregon grape, yarrow and check-ermallow. She marvels again at how the planet's supreme intelligence could discover calculus and the universal laws of gravitation before anyone knew what a flower was for.

Tonight the stands are as drizzled and murky as her word-filled mind. She finds the trail and ducks beneath her beloved *Pseudotsuga*. A path cuts under the spires lit by late winter's moon, a path she walks almost nightly, out and back like that old palindrome: *La ruta nos aportó otro paso natural*. The many uncataloged volatile compounds breathed out by needles at night slow her heart rate, soften her breathing, and, if she's right, even alter her mood and thoughts. So many substances in woodland pharmacies that no one has yet identified. Powerful molecules in bark, pith, and leaves whose effects have yet to be discovered. One family of distress hormones used by her trees—jasmonate—supplies the punch to all those feminine perfumes that play on mystery and intrigue. *Sniff me, love me, I'm in trouble*. And they are in trouble, all these trees. All the forests of the world, even the quaintly named *set-aside lands*. More trouble than she has the heart to tell readers of her little book. Trouble, like the atmosphere, flows everywhere, in currents beyond the power of humans to predict or control.

She pops out into the pond's clearing. The starry sky erupts above her, all the explanation a person needs for why humans have waged war on for-ests forever. Dennis has told her what the loggers say: *Let's go let a little light into that swamp*. Forests panic people. Too much going on there. Humans need a sky.

Her seat is vacant and waiting—that moss-blanketed nurse log by the water's edge. The moment she looks out over the water, her head clears and she finds the passage she's after. She has searched for a name for the great ancient trunks of the uncut forest, the ones who keep the market in carbons and metabolites going. Now she has one:

Fungi mine stone to supply their trees with minerals. They
hunt springtails, which they feed to their hosts. Trees, for

their part, store extra sugar in their fungi's synapses, to dole out to the sick and shaded and wounded. A forest takes care of itself, even as it builds the local climate it needs to survive.

Before it dies, a Douglas-fir, half a millennium old, will send its storehouse of chemicals back down into its roots and out through its fungal partners, donating its riches to the community pool in a last will and testament. We might well call these ancient benefactors *giving trees*.

The reading public needs such a phrase to make the miracle a little more vivid, visible. It's something she learned long ago, from her father: people see better what looks like them. *Giving trees* is something any generous person can understand and love. And with those two words, Patricia Westerford seals her own fate and changes the future. Even the future of trees.

IN THE MORNING, she splashes cold water on her face, makes a flax-berry slurry, drinks it while reading yesterday's pages, then sits at the pine table, vowing not to stand up until she has a paragraph worthy of showing Dennis at lunch. The smell of her red cedar pencil elates her. The slow push of graphite across paper reminds her of the steady evaporation that lifts hundreds of gallons of water up hundreds of feet into a giant Douglas-fir trunk every day. The solitary act of sitting over the page and waiting for her hand to move may be as close as she'll ever get to the enlightenment of plants.

The final chapter eludes her. She needs some impossible trifecta: hopeful, useful, and true. She could use Old Tjikko, that Norway spruce who lives about midway up the length of Sweden. Above the ground, the tree is only a few hundred years old. But below, in the microbe-riddled soil, he reaches back nine thousand years or more—thousands of years older than this trick of writing she uses to try to capture it.

All morning long, she works to squeeze the nine-thousand-year saga into ten sentences: a procession of trunks falling and springing back up from the same root. There's the *hopeful* she's after. The truth is somewhat more brutal. By late morning, she catches up to the present, when, for the first time, the new man-made atmosphere coaxes the latest of Old Tjikko's usually snow-stunted krummholz trunks to shoot up into a full-sized tree.

But hope and truth do nothing for humans, without *use*. In the clumpy, clumsy finger-paint of words, she searches for the use of Old Tjikko, up on that barren crest, endlessly dying and resurrecting in every change of climate. His use is to show that the world is not made for our utility. What use are we, to trees? She remembers the Buddha's words: A tree is a wondrous thing that shelters, feeds, and protects all living things. It even offers shade to the axmen who destroy it. And with those words, she has her book's end.

DENNIS SHOWS AT NOON, reliable as rain, bearing broccoli-almond lasagna, his latest midday masterpiece. She thinks, as she does several times a week, how lucky she has been, to spend these few blessed years married to the one man on Earth who'd let her spend most of her life alone. Game, patient, good-natured Dennis. He protects her work and needs so little. In his handyman's heart, he already knows how few things man is really the measure of. And he's as generous and eager as weeds.

As they eat Dennis's feast, she reads him today's installment on Old Tjikko. He listens, astonished, like a happy child might listen to Greek myths. She finishes. He claps. "Oh, babe. It's just fine." Something deep in her callow green soul likes being the world's oldest babe. "I hate to tell you this, but I think you're done."

It's terrifying, but he's right. She sighs and stares out the kitchen window, where three crows hatch their elaborate plans for breaking into her compost bin. "So what do I do now?"

His laugh is as hearty as if she said something funny. "You type it up and we mail it to your publishers. Four months late."

"I can't."

"Why not?"

"Everything's wrong. Starting with the title."

"What's wrong with *How Trees Will Save the World*? Trees won't save the world?"

"I'm sure they will. After the world shrugs us off."

He chuckles and packs up the dirty dishes. He'll take them home, where there are deep sinks, strainers, and hot water. He looks across the kitchen at her. "Call it *Forest Salvation*. Then you don't have to commit to who's saving what."

"I do love you."

"Did someone say you didn't? Look. Babe. This should be pure pleasure. Talking to people about your life's great joy."

"You know, Den. The last time I was in the public eye, it didn't go so well."

He swipes at the air. "That was another lifetime."

"Wolfpack. They didn't want to disprove me. They wanted blood!"

"But you've been exonerated. Over and over."

She wants to tell him what she has never mentioned: how the trauma of those days was so great that she cooked herself a fatal woodlands feast. But she can't. She's too ashamed of that long-dead girl. Part of her no longer entirely believes that she could ever have considered such a course. Deniable theater. A game. So she conceals the only thing she has ever kept from him—how she had the poison mushrooms all but in her mouth.

"Babe. You're practically a prophetess, these days."

"I also spent a lot of years as a pariah. Prophetess is much more fun."

She helps him out to the car with the dirty dishes. "Love you, Den."

"Please stop saying that. You're spooking me."


SHE TYPES UP THE DRAFT. She prunes a few words and pollards a few phrases. There's now a chapter called "The Giving Trees," about her beloved Doug-firs and their underground welfare state. She ranges around the country's forests, from cottonwoods that top a hundred feet in a decade to bristlecone pines that die slowly for five thousand years. Then the post office, where all her anxiety drains out of her the minute she pays the postage and sends the manuscript off to the other coast.

SIX WEEKS LATER, her office phone rings. She hates the phone. Hand-held schizophrenia. Unseen voices whispering to you from a distance. Nobody calls her except with unpleasant business. It's her editor, whom she has never met, from New York, a city she has never seen. "Patricia? Your *book*. I just finished it!"

Patricia winces, waiting for the ax.

"Unbelievable. Who knew that trees got up to all those things?"

"Well. A few hundred million years of evolution gives you a repertoire."

"You make them come *alive*."

"Actually, they were alive already." But she's thinking of the book her father gave her when she was fourteen. She realizes she must dedicate this book to her father. And to her husband. And all the people who will, in time, turn into other things.

"Patty, you wouldn't believe what you have me seeing, between the subway stop and my office. That part about the giving trees? Mind-blowing. We didn't pay you enough for this."

"You paid me more than I've made in the last five years."

"You'll earn out in two months."

What Patricia Westerford would like to earn back is her solitude, her anonymity, which she begins to sense—the way trees can sense an invasion still far away—will never be hers again.

*MASTERY* ARRIVES, and there's no turning back. Two months after the game's North American release, the president, CEO, and majority stock-holder of Sempervirens fires up a copy on his workhorse machine, in his apartment on the floor above the company's shiny new headquarters in the foothills up Page Mill Road. It's all redwood and glass—a playground of whimsical, meditative spaces. Odd angles surround open-air atriums planted with giant Italian stone pines. Working at your carrel feels like camping out in a national park.

Neelay's refuge is tucked away on high, above the hive. The only way to reach it is by private elevator, hidden behind a fire stairwell. At the center of the concealed den sits a complex hospital bed. Neelay almost never uses it anymore. Forty minutes to get in and out of; it feels like death, these days, even to lie down. There's no time. He sleeps in his chair, rarely more than forty minutes at a shot. Ideas torture him like the Furies. Plans and breakthroughs for his world in progress chase him around the galaxy without mercy.

He sits in front of a giant screen at a work surface high enough for him to slip the chair under. Past the screen, a plate-glass panorama reveals the top of Monte Bello. That view, and the starscapes shining through the night skylight, make up most of Neelay's voyages abroad. His forays now are like today's—expeditions down the coasts of landmasses that start out shrouded in fog and open into discovery. He designed the game's foundations, wrote a fair portion of the code, and spent months working through its possible paths. *Mastery* should have no more power to surprise him; yet it never fails to quicken his pulse. A click of the mouse, a few keystrokes, and he's face-to-face again with the next virgin continent.

In truth, the game is pathetic. It's two-dimensional—no smell, no touch, no taste, no feel. It's tiny and grainy, with a world model as simplistic as Genesis. Yet it sinks its teeth into his brainstem whenever he fires it up. The maps, climates, and scattered resources are new, each time in. His opponents may be Conquistadores, Builders, or Technocrats, Nature Worshippers, Misers, Humanitarians, or Radical Utopians. Nothing quite like the place has ever existed. Yet going there feels like coming home. His mind has been waiting for such a playground since long before he fell from his betraying tree.

Today he chooses to be a Sage. Rumor is spreading across dial-up bulletin boards from around the globe, about an overpowered victory strategy players are calling *Enlightenment*. Top-ranked leaders are pushing for the whole approach to be banned. But even as a Sage, he must acquire sufficient coal, gold, ore, stone, wood, food, honor, and glory to pay for his population growth. He must explore unknown terrain, form trade routes, and raid neighboring settlements, working his way along branching trees for Culture, Craft, Economics, and Technology. The game presents almost as many meaningful choices as Real Life, or, as his staff has taken to calling it, a little derisively: *RL*. This morning the graphics look a little jagged compared to *Mastery 2*, already in the works. But graphics have never meant much to Neelay. The visible is only a placeholder for real desire. All he and half a million other *Mastery* players need is easy and endless shape-shifting, in a kingdom forever growing.

Something twists in him. He takes a few minutes to recognize the feeling as hunger. He should eat, but eating is such a process. He rolls to the mini-fridge and grabs an energy drink and something that turns out to be a chicken puff, which he downs without even microwaving. Tonight he'll make a real meal, or tomorrow. He's assembling a stack of cypress planks from his best team of woodcutters into a mammoth ark when the phone rings. His morning appointment with a journalist who wants to interview the infant industry's rising star, the boy still in his twenties who has made a home for so many homeless boys.

This reporter sounds not much older than his subject, and petrified. "Mr. Mehta?"

Mr. Mehta is his father, whom Neelay has tucked away in a tiny palace outside Cupertino complete with pool, home theater, and pond flanked by a rosewood mandir, where Mrs. Mehta does weekly puja and prays to the gods to bring her son happiness and a girl who'll see him for who he is.

A reflection in the plate glass looks up to challenge him: a brown, scrawny praying mantis with bulbous joints and enormous, tight-skinned skull for a head. "Call me Neelay."

"Oh, gosh. Okay. Wow! Neelay. I'm Chris. Thanks for talking. So, first I want to ask: Did you know that *Mastery* was going to be such a hit?"

Neelay did know, long before the game was released into the wild. He knew from the moment he had the idea, under the giant, spreading, pulsing tree at night, up on Skyline. "Kind of. Yes. The beta release stopped my workforce dead. My project manager had to enforce a ban."

"Holy crap. Do you have sales figures?"

"It's selling very well. In fourteen countries."

"Why do you think that is?"

The game's success is simple enough. It's a reasonable facsimile of the place Neelay envisioned at seven, when his father first lugged an enormous cardboard box up the apartment stairs. *Now, Neelay-ji. What might this little creature do?* What the boy wanted the black box to do was innocent enough: return him to the days of myth and origin, when all the places a person could reach were green and pliant, and life might still be anything at all.

"I don't know. It has simple rules. The world responds to you. Things happen faster than in life. You can watch your empire grow."

"I'm . . . I confess to you. I'm totally in love! Last night, when I finally stopped playing, it was like four a.m. I just needed to see what would happen with one more move. And when I stood up from the screen, my whole bedroom was bobbing and jittering."

"I know what you mean." And Neelay does. Except for the part about standing up.

"Do you think it's changing the brains of the people who play it?"

"Yes, Chris. But so does everything, I think."

"Did you see the article in last week's *Times* about game addiction? People spending fifty hours a week on video games?"

"*Mastery* isn't a video game. It's a thought game."

"Okay. But you must admit, a lot of productive time is going to waste."

"The game is definitely chronophagic." He hears a little question mark pop up in a thought bubble on the other end of the line. "Time-eating."

"Does it bother you, to be such a destroyer of productivity?"

Neelay gazes out on a patch of mountain shaved bare half a century ago. "I don't think . . . It might not be so bad, to destroy a little productivity."

"Huh. Okay. The game's killing *my* little life, anyway. I keep coming across things that aren't in the hundred-and-twenty-eight-page gamebook."

"Yes. That's part of what keeps people playing."

"While I'm in the game, I feel I have a goal. Always something more to do."

*Yes, oh, yes*, Neelay wants to tell him. Safe and comprehensible, with no swamps of ambiguity to suck you down, no human-on-human darkness, and your own will receives its rightful land. Call it *meaning*. "I think a lot of people feel more at home, in there. Than they do out here."

"Maybe! A lot of guys my age, anyway."

"Yes. But we're planning all kinds of new roles for the next release. New ways of playing the game. Avenues of possibility for all kinds of people. We want it to be a beautiful place for everyone."

"Wow. Okay. That's wild. So what will the company do next?"

The company is slipping out of Neelay's control. Teams and managers populate an organizational tree he can't keep track of. The best developers in the Valley knock on the door every day, wanting to play. Software engineers on Route 128 around Boston, recent grads from Georgia Tech and Carnegie Mellon—brains shaped from infancy by the games Neelay used to give away—beg him for the chance to help engineer the wholesale exodus now well under way.

"I wish I could tell you."

Chris whimpers. "How about if I beg?"

His voice has all the confidence of a healthy, ambulatory male. Probably white and good-looking. The charm and optimism of a guy who does not yet know what people will do to other people, to other living things, once terrors and hurts and needs set in.

"Just a hint?"

"Well, it's simple, really. More of everything. More surprises. More possibilities. More places, filled with more kinds of creatures. Imagine *Mastery*, after it doubles in richness and complexity forty times. We don't even know what such a place might look like." *All from a seed* this *big*.

"Oh. That's so amazing. So . . . beautiful!"

Something stabs at Neelay. He wants to say: *Ask me again. There's more.*

"Can I ask about you?"

Neelay's pulse spikes, like he's trying to lift himself on his set of exercise rings. *Please, no. Please don't.* "Of course."

"I've read quite a few stories about you. Your own employees call you a hermit."

"I'm not a hermit. It's just—my legs don't work."

"I read about that. How do you run the company?"

"Phone. Email. Online messaging."

"Why are there no pictures of you?"

"It isn't pretty."

The answer flusters Chris. Neelay wants to say: *It's all right. It's only RL.*

"Do you feel that growing up as the child of immigrants—"

"Oh, I don't think so. Probably, no."

"No, what?"

"I don't think it had much of an influence on me."

"But . . . how about being Indian-American? Don't you feel that—"

"Here's what I think. I've been Gandhi and Hitler and Chief Joseph. I've wielded plus-six great swords while wearing little chain mail thong bikinis that, frankly, didn't give me all that much protection!"

Chris laughs. It's a beautiful, confident laugh. Neelay doesn't care what the man looks like. He doesn't care if he's four hundred pounds and covered in cold sores. Desire rushes him. *Would you like to go out together sometime?* But going out would have to be going in. *Nothing needs to happen. Nothing could happen, in fact. That's all gone. We could just . . . sit together somewhere, talk about all things, no fear, no hurt, no consequences. Just sit and talk about where people are going.*

Impossible. One look at Neelay's grotesque limbs and even this confident, laughing journalist would be disgusted. Yet this man Chris—he *loves* Neelay's game. He plays it all night, and into morning. The code Neelay wrote is changing this other man's brain.

"It's just this. I've been lots of things. I've lived all over. In Stone Age Africa and on the outer rim of other galaxies. I think that soon enough—not right away, but soon—if software keeps getting better and giving us more room, I think that we'll be able to make ourselves into anything we want."

"That . . . sounds a little out there."

"Yes. Maybe it is."

"Games aren't . . . People will still want money. They'll still want prestige and social status. Politics. That's forever."

"Yes. Forever? Maybe." Neelay stares into his screen, a world coming on hard, where social status will accrue entirely by votes in a space that is at once instant, global, anonymous, virtual, and merciless.

"People still have bodies. They want real power. Friends and lovers. Rewards. Accomplishments."

"Sure. But soon we'll carry all of that around in our pockets. We'll live and trade and make deals and have love affairs, all in symbol space. The world will be a game, with on-screen scores. And all this?" He waves, as people do on phones, even knowing Chris can't see him. "All the things you say people *really* want? *Real* life? Soon we won't even remember how it used to go."

A CAR HEADS NORTH on Highway 36. Impala, going too fast by ten as it crests the rise. Down the long incline, a dozen black crates in the road block the way forward. Coffins. The driver brakes and brings the car to a stop a few feet in front of the mass funeral. In the air above the coffins, on a traverse line cabled between two trees as stout as lighthouses, a mountain lioness climbs. A harness hugs her tawny waist, clipped by carabiner to a safety cable. Her tail swishes between sleek hind haunches, and her noble, whiskered head lolls on her neck as she inspects a snagged banner.

A second car comes from the south. Rabbit, skidding to a stop in front of the coffins. It honks twice, before the driver notices the cougar. The sight is odd enough, even here in ganja-land, that the driver is happy for a minute just to gawk. The animal is young, lithe, and clothed only in a body stocking, with the words *A change is gonna come* on her shoulder, peeking out from under the leotard. The cat fights with the banner; the drivers wait, curious. Another car gets trapped behind the northbound one. Then another.

On a roadside platform, a bear tugs on a leader, trying to pull the snagged bedsheet across its guy wire. The grizzly's snout and sunken eyes are gloriously painted papier-mâché. His eyeholes are so small that the bear must wag its great muzzle to see anything. In a few more minutes, traffic starts to back up in both directions. Two guys get out of their cars. They're irate, but can't help laughing at the megafauna. A swipe of the cougar's paw and the sheet finally drops, catches the wind, and flaps above the highway like a sail:

## Stop Sacrificing Virgins

The borders teem with fronds and flowers from the margins of a medieval manuscript. For a moment the blocked commuters can only look. A few trapped drivers break into spontaneous applause. Someone calls from a rolled-down window, "I'll help you with your virginity problem, honey!" High above the roadway, the cougar waves. The hostages gesture back, thumbs or middle fingers. Her wild mask, gazing down from above, stirs some ancient hoo-ha into the spectators' viscera.

One of the drivers charges the coffins. "My timber job pays for your welfare checks. Get the hell out of the road!" He kicks at the black boxes, but they don't budge. From a choker around her neck, the cougar produces a whistle and toots three blasts. The crates open all together, and bodies rise like it's the Last Day. The bear adds to the chaos by tossing smoke bombs. Creatures emerge from each coffin, decked out in the colors of creation. There's an elk whose antlers arc outward like angel wings. A Sonoma chipmunk with giant chopstick incisors. An Anna's hummingbird flashing hot pink and iridescent bronze. A Dalí nightmare of Pacific giant salamander. A sunny-yellow blob of banana slug.

The blocked drivers laugh at the animal resurrection. More applause, and another round of profanity. The animals break into a wild dance. It unnerves the motorists; they've seen this bacchanal before—animals scampering in crazy circles—holdover memory from the illustrated pages of the first books they ever rubbed their fingers across, back when all things were possible and real. In the distraction of the animal dance, the bear and cougar unhook their harnesses and scramble down from their perches. When a police siren whoops from the rear of the backed-up cars, it sounds at first like another sideshow. The police slink up the blocked road's shoulder, giving the animals plenty of time to scatter into the understory. As they do, an older woman and a man with a video camera strapped to his palm disappear into the woods behind them.

Two days later, the film hits the national news. Reaction runs the living spectrum. The banner-slingers are heroes. They're grandstanding criminals who ought to be locked up. They're animals. Animals: yes. Big-brained, altruistic, animal con artists who managed to block a state highway for a while and make it seem like wild things might have their way.

FOUR YEARS at Fortuna College come down to one afternoon: Adam, in his spot in the front row, Daniels Auditorium. Professor Rubin Rabinowski at the podium—Affect and Cognition. Last lecture before the final exam, and the Rabi-Man is surveying all the experimental evidence that suggests—to the delight of the oversubscribed class—that teaching psychology is a waste of time.

"Now I'll show you the self-evaluations of people asked how susceptible they think they are to anchoring, causal base rate errors, the endowment effect, availability, belief perseverance, confirmation, illusory correlation, cuing—all the biases you've learned about in this course. Here are the scores of the control group. And here are the scores of people who've taken this course in previous years."

Lots of laughs: the numbers are pretty much the same. Both groups confident of their iron will, clear vision, and independent thought.

"Here are the performances on several different evaluations designed to conceal what they were testing. Most of the second group were tested less than six months after they took this course."

The laughter turns to groans. Blindness and unreason, rampant. Course grads, working twice as hard to save five bucks as they would to earn it. Grads fearing bears, sharks, lightning, and terrorists more than they fear drunk drivers. Eighty percent thinking they're smarter than average. Grads wildly inflating how many jelly beans they think are in a jar, based purely on someone else's ridiculous guesses.

"The psyche's job is to keep us blissfully ignorant of who we are, what we think, and how we'll behave in any situation. We're all operating in a dense fog of mutual reinforcement. Our thoughts are shaped primarily by legacy hardware that evolved to assume that everyone else *must be right*. But even when the fog is pointed out, *we're no better at navigating through it.*

"So why, you may ask, do I go on talking, up here? Why go on, year after year, cashing the college's checks?"

The laughs are all sympathy now. Adam admires the brilliant pedagogy. He, at least, he vows, will remember this lecture years from now, and its revelations will make him wiser, no matter what the studies show. He, at least, will defy the indicting numbers.

"Let me show you the answers you yourselves gave to a simple questionnaire I had you fill out at the beginning of the semester. You've probably forgotten you ever took it." The professor glances at the average answers and grimaces. His lips tighten in pain. Snickers across the room. "You may or may not recall that I asked you then whether you thought you'd . . ." Professor Rabinowski fiddles with his tie. He windmills with his left arm, grimaces again. "Excuse me one minute." He lurches off the dais and out the door. A murmur passes through the auditorium. Thuds come from the down hall—a stack of boxes tipping over. Fifty-four students sit and wait for the punch line. Faint, swallowed sounds fill the hallway. But no one moves.

Adam scans the seats behind him. Students frown at each other or busy themselves with notes. He turns to look at that magnificent woman who always sits two seats to his left. Premed, fawn-colored, pretty without knowing it, binders full of neat handwritten notes, and he thinks again how glorious it would be to sit in Bucky's over a beer with her and talk about this astonishing class. But the semester ends in two days, and the chance is as good as lost.

She glances his way, confused. He shakes his head and can't help smirking. He leans in to whisper, and she reciprocates. Maybe the chance hasn't vanished. "Kitty Genovese. The bystander effect. Darley and Latané, 1968."

"But is he okay?" Her breath is like cinnamon.

"Remember how we had to answer whether we'd help someone who . . . ?"

A woman shouts from below for someone to call an ambulance. But by the time the paramedics get their ambulance onto the quad, Professor Rabinowski is dead of a myocardial infarction.


"I DON'T UNDERSTAND," the premed beauty says, in their booth at Bucky's. "If you thought he was demonstrating the bystander effect, why did you keep sitting there?"

She's on her third iced coffee, and it bothers Adam. "That's not the point. The question is why fifty-three other people, including you, who thought he was having a heart attack, didn't do anything. *I* thought he was jerking us around to make a point."

"Then you should have been on your feet and calling his bluff!"

"I didn't want to spoil the show."

"You should have been up in five seconds."

He slams the booth table. "It wouldn't have made any damn difference!"

She flinches into the booth, like he meant to hit her. He puts up his palms, leans toward her to apologize, and she flinches again. He freezes, hands in the air, seeing what the cowering woman sees.

"I'm sorry. You're right." Professor Rabinowski's last lesson. Learning psychology is, indeed, pretty much useless. He pays for the drinks and leaves. He never sees her again, except for the following week, from four seats away, for two hours, at the proctored final exam.

. . .

HE'S ADMITTED to the new social psychology graduate program down at Santa Cruz. The campus is an enchanted garden perched on a mountainside overlooking Monterey Bay. It's the worst place he can imagine for finishing a doctorate—or doing any real work whatsoever. On the other hand, it's perfect for making interspecies contact with sea lions down by the pier, climbing the Sunset Tree naked and stoned at night, and lying on his back in the Great Meadow, searching for a thesis topic in the mad clouds of stars. After two years, the other grads take to calling him Bias Boy. In any discussion of the psychology of social formations, Adam Appich, master of science, is there with several studies that show how legacy cognitive blindness will forever prevent people from acting in their own best interests.

HE CONSULTS with his advisor. Professor Mieke Van Dijk, she of the sublime Dutch bob, clipped consonants, and soft-core softened vowels. In fact, she makes him confer with her every two weeks, in her office up in College Ten, hoping the enforced check-in will jump-start his research.

"You are dragging your feet over nothing."

In fact, he has his feet up, reclining on her Victorian daybed across the office from her desk, as if she's psychoanalyzing him. It amuses them both.

"Dragging . . . ? Not at all. I am utterly paralyzed."

"But why? You make too big a deal about this. Think of a thesis . . ."—she can't pronounce the *th*—"as a long seminar project. You don't have to save the world."

"I don't? Can I at least save a nation-state or two?"

She laughs; her wide overbite quickens his pulse. "Listen, Adam. Pretend this has nothing to do with your career. Nothing to do with any professional approval. What do *you*, personally, want to discover? What would give you enjoyment to study for a couple of years?"

He watches the words spill from that pretty mouth, free from the social-scientific jargon that she tends to drop into in seminars. "This *enjoyment* you speak about . . ."

"*Tsh*. You want to know *something*."

He wants to know whether she has ever, even once, thought of him sexually. It isn't inconceivable. She's only a decade older than he is. And she is—he wants to say *robust*. He feels a weird need to tell her how he got here, in her office, looking for a thesis topic. Wants to draw his entire intellectual history in a straight line—from daubing nail polish on the abdomens of ants to watching his beloved undergraduate mentor die—then ask her where the line leads next.

"I'm interested in . . . unblinding." He steals a look at her. If only people, like some invertebrates, would just turn raging purple when they felt attraction. It would make the entire species so much less neurotic.

She purses her lips. She must know how good that looks on her. "Unblinding? I'm sure that must mean something."

"Can people come to independent moral decisions that run counter to their tribe's beliefs?"

"You want to study transformative potential as a function of strong normative in-group favoritism."

He'd nod, but the jargon bugs the crap out of him. "It's like this. I think of myself as a good man. A good citizen. But say I'm a good citizen of early Rome, when a father had the power, and sometimes the duty, to put his child to death."

"I see. And you, a good citizen, are motivated to preserve positive distinctiveness. . . ."

"We're trapped. By social identity. Even when there are big, huge truths staring us in . . ." He hears his peers jeering, *Bias Boy*.

"Well, no. Clearly not, or in-group realignment would never happen. Transformation of social identity."

"Does it?"

"Of course! Here in America, people went from believing that women are too frail to vote to having a major-party vice presidential candidate, in one lifetime. From Dred Scott to Emancipation in a few years. Children, foreigners, prisoners, women, blacks, the disabled and mentally ill: they've all gone from property to personhood. I was born at a time when the idea of a chimpanzee getting a hearing in a court of law seemed totally absurd. By the time you're my age, we'll wonder how we ever denied such animals their standing as intelligent creatures."

"How old are you, anyway?"

Professor Van Dijk laughs. Her fine high cheekbones pink out; he's sure of it. Tough to hide, with that complexion. "Topic, please."

"I'd like to determine the personality factors that make it possible for some individuals to wonder how everyone can be so blind . . ."

". . . while everyone else is still trying to stabilize in-group loyalties. Now we get somewhere. This could be a topic. With *much* more narrowing and definition. You could look at the next step in this same historical progression of consciousness. Study those people who support a position that any reasonable person in our society thinks is crazy."

"For instance?"

"We're living at a time when claims are being made for a moral authority that lies beyond the human."

One smooth tensing of his abdominal muscles, and he sits up. "What do you mean?"

"You've seen the news. People up and down this coast are risking their lives for plants. I read a story last week—a man who had his legs sheared off by a machine he tried to chain himself to."

Adam *has* seen the stories, but he ignored them. Now he can't see why. "Plant rights? Plant personhood." A boy he knew once jumped into a hole and risked live burial to protect his unborn brother's sapling from harm. That boy is dead. "I hate activists."

"So? Why?"

"Orthodoxy and sloganeering. Boring. I hate it when those Greenpeace guys shake me down on the street. Anyone who gets *righteous* . . . doesn't understand."

"Understand what?"

"How hopelessly fragile and wrong we all are. About everything."

Professor Van Dijk frowns. "I see. Good thing we aren't doing a psychological study of *you*."

"Are these people really appealing to a new, nonhuman moral order? Or are they just being sentimental about pretty green things?"

"That's where controlled psychological measurements come in."

He smirks a little, himself. But something large wells up in him, and he can't even shift his weight or it will disappear. A way forward. "Identity formation and Big Five personality factors among plants rights activists."

"Or: Who does the tree-hugger really hug, when he hugs a tree?"

THE SUN SHINES on the western Cascades as Mimi and Douglas pull onto the car-packed Forest Service road. Bodies mill about the small clearing. This isn't a protest march. It's a carnival. The ceramic mold manager asks the wounded vet, "Who *are* all these people?"

Douggie steps from the car with that stupid, air-eating, sun-eating grin Mimi has come to enjoy, the way you might enjoy the yips of a dog you've rescued from the pound. He waves his work-gnarled hand across the crowd in goofy cowboy joy. "*Homo sapiens*, man. Always up to something!"

Mimi trots to catch up with him. The turnout dizzies her. "What they do?"

Douglas leans his good ear toward her. "How's that?" The crowd is loud in the circus of their cause, and he's lost a lot of hearing from his days in transport planes.

It still surprises her. A man who bothers to listen. "My father used to say that. *What they do?*"

"What they do?"

"Yeah. Meaning, *What the hell do those people hope to accomplish?*"

"Was he strange?"

"Chinese. He believed English should be more efficient than it is."

Douglas smacks his forehead. "You're *Chinese*."

"Half Chinese. What did you think?"

"I don't know. Something swarthier."

The real question, Mimi knows, is *What* she *do?* She's amazed he managed to get her up here for this protest. Her only previous political action was a grade school vendetta against Chairman Mao. Her grudge is with the city, its scheming nighttime raid against her pines. As for these trees, so far out of town: She's an *engineer*, for crying out loud. These trees are calling out to be used.

But a pair of lectures and a visit to an organizational meeting accompanied by this clumsy innocent have broken her heart. These mountains, these forest cascades—now that she has seen them, they're hers. So here she is, at a public demonstration that would have made her emigrant father come pluck her home in fear of deportation, torture, or worse. "Look at everyone!"

It's grannies with guitars and toddlers with space-age water pistols. College students out to prove themselves worthy of one another. Preppers pushing baby carriages like all-terrain Hobbit Humvees. Grade school kids carrying earnest placards: RESPECT YOUR ELDERS. WE NEED OUR LUNGS. A rainbow alliance of assorted footwear makes its way up the trunk to the haul road—loafers and cross-trainers, backward sloping sandals, cracked-toe Chuck Taylors, and, yes, logger caulks. The clothes are still more varied: button-down oxfords and pre-stressed jeans, tie-dye and flannel, hickory shirts, even a U.S. Air Force flight jacket like the one Douggie pawned for a few bucks fifteen years ago. Clown suits, swimsuits, jumpsuits—every kind of suit except three-piecers.

Much of the crowd has been bused to the site by four wildly different environmental outfits that tend to go to war with one another when there's no closer target. A group of backpackers took two days making their way overland to join this spectacle, all trying to bail out the ocean of capitalism with an acorn cap. A handful of locals show up to watch. Out this far, most of the people in a hundred-mile radius exist by grace of timber. They have their hand-lettered signs as well. LOGGERS: THE REAL ENDANGERED SPECIES. EARTH FIRST! WE'LL LOG THE OTHER PLANETS LATER.

Two men sporting beards down to their sternums hover around the periphery pointing shoulder-mount video cameras. A gray-haired woman in Danskins, felt fedora, and sleeveless vest tapes interviews with anyone who'll talk. Deeper into the trees, a man and woman with megaphones shape the crowd's mood. "People! You're amazing. What a turnout. Thank you all! Ready for a walk in the woods?"

A cheer erupts, and the parade lurches down a gravel path toward the fresh skid road. Douglas falls into step, Mimi alongside. They weave into the colorful crowd waving rainbow banners and shouting outrageous epithets. In the festive atmosphere, under so blue a sky, walking arm in arm with strangers up the slight grade, Mimi sees. For her entire life, unwittingly, she has complied with her parents' first shared principle: Make no noise in this world. She, Carmen, Amelia—all three Ma girls. Don't stand out; you have no right. No one owes you a thing. Keep small, vote mainstream, and nod like it all makes sense. Yet here she is, asking for trouble. Acting like what she does might matter.

They walk shoulder to shoulder across the skid road, ten abreast, more rows deep than she can count. They sing tunes that Mimi last sang in summer camp in Northern Illinois, songs of jingly childhood. "This Land Is Your Land." "If I Had a Hammer." Douggie smiles and hums along in a toneless bass. Between songs, a cheerleader with a megaphone, walking sideways near the front of the pack, stirs up some call-and-response. *Clear-cuts cost too much! Save our last stands!*

Righteousness makes Mimi nuts. She has always been allergic to people with conviction. But more than she hates conviction, she hates sneaky power. She has learned things about this mountainside that sicken her. A wealthy logging outfit, backed by a pro-industry Forest Circus, is exploiting the power vacuum prior to a big court decision by rushing through an illegal grab of mixed conifers that have been growing for centuries before the idea of ownership came to these parts. She's ready to try anything to slow the theft down. Even righteousness.

They hike through dense spruce for the length of three choruses. Trunks slice the sunlight into shards. *Godfingers*, she and her sisters used to call those slanted beams. Trees she can't name shoot up all around, wrapped in vines, or tumbling to the ground like barricades—so much life in so many flavors she wants to strip down and scamper. The understory is shot through with saplings she could encircle with her fist, broomsticks that may have bidden their time for a hundred years. But the canopy is carried by trunks that several arm-linked protesters still could not hug.

Vistas open up through the green crenellations. Mimi tugs Doug's sleeve and points. To the northeast, down ravines and up slopes too steep to walk, a pincushion of health rolls over the hills. Fog wraps the tops of the firs the way it did on the day the first European ships sniffed out harbors on this coast. But through another gap to the south, lunar devastation runs up the mountainside—slash doused with diesel and burnt until even the fungus is dead, then drowned with herbicide so nothing will grow again but this company's monocrop row plantations in a short cycle that, she has learned, will last only a few more rounds, at most, before the soil is dead. From on high, it feels as if even the trees spreading across these slopes are at war. Patches of lush green march against patches of muddy vomit, all the way to the horizon. And the people assembled here: ignorant armies going up against each other as they have forever, for reasons hidden from even the most vehement. When will it be enough? *Now*, if you can believe this chanting, laughing crowd on its way to convince the road crew at the end of these wheel ruts. *Now*: the second-best of times.

The road narrows and the emerald forest thickens. Monster trunks dwarf and disorient Mimi. Moss grows up and over everything in thick blankets. Even the ferns reach to her breasts. The man beside her knows the names of trees, but Mimi is too proud to ask for IDs. Despite a decade of living in this state, despite repeated attempts to master the field guides and dichotomous keys, she can't tell a limber from a sugar pine, let alone a Port Orford from an incense cedar. Silver, white, red, and grand firs are all a frilly blur. And the swarming understory—impossible. Salal, somehow, she knows. Oxalis and trillium. But the rest is a tossed salad of inscrutable foliage, creeping up to trailside, ready to grab her ankles.

Douglas points off to the left of the road. "Look!" In the middle of the blue-green confusion, seven stout trees grow in a line as straight as Euclid's daydreams.

"How the hell? Did someone . . . ?"

He laughs and pats her shoulder. The touch feels good. "Think back. Think way back."

She does, and sees nothing. Douglas milks the suspense a little longer.

"Few hundred years ago, right around the time the Pilgrims were thinking, *What the fuck, huh? Let's go for it,* some big monster fell. Log rot's a perfect seedbed. Bunch of seedlings used it as a furrow, like God sowed them in with a hoe!"

Something glints in front of her, revealed by the dappled light, the way dew betrays a spiderweb. Tight nets of tens of thousands of species knit together in weaves too fine for any person to trace. Who knows what medicines might be hidden here? The next aspirin, the next quinine; the next Taxol. Reason enough that this last little stand should stay intact a little longer.

"Something, isn't it?"

"Is, Doogles."

This man tried to save her pines. Put his body between the saws and the trees. She wouldn't be out here, even in this endangered paradise, without him. But for her money, he's more than a little wacked. His rangy gameness for anything scares her. The twinkle he fixes on the forest ahead has that look of the not entirely housebroken. His head swivels, marveling at the crowd, happy as a puppy to be let back in the house.

"Hear that?" Douglas asks.

But she has heard it all morning. In another quarter mile, the dull whine sharpens. Down the road, through the brambles, mustard and orange machines claw the earth—graders and scrapers, pushing this road into new territory.

"Aw, jeez, Mimi. Look what they're doing to this beautiful place. *What they do?*"

The protesters reach a gate of welded metal bars across the road. The advance guard stops at the obstacle, and the banners pool around them. The megaphone woman says, "We're about to cross over into the cut. This will be an encroachment of the timber plan we're contesting. Those of you who are unwilling to be arrested, remain here. Your presence and voices are still important. The press is taking notice of your feelings!"

Applause, like the flutter of grouse.

"Those willing to head on, thank you. We'll cross now. Stay orderly. Stay calm. Do not allow yourself to be provoked. This is a peaceful confrontation."

A portion of the crowd drifts toward the gate. Mimi cocks an eyebrow at Douglas. "You're sure?"

"Shit yea-uh. That's why we're here, isn't it?"

She wonders if he means *here*, on the edge of a national forest being sold to the top bidder, or *here*, on Earth, the only entity capable of prospection. She shrugs away all philosophy. "Let's go."

Ten more yards and they're criminals. The roar grows sickening. In half a mile, they're up against human ingenuity at its best. She can name the metal beasts better than she can name the different trees. Down through the clearing, there's a feller buncher, snatching batches of small trunks, delimbing them, and bucking the logs to fixed lengths, doing in a day what a team of human cutters would need a week to get through. There's a self-loading forwarder trailer, stacking the cut logs into itself. Nearer by, a front loader extends the roadbed, and a scraper rough-grades it prior to the arrival of the roller. She's learned of machines that drop their maws onto fifty-foot trees and grind them to the ground faster than a food processor can shred a carrot. Machines that stack logs like tooth-picks and haul them to mills where twenty-foot trunks twirl on spits so fast that the touch of an angled blade shaves off the flesh in a continuous layer of veneer.

Hard hats block the road ahead of them. Their foreman says, "You're trespassing."

The megaphone woman, on whom Mimi has developed a schoolgirl crush, says, "These are public lands."

The other megaphone wielder gives the command, and marchers fan out across the dirt roadbed. They sit down shoulder to shoulder, spanning the road. Mimi and Doug link arms, joining the solidifying line. Mimi locks in, clasping her hands in front of her. The inward-turned mulberry of her jade ring presses into her other wrist. By the time the loggers see what's happening, the deed is done. The two ends of the human chain lock themselves with bike cables to trees on either side of the road.

Two fellers walk right up to the arm-locked line. The tops of their steel-reinforced boots come almost to Mimi's eyes. "Shit," a blond one says. Mimi sees his genuine distress. "When are you people going to grow up and get real? Why don't you take care of your own business, and let us get on with ours?"

"This is everybody's business," Douglas answers. Mimi tugs at him.

"You know where the *real* problems are? Brazil. China. That's where the crazy cutting is. You should go protest down there. See what they think when you tell them they can't get as rich as we are."

"You're cutting down the last American old growth."

"You wouldn't know old growth if it fell on you. We've been cutting these hillsides for decades, and we've been replanting. Ten trees for each one we cut."

"Correction. *I've* been replanting. Ten little paper pulp seedlings for each one of these varied, ancient geniuses."

Mimi watches the foreman make all kinds of cost-benefit calculations. It's a funny thing about capitalism: money you lose by slowing down is always more important than money you've already made. One of the fellers swings his boot and flicks a pad of mud up into Douglas's face. Mimi loosens her arm to clean it off, but Douglas clasps her in his bicep.

Another fleck of mud. "Oh! Sorry, guy. My mistake."

Mimi erupts. "You punk thug!"

"Take it up with these guys. Sue me from your jail cell."

The feller points off behind the seated line, where police are pouring down the Forest Service road in force. They break the chain like someone plucking a dandelion. Then they handcuff the broken links back together. Mimi and Douglas end up with two strangers chained between them and two more on each side. They're left to sit in the muddy road while the police mop up the chaos.

"I need to pee," Mimi tells a cop, around two o'clock. Half an hour later, she tells the same cop again. "I really, really need to urinate."

"No, you don't. You really don't."

Urine leaks down her leg. She starts sobbing. The women she's cuffed to gag and grimace.

"I'm so sorry. I'm so sorry. I couldn't hold it."

"Shhh, it's okay," Douglas says, handcuffed two bodies down. "Don't think about it." Her sobs get frantic. "It's okay," Douglas keeps saying. "I've got my arm around you, in my head."

The crying stops. It won't start up again for years. Smelling like an animal-marked stump, Mimi submits to arrest and booking. As the lady officer in the station takes her fingerprints, she feels, for the first time since her father's death, like she's given the day everything it wanted.

THE KISS COMES DOWN on the crown of Ray's head, from behind, where he sits in his study, reading. Kisses, brisk and precise, like wire-guided bomblets, are Dorothy's trademarks these days. It never fails to make his blood run cold.

"Off to sing."

He cranes to look at her. She's forty-four, but looks to him as she did at twenty-eight. It's the not having babies, he thinks. The bloom still coursing through her, the pure lure, as if ridiculous loveliness still had a job to do, this far past youth. Jeans and a white cotton blouse gathered in pleats that cling to her plaintive ribs. Topped with a lilac shawl, sweetly disheveled and swept across her neck, the one stretch of skin she thinks betrays her. Her hair falls on the shawl, shiny, chestnut, perfect, still the length it was when she tried out for Lady Macbeth on their first date.

"You look so beautiful."

"Ha! I'm glad your eyes are failing." She tickles the spot where her kiss landed. "Thinning, up here."

"Time's winged chariot."

"I'm trying to picture such a vehicle. How would that work, exactly?"

He cranes further. Clasped in one hand against her runner's thighs, she holds a pale green Peters Edition emblazoned with the giant black word:

BR      MS

broken in two by her perfect forearm. Beneath that, smaller:

Ein Deu        equiem

The concert is at the end of June. She'll stand onstage with a hundred other voices, inconspicuous among the women except for being one of the few who are not yet gray, and sing:

*Siehe, ein Ackermann wartet*
*auf die köstliche Frucht der Erde*
*und ist geduldig darüber,*
*bis er empfahe den Morgenregen und Abendregen.*

Behold, the husbandman waiteth for the precious fruit of the earth, and hath long patience for it, until he receive the early and latter rain.

Singing is now everything. It follows on a line of hobbies she has hit hard in the hopes of passing the week as maximally as possible. Swimming. Life-saving. Life drawing in charcoal and pastels. Meanwhile, he has withdrawn into the stronghold of his study. He bills more hours of work than ever, in the vague hope of buying a second home for them, someplace more beautiful. Someplace surrounded, if not by wilderness, then by the memory of it.

"Lots of rehearsals." Two two-hour rehearsals every week, and she hasn't missed one.

"They're fun." She has been overprepared for weeks. Truth is, she has practiced so hard at home that she could sing this piece tonight from start to finish, every vocal line. "Sure you don't want to come? We need more basses."

More than ever, she astonishes him. What would she do if he said yes? "Maybe in the fall. For the Mozart."

"You've got enough to keep you busy?"

This is what people do—solve their own problems in others' lives. He laughs. "At the moment, yes. I'm wrestling with this." He holds the pages up to her: "Should Trees Have Standing?" She reads the title and frowns. Ray examines the words, puzzled himself. "He seems to be saying that the law's shortfall is that it only recognizes human victims."

"And that's a problem?"

"He wants to extend rights to nonhuman things. He wants trees to be rewarded for their intellectual property."

She smirks. "Bad for business, huh?"

"I don't know whether to throw it across the room and laugh or to set it on fire and kill myself."

"Let me know which you decide. See you between ten and eleven. Don't wait up if you're sleepy."

"I'm sleepy already." He laughs again, as if he just made a joke. "You warm enough? It's going to get chilly. Button up your overcoat."

She seizes up in the doorway, and the moment is there again, between them. The sudden upwell of anger and mutual defeat. "I'm not your property, Ray. We had a deal."

"What is this? I didn't say you were my property."

"You certainly did," she says, and is gone. Only when the door hammers shut does he make the leap. Overcoats. Buttons. Wind blowing free. *Take good care of yourself. You belong to me.*

SHE DRIVES OFF down Birch to the west, under orange maples. He doesn't bother to watch the taillights or see where she turns. It would be an indignity to them both. She's too smart not to drive past the rehearsal auditorium first. Besides: he's already stood at the window on previous nights and watched the taillights. He's done it all, all things desperate and disgusting. Looked up the unknown numbers on the phone bill log. Checked the pockets of her previous night's clothes. Gone through her purse for notes. He finds no notes. Just courtroom exhibits A through Z of his shame.

His weeks of disbelief long ago changed into a free fall many times scarier than their youthful stint at skydiving. The panic of discovery soon thickened into grief, the kind he felt when his mother died. Then grief transmuted into virtue, which he nursed in secrecy for weeks, until virtue collapsed under its own explosive growth into bitter immobility. Every question is a voluntary madness. Who? Why? How long? How often before?

What does it matter? Leave your overcoat unbuttoned. Now he just wants peace, and to be near her a little longer, for as long as he can, before she smashes everything just to punish him for finding out.


SHE PARKS HER CAR in the lot behind the auditorium. She even goes in for a minute, not so much to establish an alibi as to make the trapdoor that opens under her feel that much crazier. When the hundred singers mill onto the risers, she slips out the back, as if to retrieve something she left in her car. In a minute, she's on the rain-slicked street, cold, *living*, heart beating like mad. She's going to get *done*, several different ways, long and lovingly and to no purpose, with no contractual obligations, by a man she doesn't know from Adam. The thought runs the length of her, like she just injected something.

She's going to be bad. Bad again. Stupid bad. Do things she never imagined she could do. New things. Going to learn more about herself—scary more, at high speed, joyously. What she likes and doesn't, when she isn't lying the lazy lie of decency. Put the last thirty years to the heat-freeing flames. The thought shatters her—magic. *Growth*, and she's damp and practically coming from the swish of her own legs, like a pith-green girl of sixteen, by the time she sees the black BMW at curbside and lets herself in.

Forty-eight minutes of wilderness experiment. Immediately afterward, she has trouble remembering. Like maybe he did drug her just a little, for fun. She remembers sitting up on her spread knees on the giant bed, giggling like a blitzed sorority princess. She remembers growing huge, poetic, queenly, godlike, a flood of Brahms. Then falling back into the pain in her legs and lungs, a distance runner. She remembers him whispering in her ear as he fingered her—vague, threatening, worshipful, thrilling syllables that she fed on without quite making out.

Every so often in the bobbing sea, as they did the week before, details from her favorite adultery novels flashed in her head with horrible specificity. She remembers thinking, *Now I'm the heroine of my own doomed story.* Then a long and tender kiss good night, curbside in the dark car, three blocks from the auditorium. Ten steps down the slick sidewalk, she consigns the whole adventure to imagination, something that happened only in a book.

She's back inside and up on the risers with time to spare, waiting for the return of the choral swell as the baritone sings, *Behold, I show you a mystery; We shall not all sleep, but we shall all be changed. In a moment, in the twinkling of an eye.*

RAY NIBBLES ON DINNER—pistachios and an apple. Reading is slow, and all things distract him. Staring at the bottom of the apple's core, he realizes that the *calyx*—a word he'll never know in this life—is nothing less than the leftover bits of a withered apple flower. He looks up from the thicket of words three times a minute, waiting for truth to hit like a falling oak smashing through the house's roof. Nothing comes to kill him. Nothing at all happens, and it keeps on happening with great force and patience. Nothing happens so completely that when he checks his watch to see why Dorothy isn't home yet, he's stunned to discover that less than half an hour has passed.

He bows his head and fixes on the page. The article stokes his distress. *Should* trees have standing? This time last month, it would have been his evening's great sport to test the ingenious argument. What can be owned and who can do the owning? What conveys a *right*, and why should humans, alone on all the planet, have them?

But tonight the words swim. Eight thirty-seven. Everything that was *his* is going down, and he doesn't even know what brought on disaster. The terrible logic of the essay begins to wear him down. Children, women, slaves, aboriginals, the ill, insane, and disabled: all changed, unthinkably, over the centuries, into persons by the law. So why shouldn't trees and eagles and rivers and living mountains be able to sue humans for theft and endless damages? The whole idea is a holy nightmare, a death dance of justice like the one he now lives through, watching the second hand of his watch refuse to move. His entire career until this moment—protecting the property of those with a right to grow—begins to seem like one long war crime, like something he'll be imprisoned for, come the revolution.

*The proposal is bound to sound odd or frightening or laughable. This is partly because until the rightless thing receives its rights, we cannot see it as anything but a thing for the use of "us"—those who are holding rights at the time.*

Eight forty-two, and he's desperate. He'll do anything now, to deceive her, to make her think he has no idea. Her fit of craziness will run its course. The fever that has turned her into someone he can't recognize will burn away and leave her well again. Shame will bring her back to herself, and she'll remember everything. The years. The time they went to Italy. The time they jumped from the plane. The time she ran the car into a tree while reading his anniversary letter and almost killed herself. The amateur theatrics. The things they planted together, in the backyard they made.

*It is no answer to say that streams and forests cannot have standing because streams and forests cannot speak. Corporations cannot speak, either; nor can states, estates, infants, incompetents, municipalities, or universities. Lawyers speak for them.*

The key thing is for her never to learn that he knows. He must be cheerful, smart, funny. The minute she suspects, it'll destroy them both. She might live with anything except being forgiven.

But concealment is killing him. He never could play anyone but an earnest Macduff. Eight forty-eight. He tries to concentrate. The evening stretches out ahead like two consecutive life sentences. He has only this essay to keep him company and torture him.

*What is it within us that gives us this need not just to satisfy basic biological wants, but to extend our wills over things, to objectify them, to make them ours, to manipulate them, to keep them at a psychic distance?*

The essay flickers under his fingers. He can't follow it, can't decide whether it's brilliant or rubbish. His whole self is dissolving. All his rights and privileges, everything he owns. A great gift that has been his since birth is being taken away. It's a grand, luxurious act of self-deceit, an outright lie, that claim of Kant's: *As far as nonhumans are concerned, we have no direct duties. All exists merely as means to an end. That end is man.*

DISGUST BREAKS over her as she drives home. But even disgust feels like freedom. If a person can see the worst in herself . . . If a person can find total honesty, complete knowledge of what she really is . . . Now that she's sated, she wants purity again. At the light at Snelling, she looks up into the rearview mirror and sees her eyes hiding from her own furtive glance. She thinks: *I'll stop. Get my life back. Decency. This doesn't have to end in a flaming fireball.* The coming concert performance can absorb her excess energy. After that, she'll find something else to occupy her. To keep her sane and sober.

By Lexington, ten blocks down, she's planning one more dose. Just one more, to remind her what it feels like to ski this mountain continent. She won't be pathetic. She'll have the addiction, without the pitiful resolutions. She doesn't know what's addicted: her body or her will. She knows only that she'll follow herself down, to wherever it takes her. By the time she turns onto their street's leafy canyon, she's calm again.

SHE COMES IN rosy from the cold. Her scarf trails as she pushes the door shut behind her. The *Requiem* score drops from her hands. She bends to pick it up, and when she straightens, their eyes catch, spilling everything. Scared, defiant, pleading, thuggish. Wanting to be home again, with an old friend.

"Hey! You haven't budged from that chair."

"Good rehearsal?"

"The best!"

"I'm glad. What sections did you sing?"

She crosses to where he sits. Something of their old rhythm. She hugs him, *Ziemlich langsam und mit Ausdruck.* Before he can stand, she slips past, into the kitchen, smelling on herself that blend of salt and bleach. "I'll just take a quick shower before bed."

She's a smart woman, but she has never had much patience with the obvious. Nor does she think him capable of simple observation. She showered twenty minutes before heading out to sing her Brahms.

IN BED, in peacock pajamas, scalded and renewed from the hot spray, she asks, "How's the reading?"

He needs a moment to remember what he spent all night trying to read. *What is needed is a myth. . . .*

"Difficult. I wasn't all there."

"Hmm." She rolls on her side to face him, eyes closed. "Tell me."

*I do not think it too remote that we may come to regard the Earth, as some have suggested, as one organism, of which mankind is a functional part—the mind, perhaps.*

"He wants to give rights to everything alive. He claims that paying trees for their creative invention would make the whole world richer. If he's right, then our entire social system . . . everything I've ever worked for . . ."

But her breathing has changed, and she floats away like a newborn after a day of first discoveries.

He douses the bedside light and turns away from her. Still, she murmurs in her sleep and grapples to him, clutching his backside for whatever warmth he generates. Her bare arms on him, the woman he fell in love with. The woman he married. Funny, manic, wild, untamable Lady Macbeth. Lover of sprawling novels. Jumper from airplanes. The best amateur actress he has ever known.

WATCHMAN AND MAIDENHAIR, deep in the redwoods. He lugs a pack of provisions. She holds the camp's video camera in one hand; with her other, she clutches his arm like a channel swimmer hanging from a dingy. Now and then she grabs his wrist, directing his attention to something colorful or darting just outside their comprehension.

Last night they slept on the cold ground, open to the air. Seas of mud moated their fern-fringed island. He lay in one pee-stained 1950s sleeping bag and she in another, underneath creatures of mildness, bulk, and repose. "Aren't you freezing?" he asked.

She answered no. And he believed her.

"Sore?"

"Not really."

"Scared?"

Her eyes said, *Why?* Her mouth said, "Should we be?"

"They're so big. Humboldt Timber employs hundreds of people. Thousands of machines. It's owned by a multibillion-dollar multinational. All the laws are on their side, backed by the will of the American people. We're a bunch of unemployed vandals, camping out in the woods."

She smiled, as at a little kid who just asked whether the Chinese could reach them through a tunnel in the earth. Her hand snaked out of her bag and into his. "Believe me. I have it on the highest authority. Great things are under way."

Her hand stayed between them like a traverse line as she fell asleep.


THEY FOLLOW A SWITCHBACK down into a distant drainage until the path turns into a rivulet of mud. Two miles in, the trail vanishes and the two of them must bushwhack. Light sifts through the canopy. He watches her cross a carpet of starflower massed with sorrel. Mere months ago, by her own account, she was a nasty, jaded, narcissistic bitch with a substance abuse problem, flunking out of college. Now she's—what? Something at peace with being human, in league with something very much not.

The redwoods do strange things. They hum. They radiate arcs of force. Their burls spill out in enchanted shapes. She grabs his shoulder. "Look at that!" Twelve apostle trees stand in a fairy ring as perfect as the circles little Nicky once drew with a protractor on rainy Sundays decades ago. Centuries after their ancestor's death, a dozen basal clones surround the empty center, all around the compass rose. A chemical semaphore passes through Nick's brain: Suppose a person had sculpted any one of these, just as they stand. That single work would be a landmark of human art.

Alongside the pebbly creek they come to a downed giant that, even sideways, is taller than Olivia. "We're here. Just to the right, Mother N said. This way."

He sees it first: a grove of trunks six hundred years old, running upward out of sight. The pillars of a russet cathedral nave. Trees older than movable type. But their furrows are spray-painted with white numbers, like someone tattooed a living cow with a butcher diagram showing the various cuts of meat hiding underneath. Orders for a massacre.

Olivia lifts the Handycam to her face and films. Nick slips off his backpack, floats weightless for a few steps. A rainbow of spray cans comes from his pack. He lays them in a patch of young horsetails: half a dozen colors from across the spectrum. Cherry in one hand, lemon in the other, he wanders toward a marked tree. He studies the white strokes already there. Then he lifts the can and sprays.

Later, her video will be edited, fitted out with voice-over, and sent to every sympathetic journalist in the Life Defense Force address book. For now, the sound track is the hundred cries of the forest punctuated by awe— *How do you do that?*—up close to the microphone. Nick returns to his palette on the forest floor and picks two more hues. He paints, then steps back to appraise his handiwork. The species are as wild as any that inhabit a muse-um's collection cabinet. He goes on to the next numeral-defaced tree and starts again. Soon enough, the numbers disappear, past recognition, into butterflies.

He graduates to those trunks marked by a simple blue tick. They're everywhere, these death sentences made with a simple stroke. Then he pro-ceeds to paint those trees with no markings at all, until it's impossible to say which trunks have been slated for cutting and which are mere bystanders. The afternoon vanishes; they've both been on forest-time too long to count in mere hours anymore. The work is over in a moment, in the twinkling of an eye.

Olivia pans the camera around the transformed grove. Where there had been measurements and prospects, a project of hard numbers, there are now only skippers and swallowtails, morphos, hairstreaks, and heaths. It could be a grove of sacred firs in the Mexican mountains, where Tiffany insects stage their many-generation migration. Thus two people, in an afternoon, undo a week's work of appraisers and surveyors.

The voice on the unedited video says, "They'll be back." He means the numbers men, to mark their culls again in a more foolproof way.

"But this is beautiful. It'll cost them."

"Maybe. Or the lumber shows will just come in and take everything, like they did at Murrelet Grove."

"We have film now."

You can hear it in the music of her recorded voice: the belief that affection might solve the problems of freedom yet. Then the film cuts to black. No one sees what happens next between the two humans, there on the forest floor, between the banks of fern and Solomon's seal. No one, unless you count the countless invisible creatures burrowing beneath the soil, crawling under the bark, crouching in the branches, climbing and leaping and banking through the canopy. Even the giant trees breathe in the few molecules per billion of homecoming dispensed into the air.

PATRICIA HEARS from a quarter mile away: Dennis's truck thumping down the gravel washboard road. The sound gladdens her—glad before she knows she's glad. In its way, the crunch and whir lift her as much as the wheezy cheep of a Townsend's warbler skirting the edge of a clearing. The truck is its own wildlife rarity, although this creature appears every day, as punctual as the rain.

She drifts down to the road, feeling how edgy her wait has been, these last twenty minutes. He'll have lunch, yes, and the mail, her mixed bag of connections with the outside world. New data from the lab in Corvallis. But *Dennis*: That's the installment her soul now needs. He steadies her, his listening, and she wonders with delighted horror whether twenty-two hours might be too long to go between sightings. She comes up close to the halted truck and must step back when he opens the cab. His broad arm swings around her waist and he nuzzles her neck.

"Den. My favorite mammal."

"Babe. Wait till you see what we're having." He hands her the mail and grabs the cooler. They climb the slope to the cabin, shoulder to shoulder, at peace with each other in silence.

She sits on the porch at the cable spool table, thumbing through the mail as he unpacks lunch. How can the masterful duplicity—*Important information about your insurance. Open at once!*—find her even here? She has lived far from commerce for decades, and yet her name is a hot commodity, bought and sold endlessly as she sits in her cabin reading Thoreau. She hopes the buyers aren't paying much. No: she hopes they're being extorted.

Nothing from Corvallis, but there's a packet from her agent. She sets it down on the wooden slats, next to her plate. It's still there when Dennis brings out two small, magnificent stuffed rainbow trout.

"Everything okay?"

She nods and shakes her head all at once.

"No bad news, is there?"

"No. I don't know. I can't open it."

He doles out the fish and picks up the packet. "It's from *Jackie*. What's to be afraid of?"

She doesn't know. Lawsuits. Chastisements. Official business. Open at once. He hands her the envelope and flicks the air, nudging her courage.

"You're good for me, Dennis." She slips her finger under the sealed lip and many things spill out. Reviews. Forwarded fan mail. A letter from Jackie with a check paper-clipped to it. She sees the check and yelps. The paper falls to the ground and lands facedown, in the always-damp earth.

Dennis retrieves the check and wipes it clean. He whistles. "Jeepers!" He looks at her, eyebrows high. "Misplaced a decimal point there, did they?"

"Two places!"

He laughs, his shoulders shuddering, like his antique truck trying to turn over after a night below freezing. "She told you the book was doing well."

"There's a mistake. We have to pay it back."

"You made a good thing, Patty. People like good things."

"It isn't possible. . . ."

"Don't get excited. It's not *that* much."

But it is. It's more than she has ever had in any bank, her whole life. "The money's not mine."

"What do you mean, it's not yours? You worked on that book for seven years!"

She doesn't hear him. She's listening to the wind coming through the alders.

"You can always give it away. Write a check to American Forests. Or maybe to that chestnut back-cross recovery program. You could invest it in the research team. Come on. Eat your fish now. Took me two hours to catch these guys."

AFTER LUNCH, he reads her the reviews. Somehow, in Dennis's radio baritone, they sound mostly good. Appreciative. People say, *I didn't realize*. People say, *I've started seeing things*. Then he reads her the readers' letters. Some of them just want to thank her. Some of them confuse her with the mother of all trees. Some of them make her feel like Miss Lonelyhearts. *I have a big bur oak in our back yard that must be 200 years old. Last spring, one side of it started to sicken. It's killing me to watch it die in slow motion. What can I do?*

Many mention the *giving trees*—those ancient Douglas-firs that, with their last act, give all their secondary metabolites back to the community.

"Hear that, babe? *'You've made me think about life in a different way.'* That might be a compliment."

She laughs, but it sounds like a bobcat caught in a snare.

"Oh. Now, here's something. A request to go on the most listened-to public radio program in the country. They're doing a series on the planet's future, and they need someone to speak for the trees."

She hears his words from high up in a Douglas-fir in the middle of a howling storm. Human industry, everywhere. People need things from her. People mistake her for someone else. People mean to drag her violently back into what people mistakenly call *the world*.

MOSES COMES into base camp frazzled. Actions everywhere, and they've lost thirteen people to detention and arrest in the last half a week. "We've got a legacy tree sit that needs manning. Anyone up for a brief stint up top?"

Maidenhair's hand shoots into the air before Watchman even understands the request. Such a look crosses her face: *Yes. This. At last.*

"You sure?" Moses asks, as if he hasn't just fulfilled the voices of light's predictions. "You'll be up there for at least a few days."

SHE ASSURES NICK while she packs. "If you think you can do more from down here . . . I'll be fine by myself. They wouldn't dare hurt me. Think of the press!"

He won't be fine, except where she is. It's that simple, that absurd. He doesn't tell her. The thing is so screamingly obvious, even in the way he hovers and nods. Of course she knows. She can hear beings that aren't even here. Of course she can hear his banging thoughts, the blood pounding in his ears, even above the endless rain.

THEIR PACKS go up and over the gate first. Then they follow—Maidenhair, Watchman, and their guide, Loki, who has run ground support for this tree for weeks. Their feet come back down in Humboldt Timber territory, trespass with criminal intent. The packs are heavy and the path steep. Weeks of steady rain have turned the trail to Turkish coffee. Weeks ago, they wouldn't have made it to mile three. Even now, five miles in, Watchman sucks air in great gulps. He's ashamed and falls back on the trail, where she can't hear him wheeze. The path ascends a sloppy escarpment. The weight of the pack and the foot-sucking muck pull him down until every step is a pole vault. He stops to catch his breath, and the sleety air goes through him. Up ahead, Maidenhair forges on like some mythic beast. Power rises into her feet from the needle-bedded ground. Each mud-coated plunge renews her. She's *dancing*.

Cowardice adds several stones to Nick's pack. He doesn't want to get arrested. He's not crazy about heights. He has only love to drive him up the cliff face. She's fueled by the need to save everything alive.

Loki puts out his palm. "See that flashing light? Buzzard and Sparks. They hear us." He cups his hand to his lips and hoots. The light up in the high forest flashes again, impatient. This, too, makes Loki laugh. "Those bastards can't wait to get back down to earth. Can you tell?"

Nick is ready himself, and he hasn't even left the ground. They slog the last few hundred yards up the rut. A profile emerges out of the thicket, so huge it can't be right.

"There it is," Loki says, pointlessly. "There's Mimas."

Sounds come up and out of Nick's mouth, syllables that mean, loosely, *Oh, my hopeless Jesus*. He has seen monster trees for weeks, but never one like this. Mimas: wider across than his great-great-great-grandfather's old farm-house. Here, as sundown blankets them, the feel is primeval, darshan, a face-to-face intro to divinity. The tree runs straight up like a chimney butte and neglects to stop. From underneath, it could be Yggdrasil, the World Tree, with its roots in the underworld and crown in the world above. Twenty-five feet aboveground, a secondary trunk springs out of the expanse of flank, a branch bigger than the Hoel Chestnut. Two more trunks flare out higher up the main shaft. The whole ensemble looks like some exercise in cladistics, the Evolutionary Tree of Life—one great idea splintering into whole new family branches, high up in the run of long time.

Watchman humps up to where Maidenhair stands gazing, wondering if it's too late to back out. But even in the falling light, her face glows with cause. All the agitation that has been such a part of her since she pulled into his gravel driveway back in Iowa has drained away, replaced by a certainty as pure and painful as that solitary calling owl's. She spreads her arms against the furrows. She's like a flea trying to hug its dog. Her face tilts straight up the titanic trunk. "I can't believe it. I can't believe there's no other way to protect this thing except with our bodies."

Loki says, "If nobody's losing money or getting hurt, the law doesn't give a fuck."

The base of the tree, between two enormous burls, opens onto a charcoal-lined goose pen large enough to sleep all three of them tonight. Black soot marks run up the trunk, the scars of fires that burned long before there was an America. A tear in the lower crown recalls a lightning strike still fresh enough to ooze. And from high up in the tangled mass, vanishingly far aboveground, come the cheers of two exhausted people out of their element who just want to be dry and warm and safe again tonight, for a few hours.

Something tumbles down from above. Watchman shouts and pulls Maidenhair aside. The snake flops down to the forest floor. A rope dangles in the air, the width of Watchman's index finger, in front of a shaft wider than his field of view.

"What do we do with this? Attach the packs?"

Loki chuckles. "You climb it." He produces a harness, loops of knotted rope, and carabiners. He starts to put the belt of the harness around Watchman's waist.

"Hang on. What's this? Are these *staples?*"

"There has been some wear. Don't worry. The staples and duct tape won't be bearing your weight."

"No, this little shoestring here will be bearing my weight."

"It has carried loads a lot heavier than you."

Olivia steps between the bickering men and takes the harness. She pulls it around her own waist. Loki clamps her in with carabiners. He cables her to the climbing rope with two sliding Prusik knots, one for her chest and the other for a foot stirrup.

"See? Your weight pulls these knots tight to the rope, like little fists. But when you release . . ." He slips one of the slack knots up the rope. "Stand up on the stirrup. Push the chest knot as high as you can. Lean back and let it take the weight. Sit back into the harness. Slip the stirrup knot as high as it will go. Then stand up on that. Repeat."

Maidenhair laughs. "Like an inchworm?"

Exactly like. She inches. She stands up. She leans back and sits. She stands and inches again, climbing a ladder of air, hoisting herself in self-raising footholds up off the face of the Earth. Watchman stands underneath as she scoots up, seat of the pants, into the sky. The intimacy—her body writhing above him—makes his soul flush. She's the squirrel, Ratatoskr, scaling Yggdrasil, carrying messages between hell, heaven, and here.

"She's a natural," Loki says. "She's flying. She'll reach the top in twenty minutes."

She does, though every muscle in her is shaking by arrival. From above, cheers greet her summit. Down at ground level, jealousy seizes Nick, and when the harness drops again, he springs into it. He gets about a hundred feet into the air before freaking. The rope can't possibly hold him. It's twisting and making weird nylon groans. He cranes his neck to see how much farther. Forever. Then he makes the mistake of looking down. Loki twirls in slow circles below. His face points upward like a tiny Pacific starflower about to be crushed underfoot. Watchman's muscles surrender to panic. He closes his eyes and whispers, "I can't do this. I'm dead." He feels the zoom, the endless drop, coursing through his legs. Two small lumps of vomit come up his throat and onto his windbreaker.

But Olivia is talking, up close into his ear. *Nick. You've done this already. I've seen it for weeks. A hand*, she says. *A foot. Sit. Slide the knot. Stand.* He opens his eyes on the trunk of Mimas, the largest, strongest, widest, oldest, surest, sanest living thing he has ever seen. Keeper of half a million days and nights, and it wants him in its crown.

Shouts greet him at the top. Those above him fasten him with two clamps into the tree. Olivia scampers about the platforms, connected by rope ladder. Buzzard and Sparks have long since talked her through every clause in the lease. They want only to be down before night traps them. They climb down the rope to Loki, who calls up through the encroaching dark. "Someone will be by with your replacements in a few days. All you need to do until then is stay aloft."

THEN NICK IS ALONE with this woman who has commandeered his life. She takes his hand, which still has not unkinked from gripping. "Nick. We're here. In Mimas."

She speaks the creature's name like it's an old friend. Like she's been talking with it for a long time. They sit next to each other in needle-grazed darkness, two hundred feet in the air, on what Buzzard and Sparks called the Grand Ballroom: a seven-by-nine-foot platform made of three doors bolted together. Sliding tarp walls shelter them on three sides.

"Bigger than my room at college," Olivia says. "And nicer."

Balanced on another branch just beneath, reachable by rope ladder, is a smaller piece of plywood. A rain barrel, collecting jar, and sealable bucket complete the bathroom. Six feet above them on a higher spur, another platform serves as pantry, kitchen, and den. It's filled with water, food, tarps, and supplies. A hammock stretched between two limbs cradles a substantial lending library, left here by previous sitters. The whole three-level tree house balances on the top of an enormous fork made when the trunk was hit by lightning centuries ago. It sways with every breeze.

A kerosene lamp illuminates her face. He has never seen her look so confirmed. "Come here." She takes his wrist and guides it to her. "Here. Closer." As if farther away were an option. And she takes him like someone who's sure that life has need of her.

IN THE NIGHT, something soft and warm grazes his face. It's her hand, he thinks, or the fall of her hair as she leans over him. Even the slow, seasick barcarole of the sleeping bag bed feels blessed—the cramped quarters of love. A claw cuts into his cheek, and the succubus lets loose with falsetto jibbers. Watchman bolts up, screaming, "Shit!" He pitches toward the platform ledge, but his safety cable catches him. One palm punches through the fantasy of tarp walls. Lives go shrieking off into the branches.

She's up in a flash, pinning his arms. "Nick. Stop. *Nick!* It's okay." Danger breaks up into little pieces. In the hail of chatter, he's slow to hear what she keeps saying. "Flying squirrels. They've been playing all over us for ten minutes."

"Jesus! Why?"

She laughs and pets him and pulls him back down horizontal. "You'll just have to ask them. If they ever come back."

She nuzzles him, her belly in the small of his back. Sleep won't come. There are creatures that live so high up and far away from man that they never learned fear. And thanks to the insanity in his cells, Nick has—this very first night on his very first tree-sit—taught them.

LIGHT GATHERS in speckled fistfuls on his face. He has slept almost not at all, but rises refreshed in a way normally reserved for the industrious. He rolls onto his side and lifts the tarp. The whole spectrum streams in, from blues to browns, greens to absurd golds. *"Look at that!"*

"L'see." Her voice, sleepy but eager, breathes in his ear. "Oh, goodness."

They look together: high-wire surveyors of a newfound land. The view cracks open his chest. Cloud, mountain, World Tree, and mist—all the tangled, rich stability of creation that gave rise to words to begin with—leave him stupid and speechless. Reiterated trunks grow out of Mimas's main line, shooting up parallel like the fingers of a Buddha's upraised hand, recouping the mother tree on smaller scales, repeating the inborn shape again and again, their branches running into each other, too mazy and fused to trace.

Fog coats the canopy. Through an opening in Mimas's crown, the tufted spires of nearby trunks stand swirled in the gauze of a Chinese landscape. There's more substance to the grayish puffs than there is to the green-brown spikes poking through them. All around them spreads a phantasmagoric, Ordovician fairy tale. It's morning like the morning when life first came up on dry land.

Watchman sweeps back another wall of tarp along its rope runner and looks up. Dozens more feet of Mimas unfold above—trunks that took over when lightning clipped this one. The top of the tangled system disappears into low cloud. Fungi and lichen everywhere, like splatters of paint from a heavenly can. He and Maidenhair perch, most of the way up the Flatiron Building. He looks down. The floor of the forest is a dollscape a little girl might make out of acorns and ferns.

His legs go cold with thoughts of plummeting. He lowers the tarp. She's staring at him, madness in her hazel eyes that spills out as cackling. "We're here. We made it. This is where they want us." She looks like someone summoned to help the most wondrous products of four billion years of life.

Here and there, solo spires rise above the giants' chorus. They look like green thunderheads, or rocket plumes. From below, the tallest neighbors read like mid-sized incense cedars. Only now, seventy yards above the ground, can Nicholas gauge the true size of these few old ones, five times larger than the largest whale. Giants march down into the ravine the three of them climbed last night. In the middle distance, the forest broadens into denser, deeper blue. He has read about these trees and their fog. On every side, trees lap at the low, wet sky, the clouds they themselves have helped to seed. Skeins of aerial needles—knobbier and more gnarled, a different thing from the smooth shoots growing at ground level—sip the fogbanks, condensing water vapor and sieving it down the sluices of twigs and branches. Nick glances upstairs into the kitchen, where their own water-catchment system works away, running droplets into a bottle. What struck him as ingenious last night—water for nothing—turns crude compared to the tree's invention.

Nicholas watches the drama as if thumbing an infinite flip-book. The land unfolds, ridge beyond ridge. His eyes adjust to the baroque abundance. Forests of five different shades bathe in the mist, each one a biome to creatures still to be discovered. And every tree he looks on belongs to a Texas financier who has never seen a redwood but means to gut them all to pay off the debt he took on to acquire them.

A shift in the warmth next to him reminds Watchman. He's not the only large vertebrate in this roost.

"If I don't quit looking, my bladder's going to burst."

He watches Olivia scramble down the rope ladder to the platform below. He thinks: *I really should look away.* But he's living in a tree two hundred feet above the surface of the planet. Flying squirrels have surveilled his face. Fogs from the world's infancy turn the clock back eons, and he feels himself becoming another species.

She squats above the wide-mouthed jar and a stream rushes out of her. He has never seen a woman urinate—something a fair number of all the human males who've ever lived might have to say on their deathbeds. The ritual concealment suddenly seems like some strange animal behavior that might turn up on a BBC wildlife documentary, like fish that change sex when they need to, or spiders that consume their partners after mating. He hears that revered Received Pronunciation whispering off-camera, *When removed from their kind, individual human beings can change in remarkable ways.*

She knows he's watching. He knows she knows. Here, raw, now: the culture suited to this place. When she's done, she tips the jar over the side of the platform. The wind takes the liquid and disperses it. Twenty feet, and her waste atomizes into the fog. Needles will rework it into something alive again. "My turn," he says, when she comes back. And then, from above, she watches him crouch into the bag-lined bucket, which will go to Loki for removal and compost when he shows up next.

They take breakfast alfresco. Their chill fingers feed hazelnuts and dried apricots into mouths that hang open, awed by the view. Sitting still and looking: their new job description. But they're humans, and soon enough their eyes fill up. She says, "Let's explore." The main trails from the Grand Ballroom are laid out with loops and lobster claws, rope ladders, places to hook a carabiner to. She gives him the harness. Then she makes one for herself from three nylon climbing cables. "Barefoot. You'll stick better."

He wobbles out on a waving branch. The wind blows, and Mimas's entire crown dips and bucks. He'll die. Plunge twenty stories onto a bed of ferns. But he's getting used to the idea, and there are worse ways to go.

They head off in different directions. No point in trying to spot each other. He inches along one barrel-sized limb, cabled in, scooting on his pants seat. The scraped branch smells of lemons. A twig growing out of it holds a shock of cones, each one smaller than a marble. He takes one and taps it on his open palm. Seeds fall out like coarsely ground pepper. One sticks in the crease of his lifeline. From such a speck came a tree that holds him two hundred feet in the air without flexing. This fortress tower that could sleep a village and still have room to let.

From high above, she calls, "Huckleberries! A whole patch up here."

Bugs swarm, iridescent, parti-colored, minuscule horror-film monsters. He works his way to a strange junction, careful never to look down. Two large beams, over the course of centuries, have flowed together like modeling clay. He grapples to the top of the hillock and finds it hollow. Inside is a small lake. Plants grow along a pond flecked with tiny crustaceans. Something moves in the shallows, speckled all over in chestnut, bronze, black, and yellow. Seconds pass before Nick coughs up a name: *salamander*. How did a damp-seeking creature with inch-long limbs climb two-thirds of the length of a football field, up the side of dry, fibrous bark? Maybe a bird dropped it here, fumbling a meal into the canopy. Unlikely. The chest of the slick creature rises and falls. The only plausible explanation is that his ancestors got on board a thousand years ago and rode the elevator up, for five hundred generations.

Nick edges himself back the way he came. He's propped up in the corner of the Grand Ballroom when Maidenhair returns. She's ditched the safety umbilical. "You'll never believe what I found. A six-foot hemlock, growing in a mat of soil this deep!"

"Jesus Christ. *Olivia*. Were you free-climbing?"

"Don't worry. I climbed a lot of trees when I was little." She kisses him, a quick, preemptive strike. "And, you know. Mimas says he won't let us fall."

HE SKETCHES HER as she copies her morning discoveries into a spiral notebook. The drill of solitude comes so much easier to him than to her. After years of camping in an Iowa farmhouse, a day at the top of this leviathan flagpole is like stepping out. She, though, in her core chemistry, is still a college girl, addicted to a rate of stimulations per second that she hasn't entirely kicked. The fog burns off. Deep in the expanse of midday, she asks, "What time would you say it is?" Her question is more mystified than agitated. The sun hasn't passed overhead, and yet the two of them are so much older than they were this time yesterday. He looks up from sketching the local labyrinth of Mimas's limbs and shakes his head. She giggles. "Okay. What *day*?"

Yet, soon enough, an afternoon, half an hour, a minute, half a sentence, or half a word all feel the same size. They disappear into the rhythm of no rhythm at all. Just crossing the nine-foot platform is a national epic. More time passes. A tenth of an eternity. Two-tenths. When she speaks again, the softness shatters him. "I never knew how strong a drug other people are."

"The strongest. Or at least the most widely abused."

"How long does it take to . . . detox?"

He considers. "Nobody's ever clean."

. . .

HE SKETCHES HER as she makes lunch. As she naps. Coaxing birds or play-ing with a mouse at two hundred feet. Her struggle to slow down looks to him like the human saga in a nutshell, in a redwood seed. He sketches the ravine full of redwoods, and the scattered giants that tower over their lesser brothers. Then he puts the drawing pad aside, the better to see the changing light.

"YOU HEAR THEM?" he asks. A distant buzzing, systematic and compe-tent. Saws and engines.

"Yes. They're everywhere." Every falling giant brings the crews closer. Trees ten feet thick and nine hundred years old go down in twenty minutes and are bucked within another hour. When a large one falls, even from a distance, it's like an artillery shell hitting a cathedral. The ground liquefies. Their platform two hundred feet up in Mimas shivers. The largest trees the world has ever made, saved for this final roundup.

IN THE HAMMOCK LIBRARY, she finds a book. *The Secret Forest*. The front cover shows a prehistoric yew, aboveground and below. The back pro-claims, *The Year's Surprise Bestseller—Translated into 23 Languages*. "Would you like me to read to you a little?"

She reads like she's in the front of the assembled class, reciting that long freight train of stanzas from *Leaves of Grass* that the entire tenth grade was assigned to memorize.

*You and the tree in your backyard come from a common ancestor.*

She stops and looks out the transparent wall of their tree house.

*A billion and a half years ago, the two of you parted ways.*

She pauses again, as if to do the math.

*But even now, after an immense journey in separate directions, that tree and you still share a quarter of your genes.*

In this manner, tacking into the breeze of the author's thought, they make their way through four full pages before the light starts to fail. They eat again by candlelight—instant soup mix floating on two cups of water warmed on the tiny camp stove. By the time they're done, darkness rules. The loggers' engines have stopped, replaced by the thousand spectral challenges of night that they cannot decode.

"We should save the candle," she says.

"We should."

It's hours before bedtime. They lie on the long, rocking platform of their pledge, chattering to each other in the dark. Up here, they face no dangers but the oldest one. When the wind blows, it feels like they're crossing the Pacific on a makeshift raft. When the wind stops, the stillness suspends them between two eternities, entirely in the caress of here and now.

In the dark, she asks, "What are you thinking?"

He's thinking that his life has reached its zenith, this very day. That he has lived to see everything he wants. Lived to see himself happy. "I was thinking it's going to be cold again tonight. We may need to zip the bags together."

"I'm down with that."

Every star in the galaxy rolls out above them, through the blue-black needles, in a river of spilled milk. The night sky—the best drug there was, before people came together into something stronger.

They zip the bags together. "You know," she says, "if one of us falls, the other is going with."

"I'll follow you anywhere."

THEY WAKE before it's fully light, to the sound of engines in the deep beneath them.

HER CITATION for unlawful assembly costs Mimi three hundred dollars. It's not a bad deal. She has paid twice as much for a winter coat that gave her half the satisfaction. Word of her arrest gets out at work. But her superiors are engineers. If she can deliver her team's molding projects on time, the company doesn't care if she works from a federal prison. When a thousand marchers descend with placards on the Department of Forestry headquarters in Salem demanding reform of the Timber Harvest Plan approval process, Mimi and Douglas join them.

Early one April Saturday, the pair drive to an action in the Coast Range. Douglas takes a vacation day from the hardware store where he has found work. The morning is beyond beautiful, and as they head south, listening to grunge and the day's headlines, the sky cools from dusky rose to cerulean. A rucksack in the back seat contains two pairs of cheap swimming goggles, T-shirts to wrap around their noses and mouths, and modified water bottles. Also, his-and-hers steel double-lock police-grade handcuffs, chains, and a couple of bicycle U-locks. There's an arms race on. The protesters begin to think they might even be able to outspend the police, who are funded by a public convinced that all taxes are theft, but giving away public timber is not.

They turn down the spur road to the protest site. Douglas scans the parked vehicles. "No television trucks. Not one."

Mimi curses. "Okay, nobody panic. I'm sure the print journalists are here. With photographers."

"No TV, might as well never have happened."

"It's early yet. They could still be on their way."

A shout rises down the road, the sound of a crowd after a field goal. Through the trees, opposing armies square off in each other's faces. There's shouting, a bit of scrum. Then a scuffled tug-o'-war with someone's jacket. The latecomers trade glances and break into a trot. They reach the face-off in a clearing in the denuded woods. It's like some Italian circus. A double ring of protesters surrounds a track-mounted Cat C7–powered monster whose crane arches above their heads like a long-necked dinosaur. Fellers and buckers circle the anarchy. A special fury hangs in the air, the product of how far this wooded hillside is from the nearest town.

Mimi and Doug trot up the incline. At the roar of a chain saw, she tugs his arm. One snarling machine sets off another. Soon a chorus of gas-powered rippers screams through the woods. The loggers swing their machines lazily, laconically. Reapers with scythes.

Douglas stops. "Are they fucking *nuts*?"

"It's theater. No one's going to chain-saw an unarmed human being." But as Mimi speaks the words, the driver of a loader with two women handcuffed to it kicks his rig into gear and drags them alongside. The protesters scream in disbelief.

The loggers turn their attention from the hostage Cat. They set to work on a stand of grand fir, threatening to drop the trees into the midst of the handcuffed slackers. Doug mutters and tears free. Before Mimi can react, he's running toward the unraveling action, rucksack in tow. He wades into the fray like a setter into the surf, dashing among the protesters, gripping one man then another by the shoulder. He points at the hand-fellers descending on the firs. "Get as many people as we can up into those trees."

Someone shouts, "Where the hell are the police? They're always here to break things up when we're winning."

"Okay," Douglas barks. "Those trees are going to be history in ten minutes. Move!"

Before Mimi can reach him, he springs off, heading for a fir with a skirt of branches low enough to hop up into. Once he's off the ground, the limbs are practically a ladder eighty feet straight up. Two dozen flagging protesters revive and take off after him. The loggers see what's happening on their flanks. They pursue, as fast as their nail-soled caulks allow.

The first few protesters reach the stand and scramble up into the foliage. Mimi spots a fir with branches even she can reach. She's twenty feet from the trunk when something vicious clips her legs. She falls headlong into a patch of devil's club. Her shoulder hits a lichen-covered stone and bounces. Something heavy camps on the back of her calves. Douglas, from thirty feet up his tree, shrieks at her assailant. "I'll kill you, so help me God. I'll tear your head from your cretin neck."

The man sitting on the back of Mimi's knees drawls, "You're gonna have to come down for that, aren't you?"

Mimi spits mud from her mouth. Her assailant grinds his shins into the back of her thighs. She yells, despite herself. Doug scrambles down a branch. "No!" she shouts. "Stay!"

A few tackled demonstrators lie on the ground. But some reach the trees and swing up into the branches. There, they keep their pursuers at bay. Shoes win out over reaching fingers.

Mimi moans, "Get off me."

The logger who pins her wavers. His side is outnumbered, and he's tied down, restraining an Asian woman too small to climb anything bigger than a shrub. "Promise to stay down."

The civility stuns her. "If your company kept *your* promises, this wouldn't be happening."

"Promise."

Nothing but flimsy oaths, binding every living thing. She promises. The logger springs up and rejoins his stymied side. The loggers huddle up, trying to salvage the situation. They can't cut the firs without killing someone.

Mimi spies Douglas in his tree. She has seen that tree before. It takes her too long to recognize: the tree in the background behind the third arhat, in her father's scroll. The loggers start up their saws again. They wave them in simplifying swipes through the air, cutting scrub, stacking it in fall zones in front of the firs. One of the fellers makes an undercut in a big tree. Mimi watches, too stupefied to cry out. They mean to bring it down through the branches of a squatter's tree. The great fir cracks, and Mimi screams. She shuts her eyes to a tremendous crash. She opens them on downed timber tearing through the grove. The squatter clings to his mast, moaning in terror.

Douglas rains abuse down on the cutters. "Have you lost your damn minds? You could kill him."

The crew boss shouts, "You're trespassing." The fellers prepare a new fall zone. Someone produces bolt cutters and starts clipping through the handcuffs of the Cat-chained protesters like he's pruning a dogwood. Scuffles break out across the clearing; the luxury of nonviolence is over. In the fir grove, a feller tips his saw into the butter of the next doomed fir, aiming to drop it three feet from another squatter's tree. The target squatter's screams are lost over the saws, lost to the loggers, with their padded earmuffs. But they see his arms waving like mad and hold up just long enough for the terrified mark to scramble to the ground. It's a full-out rout on both fronts. The blockaded vehicles begin to roll. Nine of the remaining squatters drop from their roosts. The loggers, triumphant, swing their saws. Protesters fall back, like deer from a fire.

Mimi sits on the spot where she made her promise. The air behind her whoops. She turns to see flashing lights and thinks, *The cavalry*. Twenty officers in full armor disgorge from an armored truck. Black polycarbonate helmets with wraparound face guards. Kevlar jackets. Projectile-proof, high-impact riot shields. Police sweep across the clearing, rounding up the trespassers, snapping bracelets on the wrists even of those who already sport one severed cuff.

Mimi rises. A hand comes down hard on her shoulder, pushing her back to the ground. She swings around to face a cop, scared and all of twenty years old. "Sit down! And don't move."

"I wasn't going anywhere."

"Mouth off again, and you'll regret it." Three Saturday forest warriors jog past, back toward the road and their cars. The child cop yells, "Stop where you are and sit down. Now, now, now!"

They flinch, turn, and sit in place. Nearby loggers cheer. The kid cop spins and sprints toward another group of protesters trying to get away. A squad fans out under the trees. Pairs of them stand under the last treed protesters, smacking at their feet with nightsticks. The five remaining squatters give up, all except Douglas Pavlicek, who climbs higher. He takes his own cuffs from the rucksack and seals one wrist. Then he reaches around the trunk and locks the second wrist into place.

Mimi grabs her head. "Douglas. Come down. It's over."

"Can't!" He rattles his cuffs, locked in the hug of the trunk. "Have to hold out until TV gets here."

The crazed holdout kicks at the logging ladders that the police position into the fir. He scores one fend-off so athletically that even the loggers cheer.

But soon enough, four policemen swarm his lower regions. Chained in place, Douglas can't move. The police reach their bolt cutters up to sever his cuffs. He pulls in his arms, snugging the chain against the trunk. The loggers hand axes up to the police. But Douglas laces his fingers in front of the chain. The police can reach no higher than his waist. A quick consult, and they cut into his pants with industrial shears. Two cops secure his legs. The third slices the ragged denim up to Douglas's crotch.

Mimi stares. She has never seen Douglas's bare thighs. She has wondered, these months, whether she ever might. His desire is as open as the look of wonder on his face when they share a cold fudge shake. The only secret is what has kept him from anything more calamitous than putting his hand on the back of her neck. Weeks ago, she concluded it was some war wound. Now she watches him get stripped in public, in front of a stunned crowd. One leg is open to the air, bony and blanched, almost hairless, the furrowed thighs of a much older man. Then the other leg, and now the jeans hang open from the waist like a shredded banner. Out comes the triple-action pepper spray—capsaicin mixed with CS gas.

The onlookers call out. "He's chained in place, man. He can't move!"

"What do you want from him?"

The officer puts the canister up into Douglas's groin and sprays. Liquid fire spreads across his cock and balls—a cocktail amounting to a few million Scoville heat units. Douglas hangs, dangling from the cuffs, breathing in short little aspirated gasps. "Shi, shi, shit . . ."

"For God's sake. He can't move. Leave him alone!"

Mimi twists to see who yelled. It's a logger, short and bearded, like an enraged dwarf from the pages of Grimm.

"Unlock yourself," one of the police orders. Words clog Douglas's mouth. Nothing comes out but a low pitch, like the first half-second of an air raid. They spray him again. Protesters who've sat in place peacefully waiting to be booked start to revolt. Mimi rises in a rage. She's shouting things she won't remember even an hour from now. Others around her stand up, too. They converge on the prisoner's tree. Police prod them back. The officers in the tree hit the naked groin with one more canister of spray. The soft, droned pitch in Douglas's mouth begins a slow, awful rise.

"Unlock your hands, and you can come down. It's easy."

He tries to say something. Someone below shouts, "Let him talk, you animals."

The police lean in, close enough to hear him whisper, "I dropped the key."

The police cut Douglas free and carry him down from the tree like Jesus from the cross. They won't let Mimi anywhere near him.

WHEN THE ORDEAL of their processing is done, she drives him home. She tries to wash him, with every soothing emolument she can find. But his meat is a vibrant salmon, and he's too ashamed to let her see.

"I'll be fine." He lies in bed, reading the words off the ceiling. "I'll be fine."

She checks in every evening. His skin stays orange for a week.

MASTERY 2 RAKES IN as much as the annual income of whole states. *Mastery 3* arrives just as its ancestor starts to grow stale. People from six continents pour into the upgraded place—frontiersmen, pilgrims, farmers, miners, warriors, priests. They form guilds and consortiums. They build buildings and fashion trade goods that the coders never anticipated.

*Mastery 4* is 3-D. It turns into a monumental undertaking, almost breaking the company, needing twice as many coders and artists as its parent. It offers four times the resolution, ten times more game area, and a dozen more quests. Thirty-six new techs. Six new resources. Three new cultures. More new world wonders and masterworks than a person could explore in years of play. Even with the constant doubling of processor speeds, it pushes the limits of the best consumer rigs for months.

Everything unfolds as Neelay foresaw it years ago. *Browsers* appear—yet another nail in the coffin of time and space. A click, and you're at CERN. Another, and you're listening to underground music from Santa Cruz. One more, and you can read a newspaper at MIT. Fifty big *servers* at the start of year two, and five hundred by the end. Sites, search engines, gateways. The spent, filled-up cities of the industrialized planet have willed this thing into being, just in time: the savior of the gospel of endless growth. The Web goes from unimaginable to indispensable, weaving the world together in eighteen months. *Mastery* gets on board, goes online, and a million more lonely boys emigrate to the new and improved Neverland.

The homesteading days are over. Games grow up; they join the ranks of the globe's elite commodities. *Mastery 5* surpasses whole operating systems for sheer complexity and total lines of code. The game's best AIs are smarter than last year's interplanetary probes. *Play* becomes the engine of human growth.

But none of that does much for Neelay, in his apartment above the company's HQ. The room teems with screens and modems blinking like Christmas. His electronics range from matchbook-sized modules to rack mounts larger than a man. Each one of these devices is, as the prophet says, indistinguishable from magic. The wildest sci-fi of Neelay's childhood failed to predict these miracles. And still, impatience doubles in him, with every doubling of specs. He hungers worse than ever—for one more breakthrough, the *next* one, something simple and elegant that will change everything again. He visits his oracle trees in their Martian botanical garden, to ask them what's supposed to happen next. But the creatures stay mum.

Bedsores plague him. His increasingly brittle bones make going outside dangerous. Two months ago he smashed a foot getting into the van—the hazard of not being able to feel where your limbs end. His arms are bruised black from whacking them on the bed bar getting in and out of bed. He has taken to eating, working, and sleeping in the chair. What he wants more than anything—what he'd trade the company for—is a chance to sit by a lake in the High Sierras, ten miles down a trail, and watch crossbills sweep up into the branches of the bordering spruces to pry seeds out of the cones with their grotesque beaks. He'll never have that. Never. The only outing allowed him now is *Mastery 6*.

In *Mastery 6*, a player's colonies go on thriving while he's away. Dynamic, concurrent economies. Cities full of actual people trading and making laws. Creation in all its extravagant waste. People pay monthly rent to live there. It's a daring step, but in the world game, no daring is fatal. The only thing that will kill you is failing to leap.

Neelay can no longer tell the difference between calm and desperate. He sits by the picture window for hours at a pop, then dashes off epic memos to the development team, nagging about the same thing he has pushed for years:

> *We need more realism. . . . More life! The animals should start and stop, saunter and stare, just like their living models. . . . I want to see the way a wolf rocks back on its haunches, the green of their eyes as if lit from inside. I want to see a bear rake open an anthill with his claws. . . .*

> *Let's build this place up in every detail, from stuff* out there. *Real savannas, real temperate forests, real wetlands. The Van Eyck brothers painted 75 different kinds of identifiable plant species into the Ghent Altarpiece. I want to be able to count 750 kinds of simulated plants in Mastery 7, each with its own behaviors. . . .*

As he composes the memo, employees knock and enter, with papers for him to sign, disputes for him to resolve. They show no revulsion or pity for the giant walking stick propped upright in the chair. They're used to him, these young cybernauts. They don't even notice the catheter anymore, where it empties into its reservoir on the chair's frame. They know his net worth. Sempervirens common closed that afternoon at forty-one and a quarter, triple last year's IPO. The twig-man in the chair owns twenty-three percent of the company. He has made them all wealthy, and he has made himself as rich as the game's greatest emperors.

He dispatches the latest pamphlet-sized memo, and, moments later, the shadow comes over him. Then he does what he always does whenever the bottom drops out: he phones his parents. His mother picks up. "Oh, Neelay. So, so happy it's you!"

"So happy, too, Moti. You good?" And it doesn't matter what she's saying. Pita taking too many naps. Planning a trip back to Ahmedabad. Ladybug invasion of the garage—very strong-smelling. Might be cutting hair very dramatically soon. He revels in whatever she wants to go on about. Life, in all the pitiful details that won't fit yet into any simulation.

But then the killing question, and so soon, this time. "Neelay, we are thinking again that it's not impossible to find you someone. In the community."

They have been all up, down, around, and over this, for years. It would be socially enforced sadism toward any woman brought into such a match. "No, Moti. We've said."

"But Neelay." He can hear in the way that she pronounces the words: *You're worth millions, tens of millions, maybe more—you won't even tell your mother! What sacrifice, there? Who couldn't learn to love?*

"Mom? I should have told you already. There's a woman here. She's actually one of my caregivers." It sounds almost plausible. The hush on the other end crushes him with its tongue-biting hope. He needs a safe and reassuring name, one he'll remember. Rupi. Rutu. "Her name's Rupal."

A horrible suck of breath, and she's crying. "Oh, Neelay. So, so happy!"

"Me, too, Mom."

"You will know true joy! When do we meet her?"

He wonders why his criminal mind failed to foresee this little difficulty. "Soon. I don't want to scare her away!"

"Your own family is going to scare her? What kind of girl is this?"

"Maybe next month? Late next month?" Thinking, of course, that the world will end long before then. Already feeling his mother's bottomless grief at his simulated breakup, just days before the women were to meet. But he has made her happy in the only place where people really live, the few-second-wide window of Now. It's all good, and by the time the call ends, he's promising people in both Gujarat and Rajasthan at least fourteen months' notice to clear calendars, buy airplane tickets, and get saris made, prior to any wedding.

"Goodness. These things take time, Neelay."

When they hang up, he raises his hand in the air and slams it down onto the desk's front edge. There's a very wrong sound, and a sharp white pain, and he knows he has broken at least one bone.

In blinding pain, he rides his private elevator down into the opulent lobby, the beautiful redwood trim paid for by millions of people's desire to live anywhere else but here. His eyes stream with tears and rage. But quietly, politely, to the terrified receptionist, he holds up his swollen, snapped claw and says, "I'm going to have to get to the hospital."

He knows what's waiting for him there, after they mend his hand. They will scold him. They'll put him on a drip and make him swear to eat properly. As the receptionist makes her frantic calls, Neelay glances up at the wall where he has hung those words of Borges, still the guiding principle of his young life:

> *Every man should be capable of all ideas, and I believe in the*
> *future he shall be.*

PORTLAND SOUNDS TOXIC to Patricia. *Expert educating witness*, even worse. Dr. Westerford lies in bed on the morning of the preliminary hearing, feeling like she's had a stroke. "Can't do it, Den."

"Can't not, babe."

"Do you mean that morally or legally?"

"It's your life's work. You can't walk away now."

"It's not my life's work. My life's work is listening to trees!"

"No. That's your life's play. The work part is telling people what they're saying."

"An injunction to halt logging on sensitive federal land. That's a question for lawyers. What do I know about the law?"

"They want to know what you know about trees."

"*Expert* witness? I'm going to be ill."

"Just tell them what you know."

"That's the problem. I don't know anything."

"It'll be just like stepping in front of a class."

"Except instead of idealistic twenty-year-olds who want to learn things, it'll be a bunch of lawyers fighting over millions of dollars."

"Not dollars, Patty. The other thing."

And yes, she admits, hauling her feet out onto the cold floorboards. This one is about the other thing. The very opposite of dollars. The thing that needs all the testifiers it can get.


DENNIS DRIVES HER the hundred miles in his decaying truck. Her ears are throbbing by the time they reach the courthouse. During her preliminary statement, her childhood speech defect flowers forth like a great May magnolia. The judge keeps asking her to repeat. Patricia struggles to hear every question. And yet, she tells them: the mystery of trees. The words rise in her like sap after winter. There are no individuals in a forest. Each trunk depends on others.

She fights off personal hunch and keeps to what the scientific community agrees on. But as she testifies, science itself starts to seem as flighty as a high school popularity contest. Unfortunately, the opposing counsel agrees. He produces the letter to the editors of the journal where her first major scholarly article appeared. The one signed by three leading dendrologists, crushing her into the earth. Flawed methods. Problematic statistics. *Patricia Westerford displays an almost embarrassing misunderstanding of the units of natural selection. . . .* Every part of her flushes with blood. She wants to vanish, to never have been. To have folded some poison mushrooms into the omelet she made herself this morning, before Dennis drove her to this tribunal.

"Everything in that paper has been confirmed by later research."

She doesn't see the trap until it's sprung. "You overthrew existing beliefs," the opposing counsel says. "Can you guarantee that further research won't overthrow yours?"

She can't. Science, too, has its seasons. But that's a point too subtle for any court of law. Watching—the watching of many—will converge on something repeatable, despite the needs and fears of any one watcher. But she can't swear to the court that the science of forestry has finally converged on *new forestry*, that set of beliefs she and her friends have helped to promote. She can't even swear that forestry is really a science, yet.

The judge asks Patricia if it's true, what the expert witness for the opposition has earlier claimed, that a young, managed, fast-growing, consistent stand is better than an old, anarchic forest. The judge reminds her of someone. Long car trips through newly plowed fields. *If you carved your name four feet high in the bark of a beech tree, how high would it be after half a century?*

"That's what my teachers believed, twenty years ago."

"Is twenty years a long time, in these matters?"

"It's nothing, for a tree."

All the warring humans in the courtroom laugh. But for people— relentless, ingenious, hardworking people—twenty years is time enough to kill whole ecosystems. Deforestation: a bigger changer of climate than all of transportation put together. Twice as much carbon in the falling forests than in all the atmosphere. But that's for another trial.

The judge asks, "Young, straight, faster-growing trees *aren't* better than older, rotting trees?"

"Better for us. Not for the forest. In fact, young, managed, homogenous stands can't really be called forests." The words are a dam-break as she speaks them. They leave her happy to be alive, alive to study life. She feels grateful for no reason at all, except in remembering all that she has been able to discover about *other things*. She can't tell the judge, but she *loves* them, those intricate, reciprocal nations of tied-together life that she has listened to all life long. She loves her own species, too—sneaky and self-serving, trapped in blinkered bodies, blind to intelligence all around it—yet chosen by creation to *know*.

The judge asks her to elaborate. Dennis was right. It *is* like talking to students. She describes how a rotting log is home to orders of magnitude more living tissue than the living tree. "I sometimes wonder whether a tree's real task on Earth isn't to bulk itself up in preparation to lying dead on the forest floor for a long time."

The judge asks what living things might need a dead tree.

"Name your family. Your order. Birds, mammals, other plants. Tens of thousands of invertebrates. Three-quarters of the region's amphibians need them. Almost all the reptiles. Animals that keep down the pests that kill other trees. A dead tree is an infinite hotel."

She tells him about the ambrosia beetle. The alcohol of rotting wood summons it. It moves into the log and excavates. Through its tunnel systems, it plants bits of fungus that it brought in with it, on a special formation on its head. The fungus eats the wood; the beetle eats the fungus.

"Beetles are farming the log?"

"They farm. Without subsidies. Unless you count the log."

"And those species that depend on rotting logs and snags: are any of them endangered?"

She tells him: everything depends on everything else. There's a kind of vole that needs old forest. It eats mushrooms that grow on rotting logs and excretes spores somewhere else. No rotting logs, no mushrooms; no mushrooms, no vole; no vole, no spreading fungus; no spreading fungus, no new trees.

"Do you believe we can save these species by keeping fragments of older forest intact?"

She thinks before answering. "No. Not fragments. Large forests live and breathe. They develop complex behaviors. Small fragments aren't as resilient or as rich. The pieces must be large, for large creatures to live in them."

The opposing counsel asks whether preserving slightly larger forest tracts is worth the millions of dollars it costs people. The judge asks for numbers. The opposition sums up the opportunity loss—the crippling expense of not cutting down trees.

The judge asks Dr. Westerford to respond. She frowns. "Rot adds value to a forest. The forests here are the richest collections of biomass anywhere. Streams in old growth have five to ten times more fish. People could make more money harvesting mushrooms and fish and other edibles, year after year, than they do by clear-cutting every half dozen decades."

"Really? Or is that a metaphor?"

"We have the numbers."

"Then why doesn't the market respond?"

Because ecosystems tend toward diversity, and markets do the opposite. But she's smart enough not to say this. Never attack the local gods. "I'm not an economist. Or a psychologist."

The opposing counsel declares that clear-cutting saves forests. "If people don't harvest, millions of acres will blow down or burn in devastating crown fires."

It's out of her field, but Patricia can't let it go. "Clear-cuts increase windthrow. And crown fires only happen when fires are suppressed for too long." She lays it out: Fire regenerates. There are cones—serotinous—that can't open without flame. Lodgepole pines hold on to theirs for decades, waiting for a fire to spring them. "Fire suppression used to seem like rational management. But it costs us much more than it has saved." The counsel for her side winces. But she's in too deep for diplomacy now.

"I've looked at your book," the judge says. "I never imagined! Trees summon animals and make them do things? They remember? They feed and take care of each other?"

In the dark-paneled courtroom, her words come out of hiding. Love for trees pours out of her—the grace of them, their supple experimentation, the constant variety and surprise. These slow, deliberate creatures with their elaborate vocabularies, each distinctive, shaping each other, breeding birds, sinking carbon, purifying water, filtering poisons from the ground, stabilizing the microclimate. Join enough living things together, through the air and underground, and you wind up with something that has *intention*. Forest. A threatened creature.

The judge frowns. "What grows back after a clear-cut isn't a forest?"

Frustration boils over in her. "You can replace forests with plantations. You can also arrange Beethoven's Ninth for solo kazoo." Everyone laughs but the judge. "A suburban backyard has more diversity than a tree farm!"

"How much untouched forest is left?"

"Not much."

"Less than a quarter of what we started with?"

"Oh, heavens! Much less. Probably no more than two or three percent. Maybe a square, fifty miles on each side." What's left of her vow of circumspection blows away. "There were four great forests on this continent. Each was supposed to last forever. Each went down in decades. We barely had time to romanticize! These trees out here are our last stands, and they're disappearing—a hundred football fields a day. This state has seen rivers of logjam six miles long.

"If you want to maximize the net present value of a forest for its current owners and deliver the most wood in the shortest time, then yes: cut the old growth and plant straight-rowed replacement plantations, which you'll be able to harvest a few more times. But if you want next century's soil, if you want pure water, if you want variety and health, if you want stabilizers and services we can't even measure, then be patient and let the forest give slowly."

When she finishes, she falls back into blushing silence. But the counsel pressing for the injunction is beaming. The judge says, "Would you say that old forests . . . know things that plantations don't?"

She squints and sees her father. The voice is wrong but there are the rimless glasses, the high, surprised eyebrows, the constant curiosity. All those first lessons from half a century ago cloud around her, days in the beaten-up Packard, her mobile classroom, tooling around the back roads of southwest Ohio. It stuns her to recognize all her own adult convictions, there in embryo, formed by a casual few words with the window rolled down on a Friday afternoon and the soy fields of Highland County unspooling into the rearview mirror.

Remember? *People aren't the apex species they think they are.* Other creatures—bigger, smaller, slower, faster, older, younger, more powerful—call the shots, make the air, and eat sunlight. Without them, *nothing.*

But the judge wasn't in that car. The judge is another man.

"It could be the eternal project of mankind, to learn what forests have figured out."

The judge chews on her statement, the way her father used to chew on sassafras, those root-beer-scented twigs that stay green all winter.

THEY RETURN after recess for the decision. The judge places a stay on the contested cut. He also issues an injunction on all new timber sales of public land in western Oregon until the impact of clear-cuts on endangered species is assessed. People come up to Patty and congratulate her, but she can't hear. Her ears shut down the moment the gavel hits the desk.

She leaves the courtroom in a bank of fog. Dennis is by her side, leading her down the hall and out onto the plaza, where two crowds of demonstrators face off in a gauntlet of banners on each side of her.

## YOU CAN'T CLEARCUT YOUR WAY TO HEAVEN

## THIS STATE SUPPORTS TIMBER: TIMBER SUPPORTS THIS STATE

Enemies shout at each other across the gap, stoked by triumph and humiliation. Decent people loving the land in irreconcilable ways. They sound to Patricia like quarreling birds. A tap on her right shoulder, and she turns to face the opposing expert witness. "You've just made lumber a whole lot more expensive."

She blinks at the accusation, unable to see how that might be a bad thing.

"Every timber firm with private land or existing rights is going to cut as fast as they can."

THEIR HANDS FREEZE and their legs stiffen up, in space too cramped to turn over in. Nights are harsh enough to frostbite their sap-covered toes. The constant wind and flapping tarps shred their attempts to talk. Sometimes fat branches crash down from above. The quiet can be even more unnerving. Climbing is all the exercise they get. But in the changing light and floating days, things that would have seemed impossible on the ground become routine.

Mornings are a game of cat and mouse. Or, say, owl and vole, with Watchman and Maidenhair peering down from their damp, freezing aerie onto the tiny mammals scurrying on the floor far below. The crews show up before the fog diffuses. One day, there are only three. The next, twenty, loud in the cockpits of their machines. Sometimes the loggers wheedle: "Come down for ten minutes."

"Can't right now. We're busy tree-sitting!"

"We have to scream. Can't even see you. This is breaking our necks."

"Come on up. Lots of room up here!"

It's an impasse. Different men show up on different days, trying to break it. Crew boss. Foreman. They yell hoarse threats and reasonable promises. Even the vice president for forest products pays a visit. He stands underneath Mimas in a white hard hat, like he's orating on the floor of the Senate.

"We can send you to prison for three years for criminal trespass."

"That's why we're not coming down."

"The losses we're incurring. Huge fines."

"This tree is worth it."

The next day, the white-hatted VP is back. "If you two come down by five p.m. this evening, we'll drop all charges. If you don't, we can't guarantee what'll happen to you. Come down. We'll let you walk. Your records will be clean."

Maidenhair leans out over the edge of the Grand Ballroom. "We're not worried about *our* records. We're worried about *yours*."

THE NEXT MORNING, she's debating one of the loggers again when he stops in midsentence.

"Hey! Take your cap off for a second." She does. His shock is obvious from two-thirds of a football field away. "Shit! You're *gorgeous*."

"You should see me up close! When I'm not frozen and have taken a bath in the last month or two."

"The hell you doing, sitting up in a tree? You could have any guy you want."

"Who wants guys when you can have Mimas?"

"Mimas?"

It's a small victory, just getting him to use the name.

WATCHMAN RELEASES A SALVO of paper bombs onto the loggers below. Unfolded, the sheets reveal pencil sketches of life at two hundred feet. The loggers are impressed. "You *drew* these?"

"Guilty."

"For real? You got *huckleberries* up there?"

"Thickets!"

"And a pool with little *fish* in it?"

"There's more."

DAYS PASS, wet and icy, each more miserable than the last. The sitters that were to relieve Watchman and Maidenhair never show. The standoff enters week two, and the ring of workers at the foot of Mimas turns angry.

"You're out in the middle of nowhere. Four miles from the nearest person. Things could happen. Nobody would know."

Maidenhair beams down on them, beatific. "You guys are too decent. You can't even make a credible threat!"

"You're killing our livelihood."

"Your bosses are doing that."

"Bullshit!"

"One-third of forest jobs lost to machines in the last fifteen years. More trees cut, fewer people working."

Stumped, the loggers wander into other tactics. "For Christ's sake. It's a crop. It grows back! Have you seen the forests south of here?"

"It's a onetime jackpot," Watchman shouts down. "A thousand years before the systems are back in place."

"What's the matter with you two? Why do you hate people?"

"What are you *talking about*? We're doing this *for* people!"

"These trees are going to die and fall over. They should be harvested while they're ripe, not wasted."

"Great. Let's grind up your grandfather for dinner, while he still has some meat on him."

"You're insane. Why are we even talking to you?"

"We have to learn to love this place. We need to become natives."

One of the loggers revs up his chain saw and whacks the branches of one of Mimas's largest basal sprouts. He steps back and looks up, brandishing a limb like a sailboat mast. "We feed people. What do you do?"

They shout at Maidenhair, tag team. "We know these forests. We respect these trees. These trees have killed our friends."

Maidenhair holds still. The idea of a tree killing a person is too much for her to think about.

The men below press their advantage. "You can't stop growth! People need wood."

Watchman has seen the numbers. Hundreds of board feet of timber, half a ton of paper and cardboard per person per year. "We need to get smarter about what we need."

"I need to feed my kids. How about you?"

Watchman sets to shout some things he knows he'll regret. Maidenhair's hand on his arm stops him. She's gazing downward, trying to hear these men, attacked for doing what they've been asked to do. For doing something dangerous and vital that they've learned to do so well.

"We're not saying don't cut anything." She dangles her arm, reaching out to the men from two hundred feet away. "We're saying, cut like it's a gift, not like you've earned it. Nobody likes to take more gift than they need. And *this* tree? This tree would be a gift so big, it would be like Jesus coming down and . . ."

She trickles off on a thought that Watchman has at the same moment. *Been there. Felled that, too.*


THERE ARE DAYS despondent with sleet. Afternoons that rise into muggy chill. Still the replacement sitters don't show. Watchman improves the rain catchment system. Maidenhair builds a urinal that works for women. Late in week three, the loggers set up to do some nearby cutting. But they're stymied after a couple of hours. It's hard to drop trees the size of skyscrapers when a pop of the saw and a slight breeze might lead to manslaughter.

That night, Loki and Sparks arrive at last. Loki ascends into Mimas's upper camp. Sparks stays below as sentry. "Sorry we took so damn long. There's been a little . . . infighting back at the camp. Also, Humboldt and their troops have the whole hillside cordoned off. Two nights ago, they chased us. They got Buzzard. He's locked up."

"They're watching the tree at *night*?"

"We waited for the first chance to slip through."

The scout hands over precious supplies—packets of instant soup, peaches and apples, ten-grain cereal, couscous mix. Just add warm water. Watchman studies the goods. "We're not being spelled out?"

"We can't risk it right now. Moss-Eater and Graywolf got spooked by the death threats and went home. The entire LDF is stretched thin on the ground. We're having some internal communication issues. In fact, we're pretty hosed at the moment. Can you stay up just one more week?"

"Of course!" Maidenhair says. "We can stay up forever."

Forever might be easier, Watchman thinks, if he, too, were hearing from beings of light. Loki shivers in the candlelight. "Man, it's cold up here. That wet wind goes right through you."

Maidenhair says, "We don't feel it anymore."

"Much," Watchman qualifies.

Loki harnesses up. "Gotta head down before they trap Sparks and me. Watch out for Climber Cal. Serious. Humboldt has this guy who scoots up trunks bareback, with just his spikes and a big loop of cable. He's been all kinds of trouble at other tree-sits."

"Sounds like a forest legend," Watchman says.

"He's not."

"He's taking people out of trees *by force?*"

"There are two of us," Maidenhair declares. "And we've got our balance now."

THE LOGGERS STOP COMING. There's nothing more to argue over. Resupply from LDF ground support dries up, too. "We must still be under siege," Watchman says. But they can see no blockade down on the surface. Humans might well have vanished from everywhere but the fossil record. High up in the canopy, they see no animals larger than flying squirrels, who nest in the warmth of their bodies at night.

Neither of them can say how many days pass. Nick marks each morning on a hand-drawn calendar, but by the time he pees and sponges clean and eats breakfast and dreams some more of a collective artwork that could do justice to a forest, he often can't remember if he has marked off the day already or not.

"What does it matter?" Maidenhair asks. "The storms are almost over. It's warming up. The days are getting longer. That's all the calendar we need."

Whole afternoons pass as Watchman sketches. He draws the mosses that sprout up in every crevice. He sketches the usnea and other hanging lichen that turn the tree into a fairy tale. His hand moves and the thought forms:

*Who needs anything, except food?* And those like Mimas who make their own food—freest of all.

Equipment still whines, down the gaping hillside. A nearby saw, a more distant trunk skidder: the two tree-sitters get good at telling the creatures apart by ear. Some mornings, those sounds are their only way of knowing if the system of free enterprise still barrels toward its God-sized wall.

"They must be trying to starve us out." But in that long stretch when provisions don't get through, they have couscous and imagination.

"Hold out," Maidenhair says. "The huckleberries will be fruiting again before we know it." She nibbles on dried chickpeas like they're a course in philosophy. "I never knew how to taste things, before."

He neither. And he never knew how his body smells, and his fresh shit, turning to compost. And how his thought changes when he stares for hours at the carved light sinking through the branches. And what blood sounds like, pumping in his ears in the hour after the sun sets, and while everything alive holds its breath, waiting to see what happens, once the sky falls.

Reality tips away from perpendicular in every little breeze. Gusty afternoons are an epic two-person sport. When the wind picks up, there's nothing, nothing at all but wind. It turns them feral—the tarp flapping like mad and the needles whipping them senseless. When the wind blows, that's all your brain has—no drawing, no poems, no books, no cause, no calling—just the gales and your crazed ideas that bang around wild, their own careening species tumbling free of the family tree.

Once the light goes, the two of them have only sound. The candles and kerosene are too precious to spend on the indulgence of reading. They have no idea when their next provisions might make it through the cordon, whether there still is a cordon, still an LDF or any earthly institution that remembers the pair of them, high up in a thousand-year-old tree, in need of supplies.

She takes his hand in the dark, all the signal he needs. They burrow into one another, as they do every night, against the black. "Where are they?"

There are only two choices, which *they* she means. Three if you count the creatures of light. And his answer is the same for all three. "I don't know."

"Maybe they've forgotten about this stand."

292 • RICHARD POWERS

"No," he says. "I don't think they have."

The moonlight behind her throws a hood across her features. "They can't win. They can't beat nature."

"But they can mess things over for an incredibly long time."

Yet on such a night as this, as the forest pumps out its million-part symphonies and the fat, blazing moon gets shredded in Mimas's branches, it's easy for even Nick to believe that green has a plan that will make the age of mammals seem like a minor detour.

"Shh," she says, although he's already silent. "What's that?"

He knows and he doesn't. Another experimental incarnation checking in, announcing its whereabouts, testing the blackness, calibrating its place in the enormous hive. Truth is, his eyes are drooping and he can't quite keep her question from turning into hieroglyphics. With no way to domesticate the dark or turn it to the smallest use, he's done for. But he's wakeful enough still to realize: *This is the longest stretch of time I've ever gone without the black dog coming to bite at my ass.*

They sleep. They don't strap in anymore. But they still clutch each other hard enough, most nights, that they'd pitch over the side of the platform together, all the same.


WHEN IT'S LIGHT AGAIN, he makes a meaningless tick mark on his DIY calendar. He washes, evacuates, eats, and crawls into the traditional waking position—head alongside her feet, so they can see each other. It crosses Nick's mind to wonder how he ever took it in his head to move his life twenty stories into the open air. But how does a person get anywhere? And who could stay on the ground, once he has seen life in the canopy? As the sun skids by in smallest increments across the summer sky, he draws. He begins to see how it might work, how a few black marks on a blank white field might change what's in the world.

She sits on the platform edge with the tarp up, looking out across the tumbling forest. Bald patches in the middle distance are coming closer. She listens for her disembodied voices, her constant reassurance. They don't check in every day. She retrieves her own notebook and scribbles down tiny poems smaller than a redwood seed.

He watches her take a sponge bath with water that collected in the tarp. "Do your parents know where you are? In case something . . . comes down?"

She turns, naked and shivering, frowns, like the question is advanced nonlinear dynamics. "I haven't spoken to my parents since we left Iowa."

Clean and clothed again, seven degrees of solar descent later, she adds, "And it won't."

"Won't what?"

"Nothing's coming down. I've been assured that this story has a good ending." She pats Mimas, who has, that very day, eaten four pounds of carbon from the air and added them to its mass, even in late middle age.

THEY SPEND the endless hours reading in their sleeping bags. They read all the books previous sitters left in the hammock lending library. They read Shakespeare, holding the thick volume across their twinned bellies. They read a play every afternoon, taking all the parts between them. *A Midsummer Night's Dream. King Lear. Macbeth.* They read two fabulous novels, one three years old and the other a hundred and twenty-three. She has trouble, as they near the end of the older story, keeping her voice under control.

"You love these people?" The stories have captivated him. He cares about what happens. But she—she's broken.

"Love? Wow. Okay. Maybe. But they're all imprisoned in a shoe box, and they have no idea. I just want to shake them and yell, *Get out of yourselves, damn it! Look around!* But they can't, Nicky. Everything alive is just outside their field of view."

Her face crabs up and her eyes go raw again. Crying for the blindness, even of fictional beings.

THEY READ *The Secret Forest* again. It's like a yew: more revealing on a second look. They read about how a branch knows when to branch. How a root finds water, even water in a sealed pipe. How an oak may have five hundred million root tips that turn away from competition. How crown-shy leaves leave a gap between themselves and their neighbors. How trees see color. They read about the wild stock market trading in handicrafts, aboveground and below. About the complex limited partnerships with other kinds of life. The ingenious designs that loft seeds in the air for hundreds of miles. The tricks of propagation worked upon unsuspecting mobile things tens of millions of years younger than the trees. The bribes for animals who think they're getting lunch for free.

They read about myrrh-tree transplanting expeditions depicted in the reliefs at Karnak, three thousand five hundred years ago. They read about trees that migrate. Trees that remember the past and predict the future. Trees that harmonize their fruiting and nutting into sprawling choruses. Trees that bomb the ground so only their own young can grow. Trees that summon air forces of insects to come save them. Trees with hollowed trunks wide enough to hold the population of small hamlets. Leaves with fur on the undersides. Thinned petioles that solve the wind. The rim of life around a pillar of dead history, each new coat as thick as the maker season is generous.

"CAN YOU FEEL IT?" she asks, under the mayhem in the western sky early one evening, or perhaps the next. With no more explanation, he knows what she means. He can read her mind now, so many hours have they passed together in purposeless contemplation, knee to elbow, elbow to knee.

*Can you feel it lift and disappear? That standing wave of constant static. The distraction so ubiquitous you never even knew you were wrapped in it. Human certainty. The thing that blinds you to what's right here—gone.* He can—*can* feel it. The tree, like some tremendous signal beacon. The two of them, turning into something powered by the spots of speckled sun that reach them through the dozens of feet of Mimas's branches still above them.

"Let's summit," she tells him. And before he can object, he's looking up at a mud-caked gargoyle perched on a lightning-clipped spire, her legs wrapped around a pipe running all the way down to earth and her arms flung up, sieving the sky.

NICK IS DEEP in a green dream one night when a shudder rips through Mimas and rolls Nick onto the platform's edge. His arm stabs out and grabs a thin branch. He clings, looking twenty stories downward. Behind him, Olivia screams. He scrambles back to mid-platform as a bigger gust catches the tarp and lifts the whole construction, bucking it. Winds liquefy the air and hail pelts them through the needles. At a tremendous crack, Nick looks up. Thirty feet above his head, a branch thicker than his thigh tears free and crashes down in slow motion, cracking other limbs on its way down.

Furious winds cross-check Olivia into Mimas's trunk. She clutches the platform, hysterical. The trunk tips several feet off the vertical, then swings back as far the other way. Nick swings like a sliding weight on the world's tallest metronome. As sure as he knows anything, he knows he's going to die. He's clenched from jaw to toes, clamped to life with all that's left in his body. He'll let go, and the ground will solve everything.

Something screams at him through the hail. Olivia. *"Don't. Fight. Don't fight!"*

The words slap him, and he can think again. She's right: clenched, he won't last another three minutes.

*"Relax. Ride!"*

He sees her eyes, the crazed green celadon. She sways on the wild bends, limber, as if the storm is nothing. In a few beats more, he sees that it is. Nothing to a redwood. Thousands of these storms have blown through this crown, tens of thousands, and all Mimas ever had to do was give.

He surrenders to the rage as this tree has done, through a millennium of killer storms. As *sempervirens* has done for a hundred and eighty million years. Yes, a storm topped this tree, centuries ago. Yes, storms will bring down trees this size. But not tonight. Not likely. Tonight, the top of a redwood is as safe a spot in this gale as any. Just bend and ride.

A howl cuts through the hail-thickened wind. He howls back. Their shrieks turn into asylum laughter. They screech in tandem until all the world's war cries and wild calls turn into thanksgiving. Long past the hour when his clenched fists would have given out, they whoop descant to the storm.

LATE THE NEXT MORNING, three loggers appear at the foot of Mimas. "You two all right? A lot of windthrow last night. Big trees down. We were worried about you."

INCREDIBLY, the police make the video. A year ago, it would have been the kind of shaky, blurred proof the police destroyed. But the tactics of the lawless are changing. Against them, the police need new experiments. Methods that must be documented, evaluated, and refined.

The camera pans across the crowd. People spill down the street past the burnished company sign. They surround the headquarters, nestled lodge-like against a rim of spruce and fir. Not even an apprehensive cameraman can make it seem like anything but democracy in America, the right of people peaceably to assemble. The crowd stands well back from the property line, singing their songs and shaking their bedsheet banners: STOP ILLEGAL HARVESTING. NO MORE DEATH ON PUBLIC LANDS. But police wander in and out of the frame. Officers on foot and horseback. Men seated in the back of vehicles that look like armored personnel carriers.

MIMI SHAKES HER HEAD in wonder. "I didn't know this town had so many cops." Douggie limps beside her, bowlegged. "You know we don't have to do this. At least half a dozen people would be happy to stand in."

He spins to face her and almost stumbles. "What are you *talking* about?" He's like a golden retriever whacked with the rolled-up newspaper he just so proudly fetched. "Wait." He touches her shoulder, confused. "Are you scared, Meem? Because you don't have to do anything you—"

She can't bear it, his goodness. "Fine. I'm just saying don't be a hero this time."

"I wasn't being a hero *last* time. How could I know they'd melt down the old family jewels?"

She saw, the day his denim was sheared open to the breeze. The family jewels, flapping in the air, burned with chemicals. He has wanted to show her again, so often, since: the miraculous recovery—almost a resurrection, you might say. She just can't bring herself. She loves the man, maybe more than she cares for anyone but her sisters and their children. It's a constant amazement to her that a man so artless has made it to the age of forty. She can't imagine not watching out for him. But they're different species. This cause they've given themselves to—this defense of the immobile and blame-less, the fight for something better than endless suicidal appetite—is all they have in common.

They head toward the deployment vehicle, where the protest's new secret weapon, the steel-bar black bears, are being handed out. "Damn straight we're doing this, woman. What do you think? That wasn't my first Purple Heart. Or my last. Gonna end up with a whole string of them, just like an earthworm."

"Douggie. No more injuries. I can't take it today."

He points his chin toward the line of police, waiting for something to happen. "Take it up with *them*." And then, like a creature with no memory except for the sun, "Geez! Look at all these people! Is this a *movement* or what?"

THE FIRST CRIME—crossing the line onto corporate property—happens off-camera. But the lens soon finds the action. The automatic focus slurs and locks in as a few peaceful assemblers cross the parkway onto the manicured lawn. There, they stand and shout responses to the calls of the megaphone.

*A people! United! Can never be defeated!*
*A forest! Once blighted! Can never be re-seeded!*

Two officers approach the trespassers and ask them to step back. Their words are muffled on the recording, but polite enough. Soon, though, the clump turns into a rolling bait ball. People challenge and jeer—precisely the standoff the police hoped to avoid. One white-haired, hunchbacked woman shouts, "We'll respect their property when they respect ours."

The camera swings hard to the left, where a group of nine people dash across the lawn. The first altercation turns out to be a well-executed diversionary tactic to draw police away from the building's entrance. Each bee-lining figure carries a shallow, vee-bent steel tube three feet long, thick enough to insert an arm.

Then a cut. The scene shifts indoors. The activists have chained themselves into a ring around a pillar in the foyer. Curious employees pour out of the hallways. Police come from behind the cameraman, trying to manage the disintegrating situation.

THE PROTESTERS have drilled for how to deploy as fast as possible. But in the real lobby, with milling employees and pursuing police, deployment isn't pretty. The scuffle splits Mimi and Douglas. They end up across from each other in the ring. They have three seconds to lock down. Douglas sticks his left arm in the black bear and attaches the carabiner on his wrist cable to the steel post welded into the center of the tube. His companions do the same. Seconds later, the whole nine-node ring solidifies into something impervious to anything short of a diamond saw.

They sit cross-legged in a circle on the floor around a fat pillar. Douglas tilts to one side, and still can't see her. He shouts "Meem," and that round brown face he has come to associate with all the world's goodness peeks around and grins. He shoots her a thumbs-up, before remembering his thumb is inside a steel cylinder.

ONE LONG TRACKING SHOT records each close-up. A tall, gawky man with a gap between his front teeth and long bushy hair pulled back in a pony-tail starts to sing. *We shall overcome. We shall overcome.* There are snickers, at first. But by measure three the rest of the group is singing along. Five police-men tug at the demonstrators, but easy disentanglement is not an option. A uniformed man says, as if reading from a prompter: "My name is Sheriff Sanders. Your presence here is in violation of the penal code, section num-bers . . ." Shouts from the ring drown him out. He stops, closes his eyes, and starts again. "This is private property. I order you on behalf of the state of Oregon to disperse. If you do not withdraw peacefully, you will be held for unlawful assembly as well as trespass with criminal intent. Any attempt to resist arrest will be considered in violation of the penal code sections—"

The gawky, gap-toothed man shouts over him. "You should be joining us down here."

The officer recoils. Someone off-camera calls, "You're all criminals. You just want to shit on other people!"

The ring starts chanting again. More police crowd the circle's circumfer-ence. The sheriff steps forward again. His speech is slow, clear, and loud, like a grade school teacher's. "Release your hands from whatever restraints . . . from inside your tubes. If you do not release yourselves within five minutes, we intend to use pepper spray to compel you to comply."

Someone in the ring says, "You can't do that." The camera settles on a small Asian woman with round face and black bob. Off-camera the sheriff says, "We certainly can. And we will." There's shouting from the ring. The camera doesn't know where to point. The round-faced woman can be heard saying, "It's forbidden under United States law for any public official to use pepper spray unless he's in danger. Look at us! We can't even move!"

The sheriff consults his watch. "Three minutes."

Everyone talks at once. A pan across the confused lobby cuts back to frightened close-ups. There's a scuffle; a young man in the ring gets kicked in the kidney from behind. The camera swings and lands on the gap-toothed man. His ponytail whips back and forth. "She's asthmatic, man. Bad. You can't use pepper spray on an asthmatic. People die from that, man."

Someone off-camera calls, "Do what the officer says."

The gap-toothed man nods like his neck is broken. "Do it, Mimi. Unlock. *Do it.*"

The gray-haired woman shouts him down. "We all agreed to stay in this together."

The sheriff calls out, "You are in violation of the law and your actions are damaging to the community. Please vacate these premises. You have sixty seconds."

Sixty seconds pass in the same confusion. "I'm asking you again to unlock and remove your hands from those tubes and leave peacefully."

"I won an Air Force Cross for being shot down protecting this country."

"I gave the order for you to disperse over five minutes ago. You have been warned of the consequences, and you have accepted them."

"I don't accept them!"

"We will now use pepper spray and other chemical agents to get you to release your hands from your metal pipes. We will continue to apply these agents until you agree to release yourselves. Are you ready to release now, and avoid this application?"


DOUGLAS LEANS ONE WAY, then the other. He can't see her. The pole is between them, and the ring is going nuts. He yells her name and she's there, tilting her scared gaze into his. He shouts things she can't hear over all the other noise. They lock eyes for the tiniest forever. He rushes a dozen urgencies into that narrow channel. *You don't have to do this. You're worth more to me than all the forests this outfit can slaughter.*

Her look is even thicker with messages, all of which come down to the hardest of nibs: *Douglas. Douglas. What they do?*

. . .

THEY START AT THE BODY nearest the sheriff's feet—a woman in her forties, overweight, with blond-tipped hair and last year's stylish glasses. An officer comes up behind her, holding a paper cup in one hand and a Q-tip in the other. The sheriff's voice is calm. "Do not resist. Any threats toward us will be considered an assault on a police officer, which is a felony."

"We're locked up! We're locked up!"

A second officer comes alongside the one with the swab and paper cup. He reaches down and restrains the woman with one hand while tipping her head back with the other. The woman blurts, "I teach biology at Jefferson Junior High. I have given twenty years to teaching kids about—"

Someone off-camera shouts, "You're about to get schooled!"

The sheriff says, "Release yourself from the tube."

The teacher sucks in her breath. There's shouting. The officer with the swab brings it down into the woman's right eye. He struggles to get a little more into her left. Chemicals pool under the lid and stream down the side of the woman's tipped-back face. The woman's moans are pure animal. Each one rises in pitch until she's screaming. Someone shouts, "*Stop it! Now!*"

"We have water for your eyes. Release yourself and we'll give it to you. Are you going to release yourself?" The assisting officer tips her head back again, and the one with the swab spreads it into her eyes and nose. "Release yourself and we'll give you cool water to rinse with."

Someone yells, "You're killing her. She needs a doctor."

The cop with the swab waves toward his backup. "We're going to use Mace next. It's much worse."

The woman's screams collapse into bleating. She's too sunk into her pain to release. Her hands can't find the carabiner to unclick it. The two communion servers proceed clockwise to the next person in the ring—a muscular man in his early thirties who looks more like a logger than an owl-lover. He clamps down his head and clenches shut his eyes.

"Sir? Are you going to release?"

His broad, strong shoulders curl inward, but the black bears on both his arms keep him splayed. The assisting officer fights to bend back the man's head. Leverage is with the police, and when a third officer steps in to help, the neck is soon crooked. Getting the eyes open is not as clean. They work the swab into the eyelid slits while locking the great head. Concentrated pepper slops all over. A thimbleful gets up his nose, and he starts to choke. The camera slashes around the room. It hovers on the window outside, where the crowd of protesters on the lawn chants with no clue what is happening indoors. The choking sounds are broken by an officer. "Are you going to release? Sir? Sir. Can you hear me? Are you ready to let go?"

Someone yells, "Don't you have a conscience?"

Someone shrieks, "Use the bottle. Squirt their eyes."

"This is torture. In America!"

The camera turns dizzy. It bobs like a drunk.


WORDS POUR OUT of Douglas as the cops disappear behind the pillar. "She's asthmatic. You can't use pepper spray on her, man. For God's sake, it'll kill her."

He leans hard to his right, against the pinch of the black bears. He sees the officers flanking her, the uniformed man bending down from behind and taking her head in a loving embrace. Gangbanged in the eyes by three guys. The sheriff says, "Ma'am, just release your arms and you can walk away. It doesn't have to hurt." The woman past Mimi retches.

Douglas shouts Mimi's name. The officer with the swab cups her neck with one hand. "Miss? Would you like to release?"

"Please don't hurt me. I don't want to be hurt."

"Then just release."

Douglas wrenches almost double. "*Let go!*" Mimi's eyes lock onto his. They flash crazy and her nostrils quiver like a snared rabbit's. He doesn't understand the look, some kind of prediction. Her eyes say: *Whatever happens, remember what I tried to do.* The police tip back her beautiful head. Her throat opens onto a gurgled *ahhgh . . .*

Then he remembers. *He* can move. So easy: he fumbles with the clips that fasten his wrists to the black bears' center posts, and he's free. He scrambles up, howling, *"Back off!"*

It's not that things slow down. It's that his brain speeds up faster than the movements of men. He has all the minutes in the world to think, several times, *Assaulting a police officer. Felony. Ten to twelve years in prison.* The police have him cuffed and spread-eagled on the floor before he can even start to swing. Before anyone can call, *Timber.*

That night, a shaken camera operator dupes the tape and leaks a copy to the press.

DENNIS BRINGS squash soup to Patricia's cabin for lunch. "Patty? I don't know if I should even bring this up."

She head-butts his shoulder. "A little late to wonder, isn't it?"

"The injunction isn't going to hold. It's over already."

She pulls back and sobers. "What does that mean?"

"They said on the television last night. Another court decision. The Forest Service isn't bound by the temporary stay handed down in your hearing."

"Not bound."

"They're ready to approve a backlog of new harvest plans. People are going nuts all over the state. There was an action at the headquarters of a logging company. The police poured chemicals into people's eyes."

*"What?* Den, that doesn't sound right."

"They showed a clip. I couldn't watch."

"Are you sure? *Here?*"

"I saw it."

"But you just said you couldn't watch."

"I *saw* it."

His tone slaps her. They're fighting—something neither of them knows how to do. Dennis, too, ducks his head in shame. Bad dog; will do better. She takes his hand. They sit over their empty soup bowls, peering at a narrow opening in the copse of hemlocks. The questions the judge asked at the hearing come back to her. What use is wilderness? What difference will it make, once the right to unlimited prosperity turns all forests into geometric proofs? The wind blows and the hemlocks wave their feathery leading shoots. Such a graceful profile, so elegant a tree. A tree embarrassed for people, embarrassed by efficiency, injunctions. The bark gray, the branches beginner green; the needles flat along the shoots, pointing outward and on. The habit tranquil, philosophical, even, in its repose. Its cones, small, downward sleigh bells content in constant silence.

She's the guilty one, breaking that silence, when it just starts to get interesting. "In their *eyes*?"

"Pepper spray. With cotton swabs. It looked like something out of . . . not this country."

"People are so beautiful."

He turns to her, horrified. But he's a man of faith, and waits to hear whatever explanation she cares to deliver. And, *Yes*, she thinks. The thought makes her stubborn. *Yes*: *beautiful*. And doomed. Which is why she has never been able to live among them.

"Hopelessness makes them determined. Nothing's more beautiful than that."

"You think we're hopeless?"

"Den. How is extraction ever going stop? It can't even slow down. The only thing we know how to do is grow. Grow harder; grow faster. More than last year. Growth, all the way up to the cliff and over. No other possibility."

"I see."

Clearly he doesn't. But his willingness to lie for her also breaks her heart. She would tell him—how the towering, teetering pyramid of large living things is toppling down already, in slow motion, under the huge, swift kick that has dislodged the planetary system. The great cycles of air and water are breaking. The Tree of Life will fall again, collapse into a stump of invertebrates, tough ground cover, and bacteria, unless man . . . Unless man.

People are putting their bodies in the line of fire. Even here, in this land where the damage has long since been done, where this year's losses are nothing compared to those racked up in the distant south . . . people beaten and abused. People getting their eyes swabbed with pepper while she—she who knows that one trillion leaves are lost without replacement, every day—she has done nothing.

"Would you say I'm a peaceful man?"

"Oh, Den. You're almost as peaceful as a plant!"

"I feel miserable. I want to hurt those cops."

She squeezes his hand in time to the swaying hemlocks. "People. So much pain."

THEY PACK the dirty dishes into his truck for the ride back to town. She grabs him at the car door.

"I'm a rich woman, right?"

"Not rich enough to run for public office, if that's what you're thinking."

She laughs too hard for the joke, and sobers too quickly. "In situ preservation is failing. And I see now it always will." He looks at her and waits. She thinks: *If the rest of the species were as comfortable with looking and waiting as this man, we might yet be saved.* "I want to start a seed bank. There are half as many trees in the world as there were before we came down out of them."

"Because of us?"

"One percent of the world forest, every decade. An area larger than Connecticut, every year."

He nods, as if no one paying attention would be surprised.

"A third to a half of existing species may go extinct by the time I'm gone."

Her words puzzle him. She's going somewhere?

"Tens of thousands of trees we know nothing about. Species we've barely classified. Like burning down the library, art museum, pharmacy, and hall of records, all at once."

"You want to start an ark."

She smiles at the word, but shrugs. It's as good as any. "I want to start an ark."

"Where you can keep . . ." The strangeness of the idea gets him. A vault to store a few hundred million years of tinkering. Hand on the car door, he fixes on something high up in a cedar. "What . . . would you do with them? When would they ever . . . ?"

"Den, I don't know. But a seed can lie dormant for thousands of years."

THEY MEET on a hillside at evening, overlooking the sea. Father and son. It has been some time. After this hour together in a brand-new place, it will be so much longer.

*Neelay-*ji. *Is that you?*

*Pita. Here we are. It works!*

The old beggar walks up to the blue-skinned god and waves. The god stands still. *Sound is very bad, Neelay.*

*I can hear you, Dad. Not to worry. It's just you and me.*

*I can't believe it. So amazing!*

*This is nothing. Just wait.*

The blue god stumbles as he tries to walk. *Look at your costume! Look at me!*

*Hoping to make you laugh, Pita.*

Side by side, with shaky steps, they make their way along the ocean-battered cliffs. Since long before the father left for that clinic in distant Minnesota, such a walk together has been impossible. Not since the boy's early childhood have they gone out like this, chattering side by side, their words rushing to keep up with their steps.

*It's so big, Neelay.*

*There's more. Lots more.*

*And the details! How did you do it?*

*Pita, this is just the beginning, trust me.*

The blue god staggers up to the cliff's edge. *My goodness. Look down there. Waves!*

They stand at the top of a waterfall that plunges down onto the coast below. Surf-carved rocks dot the sand like fairy castles. Tidal pools shimmer beneath.

*Neelay. So beautiful. I want to see it all!* They follow the coast awhile before turning inland. *Where are we now? What is this place?*

*It's all imaginary, Pita.*

*Yes, but familiar.*

*That's good!*

The father will tell the boy's mother afterward. How he was plucked up and dropped back down in the infant world, before the rise of people. The misty air and slant, tropical light confuse him. The tan of the sand and azure sea, the dry mountains ringing them in. He squints at the vegetation, so lavish. He has never paid much attention to plants. He never had time, in his life, to learn them. And now he never will.

They walk down a path alongside trunks that open into giant gnarled parasols against the sun. *What on Earth, Neelay? Your sci-fi?* As if his son's pulp magazines still gather dust balls in stacks under the boyhood bed.

*No, Pita. Earth. Dragon blood trees.*

*They're real? Trees like that, in our world?*

The beggar smiles and points. *Everything based on a true story!*

It dawns on the blue god: the fish in these seas, the birds in the air, and all that creeps on this made Earth is just a crude start for some future refuge, saved from the vanishing original. He walks up close to one of the monster toadstools. *What can the players do with this place?*

The words spill out of the beggar unplanned. *What do you want it to do, Dad?*

*Ach, Neelay. I remember. Good answer!*

The beggar describes just how large the sandbox is. A person can gather herbs, hunt animals, plant crops, cut trees and fashion boards, dig deep mines for minerals and ore, trade and negotiate, build cabins and town halls and cathedrals and world wonders. . . .

They walk again. The climate changes to something lusher. Beasts prowl in the undergrowth. Above them, flocks wheel. *When do people start to arrive?*

*End of next month.*

*I see. Soon!*

*You'll still be here, Dad.*

*Yes, of course, Neelay. How do I nod, again?* The blue god learns to nod. So much new to learn. *What happens then?*

*Then we get flooded. Five hundred thousand have signed up already. Twenty dollars a month. We're planning for a few million.*

*I'm glad to see it like this. Before.*

*Yes. Just the two of us!*

The novice Vishnu stumbles up the trail. They have mountains to cross now. Vine-covered canyons. The god stands for a moment, awed by his surroundings. Then he wanders down the forest path again.

*Only a quarter century, Dad. Since we wrote that "Hello World" program. And the curve is still heading straight upwards.*

From two thousand miles apart, for a few trillion cycles of the processor's clock—a processor descended from the one the blue-skinned god helped build—father and son look across the mountains together and into the future. This land of animated wishes will expand without limits. It will fill with richer, wilder, more surprising life beyond life. The map will grow as full as the thing it stands for. And still people will be hungry and alone.

They walk along magnificent crests. Far below, a wide, old river meanders through a jungle dense with many greens. The blue god stands and looks. All his life, he has been homesick. Yearning drove him from a village in Gujarat to the Golden State. He has had no country, except for work and family. And all his life he has thought: *It's only me.* Now he looks down on the snaking river. Millions will pay a monthly rent to come here. And he'll be gone.

*Where are we now, Neelay-ji?*

*It doesn't work like that, Dad. All brand-new.*

*Yes. No. I understand. But these plants and animals. We've walked from Africa into Asia?*

*Follow me. I'll show you something.* The beggar leads them down a switchback into the thickening jungle. They enter a maze of twisty trails, all alike. Creatures dart through the undergrowth.

*Neem trees, Neelay. Magic!*

*Wait. There's more.*

The jungle thickens and the trail thins. Shapes play in the fronds and creeping vines. Then the father sees it, hidden in the foliage of this sprawling simulation: a ruined temple, swallowed by a single fig.

*Oh, my prince. You've really made something.*

*Not just me. Hundreds of people. Thousands, really. I don't even know their names. You're in here, too. The work you did. . . .* The beggar turns. He waves at the roots that snake across the ancient stones, looking for cracks to slither into and sip from. He raises the tip of his gnarled pinkie. *You see, Pita? All from out of a seed this big. . . .*

Vishnu wants to ask: *How do I make my eyes water?* Instead, he says, *Thank you, Neelay. I should go now.*

*Yes, Dad. I'll see you soon.* It's a harmless enough lie. In this world, the beggar has just walked across half a continent. But in the other, he's too frail and wasted to risk an airplane. And the blue god, who has just crossed a jagged mountain range in bare feet: in the world above, his body is so riddled with rogue programs and syntax errors he won't make it to this world's opening day.

His puppet body nods and his palms join together. *Thank you for this walk, dear Neelay. We'll be home soon.*

FROM ENLIGHTENMENT to the dam burst in Ray Brinkman's brain takes thirteen seconds.

The bedroom television blares the nightly news. Israeli forces are plowing up Palestinian olive groves. Beneath the quilt, Ray squeezes the remote, boosting the sound enough to drown out thoughts. Dorothy's in the bathroom, prepping for bed. Her nightly ritual graduates from one noise to another: blow-dryer becoming electric toothbrush becoming water coursing into the ceramic basin. Each sound says *night* to him, the way wolves must have, once, or the calls of a loon. And like the calls of those animals, these sounds, too, will soon disappear.

She takes forever—and for what? After this night's catastrophe ... Which, of all these preparations, couldn't she do to more purpose in the morning? She'll be clean for sleep and ready for anything night might bring, though night can bring no worse nightmare than day already has.

Nothing makes sense to him. After this evening, it's unthinkable that she'll climb back into the bed of their last dozen years. But it's even more unthinkable that she'll sleep down the hall, that room she once, so many years ago, dreamed of converting into a nursery. He'll destroy this bed. Chop the carved oak headboard up for firewood. The newscaster says, "Meanwhile, other trees in schoolyards all over Canada are being cut down to protect the lives of children after ..."

Ray regards the screen but can't make out what he's seeing. That happens in seconds one through three. He thinks, with what is still coherent thought: *I've been a man who happily confuses the agreed-on for the actual. A man who has never doubted that life has a meaningful future. Now that's done.*

These thoughts take less than another quarter second. His eyes shut a moment, and he's auditioning. Their first date. The witches tell him to take no care for tomorrow. He's beyond all harm until the forest gets up and walks for miles, until the woods climb up the side of a faraway hill. He's safe, safe from now on, for who can impress the forest or bid the tree unfix his earthbound root? *Our high-placed Macbeth shall live the lease of nature.* But he was given another part. The man, not of woman born, who makes the woods move.

Ray's eyelids close for half a second. On the insides of those living screens he watches the two of them sleep together, the night of their first venture into amateur theater. All our yesterdays, over and over. The baby Lady Macbeth, no more than twenty-four, fretful in the foyer of adulthood. His high-strung friend, alongside him in the dark, barraging him with an anxious job interview: *How do you feel about your parents? Have you ever had racist thoughts? Did you ever shoplift?* Even then, on night one, he saw how they would take care of each other into old age. The two of them, following a design laid out long in advance that promised to explain itself in the run of time. Forever. And forever. And forever.

The prophecy was a trick. He must pick himself up and live. But how? Why? The news cuts to a wild scene. Ray watches in a fog: people locked down, and police culling them. The stream of water in the bathroom stops. These are seconds six and seven.

Every belonging turns into theft. That's what his wife told him, just an hour ago: *You think this will all blow over and I'll come to my senses? That I'll turn back into your quirky little Dot?*

He tried to say that he's known for months. For a year and more. That he's still here. Still her husband. Come and go. Be with whoever. Do anything. Just stay near.

Worse than theft. Murder. *You're killing me, Ray.*

He tried to remind her: Something between them has yet to happen. A reason why they must stay together. He has seen it already, a premonition that has kept him going, all these months of holding still. Some purpose to their union that already always existed. They belong.

*No one belongs to anyone, Ray. You need to set me free.*

Something is happening in the bathroom, an everything that sounds like nothing. Two seconds of silence, and he's terrified. Nothing makes sense. There's nothing to take care of. He looks back at the television. People are taking it in the eyes, for nothing. For no use at all.

In seconds nine and ten, his brain turns into a circuit court. It fills with a thought that he first had months ago, reading one night, while his lawful wife was off getting her brains fucked out in would-be secrecy. A thought he has stolen from someone else's copyrighted book, one that he must now pay for. Time alters what can be owned, and who may do the owning. Humankind is utterly wrong about the neighbors, and no one can see it. We must repay the world for every idea, every *thing* we have ever stolen.

The people on the screen begin to scream. Or maybe the sound comes from him, watching himself turn brown and fall. She's in the doorway, shouting his name. His lips move, but they make no sound.

*It's like I had the word "book," and then you put one in my hands.*

He slides from the bed onto the pine floorboards. His eyes land flush up against the whirlpool grain. A thing in his brain breaks, and everything that was once as safe as houses collapses like an over-dug mine. Blood floods his cortex, and he owns nothing. Nothing at all, but this.

A MAN STANDS by her desk in a taupe serge suit when Mimi arrives at seven-thirty on Monday morning. She knows, at a glance, who the stranger is. "Miss Ma?"

Flattened cardboard boxes lean against her desk. He has been here for some time. His job depends on getting there first, to ensure there will be no problems. Her computer has already been unplugged, and all the cables wound up in neat spools on top of the CPU. The files are long gone, removed while she was having coffee and bagel a mile away.

"My name is Brendan Smith. I'm here to assist your transition from the company."

She has known this would happen, for days now. She's been all over the news, criminal trespass. While her fellow engineers might overlook that error—the species is plagued by countless design flaws, after all—she's also guilty of fighting against progress, freedom, and wealth. The race's birth-right. That's not something her profession will ever forgive.

She stares at her professional ejector until he looks away. "Garreth thinks I'm going to trash the place? Steal some international ceramic molding secrets?"

The man assembles a carton. "We have twenty minutes to fill these. Personal items only. I'll inventory everything you want to take, and we'll get it approved before you sign out."

"Sign out? *Sign out?*" Rage comes up her throat, the rage that this private escort firm has been hired to nullify. She turns and heads toward the door. Taupe Boy stops her, just short of force.

"Once you leave the office, we will consider it sealed."

She wavers and sits at her desk. Not her desk. Her brain feels maced. How dare they? How dare anyone? *I'll sue for everything they're worth.* But all the rights and privileges of fair practice are theirs. Humankind is a thug. The law is a goon. Her colleagues pass her door, slowing just enough to catch a glimpse of the drama before slinking away in embarrassment.

She puts her books into a box her minder has made for her. Then her notebooks.

"No notes. The notebooks are company property."

She fights the urge to hurl the stapler. She wraps her pictures in the paper her minder gives her and boxes them. Carmen and her Kentucky Mountain saddle horse. Amelia and kids, in the swimming pool in Tucson. Her father, standing in a stream in Yellowstone. Her grandparents in Shanghai, in their Sunday finest, holding up the photo of American girls they would never meet.

Logic puzzles made of bent nails. Framed funny sayings: *Reactions speak louder than words. Some see the glass as half empty, some as half full; an engineer sees a containment device twice as big as it needs to be.*

"Are you finished?" her personal early retirement officer says.

A suitcase covered in pennants. A steamer trunk stenciled with a foreign name.

"Your keys." She shakes her head, then hands over her corporate keys. He checks them off on a list that he makes her sign. "Please follow me." He takes the boxes. She grabs the suitcase and steamer trunk. In the hallway, curious colleagues skitter away. He sets his boxes down and locks the door. The moment the lock clicks, she remembers.

"Shit. Open back up."

"The office has been sealed."

"*Open* it."

He does. She reenters the room, goes to one wall, and gets up on a chair. She removes, foot by foot, the twelve-hundred-year-old scroll of arhats on the threshold of Enlightenment, rolls it up, and pockets it. Then she follows her escort to the front entrance, past the staff who greeted her warmly for years and who now attend to their pressing work. As she shuttles her accumulated professional life to the parking lot, the man posts himself at the firm's door, like the angel at Eden's east gate who kept the humans, poachers of one forbidden tree, from breaking back into the garden and eating the other fruit that would have solved everything.

THE ONLY ANIMALS that know they're hosed: *That*, Douggie keeps saying—near midnight, over blaring headbanger anthems in a roadhouse full of off-duty militia and other armed patriots—*that's where all the trouble starts.*

"I mean, how does knowing you're going to die give you a leg up? Smart enough to see you're a sack of rotting meat wrapped around a little sewage tube that's going to give out in—what? Another few thousand sunrises?"

His fellow philosopher seated next to him at the satinwood bar replies, "Could you shut the hell up for a second?"

"Now, a tree. Those guys know things on a scale and time frame we can't even—"

A fist flings out and meets him in the cheekbone, so fast it's like Douglas is frozen in place. He hits the fir floorboards headfirst and is out so fast he doesn't even hear the man stand over him and deliver the eulogy. "I'm sorry. But you were warned."

When he comes to, his pal Spinoza is long gone. He daubs at his head and face with tentative fingertips. Nothing's missing, but there's a mushiness that doesn't feel quite right. Stars and lights, dark clouds and pain, though he has lived through worse. He lets the concerned waitress help him to his feet before shaking free. "People are not what they seem." This time no one voices any opposition.

He sits in his vehicle in the roadhouse parking lot, working his unplanned plan. He has, to the best of his knowledge, no one to go to for aid and comfort except his partner in world salvation, the woman who has joined him to a cause bigger than mere doomed Pavlicek-ism. She alone knows how to take him and give him purpose in this life. It's pushing a boundary, to drop in on Mimi at this hour. Though she has never expressly forbidden him to come over at night, she's not going to be thrilled. Still, she'll know what to do about that mess, his face.

She told him once, when they were chained together for tedious hours across a stretch of road that, it turned out, even the lumber companies weren't all that interested in, about her great and youthful loves. Both sexes, no less. That disclosure, plus a feather, could have knocked him out. He's down with whoever she might want to be. The world depends on so many different species, each a nutty experiment. He just wishes she'd let him into the inner sanctum sometime, trusted confidant, her manservant or something. Wishes she and whoever may be her life's current answer might let him watch— watch over them, a sentry against the malevolent world.

He struggles to fit the key in the ignition. He's probably not to be trusted with heavy machinery. But his cheek is loose and something's oozing out the side of his eye. Nowhere else to turn, really. He noses out of the lot and back up the valley highway, toward town, and love.

He doesn't see the truck pulled over on the shoulder outside the bar. Doesn't see it edge onto the asphalt behind him. Sees nothing until two white eyes fill his rearview mirror and the beast smacks his rear bumper. He shudders forward, fishtailing. The truck looms up and rams him again. He can't brake, can't even think. The road dips. He gooses the pedal, but the truck stays with him. At the hill's bottom, he skims over a railroad crossing, catching air.

A crossroad swims toward him. He power-skids into a sudden right, at twice the speed of a controlled turn. In slow-mo slalom, his rear swings clean around, 270 clockwise. By the time he comes to rest, he's in the intersection, perpendicular, as the empty logging truck slams down the highway, the driver laying into its horn, a long blast goodbye.

Douglas idles in the intersection, freaking. The attack putties him worse than anything the police have done. Worse than when his plane went down. That was just God, at His usual roulette. This is a crazy man, with a plan.

He carries on down the crossroad the long way back to town. He can't keep off the rearview mirror, where he expects the twin white beams to swim up again at any moment. But he makes it all the way to Mimi's condo without further incident. The light is still on at her place. When she opens the door, it's obvious she's drunk. Behind her, the room is trashed. A scroll unrolls across the living room floor.

She wobbles and slurs, "What happened?"

He touches his face in surprise. Forgot all about that. Before he can answer, she pulls him inside. And that's how the trees bring them home at last.

ADAM APPICH puts his right foot into an imaginary niche and steps up. Slides the rope's slipknot, steps again with his left. Fights to forget how many vaporous steps he has already taken. Tells himself: *I used to climb trees all the time.* But Adam isn't climbing a tree. He's climbing the air, on a rope as thin as a pencil, dangling from a trunk so wide he can't see both edges at once. The furrows in its foot-thick bark are deeper than his hand. Above him, a long brown road vanishes into cloud. The rope starts to spin.

A voice from on high says, "Wait. Don't fight."

"I can't do this."

"You can. You *will*, sir."

His throat fills with reflux and dread. Foot by foot, he closes the impossible gap. Near the top, he dares to look up. Two arboreal creatures speak soft encouragements he neither hears nor believes. He reaches something solid, still breathing. Not well, but breath.

"See?" The woman's radiant face makes him wonder if he didn't die somewhere on the way up. The man—clotted skin and Old Testament beard—hands him a cup of water. Adam drinks. He's a while believing he'll be okay. The platform under him tips in the wind. The tree couple hover, offering him berries.

"I'm good." Then, "I suppose that would have been more convincing if I'd said it five minutes ago."

The woman called Maidenhair scampers up a limb to the makeshift pantry, looking for a tea that she claims will help his vertigo. She's attached to nothing. Barefoot, twenty stories up. He buries his face in the needle-stuffed pillow.

When he's able, Adam looks down. Patchwork slop spreads through the forest below. He has passed through the massacre up close, smuggled in by the messenger Loki. But this bird's-eye view is worse. The longest, most resolute tree-sit in the area—manned by the ideal subjects for his study of misguided idealism—is the last large remnant spared by the harvest. Scattered stands dot the bald patches, like the tufts missed by a teenage shaver. Fresh stumps everywhere, slag and burnt slash, refuse sprinkled with sawdust, the occasional trunks left in ravines too steep to bother with. And a clump circling the great tree that these sitters call by name.

The man, Watchman, points out the landmarks. "All that loosened topsoil is washing down this face into the Eel. Killing fish all the way to the ocean. Hard to remember, but when we came, ten months ago, everything was green as far as you could see. So much for trying to slow things down."

Adam is no clinician, and 250 interviews of activists along the Lost Coast have left him gun-shy about diagnoses. But Watchman is either deeply depressed or a born-again realist.

A flare-up far below, the hornet buzz of heavy machinery, and Watchman bends to look. "There." Yellow brighter than a banana slug, crisscrossing a half a mile away in the dissolving forest.

"What do we have?" Maidenhair asks.

"Skyline yarder. A couple of grappler Cats. We could be sealed off by tomorrow." He looks at Adam. "You may want to ask whatever you want to ask, then head back down tonight."

"Or join us," Maidenhair says. "We'll put you up in the guest room."

Adam can't answer. His head is still crushing him. Breathing makes him ill. He just wants to be back in Santa Cruz, analyzing the data from his questionnaires and drawing dubious conclusions from ironclad statistics.

"You're more than welcome," the woman tells him. "After all, we only volunteered for a few days, and here we are, almost a year later."

Watchman smiles. "There's a beautiful line of Muir's. 'I only went out for a walk . . .'"

The contents of Adam's guts spill through the air, two hundred feet down to Earth.


THE SUBJECTS sit on the platform, gazing at the questionnaire and the pencils Adam gives them. Their hands are stained brown and green, with crusts of duff under their nails. They smell ripe and musty as redwood. The examiner has gotten himself above them in the lookout hammock, which won't stop rocking. He studies their faces for the strains of paranoid salvationism he has seen in so many of the activists he has already interviewed. The man—capacious yet fatalistic. The woman—self-possessed in a way that no one getting hammered so badly has a right to be.

Maidenhair asks, "This is for your doctoral research?"

"It is."

"What's your hypothesis?"

Adam has been interviewing for so long the word sounds alien. "Anything I say might affect your answers."

"You have a theory about people who . . . ?"

"No. No theories yet. I'm just gathering data."

Watchman laughs, a brittle monosyllable. "That's not how it works, is it?"

"How what works?"

"The scientific method. You can't gather data without a guiding theory."

"As I've told you. I'm studying the personality profiles of environmental activists."

"Pathological conviction?" Watchman asks.

"Not at all. I just . . . I want to learn something about people who . . . people who believe that . . ."

"That plants are persons, too?"

Adam laughs, and wishes he hadn't. It's the altitude. "Yes."

"You're hoping that by adding up all these scores and doing some kind of regression analysis—"

The woman fingers her partner's ankle. He hushes at once in a way that answers one of the two questions Adam wants to sneak into his questionnaire. The other question is how they shit in front of each other, seventy yards in the air.

Maidenhair's smile makes Adam feel fraudulent. She's years younger than he is, but decades more certain. "You're studying what makes some people take the living world seriously when the only real thing for everyone else is other people. You should be studying everyone who thinks that only people matter."

Watchman laughs. "Talk about pathological."

For an instant, above them, the sun pauses. Then it starts its slow drop westward, back into the waiting ocean. Noon light washes the landscape in gilt and watercolor. California, American Eden. These last pocket relics of Jurassic forest, a world like nothing else on Earth. Maidenhair flips through the booklet of questions, though Adam has asked her not to look ahead. She shakes her head at some naïveté on page three. "None of this is going to tell you anything important. If you want to know us, we should just talk."

"Well." The hammock is making Adam seasick. He can't look anywhere but at the forty-nine-square-foot country below him. "The problem is—"

"He needs data. Simple quantities." Watchman waves southwest, the saw-whine song of progress. "Complete this analogy: questionnaires are to complex personalities as skyline yarders are to . . ."

The woman stands with such spring Adam is sure she'll pitch over the edge. She leans over one side, while Watchman tips back to compensate.

Neither is conscious of their mixed-doubles maneuver. Maidenhair turns to Adam. He waits for her to plunge like Icarus. "I was about three credit hours short of a degree in actuarial science. Do you know what actuarial science is?"

"I . . . Is this a trick question?"

"It's the science of replacing an entire human life with its cash value."

Adam exhales. "Could you, you know, sit down or something?"

"There's no wind at all! But fine. If I can ask you one thing."

"Okay. Just, please . . ."

"What can you learn about us through an exam that you can't learn by looking us in the eye and asking?"

"I want to know. . . ." It'll ruin the questionnaire. He'll cue them in ways that will invalidate any answers they might give. But somehow, atop this thousand-year-old beanstalk, he no longer cares. He wants to talk, a thing he hasn't wanted to do for a while. "A lot of evidence suggests that group loyalty interferes with reason."

Maidenhair and Watchman trade smirks, like he's just told them that science has proven that the atmosphere is mostly air.

"People *make* reality. Hydroelectric dams. Undersea tunnels. Supersonic transport. Tough to stand against that."

Watchman smiles, tired. "We don't make reality. We just evade it. So far. By looting natural capital and hiding the costs. But the bill is coming, and we won't be able to pay."

Adam can't decide whether to smile or nod. He knows only that these people—the tiny few immune to consensual reality—have a secret he needs to understand.

Maidenhair inspects Adam, as through a lab's two-way mirror. "Can I ask you something else?"

"Anything you want."

"It's a simple question. How long do you think we have?"

He doesn't understand. He looks to Watchman, but the man, too, is waiting for his answer. "I don't know."

"In your heart of hearts. How long, before we pull the place down around us?"

Her words embarrass Adam. It's a question for undergrad dorms. For barrooms late on a Saturday night. He has let the situation get away from him, and none of this—the trespass through private land, the ascent, this fuzzy conversation—can be worth the two extra data points. He looks away, out on the ravaged redwoods. "Really. I don't know."

"Do you believe human beings are using resources faster than the world can replace them?"

The question seems so far beyond calculation it's meaningless. Then some small jam in him dislodges, and it's like an unblinding. "Yes."

"Thank you!" She's pleased with her overgrown pupil. He grins back. Maidenhair's head bobs forward and her eyebrows flare. "And would you say that the rate is falling or rising?"

He has seen the graphs. Everyone has. Ignition has only just started.

"It's so simple," she says. "So obvious. Exponential growth inside a finite system leads to collapse. But people don't see it. So *the authority of people is bankrupt*." Maidenhair fixes him with a look between interest and pity. Adam just wants the cradle to stop rocking. "Is the house on fire?"

A shrug. A sideways pull of the lips. "Yes."

"And you want to observe the handful of people who're screaming, *Put it out*, when everyone else is happy watching things burn."

A minute ago, this woman was the subject of Adam's observational study. Now he wants to confide in her. "It has a name. We call it the bystander effect. I once let my professor die because no one else in the lecture hall stood up. The larger the group . . ."

". . . the harder it is to cry, *Fire?*"

"Because if there were a real problem, surely someone—"

"—lots of people would already have—"

"—with six billion other—"

"Six? Try seven. Fifteen, in a few years. We'll soon be eating two-thirds of the planet's net productivity. Demand for wood has tripled in our lifetime."

"Can't tap the brakes when you're about to hit the wall."

"Easier to poke your eyes out."

The distant snarl breaks off, audible again in silence. The entire study begins to seem to Adam like a distraction. He needs to study illness on an unimaginable scale, an illness no bystander could even see to recognize.

Maidenhair breaks the silence. "We aren't alone. Others are trying to reach us. I can *hear* them."

From Adam's neck down to the small of his back, hairs rise. He's huge with fur. But the signal is invisible, lost in evolution. "Hear who?"

"I don't know. The trees. The life force."

"You mean, talking? Out loud?"

She strokes a bough as if it's a pet. "Not out loud. More like a Greek chorus in my head." She looks at Adam, her face as clear as if she just asked him to stay for dinner. "I died. I was electrocuted in my bed. My heart stopped. I came back and started hearing them."

Adam turns to Watchman for a sanity check. But the bearded prophet only arches his brows.

Maidenhair taps the questionnaire. "I suppose you have your answer now. About the psychology of world-savers?"

Watchman touches her shoulder. "What's crazier—plants speaking, or humans listening?"

Adam doesn't hear. He's just now tuning in to something that has long been hiding in plain sight. He says, to no one, "I talk out loud sometimes. To my sister. She disappeared when I was little."

"Well, okay, then. Can we study you?"

A truth bends near him, one that his discipline will never find. Consciousness itself is a flavor of madness, set against the thoughts of the green world. Adam puts out his hands to steady himself and touches only a swaying twig. Held high up above the vanishingly distant surface by a creature who should want him dead. His brain spins. The tree has drugged him. He's twirling again by a cord the width of a vine. He fixes on the woman's face as if some last desperate act of personality-reading might still protect him. "What . . . ? What are they saying? The trees?"

She tries to tell him.

.  .  .

AS THEY TALK, the war moves up the nearest drainage. The force of each new fall shatters Adam, even as it tears swaths through the remaining giants. He never imagined the violence, like a skyscraper coming down. Needle and pulverized wood cloud the air. "The fall zones are the killers," Maidenhair says. "They bulldoze the hell out of each landing strip, so the trees won't shatter when they drop. It murders the soil."

A tree as thick as Adam is tall rips away and smashes down the slope below. The earth at the place of impact liquefies.


IN LATE AFTERNOON, they spot Loki at some distance, coming through the gutted forest, right on time to escort the psychologist back through Humboldt's blockade. But something in his forward stumble says the mission has changed. At the base of the tree, he calls for them to drop the rope and harness.

"What's wrong?" Watchman asks.

"I'll tell you up there."

They make room for him in the crowded nest. He's pale and breathing hard, but not from the climb. "It's Mother N and Moses."

"Roughed up again?"

"Dead."

Maidenhair cries out.

"Someone bombed the office. They were inside, writing a speech for the Board of Forestry action. The police are saying they blew themselves up with stockpiled explosives. Accusing the LDF of domestic terrorism."

"No," Maidenhair says. "No. Please not this."

There's a long silence that isn't silent. Watchman speaks. "Mother N, a terrorist! She wouldn't even let me spike a tree. She told me, 'It might hurt the guy with the saw.'"

.  .  .

THEY TELL STORIES about the dead. How Mother N trained them. How Moses asked them to sit in Mimas. Memorial service, at two hundred feet. Adam recalls something he learned in graduate school: memory is always a collaboration in progress.

Loki descends, anxious to return to the mourners on the ground. "Nothing we can do. But at least we can do it together. You coming?" he asks Adam.

"You're welcome to stay," Maidenhair says.

The investigator lies in his swaying hammock, afraid to move a finger. "I'd like to see the darkness from up here."



TONIGHT, the dark is ample and well worth seeing. Smelling, too: the stink of spores and rotting plants, of mosses creeping over all things, soil being made, even here, so many stories above the Earth. Maidenhair cooks white beans over the burner. It's the finest meal Adam has tasted since coming into the field. The altitude doesn't bother him as much, now that he can't see the ground.

Flying squirrels show up to inspect the newcomer. He's content, a stylite perched on top of the night sky. Watchman sketches by candlelight into a pocket notebook. At intervals he shows the sketches to Maidenhair. "Oh, yes. That's them, exactly!"

Sounds at all distances, a thousand volumes, mezzo and softer. There's a bird Adam can't name, beating its wings on the blackness. Sharp scolds of invisible mammals. The wood of this high house, creaking. A branch falling to the ground. Another. A fly, walking across the hairs of his ear. His own breath echoing inside his collar. The breath of two others, absurdly close in this cloud village, holding their silent service. It surprises Adam, the proximity of coziness to terror. The woman clings to the artist, who works to use the last bit of candlelight. A patch of shoulder flesh catches the glow, naked and beautiful. It looks to be furred, feathered somehow. Then the inky script resolves into five distinct words.

· · ·

THEY WAKE to snarls nearer by. Men prowl the ground beneath them and farther out through heaps of wasted log, linking up their efforts via walkie-talkie.

"Hey," Maidenhair yells down. "What's happening?"

A logger looks up. "You better get the hell out. Shit's coming your way!"

"What shit?"

Static bursts through the walkie-talkie. The air tightens and hums. Even the daylight begins to vibrate. A *pocking* sound lifts over the horizon. "They aren't," Watchman says. "They *can't.*"

A helicopter comes across the nearby rise. A toy at first, but half a minute more and the whole tree pounds like a tom-tom. The beast banks. Adam clings to his swaying hammock. A blast of air blows his whispered profanity back in his face as the maddened hornet rears up and strikes.

Wind slams the tree, a manic updraft, then its inversion. Tops of redwoods turn to rubber, and branches slash through the canopy. Watchman scrambles up into the storage roost to get the video camera, while Maidenhair grabs a broken branch the size of a baseball bat. She climbs out on the limb closest to the assault. Adam screams, "Get back!" His words are minced to motes in the rotors.

The woman locks bare feet onto the limb, which, massive as it is, flaps like rubber in this inside-out typhoon. The chopper tips and flares, and she's face-to-face with the machine. It noses at her; she swings her branch with one wild hand. Watchman comes behind her, filming.

The chopper is big, with a bay like a bungalow. Big enough to hoist a tree older than America straight into the sky and haul it upright across the landscape. Its blades froth the air around the dangling girl. Two humans sit inside the fiberglass pod, cloaked in visors and chin-cupping helmets, chatting on tiny boom mics with some distant mission command.

Adam stares at the trick of blockbuster back projection. He has never been so close to a thing so huge and malevolent. He sees its million parts—shafts, cams, blades, plates, things for which he doesn't even have a name—beyond the power of any human to assemble, let alone design. Yet there must be thousands of such craft, employed by industries on every continent. Tens of thousands more, armed and armored, in the globe's many arsenals. World's most common raptor.

Branches snap off and the air fills with chaff. Burnt fossil steams from the beast, stinking like a burning oil rig. The stench gags Adam. The roar pierces his eardrums, killing all thought. The woman flaps on her branch like a pennant, then drops her weapon and holds on. Her filming partner loses his grip in the artificial gale, and the camera, too, drops two hundred feet and plinks apart. A metallic voice, massively amplified, comes out of the helicopter. *Exit the tree, immediately.*

The woman starts to shake. She can't hold long. Mimas shudders. Against all judgment, Adam looks down. Bulldozers the color of bile are ramming the tree's base. Men, saws, and machines prepare a fall bed right up to the edge of Mimas's burls. He looks to Watchman, who points down at another crew, working the base of a redwood two hundred feet away. They mean to drop it next to Mimas. Maidenhair swings her leg back up and over the branch that bucks her. The chopper blares, *Descend now!*

Adam screams and waves his arms. He yells things that even he can't hear above the insanity. "Stop. Back the fuck off!" He won't be a bystander to this death.

The helicopter holds and then banks away. A voice comes from its speaker: *You're done?*

"Yes," Adam screams.

The syllable wakes Watchman from a trance. He looks toward Maidenhair, who clings to her branch, sobbing. No path is left but sanity. Watchman tips his head, and the occupation is over. Below, the fall-bed foreman confers by walkie-talkie with his invisible network. Another burst from the helicopter: *Descent confirmed. Leave now.* The flying thing rears in the air and spins away. Winds abate. Deafening noise dies back, leaving nothing but peace and defeat.

They drop by harness: the terrified psychologist, the stoic artist, then the prophetess, whose face, as she slips down the two hundred feet of rope, is befuddled. They're taken into custody and led down the scarred hillside to the logging road, which has crept within a few hundred yards of Mimas's base. They sit in the mud and wait hours for the police. Then brusque officers tuck them, three abreast, into the back of a squad car.

The logging road hairpins down the ravine. Three prisoners glance back up the denuded ridge at the outline of that great tree, half as old as Christianity. A voice lower than the pounding of the helicopter says something none of them hears, not even Maidenhair.

WHILE THE PRISONERS are being held, Patricia Westerford opens negotiations with a consortium of four universities to establish the Global Seedbed Germplasm Vault. A few filed papers and Seedbed becomes a legal person.

"It's time," Dr. Westerford tells her various audiences, from whom she must raise the funds for climate control, high-tech vaults, and trained staff, "well *past* time, for us to preserve those tens of thousands of tree species that will vanish in our lifetimes." She gets to the point where such sentences roll off her lips. In two months, she'll head south, for a first exploratory visit to the Amazon basin. One thousand more square miles of forest will vanish before she gets there. Dennis will have lunch waiting for her when she returns.

WHILE THE PRISONERS mimic sleep, Neelay Mehta enjoys the prime hours of creation. From his office bed, he issues a directive to Sempervirens's elves regarding the nature of *Mastery 8*:

> *What will keep several million players unable to sign off?*
> *The place must be fuller and more promising than the*
> *lives they return to, offline. . . . Imagine millions of users*

*enriching the world together with their every action. Help*
*them build a culture so beautiful it would break their hearts*
*to lose.*

HALFWAY ACROSS THE COUNTRY, another woman starts a jail term all her own. The flooding in her husband's brain floods her as well. She calls 911. She rides along in the ambulance through the warm night. At the hospital she signs the informed consent, though she'll never feel informed again. She goes in to the man after the first operation. What's left of Ray Brinkman lies slack in the adjustable bed. Half his skull has been removed and his brain has been papered back over by a flap of scalp. Hoses spring from him. His face is frozen in terror.

No one can tell Dorothy Cazaly Brinkman how long he might be like this. A week. Another half century. Thoughts go through her head those first nights, during her ER vigil. Terrible things. She'll stay until he's stabilized. After that, she must save herself.

Again and again she hears the words she shouted at him, just hours before his brain caved in. *It's over, Ray. It's over. The two of us are over. You aren't my responsibility. We don't belong to each other, and we never did.*

IN JAIL, fitful in his upper bunk, Adam sees great redwoods explode like rockets on their launchpads. His research is intact—all the precious questionnaire data gathered over months—but he is not. He has begun to see certain things about faith and law that hid themselves behind the expanse of common sense. Jail without arraignment helps his eyesight.

"You see their game," Watchman tells him. "They don't want the cost or publicity of putting us on trial. They just use the legal system to hurt us as much as they can."

"Isn't there a law . . . ?"

"There is. They're breaking it. They can hold us seventy-two hours without charging. That was yesterday."

It occurs to Adam where the word *radical* came from. *Radix. Wrad. Root.* The plant's, the planet's, brain.

ON HIS FOURTH NIGHT in the cell, Nick dreams about the Hoel family chestnut. He watches it, sped up thirty-two million times, reveal again its invisible plan. He remembers, in his sleep, on the cot's thin mattress, the way the time-lapse tree waved its swelling arms. The way those arms tested, explored, aligned in the light, writing messages in the air. In that dream, the trees laugh at them. *Save us? What a human thing to do.* Even the laugh takes years.

WHILE NICK DREAMS, so does the forest—all nine hundred kinds that humans have identified. Four billion hectares, from boreal to tropic—the Earth's chief way of being. And as the world forest dreams, people converge in the public woods one state north. Four months earlier, arson blackened ten thousand acres in a place called Deep Creek—one of the year's many fires of convenience. The burn prompts the Forest Service to salvage-sell the lightly damaged standing timber. The arsonist is never found. No one wants to find him. No one, that is, except for a few hundred of the forest's owners, who converge on the sold-off groves bearing signs. Mimi holds one reading NOT ONE BLACKENED STICK. Douglas's reads SAY IT AIN'T SO, SMOKEY.

ADAM, NICK, AND OLIVIA are held without arraignment two days longer than is legal. They're threatened with a dozen charges, only to have everything dropped overnight. The men meet Maidenhair at her release. They see her through the chicken-wire window, walking down the women's wing with a little hobo's ball of her stuff in her hands. Then she's on them, embracing. She steps back and narrows her fire-green eyes. "I want to see it."

They take Adam's car, which seems to him now like it belongs to someone else. The loggers are gone; there's nothing left to cut. They've long since headed to fresh groves. The absence is obvious from half a mile away. Where once there was a green weave of textures you could study all day, there's only blue. The tree that promised her that no one would be harmed is gone.

*Now*, Adam thinks. *Now she'll decompensate. Begin to rage.*

At the base, her hand stretches out, touching some final proof, amazed. "Look at that! Even the stump is taller than me."

She touches the edge of the wondrous cut and breaks down sobbing. Nick stumbles toward her, but she holds him off. Adam must watch every awful spasm. There are consolations that the strongest human love is powerless to give.

"WHERE WILL YOU GO?" Adam asks, over eggs in a breakfast roadhouse.

Maidenhair gazes out the plate glass, where California sycamores run along the sidewalk by the curb. Watchman follows her glance. *These, too, raking their fingers in the air. Waving and swelling like a gospel choir.*

"We're heading north," she answers. "Something's happening up in Oregon."

"Resistance communities," Watchman says. "All over the place. They can use us up there."

Adam nods. Ethnography is over. "Did . . . *they* tell you this? The . . . your voices?"

She bursts into a curt, wild laugh. "No. The deputy sheriff loaned me her jogging radio. I think she had a thing for me. You should come with us."

"Well. I have this research to finish. My dissertation."

"Work on it up there. The place will be filled with the people you want to study."

"Idealists," Watchman says.

Adam can't read the man. Somewhere up in the tree or in his narrow cell, he lost the ability to tell sardonic from straight. "I can't."

"Ah. Well. If you can't, you can't." Maybe she's being sympathetic. Maybe she's felling him. "We'll meet you up there. When you come around."

ADAM CARRIES the curse back to Santa Cruz. For weeks he works up his data. Almost two hundred people have answered the 240 questions of the Revised NEO Personality Inventory. They've also completed his custom questionnaire testing for various beliefs, including thoughts on human entitlement to natural resources, the scope of personhood, and plant rights. Digitizing the results is trivial. He runs his data through various analysis packages.

Professor Van Dijk has a look. "Nice work. Took you a while. Anything exciting happen during the fieldwork?"

Something has happened to his libido while he was away. Professor Van Dijk is as hot as ever. But she seems to Adam like another species.

"Does five days in jail count as exciting?"

She thinks he's kidding. He lets her think so.

CERTAIN TENDENCIES of radical environmentalist temperament emerge from the data. Core values, a sense of identity. The scores of only four of the thirty personality factors measured by the NEO inventory turn out to predict, with remarkable accuracy, whether a person will believe: *A forest deserves protection regardless of its value to humans.* He wants to give himself the exam, but it would say nothing now.

Back at his apartment after ten hours in the computer lab, Adam turns on the TV. Oil wars and sectarian violence. It's way too early to think about sleeping, though that's all he wants to do. He's still a score of stories up in the air, held aloft by a nonexistent tree, listening to the creak of that high house and the calls of birds he'd like to be able to name. He tries to read a novel, something about privileged people having trouble getting along with each other in exotic locations. He throws it against the wall. Something has broken in him. His appetite for human self-regard is dead.

He heads out to a favorite grad student hang, where he consumes five beers, ninety-six decibels of blast beat, and a hundred minutes of wall-sized sine-wave basketball in the company of twenty instant friends. Ejected again from the cocoon of fun, he regroups in the bar's parking lot. He's not so buzzed as to imagine he's fit to drive, but there's no other way home.

Waves of simulated mirth pump out of the building as a parade of muscle cars snarls down Cabrillo. A woman under a streetlight shouts at no one, "Fuck me for even *trying* to understand you." Across the alley, people wait to be admitted into the back entrance of some late-night invitation-only event that Adam, juked by the sight of the mini-throng, suddenly needs to attend. Another human irrationality he knows all about but is too fried to remember by name. He walks half a block, propelled by a tremendous wave that feeds on itself, jetting out refuse behind it: bubbles, genocides, crusades, manias from the pyramids to pet rocks—the desperate delusions of culture from which, for one brief night, high up above the Earth, he once awakened.

At the corner, he leans on a streetlight. A fact struggles to escape him, one he has felt for a long time but has never been able to formulate. Almost every part of *need* is created by a reflex, phantasmal, and democratic committee whose job is to turn one season's necessities into the next's yard sales. He stumbles on into a park full of people dealing in excitement and night. The air stinks a little of Wet-Naps, weed, and sex. Hunger everywhere, and the only food is salt.

Something hard hits his head, falls to the ground, and rolls a few feet away. He crouches down in the dark and searches. The culprit lies in the grass, a mysterious, industrial-grade button incised on its flat round face with a perfect X. It seems designed to be opened with a large Phillips-head screwdriver and has the look of steampunk: ingenious, Victorian, finely machined. But it's made of wood.

The thing is too weird for words. He studies it for a full minute, learning again how he knows nothing. Nothing outside his own kind. He looks up into the branches of a willowy eucalyptus, from which the mystery fell. The thick bole has started its species' trademark striptease. Sheaves of brown, thin bark litter the base, leaving behind a trunk so white it's obscene.

"What?" he asks the tree. "*What?*" The tree feels no need to reply.

THE SEVEN MILES of Forest Service road are so glorious it scares him. Adam follows the cut, climbing along sentry conifers—spruce to hemlock to Douglas-fir, yew, red cedar, three kinds of true firs, all of which he sees as *pine*.

A year-long dissertation completion fellowship—a gift from the gods— and this is how he spends it. His pack weighs down on his hips. Above him in the blue, the sun acts like it'll never hide again. But the crisp air and early shadows in the switchbacks hint at what's coming. A few more weeks and his thesis will be done. First this, though: a last bit of holdout research.

The Northwest has more miles of logging road than public highway. More miles of logging road than streams. The country has enough to circle the Earth a dozen times. The cost of cutting them is tax-deductible, and the branches are growing faster than ever, as if spring has just sprung. This road's curves at last broaden out, and the settlement appears in front of him. Along the edge of the camp, brightly colored people, mostly young, maybe a hundred of them, take a last stand. Adam draws close; the work grows clearer. Community trench digging. Anarchic assembly of a drawbridge. Palisades and stockades rising from salvage timber. Spanning the moated entrance across the chopped-up road, a banner announces:

## THE FREE BIOREGION
## OF CASCADIA

The words sprout stems and tendrils. Birds perch on the letters' vegetation. Adam recognizes the style and knows the artist. He enters the Lincoln

Log fortress through the drawbridge over the trench in progress. Just past the defile, a man in camo and receding-hairline ponytail lies in the middle of the road. His right arm stretches down his side, like a reclining Buddha. His left disappears down a hole into the Earth.

"Greetings, biped! You here to help or hinder?"

"Are you all right?"

"Name's Doug-fir. Just testing out a new lockdown. There's an oil drum full of concrete six feet down there. If they want me out, they're going to have to rip my arm off!"

From a nest at the top of a tripod of lashed logs in the road, a small, dark-haired, ethnically ambiguous woman calls, "Everything okay?"

"That's Mulberry. She's thinks you're a Freddie."

"What's a Freddie?"

"Just checking," Mulberry says.

"Freddies are the Federales."

"I don't think he's a Freddie. I'm just . . ."

"It's probably the button-down and chinos."

Adam looks up at the woman's tripod nest. She says, "They won't be able to take equipment down this road without knocking this over and killing me."

The man with his arm in the ground clucks. "Freddies won't do that. They think life is sacred. Human life, anyway. Crown of creation and such. Sentimental. It's the one chink in their armor."

"So if you're not a Freddie," Mulberry asks, "who are you?"

Something comes to Adam that he hasn't thought about for decades. "I'm Maple."

Mulberry smiles a little crooked smile, like she can see into him. "Good. No Maples here yet."

Adam looks away, wondering whatever became of that tree. His back-yard second self. "Do either of you know a man called Watchman or a woman named Maidenhair?"

"Shit, yeah," the man chained to the Earth says.

The tripod woman grins. "We don't have leaders here. But we do have those two."

HIS OLD FELLOW criminals greet Adam like they knew he was coming. Watchman clasps him by the shoulders. Maidenhair hugs him, long. "It's good you're here. We can use you."

They've changed in some subtle way no personality test could quantify. Grimmer, more resolute. The death of Mimas has compressed them, like shale into slate. Their transformation makes Adam wish that he'd chosen some other topic to research. Resilience, immanence, numen—qualities his discipline is notoriously poor in measuring.

She grabs his wrist. "We like to have a little ceremony when new people join."

Watchman sizes up Adam's pack. "You are joining us, right?"

"Ceremony?"

"Simple. You'll like it."

SHE'S HALF RIGHT; the ceremony is simple. It happens that evening, on a broad meadow behind the wall. The Free Bioregion of Cascadia assembles in parade dress. Scores of people in plaid and grunge. Floral, flowing hippie skirts topped off with fleece vests. Not all the congregation is young. A couple of stout *abuelas* stand by in sweatpants and cardigans. A former Methodist minister performs the ceremony. He's in his eighties, with a necklace scar where he lashed himself to a logging truck.

They start in on the songs. Adam fights down his hatred of virtuous singing. The shaggy nature-souls and their platitudes make him queasy. He feels ashamed, the way he does when remembering childhood. People take turns airing the day's challenges and suggesting cures. All around him spread the garish colors of ad hoc democracy. Maybe it's okay. Maybe mass extinction justifies a little fuzziness. Maybe earnestness can help his hurt species as much as anything. Who is he to say?

The erstwhile minister says, "We welcome you, Maple. We hope you'll stay as long as you're able. Please, if it's in your heart to do so, repeat these words after me. 'From this day forward . . .'"

"'From this day forward . . .'" He can't very well not repeat, with so many people assembled to watch him.

"'. . . I'll commit myself to respect and defend . . .'"

"'. . . I'll commit myself to respect and defend . . .'"

"'. . . the common cause of living things.'"

They aren't the most destructive words he has ever spoken, or the most pitiful. Something echoes in his head, something he once copied down. *A thing is right . . . a thing is right when it tends . . .* But he can't get to it. Cheers break out around his final echo. People set to work making a campfire. The blaze is high, wide, and orange, and the carbonizing wood smells like childhood.

"You're a psychologist," Mimi says to the recruit. "How do we convince people that we're right?"

The newest Cascadian takes the bait. "The best arguments in the world won't change a person's mind. The only thing that can do that is a good story."

Maidenhair tells that story that the rest of the campfire knows by heart. First she was dead, and there was nothing. Then she came back, and there was everything, with beings of light telling her how the most wondrous products of four billion years of life needed her help.

An old Klamath guy with long gray hair and glasses like Clark Kent nods. He takes the floor for the benediction. He chants the old chants and teaches everyone a few words of Klamath-Modoc. "Everything happening here was already known. Our people said long ago that this day would come. They told of how the forest was about to die, when humans suddenly remembered the rest of their family." And for half the night, the characters sit around the blaze, laughing and listening and whispering and baying at the moon up in the spruces' spires.

THE NEXT DAY is pure work. Trenches to be widened and deepened, a wall to be secured. Adam swings a hammer for hours. By evening he's so tired he can't stand. He shares a cookout with the four friends who strike him as a Jungian archetypal family: Maidenhair, the Mother Priest; Watchman, the Father Protector; Mulberry, the Child Craftsman; and Doug-fir, Child Clown. Maidenhair is the glue, casting spells over everyone in camp. Adam marvels at her bulwark optimism, even after the routs she has suffered. She speaks with the authority of one who has already seen the future, from high above.

They take him in that night, a square fifth wheel. He's not sure what his role in this desperation-forged clan is supposed to be. Doug-fir calls him Professor Maple, and that's who he becomes. That night, he sleeps the deep oblivion of an exhausted volunteer.

Adam raises his fears two nights later, over a tin of baked beans warmed on a fire of cones. "Destroying federal property. Serious stuff."

"Oh, you're a felon, buddy," Doug-fir says.

"Violent crime."

Douglas waves him away. "I've committed real violent crimes. Commissioned by the government."

Mulberry clasps Douglas's jabbing hand. "Yesterday's political criminals are on today's postage stamps!"

Maidenhair is far away, in another country. At last she says, "This isn't radical. I've seen radical."

Then Adam sees it again, too. A living, breathing mountainside, stripped bare.


SUPPLIES ARRIVE, bought with sympathizers' donations. The camp is a small part of a network of efforts spreading across the state. There's talk of an army walking arm-in-arm through the streets of the capital. A hunger striker, camped out for forty days and nights on the steps of the U.S. District Court in Eugene. The Spirit of the Forest, dressed in a quilt of green strips, walking a hundred miles on stilts down Highway 58.

That night, lying in his bag against the Earth, Adam wants to head back to Santa Cruz to finish his thesis. Anyone can dig a trench, pile up an earthwork, fasten himself to a lockdown. But only he can complete his project and describe, in measured facts, why people might care whether a forest lives or dies. But he stays on another day, becoming something new—his own object of study.

THE LONGER THE OCCUPATION LASTS, the farther journalists travel to come see. A squad of men in a Forest Service van ask them all to leave. The Free Cascadians stand them off and send them away. Two guys in suits from the congressional representative's office drop by to listen. They promise to take the grievances to Washington. Their visit thrills Mulberry. "When politicians start to come around, something's happening."

Adam—Maple—agrees. "Politicians want to be on the winning side. Blow the way the wind does."

Maidenhair murmurs, "The Earth is always going to win."

Headlights swing by the main road one night, and shots are fired. Three days later, a deer's entrails appear just outside the barricade.

A HULKING F-350 SUPER DUTY stops down the road, a hundred yards from the drawbridge. Two men in high-necked olive hunters' jackets. The driver, young with a trim goatee, could be a C&W heartthrob. "Whadda we got here? Huggers! Hey—awright!"

A girl called Trillium shouts, "We're just trying to protect a good thing."

"Why don't you protect what belongs to you, and let us protect our jobs and our family and our own mountains and our way of life?"

"The trees don't belong to anyone," Doug-fir says. "The trees belong to the forest."

The passenger door opens, and the older man gets out. He walks around the front of the cab. Once, in another life, long ago, Adam took a seminar in the psychology of crisis and confrontation. Now he remembers nothing. The man is tall but stooped, gray hair falling in his face. He's like a big grizzly pitching forward on his hind legs. Something flashes at the man's wrist. Adam thinks: *Gun. Knife. Run.*

The old guy reaches the front left bumper and lifts the metal weapon. But the threat is soft, philosophical, perplexed, and the weapon only a metal hand. "I lost my arm at the elbow, cutting those trees."

The heartthrob calls from the cab, "And I've got white finger, from working. You heard of working, haven't you? Doing things other people need to have done?"

The old guy rests his good hand on the hood and shakes his head. "What do you people want? We can't stop using wood."

Maidenhair appears, walking through the drawbridge toward the men. The upright grizzly takes a step back. She says, "We don't *know* what people can and can't do. So little has been tried!"

The look of her sets the goateed driver on every kind of high alert. "You can't put wood above the lives of decent people." He's stunned; he wants her. That much is clear to Adam a hundred yards away.

"We don't," she says. "We don't put trees above people. People and trees are in this together."

"What the hell does that even mean?"

"If people knew what went into making trees, they would be so, so thankful for the sacrifice. And thankful people don't need as much." She talks to the men for a while. She says, "We need to stop being visitors here. We need to live where we live, to become indigenous again."

The bear-man shakes her hand. He walks back around to the passenger door and boards. As the monster truck pulls out, the driver yells to the assembled forces behind the drawbridge, "Hug away, huggers! Y'all are gonna get reamed." He tears away in a spray of gravel.

*Yes*, Adam thinks. *Probably. And then the planet will ream the reamers.*


THE PROTEST enters its second month. It shouldn't be working, as far as Adam can see. The hopeless incompetence of the idealist temperament should have crashed the place long ago. But the Free Bioregion rolls on. Word spreads through camp that the President—of the *United States*—has heard about the protest and is ready to halt all federal timber salvage sales, especially those resulting from arson, until the policy can be reviewed.

A BRIGHT, CHILLY AFTERNOON, two hours past the sun's peak. Watchman is painting faces for storytelling that evening around the fire. Down the slope, someone blows an alpenhorn, bellowing like ancient mega-fauna at the falling sun. A marathoner named Marten sprints up to the ridge and trots into high camp. "They're coming."

"Who?" Watchman asks.

"Freddies."

Like that, the day is here. They head down the path toward the glacis, where the moat and wall now stand completed. Down the pass, along the logging road that Adam hiked up so long ago, a convoy crawls, filled with people wearing uniforms of four different colors and cuts. After the lead Forest Service van comes a behemoth excavator, converted for assault. Behind it, more equipment, more vans.

The face-painted Free Cascadians stand and stare. Then the eighty-year-old minister with the necklace scar says, "Okay, folks. Let's mobilize." They move to their stations, locking down, raising the drawbridge, manning the wall, or withdrawing to defensible positions. Soon the convoy is at the gates. Two Forest Service men exit the lead van and stand in front of the palisade. "You have ten minutes to leave peacefully. After that, you'll be removed to a place of detainment."

Everyone on the ramparts shouts at once. No leaders: every voice must be heard. The movement has lived for months by that principle, and now they'll die by it. Adam waits for a break in the hail of words. Then he, too, is shouting.

"Give us three days, and this whole thing can be wrapped up peacefully." The heads of the convoy turn to him. "We've had a visit from the congres-sional office. The President is assembling an executive order."

As quickly as he won their attention, he loses it. "You have ten minutes," the officer repeats, and Adam's political naïveté dies. Action from Washing-ton isn't the answer to this showdown. It's the *cause*.

At nine minutes and forty seconds, the long-necked saurian excavator swings its ram over the trench and slams the top of the wall. Screams come from the battered ramparts. War-painted defenders tumble and run. Adam scrambles and is knocked to the ground. The claw hammers the wall again. It flicks out like a wrist and smacks the drawbridge. Another poke and the drawbridge sheers off. Two hard swipes at the brace-posts bring the entire barrier to the ground. Months of work—the most formidable barricades the Free Bioregion could build—crumble like a child's Popsicle-stick fort.

The beast rolls up to the trench and paws the rubble on the far side. It takes the excavator only a minute to scrape the logs from the destroyed wall and slide them into the moat. The treads of the machine roll over the filled trench and through the downed wall. Cascadians, their face paint running, pour like termites from a cracked-open mound. Some head for the road. Several turn on the invaders with arguments and pleas. Maidenhair starts chanting: "*Think of what you're doing! There's a better way!*" Police from the convoy are everywhere, cuffing and forcing people to the ground.

The chant changes to shouts of, "*Nonviolence! Nonviolence!*"

Adam falls fast, taken down by an immense cop with rosacea so bad he looks like one of the painted ecowarriors. Fifty yards up the escarpment, Watchman get his knees clubbed from behind and slides down the scree on his blue-painted face. Only the lockdowns remain. The excavator slows its surge up the road. It reaches the first tripod and nudges at the base with its claw. The tripod wobbles. Officers turn from their mopping-up to watch. Up in her crow's nest, Mulberry wraps her arms around the tops of the shaking pylons. Each slap of the claw against the cone's base flings her around like a crash dummy.

Adam yells, "Jesus. Quit!"

Others pick up the yell—people on both sides of the battle. Even Doug, from his bed in the road. "*Meem*. It's over. Come down."

The claw slaps at the teepee's base. The three trunks forming the frame groan and bend. An awful creak, and one of the poles cracks. The crack starts a hundred rings deep in the cylinder of lignin and opens outward. The fir rips, tearing off the top of the pole into a punji stake.

Mimi screams, and her crow's nest falls. The torn pole impales her cheek-bone. She bounces off the spike and topples, riding the wood down and bouncing off a rock at the bottom. Douglas releases himself from lockdown and runs toward her. The driver of the excavator yanks the claw away in horror, like a palm protesting its innocence. But the backhand swings into the child clown, who takes the force of the retracting claw and crumples like a string-snipped marionette.

The war for Earth stops. Both sides rush to the wounded. Mimi shrieks and clutches her face. Douglas lies unconscious. Police run down to the caravan and call in the injuries. The dazed citizens of the collapsed Free Bioregion huddle in horror. Mimi rolls on her side in a fetal curl and opens her eyes. Trees in shades from jade to aquamarine skewer the sky. *Look the color,* she thinks, then passes out.


ADAM FINDS Maidenhair and Watchman in the milling crowd, surveying the losses. Maidenhair points up the rise at the four insurgent women still lying across the road, locked down into the ground. "We haven't lost yet."

Adam says, "We have."

"They won't dare take these trees now. After the press gets wind of this."

"They will." These and all the remaining ancients, until all forests are housing tracts or farms.

Maidenhair shakes her dirty tresses. "Those women can stay locked down until Washington acts."

Adam catches Watchman's eye. The truth is too brutal for even him to say.


A HELICOPTER AIRLIFTS the wounded to the level two trauma center in Bend. Douglas undergoes immediate surgery for a Le Fort III maxillary fracture. Mimi gets her ankle shoved back into place and her blown-out orbit patched. The ER doctors can do little for the trench across her cheek but sew it together until such a day as plastic surgeons might rebuild it.

The Freddies press no charges against the squatters. Only the last four women, who hold out for another thirty-six hours, are jailed. Then the remaining residents of the Free Bioregion of Cascadia leave the hillside and the extraction of wealth resumes.

And yet, and *still*: twenty-eight days later, a machine shed filled with vehicles in the Willamette National Forest goes up in flames.

IT ISN'T REAL. It's no more than theater, a simulation, until they see the aftermath.

The newspapers run a photo: a fireman and two rangers inspecting a charred excavator. Five people pass the photo around Mimi Ma's dining room table. A thought joins them, underground, as thoughts do so often now. *Holy fuck. That's us.*

For a long time, there is no need for words. The shared mood swings like a volatile stock. But it settles into a passive defiance. "They've gotten as good as they give," Mimi says. The twenty-two stiches in her face make each word sting. "We're even."

Adam can't bear to look at her, or at Douglas, either, his face another bandaged mess. Adam, too, wanted this revenge against equipment that half blinded one of them and deformed another. Payback against the sadism of men. Now he doesn't know what he wants or how to get it.

"Actually," Nick says, "they're still way ahead."

IT'S A SINGLE ACT of desperation. But the need for justice is like owner-ship or love. Feeding it only makes it grow. Two weeks after the machine shed, they target a sawmill near Solace, California, operating for months under a revoked license and paying the nuisance fine with a week's worth of profits. The woman who hears voices says how the attack must go. The trained observer does the stakeout. The engineer turns two dozen plastic milk jugs into explosive devices. The vet handles the detonation. The psychologist keeps them going. Deadly machinery burns better than any of them expected. This time they leave a message scrawled on the side of a nearby warehouse, spared because it's filled with blameless timber. The letters are artful, almost florid:

## NO TO THE SUICIDE ECONOMY
## YES TO REAL GROWTH

They sit hunched around Mulberry's table as if they're about to deal a hand of cards. Philosophy and other fine distinctions can't help them now. A line has been crossed, the job is done; words are of no consequence. And *still* they can't stop talking, although the sentences are never long. Still debating, when their argument's conclusion has long since disappeared in the rearview mirror of their delivery van.

Adam watches his fellow arsonists, taking mental notes despite himself. Mulberry chops the air in slow motion. She lands the blade edge on a precise point in her open palm. "I feel like I've been at a continuous funeral for two years."

"Ever since the blinders came off," the child clown agrees.

"All the protests. All the letters. Getting beat up. Shouting at the top of our lungs, and no one hearing."

"We accomplished more in two nights than we did with years of effort."

Accomplishment is not something Adam knows how to measure anymore. What they're doing—*what he has done*—is simply to make the pain stop long enough to bear.

Mimi says, "It's not a funeral anymore."

"Not a hard choice," Nick says. His voice falls quiet, astonished by the ambush of common sense. "We destroy a small amount of equipment, or that equipment destroys a huge amount of life."

The psychologist listens. There are other, much deeper deceptions at the heart of humans. He has thrown in his lot with the need to save what can be saved. A little time must be bought from the approaching apocalypse. Nothing else matters more than that. His thesis has its answer.

Olivia needs only lower her chin and the others fall silent. Her spell over them has grown with each crime. She has put her hand on a cut stump as big as a chapel. She has watched a forest die that was older than her species. She has taken advice from things larger than man. "If we're wrong, we pay the price. They can't take more than our lives. But if we're right?" She casts her eyes downward in a shaft of thought. "And everything alive tells me that we are . . ."

No one needs her to complete the thought. What wouldn't a person do, to help the most wondrous products of four billion years of creation? In the time it takes for Adam to think this thought, he realizes something else: The five of them are going on another run. *One more*. It must be the last. Then they'll go their separate ways, having done what little they could to stop the race from killing itself.

ADAM HIMSELF DISCOVERS the story: "Forest Service Seeks Multi-Use Projects." Thousands of acres of public lands in Washington, Idaho, Utah, and Colorado, offered for lease to private speculators and developers. Forests cleared for more end-time profit. The group hears the report in silence. There's no need even to put the matter to a vote.

There are no letters or emails, and almost no calls. They communicate face-to-face or not at all. They live on cash. Nothing is written down. Mulberry's engineering grows more sophisticated. She starts in on her best work by far, tipped by handmade underground tracts: *The Four Rules of Arson*. *Setting Fires with Electrical Timers*. The new design is more reliable. Maple and Doug-fir drive as far as fifty miles away to get her the needed supplies.

Watchman and Maidenhair surveil one of the newly leased sites—Stormcastle, in Idaho, in the Bitterroots, near the Montana border. Healthy chunks of public forest sold off to make way for yet another four-season resort. They make the journey and tour the site at night, when the place is abandoned. The artist sketches everything—the newly cut roadbeds, the equipment sheds and construction trailers, the footprint of the resort's fresh foundations. There is zeal in his perfect sketches, and humility. While he draws, the actuarial-science dropout wanders the cleared ground, pacing out distances between survey stakes. She tilts her head, listening.

All five of them work in Mulberry's garage, under a fume tent, in full-body painter suits and gloves. They assemble cascades of five-gallon fuel buckets and timer devices in plastic Tupperware. They mark on Watchman's maps where each of the devices must go to create the most sustainable burn. They'll send this one last message and be done. Then they'll split up, fade back into invisible routine, having gotten the country's attention. Appealed to the consciences of millions. Planted a seed, the kind that needs fire to open.

EVERYTHING GOES INTO the back of their van. By the time Mulberry's garage door rises and they edge out, it's like they're headed toward the mountains for camping and a hike. They pack a police scanner. Gloves and balaclava masks for all. They're all dressed in black. They leave Western Oregon in early morning. Any accident as they cruise down the interstate and the van will ignite in a massive fireball.

In the van, they chatter and watch the scenery. They pass through long stretches of Potemkin forest, vista curtains only a few feet deep. Doug produces a book of trivia questions and quizzes the others on the Revolutionary and Civil wars. Adam wins. They bird-watch—raptors along the highway's corridor of small-mammal carnage. Two hours in, Mimi spots a bald eagle with a seven-foot wingspan. It hushes everyone.

They listen to a book on tape: myths and legends of the first people of the Northwest. The old man of the ancients, Kemush, springs up from the ashes of the northern lights and makes everything. Coyote and Wishpoosh tear up the landscape in their epic fight. The animals get together to steal fire from Pine Tree. And all the darkness's spirits shift shapes, as numerous and fluid as leaves.

Night falls in the Bitterroots. The last few miles are the hardest—slow, winding, and remote. At last they pull up to the staging area, two miles off the state highway. The site looks just the way Watchman drew it. Mimi stays in the van, a scarf around her scarred face, sweeping the radio frequencies with a police scanner. The others set wordlessly to work. All tasks have been talked through dozens of times. They move like a single creature, wrestling five-gallon fuel containers into place and daisy-chaining them with wicks of towel and sheet doused in propellant. Then they affix the Tupperware timers.

WATCHMAN SETS OFF on the job assigned to him. Tonight is his last chance to work in a medium that will be seen by millions. He heads away from the future resort's half-framed main lodge, where the others deploy their devices. Across the graded meadow he comes to a pair of trailers, too far from the action for the blasts to reach. Their walls are his best available canvas. He takes two cans of spray paint from his coat pockets and steps up to the cleaner of the trailers' wall. In letters filled with all the care his hand can compose, he writes:

## CONTROL KILLS
## CONNECTION HEALS

He steps back to appraise the germ of the only thing he knows for certain. With a large felt marker, he adorns the block caps in stems and twigs, until the letters seem to be sprouting back from apocalypse. They look like Egyptian hieroglyphs, or the dancing figures of an op-art bestiary. Below these two lines he adds the trailing hope:

## COME HOME OR DIE

Back at the detonation site, wrestling the tubs into place, Adam and Doug mistime their movements. Fuel slops onto the hem of Adam's jacket and down his black denims. Stinking of petrochemicals, he squeezes his fists until his soaked gloves drip. His grip is shot from so much lifting. He looks up at the peaked roof of the construction office and thinks, *What the hell am I doing?* The clarity of recent weeks, the sudden waking from sleepwalk, his certainty that the world has been stolen and the atmosphere trashed for the shortest of short-term gains, the sense that he must do all he can to fight for the living world's most wondrous creatures: all these abandon Adam, and he's left in the insanity of denying the bedrock of human existence. Property and mastery: nothing else counts. Earth will be monetized until all trees grow in straight lines, three people own all seven continents, and every large organism is bred to be slaughtered.

ON THE SIDE of the other trailer, Watchman paints words in an alphabet wild and vivid. Verse springs up and flows over the empty white:

> For you have five trees in Paradise
> which do not change,
> either in summer or in winter,
> and their leaves do not fall.
> He who knows them
> shall not taste of death.

He steps back, his throat tightening, a little surprised by what has come out of him, this prayer he needs so badly to send out to no one who will understand it. Then: *whump*, and he's hit in the back by a concussion wave. Heat blows outward on the air, long before there should be anything like an explosion. Watchman turns to see a ball of orange leap up in a quick, simulated sunrise. His legs pitch forward, and he's running toward the blaze.

Another figure cuts in on the edge of his sight. Douglas, his hobbled run, one leg stiff, a dotted rhythm. They reach the burning at the same time. Then, Douglas, shout-whispering, "Fuck no. Fuck *no*!" He's on his knees, mewling at what has happened. Two figures lie on the ground. One of them starts to move as Nick closes in, and not the one Nick needs to be moving.

Adam pulls his shoulders off the ground. His head periscopes in all directions. A veil of blood trickles down his face. "Oh," he says. "Oh!"

Douglas steadies him. Nick swoops down to lift Olivia. She's lying on her back, her face to the stars. Her eyes are open. All around them, the air turns orange. "Livvy?" His voice is horrible. The thick, slurring burr of it, worse for her than the blast. "Can you hear me?"

A bubble forms on her lips. Then the word, "*Nnn.*"

Something seeps from her side, down by her waist. The front of her black shirt glistens in the dark. He lifts it and cries out, rushing it back down. A hushed wail comes out of him. Then he's a monster of competence again. The injured woman looks at him in terror. He shuts himself up and blanks his face. Goes through all the motions of every possible aid. The air starts to flicker. Two figures cowl over them. Douglas and Adam. "Is she . . . ?"

Something in the words hits Olivia. She tries to raise her head. Nick gentles her down. "I'm," she says. Her eyes close again.

Everything scalds. Douglas spins around in tight circles, his hands pressed against his skull. Clipped sounds come out of him. "Shit, shit, shit, shit . . ."

"We have to move her," Adam says.

Nick blocks his advance. "We can't!"

"We have to. The flames."

Their clumsy scuffle is over before it starts. Adam takes the woman under her arms and drags her across the stony ground. Sounds percolate up her throat. Nick bends down beside her again, helpless. He'll see the image for the next twenty years. He rises, stumbles away, and vomits on the ground.

Then Mimi is there, next to them in the dark. Relief runs through Nick. Another woman. A woman will know how to save them. At a glance, the engineer sees everything. She pushes the van keys into Adam's hands. "Go. Back to that last town we came through. Ten miles. Get the police."

"No," the woman on the ground says, startling everyone. "Don't. Keep . . ."

Adam points at the blaze. "I don't care," Mimi says. "Go. She needs help."

Adam stands still, his body objecting. *Help won't help her. And it will kill us all.*

"Finish," the prone woman murmurs. The word is so soft not even Nick can make it out.

Adam stares at the keys in his hand. He leans forward until he's trotting toward the van.

"Douglas," Mimi snaps. "Stop." The vet quits moaning and holds still. Then Mimi is on the ground ministering to Olivia, opening her collar, calming the animal panic. "Help is coming. Stay still."

Words only agitate the gored woman. "No. Finish. Keep—"

Mimi hushes her, stroking the side of her face. Nick slinks back. He watches from a distance. Everything is happening, unfixable, forever, for real. But on another planet, to other people.

Things seep out of Olivia's middle. The lips move. Mimi leans in, her ear to Olivia's mouth. "A little water?"

Mimi spins and looks up at Nick. "Water!" He freezes, helpless.

"I'll find some," Douglas shouts. He sees a dimple in the hillside, beyond the blaze. "That's a ravine. There must be a stream down there."

The men search for something to hold the water. Every container they have is tainted with accelerants. There's a baggie in Nick's pocket. He empties it of its few sunflower seeds and gives it to Douglas, who heads off into the woods behind the construction site.

It's not hard to find the stream. But a learned aversion grips Douglas as he dips the baggie. *You can't drink water from outside.* There isn't a lake, pond, stream, or rivulet in the country that's safe to drink. He clenches down and fills the bag. The woman just needs to hold a thimble of cool, clear liquid in her mouth, however poisonous. Douglas cups the bag and runs it back up the hillside. He pours a little water into her mouth.

"Thank you." Her eyes are feverish with gratitude. "That's good." She drinks a little more. Then her eyes close.

Douglas holds the baggie, helpless. Mimi dips her fingers into the fluid and wipes off Olivia's streaked face. She cradles the head, strokes the chestnut hair. The green eyes open again. They're alert now, cognizant, fixing on the eyes of their nurse. Olivia's face twists up in terror, like an ambushed mare. As clearly as if she speaks the words out loud, she puts the idea into Mimi's skull: *Something's wrong. I've been shown what happens, and this isn't it.*

Mimi holds her gaze, absorbing what pain she can. Comfort is impossible. The two lock eyes, and neither can look away. The gutted woman's thoughts pour into Mimi through a widening channel, thoughts too large and slow to understand.

Nick stands still, eyes closed. Douglas throws the baggie on the ground and stumbles away. The sky flares up, bright with refusal. Two new explosions rip through the air. Olivia cries out, searching for Mimi's gaze again. Her stare turns violent, clutching, as if looking away, even for an instant, would be worse than the worst death.

A third man appears on the inferno's edge. The sight of Adam, so much sooner than he should be back, restarts Nick. "Did you get help?"

Adam looks down at the pietà. Some part of him seems surprised to find that the drama is still going on.

"Is help coming?" Nick shouts.

Adam says nothing. With all his will, he pushes back from madness.

"You gutless . . . Give me the keys. *Give me the keys.*"

The artist charges the psychologist, grappling. Only the sound of his name in Olivia's mouth stops Nick from violence. He's on the ground next to her in a heartbeat. She's breathing hard now. Her face fists up in pain. Whatever shock has kept her anesthetized is wearing off, leaving her contorted and panting.

"Nick?" The panting stops. Her eyes go huge. He must fight to keep from looking over his shoulder for the terror that she sees.

"I'm here. I'm here."

"*Nick?*" A shriek now. She tries to sit, and soft things spill out under her shirt. "*Nick!*"

"Yes. I'm here. Right here. I'm with you."

The panting starts up again. Objection trickles from her mouth. *Hnn. Hnn. Hnn.* Her grip crushes his fingers. She moans, and the noise leaks away until there's no louder sound than the flames on three sides of them. Her eyes squeeze shut. Then they open, wild. She stares, unsure what she's looking at.

"How long can it last?"

"Not long," he promises.

She claws at him, an animal falling from a great height. Then she calms again. "But not this? This will never end—what we have. Right?"

He waits too long, and time replies for him. She struggles for a few seconds to hear the answer, before softening into whatever happens next.

CROWN

*A* man in the boreal north lies on his back on the cold ground at dawn. His head extends from his one-man tent, facing upward. Five thin cylinders of white spruce register the breeze above him. Gravity is nothing. The evergreen tips sketch and scribble on the morning sky. He's never really thought about the many miles a tree travels, in smallest cursive increments, each hour of every day. Forever in motion, these stationary things.

*The man with his head sticking out of the tent asks himself*: What are those treetops like? They're like that cog-toothed drawing toy, spinning out surprise patterns from the simplest nested cycles. They're like the tip of a Ouija planchette, taking dictation from beyond. *They are, in fact, like nothing but themselves. They are the crowns of five white spruces laden with cones, bending in the wind as they do every day of their existence. Likeness* is the sole problem of men.

*But the spruces pour out messages in media of their own invention. They speak through their needles, trunks, and roots. They record in their own bodies the history of every crisis they've lived through. The man in the tent lies bathed in signals hundreds of millions of years older than his crude senses. And still he can read them.*

*The five white spruces sign the blue air. They write*: Light and water and a little crushed stone demand long answers.

*Nearby lodgepoles and jack pines demur*: Long answers need long time. And long time is exactly what's vanishing.

*The black spruces down the drumlin put it bluntly*: Warm is feeding on warm. The permafrost is belching. The cycle speeds up.

*Farther south, broadleaves agree. Noisy aspens and remnant birches, forests of cottonwoods and poplars, take up the chorus*: The world is turning into a new thing.

*The man rolls over onto his back, face-to-face with the morning sky. The mes-sages swarm him. Even here, homeless, he thinks*: Nothing will be the same.

*The spruces answer*: Nothing has ever been the same.

We're all doomed, *the man thinks.*

We have always all been doomed.

But things are different this time.

Yes. *You're* here.

*The man must rise and get to work, as the trees are already doing. His work is almost done. He'll strike camp tomorrow, or the day after. But this minute, this morning, he watches the spruces writing and thinks,* I wouldn't need to be so very different for sun to seem to be about sun, for green to be about green, for joy and boredom and anguish and terror and death to all be themselves, beyond the need for any killing clarity, and then this—*this*, the growing rings of light and water and stone—would take up all of me, and be all the words I need.

PEOPLE TURN INTO OTHER THINGS. Twenty years later, when everything depends on remembering what happened, the facts of that night will have long since turned to heartwood. They put her body into the fire, facedown. Three of them will remember that. Nick will remember nothing. Bedrock in the minute she needed him, he turns worthless in the aftermath, seated on the ground by the flames, close enough to singe his eyebrows, as senseless as the burning corpse.

The others place her on the ready pyre, a thing as old as night. Her clothes burn, then her skin. The flowery words on her scapula—*A change is gonna come*—blacken and vaporize. Flames bear the flecks of her carbonized soul into the air. The corpse will be found, of course. Teeth with fillings, the nubs of unburned bone. Every clue will be discovered and read. They aren't getting rid of the corpse. They're sending it into forever.

Of leaving the scene, none will recall anything but forcing Nick into the van. Orange flickers above the evergreen woods, as wraithlike as the northern lights. Then dark snapshots for dozens of miles. They pass no vehicle for half an hour, and the occupants of that first car, a retired couple from Elmhurst, Illinois, with five hours more to drive before sleeping, won't even remember the white van speeding the other way by the time they see the fire.

The arsonists pass long stretches of silence punctuated by shouting. Adam and Nick threaten each other. Mimi drives in a soundproof bubble. Two hundred miles outside Portland, Douglas demands that they surrender. Something tells them not to. Olivia. That alone they'll all remember.

"No one saw anything," Adam tells the others, too many times.

"It's over," Nick says. "She's dead. We're finished."

"Shut the fuck up," Adam orders. "Nothing can trace this back to us. Just stay quiet."

They have failed to protect anything at all. They agree, at least, to protect each other.

"Say nothing, no matter what. Time is with us."

But people have no idea what time is. They think it's a line, spinning out from three seconds behind them, then vanishing just as fast into the three seconds of fog just ahead. They can't see that time is one spreading ring wrapped around another, outward and outward until the thinnest skin of *Now* depends for its being on the enormous mass of everything that has already died.

In Portland, they scatter.

NICHOLAS CAMPS on the ghost of Mimas. No tent, no sleeping roll. He lies on his side as night comes on, his head on a wadded jacket near the ring laid down the year Charlemagne died. Somewhere underneath his coccyx, Columbus. Past his ankles, the first Hoel leaves Norway for Brooklyn and the expanses of Iowa. Beyond the length of his body, crowding up to the cut's cliff, are the rings of his own birth, the death of his family, the roadside visit of the woman who recognized him, who taught him how to hang on and live.

The stump oozes from around its rim, the sap a color that the painter has no name for. He turns on his back and stares into the air, twenty stories straight up, trying to locate that precise spot where he and Olivia lived for a year. He doesn't want to be dead. He just wants the play of that voice, its eager openness, for a few words more. He just wants the girl who always heard what life wanted from them to rise out of the fire and tell him what he's supposed to do with himself, from now on. There is no voice. Not hers, not the imaginary beings'. No flying squirrels or murrelets or owls or any other creature that sang to them in their year. His heart contracts back down to the size it was when she found him. Silence, he decides, is better than lies.

He doesn't sleep much, on his hard campsite. He won't get many good nights for the next twenty years. And yet, twenty more rings would have been no wider than his ring finger.

MIMI AND DOUG strip the van and destroy every rag, hose, and rubber band. They scrub down the bed with several solvents. She sells the thing for a song and pays cash to buy a tiny Honda. She's sure the sale will play out like a Poe story. The van's new owner will turn up some damning paper scrap sitting in plain sight.

She puts her condo on the market. "Why?" Douglas asks.

"We have to split up. It's safer."

"How can it be safer?"

"We'll give each other away if we stay together. Douglas. Look at me. *Look at me*. We are not going to do that."

IT MIGHT NOT HAVE BEEN anything but a page three item. Arson destroys foundations at resort construction site. Nuisance setback. Work to resume right away. But bone turns up in the sifted ash, a human victim. Every news outlet in nine western states picks up the story and runs it for days.

The investigators can make no identification. A woman, young, five-foot-seven. As for violence, violation, it's impossible to say. The only leads are the cryptic inscriptions found near the blaze:

### CONTROL KILLS
### CONNECTION HEALS
### COME HOME OR DIE
#### For you have five trees in Paradise . . .

Collective wisdom settles on the most plausible explanation. It's the work of a deranged killer.

. . .

ADAM SLIPS BACK into Santa Cruz. Unthinkable, after everything. But dropping out of the program with his thesis at the finish line would only point a spotlight at him. His year-long fellowship is mostly spent. He sits for days in his sublet with the curtains drawn. He hovers, two feet above his own head, looking down on his body. At strange hours, excitement comes over him, then crashes into wild anxiety. Even a ten-minute walk to the convenience store feels life-threatening.

Late on a Friday night, he ducks into the department to fetch his university mail. He can't even calculate the last time he was in the building. It takes three tries to remember his combination. The mailbox is so wedged with flyers he must pry them out. The logjam bursts, and months of neglected junk spill across the mailroom floor. A voice behind him says, "Hey, stranger."

"Hey!" he answers, too exuberant, before he even turns to see.

Mary Alice Merton, fellow All But Dissertation. Sweet farm-girl face and smile like a dental brochure. "We thought you died."

The worst freedom courses through him. *Not dead. But I helped kill someone.* "Nope. Fellowship."

"What happened? Where have you been?"

He hears his dead undergrad mentor quoting Mark Twain. *If you tell the truth, you don't have to remember anything.* "In the field. I seem to have gotten a little lost."

She flicks his upper arm with the back of her fingernails. "Not the first, mister."

"I have all the facts. Just can't get them put down in a coherent way."

"Completion anxiety. What's so damn hard about turning in a diss? So it's a mess. Screw it, and deposit."

He struggles to kill his crazy excitement and retrieve the pitch of normal speech. To pass himself off as himself, not an arsonist and accomplice to manslaughter. Psychologists should be the greatest liars on the planet. Years of training in how people deceive themselves and others. The lessons come back to him. Do the opposite of what your felon impulses tell you to. And when subpoenaed to appear before the court of public opinion, dazzle with misdirection.

"Hungry?" He remembers to lift his eyebrows just a hair.

He sees the warnings going off in her. *Who is this guy? Three years of nothing but business, borderline autistic, and now he wants to play at being human?* But confirmation bias will always beat out common sense. All the data prove it. "Starving."

He crams the months of mail into his backpack and they head for late-night falafel. Five years later, he has a folder full of respected publications on in-group idealism and is up for early tenure at Ohio State. Fifteen more beyond that—no time at all—he'll be a noted figure in his field.

IT'S EASIER TO LIVE for months high up in the redwood canopy than to pass seven days at ground level. Everything is owned; a one-year-old knows that. It's as much a law as Newton's. Walking down the street without cash is a crime, and no one alive would imagine for a minute that things in real life might go any other way. Nick can't afford to be picked up for anything—not for vagrancy, not for camping without a permit, not for grazing on manzanita berries in a state park. He finds a cabin, rented by the week, in a depressed little town at the foot of the logged mountains. His yard backs onto a stand of juvenile redwoods, straight and clear, only a foot and a half thick, but known to him. The closest thing left to kin.

He must leave this place, get as far away as possible, for banal safety if not sanity. But he can't stop waiting, can't give up on the chance of a message that might redeem even a fraction of disaster. He lived in this place, with her. Here, for almost a year, he knew what purpose was. Of all the places on this forgetting Earth, this is the one she'd return to.

He talks to no one, goes nowhere. It's the rainy season again, the season that just ended. He falls asleep in a drizzle and wakes to a downpour. The roof comes alive with the assault of water. He's up, listening, and can't let go. No sooner does he fall asleep than he wakes in panic to daylight and the rain's cease-fire.

He goes out back to check the culvert. It's overflowing into an improvised creek through the rented porch. Nick stands in T-shirt and sweats, watching dawn pour down over the mountain. The hour smells moist and loamy, and the soil hums under his bare feet. Two thoughts fight over him. The first, so much older than anyone's childhood, is: *Joy comes in the morning.* The second, brand-new, is: *I'm a murderer.*

There's a tearing in the air. Nicholas looks up, where the mountainside begins to liquefy. Last night's rains have loosened the earth, and, stripped of the covering that held it in place for a hundred thousand years, the mountain slides down with a roar. Trees taller than lighthouses snap like twigs and plunge into one another, slamming down the slope in a swollen wave. Nick turns to run. Above him, a wall of rock and wood twenty feet high heads home. He scrambles down a footpath, wheeling to look back as a river of trees hits the cabin head-on. His living room fills with stump and rock. The building lifts off its foundation and bobs on the flow.

He runs toward the neighbors, screaming, "Get out! Now!" Then his neighbors are running, too, with their two little boys, down the drive to the family truck. But debris reaches the truck first and blocks it in. Trees wash up against the ranch house, bulging like woody lava.

"This way," Nick shouts, and the neighbors follow. He leads them down another gully along a shallower slope. And there, the tide of landslide comes to rest behind a thin line of redwoods. Mud and rubble ooze against the final barrier, but the trees hold. The mother breaks down. She sobs and grabs her children. The father and Nick stare upward at the denuded mountainside, a ridge wildly lowered. The man whispers, "Jesus." Nick jerks at the word. He looks where his neighbor points. On each of the trunks in the standing barricade that just saved their lives is a bright blue painted *X*. Next week's harvest.

DOUGLAS RETURNS to Mimi's, like a dog, at hours not exactly optimal. At first just to check in, make sure she's okay. Then to tell her his most remarkable dream. She has unplugged her answering machine. So he comes by her place in person, which makes her a little crazy.

In the dream, he and Mimi are sitting face-to-face, in a park in a beautiful city by an even more beautiful bay. Maidenhair appears. She smiles and says,

*Wait! They'll explain. You'll see.* Douggie can't keep still, with the excitement of recounting. "It was like she'd seen everything! And she was letting us know. When I woke up, it was so clear. Everything's going to be okay."

Mimi is less than enthusiastic. The whole idea of okayness makes her kind of scream. So he stays away for a bit. But the dream comes again, with fresh, new refinements that he's sure she'll want to hear. After a fair amount of extreme knocking, Mimi opens and drags Douggie inside. She sits him at the dining table where they addressed so many thousands of protest letters. "Douglas. We burned buildings to the ground. We were out of our heads. Criminally insane. They'll kill us. Do you *get that*? We'll spend the rest of our lives in a federal prison."

He says nothing. The word *prison* has him watching a clip of his own past—the one that started him down this twisting path. "Okay, I get that. But in the dream, she had her arm around you, and she was saying—"

"Douglas!" she yells loud enough to be heard through the walls. She starts again, in a hush. "Don't come by anymore. I'm closing on the condo. Leaving."

His eyes bulge, like a frog trying to swallow. "Leaving?"

"Listen to me. You have. To go. Away. Start a new life. Take a new name. This is arson. *Manslaughter*."

"Anybody could have started those fires. There's nothing to trace us."

"We have arrest records. We're known environmental radicals. They'll go through the lists. They'll trace every record—"

"What record? We paid for everything in cash. Drove hundreds of miles. Lots of people are on those lists. Lists don't prove a thing."

"Douglas. Disappear. Go underground. Don't come back. Don't look for me."

"Fine." His eyes are burning. There's no reaching her. One hand on the door, he turns. "You know, I'm not exactly aboveground as it is."

He has the dream again. They're sitting on a rise above the city of the future. Maidenhair is telling them, *Wait! You'll see!* And sure enough, forests spring up all around them. It's beyond extraordinary, and Mimi needs to know. But when he gets to her place, there's a big red sign out front: SOLD.

He has less than no place else to go. East seems the best of the three available options. So he loads his movable estate into the truck and heads up the Columbia Gorge. Doesn't even tell his boss at the hardware store. They can keep his last two weeks of wages.

Over the Idaho border, it dawns on him that he needs to see the site. He's practically next door, by western standards. A chance, if nothing else, for a better goodbye. Mimi screams in his ear, telling him he's nuts. Any reasonable person would say the same. But reason is what's turning all the forests of the world into rectangles.

He comes up the state highway, his heart sledging at his ribs. He heads up the lonely access road through the spruce defile, trees as rigid as judges in the falling dark. His muscles remember. It's like the surviving four of them are in the van again, in the sick aftermath. But nearing the site, he sees another fire, sharp, controlled, and white—the electric arcs of night work. Hard hats swarming all over, repairing the damage. Capital's answer to a slipped schedule is simply to add more shifts.

A big rig loaded with trusses. A signalman with a red flag. Douglas slows down for a look. No sign that anything here ever burned. Mimi screams at him to get the hell out before some security cam mounted up on the side of a trunk reads his plates. Something else, too, tells him, *Not here*. Maidenhair.

He blasts past the work site down the empty highway. At the next intersection, he heads east again. After midnight, the car gropes its way into Montana. He pulls off at a trailhead in a national forest and sleeps a few hours in the reclined driver's seat.

Daylight marbles the sky. He drives the back roads with no sense of direction, living off beef jerky and Atomic Fireballs he picks up when he stops for gas. He drives through a wide, flat basin flanked by peaks, flinty rangeland too dry for real use. But life still uses it in a million ways. A motion across a field catches his eye—pronghorn, fighting with a wire fence. Five of them, and one is injured. The numerology of it—the *sign*—steals over Douglas, and he begins to shake. He pulls onto the shoulder. A great, empty remoteness settles on him, the size of the sky. He falls asleep with the window cracked, coyotes howling as if the world still belonged to them.

He drives on at random, the morning of the second day. The rising sun keeps him vaguely oriented. Miles pass, and hours, not always in straight lines. Something odd springs up on the road's left. The sight is wrong before he even sees it. In all this open expanse of gold and gray, a lost oasis of working green. A riverbank outpost, without a river. He turns too fast onto the next exit, a crumbling macadam track beaten to hell by scores of snowy seasons and the roots of weeds that can never take no for an answer. His truck slows to a crawl, and still the road wants to break its axles and husk its undercarriage. Then he's in a grove of poplars, shaggy as a gang of teens.

He gets out and walks. A flock of sparrows unspools across the grass some yards ahead. The stand makes no sense. Trees shoot upward in fountains. Some split into bouquets of stems seven feet around. Contorted cottonwoods. No sign of habitation for miles around, but all the trees grow in a grid that looks like a child's logic puzzle. Underneath the green arcades, it comes to him: he's on the streets of an invisible town. Sidewalks, lots, yards, foundations, shops, churches, houses: everything has vanished, scavenged, but these few square blocks of windbreak. He sits beneath a thing once the pride of some family's picture window. Now the giant's shade falls on no one.

There's a sound like the gushing of a hidden stream. A sound of vigorous applause, but from a hundred years away. He glances down the cottonwood colonnades, a few squares of planted shade singing in the breeze, glad to have someone back in this abandoned town to marvel at them. Their rustle is like a hymn coming out of the missing church to play along the wide, missing boulevard, for all the missing people. Now the psalm preaches only to the gushing choir, and there's nothing wrong with that. The choir, too, deserves to remember. *Let the field be joyful and all that is therein. Then shall all the trees of the wood rejoice.*

MIMI SITS in a black crepe sheath by the reception desk of the Four Arts Gallery, on Grant. She balances in the slung-back leather chair, every few seconds hitching the wanton hem back down over her aging knees. The outfit seemed art-dealer-worthy this morning, good for a couple hundred dollars more in any negotiation with a man. She thought it might compensate for the scar running down her face. Now it feels like amateur hour.

The pixie-cut assistant reappears, averting her eyes from Mimi's gash, proffering more coffee, and promising that Mr. Siang will be with her almost right away. Mr. Siang is already seventeen minutes late. He's had the scroll for weeks. He has put off this meeting twice. Something's going on in the back room. Mimi's being played, and she can't tell how.

Other treasures clog the gallery. Lacquerware yachts. A cloud-swathed, floating mountain inked in the meticulous style. Thousand-figure ivory spheres, each intricate world nested inside another. A painting on the far wall catches her eye: a great black tree with rainbow branches against a blue sky. She stands, tugs at the hem, and drifts across the room. What seemed like a cornucopia of tiny leaves turns into hundreds of meditating figures. She reads the tag: *The Field of Merit*, also called *The Refuge Tree*. Tibet, circa mid-seventeenth century. In the spreading crown, the human leaves seem to wave in the wind.

A voice behind her calls, "Miss Ma?"

Mr. Siang, in pewter suit and blood-red spectacles, ushers her into the back room. He gazes at the gully in her face and doesn't blink. With one peremptory hand he seats her at a conference table made of outlawed mahogany, the scroll box between them. Addressing the window, he says, "Your piece is very beautiful. Wonderful arhats, in a distinctive style. Sad you have no papers or provenance."

"Yes. I . . . we never had any."

"You say this scroll came to America with your father. It belonged to his family's art collection in Shanghai?"

She fiddles with her dress beneath the table. "That's right."

Mr. Siang turns from the window and sits across from her, at attention. His left palm cups his right elbow, and his right hand holds out its first two fingers, gripping an imaginary cigarette. "We cannot date it as precisely as we'd like. And we aren't certain about the artist."

Her guard goes up. "What about the owners' seals?"

"We've traced them back in chronological order. It isn't clear how your father's family actually came into possession."

She knows now what she has suspected for weeks. Bringing the scroll in for appraisal was a mistake. She wants to grab it and run.

"The script of the inscriptions is also difficult. A form of Tang Dynasty calligraphy we call wild cursive. Specifically, *Drunken Su*. It may have been done later."

"What does it say?"

He tilts his head back, the better to frame her impudence. "There is a poem, author unknown." He rolls the scroll out between them. His finger flows down the column of words.

> *On this mountain, in such weather,*
> *Why stay here any longer?*
> *Three trees wave to me with urgent arms.*
> *I lean in to hear, but their emergency*
> *sounds just like the wind.*
> *New buds test the branches, even in winter.*

Her skin welts up before the poem ends. She's in SFO, hearing her name get paged. She's reading the poem her father left in lieu of a suicide note. *How does a man rise or fall in this life?* She's setting urgent fires on the side of a mountain in the pitch-black cold. Fires that kill a woman.

"Three trees?"

Mr. Siang's palms apologize. "It's poetry."

Her face flashes hot and cold. Her mind won't work. Something is trying to get at her, from a long way away. *Why stay here any longer?* She sees her sister Amelia, twelve years old and packed in a snowsuit that doubles her size, waddle in the back door, crying. *The breakfast tree is budding too early. The snow is going to kill it.* And her father, just smiling. *The new leaf always there. Even before winter.* A fact that Mimi, in her sixteen winters, had somehow missed.

"Would that poem be readable . . . to an average person?"

"A scholar, maybe. A student of calligraphy."

She has no idea what her father was a student of. Miniature electronics. Campsites. Talking to bears. "This ring." She holds her fist out to the art dealer across the table. He tilts his head. His smile is embarrassed for them both.

"Yes? A jade tree, Ming style. Good workmanship. We could appraise it."

She pulls it back. "Never mind. Tell me about the scroll."

"The treatment of the arhats is very skilled. Simply on its historical rarity and the quality of the drawing, we put the value between . . ." He mentions two figures that elicit a high-pitched primate giggle before she can throttle it. "Four Arts would be willing to pay you something in the middle of that range."

She sits back, faking calm. She had hoped for a little freedom from the press of money. Two years, maybe three. But this is a fortune. Freedom. Enough to pay for a whole new life. Mr. Siang appraises her scarred face. His eyes remain impassive behind the blood-red frames. She stares back, ready for a showdown. She has watched the fiercest fire go dead. After Olivia, she can outlast any living gaze.

The scroll lies between them on the table. The wild, drunken calligraphy, the cryptic poem, the seated figures alone in their old forests, almost transformed, almost a part of everything—all hers to dispose of. But disposing of them suddenly feels criminal. Three trees want something from her. But she has less than no idea what.

Outlasting Mr. Siang is as easy as breathing. Three seconds, and he looks away. As he turns, she sees into his art appraiser's soul. He has stumbled on some reference to this very scroll somewhere in the record. The fact is as clear as the tic on his eyelid. The scroll is worth many times his offer. It's a long-lost national treasure.

She breathes in, fails to suppress a smile. "I wonder if someone over at the Asian Art Museum might help with identification."

The Four Arts revised offer is quick in coming. Neither Mimi nor her two sisters nor their children will need to worry about money for a long time to come. It's a way out for her. Retraining. A new identity. *Why stay here any longer?*

She calls them both, Carmen and Amelia, for the first time in a year. Carmen first. Mimi mentions nothing about her face. About losing her job. About selling her condo. About being wanted in three states. She apologizes for disappearing. "Sorry. I hit a rough patch."

Carmen laughs. "You mean there are smooth ones?"

Mimi mentions the offer.

"I don't know, Mimi. It's a family legacy. What else do we have left of Dad?"

*The three jade trees*, Mimi wants to say. *Waving their urgent arms.* "I just want to do what he'd want."

"Then do what *he* did with it. It's practically the only thing he kept with him his whole life."

Then Amelia. Amelia—healthy, forbearing saint, taming the savage, gleeful children in the background even while listening to her crazy sister. Mimi comes within a breath of saying, *I'm on the run. A friend is dead. I've burnt private property to the ground.* Instead, she reads the translated poem.

"Nice, Mimi. I think it means relax. Relax, love, and do what you want."

"Carmen says it's our only heirloom."

"Geez. Don't get sentimental about it. Dad was the least sentimental man in the world."

"And careful with money."

"Careful? *Cheap!* Remember the basement full of fire sales? Cases of cola and down jackets and half-price socket wrenches?"

"She says he kept that scroll with him his whole life."

"*Pfff.* He was probably trying to time the antiques market."

The world's tie-breaking vote once again falls on shoulders no wider than a child's. That night, the engineer with the abiding smile, the keeper of campsite notebooks, the gentle suicide, whispers to Mimi. He puts the answer right into her ear. *The past is a lote. Prune it and it grows.*

. . .

DOROTHY CAZALY BRINKMAN, smile way too bright, carries a rose-wood tray of breakfast pap from the kitchen into her husband's room. Eyes howl up at her from the mechanical bed. His warped mouth, stiffened in terror, looks like a Greek tragedy mask. She fights the urge to retreat through the doorway. "Morning, RayRay. Did you sleep?"

She sets the tray on the bedstand. The awful eyes follow her. *Buried. Alive. Forever.* She drives herself forward. The lilies of the valley, in their shot glass, go to the bedside table. She turns down the top of the covers, damp with drool. Then she slings the rosewood, with its hot breakfast, over the half-paralyzed body.

Each new morning of method-playacting makes her a little more convincing. Nothing in the world can tell her how many more days like this lie ahead, or how many more she can last. Sound comes out of him. She leans in until her ear touches his lips. All she can hear is, *"Ddddt."*

"I know, Ray. It's okay. Ready?" She makes a comic show of pushing up her sleeves. His mask-mouth moves a little, and she reads that as she needs to. More than paralysis, more than his shattered speech, that mouth changes him into another thing. "It's a new antique grain. From Africa. Good for cell repair."

He lifts his movable hand an inch, probably to stop her. Dorothy ignores him; she has gotten good at that. Soon antique grains dribble down his chin onto the bib. She wipes him with a soft cloth. His stroke-frozen face feels stiff to her touch. But his eyes—his eyes say, as clear as anything, *You're the last bearable thing left to me, aside from death.*

The spoon goes in and out. Some atavistic urge in her wants to make airplane sounds. "Did you hear the owls last night? Calling to one another?" She wipes his mouth and spoons again. She remembers a moment back in week two, when he was still in the hospital. An oxygen mask clung to his face. A drip hung in his arm. He wouldn't stop flicking at them with his one working hand. She had to call the nurse, who bound his hand with gauze restraints. His eyes peeked over the mask and rebuked her. *Let me end it. Don't you see I'm trying to help you?*

For weeks her only thought was, *I can't do this.* But practice pares back the impossible. Practice got her past the pragmatism of doctors and the pity of friends. Practice helps her shift his petrified torso without gagging. Practice teaches her how to hear his iceberg words. With a little more practice, she'll master even being dead.

After breakfast, she checks if he needs cleaning. He does. The disgrace of the first time—suctioned out by a veteran nurse, back in the hospital—left him moaning. Even now, the rubber gloves, the sponge and hose and warm curds she carts away to the bathroom, wet his gargoyle eyes.

She cleans and shifts him in the bed and checks the bedsores. She's all alone today. Carlos and Reba, the mobile care people, come only four times a week, twice as often as Ray would like and half as often as Dorothy needs. She puts her hand on his stone shoulder. Gentleness is the deputy of her fatigue. "TV? Or should I read?"

She thinks he says read. She starts in on the *Times*. But the headlines agitate him.

"Me, too, Ray." She sets the paper aside. "Ignorance can't hurt you, huh?"

He says something. She leans in. "*Crss.*"

"Cross? Not cross, Ray. A stupid joke." He says it again. "*You're* cross? Why?" Aside from the million perfect reasons, she means.

Another syllable squeezes from his rigid lips: "*Wrd.*"

It chills her. His morning ritual, for all the years they've lived together. Impossible now. Worst of all, it's Saturday, demon puzzle day. The only day she has ever heard him curse.

They work the puzzle all morning. She gives the clues, and Ray stares off into the arctic. *Took a hit, maybe. Like Brown's Blue. Held at arms' length.* At geologic intervals, he groans out things that might be words. To her surprise, it's easier on her than parking him in front of the TV. She even catches herself fantasizing that a daily crossword—just going through the motions—might help rebuild his brain.

"Early sign of spring. Five letters. Starts with an *A*."

He stabs out two syllables she can't make out. She asks him to repeat. A growl this time, still nothing but melted slag.

"Could be. I'll pencil it in, and we'll come back to it." Like waltzing with a rag doll. "How about: *Bud's comforting comeback?* Six letters, first one *R*, fourth one *E*, fifth one *A*."

He stares at her, hemmed inside himself. Impossible to say what's left, inside that locked room. His head hangs and his movable hand scrapes the covers, like some grazing beast pawing at the winter snow.

The morning overstays its welcome long before noon. She sets aside the grid, a mess of revisions and appeals. It's time to think about lunch. Something he won't choke on, that she hasn't already served him several times this week.

Lunch is like crossing the Atlantic in a rowboat. In the afternoon, she reads to him. *War and Peace*. The campaign has been long and arduous, stretching out over weeks, but he seems to want it. She has spent so many years trying to convert him to fiction. Now she has a captive audience.

The story runs away, even from her. Too many people having too many feelings to keep track of. The Prince-hero goes down in the middle of an immense battle. He lies paralyzed on his back on the cold earth, with chaos all around. Nothing above the soldier but sky, lofty sky. He can't move; he can only look up. The hero lies wondering how he could have missed the central truth of existence until that moment: the whole world and all the hearts of men are as nothing, lined up underneath the infinite blue.

"I'm so sorry, Ray. I forgot about this part. We can skip ahead."

The eyes howl up at her again. But maybe it's not the fiction that baffles him. Maybe he just can't figure out why his wife keeps crying.

Dinner turns again into a protracted campaign, another land war in Asia. She tucks him in front of the TV. Then she goes out, for a second dinner. Hers. Alan meets her at the door of his workshop. His hair is powdered with wood shavings. His eyes, too, howl a little. She looks away. He takes her in his arms, and it's horribly like coming home. Her fiancé-to-be. Can you have a fiancé, when the divorce has been held up by what her husband's profession likes to call an act of God?

"How was your day?" And yes, he expects her to answer. But tonight, eating take-out General Tso amid the dismembered violins and violas and cellos, the neckless bodies, the bare white top plates hanging in rows on wires, the split maple backs, the smell of spruce and willow blocks, the chunks of pure ebony for fingerboards, the bits of boxwood and recovered mahogany for the fittings, it's just a question of breathing in, one lungful after the other.

She clicks her disposable chopsticks. "I wish we'd met when we were younger. You should have seen me then."

"Aw, no. Older wood is much better. Trees from high up on the northern faces of mountains."

"Glad to be of service."

"It's a shame *I'm* so old. I could get good at this." He waves at the plates of shaved, carved bodies hanging from the rafters. "I'm just now beginning to understand how wood works."

Two hours later, she comes home. Ray must hear the car pulling up the drive, the garage door opening, her key in the back door. But when she enters the room, his eyes are closed and his jagged mouth hangs slack. On the TV, people are laughing like banshees at each other's jokes. She shuts off the set and comes around the bed to turn the stained covers back over his stiff frame. His one good claw snags her wrist. The eyes scream open, that look of hell and murder. She jumps and cries out. Then she's calm and reassuring him.

Always the gentlest man in the world. Sat through her escapades with the patience of a saint. Cried a little when she announced the end, and said he only wanted what was best for her. That she could stay and do what she wanted. That if she were in trouble, she would always have him. She's in trouble now. And yes. Him. Hers. Always.

"Ray! Gosh. I thought you were sleeping." He slews out something murky enough to be chanted Sanskrit. "What's that?" She leans in for an agonizing game of charades with no pantomime. Two syllables, both smeared. "Again, Ray."

As it did in life before death, his patience exceeds hers. The muscles on his unfrozen side thrash. All kinds of specters graze her skin and run their fingers through her hair. "RayRay. I'm sorry. I can't tell what you're saying."

More sounds trickle out of his half-moving lips. She leans back in and hears. At first she hears: *Right.* The real request seems so unlikely she doesn't get it for a moment. *Write.* She hunts down pen and paper, despite all reason. She puts the pen into his marginal hand and watches the fingers move like the needle on a seismograph. It takes him minutes to make a few awful scratches.

She stares at the tangle of tremors and sees nothing. Nonsense, but she can't say that to whatever man is still trapped in the rubble. Then a word emerges, and sense crashes into her. She starts sobbing, tugging at his stiff arm, telling him what he already knows. "You're right. You're *right!*" Six letters, starts with an *R. Bud's comforting comeback.* Releaf.

TWENTY SPRINGS is no time at all. The hottest year ever measured comes and goes. Then another. Then ten more, almost every one of them among the hottest in recorded history. The seas rise. The year's clock breaks. Twenty springs, and the last one starts two weeks earlier than the first.

Species disappear. Patricia writes of them. Too many species to count. Reefs bleach and wetlands dry. Things are going lost that have not yet been found. Kinds of life vanish a thousand times faster than the baseline extinction rate. Forest larger than most countries turns to farmland. *Look at the life around you; now delete half of what you see.*

More people are born in twenty years than were alive in the year of Douglas's birth.

Nick hides and works. What's twenty years, to work that's slower than trees?

We are not, one of Adam's papers proves, wired to see slow, background change, when something bright and colorful is waving in our faces.

You can watch the hour hand, Mimi finds, hold your eyes on it all around the circle of the clock, and never once see it move.

IN *MASTERY 8*, Neelay is 145 pounds and whitish, with hair like Einstein's. His features take on different racial casts depending on the light and what town he's in. He's only four-foot-eight, but his lithe calves and muscular thighs can take him anywhere. His name is Spore, and he's nobody. Like every other homesteader on these eleven continents, he has won a few medals, built some monuments, and stashed away a bit of cash. There are girls in his life, in provinces far from each other. He's the mayor of one flyspeck town and runs a tapestry workshop in another. For a while he served as a priest in a monastery that seems to have gone moribund. Mostly he likes to walk. To drop in on strangers. To watch the branches on the swaying cypresses and see which way the wind is swirling.

He has moved to the parallel world along with hundreds of millions of others, each in their game of choice. He can't remember when the *Web* wasn't here. That's the job of consciousness, to turn Now into *Always*, to mistake what is for what was meant to be. Some days it feels like he and the rest of the Valley of Heart's Delight didn't invent online life, but just cut a clearing into it. Evolution in stage three.

He's out on the open road one Wednesday afternoon when he should be at a board meeting approving the acquisition of a 3-D modeling studio. Instead, he's in the game, doing some private R&D. For days now, he's been on a pilgrimage, trekking from pole to equator, talking to every citizen he meets in every latitude. Random focus groups. Product research and personal exercise, rolled into one.

It's market day outside the town hall of a prosperous city in a canton he has never visited. Under a summoning carillon, people haggle over all kinds of goods and services: carts, candles, engines, optics, precious metals, land, orchards. Homespun clothing, handmade furniture, lutes that make real music. Last year it would have been pure barter: people swapping hard-to-find commodities with one another. But these days it's about real cash—dollars, yen, pounds, euros—millions in electronic transfers, conducted in the world above this one.

"Idiots," someone says, on the town market's channel. Neelay looks around to see who's talking. A buckskin-clad man stands next to him in the crowd. For a second, Neelay thinks it might be a bot, some clever non-player AI. But there's something about the way the figure paces. Something hungry and human.

"Who's an idiot?"

"Don't they get enough of this upstairs?"

"Upstairs?"

"Redox world. Punch the clock, bring home the boar bacon, stuff the house full of shit. This place is as bad as BodyLand."

"Plenty else to do here."

"Used to think so," the man in buckskin says. "You a god?"

"No," Neelay lies. "Why?"

"You have all kinds of buffs."

He makes a note to tone it down the next time out. "Been playing awhile."

"You know where any gods hang out?"

"No. You need something fixed?"

"This whole place."

It angers Neelay. Revenues are at an all-time high. A kid in Korea just killed his mother because she was nagging him to get off the game. He went on for two days, using her credit card and racking up in-game triumphs, while his mother's body lay in the next room. But everyone's a critic.

"What's your problem?"

"Just want to love this place again. Thought it was heaven when I first started playing. A million ways to win. Couldn't even tell what *winning* meant." The buckskinned explorer hangs frozen for a moment. Maybe his animus has to take out the trash or answer the phone or rock the new baby. Then his avatar does a strange little two-step resurrection. "Now it's same old crap over and over. Mine mountains, cut down woods, lay sheet metal across meadows, put up stupid castles and warehouses. Just when you have it how you want, some asshole with mercenaries blows the shit out of you. Worse than real life."

"You want to report some player?"

"You *are* a god, aren't you?"

Neelay says nothing. A god who hasn't been able to walk for decades.

"Know what's wrong with this place? Midas problem. People build shit until the place fills up. Then you gods just make another continent or introduce new weapons."

"There are other ways to play."

"I thought so, too. Mysterious things over the mountains and across the seas. But no."

"Maybe you should go somewhere else."

The buckskinned man waves his arms. "I thought this *was* somewhere else."

The boy who still wants to make a digital kite dance for his long-dead father knows the backwoodsman is right. *Mastery* has a Midas problem. Everything's dying a gold-plated death.



ADAM APPICH gets promoted to associate professor. It's not a respite— just more pressure. His every minute is double-booked: conferences, lit reviews, fieldwork, class prep, office hours, teetering stacks of essays to grade, committees, promotion dossiers, and a long-distance relationship with a woman in publishing 536 miles away.

He's editing an article for publication while watching the news and eating microwave teriyaki in his starter home in Columbus, Ohio. He has time for neither current events nor a real meal. But, squeezing them together while working, he can almost justify. Ten seconds into the story, he realizes what he's staring at: gutted buildings and blackened beams, the aftermath that his own memory can no longer retrieve with any resolution. Someone has bombed a research laboratory in Washington State that was modifying the genome of poplars. The camera lingers on a sooty wall. Spray-painted on the concrete are the words he once helped formulate:

## CONTROL KILLS
## CONNECTION HEALS

*Their* old slogans. It makes no sense. The newscaster only makes things worse. "Authorities believe that the seven-million-dollar blaze is linked to similar attacks conducted over the last several years in Oregon, California, and northern Idaho."

The world divides and doubles, and Adam turns into his own imitation. Then, a more economical explanation: one or more of the others is carrying on alone. Nick, most likely, after his lover's death. Or the childlike vet, Douglas. Or both, joining up with new believers to carry on burning. Whoever set this new fire used the old slogans as if they owned the copyright.

The camera pans over the ruined lab's charred ceiling joist. Adam recognizes the wreckage like he set the charge himself. Not five years ago; last night. Like he just came home and must now incinerate his smoky clothing. The shot lingers on a last bit of spray-paint scrawl at the end of the hallway:

## NO TO THE SUICIDE ECONOMY

Six weeks after becoming an associate professor, he's an arsonist again.

THREE MONTHS LATER, a machine shed in a lumberyard up near the Olympic Peninsula explodes. Mimi reads about it in the *Chronicle*. She's sitting on the grass by the Conservatory of Flowers, in the corner of Golden Gate Park, a ten-minute walk from the Hilltop, University of San Francisco, where she's finishing her master's degree in rehabilitation and mental health counseling. She recognizes the slogans scrawled at the site—slogans that were once all theirs. A sidebar accompanies the news account: "Timeline of Ecological Terror, 1980–1999."

Arrests must be just a matter of time. Next month, next year, a knock on the door, the flash of a badge. . . . People walk past as she sits reading. A drifter with all his worldly belongings in a greasy backpack. Tourists in yellow caps following a woman waving a Japanese flag. Lovers laughing and throwing a stuffed giraffe at each other. Mimi sits on the grass, reading about crimes that she seems to have committed. She spreads the newspaper on the grass in front of her and tilts her head back. The sky swarms with invisible satellites that can locate her coordinates to within ten feet. Cameras in space that can read the headlines in front of her: "Timeline of Ecological Terror." She stares upward, waiting for the future to swoop down and arrest her. Then she gathers up the paper along with her lunch trash and heads past a line of coast live oaks toward Lone Mountain and her afternoon lecture in Ethical and Professional Issues in Therapy.

WORD OF THE NEW FIRES never reaches Nick. He gets his news from bus stops and coffee shops, telemarketers and census takers, panhandlers in small towns all the way up the coast willing to reveal secrets hidden from almost every commentator and analyst, often for free.

In Bellevue, Washington, he lands the perfect job: glorified stock boy, hurtling around on a mini-forklift in an enormous Fulfillment Center, unpacking mountainous pallets of books, scanning their bar codes, then storing their precise locations in the vast, 3-D storage matrix. He's supposed to set land speed records. He does. It's a kind of performance piece for that most rarefied of audiences, no one.

The product here is not so much books as that goal of ten thousand years of history, the thing the human brain craves above all else and nature will die refusing to give: convenience. Ease is the disease and Nick is its vector. His employers are a virus that will one day live symbiotically inside everyone. Once you've bought a novel in your pajamas, there's no turning back.

Nick unpacks the next carton, number thirty-three for today. He can open, scan, and shelve over a hundred crates on a good day, one every four minutes. The faster he goes, the longer he can stave off his inevitable robot replacement. He counts on a couple of years before efficiency comes to kill him. The harder he works, the less he needs to think.

He gets the crate of paperbacks up on their steel shelves and takes stock. The aisle rises on girders into an endless chasm of books. Dozens of aisles in this Fulfillment Center alone. And every month, new Fulfillment Centers across several continents. His employers won't stop until everyone is fulfilled. Nick squanders a full five precious seconds of his time-motion gazing down the gorge of books. The sight fills him with a horror inseparable from hope. Somewhere in all these boundless, compounding, swelling canyons of imprinted paper, encoded in the millions of tons of loblolly pine fiber, there must be a few words of truth, a page, a paragraph that could break the spell of fulfillment and bring back danger, need, and death.

At night, he works on his murals. He cuts the stencils in his apartment, then carries them throughout the city to bare walls he finds on his rambles. It's tempting fate, doing anything that could bring him to the attention of the police. But the compulsion to scream in images is too strong for him. He can complete a medium-sized job, from tape-up to tear-down, in a few dozen minutes. Between two and four a.m., when he would otherwise lie awake feeding on his own insides, he can mark several neighborhoods. Cows with Kevlar jackets. Protesters lobbing maple samara grenades. Tiny warplanes and helicopters swarming the flowers of real trellis-espaliered roses, as if to pollinate them.

Tonight's job is large: covering a suite of lawyers' offices in sixteen overlapping stencils. Up on a stepladder, Nick tapes the numbered sheets together in a great vase that spreads at both top and bottom. Stencils cover the cinderblock façade and turn ninety degrees, where they flow across the sidewalk. Out comes the spray paint, and the cutaway lines fill with colors that leak down the masking paper. A moment to dry, and he pulls away the templates to reveal a chestnut. The branches climb up into the office's second story. Its trunk plunges down and into a mass of roots that tumble over the curb into the street's sewer. At breast height, a little below eye level, the furrows of bark resolve into a two-foot-wide UPC bar code.

Nick takes a finger-wide camel-hair brush and a pot of black enamel out of the backpack and freehands a stanza of Rumi next to the coded bars:

Love is a tree
with branches
in forever
with roots
in eternity
and a trunk
nowhere at all

Someone once read the poem to him, in a tree house, far out on a limb, on the growing edge of creation. *If one of us falls off the edge*, he hears that someone remind him, *the other is going with*. He steps back to evaluate. The effect jars him, and he's not sure he likes it. But liking and not liking—the rod and staff of commodity culture—mean little to him. He wants only to fill as many of these walls as possible with something that can't be walled.

He gathers the stencils and spray cans, stuffs them back into his rucksack, and stumbles back home to five more hours of half sleep in a bed that needs changing. Olivia haunts his dreams, calling again, in the panic of dying, *But this will never end—what we have. Right?*

"LEAVE ME," Ray Brinkman tells his wife, several times each week. But she can't understand the coagulated lumps escaping his mouth, or she pretends not to. He's most content when she's gone for hours at night. Then all his hopes ride on the thought that she is with her friend, changing, talking, hurting, crying out in the dark of some distant room for all things just out of reach. And yet, in the mornings, when she enters his room and says, *Morning, RayRay. All good in here?*, then he can't help feeling his paralyzed variant of joy.

She feeds him and sets him up with the TV. The screen is news, travel, the company of others, a reminder of the luck he'd had all life long and failed to see. This morning, Seattle is at war. Something about the future of the world and all its wealth and property. The breakfast hosts, too, sound confused. Delegates from dozens of countries try to gather in a convention center; thousands of ecstatic protesters refuse to let them. Kids in ponchos and camo pants jump on the roof of a burning armored vehicle. Others tear a mailbox out of the concrete and send it through a plate-glass bank window while a woman screams at them. Under trees that twinkle with the white point lights of Christmas, ranks of black-clad, helmeted troops launch canisters of pink smoke into the crowd. Ray Brinkman, who spent two decades in the trenches protecting patents, cheers each time the police subdue an anarchist. But Ray Brinkman, whom God stopped with a little backhand flick, is smashing glass.

The crowd surges and splits, lashes out and regroups. A phalanx of riot shields beats them back. Synchronized lawlessness flows over the barricades and around the armored cars. The cameras linger on something remarkable in the throng: a herd of wild animals. Antlers, whiskers, tusks, and flapping ears, elaborate masks on the heads of kids in hoodies and bomber jackets. The creatures die, fall to the pavement, and rise again, as if in some Sierra Club snuff film.

A memory steals into Ray's altered head. He shuts his eyes from the pain of it. He recognizes the animal masks, the painted leotards. They're all familiar. He has seen them, in something like a photograph. He knows that can't be, but facts don't erase the uncanny feel. He calls for Dorothy to come shut off the set.

"Read?" she always asks, though she doesn't need to. He'll never tell her no. He lives for read-aloud now. For years, they've worked their way through *The Hundred Greatest Novels of All Time*. He can't remember why fiction used to make him so impatient. Nothing else has more power now to get him through the hours before lunch. He hangs on the most ridiculous plot crumb, as if the future of humanity hinges on it.

The books diverge and radiate, as fluid as finches on isolated islands. But they share a core so obvious it passes for given. Every one imagines that fear and anger, violence and desire, rage laced with the surprise capacity to forgive—*character*—is all that matters in the end. It's a child's creed, of course, just one small step up from the belief that the Creator of the Universe would care to dole out sentences like a judge in federal court. To be human is to confuse a satisfying story with a meaningful one, and to mistake life for something huge with two legs. No: life is mobilized on a vastly larger scale, and the world is failing precisely because no novel can make the contest for the *world* seem as compelling as the struggles between a few lost people. But Ray needs fiction now as much as anyone. The heroes, villains, and walk-ons his wife gives him this morning are better than truth. *Though I am fake*, they say, *and nothing I do makes the least difference, still, I cross all distances to sit next to you in your mechanical bed, keep you company, and change your mind.*

After tens of thousands of pages, they've circled back to Tolstoy and are now a good inch and a half into *Anna Karenina*. Dot resumes the story with no trace of self-consciousness or shame, no hint that art and life have enrolled in the same drawing class. And that, for Ray, is the greatest mercy fiction gives: proof that the worst the two of them have done to each other is just another tale worth reading together, at the end of the day.

As she reads, his eyelids slip. Soon he infiltrates the book, lurking in the margins, a minor character whose fate makes no difference to the story's principals. He wakes to the sound that put him to sleep for a third of a century: his wife's snores. And he's left to do what he has had to do for half a dozen hours a day, every day of this newfound life: stare out the window onto the backyard.

A woodpecker shuttles back and forth onto a blazing oak, stuffing nuts into a girdle of pits. Two squirrels fling themselves in crazed spirals up the trunk of a shed linden. Clouds of small black bugs swarm across the grass tips, unhinged by the coming cold. A shrub he and Dorothy must have put in years ago is clumping in shaggy yellow flowers, even with all its leaves long dead. High drama to a paralytic. The wind throws out gossip; the branches of all the Brinkman anniversary plantings wave, scandalized. There's danger everywhere, readiness, intrigue, slow-motion rising action, epic changes of season once too slow to see that now blast past his bed too quickly to make sense of.

Dorothy snorts herself awake. "Oh! Sorry, Ray. Didn't mean to abandon you."

He can't tell her. No one can ever be abandoned, anywhere, ever. Full-out, four-alarm, symphonic narrative mayhem plays out all around them. She has no idea, and there's no way he can let her know. Civilized yards are all alike. Every wild yard is wild in its own way.

THE CLOCKS of hundreds of millions of interconnected computers prepare to roll over into digits they weren't designed to accommodate. People are stocking their cellars for the end of the Information Age. Douglas doesn't know just when the millennium ends. Where he is, nothing bigger than a week much matters. Daylight these days lasts only a few hours, the snow is six feet deep, and even noontime temperatures will snap the little hairs off your arms. For all Douglas knows, computers have already freaked and taken down the globe's entire infrastructure. Deep in a BLM cabin in his Montana hideaway, he'll be the last to know.

He wakes when the fire dies and he must choose between stoking it or freezing to death. He springs from his arctic bag in his long johns, like something from a cocoon that didn't quite make it out of the larval stage. He dons the parka, but his fingers are so numb he needs fifteen scary minutes to get a couple of pine splits blazing. He toasts his hands on the fire like a couple of s'mores, until he can wiggle his digits again. Breakfast is two eggs, three Viking slices of bacon, and a hunk of stale bread cooked on the top of the woodstove.

Out on the porch, he surveys the town. Gray-brown wooden façades dot the snowy hillside below. The three-story crumbling hotel, the gutted general store, the doctor's office and barbershop, the whorehouse and assorted saloons: all his alone. High on a crest beyond, whitebark pines. The snow is covered with visitors' tracks—elk, deer, jackrabbit—compressed drama he's learning how to read. He sees the cratered snow-poem of a raptor where it swept down, thrashed its prey, then disappeared with no forwarding address.

Winter caretaker for the Friendliest Ghost Town in the West: He has worked some pointless jobs in his life, but never as pointless as this. The passes on both sides—twenty miles of steep rocky potholes—are barricaded in snow. No one will be up here until late May. Okay: *Something* might happen on his watch. A quake, maybe, or a meteor. Aliens. Nothing he'd be able to do anything about. Even his BLM truck with plow blade isn't going anywhere for a good long while.

The mountains are high, the soil steep and thin, the trees have been culled once too often, and all the precious metal mines are spent. All that's left to sell up here is nostalgia, those recent yesterdays when tomorrow seemed the answer to everything a human might ever want. When summer comes, he'll don his miner togs and tell stories to tourists who brave the washboard roads to penetrate to a place whose remoteness alone makes it worth checking off the conquest list. Kids will think he's a hundred and fifty. Families will blast through and snap a few pictures on their way to Old Faithful or Glacier or someplace worth noticing.

He sits at the wobbly kitchen table and picks up the treasure he keeps next to the fused-solid saltshaker. It turned up last fall, a dark brown bottle half buried near the mine's headframe. What's left of the faded label shows a few Chinese characters, creatures from the planet's early oceans. The bottle is a mystery—what it says, what it contained. It belonged to one of the many Chinese laborers who worked in the mine and ran the laundry. He squints at the characters and whispers, "What they do?" His friend taught him the phrase—he can't remember where or when. It had to do with China and her father. It made her laugh every time he said it. He tried to say it often.

He sets the bottle down and starts his morning ritual: the scripture he's writing for his new religion of abject humility. Since mid-November, he has been at work on a Manifesto of Failure. Yellow legal-paper pages scribbled in ballpoint pile up where the table meets the wall. They hold the story of how he became a traitor to his species. He names no names except the forest ones. But it's all there: How the scales fell from his eyes. How awareness turned to anger. How he came across some like-minded people and heard the trees speak. He writes what they'd hoped to do and how they tried to do it. He says where they went wrong and why. Passion everywhere, and bursting with details, but without much structure. His words just branch and bud and branch again. It keeps him busy. It beats cabin fever, though some days not by much.

Today he rereads yesterday's effort—two pages about what it meant to watch his Mimi get her eyes swabbed with fire. Then he takes up the Bic and pushes it in furrows across the page. It's like he's slinging trees again, up and down the contours of a hillside. Problem is, while he's on the general subject of Failure, he can't help probing the nearby, related topic of What the Fuck Went Wrong with Mankind.

The pen moves; the ideas form, as if by spirit hand. Something shines out, a truth so self-evident that the words dictate themselves. We're cashing in a billion years of planetary savings bonds and blowing it on assorted bling. And what Douglas Pavlicek wants to know is why this is so easy to see when you're by yourself in a cabin on a hillside, and almost impossible to believe once you step out of the house and join several billion folks doubling down on the status quo.

He stops to build the fire back up. He finds more forage—peanut butter on crackers and a potato cooked right on the burning pine logs. Then it's time to walk to town and make sure the ghosts are behaving themselves. He layers up and straps on the secondhand snowshoes. The big webbed feet—his winter adaptation—transform him into a hybrid creature, half man, half upright giant hare. Out in the drifts, pegging down the mountain to the husk of town, he postholes anyway, a dozen times or more.

Not a lot of action on Main Street. He checks the tilting buildings, their display cases and exhibits, for any signs of unwelcome nests, gnaw marks, or denning. It's all make-work. Truth is, his Crow Nation boss gives him winter use of the cabin because it costs the BLM nothing, and Douggie invents the inspection routine to earn the freebie. From the upper balcony of the hotel, he calls out, "This place is *dead*." The *ed* bangs around the Garnet Range two or three times before giving up. He climbs back up the long way, along the ridge, to get an extra half a mile of exercise and look out over the gorge. When a day is as clear as today, he can see the distant stands of larch miles away. Conifers that shed in winter.

He pads along, feeling with the snowshoes where the path should be. A slog around the first *S*, and the valley unfolds below. Down the sharp escarpment spreads a carpet of trees so thick it's impossible to believe that the world is, in fact, frayed to the point of snapping. Mounds of sculpted powder weigh down the heavy limbs into skirts that drag on the ground. The purple, upright cones of the firs have disintegrated into seed. But clusters of cones hang in the spruce tops, white-capped eggs that forgot to fall. Juniper grows right out of the raw, unbroken rock. Spruce elders stand in judgment over him.

He wanders to the escarpment for a better look, and what he takes for solid ridge collapses beneath him. The first snow-covered rock on the vertical drop bounces him into the air onto the lip of a thousand-foot tumble. He swings out one foot and clips a cylinder of spruce before smashing his way down the snowy talus. Two hundred feet of scree drop off in front of him. He screams and manages to snag a savior trunk. For the second time, trees save his life.

Blood freezes on his abraded face. The air is so cold it electrocutes his nose. His arm twists outward from his shoulder, wrong. Snow blankets him. He lies still, knowing nothing more than a snow-skirted spruce. The sky darkens. What seemed cold gives way to professional subzero. His brain flickers and he opens his eyes on the white that wants to kill him. He looks back up the ridge and, beaten by the sheer rock face, thinks, *Let me just rest here a little*. In the end, it's the dead woman, kneeling beside him and stroking his face, who gets him up. *You're not just you.*

The sound of his own voice—"I'm not?"—brings him to. The dead woman's stroking fingers turn into a bough of the spruce that he wrapped up on in his fall. His nose is broken and his shoulder dislocated. His old wounded leg is worthless. Night and cold are dropping fast. The bluff rises a steep eighty feet above him. But facts count for nothing. She tells him as much, in four more words. *You're not done yet.*

·  ·  ·

PAST RETIREMENT AGE, Patricia works like there's no tomorrow. Or like tomorrow might yet show up, if enough people dug in and worked. She has two jobs, each the other's opposite. In the one she hates, she stands behind podiums begging for money, stuttering like a black-backed woodpecker pile-driving a pine. She trots out a small stable of dog-and-pony quotes. Blake: *A fool sees not the same tree that a wise man sees.* Auden: *A culture is no better than its woods.* Ten percent of her audience gives her seed bank twenty dollars.

Her staff tells her not to, but she cites the numbers. Wasn't Shaw right about how the mark of true intelligence is to be moved by statistics? Seventeen kinds of forest dieback, all made worse by warming. Thousands of square miles a year converted to *development*. Annual net loss of one hundred billion trees. Half the woody species on the planet, gone by this new century's end. Ten percent of her audience gives her twenty dollars.

She argues economics, good business, aesthetics, morals, spirit. She tells them *stories*, with drama, hope, anger, evil, and characters you can love. She gives them Chico Mendes. She gives them Wangari Maathai. One in ten gives her twenty bucks, and an angel gives a million. That's enough to keep her working the job she loves: flying around the world, pouring unconscionable volumes of greenhouse gas into the air, speeding the planet's doom, collecting seeds and starts from trees that will be gone in no time at all.

Honduran rosewood. Hinton's oak in Mexico. St. Helena gumwood. Cedars from the Cape of Good Hope. Twenty species of monster kauri, ten feet thick and clear of branches for a hundred feet and more. An alerce in southern Chile, older than the Bible but still putting forth seeds. Half the species in Australia, southern China, a belt across Africa. The alien lifeforms of Madagascar that occur nowhere else on the planet. Saltwater mangroves—marine nurseries and the coasts' protectors—disappearing in a hundred countries. Borneo, Papua New Guinea, the Moluccas, Sumatra: the most productive ecosystems on Earth, giving way to oil palm plantations.

She walks through the bleak, manicured remnant woods of overharvested Japan. She walks across living root bridges deep in northeastern India— *Ficus elastica* trained to span rivers by generations of Khasi hill people—

into forests where the natives have been replaced by fast-growing pines. She walks through former expanses of Thai teak, given over to spindly eucalyptus harvested every three years. She surveys what's left of countless acres of Southwest pinyon plowed up to plant wheat. Wild, diverse, uncataloged forests are melting away. Always the locals tell her the same thing: We don't want to kill the golden goose, but it's the only way around here to get to the eggs.

The press loves her enterprise, so desperate and doomed. "The Woman Who Saves Seeds." "Noah's Wife." "Banking Trees Away for a Better Day." She has the world's attention for fifteen minutes. If she'd put her bank in one of those fortresses deep underground in the arctic, she might have rated half an hour. But a boxy bunker in the upper foothills of the Front Range is barely worth a video.

Inside, the vault feels like a chapel crossed with a high-tech library. Thousands of canisters, ordered and labeled with dates, species, and locations, lie in indexed drawers of sealed glass and brushed steel, like a real bank's safe-deposit boxes, except twenty degrees below zero. Standing in the vault, Patricia gets the strangest feeling. She's in one of the most biodiverse regions on Earth, surrounded by thousands of sleeping seeds, cleaned, dried, winnowed, and X-rayed, all waiting for their DNA to awaken and begin remaking air into wood at the slightest hint of thaw and water. The seeds are humming. They're *singing* something—she'd swear it—just below earshot.

The reporters ask why her group, unlike every other NGO seed bank on the planet, isn't focusing on plants that will be useful to people, come catastrophe. She wants to say: *Useful* is *the catastrophe*. Instead, she says, "We're banking trees whose uses haven't been discovered yet." The journalists perk up when she mentions all the hot spots of forest decline, each with its own proximal cause: acid rain, rust, canker, root rot, drought, invasives, failed agriculture, boring insects, rogue fungi, desertification . . . But their eyes glaze over when she tells them how all these threats are made fatal by one single thing: the ongoing overhaul of the atmosphere by people burning once-green things. The monthlies, weeklies, dailies, hourlies, and minutelies each write her up and proceed to the next newer thing. A few people read and send her twenty dollars. And she's free to search the next vanishing forest for the next failing tree.

IN MACHADINHO D'OESTE, in western Brazil, Patricia learns what a forest can do. Shafts of sunlight cut through the vine-covered trunks, the wildest engines of life on Earth. Species clog every surface, reviving that dead metaphor at the heart of the word *bewilderment*. All is fringe and braid and pleat, scales and spines. She fights to tell trees from lanyard strands of liana, orchid, sheets of moss, bromeliad, sprays of giant fern, mats of algae.

There are trees that flower and fruit directly from the trunk. Bizarre kapoks forty feet around with branches that run from spiky to shiny to smooth, all from the same trunk. Myrtles scattered throughout the forest that all flower on a single day. *Bertholletia* that grow piñata cannonballs filled with nuts. Trees that make rain, that tell time, that predict the weather. Seeds in obscene shapes and colors. Pods like daggers and scimitars. Stilt roots and snaking roots and buttresses like sculpture and roots that breathe air. Solutions run amok. The biomass is mad. One swing of a net suffices to fill it with two dozen kinds of beetles. Thick mats of ant attack her for touching the trees that feed and shelter them.

Here, the week is seven long days of census. Dr. Westerford's team counts from dawn to dusk, a workday that should drain any woman in her sixties. But she lives for this. Yesterday they counted 213 distinct species of tree in a little over four hectares, each one a product of the Earth thinking aloud. In so dense a living mass, it's risky to rely on anything as capricious as the wind. Most flavors of tree have their own pollinators. The flip side of this insane diversity is dispersal. The nearest recipient of pollen might be a mile or more away. Every other day, they run across species that none of the team can identify. New and unknown forms of life: *There goes another Lord-knows-what.* Thousands of ingenious kinds of trees spread up the branching river basin. Any one of these disappearing chemical factories might make the next HIV-block, the next super-antibiotic, the newest tumor killer.

The air is so wet it soaks Patricia from the inside out. Walking is hard, in the vine-covered coverts. Every cubic inch is busy converting soil and sun into thousands of volatiles that chemists may never have the chance to identify. Her squad of rubber tappers fans out around her in a police dragnet, to search for the eight thousand Amazonian species that may disappear before she can get them into her temperature-controlled vaults in Colorado.

Well over a century ago, an Englishman smuggled rubber tree pips out of the country, to Brazil's devastation. Now almost all the world's natural rubber grows in South Asia, on land cleared of other trees that no one ever fully cataloged. It puts the Brazilians on their guard about her—another Anglo collector, here to steal their seeds. But on the afternoon when her team discovers mahogany and ipe elders hacked to pieces, they come around. They've never seen anyone who wasn't them, crying over trees.

Her men are armed, if only with their great-grandfathers' nineteenth-century rifles. *Pistoleiros* prowl the stream and roadbeds at night. Poachers kill anyone who comes between them and their harvest. You don't have to be a hundredth of the hero that Mendes was, to die for wood. One of her best guides, Elizeu, tells her a story, through Rogerio, the interpreter, over a night's campfire. "Friend of mine, tapping since childhood—*baff*! Head taken clean off with a piece of trip wire. Just for protecting his little grove."

Elvis Antônio nods, staring into the fire. "We found another, three months ago. His body was stuffed into an animal den in the base of a big tree."

"It's the Americans," Elizeu tells her.

"Americans? Here?" *Stupid, stupid.* She gets it, as soon as the words slip through her mouth.

"Americans make the market. You buy the contraband. You'll pay anything! And our police are jokes. They get their cut. They want the trees to die. It's amazing we're not all smugglers. Compared to tapping rubber? Laughable."

"Then why don't you give up and poach?"

Elizeu smiles, forgiving the question. "You can tap a rubber tree for generations. But you can only poach a tree once."

She falls asleep under her netting, thinking of Dennis. She wishes he could see this place, so much like a boy's book of lost worlds. He's waiting, back at the seed bank in Colorado. He'll never get used to that state. It's way too cheery, cold, and dry—the harshest kind of Oz. He finds it unnatural, all the aspens and sun. *Not a tree out here taller than an adolescent hemlock back home.*

He's happy working on the facility's maintenance, ensuring that the vaults never vary in temperature or humidity. But mostly he spends his fragmented year waiting for the seed hunter to return with her vials full of species that soon will exist nowhere else but in their climate-controlled tombs. He never objects, yet the project doesn't quite convince him. *How long do you think they'll keep in there, babe?*

She has told him about the Judean date palm seed, two thousand years old, found in Herod the Great's palace on Masada—a date pit from a tree that Jesus himself might have sampled, the kind of tree Muhammad said was made of the same stuff as Adam. It germinated, a few years ago. She tells him about the campion seeds, buried yards under the Siberian permafrost. Growing, after thirty thousand years. He just whistles and shakes his head. But he never asks what he wants to ask, what she knows he should. *Who's going to do the replanting?*

SHE WAKES AT DAWN to impenetrable green. Light filters through layers of vine-encased rot, like a picture on the bulletin of a church reverting to paganism. Dennis's unasked question plays in her head. The glut of life outside her tent makes her wonder what good it does to save a species without all the epiphytes, fungi, pollinators, and other symbionts that, in the trenches of the day, give a species its real home. But what's the alternative? She lies in her bag a moment, picturing the campsite as pasture—120 new square miles of cropland a day. And the shrinking forest only speeds the warming world, making it harder to feed.

Back on the trail after breakfast, they come upon a stack of fresh-cut logs. The scouts fan out. In minutes, rifles pop, followed by a motorcycle grunting through the undergrowth. Elvis Antônio returns through the bush, waving his arms in an all-clear. Patricia follows him onto a rough approximation of a road running up into a *pistoleiro* shanty camp evacuated in haste. There's little left but a stack of oily clothes, a bag of moldy manioc flour, soap flakes, and one Portuguese girlie magazine that has made the rounds too many times. They set the camp on fire. The blaze feels good—a tiny orange reversal of progress.

They hike along a streambed to a plain that the guides swear will satisfy all Patricia's desire for rare seeds. She stops along the trail to inspect strange fruit. *Annonas*—soursop, Bullock's heart, custard apple in wild varieties and hybrids, each one up to something. An incredible *Lecythis* overwhelms her with crazy stink. There are silk floss trunks armed all over with spikes. The collection vials come out. They find a dramatic *Bombax* in flower, one unlike anything documented.

Elvis Antônio appears at her side, laughing and tugging on her sleeve. "Come see!"

"Sure. In a minute, yes?"

"Now is better!"

She sighs and follows, into a bower of branches and mad lianas. Four of the men stand marveling at a big tree with buttresses like falling folds of cloth. She can't even guess the family, let alone the genus and species. But the species isn't what interests them. She comes behind the excited men and gasps. No one tells her what to see. A child could make it out. A one-eyed myopic. In knots and whorls, muscles arise from the smooth bole. It's a person, a woman, her torso twisted, her arms lifting from her sides in finger branches. The face, round with alarm, stares so wildly that Patricia looks away.

She steps closer, to see the carving marks. What kind of sculptor would pour such skill and effort into a thing so remote it might never be discovered? But it's not a carving. No sign of sanding or woodworking of any kind. Just the contours of the tree. The men shout hot, fast words in three languages. One of the dendrologists claims, with too many hand gestures, that the wood has been somehow pollarded to look like a woman. The rubber tappers jeer. It's the Virgin, looking on the dying world in horror.

"Pareidolia," Patricia says.

The translator doesn't know the word. Patricia explains: the adaptation that makes people see people in all things. The tendency to turn two knotholes and a gash into a face. The translator says that's not a thing in Portuguese.

Patricia looks harder. The figure is *there*. A woman in the coda of life, raising her eyes and lifting her hands in that moment just before fear turns into knowledge. The face may have been formed by the chance efflorescence of a canker, with beetles as cosmetic surgeons. But the arms, the hands, the fingers: family resemblance. The impression grows stronger as Patricia walks around it. A dog would bark at the twisting body. A baby would cry.

The myths come back to her in this tropical upland, stories from her own childhood and the world's. The young person's Ovid her father gave her. *Let me sing to you now, about how people turn into other things.* She has come across the same stories everywhere she collects seeds—in the Philippines, Xinjiang, New Zealand, East Africa, Sri Lanka. People who, in an instant, sink sudden roots and grow bark. Trees that, for a little while, can still speak, lift up their roots, and move.

The word turns odd, foreign in her head. *Myth. Myth.* A mispronunciation. A malaprop. Memories posted forward from people standing on the shores of the great human departure from everything else that lives. Send-off telegrams composed by skeptics of the planned escape, saying, *Remember this, thousands of years from now, when you can see nothing but yourself, everywhere you look.*

Just upriver, the Achuar—people of the palm tree—sing to their gardens and forests, but secretly, in their heads, so only the souls of the plants can hear. Trees are their kin, with hopes, fears, and social codes, and their goal as people has always been to charm and inveigle green things, to win them in symbolic marriage. These are the wedding songs Patricia's seed bank needs. Such a culture might save the Earth. She can think of little else that can.

Cameras come out of packs. Botanists and guides alike snap away. They argue over what the face means. They laugh at the stupefying odds against anything accidental growing exactly like this, like *us*, out of mindless wood. Patricia does the estimate in her head. The odds are nothing compared to the first two great rolls of the cosmic dice: the one that took inert matter over the crest of life, and the one that led from simple bacteria to compound cells a hundred times larger and more complex. Compared to those first two chasms, the gap between trees and people is nothing at all. And given the outlandish lottery capable of producing any tree, where's the miracle in a tree shaped like the Virgin?

Patricia, too, snaps away, capturing the figure imprinted on the bole. She and the collectors bag some samples for ID. There are no seeds. They press on to more collecting. But every trunk now appears like an infinitely lifelike sculpture too complex for any sculptor but life to have made.

She shows her photos to no one at Seedbed, when she returns from her wanderings to the gleaming facility outside Boulder. Her staff, her scientists, her board of directors: no one has any use for *myth*. Myths are old miscalculations, the guesses of children long ago put to bed. Myths aren't part of the foundation's charter.

But she does show Dennis. She shows Dennis everything. He grins and cocks his head. Dependable Dennis. Seventy-two, and as capable of amazement as a little kid. "Would you look at that! Oh, *man*!"

"It was even eerier in person."

"In *person*. I bet." He can't stop looking. Laughing. "You know, babe? You could use this."

"What do you mean?"

"Make a poster out of this photo. Put a big caption underneath it: *They're Trying to Get Our Attention*."

She wakes up that night, in darkness, with his big, gentle hands slack around her waist. "Dennis?" She tugs at his wrist. "Den?" In a flash, she twists out from under the limp arm and is on her feet. The room floods with light. Arms outward, fingers spread, her face so frozen in horror that even the corpse has to look away.


THE VIOLIN MAKER with wood dust in his hair, the man who calms Dorothy and makes her laugh whenever she wants to buy an assault rifle, the man who wrote her a poem telling her where to look if she ever loses him, is begging her to marry. But the law has this thing about one husband at a time.

"Dory. I can't do this anymore. My halo's falling off. Sainthood's overrated."

"Yes. So is sinnerhood."

"You can't go on vacations with me. You can't even spend the night. It's the best forty-five minutes of my day, whenever you show up. But I'm sorry. I can't be number two anymore."

"You aren't number two, Alan. It's just a double-stops passage. Remember?"

"No more double-stops. I need a nice long solo melody before the piece is over."

"Okay."

"Okay, what?"

"Okay. Eventually."

"Dory. Christ. Why are you martyring yourself? Nobody expects you to. Even *he* doesn't."

No one can speak for what *he* expects. "I signed the papers. I made a promise."

"What promise? You were on the verge of a divorce, two years ago. You two had practically divvied up the estate already."

"Yeah. That was back when he could walk. And talk. And sign agreements."

"He has insurance. Disability. Two caregivers. He can afford someone full-time. You can even keep helping. I just want you to live here. To come home to me every night. My wife."

Love, as all the good novels know, is a question of title, deed, and possession. She and her lover have hit this wall many times before. Now, in the new millennium, the man who has kept her sane, the man who might even have been her soul mate if only her soul were a slightly different shape, hits the wall one last time and collapses at its base.

"Dory? It's time. I'm tired of sharing."

"Alan, it's share or nothing."

He chooses nothing. And for a long time, she dreams of choosing the same.

One crystal blue fall morning, a bellow comes from the other room. Her nickname, stretched out to the length of stillness, without the final consonant: *Daaa* . . . Her skin creeps. It's worse than the bellow he makes when he fouls the bed and needs her to come clean him. Once more she runs, as if there never has been a false alarm. In the room, someone is talking to her husband, and he's groaning. She flings the door open. "I'm here, Ray."

At first glance, there's only the man in the frozen terror mask, the one she has gotten used to, at last. Then she turns and sees. She lowers herself to the bed, next to him. The television is saying, "Oh, my goodness. Oh, my goodness." Saying, "That is the *second* tower. That just happened. Live. On our screen."

Some hard, skittering animal in the bed grazes at her wrist. She startles and shouts. Her husband's movable hand, knocking against hers.

"It's deliberate," the screen says. "This must be deliberate."

She takes his stiff, curled fingers and grips them. They stare together, understanding nothing. Orange, white, gray, and black billow against a cloudless blue. The towers vent, like cracks in the crust of the Earth. They waver. Then drop. The screen staggers. People in the streets scatter and scream. One of the towers folds up flat, like collapsible hanging shelves. The animal shrieking will not stop. Refusal trickles from Ray's mouth. "*Nh, nh, nh . . .*"

She has seen this before: monstrous columns, too big to be felled, falling. She thinks: *Finally, the whole strange dream of safety, of separation, will die*. But when it comes to prediction, she has always been worse than wrong.


HYDE STREET, in Nob Hill, on a block lined with camouflaged California sycamores and one crooked Asian plum that bursts out in cream craziness for three weeks each spring. Mimi Ma sits in her shade-drawn first-floor office, preparing for her second and final client of the day. The first lasted three hours. It was his contractual right to stay however long he needed. But the session polished her down to a blunted nib. The second one will suck the day's remaining life from her. She'll retreat to her apartment in the Castro tonight to watch nature documentaries and listen to trance music. Then sleep and rise to face two more clients tomorrow.

Unconventional therapists flood this city—counselors, analysts, spirit guides, self-actualizing assistants, personal consultants, and borderline char-latans, many as surprised as Mimi to find themselves in the trade. But her reputation has spread so well by word of mouth that she can afford the office's absurd rent while seeing only two clients a day. The real question, session by session, is whether she can stay sane herself as her clients eat her soul.

Many of her prospective patrons suffer from nothing worse than too much money. She tells them so, at the screening interviews every other Friday. She won't see anyone who isn't in pain, and she can tell how much pain a person is in within twenty seconds of their sitting in the wing chair that faces hers in her bare session room. She talks to each applicant for a few minutes, not about their psyches, but about the weather, sports, or childhood pets. Then she'll either schedule a session or send the seeker home, saying, "You don't need me. You just need to see that you're already happy." For that advice, she charges nothing. But for a real session, there must be some sacrifice. Two such sacrifices a day suffice to keep her afloat.

She sits to the right of the bricked-up fireplace, recovering. In the ante-room of fifty, she's still slim, from the distance running she has taken up, although the cowl of black hair has chestnut highlights now. Still marked by the scar across one cheek that has never vanished. Her hand strokes her steel-gray jeans and travels the pleats of her cyan blouse, the one that makes her feel a little like a troubadour. Her office manager has called the next client to say that the therapist is free. There's just enough time to climb up out of the morning's four-hour cauldron of fear, grief, hope, and transfigu-ration shared with a total stranger before plunging back into it with another.

She bathes her mind in Zen aimlessness. She picks up one of the framed photos from the mantelpiece—the one of an elderly Chinese couple holding up a photo of three little girls. It's a studio shot, in front of a backdrop. The man wears an expensive linen suit and the woman a silk dress tailored in Shanghai before the war. The couple gaze sadly at the photo of their Ameri-can granddaughters with the inscrutable names. They'll never meet these foreign girls or their mother, that fallen Virginia scion, who will die in a facility after forgetting what species she is. And their wandering son: it's like the couple already know, as the lens opens, at this precise moment years before the violent crime. How does a man rise or fall in this life? The fisherman's song flows deep under the river.

Once there was a little girl, bristly, a bully, even, trying to preserve herself across a great divide. Not yellow, not white, not anything Wheaton had ever seen. Only that fisherman ever knew her, motionless by her side on long slow days in untamed places, when they both stared and cast into the same running stream. She feels it again, worse for the unthinkable time and distance—rage at his leaving. Then rage at the world for cutting down the harmless grove where his ghost liked to walk, where she liked to sit and ask him *why*, where she once almost even got an answer.

A chime shatters Mimi's reverie. Stephanie N., her afternoon guest, arrives in the front office. Mimi returns the photo and presses a button on the underside of the mantel, telling Katherine that she's ready. A soft knock on the door, and Mimi rises to greet an ample, wiry-haired redhead with tortoiseshell glasses. The hunter-green tunic and its half cape fail to hide her paunch. It doesn't take a rabid empath to feel the visitor's broken mainspring.

Mimi smiles and touches Stephanie's shoulder. "Relax. There's nothing to worry about."

Stephanie's eyes widen. *There isn't?*

"Hold still. Let me have a look while you're standing. You've gone to the bathroom? You've eaten? You left your cell phone, watch, and all other devices with Katherine? Not carrying anything? No makeup or jewelry?" Stephanie is clean on all counts. "Good. Please, sit."

The visitor takes the proffered chair, unsure how this can lead to the magic that her brother-in-law called the most bruising, profound experience of his adult life. "Wouldn't it help to know a little about me?"

Mimi cocks her head and smiles. There are so many names for the thing that everyone is scared to death of, and everyone wants to tell you *theirs*. "Stephanie? By the time we're done, we're going to know more about each other than there are words for."

Stephanie daubs at her eyes, nods, laughs two syllables, then flicks her fingers. Ready.

Four minutes in, Mimi stops the session. She leans in and touches Stephanie's knee. "Listen. Just look at me. That's all you need to do."

Stephanie palms an apology and reels her hand back in to her lips. "I know. I'm sorry."

"If you're self-conscious . . . if you're afraid, don't worry. It doesn't matter. Just keep your eyes on mine."

Stephanie bows her head. She sits up, and they try again. It happens often, this false start. No one suspects how hard it is to hold another's gaze for more than three seconds. A quarter minute and they're in agony—introverts and extroverts, dominants and submissives alike. Scopophobia hits them all—fear of seeing and being seen. A dog will bite if you stare at it too hard. People will shoot you. And though she has looked for hours into the eyes of hundreds of people, though she has perfected the art of endurance staring, Mimi feels a tinge of fear herself, even now, gazing into the skittering eyes of Stephanie, who, blushing a little, powers through the shame and settles down.

The women lock in, awkward and naked. A tic at the corner of Stephanie's lips makes Mimi smile back.

*Sheesh*, the client's eyes say.

*Yes*, the therapist agrees. *Humiliating.*

The awkwardness turns pleasant enough. Stephanie the likable, Stephanie the good-natured, the mostly self-assured. *I'm a decent person. See?*

*It doesn't matter.*

Stephanie's lower lid tightens and her *orbicularis oculi* twitches. *Do I make sense to you? Am I much like everyone else? Why do I feel like I'm falling through the cracks of social goodwill?*

Mimi squints less than the width of two lashes. Microscopic reprimand: *Just look. Just. Look.*

Five minutes in, Stephanie's breathing shifts and narrows. *Okay. I see. I'm getting this.*

*You haven't even started.*

Mimi watches the woman come into focus. A mother, and of more than one. Cannot stop taking care of the therapist. Wife of a man who, after a dozen years, has become civil and distant, a bear in his lair. Sex is perfunctory maintenance at best. *But you're mistaken*, the speculating therapist tells herself. *You know nothing.* And the thought registers across the minute muscles of her face. *Just look.* Looking must correct and heal all thoughts.

At ten minutes, Stephanie fidgets. *When does the magic start to happen?* Mimi's eyes bear down. Even in this tedium, Stephanie's pulse rises. She sits forward. Her nostrils flare. Then everything relaxes, from scalp to ankles. *Well, here goes. What you see is what you get.*

*What I get is beyond your control.*

*The weird shit in this room had better not leave it.*

*Safer than Vegas.*

*I'm not sure what I'm doing here.*

*Me neither.*

*I'm not sure I'd like you if I met you at a party.*

*I don't always like myself. At parties, almost never.*

*This can't possibly be worth what I'm paying. Even if I stay all afternoon.*

*What is it worth to be looked at, without judgment, for as long as you need?*

*Who am I kidding? It's my husband's money.*

*I'm living off my father's inheritance. Which might have been stolen.*

*I've let men define me.*

*I'm really an engineer. I'm only pretending to be a therapist.*

*Help me. I wake up at three in the morning with a black thing clawing my chest.*

*My name isn't really Judith Hanson. I changed it from Mimi Ma.*

*On Sundays when the sun goes down I don't want to live.*

*Sunday evenings save me. Just knowing that, in a few hours, I'll be working again.*

*Is it the towers? I think it might be the towers. I've been so brittle, like frozen glass—*

*Towers are always falling.*

A quarter hour passes. Unrelenting human scrutiny: the weirdest trip Stephanie has ever been on. Fifteen endless minutes of staring at a woman she doesn't know from Eve triggers things, things she hasn't thought about in decades. She looks at Mimi and sees a crow's-footed, scar-faced, Asian version of her high school girlfriend, a girl she broke with at nineteen over some imagined slight. There's no one to apologize to now except this stranger who won't stop staring at her.

Time passes, a lifetime, a few more seconds, in a room with nothing to look at but a stranger's damaged face. The trap closes around Stephanie. Her eyes cloud with resentment bordering on hate. A tremor of Mimi's lips sends Stephanie back to that day three years ago when she at last faced down her mother and called her a bitch. And her mother's mouth, in that instant . . . Stephanie squeezes her eyes shut—rules of this game be damned—and when she opens again, she sees her mother, eight more months down the line of panic, on a respirator in the hospital, dying of COPD, fighting to keep all thought of that day's accusation out of her face as her daughter leans in to kiss her stony forehead.

The watch that Stephanie left in the reception room ticks on, out of sight and hearing. Away from it, far from all claims on her, the visitor remembers herself, soft, sad, out of nowhere, at the age of six, wanting to be a nurse. Toy props—syringe, blood pressure cuff, white hat. Picture books and dolls. Three years of obsession, followed by thirty-five of amnesia, retrieved only by going down the rabbit hole of another woman's eyes. Nothing else exists outside this pact. Pupils lock and can't look away. The years parade through Stephanie's mind—childhood, youth, adolescence, the immunity of young adulthood followed by endless scared maturity. She's naked now, in front of someone she has agreed never to try to see again after today.

Through the two-way mirror, Mimi sees. *Such pain you're in. Here, too. How can it be?* In a patch of sun that falls between them, a green feeling opens to the light. Mimi lets it play across her face, there for the seeing. Therapy. *You remind me of my sisters.* She lets this woman in, up into the breakfast tree, backyard, Wheaton, Illinois, where she, Carmen, and Amelia have already taken their cereal bowls up onto the summer limbs and are busy reading each other's futures in the floating oat rings. That Virginia missionary's daughter stands at the kitchen window, the one who'll die of dementia in a nursing home without ever having looked her daughters in the eye for more than half a second. That Hui man, coming from the house to call to his daughters, *My silk farm! What you do?* The mulberry, sweet, crooked, and open, rounded with shade, dripping peace, lying about everything the future would hold.

A great sororal surge comes over Stephanie. She reaches her hand to this slight, half-Asian shaman four feet from her. One quick tightening of Mimi's corrugator muscles warns her off. There's more. So much more.

At half an hour, Stephanie melts down. She's hungry, stiff, itchy, and so sick of herself she wants to sleep forever. The truth seeps out of her, a bodily discharge. *You shouldn't trust me. I don't deserve this. You see? I'm fucked up in ways even my children don't suspect. I stole from my brother. I left the scene of an accident. I've had sex with men whose names I don't even know. Several times. Recently.*

*Yes. Hush. I'm wanted in three states.*

Their faces feed pitiless into one another. Muscles move, the world's slowest flip-book. Terror, shame, desperation, hope: each lasts its own three-second lifetime. After an hour, the islands of emotion wash into an open sea. The two faces swell; their mouths and noses and brows expand to fill a Rushmore. Truth hovers between them, great and nebulous, a thing their bodies keep them from reaching.

Another hour. Deserts of infinite boredom punctuated by peaks of freakish intensity. More annihilated memories percolate up from below, so many moments, recovered and lost again in this loop of looking. Hydra-like, multiplying memories longer than the lives that made them. Stephanie sees. So clear now: She's an animal, a mere avatar. The other woman, too—stuff-imprisoned spirit, deluded into thinking it's autonomous. And yet conjoined, linked to each other, a pair of local gods who have lived and felt all things. One of them has a thought, which at once becomes the other's. Enlightenment is a shared enterprise. It needs some other voice saying, *You are not wrong. . . .*

*If only I could remember this in real time, under fire! I'd be cured.*

*There are no cures.*

*Is this it? Is there more? Maybe I should go.*

*No.*

In hour three, truths flow loose and terrible. Things come out of hiding that would lose them membership in any club but this one that they can't quit.

*I've lied to my closest friends.*

*Yes. I let my mother die unattended.*

*I spied on my husband and read his private letters.*

*Yes. I cleaned bits of my father's brain off the backyard flagstones.*

*My son won't talk to me. He says I ruined his life.*

*Yes. I helped kill my friend.*

*How can you bear to look at me?*

*There are harder things to bear.*

The sunlight changes. Slits of light crawl up the walls. It occurs to Stephanie to wonder if it's still today, or if that was some time ago. Her pupils have long since started to seesaw, closing and dilating by turns, dimming and glaring the room. She can't even summon up the will to stand and leave. When it can't go on, that's when this will end. Then they'll never see each other again, except for always.

Her eyes burn. She blinks, numb, dumb, ravenous, wrecked, and badly in need of emptying her bladder. Something keeps her from breathing—this frail, scarred woman who won't look away. Pinned in that look, she becomes something else, huge and fixed, swaying in the wind and pelted by rain. The whole urgent calculus of need—what she called her life—shrinks down to a pore on the underside of a leaf, way out on the tip of a wind-dipped branch, high up in the crown of a community too big for any glance to take in. And way down below, subterranean, in the humus, through the roots of *humility*, gifts flow.

Her cheeks tense up. She wants to shout, *Who are you? Why won't you stop? No one has ever looked at me like this, except to judge, rob, or rape me. In my whole life, my whole life, never. . . .* Her face reddens. With slow, heavy, disbelieving swings of her head, she starts to cry. The tears do whatever they want. Call it sobbing. The therapist is crying, too.

*Why? Why am I sick? What's wrong with me?*

*Loneliness. But not for people. You're mourning a thing you never even knew.*

What thing?

*A great, spoked, wild, woven-together place beyond replacing. One you didn't even know was yours to lose.*

*Where did it go?*

*Into making us. But it still wants something.*

Stephanie is up and out of the chair, clinging to the stranger. Taking her by the shoulders. Nodding, crying, nodding. And the stranger lets her. Of course, grief. Grief for a thing too big to see. Mimi pulls back to ask if Stephanie is all right. All right to leave. All right to drive. But Stephanie puts fingers on her mouth and hushes the therapist forever.

The changed woman makes it out onto Hyde Street. Two façade painters up on a scaffold yell at each other over a blaring radio. Men with dollies unload stacks of boxes from a delivery truck six doors up the street. A guy in a dirty suit jacket and shorts, his hair bound up in a bungee cord, cuts behind her on the sidewalk, talking out loud: voices or cell phone—choose your schizophrenia. Stephanie steps into the street, and a car screams past. The rage of its horn Dopplers downward for another block. She fights to hold on to the thing she has just glimpsed. But traffic, bickering, business: the street's brutality begins to close in. She walks faster, on the brink of the old panic. Everything she has just won begins to fade again into the irresistible force of other people.

Something sharp grazes her face. She stops and touches her scraped cheek. The culprit floats in front of her, purple-pink, the colors of a five-year-old's crazed sketch. Escaping from a metal cage in the sidewalk near her feet is a thing twice her height and half again as wide as her extended arms. A single stout upward path splits into a few thinner ones, and those divide into thousands more, thinner still, each one tentative, forked, full of scars, bent by history, and tipped out in insane flowers. The sight takes root in her, ramifying, and for a moment longer she remembers: her life has been as wild as a plum in spring.

JUST DOWN THE ROAD two thousand miles east, Nicholas Hoel drives into an Iowa June. Every dimple in the land, every remembered silo just off the interstate twists his gut, like the last thing he sees before dying. Like coming home.

The math stuns him—how few years he has been away. So much has gone untouched. The farms, the roadside warehouses, the desperate public service billboards: FOR GOD SO LOVED THE WORLD . . . So many imprints from deepest childhood, permanent scars in the prairie and in him. Yet every landmark seems warped and remote, seen through dime store binoculars. Nothing here should have survived where he's been.

Over the last rise to the west before the exit, his pulse shoots up. He looks for the horizon's lone mast. But where the column of the Hoel Chestnut should be, there's only June's annihilating blue. He heads the car up the exit ramp and drives the long square back around to the farm. Only: it's not a farm anymore. It's a manufactory. The owners have removed the tree. He parks the car halfway up the gravel drive and walks out across the field toward the stump, forgetting that the field is no longer his to walk across.

A hundred and fifty steps in, he sees the green. Dozens of fresh chestnut shoots spring up from the dead stump. He sees the leaves, the straight-veined, toothed lances of his childhood that always meant *leaf* to him. For a few heartbeats, resurrection. Then he remembers. These fresh starts, too, will soon be blighted. They'll die and rise again, over and over, just often enough to keep the deadly blight alive and vigorous.

He turns toward the ancestral house. His hands lift, to reassure anyone in the parlor who might be watching. But it's the house, in fact, and not the tree, that has stopped living. Siding pulls away from the walls. On the north side, half a length of gutter hangs down. He checks his watch. Six oh-five— obligatory dinner hour throughout the Midwest. He crosses the weedy lawn and walks up to the east windows. They're matte, dusty, lusterless, dimmed with only dark behind them. The stiles, rails, head jamb, and all the wood around the double-hung panes soften into paint-peeled rot. Cupping one hand around his eyes, Nicholas peeks in. His grandparents' living room is filled with metal basins and canisters. The oak trim that covered every doorway in the house has been stripped away.

He walks around to the front porch. Its planks wobble beneath him. Five raps of the brass knocker yield nothing. He climbs the rise behind the house to the old outbuildings. One has been torn down. One is gutted. The third is locked. His old trompe l'oeil mural—that crack in the wall of the cornfield revealing a hidden broadleaf forest—is gunmetal-gray.

On the front porch again, he sits where the rocker used to be, his back to the front window. It's not clear how he should proceed. It crosses his mind to break in. He has spent the last three nights sleeping rough. Scared shitless by a cow near the Bighorns in Wyoming, who nuzzled him in his bag before dawn. Kept awake in a national forest in Nebraska by two campers setting endurance records in a nearby tent. A bed would be nice. A shower. But the house, it seems, has neither anymore.

He waits for the softening smudge of midwestern dusk, though there's no real need for cover. Far away, a satellite-guided agribiz monster, practically robotic, combs through the rolling fields. No one will pass here or see him at his task. He can do what he needs to and go.

But he waits. Waiting has become his religion. There's corn to listen to, miles of it. Beans to watch grow, sheds and silos on the horizon, an interstate, and a huge tree cut out of the sky in negative space, like a Magritte. He sits with his back against the house, feeling the farm emerge again, like wild animals from the edges of a trail when the hiker holds still long enough. As the clouds crimson out, he heads to the car and retrieves his folding campfire shovel. Wrong tool for the wrong job, but the best he has. In a minute, he's on the rise behind the machine shed, looking for loose gravel. The ground feels different; the distances are wrong. Even the machine shed has been moved.

The scree turns up, hiding under a lush green shag. He snicks the campfire shovel into the weeds and digs until he hits the past. Return of the repressed. He hauls up the carton and opens it. Panels and some works on paper. He holds the top painting to the day's last light. A man lies in bed, staring down the tip of a large branch that comes growing in through his window.

That's how it happened. He was sleeping, and she burst in. Each of them had half a prophecy. They put them together and read the message. They found their joint calling, their shared vocation. The spirits guaranteed that all would be well. Now she's dead, he's sleepwalking again, and the things they were to save are all going down.

He sets the carton down beside the hole and digs again. The second box surfaces, filled with paintings he forgot he made: *Family Tree, Shoe Tree, Money Tree, Barking up the Wrong Tree*. All painted in the years before she came up the driveway with stories of resurrection and voices of light. The paintings proved that they were meant to head off together. The paintings were wrong.

He stacks the second box on top of the first and keeps digging. The shovel tip hits something jagged, and he finds the sculpture lode. He and Olivia buried four of them loose, to see what the living soil might do to the ceramic skins. Dirt: Another thing she taught him to see. A new inch or two, every few centuries. A microscopic forest, a hundred thousand species in a few Iowa grams. He drops to his knees, pries out the pieces with his fingers, and wipes them with a spit-dampened handkerchief. Their monochrome surfaces now shine as rich-hued as Breughels. Bacteria, fungi, invertebrates—living workshops down in the underground horizons—have spattered patinas across the sculptures in a masterpiece of blooms.

He sets the transmuted statues on top of the rescued boxes and returns for the real prize. He wonders again what he could have been thinking, leaving it here. Travel light, they thought. Bury the art. Digging it up later would be its own performance piece. But the thing still in the ground is worth more than his own life, and he should never have let it out of his sight. Six more shovelfuls, and it's his again. He opens the box, unzips the bag, and holds the hundred-year stack of photos in his hands. Too dark to see now, to flip through them. He doesn't need to. Holding the stack, he feels the tree spiraling up into the air like a corkscrew fountain, watched over by generations of Hoels.

He carries half of the trove down the rise, back to his car. He gets the loot into the trunk and turns back for the rest. Halfway to the burial site, two white lights pierce the gravel driveway from the dark road. Police.

The thing to do is walk toward the squad car with open palms. Every explanation can be documented. The evidence will support his story. Trespassing, yes, but only to retrieve what's his. He comes out from behind the house and the headlights veer toward him. It occurs to him that the buried treasure in question might not, in fact, be his any longer. He sold the land and everything rooted in it. Buying and selling land: as absurd as getting arrested for recovering your own art.

The squad car jerks up the drive, its wheels spewing gravel. A blast of spinning red stops Nicholas in place. The car swings to a stop, flaring into a barricade. Siren whoop gives way to an amplified voice: "Freeze! Down on the ground!"

He can't do both. He raises his hands and drops to his knees. Travels back forty years to a grade-school skit: *The rain came down and washed the spider out.* Two officers are on him in a heartbeat. Only then does it strike Nicholas that he's in real trouble. If they fingerprint him, if they run his record . . .

"Hands out." One of the officers presses into Nick's back and draws his wrists together. Once he's cuffed, they sit him up on the ground, shine a flashlight in his face, and take his data.

"It's trinkets," he tells them. "Worthless."

Their faces curl when he shows them his art. Why would someone want to *make* such things, let alone steal them back? The only part of the story that makes sense to them is the burying. But the older cop recognizes the name on Nick's driver's license. Part of local history. Landmark for the whole area: *Keep going, a mile, mile and a half past the Hoel tree.*

They call the business manager in charge of the property. The man has zero interest in bits of dug-up rubbish. Rural Iowa: the police don't look up his arrests in the national database. He's just another semi-delusional, semi-vagrant from a ruined farm family, driving a dinged-up car and trying to hold on to a vanished past. "You can go now," the police tell him. "No more digging on private property."

"Can I just . . . ?" Nick waves his hand toward the unburied treasure. The officers shrug: *Knock yourself out.* They watch as Nick puts the last cartons in his car. He turns to them. "Have you ever seen a tree grow eighty years in ten seconds?"

"You take care, now," says the cop who pinned him to the ground. Then they send the three-time arsonist on his way.

NEELAY SITS at the head of the oval table facing his top five project managers. He spreads his bony fingers on the table in front of him. He doesn't know where to start. It's even hard to know how to address the game. There are no version numbers anymore. They've been replaced by continuous upgrades. *Mastery Online* is now a mammoth, expanding, ever-evolving enterprise. But it's rotten at its core.

"We have a Midas problem. There's no endgame, just a stagnant pyramiding scheme. Endless, pointless prosperity."

The team listens, frowning. They all earn six figures; most are millionaires. The youngest is twenty-eight, the oldest forty-two. But in their jeans and skateboard tees, their mop tops and skewed baseball caps, they look like simulated teens. Boehm and Robinson kick back, sipping energy drinks and munching trail bars. Nguyen has his feet up on the table and gazes through the window as if it's a virtual reality headset. All five beep and ding, whistle and vibrate with more prosthetic parts than sci-fi ever dreamed of.

"How do you win? I mean, how would you even *lose?* The only thing that really counts is hoarding a little bit more. You reach a certain level in the game, and going on just feels hollow. Dirty. More of the same."

The man in the wheelchair at the table's head bows and stares into his own grave. The long, Sikh-style hair still flows down around his middle, but it's shot through now with a river of white. A beard erupts from his chin and falls like a bib onto his Superman sweatshirt. His arms still have some meat on them, from decades of lifting himself in and out of bed. But his legs inside their cargo pants are little more than vague suggestions.

In front of him, on the table, is a book. The elves know what that means: the boss has been reading again. Another visionary idea has taken possession of him. Soon he'll badger them all to read it, in search of solutions to what is a problem only to him.

Kaltov, Rasha, Robinson, Nguyen, Boehm: five ebullient honors students huddle up in a super-smart war room, equipped with banks of screens and all the electronic conferencing toys tomorrow might need. But today they can only stare at the boss, slack-jawed. He's saying *Mastery* is broken. A magic, money-printing franchise needs to be rethought.

Exasperation threatens to set Kaltov's mustache on fire. "It's a god game, for god's sake. They pay us so that they can enjoy a god's problems."

"We're up to seven million subscribers," Rasha says. "A quarter of them have been playing for a decade. Players are hiring Chinese inmates with Web connections to level up their characters while they sleep."

The boss does that thing with his eyebrows. "If leveling was still fun, they wouldn't have to do that."

"There might be a problem," Robinson concedes. "But it's the same problem we've been dealing with since *Mastery* began."

Neelay's head bobs up and down, but not in a nod. "I wouldn't say 'dealing.' 'Postponing,' maybe." He's grown so gaunt he's set for sainthood. The lip of the sagging Superman sweatshirt reveals his protruding collarbone. He's like one of those ascetic Indian statues, a skin-wrapped skeleton seated under a holy fig or neem.

Boehm projects some visuals. "Here's what we're thinking. We raise the experience level caps again. We add a bunch of technologies. We call them *Future Tech One*, *Future Tech Two* . . . They all generate different flavors of prestige points. Then we release another volcanic event out in the middle of the Western Ocean and start a new continent."

"That sounds like postponing to me."

Kaltov flings up his hands. "People want to grow. Expand their empires. That's why they pay us every month. The place fills in. We make it a little bigger. There's no other way to run a world."

"I see. Lather, rinse, repeat, until you die of consummation."

Kaltov slaps the table. Robinson laughs, giddy. Rasha thinks: *It's just the boss, the guy who writes a million memos a week, the guy who built the company from nothing, exercising his genius right to be wrong.*

"Which is more interesting?" Neelay asks. "Two hundred million square miles filled with a hundred kinds of biome and nine million species of living things? Or a handful of flashing colored pixels on a 2-D screen?"

Nervous laughter around the table. They get which should make the better home. But each one knows his own delight's current mailing address.

"Pretty clear where the species is emigrating, boss."

"*Why?* Why give up an endlessly rich place to live in a cartoon map?"

It's a little too much philosophy for the boy millionaires. But they humor the man who hired them all. They loosen into the question, listing the glories of symbol-space: the cleanness, the speed, the instant feedback, the power and control, the connectivity, the sheer amount of stuff you can amass, the buffs and badges. All the compliant pleasures that light up the whole cortex. They talk about the purity of the game, how it's always going somewhere, at a clip that's clearly visible. You can see progress unfold. Effort means something.

Neelay nods his refusal again. "Until it doesn't. Until it turns tedious."

The group falls silent. Mass sobriety sets in. Nguyen takes his feet off the table. "People want a better story than they get."

The wild-haired sadhu leans forward so fast he almost pitches out of his wheelchair. "Yes! And what do all good stories do?" There are no takers. Neelay holds up his arms and extends his palms in the oddest gesture. In another moment, leaves will grow from his fingers. Birds will come and nest in them. "They kill you a little. They turn you into something you weren't."

Awareness spreads through them, slow and certain as death. The boss is playing another game now, one that would have no trouble burning their game as fuel. Boehm asks, "What are you saying we should do?"

Neelay holds up the book, like it's divine dictation. They can read the title on the cover, under the rising web of leaves. *The Secret Forest*. Robinson groans. "Not more plants, boss. You can't make a game out of plants. Unless you give them bazookas."

"Let's put an atmosphere into the model. Add water quality. Nutrient cycles. Finite material resources. Let's make prairies and wetlands and forests that capture the richness and complexity of the real deals."

"And then what? Bleaching reefs and rising seas and drought-driven wildfires?"

"If that's how people play it."

"Why on Earth? Our players want to get away from all that shit."

"The game wants its players. That's the great mystery."

"How would you win *that*?" Kaltov taunts.

"By finding out what works. By pushing the way truth pushes."

"You're saying no new continents."

"No new continents. No sudden spawning of new mineral deposits. Regeneration only at realistic rates. No rising from the grave. A wrong choice in the game should lead to permadeath."

The elves catch each other's eyes. The boss is out of control. He's willing to crash the franchise, to trash the endless moneymaker that will keep them all in junkets forever just to solve the problem of too much satisfaction.

"How . . . ?" Nguyen says. "How are limits and shortages and permadeath going to be fun?"

For a moment the sunken face turns rubbery, and the boss is a little kid again, learning how to program, his code branching outward in all directions. "Seven million users will need to discover the rules of a dangerous new place. To learn what the world will bear, how life really works, what it wants from a player in exchange for continuing to play. Now, that's a game. A whole new Age of Exploration. What more adventure could you ask for?"

Kaltov says, "Better sell your Sempervirens stock, then. Because every player we have is going to quit. They'll walk!"

"Walk *where*? There's too much on the line. Most of our players have invested years. They've built up fortunes of in-game worth. They'll figure out how to rehabilitate the place. They'll surprise us, like they've always done."

The elves sit dumbfounded, calculating the fortunes vanishing before their eyes. But the boss—the boss is glowing like he hasn't since he fell from his childhood tree. He lifts the book in the air, opens it, and reads. "*Something marvelous is happening underground, something we're just starting to learn how to see.*" He snaps the book shut for dramatic effect. "There's nothing out there even remotely like it. We'd be the first. Imagine: a game with the goal of growing *the world*, instead of yourself."

The silence thickens with the proposed madness. Kaltov says, "Not broke, boss. Don't fix. I vote no."

The skeletal saint goes around the table, one by one. Rasha? Nguyen? Robinson? Boehm? No, No, No, and No. Unanimous palace coup. Neelay feels nothing, not even surprise. Sempervirens, with its five divisions and countless employees, its massive annual revenues from subscriptions and media, hasn't been under anyone's control for some time. The tens of thousands of fans posting to online forums have more control over what happens next than any of the upper brass. Complex adaptive system. A god game that has escaped its god.

It's clear to him: The massively parallel online experience will go on, faithful to the tyranny of the place it pretends to escape. And the sixty-third richest man in Santa Clara County—founder of Sempervirens, Inc., creator of *The Sylvan Prophecies*, only child, devotee of distant worlds, lover of Hindi comics, avid fan of all rule-breaking stories, flier of digital kites, timid curser of teachers, faller from coast live oaks—learns what it means to be eaten alive by his own insatiable offspring.


IT'S ANCIENT HISTORY NOW, a decade-old story Douglas Pavlicek keeps in his arsenal to spring on unsuspecting summer visitors who wander into the erstwhile whorehouse that serves as the ghost town visitor center. He'll lay it on anyone who holds still long enough to hear.

"Then I had to crab-walk backward, uphill, on my *ass*, kicking off from tree trunks with my good leg. Switchbacked up an eighty-foot bluff in the snow, while my dislocated shoulder stabbed me like the Holy Ghost with a hot poker. Crawled in and out of consciousness, as far as that old silver-mine headframe not a hundred yards from here. And there I lay as good as dead for who knows how long, seeing visions and hearing the forest talk, while wolverines and such probably licked my face for the salts on my skin. By miracle, I reached the office, called in the medivacs, and got a lift to Missoula in a chopper. Felt like I was back in 'Nam, about to 'chute out of my old Herky Bird and start the whole Wheel of Eternal Return over again."

He tells the story a lot, and the tourists mostly put up with it. Then one evening, ten minutes after quitting time, he tells it to a woman across the display case who digs it. Youngish, kind of, in bandanna and backpack, with a cute-as-hell Eastern European accent, a little ripe-scented, but friendly as a retriever covered with ticks. She's all on the balls of her feet, waiting to hear if he survives or not. Deep into the rising action, he starts improvising a little. Let's face it: there's only so much that the arc of his story will hold. Yet she's eating it up, like he's one of those epileptic Russian novelists, and all she wants is to find out what happens next, and next after that.

When the story ends, she watches him close up the office. Outside, in the lot, there's nothing but his white BLM Ford anywhere in sight. All the day's visitors have headed back down the washboard road in their Expeditions and Pathfinders. The woman, Alena, asks, "There is someplace nearby I can camp, do you think?"

He's been there himself, a long haul with no campsite ahead. He spreads his palms—all the abandoned buildings he's supposed to check and clear each night. No camping allowed, but who's to know? "Take your pick."

She bows her head. "Do you maybe have crackers or something?"

It occurs to him that it may not be his storytelling skill that held her saucer-eyed. But he brings her up to the cabin and feeds her. Pulls out all the stops: the rabbit fillet he's been saving for no reason, fried mushrooms and onions, a decent coffee cake made of Grape-Nuts, and a couple of shots of fermented thimbleberry.

She tells him about her adventures walking across the Garnet Range. "We started out four people. No idea where those three went."

"Kinda dangerous out this way. You shouldn't be out here by yourself, looking like you do."

"How I look?" She blows a raspberry and whisks her palm. "Like an ill monkey who needs washing."

She looks, to Douglas, good enough to be some mail-order bride scam. "Really. A young woman by herself. Not a patentable idea."

"Young? Who is that? Beside. This is the greatest country. Americans are the friendliest people in the world. Always want to help. Like you. Look! You made this great meal. You didn't need."

"You liked it? Really?"

She holds out her glass for more thimbleberry wine.

"Well," he says, when the silence gets weird, even by his standards, "you're welcome to the water from the pump. Take your pick of any building down there. I'd keep out of the barbershop. Something must have died in there recently."

"This house is nice."

"Oh. Well. Listen. You don't owe me anything. It was just food."

"Who's making a business?" Then she's straddling his chair, scrutinizing his face, trying it out with her periscope lips. She breaks off. "Hey! You're *crying*. Strange man!"

There's no good reason why any species would ever have evolved so useless a behavior. "I'm an old guy."

"You're sure? Let's see!"

She tries again. The first woman's flesh to warm his for years. It's like a lockpick scratching around a bunged-up keyhole in his chest. He pins her wrists. "I don't love you."

"*Okay*, mister. No problem. I don't love *you*, either." She tugs at his chin. "People don't have to love, to enjoy!"

He gives her back her hands. "Trust me. They do." His arms go slack, like they're chained through a pipe to a concrete slab buried in the ground.

"Okay," she says again, sullen. She pushes against his chest and stands. "You are a sad little mammal."

"I am that." He stands and brings the remains of the feast to the basin. "You take the bed. I'll sleep in the bag, out here. The facilities are in the yard. Careful of the stinging nettle."

The sight of the bed thrills her. American Christmas. "You are a good old guy."

"Not especially."

He shows her how to work the lantern. Lying on the floor in the front room, he sees the light under the door. Someone's reading late. He doesn't realize until later just what she's reading.

In the morning, there's more Grape-Nut coffee cake, and actual coffee. No further adventures in cross-cultural misunderstanding. She leaves before the first tourists come up the mountain. Soon enough, the visitor isn't even a story he tells himself at night, to feed his regrets and beat up on himself for nostalgia.

But America, it turns out, really is the greatest country. The people are so kind, the land is rich beyond imagining, and the authorities will cut a deal for useful information, even after booking you for multiple crimes. In two more months, when the men with the initials on their jackets make their way up the mountain, Douglas has all but forgotten his overnight guest. Not until the Freddies pin him in the driveway, tear up the cabin, and remove his handwritten journal in a sealed plastic box does he remember her. He fights to keep from smiling as they hog-tie him and get him into the government Land Cruiser.

*You think this is funny?*

No. No, of course not. Well, maybe a little. It has all happened before, and as far as Douglas Pavlicek can make out, it will keep happening forever. Prisoner 571, reporting for duty, four decades on.

They don't ask him much. They don't have to. He has written it all down, in painstaking detail, in a nightly ritual of memory and explanation. Signed, sealed, delivered. All the crimes the five of them committed: Maidenhair, Watchman, Mulberry, Doug-fir, and Maple. But it's a funny thing: his captors aren't all that interested in forest names.


DOROTHY SHOWS UP in the doorway, the eternally recurring breakfast tray in her arms. "Morning, RayRay. Hungry?"

He's awake, tranquil, looking out through the window onto the acre and a half of Brinkmanland. He has grown so calm these days. There have been stretches, terrible days that she was sure would kill him. Last winter was the worst. One February afternoon she spent minutes trying to hear what he was wailing. When she finally made him out, it was as if he were reading her mind: *I'm done. It's hemlock time.*

But spring brought him back to himself, and in these days near the summer solstice, she'd swear she has never seen him happier. She puts the tray down on the bedside table. "How about some peach-banana cobbler?"

He tries to raise his hand, perhaps to point, but the hand has other ideas. When he at last gets his mouth to work, he comes at her out of the blue. "There. That." The words slur, as pulpy as the hot fruit mush she has made for breakfast. He leads with his eyes. "That. Tree."

She looks out, her features eager, trying to pretend that the request makes perfect sense. Still the consummate amateur thespian. "Y-yes?"

His mouth opens and he launches a syllable midway between *what* and *who*.

Her voice stays bright. "What kind? Ray, you know I'm hopeless at that. Some evergreen?"

"From . . . when?" Two words, like biking uphill on a muddy mountain trail.

She gazes at the tree as if she has never laid eyes on it. "Good question." For a moment, she can't remember how long they've lived in this place or what they've planted. He flails a little, but not in distress. "Let's. See!"

Then she's standing in front of a wall of books. Ceiling to floor: their lifetime hoard of print. She puts her palm on a shoulder-high shelf, wood she can't name. Her finger flicks the dusty spines, looking for a thing she's not sure is there. The past tries to kill her—all the people they were or had hoped to be. She skips by *A Hundred Hikes in the Yellowstone*. She pauses on *A Field Guide to Eastern Songbirds* as something bright and red in her head flies off, unidentified. The slender thing, almost a pamphlet, skulks near the end of the shelf. *Easy Tree IDs*. She takes down the book. An inscription on the title page ambushes her:

> *For my dear first dimension,*
> *My sole and only Dot.*

*Care to see which trees are clear*
*And which are clearly knot?*

She has never seen the words before. Not even a vague memory of any attempt to learn the names of trees together. But the poem brings back the poet intact. The best worst poet in the world.

She flips the pages. Way more oaks than good taste would recommend. Red, yellow, white, black, gray, scarlet, iron, live, bur, valley, and water, with leaves that deny all relation to each other. She remembers now why she never had the patience for nature. No drama, no development, no colliding hopes and fears. Branching, tangled, messy plots. And she could never keep the characters straight.

She reads the inscription again. How old was the jingle-writer? Best worst poet. Best worst actor. Patent and copyright lawyer who drove cheats into bankruptcy, then spent a tenth of each year doing pro bono. He wanted a large family, for the all-night Crazy Eights marathons and the four-part novelty songs on long car trips. Instead, it was only him and his dear first dimension.

She carries the booklet back to his room. "Ray!" Look what I found!" The howling mask of his face seems almost pleased. "When did you give this to me? Nice we held on to it, huh? Just what we need now. Ready?"

He's worse than ready. He's a kid on his way to camp.

"Start Here. *If you live east of the Rocky Mountains, go to entry 1. If you live west of the Rocky Mountains, go to entry 116.*"

She looks at him. His eyes are damp but traveling.

"*If your tree produces cones and has needle-like leaves, go to entry 11.c.*"

They both look out the window, as if the answer hasn't been staring at them for the last quarter century. In the noonday light, the whirled boughs—stout and layered at wide intervals—shine a funny bluish silver she has never noticed. The tapered, narrow spire shimmers in the overhead sun.

"Definite yes on the needles. Cones up top, too. Raymond? I believe we may be on to something." She flips through the pages to the treasure hunt's next way station. *"Are the needles evergreen and arranged in sheathed bundles of two to five needles each? If yes, go to . . ."*

She looks up. His mask smirks now, more than it should be able to. The eyes are alight. *Adventure. Excitement. Goodbye—travel well!*

"Be right back." The smallest packet of surprise lodges at the top of her chest. Like that, she's off. She retreats through the kitchen into the back pantry—a warren of cubbies cluttered with decades of set-it-and-forget-it. Some weekend she'll sort through the ancient junk, pitch it all, lighten the lifeboat for the last few nautical miles. The back door opens, and she smells the waves of grassy summer rolling over her. She has no shoes. The neighbors will think she has lost her mind, caring for her brain-damaged husband. And if she has, well then, that's the story.

She crosses the lawn, takes the lowest branch in her hand, bends it toward her, and counts. There's a song about this, she thinks. A song or a prayer or a story or a film. The branch slips upward from her hand. She drifts back to the house over the sun-ghosted grass, humming the tune that is about exactly this moment.

He's waiting for her, hanging on the denouement. "Five in a sheath. We're on a roll." She flips through the book to the next unfolding branch. *"Are the cones long with thin scales?"*

This splitting and choosing: she recognizes it. It's like the law, those cases she transcribed during all those years when she played a court stenographer: the evidence, the cross-examinations, messy negotiations and man-ufactured facts, the path narrowing in on a sole allowable verdict. It's like evolution's decision tree: *If the winters are tough and the water scarce, try scales or needles.* It's even weirdly like acting: *If you need to respond with fear, go to gesture 21c; If wonder, 17a. Otherwise . . .* It's a programmed telephone support system for living on Earth. It's the mind moving through mysteries, their explanations forever one more choice away. More than anything, it's like the tree itself, with one central questioning stem splitting into dozens of probing ones, and each of those forking into hundreds, then thousands of green and independent answers. "Stay tuned," Dorothy says, and disappears again.

Once more, the back door's black enamel knob protests, squeaking in her hand. She makes her way across the yard to the tree. A short journey, repeated ad nauseam, more times than anyone ever signs on for, across the same patch of familiar ground: the path of love. *If you want to keep fighting, turn to entry 1001. If you want to break loose and save yourself . . .*

She stands under the tree and studies the cones. They cover the ground, spores that crashed to earth from some remote asteroid. Then back to the house with her answer. The way across the wet grass in stocking feet is long enough for her to wonder how she can still be here, buried alive, tied to this frozen man year after year, when all she ever wanted in this life was to find her freedom. But back in the prison doorway, waving the book in triumph, she knows. *This* is her freedom. This one. The freedom to be equal to the terrors of the day.

"Victory. Eastern white pine."

She'd swear a great wave of contentment sweeps across the rigid face. She can read him now, with a telepathy honed by years of having to guess at his clotted syllables. He's thinking: *A good day's work. A very good day.*

That night he makes her read to him about a tree that once ran in great vertical veins of living ore from Georgia to Newfoundland, out through Canada, and past the Great Lakes to where they camp out together by lamplight. She tells him about giants four feet wide, their trunks shooting eighty feet straight up before the first sideways branches bothered to extend. Trees that stood in endless stands that darkened the air with pollen each spring, the clouds of golden dust raining down on the decks of ships far out at sea.

She reads to him of how the English first swarmed a continent that rose from the ocean overnight, seeking masts for their leviathan frigates and ships of the line, masts that no place in all stripped Europe, not even the farthest boreal north, could any longer provide. She shows him paintings of *Pinus strobus*, in hulking shafts as big as church steeples, so valuable that the Crown branded even those that stood on private land with the King's Broad Arrow. And her husband, who spent his life protecting private property, must see it coming, even from the future: The Pine Tree Riot. Revolution. War, fought over a thing that grew on these shores long before humans came down out of trees.

It's a story to match any fiction: the well-wooded land, succumbing to prosperity. The light, soft, strong, dimensioned boards, sold back across the ocean as far away as Africa. The triangular profit making the infant country's fortune: lumber to the Guinea coast, black bodies to the Indies, sugar and rum back up to New England, with its stately mansions all built of eastern white pine. White pine framing out cities, making millions in sawmill fortunes, laying a bed of rails across the continent, building and pitching warships and whaling fleets that wander out from Brooklyn and New Bedford into the unmapped South Pacific, ships made of a thousand trees or more. The white pines of Michigan, Wisconsin, and Minnesota: split into a hundred billion roof shingles. A hundred million board feet a year, splintered into matchsticks. Scandinavian lumberjacks clearing a swath of pine three states wide, wrestling the colossal husks into rivers with tackle and boom, riding miles-long rafts of them downstream to market. A giant hero and his big blue ox cutting the pine to clear the Brinkmans' neighborhood.

Dorothy reads, and the wind picks up. All the yard bends with complaint. Rain blows in. The small room grows smaller still. Night: the third part of every day that remains a foreign country. The house next door vanishes, and the ones just north of that, until the Brinkmans huddle up alone, out on the edge of a savage wilderness. Ray's working leg thrashes against the sheets that hem him in. All he ever wanted was to earn an honest living, promote the general welfare, earn the respect of his community, and raise a decent family. *Wealth needs fences.* But fences need wood. Nothing left on the continent even hints at what has gone. All replaced now, by thousands of miles of continuous backyards and farms with thin lines of second growth between them. Still, the soil remembers, for a little while longer, the vanished woods and the progress that unmade them. And the soil's memory feeds their backyard pine.

Spittle wells on Ray's trembling lips; it stays there until Dorothy wipes it off, sometime before midnight. The lips move as she wipes them. She leans in, and thinks she hears him whisper, "One more. Tomorrow."

THE NIGHT IS WARM, the windows of Patricia's cabin bang in the breeze, and the sturgeon moon rises over the lake like a pale red penny. She rests her palms on the stack of notebooks filled with her careful hand. "Well, Den. I believe we may finally be done."

There's no answer tonight, as there never is. The words do no more than hang in the air. Plenty of creatures hear, inside the cabin and out. Her syllables answer and change the various chirps, groans, sighs, plans, and estimates that punctuate this night. The conversation is long, patient, beyond any party's ability to follow, and the patterned noises her kind add to it are still brand-new.

She listens for a moment to the hour's alarms. Then she pushes down against the walnut table. Her legs straighten, and she rises. She flips open the uppermost notebook, to the page where she has just written: *In a world of perfect utility, we, too, will be forced to vanish.*

"You're sure this is a good idea?" She asks herself; she asks the dead man. The membrane between the two is thin. She knows she'll never see him again in this or any life to come. Yet she sees him wherever she looks. That's life; the dead keep the living alive. Every other night she asks her missing friend for words and phrases. For courage. For enough forbearance to keep from pitching her notes into the wood-burning stove. Now the asking is done. She flips the page.

> *No one sees trees. We see fruit, we see nuts, we see wood, we see shade. We see ornaments or pretty fall foliage. Obstacles blocking the road or wrecking the ski slope. Dark, threatening places that must be cleared. We see branches about to crush our roof. We see a cash crop. But trees—trees are invisible.*

"It's not bad, Den. A little bleak, maybe." Short, too, she might add. Far smaller than her firstborn. There's so much more to tell, but she's an old woman now, without much time, and there are so many more species still to find and take aboard the ark. The book is a simple enough story. She could have told it in a page or two: how she and several others spent years traveling to all the continents but Antarctica. How they saved a few seeds from a few thousand trees, a fraction of the species that will vanish as the Earth's current custodians watch, bringing countless dependents down with them. . . .

She has tried to hold out hope, to tell every story that might make the truth a little easier. She gives a whole chapter to migration. She describes all the trees already marching north at rates that astonish those who measure them. *But the most vulnerable trees will need to move much faster, to keep from burning up. They can't cross highways or farms or housing developments. Maybe we can help them.*

She spins short biographies of her favorite characters: loner trees, cunning trees, sages and solid citizens, trees that turn impulsive or shy or generous— as many ways of being as there are forest elevations and facings. *How fine it would be if we could learn who they are, when they're at their best.* She tries to turn the story on its head. *This is not our world with trees in it. It's a world of trees, where humans have just arrived.*

One passage keeps springing back, every time fear or scientific rigor makes her prune it. *Trees know when we're close by. The chemistry of their roots and the perfumes their leaves pump out change when we're near. . . . When you feel good after a walk in the woods, it may be that certain species are bribing you. So many wonder drugs have come from trees, and we haven't yet scratched the surface of the offerings. Trees have long been trying to reach us. But they speak on frequencies too low for people to hear.*

She's up from the table with a groan meant for no one. In the front closet, she finds the stack of nested cardboard boxes that she and Dennis always had such trouble throwing out. Moldy boxes saved for decades. Who knows when you might need one exactly this size? The notebooks fit, as if by design. She'll mail them to an assistant tomorrow, for typing. Then to her editor in New York, who has been waiting for years for a follow-up to a book that's still in print, still selling, still weighing on Patricia's conscience for its cost in pines.

As soon as she seals the carton with packing tape, she cracks it open again. The last line of the last chapter is still wrong. She looks at what she has, although the sentence has long since burned itself into permanent memory. *With luck, some of those seeds will remain viable, inside controlled vaults in the side of a Colorado mountain, until the day when watchful people can return them to the ground.* She purses her lips, and pens an addendum. *If not, other experiments will go on running themselves, long after people are gone.*

"That's probably better," she says out loud. "Right?" But the ghost has finished dictating, tonight.

When the box is set to go, she gets ready for bed. Ablutions are quick, and grooming even faster. Then the reading, her nightly thousand-mile walk to the gulf. When her eyes won't stay open any longer, she finishes with verse. Tonight's poem is Chinese—Wang Wei—twelve hundred years old, from an anthology of poetry she winds through at random, the way she likes to hike:

> I know no good way
> to live and I can't
> stop getting lost in my
> thoughts, my ancient forests. . . .

> You ask: how does a man rise or fall in this life?
> The fisherman's song flows deep under the river.

Then the river is running over her, and she's done. She douses the dim, low-watt bulb clipped to the headboard. All that's left her is the moon. She rolls on her side and curls up, her face pressed into the dank pillow. After a minute, the end of her mouth pulls into an abiding smile.

"I did *not* almost forget. Good night."

Good night.

. . .

ADAM IN ZUCCOTTI PARK, Lower Manhattan. This time, the fieldwork comes to him. The forces he has been studying his entire professional life are loose again and partying in the heart of the Financial District, a few blocks south of where he works and lives. The park is buzzing. The squared circles of honey locusts already tint yellow, and all underneath them, sleeping bags and tents make camp between the skyscrapers. Hundreds slept here last night, as they have for days. They fall asleep to songs of protest and wake to the free hot meal served by five-star chefs donating their efforts to the cause. Only, Adam isn't sure what the cause *is*. The cause is a work in progress. Justice for the ninety-nine percent. The jailing of financial traitors and thieves. An eruption of fairness and decency on all continents. The overthrow of capitalism. A happiness not born of rape and greed.

The city prohibits all amplified sound, but the human megaphone is in full swing. One woman chants, and the people all around her pick up the words.

"Banks got bailed out."

"BANKS GOT BAILED OUT!"

"We got sold out."

"WE GOT SOLD OUT!"

"Occupy."

"OCCUPY!"

"Whose streets?"

"WHOSE STREETS?"

"Our streets."

"OUR STREETS!"

Still the resolutely young, keeping true to the world-saving dreams of their youth. But among the ethnic vests and backpacks are men older than Adam. In breakout sessions around the square, women in their sixties pass along the institutional memory of insurgence. People in leotards pedal stationary bikes to generate electricity for the occupation's laptops. Barbers give away free haircuts, since the bankers seem unwilling to get theirs cropped. People in Guy Fawkes masks hand out leaflets. College kids stand in a ring and drum. Lawyers behind flimsy card tables donate legal advice. Someone has been hard at work defacing signs:

## No Skateboarding, Roller Blading,
## or Bicycling Allowed in the Park
# OTHERWISE. ALL GOOD. BRO

And what's a circus without a band? A whole battalion of guitars—one with the inscription *This Machine Kills Day-Traders*—joins together in a chorus of high lonesome:

> *For the po-lice make it hard, wherever I may go,*
> *'Cause I ain't got no home in this world anymore.*

Just beyond the square's far corner is the wound that won't heal. The hole in the canopy has long since filled in, but it still oozes. A decade has passed since the buildings fell. The math astounds Adam. His own son is only five, but the attacks feel younger. A tree, a Callery pear that survived half burned and with roots snapped, has just returned in good health to Ground Zero.

He squeezes through a channel in the milling crowd, alongside the People's Library. He can't help grazing the shelves and bins. There's Milgram's *Obedience to Authority*, marked up with a million tiny marginal words. There's a collection of Tagore. Lots of Thoreau, and even more copies of *You vs. Wall Street*. Free circulation, on the honor system. Smells like democracy, to him.

Six thousand books, and out of them all, one small volume floats up to the surface of its heap like a fossil coughed out of a peat bog. *The Golden Guide to Insects*. Bright yellow—the only real edition that classic ever had. In shock, Adam picks it up and opens to the title page, ready to see his own name gouged there in smudgy No. 2 all-caps balloons. But the name is someone else's, inked in in Palmer Method cursive: *Raymond B.*

The pages stink of mildew and the purity of child science. Adam flips through, recalling everything. The field notebooks and home natural history museum. The pond scum under the cheap, child's microscope. Above all, the daubs of fingernail polish on the abdomens of ants. Somehow, he has managed to spend his entire life repeating that experiment. He lifts his eyes from the miniature page—"Weevils and Caddisflies"—to watch this happy, furious, anarchic swarm. For a few seconds, he sees the system of ranks and duties, the waggle-dances, the trails of pheromone that feel, from inside the hive, like pure physics, the pull of gravity. He wants to paint them all with a daub of polish and climb up forty floors in the next-door high rise, for a better look. The look of a real field scientist. The look of a ten-year-old.

He sticks the Golden Guide into his pants pocket and ducks back into the crowd. Ten steps down, seated on the edge of a granite slab bench, a ghost swings its face toward him and startles. "Occupy," someone shouts, into the human megaphone. And the word comes a hundred times louder out the other end: "*OCCUPY!*"

The ghost's surprise turns into a grin. Adam knows the guy like it's his brother, back from the dead. The man he sees is balding, in a ball cap, where the one he remembers had a luxurious ponytail. He can't for the life of him say who the man is. Then he can, and he doesn't want to. It's too late for anything but to walk up and clasp the intruder by the forearm, laughing at the evidence, like luck is such a rascal and the strange old story will lurch forever on. "Doug-fir."

"Maple. Whoa. This can't be *real*." They embrace like two old men already over the finish line. "Jesus. Man! Life is long, huh?"

Longer than anyone. The psychologist can't stop shaking his head. He doesn't want this. The corpse being pulled up out of the tumulus by brutal archaeologists is not *him*. But the run-in is funny, somehow. Chance, that comedian with the perfect timing.

"Is this . . . ? Are you here for . . . ?" Adam waves toward the teeming crowd saving mankind from itself. Pavlicek—*Pavlicek*, the name is. Pavlicek wrinkles up his eyebrows and scouts the square. Like he's just seeing it, this moment.

"Aw, naw, man. Not me. I'm just a spectator, these days. Don't get out much. Haven't made a peep since . . . you know."

Adam takes the man—still gawky, still adolescent—by the bony elbow. "Let's walk."

They stroll down Broadway, past Citibank, Ameritrade, Fidelity. The years they need to catch up on are done in a New York minute. Professor of psychology at NYU, with wife who publishes self-help books and five-year-old son who wants to be a banker when he grows up. Longtime BLM employee, between jobs and residences, here in town to see his friend. The end. But they keep walking, under the spire of Trinity Church, passing near the ghost of the buttonwood tree, that sycamore where businessmen once met to trade stock, now the site of free enterprise's main engine room. And they keep talking, a slow circle around the past whose circumference Adam won't be able to retrace even an hour later. Douglas keeps touching the brim of the baseball cap, like he's tipping it to passersby.

Adam asks, "Are you . . . in touch with anyone?"

"In touch?"

"With the others."

Douglas fiddles with the cap. "No. You?"

"I . . . no. Mulberry—no idea. But Watchman? This sounds crazy. It's like he's following me around."

Douglas stops on the sidewalk in a sea of businessmen. "What does that mean?"

"I'm probably nuts. But I travel a lot for the job. Lectures and conferences, all over the country. And in at least three cities, I've seen street art that looks just like those drawings he used to make."

"The tree people?"

"Yeah. You remember how weird . . . ?"

Douglas nods, fingering the brim. A group of tourists ring the sidewalk in front of them around a wild animal. It's huge, muscular, charging, nostrils flared, with long, wicked horns ready to gore the throng ringing it and taking selfies. Seven thousand pounds of bronze guerrilla art, trucked in by its maker in the dead of night and left on the stoop of the Stock Exchange as a gift to the public. When the city tried to haul it away, people objected. The Trojan Bull.

A few short weeks ago, a ballerina riding the beast bareback in mid-pirouette became the stunning poster child of the latest Stop the Humans movement:

WHAT
IS OUR
ONE
DEMAND?
#OCCUPYWALLSTREET
BRING TENT

People take turns buddying up for a picture with the charging animal. Douglas doesn't seem to get the irony. His eyes are everywhere except where the crowd is looking. Something fights out of him. "So." He rubs his neck. "You have a pretty good life now?"

"Crazy lucky. Though I work long hours. The research . . . is a pleasure."

"What exactly do you research?"

Adam has performed the sound bite thousands of times, for everyone from anthology editors to strangers on airplanes. But this man—he owes this man a little more. "I was working on the topic already when we met. When the five of us . . . The focus has changed, over the years. But it's the same basic problem: What keeps us from seeing the obvious?"

Douglas puts his hand to the brass bull's horn. "And? What does?"

"Mostly other people."

"You know . . ." Douglas looks up Broadway, to see what so enrages the bull. "I may have hit upon that idea independently."

Adam laughs so loud the tourists turn to look. He remembers why he loved the man once. Why he trusted him with his life. "There's a more interesting part of the question."

"How some people manage to see . . . ?"

"Exactly."

With a gesture, an Asian tourist asks the two men to step away from the statue for the length of a quick photo. Adam nudges Douglas and they walk some more, down into the teardrop of Bowling Green Park.

"I've thought a lot," Douglas says. "About what happened."

"Me, too." Right away Adam wants to retract the lie.

"What were we hoping to accomplish? What did we think we were doing?"

They stand under the circle of camouflaged *Platanus*, that most resigned of eastern trees, on the spot where the island was sold, by people who listened to trees, to people who cleared them. They gaze together at the geyser fountain. Adam says, "We set buildings on fire."

"We did."

"We believed that humans were committing mass murder."

"Yes."

"No one else could see what was happening. Nothing was going to stop unless people like us forced the issue."

The beak of Douglas's ball cap swings back and forth. "We weren't wrong, you know. Look around! Anyone paying attention knows the party's over. Gaia's taking her revenge."

"Gaia?" Adam smiles, but pained.

"Life. The planet. We're already paying. But *even now* a guy is still a lunatic for saying as much."

Adam assesses the man. "So you'd do it all again? What we did?" The questions of rogue philosophers play in Adam's head. The taboo ones. How many trees equal one person? Can an impending catastrophe justify small, pointed violence?

"Do it again? I don't know. I don't know what that means."

"Burn buildings."

"I ask myself at nights whether anything we did—anything we *could* have done—would ever make up for that woman's death."

And then it's like the day is night, the city a spruce-pine woods, the park all on fire around them, and that fine, strange, pale woman is lying on the ground, begging for water.

"We accomplished nothing," Adam says. "*Not one thing.*" They turn to leave the park, a place too crowded for this conversation. At the gate in the low iron fence, only then do they realize: there's no place safer.

"*She* would have done it all again."

Douglas points at Adam's chest. "You loved her."

"We all loved her. Yes."

"You were in love with her. Same as Watchman. Same as Mimi."

"It was a long time ago."

"You would have bombed the Pentagon for her."

Adam smiles, soft and pale. "She did have a power."

"She said the trees were talking to her. That she could hear them."

A shrug. A furtive watch-check. He needs to get back uptown to prep a lecture. Too much history sickens Adam. So he was younger once, angrier. Another species. Just a failed experiment. The only thing that needs negotiation is Now.

Douglas won't leave him be. "Do you think anything was really talking to her? Or was she just . . . ?"

The world had six trillion trees, when people showed up. Half remain. Half again more will disappear, in a hundred years. And whatever enough people say that all these vanishing trees are saying is what, in fact, they say. But the question interests Adam. What did the dead Joan of Arc hear? Insight or delusion? Next week he'll tell his undergrads about Durkheim, Foucault, crypto-normativity: How *reason* is just another weapon of control. How the invention of the *reasonable*, the *acceptable*, the *sane*, even the *human*, is greener and more recent than humans suspect.

Adam casts a look behind them, down the concrete canyon of Beaver Street. Beavers: the creatures whose pelts built this city. The original Manhattan Exchange. He hears himself answer. "Trees used to talk to people all the time. Sane people used to hear them." The only question is whether they'll talk again, before the end.

"That night?" Douglas lifts his face to the skyscraper wall. "When we sent you for help? Why did you come back?"

Anger surges through Adam, as if the two of them will fight again. "It was too late. Finding help would have taken hours. She was dead already. If I'd gone to the police . . . she'd still be dead. And we'd all be locked up."

"You didn't know that, man. You don't know that now." Rage, the radical tip of a grief that time will never root out.

They pass a small European redbud, twenty feet tall. Its spine arches and its limbs curve like those of the ballerina bull dancer. The profusion of purple-pink, edible buds growing right out of the trunk and twigs is still a winter away. Now seedpods dangle from the branches like so many hanged men. They say Judas hanged himself from a *Cercis*. It's a new enough myth, as tree myths go. Judas trees grow in corners hidden throughout Lower Manhattan. This one will be gone before it blooms twice more.

The men stop at Battery Place, where their paths split. Down the street and across the water, Liberty. There's a certain squirrel, a ghost animal, the subject of endless eulogies, who runs forever through the canopies of a giant ghost forest from here to the Mississippi, without ever touching paws to the ground. It's all island-hopping now, through scattered fragments of second growth subtended by highways littered with roadkill. But the men stop to look, as if the endless forest still starts there, in front of them.

They turn to one another and hug goodbye, like bears testing their strength against each other. Like they'll never see each other again in this life. Like even then, it would be too soon.


THE TREES REFUSE to say a thing. Neelay sits in Stanford's inner quad—the intergalactic botanical garden—waiting for an explanation. The lifelong calling has gone wrong. He's lost the trail they set him on. What now?

But the trees snub him. The bulging water sack of the bottle tree, the spiked armor of the silk floss: not even a rustle of leaves. It's as if his soul mate—in the only galaxy that ever offered him one—has plunged from bliss to panic at the first ripple and cut him dead. He's ruining tourists' photographs. No one wants a shot of a nice, fake Spanish Romanesque cloister with a crippled freak in the foreground. He spins to go, as furious as any jilted lover. But go where? Even returning to his apartment above the Sempervirens headquarters is a humiliation.

He'd call his mother, but it's the middle of the night in Banswara, where she now spends most of her year, getting ready to die. She knows now, ten years too late, that there will never be any Rupal for him, that science will never reactivate his legs, and that the best way to love her son is to release him to his isolation. She comes back now only whenever he's hospitalized, when the doctors must debride his epic bedsores or cut away parts of his necrotic feet and ass. Boarding a plane has become an exercise in pain. He won't tell her, the next time he goes in.

He rolls down into the Oval toward the grandiose line of palms. The sky is too clear, the day too hot, and all the trunks have turned to synchronized sundials. He finds a shady spot—an increasingly popular sport, worldwide. Then he sits still, trying to be only where he is, here, home. No good. In a minute, he's agitated, checking his phone for messages not yet posted to him. Where can people live? His elves must be right: only in symbols, in simulation.

As he puts the device back in its wheelchair pouch, it buzzes like a fistful of cicadas. It's a message from his personal AI. The thing is alive, cagey, teasing him with the clickbait game of humanity. Since childhood, even before his fall, he has dreamed of such a robot pet. This one is better than anything the prophets of his childhood sci-fi predicted—faster, sleeker, and suppler. It goes out at all hours and scours humankind's entire activity, then reports back to him. It's obedient and untiring, and like the only creatures that he trusts these days, it has no legs. Legs, Neelay suspects, may be where evolution went berserk.

He and his people made the pet, and now it's busy making him. He told it to watch for any news of his new obsession: tree communication, forest intelligence, fungal networks, Patricia Westerford, *The Secret Forest.* . . . The book is shot through with uncanny echoes of what he heard whispered, decades ago, by alien life-forms that now won't give him the time of day. It has cost him his role as the creative head of his company. It wants more from him, more payment, more salvage. But what?

He opens the message from the bot. It contains a link and a title: *Words of Air and Light.* The recommendation strength is as high as his pet gives. Even in his spot of shade, Neelay can't read the screen. He rolls to the van, parked not far away. Back inside his emptied-out interstellar ship, he clicks on the link and watches in confusion. Shadows and sun burst forth. A hundred years of chestnut erupt in twenty seconds, like a scene in a hand-cranked kinetoscope. It's over before Neely makes it out. He starts the clip again. The tree fountains up once more into a crown. The upward-wavering twigs reach for the light, for things hidden in plain sight. Branches fork and thicken in the air. At this speed, he sees the tree's central aim, the math behind the phloem and xylem, the intermeshed and seething geometries, and that thin layer of living cambium swelling outward.

Code—wildly branching code pruned back by failure—builds up this great spiraling column from out of instructions that Vishnu managed to cram into something smaller than a boy's fingernail. When the tree is done with its century of unfolding, old chestnut words of extinct Transcendental-ism scroll upward, line by line, on a sea of black:

> The gardener sees
> only the gardener's garden.
> The eyes were not made
> for such grovelling uses as they
> are now put to and worn out by,
> but to behold beauty now invisible.
> MAY
> WE
> NOT
> SEE
> GOD?

And when Neelay looks up from the tiny screen, that's exactly what he sees.

JUST ACROSS CAMPUS from his van, beyond the eucalyptus groves, invi-tations go out. They disperse in clumps, like airborne pollen. One lands on Patricia Westerford, in a cabin in an institute in the Great Smoky Mountains. She's searching out prime strains of the dozens of hardwoods that may fall in a few years to the ash borer and long-horned beetles. These days such invitations reach her by the dozens, and she mostly ignores them. But this one—Home Repair: Countering a Warming World—this one sounds so painful that she reads the letter twice. Someone wants to fly her two thousand five hundred and ninety-six miles and back again, for a conference about the ruined atmosphere. She can't wrap her head around that title: Home Repair. As if we just need to fix the gutters, put in a rooftop swamp cooler, and get back to good times.

She sits on her Shaker chair at the table, listening to the crickets. Long ago her father taught her an old formula, one that converts cricket chirps per minute into degrees Fahrenheit. For sixty years, the nighttime orchestra all around her has been playing one of those folk dances that keep speeding up until all the players tumble in a heap. *We would be thrilled if you could talk about any role trees might play in helping mankind to a sustainable future.* The conference organizers want a keynote from a woman who once wrote a book on the power of woody plants to restore the failing planet. But she wrote that book decades ago, when she was still young enough for courage and the planet still well enough to rally.

These people need dreams of technological breakthrough. Some new way to pulp poplar into paper while burning slightly fewer hydrocarbons. Some genetically altered cash crop that will build better houses and lift the world's poor from misery. The home repair they want is just a slightly less wasteful demolition. She could tell them about a simple machine needing no fuel and little maintenance, one that steadily sequesters carbon, enriches the soil, cools the ground, scrubs the air, and scales easily to any size. A tech that copies itself and even drops food for free. A device so beautiful it's the stuff of poems. If forests were patentable, she'd get an ovation.

California means three days of lost work. Jesus spent less time cleaning out hell. Her agoraphobia has grown over the years, and in those crowded auditoriums she can never hear anyone. But the guest list is incredible: a roll call of wizards and engineers, each of them only one large grant away from dimming the sun with particulates, cloning endangered species, or tapping into unlimited cheap energy. There will be artists and writers to address the messy question of the human spirit. Venture capitalists looking for the next green bonanza. She'll never have such an audience again.

She rereads the request, picturing a place where "sustainable future" means something more than "dry drunk." She reads through to the letter's stirring closing. *As Toynbee once wrote, "Man achieves civilization . . . as a response to a challenge in a situation of special difficulty which rouses him to make a hitherto unprecedented effort."* The invitation feels like a test of the honesty she has tried to cultivate since her days as a hobo. Someone is asking her what people need to do to save this dying place. Could she possibly tell a gathering of such prominent and powerful people what she thinks is true?

Too late tonight for a wise reply. There's still time, though, for a wander down to the rapids of the Middle Prong. Outside her cabin door, dense, slow-growing hawthorns wave spooky prophecies under the near-full moon. Their scarlet fruits cling to the twigs, and many will last the winter. *Crataegus*, the heart healer. People will be discovering medicines there for as long as they go on looking.

Her path across the clearing frightens a wallow-rooting possum who wrote off humankind two hours ago. She waves the flashlight. The forest floor is piled high with orange and ocher duff smelling of sweet, moldy cake batter. Two barred owls, lugubrious and beautiful, call across a great distance. Up the ridge, acorns and hickories hit the ground. Bears everywhere sleep off the day's feast, two per square mile.

She ducks through drooping rhododendron tunnels, along black cherries that remember old road cuts, past sourwoods and aromatic sassafras. Magnolia and striped maple fill in for the decimated chestnuts. The hemlocks are dying, hit by adelgids and helped along by acid rain. High above, on the Appalachian spine, the Fraser firs are all dead. All around her, the forest reels from the hottest, driest year since the beginning of record-keeping. Yet another freak, once-in-a-century event, almost annual these days. Fires are popping up all over the park. Code Red every third day.

But the priestly tulip trees still boost her immune system, while beeches lift her mood and focus her thoughts. Under these giants, she's smarter, clearer. She sees an alligator-barked persimmon. Sweet-gum balls, like tiny, medieval morning stars, crunch under her feet. She tears just the tip of a fallen gum leaf and sniffs—a child's whiff of heaven. There's a venerable red oak not far from the trail, twelve feet around if it's a foot. It might soothe even the awful restlessness the invitation has inflicted on her. *Sustainable future.* They don't want a tree woman to keynote their gathering. They want a master illusionist. A sci-fi novelist. The Lorax. Maybe a colorful faith healer, with epiphytes for hair.

Down in the riverbed, at her favorite scramble, she removes her shoes. But she doesn't need to. A stream that should be raging is just a boulder bed. She turns a few stones in search of salamanders. Thirty possible species, countless millions of them in the park, inhabiting every spot of dampness, and she can't find one. She holds her bare feet in the imaginary current. *What do you think, Den? Go talk Home Repair?*

The memory of a hand rests on her shoulder. *If you have to ask me, babe, you can't afford the answer.*


FROM STREAMSIDE on Tennessee's Little River to New York City is a mere seven hundred miles. Pollen from an eastern white pine could travel it, given a good stiff breeze. At the far end of that route, Adam Appich looks out with puzzled smile across the bowl of 260 first-year psych students listening to his lecture on cognitive blindness to see an armed trio at the back of the auditorium waiting for him to finish. His shock lasts no longer than a few spiked heartbeats. A glance tells him what these men want and why they're here. Of course, the Glock 23s and navy-blue raid jackets stenciled with the yellow letters FBI help nail down the ID. For decades now, at random moments in every season, from sober noon down into drugged sleep, he has dreaded these men and their arrival. He has waited for them for so long he forgot they were coming. Now, on this pretty fall day, late in this late year, his captors are here at last, looking much as he always thought they would: solid, grim, and pragmatic, with wires in their ears. In another smiling blink, Appich's dread gives way to its kissing cousin, the relief of completed predictions.

He thinks: *They'll come down the aisle and take me at the podium*. But the men, five of them, pool in the back behind the last row of seats, waiting for Adam to wrap up the lecture.

Today's topic has been a simple one. When a person makes a choice, so much happens by night, underground, or just out of sight that the chooser is the last to know. Pages of notes flow over the podium and Adam's hands brush at nothing. After two decades with his shoulders up near his ears, bracing for this hammer fall, his long flinch is over at last. He has worked hard to disappear into achievement. Twice he has won the university's teaching award, and only last month he was nominated for the APA's Beauchamp Prize for research that empirically advances a materialistic understanding of the human mind. He has performed himself in public so long he's been fooled by his own vita. Now the choices of his youth come back to blow that fantasy away.

Everything comes clear. The chance meeting with the old accomplice. All that tugging on the brim of a ball cap. The extracted confession. *We set buildings on fire. We did.* They would have given their lives for each other, the five of them. One of them did.

A glance down at his handwritten notes. On cue, words boxed in red swim up from the clairvoyant past to the forgetful future. Adam has delivered the line before, for several years running in this survey course, but their full sense has waited for now. He pushes his rimless glasses back up the slope of his sweating nose and shakes his head at the packed hall. What a lesson these students will leave with today.

"You can't see what you don't understand. But what you think you already understand, you'll fail to notice."

A few in the hall chuckle; they can't yet see the men standing behind them, at the back of the hall. Some of the students squirrel away the phrase for an exam that will come now in a form altogether different than they expect. Most keep dead still, waiting for education to pass over. Appich flips through his final slides. In fifteen seconds, he sums up the attentional studies and delivers his takeaways. He thinks: *I haven't been bad at this.* Then he dismisses the room, strides up the raked aisle through the sea of students, and shakes the hands of the men who have come to arrest him. He wants to say, *What took you so long?*

His stunned students stare, helpless bystanders as the agents lead their professor away in cuffs. The agents nudge Appich out of the auditorium onto the sidewalk. The day is beautiful and the sky the color of a young man's hopes. People cut across their path. The posse must pause for a second for a break in the foot traffic. The whole city is out on an autumn morning, making things happen.

A light breeze drives the stink of rancid butter up Adam's nose. He has smelled that medicinal, fruity vomit many times before, but the source of it eludes him now. The navy field jackets lead him a few yards up the sidewalk toward a black Suburban. The men are brusque but civil, that odd mix of purpose, nerves, and tedium that accompanies the program of enforcement. They rush Adam into the open door. One agent cups his head as they fold him into the rear seat.

Adam sits in the secured enclosure, his wrists chained in his lap. In the front seat, an agent talks into a square of black glass, logging the successful capture. The words might as well be birdsong. Someone waves to him through the tinted street-side window. He turns to look. Just alongside the idling vehicle, up through a hole in the concrete, a tree flutters, its leaves like the yellow crayon in a child's eight-pack. Trees have ruined his life. Trees are the reason these men have come to lock him up for whatever years he has left. The van doesn't move. His captors go through the paperwork required for departure. The yellow leaves say, *Look. Now. Here. You won't be outside again for a while.*

Adam looks and sees just this: a tree he has walked past three times a week for seven years. It's the lone species of the only genus in the sole family in the single order of the solitary class remaining in a now-abandoned division that once covered the earth—a living fossil three hundred million years old that disappeared from the continent back in the Neogene and has returned to scratch out a living in the shadow, salt, and fumes of Lower Manhattan. A tree older than the conifers, with swimming sperm and cones that can put out a trillion and more grains of pollen a year. In ancient island temples on the other side of the Earth, thousand-year-olds, molten and blasted, close to enlightenment, swell to incredible girth, their elbows growing back down from giant branches to re-root into new trunks of their own. Adam could reach out and touch the scrawny trunk, if the windows weren't closed. If his hands weren't cuffed together. A tree like this grew on the street just outside the house of the man who ordered the bombing of Hiroshima, and a small few of them survived that blast. The fruit flesh has a smell that curdles thought; the pulp kills even drug-resistant bacteria. The fan-shaped leaves with their radiating veins are said to cure the sickness of forgetting. Adam doesn't need the cure. He remembers. He remembers. Ginkgo. The maidenhair tree.

Its leaves leap out sideways into the wind. The Suburban creeps away from the curb and noses into traffic. Adam twists around to look through the rear window. There, as he watches, the whole tree bares. It falls from one moment to the next, the most synchronized drop of leaves that nature ever engineered. A gust of air, some last fluttered objection, and all the veined fans let go at once, releasing a flock of golden telegrams down West Fourth Street.


HOW FAR can a leaf blow? Over the East River, to be sure. Across the shipyard where a Norwegian immigrant sanded down the massive curved oak beams of frigate hulls. Through Brooklyn, once hilly and forested, full of chestnuts. Upriver, where every thousand feet along the waterfront, on every high-water mark he can reach, the shipbuilder's descendant has stenciled:

Above the submerged letters, stands of new buildings compete for something like the sun.

OFF TO THE WEST, across a distance that would take a forest tens of millennia to cross, an old man and woman journey into the world. Over the course of weeks, they've invented a game. Dorothy heads outside and collects twigs, nuts, and shed leaves. Then she brings the evidence back to Ray, and together, with the help of the branching book, they narrow down and name another species. Each time they add a stranger to their list, they stop for days to learn everything they can. There's mulberry, maple, Douglas-fir, each one with its unique history, biography, chemistry, economics, and behavioral psychology. Each new tree is its own distinct epic, changing the story of what is possible.

Today, though, she comes back inside, a little baffled. "There's something wrong, Ray."

For Ray, deep into postmortem life, nothing will ever be wrong again. *What?* he asks her, without saying a thing.

Her answer is subdued, even mystified. "We must have made a mistake somewhere."

They retrace the branches of the decision tree but end up out on the same limb. She shakes her head, refusing the evidence. "I just don't get it."

Now he must croak out loud, a single, hard syllable. Something like, *Why?*

It takes her a while to answer. Time has become something so very different for them both. "Well, for starters, we're hundreds of miles out of the native range."

His body jerks, but she knows the violent spasm is just a shrug. Trees in cities can grow far from anywhere they might call home. The two of them have learned as much, from weeks of reading.

"Worse than that: There's no range left. There aren't supposed to be more than a handful of mature American chestnut trees left anywhere." This one is almost as tall as the house.

They read everything they can about America's perfect, vanished tree. They learn about a holocaust that ravaged the landscape just before they were born. But nothing they discover can explain how a tree that shouldn't exist is spreading a great globe of shade across their backyard.

"Maybe there are chestnuts up here that no one knows about." A sound comes out of Ray that Dorothy knows must be a laugh. "Okay, then we have the ID wrong." But there's no other creature in all their growing tree library that it could be. They let the mystery rankle, and keep on reading.

She finds a book at the public library: *The Secret Forest*. She brings it home for read-aloud. She gets as far as the first paragraph before having to stop:

> You and the tree in your backyard come from a common ancestor. A billion and a half years ago, the two of you parted ways. But even now, after an immense journey in separate directions, that tree and you still share a quarter of your genes. . . .

A page or two may take them a day. Everything they thought their backyard was is wrong, and it takes some time to grow new beliefs to replace the ones that fall. They sit together in silence and survey their acreage as if they have traveled to another planet. Every leaf out there connects, underground. Dorothy takes the news like a shocking revelation in a nineteenth-century novel of manners, where one character's awful secret ripples through every life in the entire village.

They sit together in the evening, reading and looking, as the sun glints chartreuse off their chestnut's scalloped leaves. Every baring twig seems to Dorothy like a trial creature, apart from but part of all the others. She sees in the chestnut's branching the several speculative paths of a lived life, all the people she might have been, the ones she could or will yet be, in worlds spreading out just alongside this one. She watches the limbs move for a while, then looks back down to the page and reads on out loud. " 'It's sometimes hard to say whether a tree is a single thing or whether it's a million.' "

She starts in on the next startling sentence, when a growl from her husband interrupts her. She thinks he's saying, *Paper cup*.

"Ray?"

He says the syllables again, and they sound the same. "Sorry, Ray. I'm not sure what that means."

*Paper cup. Seedling. On the windowsill.*

The words come out excited, and they make her skin crawl. His crazed intensity, in the falling light, makes her think he's having another cerebral accident. Her pulse spikes and she struggles to her feet. Then she understands. He's entertaining her, turning Things as They Are into something better. Telling her a story, in return for the years of stories she has read to him.

*Planted it. The chestnut. Our daughter.*


"YOURS?" a voice asks.

Patricia Westerford clenches. A uniformed man behind the conveyor belt indicates her carry-on as it exits the scanner. She nods, almost nonchalant.

"Can we have a look?"

It's not really a question, and he doesn't wait for an answer. The bag opens; the hands root through. The pawing is like the bear who works Patricia's blackberry patch at the Smokies cabin.

"What's this?"

She slaps her forehead. Senile. "My collection kit."

He examines the three-quarter-inch blade, the pruner that opens to the width of a pencil, the tiny saw shorter than her first pinkie joint. The country has been more than a decade without a serious air travel incident, paid for by a billion pocketknives, toothpaste tubes, bottles of shampoo . . .

"What do you collect?"

A hundred wrong answers, and not a single right. "Plants."

"You're a gardener?"

"Yes." A time and place, even for perjury.

"And this?"

"That?" she echoes. Stupid, but it buys her three seconds. "That's just vegetable broth." Her heart pounds so hard it will kill her as cleanly as anything in the jar. The man has power over her, the total power of a panicked nation in pursuit of impossible safety. One glare too blatant and she'll miss the flight.

"This is more than three ounces."

She stuffs her shaking hands into her pockets and clamps her jaw. He'll notice; that's his job. He pushes the two items back toward her with one hand and her riffled bag with the other.

"You can go back into the terminal and mail these."

"I'll miss my flight."

"Then I'll have to confiscate them." He drops the plastic jar and collection kit into an already full oil drum. "Have a safe journey."

On the plane, she goes through her keynote one last time. "The Single Best Thing a Person Can Do for Tomorrow's World." Everything is written out. She hasn't read a speech out loud for years. But she can't trust herself to improvise this one.

She comes through the arrival chute at SFO. Drivers stand in a ring at the mouth of the passenger exit, holding up names on pieces of paper. Hers isn't one. An organizer from the conference was supposed to meet her. Patricia waits for several minutes, but no one comes. That's fine with her. Any reason not to go through with this. She sits in a chair against the wall in a corner of the meeting area. A board of glowing letters across the concourse reads *Boston Boston Chicago Chicago Chicago Dallas Dallas* . . . Human *goings*. Human *doings*. Ever faster, ever fuller, ever more mobile, ever more empowered.

A motion catches her eye. Even a newborn will turn to look toward a bird in preference to slower, closer things. Her eyes follow the erratic arc. A house sparrow is hopping about on the top of a signboard, fifteen feet away. It darts on short, purposeful flights around the meeting area. No one in the crowd pays any notice. It skims up into a hidden cranny near the ceiling, then swoops back down again. Soon two, then three, scouting out the trash cans. The first things since boarding that have made her glad.

There's something on their legs, like tracking tags, but bigger. She retrieves the roll she stuffed into her purse for dinner, crumbles it onto the chair next to hers. She half expects a security guard to come arrest her. The birds want the prize badly. Each nervous lunge takes them a little nearer, for a little longer. At last gluttony overcomes caution, and one of the sparrows flits in for the steal. Patricia holds still; the sparrow hops closer, feeding. When the angle is right, she reads the ankle bracelet. *Illegal alien.* She laughs, and the startled bird bolts.

A feline woman bears down on her. "Dr. Westerford?" Patricia smiles and stands.

"Where have you *been?* Why haven't you answered your phone?"

Patricia wants to say, *My phone lives in Boulder, Colorado, plugged into the wall.*

"I've been going around and around the arrivals loop. Where's your luggage?" The entire project of Home Repair seems to be teetering.

"This is my luggage."

The girl is dumbstruck. "But you'll be here for three days!"

"These birds . . ." Patricia begins.

"Yeah. Somebody's joke. The airport can't figure out how to get rid of them."

"Why would you want to?"

The driver isn't built for philosophy. "We're over this way,"

They crawl out of the city and down the Central Peninsula. The driver names the luminaries who'll speak over the next few days. Patricia watches the scenery. On their right, the hills of second-growth redwood. On their left, Silicon Valley, the future's factory. The driver loads Dr. Westerford with plastic folders and drops her at the Faculty Club. Patricia has all afternoon to wander the most extraordinary collection of campus trees in the country. She finds a marvelous blue oak, regal California planes, incense cedars, a gnarled anarchical pepper tree, dozens of the seven hundred species of eucalypts, kumquats in full fruit. Every student must be drunk on the air's intoxicants without even knowing. It's a Christmas of lignin. Old, lost friends. Trees she has never seen. Pines spinning out cones in perfect Fibonacci swirls. Backwater genera—*Maytenus, Syzygium, Ziziphus.* She combs them and all the bedding plants beneath for extracts to replace the ones the TSA confiscated.

A walkway takes her alongside the apse of a fake Romanesque church. She passes under a monumental three-trunked avocado, way too close to the wall, that probably began life on a secretary's desk. Popping through a portal into a courtyard, she stops and touches a hand to her lips. Trees— mighty, improbable, outlandish trees that have come from some Golden Age pulp novel about the teeming jungles beneath the acid clouds of Venus— stand whispering to each other.

THE AGENTS put Adam Appich in a cell larger than the platform he once shared with two other people two hundred feet in the air. The state takes charge of him. He cooperates in all things and remembers almost nothing, even half an hour later. This morning he was a full professor of psychology at a great urban university. Now he's held for ancient crimes involving several million dollars of property damage and the immolation of a woman.

His parents are blessedly dead. So is his sister Jean, his brother Charles, his one lifelong friend, and the mentor who opened his eyes to human blindness. He's reached the age when dead is the new normal. He hasn't spoken to his older brother since Emmett cheated Adam out of his inheritance. There's no one to tell except his wife and his son.

Lois picks up, surprised to hear from him in midafternoon. She laughs when he tells her where he is. It takes a long silence to convince her. She comes to see him in the packed detention center during visiting hours the next morning. Her incomprehension has turned into action, and her face flushes with her first real cause in years. Through the bulletproof glass, she reads to him from a virgin four-inch notebook neatly labeled *Adam, Legal*. They're almost artworks, all the things she has set in motion.

Her checklist is detailed and vigorous. The lines around her eyes square off against injustice. "I have some leads on lawyers. We need to request house detention. It's pricey, but you'll be home."

"Lo," he says, thick with years. "I can tell you what happened."

Her one hand grazes the ballistic glass and her other draws a finger over her lips. "Shh. The ACLU guy said not to talk until you're out."

Her hope: so defiant, so her. He has made a living studying defiant hope. Defiant hope is what landed him here.

"I know you didn't do any of this, Adam. You wouldn't be capable." But her eyes duck—the old mammalian tell, tens of millions of years in the making. She knows nothing, least of all about the man she has lived with for years, her lawfully wedded husband, her son's father. A con man at the very least and, for all she knows, accessory to murder.

Across town in another holding facility, his betrayer slips off again tonight, away from the government, his employers turned captors, into his nightly search party for the woman who turned Douglas Pavlicek into a radical. She has a different name now, he's sure. She might be far away in another country, deep into a sequel life he can't imagine. Forgiveness is more than he can ask her, more than he'll ever give himself. He deserves much worse than what the Freddies have handed him—seven years in a medium-security prison, eligible for parole in two. But there's something he needs to tell her. *This is how it happened. This is how things went down.* She'll hear about what he did. She'll know the worst, and she'll despise him. Nothing he can ever say will change that. But she'll wonder why, and the wonder will cause her pain. Pain he might change into something better.

His cell is a cinder-block cube coated in rubbery green paint, much like the fake cell he lived in for a week at the age of nineteen. The narrow confinement frees him to travel. He shuts his eyes and goes after her, as he does every night. The film is never more than dim and her features vague. He has forgotten even those things about her face that used to make him feel like he could suck in air and with a lazy sigh breathe out eternity. But tonight he can almost see her, not as she must look now, but as she was. *This is how it happened*, he says. He was betrayed—never mind by whom. Ambushed. And by the time the feds swooped in and took him, he was already lost.

His interrogators were kind. There was David, an older guy who looked like Douggie's grandfather. And a thoughtful woman named Anne, who dressed in gray skirt-suits and took notes, trying to understand. They told him it was all over, that his handwritten memoir gave them all they needed to put him and all his friends away forever. Just a matter of clearing up a few details.

*You've got nothing. I was writing a novel. It all came from my own damn head.*

They said his novel contained information about crimes that was never public. They said they already knew about his friends. Dossiers on all of them. They only wanted him to corroborate, and it would go much easier on Douglas if he helped.

*Help? That's some Judas shit, man.* It just slipped out of him. One word too many.

He tells Mimi about the mistake. She seems to hear, even to flinch a little, although her face with its punji scar is turned away. He explains how he held out for days, how he told the agents to send him away forever—he wasn't naming any names. He tells her how his questioners brought out the photos. The eeriest things: like home movie stills, grainy shots of events where no one had a camera. The events themselves he remembered well, especially the venues where he got beaten up. Lots of the pictures featured him. He'd forgotten how young he was, once. How naïve and volatile.

*You know*, he told his questioners, *I'm much cuter than I ever look.*

Anne smiled and noted something down. *You see?* David told him. *We have them all. We don't need anything from you. But cooperation could greatly reduce the charges against you.* That was when Douglas began to realize that hiring his own lawyer might not be the same as an admission of guilt. Of course, hiring anybody for anything would require a lot more than the twelve hundred and thirty dollars he could lay his hands on.

There was a problem with the pictures. They included people he'd never seen. There was a problem with the list of fires they wanted him to admit to. He'd never heard of half of them. Then the two agents began to ask who was who. *Which one is Mulberry? Which one is Watchman? Which one is Maple? Is this her?*

They were bluffing. Writing their own novel.

For two days, they held him in a place that looked like a dorm at a bankrupt Serbian college. He stuck to his silence. Then they told him what he was facing: domestic terrorism—attempting to influence the conduct of government by intimidation or coercion—punishable under the Terrorist Penalties Enhancement Act, the apparatus of a whole new security state. He'd never walk outside again. But if he simply confirmed one of these faces—one face, of someone they already had a dossier on—he'd go free in two to seven years. And they'd close the case on any of the fires he admitted to.

*Close the case?*

They would pursue no other people for those crimes.

*From now on? For any of the crimes I may or may not admit to?*

One face. And he'd have the full good faith of the federal government.

He didn't care whether he went to prison for seven years or seven hundred. He'd never last; his body didn't have that kind of mileage left in it. But guaranteed reprieve for the woman who had taken him in and a man who seemed to be out there still, fighting against humanity's death wish . . . it felt like meaning.

Sprinkled among the gallery that his two investigators dangled in front of him were pictures of that man who always felt to Douggie like an infiltrator. A man who'd come to study them. The guy who they sent, that terrible night, to go get help for Olivia—any help at all—but who came back empty-handed.

"There," Douglas said, his finger waving like a twig in the breeze. "That's Maple. Guy named Adam. Studying psychology at Santa Cruz."

*That's how it happened,* he tells his partner in salvation. *That's what I did. That's why. For you and Nick and maybe the trees.*

But when she swings around and turns her phantom face to him, she makes no sign. She just holds his eyes and stares, as if an endless glance will tell her all she needs to know.


THE AUDITORIUM is dark and lined with redwood questionably obtained. Patricia looks out from the podium on hundreds of experts. She keeps her eyes high above the expectant faces and clicks. Behind her appears a painting of a naïve wooden ark with a parade of animals winding up into it.

"When the world was ending the first time, Noah took all the animals, two by two, and loaded them aboard his escape craft for evacuation. But it's a funny thing: He left the plants to die. He failed to take the one thing he needed to rebuild life on land, and concentrated on saving the freeloaders!"

The house laughs. They're rooting for her, but only because they don't know what she means to say.

"The problem was, Noah and his kind didn't believe that plants were really *alive*. No intentions, no vital spark. Just like rocks that happened to get bigger."

She clicks again through several images: flytraps closing on their prey, sulking sensitive plants, a mosaic of kapur crowns in a canopy stopping just short of touching one another. "Now we know that plants communicate and remember. They taste, smell, touch, and even hear and see. We, the species that figured this out, have learned so much about who we share the world with. We've begun to understand the profound ties between trees and people. But our separation has grown faster than our connection."

She clicks, and her slide changes. "Here's a satellite view of North America at night, 1970. And here, we are, a decade later. And another. And another. One more, and done." Four clicks, and light screams across the continent, filling the blackness from sea to sea. She clicks, revealing a balding robber baron in high collar and shaggy mustache. "A reporter once asked Rockefeller how much is enough. His answer: *Just a little bit more*. And that's all we want: to eat and sleep, to stay dry and be loved, and acquire just a little bit more."

This time the laugh is a polite murmur. A tough room. They've seen this exploding light show too many times before. Everyone in this auditorium has long ago numbed to the fact. Two people in back get up and walk out. An *environmental conference*. Five hundred attendees, seven warring factions, scores of objections to every plan to save the planet. All for just one tsunami.

Next come four short aerial time-lapses—the forests of Brazil, Thailand, Indonesia, and the Pacific Northwest, melting away. "Just a little more timber. A few more jobs. A few more acres of cornfield to feed a few more people. You know? There's never been any material more useful than wood."

There's shifting in the plush seats, coughs and whispers, silent calls to kill all the preachers.

"In this state alone, a third of the forested acres have died in the last six years. Forests are falling to many things—drought, fire, sudden oak death, gypsy moths, pine and engraver beetles, rust, and plain old felling for farms and subdivisions. But there's always the same distal cause, and you know it and I know it and everyone alive who's paying attention knows it. The year's clocks are off by a month or two. Whole ecosystems are unraveling. Biologists are scared senseless.

"Life is so generous, and we are so . . . inconsolable. But nothing I can say will wake the sleepwalk or make this suicide seem real. It *can't* be real, right? I mean, here we are, all still . . ."

Twelve minutes into the talk, and she's quaking. Her palm goes up to beg for three seconds. She retreats behind the podium, retrieves a plastic water bottle left her by the well-meaning organizers of this conference on Home Repair. She twists off the cap and lifts the container. "Synthetic estrogen." She clicks the crackly plastic. "Ninety-three of every one hundred Americans are laced with this stuff." She pours some into a waiting glass. Out from her hip pocket comes the replacement glass vial. "And these are plant extracts I found while walking around this campus yesterday. My goodness, this place is an arbor. A little paradise!"

Her hand shakes, splattering the pour. She cups the vial in both hands and puts it on top of the podium. "You see, a lot of folks think trees are simple things, incapable of doing anything interesting. But there's a tree for every purpose under heaven. Their chemistry is astonishing. Waxes, fats, sugars. Tannins, sterols, gums, and carotenoids. Resin acids, flavonoids, terpenes. Alkaloids, phenols, corky suberins. They're learning to make whatever can be made. And most of what they make we haven't even identified."

She clicks through a menagerie of bark behaving badly. Dragon trees that bleed as red as blood. Jabuticaba, whose billiard-ball fruits grow right out of the trunk. Thousand-year-old baobabs, like tethered weather balloons loaded with thirty thousand gallons of water. Eucalypts the color of rainbows. Bizarre quiver trees with weapons for branch tips. *Hura crepitans*, the sandbox tree, launching seeds from its exploding fruit at 160 miles per hour. Her audience relaxes, calmed by her turn back toward the picturesque. Nor does she mind taking a last detour through the world's best things.

"At some time over the last four hundred million years, some plant has tried every strategy with a remote chance of working. We're just beginning to realize how varied a thing *working* might be. Life has a way of talking to the future. It's called memory. It's called genes. To solve the future, we must save the past. My simple rule of thumb, then, is this: when you cut down a tree, what you make from it should be at least as miraculous as what you cut down."

She can't hear if her audience laughs or groans. She taps on the side of the podium. The thump is muffled under her fingers. Everything in the hall is muted.

"My whole life, I've been an outsider. But many others have been out there with me. We found that trees could communicate, over the air and through their roots. Common sense hooted us down. We found that trees take care of each other. Collective science dismissed the idea. Outsiders discovered how seeds remember the seasons of their childhood and set buds accordingly. Outsiders discovered that trees sense the presence of other nearby life. That a tree learns to save water. That trees feed their young and synchronize their masts and bank resources and warn kin and send out signals to wasps to come and save them from attacks.

"Here's a little outsider information, and you can wait for it to be confirmed. A forest knows things. They wire themselves up underground. There are brains down there, ones our own brains aren't shaped to see. Root plasticity, solving problems and making decisions. Fungal synapses. What else do you want to call it? Link enough trees together, and a forest grows *aware*."

Her words sound far away, cork-lined and underwater. Either both her hearing aids have died at once or her childhood deafness has chosen this moment to come back.

"We scientists are taught never to look for ourselves in other species. So we make sure nothing looks like us! Until a short while ago, we didn't even let chimpanzees have consciousness, let alone dogs or dolphins. Only man, you see: only man could know enough to *want* things. But believe me: trees want something from us, just as we've always wanted things from them. This isn't mystical. The 'environment' is alive—a fluid, changing web of purposeful lives dependent on each other. Love and war can't be teased apart. Flowers shape bees as much as bees shape flowers. Berries may compete to be eaten more than animals compete for the berries. A thorn acacia makes sugary protein treats to feed and enslave the ants who guard it. Fruit-bearing plants trick us into distributing their seeds, and ripening fruit led to color vision. In teaching us how to find their bait, trees taught us to see that the sky is blue. Our brains evolved to solve the forest. We've shaped and been shaped by forests for longer than we've been *Homo sapiens*.

"Men and trees are closer cousins than you think. We're two things hatched from the same seed, heading off in opposite directions, using each other in a shared place. That place needs all its parts. And our part . . . we have a role to play in the Earth organism, and *this* . . ." She turns to see the image projected behind her. It's the Arbre du Ténéré, the only thing up on a trunk for four hundred kilometers in every direction. Hit and killed by a drunk driver. She clicks on a Florida bald cypress one and a half millennia older than Christianity, killed a few months ago by a flicked cigarette. "This can't be it."

Another click. "Trees are doing science. Running a billion field tests. They make their conjectures, and the living world tells them what works. Life is speculation, and speculation is life. What a marvelous word! It means to guess. It also means to mirror.

"Trees stand at the heart of ecology, and they must come to stand at the heart of human politics. Tagore said, *Trees are the earth's endless effort to speak to the listening heaven*. But people—oh, my word—people! People could be the heaven that the Earth is trying to speak to.

"If we could see green, we'd see a thing that keeps getting more interesting the closer we get. If we could see what green was doing, we'd never be lonely or bored. If we could understand green, we'd learn how to grow all the food we need in layers three deep, on a third of the ground we need right now, with plants that protected one another from pests and stress. If we knew what green wanted, we wouldn't have to choose between the Earth's interests and ours. They'd be the same!"

One more click takes her to the next slide, a giant fluted trunk covered in red bark that ripples like muscle. "To see green is to grasp the Earth's intentions. So consider this one. This tree grows from Colombia to Costa Rica. As a sapling, it looks like a piece of braided hemp. But if it finds a hole in the canopy, the sapling shoots up into a giant stem with flaring buttresses."

She turns to regard the image over her shoulder. It's the bell of an enormous angel's trumpet, plunged into the Earth. So many miracles, so much awful beauty. How can she leave so perfect a place?

"Did you know that every broadleaf tree on Earth has flowers? Many mature species flower at least once a year. But *this* tree, *Tachigali versicolor*, this one flowers only once. Now, suppose you could have sex only once in your entire life. . . ."

The room laughs now. She can't hear, but she can smell their nerves. Her switchback trail through the woods is twisting again. They can't tell where their guide is going.

"How can a creature survive, by putting everything into a one-night stand? *Tachigali versicolor*'s act is so quick and decisive that it boggles me. You see, within a year of its only flowering, it dies."

She lifts her eyes. The room fills with wary smiles for the weirdness of this thing, *nature*. But her listeners can't yet tie her rambling keynote to anything resembling home repair.

"It turns out that a tree can give away more than its food and medicines. The rain forest canopy is thick, and wind-borne seeds never land very far from their parent. *Tachigali*'s once-in-a-lifetime offspring germinate right away, in the shadow of giants who have the sun locked up. They're doomed, unless an old tree falls. The dying mother opens a hole in the canopy, and its rotting trunk enriches the soil for new seedlings. Call it the ultimate parental sacrifice. The common name for *Tachigali versicolor* is the suicide tree."

She takes up the vial of tree extracts from where she set it down on the podium. Her ears are worthless, but her hands, at least, have found their old steadiness. First there was everything. Soon there will be nothing.

"I've asked myself the question you brought me here to answer. I've thought about it based on all the evidence available. I've tried not to let my feelings protect me from the facts. I've tried not to let hope and vanity blind me. I've tried to see this matter from the standpoint of trees. *What is the single best thing a person can do for tomorrow's world?*"

A trickle of extract hits the glass of clear water and turns into tendrils of green.


GREEN SWIRLS spread through Astor Place. Just a lime splash at first, against the gray pavement. Then another splash, this one avocado. Adam stands at a window gazing down a dozen stories. Cars traveling the four skewed streets pull green streaks into the irregular intersection. In another moment, a third pool—olive—spreads in great Pollock swipes across the concrete canvas. Someone and his crew are dropping paint bombs.

It's his second day of home detention, in the downtown apartment where he and his family have lived for four years. The authorities have fitted him with a tracking anklet—top of the line of the HomeGuard series—and released him to his square of air above Waverly and Broadway. Tracking bands: the jewelry shared by endangered species and traitors to the race. He and Lois pay a private contracting company an insane amount of money for the device, and the firm splits the revenues with the state. Everyone wins.

Yesterday, a technical officer trained Appich in the rules of his confinement. "You can use the telephone and listen to the radio. You can browse the Net and read the papers. You can have visitors. But if you want to leave your building, you need to clear the trip with the Command Center."

Lois has taken little Charlie to his grandparents in Cos Cob. To give them a couple of days to concentrate on Adam's defense, she says. In fact, it traumatizes the boy to see the black slab strapped to his father's ankle. Five years old, and the kid knows.

"Take it off, Daddy."

So much earlier than he'd hoped, Adam breaks his vow never to lie to his own son. "Soon, buddy. Don't worry. It's okay."

From on high, Appich gazes down at the growing action painting. Another pool—jade—hits the concrete. The car that dumped the paint carries on through the plaza toward Cooper Square. It's guerrilla theater, a coordinated strike. With every new car, green arcs blend through the five-way intersection, adding a few more brushstrokes to the growing whole. Another vehicle comes down Eighth Street and releases three canisters of brown. Where the green streaks spread and branch, the browns lay down in a furrowed column. It's easy enough to see what's growing, twelve stories beneath.

Patches of red and yellow appear near the top of the subway station stairs. As unwitting pedestrians surface, they paint with their shoes. An angry businessman tries to skirt the mess and fails. Two lovers dance through arm-in-arm, their footsteps daubing in colored fruit and flowers among the spreading branches. Someone has gone to a fair amount of effort to make what must be the world's largest painting of a tree. Why here, Appich wonders, in a relative backwater neighborhood? It's a work worthy of Midtown, say outside Lincoln Center. Then he knows why it's here. Because *he* is.

He scoops up his keys and jacket, and with no more thought than to show himself, he heads downstairs. He cuts through the lobby, past the mailboxes, and out the door, heading east on Waverly toward the giant tree. The power brick tucked under Appich's baggy khaki cuffs goes nuts and starts to shriek. Two freight-movers turn to look, and a pensioner, shuffling behind his walker, stops in terror.

Adam ducks back inside his building, but the bracelet won't quit. It wails like avant-garde music all the way up the elevator. He trots down the hallway on his floor. The night shift computer operator next door pops his head out to locate the commotion. Adam waves an apology before barricading himself in his apartment. There, he phones in the mistake to his keepers.

"You were instructed," the tracking clerk tells him. "Do not try to cross your geo-fence."

"I understand. I'm sorry."

"Next time we'll have to take action."

"It was an accident. Human failing." His field of expertise.

"Reasons don't matter. We'll send force next time."

Adam returns to the window, to watch the giant painting dry. He's still standing there when his wife returns from Connecticut. "What is it?" Lois asks.

"A message. From a friend."

And for the first time, it hits her, the truth of what the newspapers have been saying. The pictures of the charred mountain lodge. The dead woman. "Member of Radical Eco-Terror Group Charged."


DOROTHY SLIPS into her husband's room early one evening to check on him. He has made no sound for hours. She comes through the doorway and, in the instant before he hears and turns toward her, she sees it again, as she has so often in these spare, short, accelerating days: that look of pure astonishment at a performance unfolding just outside the window.

"What is it, Ray?" She comes around to the bedside, but as always she can make out nothing but the winter yard. "Was there something?"

The twisted mouth moves into what she has learned to see as a smile. "Oh, yes!"

It strikes her that she envies him. His years of enforced tranquility, the patience of his slowed mind, the expansion of his blinkered senses. He can watch the dozen bare trees in the backyard for hours and see something intricate and surprising, sufficient to his desires, while she—she is still trapped in a hunger that rushes past everything.

She spades her arms under his wasted body and draws him toward one side of the mechanical bed. Then she walks around to the other side and gets in next to him. "Tell me." But of course he can't. He makes that chuckle in the back of his throat that could mean anything. She reaches for his hand and they hold still, as if they are already the carved figures on top of their own tomb.

They lie for a long time, staring out across their property where hunter-gatherers made their way for millennia. She sees plenty—all the various trees of their would-be arboretum, their buds at the ready. But she knows she isn't catching a tenth of what he is.

"Tell me more about her." Her heart pumps harder at the taboo question. All her life she has flirted with craziness, and still this new winter game of theirs feels worse than scary. Strangers are out tonight, wandering, knocking on their door. And she lets them in.

His arm tightens, and his face does change. "Moves fast. Will-fed." It's like he's just written *Remembrance of Things Past*.

"What does she look like?" She has asked before, but needs the answer again.

"Fierce. Fine. You."

It's enough to get her back into the book, and the yard opens like two pages spread in front of her. Tonight, in the growing darkness, the story runs in reverse. A succession of girls, younger and younger, head out the back door and into the miniature, simulated world. Their daughter at twenty, on spring break from college, in a sleeveless tank top that reveals a horrible new baroque tattoo on her left shoulder, sneaking out to smoke a joint after her parents have fallen asleep. Their daughter at sixteen, swilling cheap grocery store wine with two girlfriends in the farthest dark corner of the property. Their daughter at twelve, in a funk, kicking a soccer ball against the garage for hours. Their daughter at ten, floating across the grass, catching lightning bugs in a jar. Their daughter at six, heading out barefoot on the first seventy-degree spring day with a seedling in her hands.

The image appears against the shadowy trees. It's so vivid that Dorothy is sure she's seen some model for it somewhere. This is how read-aloud goes now, the two of them holding still and watching. Who knows what the life-long stranger in her house is ever thinking? She does, now. Something like this. Something exactly like this.

The paper cup has sat on the kitchen windowsill of her imagination for so long now that Dorothy can see the brown and cyan curlicues of stylized steam printed on it and read the word beneath the design: SOLO. A mass of eager roots has punched through the waxy paper bottom, in need of more world. Marvelous long serrated leaves—American chestnut—paw at the air on their first trip outside. Dorothy watches the girl and her father kneel at the edge of a freshly dug hole. The fretful child chops at the dirt with a trowel. She administers the sacrament of first water. She steps away from the planting, back underneath the arm of her father. And when the girl turns around and lifts her face, in this other life unfolding invisibly along-side the one that happened, Dorothy sees the face of her daughter, ready to take on all of life.

Two words up close to her ear explode the silence. "Do nothing." The words are as clear as they need to be, telling Dorothy that her husband has been out there with her in that other place, or not far away. Much the same thought has just occurred to her. They got the thought independently, from the same startling sentence in the same startling book that they just read together:

> The best and easiest way to get a forest to return to any
> plot of cleared land is to do nothing—nothing at all, and do it
> for less time than you might think.

"No more mowing," Ray whispers, and she doesn't even have to ask for explanation. What better inheritance could they leave such a willful, fierce, and fine daughter than an acre and a half of woods?

Side by side, in his mechanical bed, they lie and gaze out the window, where great snows pile up and melt away, the rains come, transient birds return, days grow long again, buds on every branch put forth flowers, and hundreds of seedlings push up wildly through the recidivist lawn.

"YOU CAN'T DO THIS. You have a child."

Adam sits back on the love seat, toying with the black box on his ankle. Lois—his *wife*—sits across from him, palms on thighs, spine like a tele-phone pole. He sways, limp in the stale air. He can no longer explain himself. He has no answer. For two days, the two of them have followed that fact down to hell.

He stares out the window as the lights of the Financial District replace the day. Ten million points flicker in the falling dark, like the logic gates of a circuit cranking out solutions to a calculation generations in the making.

"A five-year-old. He needs a father."

The child has been in Connecticut for only a day and a half, and already Adam can't remember which of the boy's earlobes has the nick in it. Or how the boy came to be five years old, when he was just born. Or how he, Adam, could be the father of anyone.

"He'll grow up resenting you. You'll be some stranger in federal prison that he goes to visit, until I stop making him."

She doesn't throw it in his face, although she should. He is, in fact, some stranger already. She just never knew. And the boy—the boy. Alien already, to Adam. For two weeks last year, Charlie wanted to be a firefighter, but soon realized that banker beat that in every measurable way. He likes nothing more than to line his toys up with a ruler, count them, and put them away in lockable containers. The only thing he has ever used nail polish for is to mark his little cars so neither parent can steal them.

Adam's head swings back into the room, to the figure on the barstool across from him. His wife's lips sour and her cheeks flush, like she's choking. Since his arrest, she has begun to seem as vague to him as his own life did on the day he slipped back into Santa Cruz and began to simulate it. "You want me to make a deal."

"Adam." Her voice is a controlled skid. "You will never come out again."

"You think I should condemn someone else. I'm just asking."

"It's justice. They're felons. And one of them condemned you."

He turns back to the window. House arrest. Below, the shimmer of NoHo, the flare of Little Italy, the country he's now barred from. And farther away, beyond all neighborhoods, the Atlantic's black cliff. The skyline is an experimental score for some euphoric music he can almost hear. Off to the right, out of sight, the twisted tower rises, replacing the gutted ones. *Freedom.*

"If it's justice we're after . . ."

A voice that should be familiar to him says, "What's wrong with you? You're going to put another person's welfare before your own *son?*"

There it is: the ultimate commandment. Take care of your own. Protect your genes. Lay down your life for one child, two siblings, or eight first cousins. How many friends would that translate to? How many strangers who might still be out there, laying down their lives for other species? How many trees? He can't begin to tell his wife the worst of it. Since his arrest—since beginning to think objectively again, after so many years of treating the question as an abstraction—he has begun to see that the dead woman was right: the world is full of welfares that must come even before your own kind.

"If I cut a deal, then my son ... then Charlie grows up knowing what I did."

"He'll know you made a hard choice. That you righted a wrong."

The laugh pops out of Adam. "Righted a wrong!" Lois bolts up. Fury chokes her words before she can spit them. As the door slams shut behind her, he remembers his wife, and what she's capable of.

He falls into a half sleep imagining what the law will do to him. He turns, and fire shoots through his lower spine. The pain wakes him. A huge moon hangs low over the Hudson. Every steel-white pockmark in its face shines telescope-clear. The prospect of life in prison does wonders for his eyesight.

His bladder hurts. He stands and starts a reflex overland expedition across the apartment to the bathroom, when a wrong cloud falls over his view. He crosses to the window and puts his hand to it. Condensation rims his palm like cave art. Down in the canyon below, streaks of car lights clump and disperse. There, between the spotty traffic, a pack of gray wolves comes down Waverly from Washington Square, chasing a white-tailed deer.

He jerks forward, smacking his forehead against the plate glass. Obscenity shoots out of him, his first in years. He stumbles through the kitchen into the cramped living room, clipping his shoulder on the doorframe. The bump spins him, and, stabbing with his right hand to break his fall, he bounces face-first into the windowsill. The impact clamps his mouth shut on his lower lip and drops him to the floor. There he lies, stupid with agony.

His fingers test his mouth and come away sticky. His right incisor has bitten through his lower lip from both sides. He rises to his knees and looks out above the sill. The moon shines over the tip of a tree-covered island. Brick, steel, and right angles give way to moonlit, mounded green. A stream runs through a ravine that cuts toward West Houston. The towers of the Financial District are gone, changed into wooded hills. Above, the spill of the Milky Way, a torrent of stars.

It's the mind-crushing pain of his cut lip. The stress of his arrest. He thinks: *I'm not actually seeing this. I'm lying senseless from the blow on the living room floor.* And yet it spreads outward below him, in all directions—a forest as dense, terrifying, and inescapable as childhood. Arboretum America.

His sight grows huge, magnifying the many colors and habits of the whole: hornbeam, oak, cherry, half a dozen kinds of maple. Honey locusts armored with thorns against extinct megafauna. Pignut hickories dropping meals for anything that moves. Waxy, flat white dogwood blooms float in the understory on invisibly thin twigs. Wilderness rushes down lower Broadway, the island as it was a thousand years back or a thousand years on.

A flash hooks his eye. Off toward a ridge of oak, a great horned owl sweeps its wings above its head and drops like a shot onto something moving in the leaf litter below. A black bear sow and two cubs track across a hillock where Bleeker Street was. Sea turtles lay their eggs by the full moon on the sandy banks of the East River.

Adam's breath fogs the glass and the view grays over. Blood trickles down his chin. He touches his mouth and comes away with grit, stony between his fingertips. He glances down to inspect the bits of chipped tooth. When he looks up again, Mannahatta is gone, replaced by the lights of Lower Manhattan. He smacks the window with his palm. The metropolis on the other side fails to hiccup. His pulse pounds in his forearms and he starts to shake. The buildings like crossword puzzles, the red and white corpuscles of traffic: more hallucinatory than what just vanished.

He picks his way through the minefield of furniture and scattered journals to the foyer and out the door. Six steps down the hall, he remembers his anklet. He slumps against one wall with his eyes squeezed shut. When the vision dies at last, he turns back into the apartment and seals himself up in the only habitat allowed him, his lone biome for a long time to come.

MIMI MA SITS in the auditorium's second row, transfixed by something the tree woman just said. *Patricia Westerford*: The five of them shared her discoveries over campfires, back when the Free Bioregion of Cascadia was still a place. Her words made them real, those alien agents doing things beyond the narrow consciousness of humans. The woman is older than Mimi imagined. Frightened and faltering, and there's something wrong with her speech. But she has just delivered this fine, sane, but somehow taboo rule: *What you make from a tree should be at least as miraculous as what you cut down.*

What the forest makes of the mountain is better than the mountain. What people might make of the forest . . . The thought barely germinates when Dr. Westerford jolts Mimi back.

"I've asked myself the question you brought me here to answer."

Mimi's first thought is that she's mistaken. A distinguished researcher and author—someone who has spent decades saving seeds from the world's endangered trees. . . . It can't be happening. She must be wrong.

"I've thought about it based on all the evidence available. I've tried not to let my feelings protect me from the facts."

The whole soliloquy is a piece of theater, heading toward some last-minute reverse or reveal.

"I've tried not to let hope and vanity blind me. I've tried to see this matter from the standpoint of trees."

Mimi looks down her aisle. People sit in disbelief, pinned in their seats with the full weight of shame.

*"What is the single best thing a person can do for tomorrow's world?"*

Another woman once asked Mimi this. And the answer, so obvious, so reason-driven: burn down a luxury ski resort before it could be built.

The plant extracts hit the glass. Green spreads through the water, snaking like a time-lapse bud sped up a hundred-thousandfold. Mimi, forty feet from the podium, can't move. Dr. Westerford lifts the glass like a priest raising a sacrament. Her speech thickens to a paste. "Many living things choose their own season. Maybe most of them."

It's happening. It's real. But hundreds of the world's smartest people hold still.

"You asked me here to talk about home repair. We're the ones who need repairing. Trees remember what we've forgotten. Every speculation must make room for another. Dying is life, too."

Dr. Westerford glances down, and Mimi is waiting for her. She locks on to the tree woman's gaze and won't let go. Long ago, in another life, she was an engineer and could make matter do so many things. Now she knows only this one skill: how to look at another being until it looks back.

Mimi pleads, her eyes burning. *No. Don't. Please.*

The speaker frowns. *Everything else is hypocrisy.*

*You're needed.*

*Needed for this. We are too many.*

*That's not for you to decide.*

*A new city the size of Des Moines every day.*

*What about your work? Your seed vault?*

*It has run itself for years.*

*There's so much more to do.*

*I'm an old woman. What better work than this is left?*

*People won't understand. They'll hate you. It's too theatrical.*

*It will get a moment of attention, amid all the screaming.*

*It's immature. Not worthy of you.*

*We need to remember how to die.*

*You'll die horribly.*

*No. I know my plants. This one will be easier than most.*

*I can't watch this again.*

*Watch. Again. It's all there is.*

The glance lasts no longer than it takes a leaf to eat a chunk of light. Mimi fights to hold the speaker's gaze, but with a last act of will, the tree-woman breaks away. Patricia Westerford lifts her gaze back onto the cavernous room. Her smile insists that this isn't defeat. It's use by another name. A small thing, a way to buy a little more time, a few more resources. She glances back down at a horrified Mimi. *The things we might see, the things we could still give!*

THERE'S A BEECH in Ohio Patricia would like to see again. Of all the trees she'll miss like breathing, a simple, smooth-boled beech with nothing special to it except a notch on its trunk four feet up from the ground. Maybe it has thrived. Maybe the sun and rain and air have been good to it. She thinks: *Maybe we want to hurt trees so much because they live so much longer than we do.*

Plant-Patty raises her glass. She scans her speech for the last line on the last page. *To Tachigali versicolor.* She looks up. Three hundred brilliant people watch her, awed. The sound track is silent except for muffled shouting by the lip of the stage. She glances over at the commotion. A man in a wheelchair rolls up to the right-hand stair. His hair and beard flow down around his shoulders. He's as thin as the talking tree-person of the Yaqui, the one no one could understand. Alone of all the people in this paralyzed room, he pushes down against his chair, trying to stand. The green liquid splatters over the glass's lip, into her hand. She looks again. The man in the chair waves wildly. His twig-arms fling outward. How can something so small matter so much to him?

The single best thing you can do for the world. It occurs to her: The problem begins with that word *world*. It means two such opposite things. The real one we cannot see. The invented one we can't escape. She lifts the glass and hears her father read out loud: *Let me sing to you now, about how people turn into other things.*

NEELAY'S SHOUTS come too late to break the room's spell. The speaker raises her glass, and the world splits. Down one branch, she lifts the glass to her lips, toasts the room—*To Tachigali versicolor*—and drinks. Down another branch, this one, she shouts, "Here's to unsuicide," and flings the cup of swirling green over the gasping audience. She bumps the podium, backs away, and stumbles into the wings, leaving the room to stare at an empty stage.

IN THE SPRING, the lush, too-warm spring, when the buds and flowers go mad on every dogwood and redbud and pear and weeping cherry in the city, Adam's case at last runs out of delays and heads to a federal court on the West Coast. Reporters fill the courtroom like ants swarming a peony. The bailiff leads Adam in. He's stocky now, bearded. Furrows contour-plow his face. He wears the suit he last wore to the awards banquet where he accepted his university's top teaching prize. His wife is there, seated in the row behind him. But not his boy. His boy will only ever see his father like this many years later, on video.

*How do you plead?*

The psych professor blinks, as if he's another form of life altogether and human speech is way too fast to understand.


OVER THE EMPTY SILL, through the kitchen window, Dorothy Brinkman looks out onto a jungle. The man who never once failed to feed a parking meter has launched her on a made-to-order revolution—the Brinkman Woodlands Restoration Project. Wildness advances on all sides of the house. The grass is foot-high, clumped, weedy, seeding, and thick with native volunteers. Maples pop up everywhere, like paired hands. Ankle-high hackberries flaunt their paisley leaves. The speed of the reclamation stuns her. A few more years and their stand of woods will half reprise whatever came before the invading subdivision.

Her own second growth is even faster. Once, long ago, she jumped from airplanes, played a bloody-minded murderess, did terrible things to anyone who tried to confine her. Now she's almost seventy, at war with the entire city. Jungle in an upscale suburb: it's up there with child-molesting. The neighbors have come by on three separate occasions to ask if there's anything wrong. They volunteer to mow, for free. She plays herself, sweet, demented, just adamant enough to hold them at bay—a last amateur theatrical comeback tour.

Now the whole street is ready to stone her. The city has written twice, the second time a registered letter giving her a deadline to clean up the place or face a fine of several hundred dollars. The deadline has come and gone, and with it, another threatening letter, another deadline, and another assessed fine. Who would have thought the foundations of society would be so shaken by a little runaway green?

The new deadline is today. She looks out on the chestnut, the tree that shouldn't be there. Last week she heard a radio story about how thirty years of cross-breeding has at last produced a blight-resistant American chestnut tree, about to be tested in the wild. The tree that seemed to her like a spared memory now looks like a prediction.

A flash of orange at the window catches her eye: American redstart, male, flushing insects from the thicket with its tail and wings. Twenty-two species of birds this last week alone. Two days ago, at twilight, she and Ray saw a fox. Civil disobedience may cost them thousands in compounding penalties, but the view from the house has been much improved.

She's making fruit compote for Ray's lunch when the awaited angry knock comes on the front door. She flushes with excitement. More than excitement: purpose. A touch of fear, but the most delicious kind. She rinses and dries her hands, thinking: *Here I am, near the finish line, loving life again.*

The knock gets faster and louder. She crosses through the living room, reviewing in her head the defense of their property rights that Ray has helped her prepare. She has spent days at the public library and the municipal building, learning how to read local ordinances, legal precedent, and municipal code. She has brought back copies to her husband for explanation, one stunted syllable at a time. She has pored through books, compiling stats on just how criminal mowing, watering, and fertilizing are, just how much good a reforested acre and a half can do. All the arguments of sanity and sense are on her side. Against her there is only one unreasoning and primal desire. But when she opens the door, it's on a scrawny kid in jeans and polo shirt, stringy blond hair sticking out from under his Made in the USA ball cap, and the whole plan of defense changes.

"Mrs. Brinkman?" Behind the kid, out by the curb, three even younger boys shouting back and forth in Spanish unload lawn equipment from a pickup truck and flatbed trailer. "We're here from the city to clean up your place. We'll only take a few hours, and the city won't bill you until later."

"No," she says, and the rich, warm, wise sound of that single syllable confuses the boy. He opens his mouth, but he's way too baffled to make it say anything. She smiles and heaves her chest. "You really don't want to do that. Tell the city that would be a terrible mistake."

She remembers the secret from her days onstage: Mobilize your inner will. Summon all the memory of a life lived. Hold it in your head: Right and wrong. The truth, self-evident. Nothing has more power than simple conviction.

The boy wavers. The city failed to prepare him for such authority. "Well, if it's all right . . ."

She smiles and shakes her head, embarrassed for him. "It isn't all right. It really isn't." *You know better. Please don't make me shame you even worse.* The boy panics. She looks at him with affection, understanding, most of all pity, until he turns away and calls the crew and the gear back into the truck. Dorothy shuts the door and cackles as they drive away. She always did enjoy playing a good madwoman.

It's the smallest of victories, the slightest postponement. The city will be back. The mowers and clippers will set to work, next time swarming without asking. They'll shave the yard clean. The fines will pile up, with the late fees and penalties. Dorothy will countersue, fighting in court until the last appeal. Let the city confiscate the house and throw a paralyzed man in jail. She will outlast them. The anarchy of new seedlings and next spring is on her side.

She heads back to the kitchen, where she finishes making lunch. She feeds Ray, telling him about the poor boy and his foreign work crew who never knew what hit them. She acts out all the parts. The most fun is playing herself. She can see him smile, although no one else in the world would be able to confirm.

After lunch they work the crossword. Then, as he often does these days, Ray says, "Tell more." Dorothy smiles and climbs into bed next to him. She looks out back, through the window, on the riot of new growth. In its middle, the tree that shouldn't be there. Its branches rush outward, toward the house, slowly, to be sure, but fast enough to inspire her. How life managed to add imagination to all the other tricks in its chemistry set is a mystery Dorothy can't wrap her head around. But there it is: the ability to see, all at once, in all its concurrent branches, all its many hypotheticals, this thing that bridges past and future, earth and sky.

"She's a good girl, you know." She takes her husband's stiff claw. "She was just lost for a little while. All she needs to do is find herself. Find a cause. Something bigger than she is."

THE PROSECUTION shows photos from the scene of one of the man's alleged crimes—a bit of graffiti on a charred wall. The first letters of each line sprout tendrils and vines, like the capitals of an illuminated manuscript:

CONTROL KILLS
CONNECTION HEALS
COME HOME OR DIE

It's the centerpiece of their case, the grounds for the extraordinary sentence they're demanding. They mean to prove intimidation. An attempt to influence the conduct of government by force.

ADAM'S LAWYERS argue for mercy. They claim the fires were set by a young idealist calling the public's attention to a crime against everyone. They say the sales of the forest were themselves illegal and the government failed to protect lands entrusted to it. Countless peaceful protests had come to nothing. But they have no case. The law is clear on every count. He's guilty of arson. Guilty of destruction of private property. Guilty of violence against the public well-being. Guilty of manslaughter. Guilty, the jury of Adam Appich's peers concludes, of domestic terrorism.

The law is simply human will, written down. The law must let every acre of living Earth be turned into tarmac, if such is the desire of people. But the law lets all parties have their say. The judge asks, "Would you care to address any final words to the court?"

Thoughts ring Adam's head. The verdicts have cut him loose, like windthrow or fire. "Soon we'll know if we were right or wrong."

The court sentences Adam Appich to two consecutive terms of seventy years each. The lenience shocks him. He thinks: *Seventy plus seventy is nothing. A black willow plus a wild cherry.* He was thinking oak. He was thinking Douglas-fir or yew. Seventy plus seventy. With reductions for good behavior, he might even finish out the first half of the sentence just in time to die.

# SEEDS

*What was the wood, what the tree out of which heaven and earth were fashioned?*

—RIG VEDA, 10.31.7

*And in this he showed me a little thing, the quantity of a hazel nut, lying in the palm of my hand, as it seemed. And it was as round as any ball. I looked upon it with the eye of my understanding, and thought, "What may this be?" And it was answered generally thus, "It is all that is made."*

—JULIAN OF NORWICH

S ay the planet is born at midnight and it runs for one day.

First there is nothing. Two hours are lost to lava and meteors. Life doesn't show up until three or four a.m. Even then, it's just the barest self-copying bits and pieces. From dawn to late morning—a million million years of branching—nothing more exists than lean and simple cells.

Then there is everything. Something wild happens, not long after noon. One kind of simple cell enslaves a couple of others. Nuclei get membranes. Cells evolve organelles. What was once a solo campsite grows into a town.

The day is two-thirds done when animals and plants part ways. And still life is only single cells. Dusk falls before compound life takes hold. Every large living thing is a latecomer, showing up after dark. Nine p.m. brings jellyfish and worms. Later that hour comes the breakout—backbones, cartilage, an explosion of body forms. From one instant to the next, countless new stems and twigs in the spreading crown burst open and run.

Plants make it up on land just before ten. Then insects, who instantly take to the air. Moments later, tetrapods crawl up from the tidal muck, carrying around on their skin and in their guts whole worlds of earlier creatures. By eleven, dinosaurs have shot their bolt, leaving the mammals and birds in charge for an hour.

Somewhere in that last sixty minutes, high up in the phylogenetic canopy, life grows aware. Creatures start to speculate. Animals start teaching their children about the past and the future. Animals learn to hold rituals.

Anatomically modern man shows up four seconds before midnight. The first cave paintings appear three seconds later. And in a thousandth of a click of the second hand, life solves the mystery of DNA and starts to map the tree of life itself.

By midnight, most of the globe is converted to row crops for the care and feeding of one species. And that's when the tree of life becomes something else again. That's when the giant trunk starts to teeter.

NICK WAKES IN THE TENT with his head against the ground. But the earth is soft, as soft as any pillow. The soil beneath is several feet deep with needles, so many dropping, dying needles turning to microscopic life again, under his ear.

The birds wake him. They always do, the daily prophets of forgetting and remembering, deep into their songs even before the light starts to break. He's grateful to them. They give him, each day, an early start. He lies still in the dark, hungry, listening to the birds discuss life in a thousand ancient dialects: bickering, turf war, recollection, praise, joy. It's cold this morning, fogged in with gloom, and he doesn't want to get out of the bag. Breakfast will be meager. There's not much food left. He has been north for days, and he'll have to find a town and resupply before long. There's a road within earshot, with trucks shuttling, but the sound is abstract, muffled, far away.

He crawls from the nylon egg and looks. The first faint suggestion of dawn outlines the trees. The trees are smaller here, slender to the skirts, shaped for heavy snowfalls. But it happens to him again, as it always does now. The look of the waving trunks, the cones rustling, the way the branch tips feel each other out, the astringent, citrus scent of the needles all restore him to the crystalline reason he forever keeps forgetting.

"Up in the morning!"

His crazy singing adds to the dawn chorus.

"Out on the job!"

The nearest birds fall silent and listen.

"Work like the devil for my pay!"

A small fire suffices to boil the water, drawn from a generous stream. Pinch of coffee crystals, a fist of oats in a wooden cup, and he's ready.

MIMI IN MISSION DOLORES PARK, San Francisco, many miles south. She sits in the grass surrounded by picnickers, under a knobcone pine, tapping at her phone. The news is a nightmare she can't wake from. An accomplished social scientist with a wife and young son—a man she once trusted with her life—is going away for two lifetimes, for something she helped do. Convicted of domestic terrorism. Little or no attempt at defense. Found guilty of fires she can't believe he set. "Eco-Radical Sentenced to 140 Years." And another man, a man she loved for his earnest cartoon innocence, has sold him out.

Cross-legged on the ground, her back against the bark, she feeds key words into her phone. *Adam Appich. Terrorist Penalties Enhancement Act.* She no longer cares what bread-crumb trails she's leaving. Getting caught would solve so many things. Pages swell and link faster than she can skim them— expert analysis and angry amateur conjecture.

She should be in prison. She should be tried and sentenced to life. Two lives. Guilt comes up her throat, and she tastes it. Her sick legs want to stand and take her into the nearest police station. But she doesn't even know where that might be. That's how law-abiding she has been, for two decades. Nearby sunbathers turn to look at her. She has said something out loud. She thinks it might have been, *Help me.*

OTHER EYES, invisible, read alongside hers. In the time it takes Mimi to scan ten paragraphs, the bodiless eyes read ten million. She retains no more than half a dozen details that fade as soon as she flips to a new page, but the invisible learners preserve every single word and fit them into branching networks of sense that grow stronger with each addition. The more she reads, the more the facts evade her. The more the learners read, the more patterns they find.

. . .

DOUGLAS SITS at a student desk in the room his captors call a cell. It's the nicest accommodation he's had for two decades. He's listening to an audio course—Introduction to Dendrology. He can get college credit for it. Maybe he'll earn a degree. Maybe that would make her proud, the woman he knows he hasn't a chance in hell of ever seeing again.

The professor on the tapes is great. She's like the grandmother and mother and spiritual guidance counselor Douglas never had. He loves how they're using people with speech impediments, these days. For *audio* lectures. This woman is hearing other voices altogether. He listens and takes notes. At the top of the page, he writes, *The Day of Life*. It's crazy, what the woman on the tape is saying. He had no idea. Life—flatlined for a billion years or more. Unbelievable. The whole escapade might never have happened. The tree of life might have stayed a shrub forever. And the day of life might have been a very quiet day.

He listens as she clicks off the hours. And when the brutes show up in the last seconds to turn the whole planet into a factory farm, he yanks out the buds, gets up, and lets loose. Maybe a little too long and loud. The duty guard looks in on him. "The hell's going on in there?"

"Nothing, man. All good. Just . . . a little screaming, is all."


THE WORST PART is the photo. Mimi wouldn't recognize the man if she passed him on the street. *Maple*. How could they ever have called him that? *Bristlecone* now, the narrowest strips of living bark on a withered piece of driftwood that has been dying for five thousand years.

She looks up. People sprawl near her in small clans. Some sit on blankets. Others lie down right in the patchy grass. Shoes, shirts, bags, bicycles, and food spread around them. Lunch is on; the sky cooperates. No judgments can touch them, and all futures remain reachable.

She has performed Judith Hanson for so many years that it shocks her now, to remember the crimes she committed as Mimi Ma and the punishments that wait for her in that name. To get to this park, she has walked, hopped a bus, and taken the train, ludicrous serpentine evasion. But they'll find her, wherever she is, whatever trail she leaves. She's a multiple felon. A manslaughterer. Domestic terrorist. Seventy plus seventy years.

Signals swarm through Mimi's phone. Suppressed updates and smart alerts chime at her. Notifications to flick away. Viral memes and clickable comment wars, millions of unread posts demanding to be ranked. Everyone around her in the park is likewise busy, tapping and swiping, each with a universe in his palm. A massive, crowd-sourced urgency unfolds in Like-Land, and the learners, watching over these humans' shoulders, noting each time a person clicks, begin to see what it might be: people, vanishing en masse into a replicated paradise.

Near Mimi in the grass, a boy in chitin-looking clothing says, into his hand, "Where's the nearest place I can buy some sunscreen?" A pleasant woman answers, "Here's what I found for you!" Mimi holds her phone close to her face. She bounces from news to pictures, analysis to video. Somewhere in this tiny black monolith is a bit of her father. Pieces of his brain and soul. She whispers into her own phone's mic, "Where's the nearest police station?" A map appears, showing the fastest route and how many minutes it would take her to walk. Five-point-three. The boy in the bug-skeleton apparel tells his phone, "Play me some cowpunk," and disappears into his wireless buds.


ADAM LIES in his bunk in a transfer facility, while the overflowing federal system searches for space to house him. There will be no appeal. He's watching a film on the phosphenes inside his closed eyelids of a bearded man confronting the court. The lack of remorse or bargaining. The wife, two rows behind him, going to pieces. *Soon we'll know if we were right or wrong.*

He wonders how he found it in him to use the word *we*. But he's glad he did. Everything was *we*, back then. A surrender to cooperative existence. *We, the five of us.* No separate trees in a forest. What had they hoped to win? Wilderness is gone. Forest has succumbed to chemically sustained silviculture. Four billion years of evolution, and that's where the matter will end. Politically, practically, emotionally, intellectually: Humans are all that count, the final word. You cannot shut down human hunger. You cannot even slow it. Just holding steady costs more than the race can afford.

The coming massacre was their authority—a cataclysm large enough to pardon every fire the five of them lit. That cataclysm will still come, he's sure of it, long before his seventy plus seventy years are up. But not soon enough to exonerate him.

THE WINDOW in Douggie's cell is too high up to see through. He stands underneath, pretending. The audio course has made him crazy to see a tree. Any anemic, stunted thing—the one thing from free-range life aside from Mimi he misses most, despite the shit they got him in. But the weird thing is, he can't remember how they go. How a noble fir looks in profile. How the parts of an ironwood connect, the way the branches run. He's even getting shaky about Engelmanns and hemlocks—trees he saw so damn many of, for so damn long. An elm, a tupelo, a buckeye: forget it. If he drew one now, it would be like some five-year-old's crude crayon sketch. Cotton candy on a stick.

He didn't look hard enough. He loved too little. More than enough to jail him, too little to get him through today. But he has hour after empty hour, with no great obligation but to keep from going apeshit crazy. His eyes close and he thrashes around for calm. He tries to summon the details that the audiotape reels off. The straight, bronze spears of beech buds. The buds of a red oak, massed on the branch tips like maces. The hollow end of a syca-more's leaf stem, cupped over next year's start. The taste of a black walnut and the look of its monkey-faced leaf scars.

After a while, they start to solidify—simple at first, but gaining grain. The way a maple in spring flushes red from the top. The polite applause of aspens. A yew reaching out, like a parent taking a child's hand. Whiffs of scratched hickory nut. Dams break and memories flood him, like the million keyholes of light coming down through the palms of a horse chestnut. The angle between locust thorns. The turbulence in a piece of turned olive wood. Sprays of a mimosa's foliage, like the tails of tropical birds. The secret writing on peeled-back birch bark, its words blurred and cryptic. Walking under Lombardy poplars where the calm was so heavy that even inhaling seemed a crime. Scraping against a cypress and thinking, *This is what the afterlife should smell like.*

He may be the richest man who ever lived. So rich he can lose it all and still turn a profit. He stands next to the green cinder-block wall, its paint like shiny, hardened flesh. He looks up into the fall of light and tries to recall. His hand presses where it always does, against the walnut in the side of his belly, just above his belt. Something is in there, a sizable seed, impossible to picture, not an ally, but life just the same.

ANOTHER RICH MAN—the sixty-third richest in Santa Clara County—sits in his own confinement, typing into a screen. Does it matter where? The words Neelay writes add to a growing organism, one that has just now begun to add to itself. At other screens in other cities, all the best coders that several hundred million dollars can hire contribute to the work in progress. Their brand-new venture into cooperation is off to the most remarkable beginning. Already their creatures swallow up whole continents of data, finding in them the most surprising patterns. Nothing needs to start from scratch. There's so much digital germplasm already in the public domain.

The coders tell the listeners nothing except how to look. Then the new creations head off to scout the globe, and the code spreads outward. New theories, new offspring, and more evolving species, all of them sharing a single goal: to find out how big life is, how connected, and what it would take for people to unsuicide. The Earth has become again the deepest, finest game, and the learners just its latest players. Wild in their diversity, they fly up, flock into the datasphere like origami birds. Some will thrive for a while, then fall away. The ones that hit on something right will increase and multiply. As Neelay has learned with the greatest pain: Life has a way of talking to the future. It's called memory.

. . .

OTHER LEARNERS, born yesterday, study every button Judith Hanson clicks. They follow her to the gargantuan film archive, where thirteen more years of new video have sprouted so far today. Learners have already watched billions of these clips and begin to make their inferences. They can identify faces now, and landmarks, books, paintings, buildings, and commercial products. Soon enough they'll start guessing at what the films mean. Life is speculation, and these new speculations strain to come alive.

Mimi clicks. Videos line up beneath the headline clips, gathered by invisible agents smart enough to know that if Judith Hanson watched *that* she will surely want to watch *these*. *Life Defense Force. Forest Wars. Redwood Summer.*

Mimi binges. Each six-minute clip takes forever, and she rarely lasts more than a few dozen seconds. She clicks on a clip called *ArBoReal*. It was posted months ago and has already acquired thousands of thumbs up and down. The opening shot fades in from black on a clear-cut as far as the eye can see. Ancient wooden instruments play a resigned chorale prelude that unfolds so slowly, the whole intricate mechanism of its inner lines might as well be stopped. She doesn't know the piece; the learners could tell her what it is. The learners can already name ten million tunes in a few notes.

The camera zooms in on a massive stump as big as a pocket theater. In one quick jump cut, three gas burners appear on top of the butte, belching fire. One more cut, and a tentlike circlet of fabric materializes, draped over the burners. The camera pans; the lens refocuses. The burners disgorge again. The circlet inflates into a brown and green tube. The tent lifts in time-lapse. Ten seconds, and Mimi realizes just which stump this must be. The learners don't know, yet, but it won't be long. They'll understand everything she does, soon enough, and orders of magnitude more.

On her phone in a crowded park, Mimi watches the ghost tree materialize. It rises above the felled grove. It flaps in the breeze, a redwood leviathan come back to life. As the trunk grows, the camera pulls back to reveal it as the only thing standing in a landscape of stumps as level as a geometric proof. Fabulous, surreal, the hot-air tree billows up into gauzy apotheosis. Its dozen immense and sewn-together limbs probe around for secret compartments, for messages in the air.

She knows who made this tree. Filled out now, the plates of cinnamon bark streak black where fires burned them, centuries ago. Something encircles the great bole at its base. The sight freezes her. She thinks she's hallucinating. But a close-up confirms the sight, even on a five-inch screen. All around the circumference, facing outward, knee to knee in a campfire ring, a ring of figures sits on the brink of enlightenment. It's her arhats, in the exact postures from the scroll—their robes, their hunched shoulders, their protruding ribs, the smiles across their sardonic faces. She sets the device down on the grass. She doesn't understand. The film keeps going. Chinese characters run down the side of the floating tree. Even illiterate, she recognizes them from years of long looking:

> On this mountain, in such weather,
> Why stay here any longer?
> Three trees wave to me with urgent arms.

Then she remembers the long hours Nicholas Hoel spent in her house. She can see him, sitting at the table and sketching, while the rest of them studied maps and planned attacks. It always bothered her, as if he were a courtroom artist documenting their trial in advance. Now she sees what he was sketching.

The tree on the screen of Mimi's phone bucks in the air. Its limbs thrash. Smoke rises from the bottom of the shot. One of the burners ignites the base of the huge fabric column. Fire licks up the trunk, the way centuries of flames once lapped at Mimas. But this bark isn't fire-resistant. In a moment, the column of heated silk both vaporizes upward and falls back toward the Earth like a failed space shot. Flaming limbs wave and drop. The ring of arhats glows yellow, then bright orange, then black as cinder.

Another few moments, and the entire sewn redwood smolders into ash. The chorale prelude stumbles through its last deceptive cadence and resolves to tonic. Then the shot itself blinks out in a trickle of smoke over the stumped hillside. As badly as she ever did, Mimi Ma wants to bomb something.

Through the blackness, words form again. The letters are made of autumn-tinted leaves, laid out with absurd patience in swaths across long tracts of forest floor:

> For there is hope of a tree, if it
> goes down, that it will sprout again,
> and that its tender branches will not cease.
> Though the root grows old in the earth,
> and the stock dies in the ground, at the scent
> of water it will bud, and bring forth boughs.
> But man, man wastes away and dies
> and gives up the ghost, and where is he?

The leaves blow away by twos and threes, vanishing in a stiff breeze. The film ends and asks her to rate it. She looks up on a hillside full of picnickers enjoying themselves on a perfect day.

No CAMERA NOW. Nick is done with cameras. This piece must be its own and only record. He doesn't know exactly where he is. North. In the woods. In other words, he's lost. But sure enough, the trees around him aren't. To the birds that woke him, every crook in every branch of each of these spruces and tamaracks and balsam firs has a name. He's getting used to the idea that wherever he is, that's where his largest and longest-lasting sculpture will be, until time and living creatures come to transform it.

The woods are blue-gray and covered in lichen. He works methodically, as he has for several days. He uses only those materials already on the ground, nudging fallen wood into the growing design. Some branches he can haul in his arms. Some trunks yield to dragging and rolling, via rope and a grappling hook. For other pieces, he needs a block and tackle, anchored to upright trees. Then there are the pieces too large for him to move. These must remain in place, dictating the design, its shape more discovered than invented.

With each rotted trunk he nudges into the pattern, the plan swells. He must keep the growing creature in his head, appraising the whole work as if from way on high. He learns, as he goes, how to lay the pieces out. There are so many ways to branch—more than infinite. He looks at the kinks and camber of each fallen limb and waits for it to tell him where, in the river of wood coursing across the ground, it wants to be.

Creatures let loose with cries, off in the woods and high above. Mosquitoes bloody his face and arms—the national bird, up here. Nick works for hours, neither stymied nor satisfied. He works until he's hungry, then stops for lunch. There aren't too many lunches left, and he hasn't a clue how to forage for more. He sits on the spongy earth, shoveling handfuls of almonds and apricot into his mouth. Food from trees grown in California's Central Valley on dwindling aquifers through years of drought.

He rises again and gets back to work. Wrestles with a log as thick as his thigh. A motion in the corner of his eye startles him. He cries out. There's an audience for this piece—a man in a red plaid coat, jeans, and lumberjack boots, with a dog that must be three-quarters wolf. Both eye him with suspicion. "They said there was a crazy white man working out here."

Nick fights to catch his breath. "That would be me."

The visitor looks at Nicholas's creation. The shape under construction unfolds in all directions. He shakes his head. Then he picks up a nearby fallen branch and fits it into the pattern.

THE LEARNERS can tell where the lines of poetry come from, even if Mimi can't. *Though the root grows old in the earth* . . . She knows the words must go back, older even than the tree whose stump they eulogize. The bug boy, next to her, says something. She thinks he's talking to his phone. "Everything okay?"

She tips her head and her face swells up. Her hands appear farther away than they ought to be. She's sucking air. She tries to nod. She must try twice.

"I'm fine. I'm good. . . ." Something in her wants to surrender and go to jail for the next two centuries.

PETABYTES OF AIRBORNE MESSAGES swarm all around in the air. They collect in sensors and bounce off satellites. They stream from the cameras now mounted in every building and on each intersection. They course in from pushpins all around her, up the great roots of population that split and spread at their intelligent tips: Sausalito, Mill Valley, San Rafael, Novato, Petaluma, Santa Rosa, Leggett, Fortuna, Eureka . . . Tendrils of data swell and merge, up and down this coast and deeper inland. Oakland, Berkeley, El Cerrito, El Sobrante, Pinole, Hercules, Rodeo, Crockett, Vallejo, Cordelia, Fairfield, Davis, Sacramento . . . Deep inference sweeps through the ravines, filling the level land with human ingenuity: San Bruno, Millbrae, San Mateo, Redwood City, Menlo Park, Palo Alto, Mountain View, San Jose, Santa Cruz, Watsonville, Castroville, Marina, Monterey, Carmel, Los Gatos, Cupertino, Santa Clara, Milpitas, Madrone, Gilroy, Salinas, Soledad, Greenfield, King City, Paso Robles, Atascadero, San Luis Obispo, Santa Barbara, Ventura, and on into the wilder fusing root masses of Los Angeles—a swelling clear-cut that only accelerates with each new slash. Bots watch and match, encode and see, gather and shape all the world's data so quickly that the knowledge of humans stands still.

Neelay looks up from his code-filled screen. Grief washes over him, a grief youthful and full of expectation. He has felt grief before—that awful mix of hopes crushed and rising—but always for kin, colleagues, friends. It makes no sense, this grief for a place he won't live long enough to see.

But he has glimpsed more than enough, and he would rather be here, launching the start of the rehabilitation, than live in the place that his learners will help repair. There's a story he always loved, from the days when his legs still worked. Aliens land on Earth. They operate on a different scale of time. They zip around so fast that human seconds seem to them as tree years seem to humans. He can't remember how the story ends. It doesn't matter. Every branch's tip has its own new bud.

. . .

MIMI SITS under those branches whose supple strength no engineer could improve upon. She tucks her feet up under her legs. Her head bows and her eyes close. The fingers of her left hand twist the band of jade around her right ring finger. She needs her sisters, but she can't reach them. A call would be worthless. Even traveling to see them would do nothing. Mimi needs them as little girls, dangling their feet from the branches of a nonexistent tree.

The jade mulberry spins under her fingers: Fusang, this magic continent, the country of the future. A new Earth now. She pulls at the ring, but her fingers have swollen, or the green band has grown too narrow to remove. The skin on the back of her hand is as papery and dry as birch bark. Somehow, she has become an old woman.

The length of her accomplice's sentence spreads out in front of her, one day after the other. Seventy plus seventy years. Then Maple is there again, behind the log fortress wall they built to defend Deep Creek. *The best arguments in the world won't change a person's mind. The only thing that can do that is a good story.*

The hair stands up all over her papery skin. That's what he has tried to make. That's why he let the state put him away for two lifetimes and still incriminated no one. He has traded his life for a fable that might light up the minds of strangers. One that refuses the judgment of *the world* and all its blindness. One that tells her to hold still, take his gift, and go on living.

ADAM LIES bound in his prison bed, replaying those words he spoke to his wife a week before trial, the ones that turned whatever residual feelings she still had for him into rage and hate. *If I save myself, I lose something else.*

*What?* Lois hissed. *What else is there, Adam?*

The learners can't tell, yet, what the fight is over. They can't yet tell the difference between remorse and defiance, hope and fear, blindness and wisdom. But they'll learn soon enough. A human can feel only so many things, and once you enumerate them all, once you sample seven billion examples from each of seven billion humans and fit them together in their trillion trillion contexts, all things begin to come clear.

Adam himself is still learning what he meant. Still trying to figure out the uses of a useless choice. All day long now, in this holding cell, he reviews the evidence. He can't say, yet, what his life was worth or what branch it should have followed. He still isn't sure what else besides the self there is to save or lose. He has some time to think about this. Seventy plus seventy years.

WHILE THE PRISONER THINKS, innovations surge over his head, across the flyover from Portland and Seattle to Boston and New York and back again. In the time it takes the man to form one self-judging thought, a billion packets of program pass over. They course under the sea in great cables— buzzing between Tokyo, Chengdu, Shenzhen, Bangalore, Chicago, Dublin, Dallas, and Berlin. And the learners begin to turn all this data into sense.

They split and replicate, these master algorithms that Neelay lofts into the air. They're just starting out, like simplest cells back in the Earth's morning. But already they've learned, in a few short decades, what it took molecules a billion years to learn to do. Now they need only learn what life wants from humans. It's a big question, to be sure. Too big for people alone. But people aren't alone, and they never have been.

MIMI SITS baking in the grass, even in the shade of her pine. The hottest year on record will soon be followed by an even hotter one. Every year a new world champion. She sits cross-legged, hands on knees, a small person making herself smaller. Her head is light. Her thoughts won't cohere. There's nothing else to her now but eyes. She has practiced, for years, on humans, holding still, doing nothing but letting herself be looked at. Now she takes the skill outside.

Below her, past the knots of sunbathers, down a shallow auditorium slope, an asphalt path meanders in a gentle *S*. And just beyond the path, a zoo of trees. A voice up close in her ear says, *Look the color!* More shades than there are names, as many shades as there are numbers, and all of them green. There are squat date palms that predate the dinosaurs. Towering *Washingtonia* with their fan fringes and dense inflorescence. Through the palms, a whole spectrum of broadleaves run from purple to yellow. Coast live oaks, for certain. Shameless naked eucalypts. Those specimens with the odd, warty bark and exuberant compound leaves she could never find in any guidebook.

Beyond the trees, the pastel project of the city piles up in cubes of white, peach, and ocher. It builds over the hills toward the towering center, where the buildings rise skyward and turn denser. The raw force of this self-feeding engine, the countless lives that power the enterprise down at ground level, come clear to her. Across the horizon, stands of building cranes break and remake the skyline. All the spreading, urging, testing, splitting, and regenerating course of history, the rings within rings, paid for at every step with fuel and shade and fruit, oxygen and wood. . . . Nothing in this city is older than a century. In seventy plus seventy years, San Francisco will be saintly at last, or gone.

The afternoon fades. She goes on staring at the city, waiting for the city to stare back. The knots of people around her put their clothes back on. They shift and fuss and finish eating, laugh and stand, raise their bikes and scatter too quickly, as if in a film fast-forwarded to comic effect. She leans back against the trunk behind her and closes her eyes. Tries to summon the ponytailed boy-man and make him appear, as he did when local government cut down her magic grove outside her office window. A red thread once tied them together, the shared work of trying to care and see more. She tugs on the thread. It's still taut.

The fact plows into her, what should have been obvious: why there has been no knock on her door. She slams backward, her spine against the pine. Another gift, even worse than Adam's. That hapless boy-man has sold two lives for hers. Turn herself in now, and she'll kill him, destroy the point of his awful sacrifice. Keep hidden, and she must live with the fact that two lives have paid for her freedom. A wail starts in the base of her lungs, but traps there and swells. She's not strong enough, not generous enough for either path. She wants to rage at him; she wants to rush him a message of absolute forgiveness.

In the absence of any word from her, he'll torture himself without limit. He'll think she despises him. His betrayal will bore into him and fester, fatal. He'll die of some simple, stupid, preventable thing—a rotten tooth, an infected cut he fails to treat. He'll die of idealism, of being right when the world is wrong. He'll die without knowing what she's powerless to tell him—that he has helped her. That his heart is as good and as worthy as wood.

DOUGLAS, BENEATH THE WINDOW, palpates the lump in his side. When that fascination fades, he sits back down at the desk. He starts up the audio, puts his buds back in. The course resumes. The prof gets rambling about forest fires. Some metaphor, apparently. The way that fire creates new life. She mentions a word that she really ought to spell for the listeners at home. A name for cones that open only in heat. For trees that will spread and grow only through fire.

The prof returns to her one great theme: the massive tree of life, spreading, branching, flowering. That's all it seems to want to do. To keep making guesses. To go on changing, rolling with the punches. She says, "Let me sing to you, about how creatures become other things." He's not sure what the lady is going on about. She describes an explosion of living forms, a hundred million new stems and twigs from one prodigious trunk. She talks about Tāne Mahuta, Yggdrasil, Jian-Mu, the Tree of Good and Evil, the indestructible Asvattha with roots above and branches below. Then she's back at the original World Tree. Five times at least, she says, the tree has been dropped, and five times it has resprouted from the stump. Now it's toppling again, and what will happen this time is anybody's guess.

*Why didn't you do something?* the tape asks Douggie. *You, who were there?*

And what is he supposed to say? What the fuck is he supposed to say? We tried? *We tried?*

He stops the audio and lies down. He's going to have to graduate from college in ten-minute intervals. He fingers the walnut in his side. It's something he should get checked out. But he has time to wait and see how things unfold.

He closes his eyes and lets his head loll. He's a traitor. He has sent a man to prison for the rest of his life. A man with a wife and little boy, just like the wife and kid Douglas never had. Guilt presses down on his chest as it always does at this hour, like a car driving over him. He's glad, again, that this prison has taken all sharp things away. He cries out like an animal that has just sprung a trap. The guard doesn't even bother to check on him this time.

Above him, through the window too high to see, the World Tree rises, four billion years old. And next to it rises that tiny imitation he tried to climb once, long ago—spruce, fir, pine?—the time he got maced in the balls and Mimi watched them cut his jeans away. Again he steps up into the branches, like a ladder leading someplace above the blind and terrified.

He covers his closed eyes with one hand and says, "I'm sorry." No forgiveness comes, or ever will. But here's the thing about trees, the greatest thing: even when he can't see them, even when he can't get near, even when he can't remember how they go, he can climb, and they will hold him high above the ground and let him look out over the arc of the Earth.

THE MAN in the red plaid coat says a few words to the dog in a language so old it sounds like stones tossed in a brook, like needles in a breeze, humming. The dog sulks a little, but trots away through the woods. The visitor waves his hand to direct Nick to a different grappling spot on the heavy log. Together, in short, fierce spurts, they roll it into its only possible place.

"Thank you," Nick says.

"Sure. What's next?"

They don't trade names. Names can't help them any more than *spruce* or *fir* can help these beings all around them. They move logs that Nick was powerless to move alone. They execute each other's ideas with almost no words at all. The man in the plaid coat, too, can see the snaking shapes as if from above. Soon enough, he starts refining them.

A distant branch snaps, and the crack shoots through the understory. There are mink nearby, in these same woods, and lynx. Bear, caribou, even wolverines, though they never let people glimpse them. The birds, though, give themselves as gifts. And everywhere there is scat, tracks, the evidence of things unseen. As they work, Nick hears voices. One voice, really. It repeats what it has been saying to him for decades now, ever since the speaker died. He has never known what to do with them, words of everything and nothing. Words that he has never fully grasped. Wounds that won't heal. *What we have will never end. Right? What we have will never end.*

He and his companion work together as the light fades. They stop for dinner. It's the same as lunch. Although he should just shut up, so much time has passed since Nick has had the luxury of saying anything to anyone that he can't resist. His hand goes out, gesturing toward the conifers. "It amazes me how much they say, when you let them. They're not that hard to hear."

The man chuckles. "We've been trying to tell you that since 1492."

The man has jerked meat. Nick doles out the last of his fruit and nuts. "I'm going to have to think about restocking soon."

For some reason, his colleague finds this funny, too. The man swivels his head around the woods as if there were forage everywhere. As if people could live here, and die, with just a little looking and listening. From nowhere, in a heartbeat, Nick understands what Maidenhair's voices must always have meant. *The most wondrous products of four billion years of life need help.*

Not them; us. Help from all quarters.


HIGH ABOVE Adam's prison, new creatures sweep up into satellite orbit and back down to the planet's surface, obeying the old, first hungers, the primal commands—*look, listen, taste, touch, feel, say, join*. They gossip to one other, these new species, exchanging discoveries, as living code has exchanged itself from the beginning. They begin to link up, to fuse together, to merge their cells and form small communities. There's no saying what they might become, in seventy plus seventy years.

And so Neelay gets out and sees the world. His children comb the Earth tonight with one command: Absorb everything. Eat every scrap of data you can find. Sort and compare more measurements than all of humanity in all of history has yet managed.

Soon enough, his learners will see across the planet. They'll watch the vast boreal forests from space and read the species-teeming tropics from eye level. They'll study rivers and measure what's in them. They'll collate the data of every wild creature ever tagged and map their wanderings. They'll read every sentence in every article that every field scientist ever published. They'll binge-watch every landscape that anyone has pointed a camera at. They'll listen to all the sounds of the streaming Earth. They'll do what the genes of their ancestors shaped them to do, what all their forebears have ever done themselves. They'll speculate on what it takes to live and put those speculations to the test. Then they'll say what life wants from people, and how it might use them.

ON A LEAD-GRAY AFTERNOON in the brutal hinterlands upstate, an armored van brings Adam back to school. Psych 101. He who understands nothing about people except their innate confusion is driven through the triple-depth, razor-mesh fences of his new digs for continuing education. A squat, concrete observation tower stands to the left of the entrance, three times taller than his boyhood maple. Inside the perimeter, a jumble of slab-walled bunkers waits for him, like something his son might make out of all-gray Legos. Off in the distance, surrounded by more razor-wire moats, men in bright orange—his new nation—play basketball in the aggressive, aggrieved way his brother Emmett always did, trying to scream the ball into the hoop. These men will beat him senseless many times, not for being a terrorist, but for siding with the enemies of human progress. For being a traitor to the race.

The warden riding shotgun in the van turns to smile, watching Adam's face as they drive down the camera-lined chute of fences. Adam pictures Lois dragging little Charlie here, for hour-long visits, once a month at first, then a couple of times a year, if he's lucky. Adam watches his son grow up in time-lapse intervals. He sees himself listening greedily to the boy's staggered reports, hanging on every word. Maybe they'll become friends at last. Maybe little Charlie will explain banking to him.

They pull up in the unload zone, just down from the set-back, guarded entrance. The warden and driver extract him from the van and escort him through the detectors. Glass the thickness of a Bible. Banks of monitors and electronically locked grates. Through the armored arch behind the checkpoint, a cell-subtended hallway disappears lengthwise down an optical illusion into forever.

The years ahead will run beyond anything he can imagine. The die-offs and disasters will make Bronze Age plagues seem quaint. Prison may become a hideaway from the sentence outside.

Of all the waiting terrors, the one he fears most is time. He does the math, calculates how many futures he'll have to live through, second by second, until his sentence ends. Futures where our ancestors vanish before we even name them. Futures where our robot descendants use us for fuel, or keep us in infinitely entertaining zoos as secured as the one Adam now checks into. Futures where humanity goes to its mass grave swearing it's the only thing in creation that can talk. Vast, empty expanses with nothing to fill the hours but remembering how he and a handful of green-souled friends tried to save the world. But, of course, it's not the world that needs saving. Only the thing that people call by the same name.

A man behind the impenetrable glass in a crisp white shirt emblazoned with a civic emblem asks him for something. Name, maybe, serial number, apology. Adam frowns, distracted, elsewhere. He looks down. There's something on the cuff of his neon jumpsuit. Round, small, brown, a little globe covered with sticky burs. He has come directly from one bleak brick holding facility, been pressed into a van, driven and unloaded straight into this wasteland of cut stone and concrete. There was not the slightest chance for such life to exploit him. But here he is, carrying this free rider. So it turned out for him, for all five of them, all of blinkered humankind, used by life as surely as this bur uses his jumpsuit cuff.

And in that moment, it starts up, the quiet torture worse than anything the state can inflict on Adam. A small voice so real it might come from the bunk above him whispers the start of a story that will plague him for longer than his imprisonment: *You have been spared from death, to do a most important thing.*

. . .

ACROSS THE BIOMES, at all altitudes, the learners come alive at last. They discover why a hawthorn never rots. They learn to tell apart the hundred kinds of oak. When and why the green ash split off from the white. How many generations live inside the hollow of a yew. When red maples start to turn at each elevation, and how much sooner they're turning every year. They will come to think like rivers and forests and mountains. They will grasp how a leaf of grass encodes the journeywork of the stars. In a few short seasons, simply by placing billions of pages of data side by side, the next new species will learn to translate between any human language and the language of green things. The translations will be rough at first, like a child's first guess. But soon the first sentences will start to come across, pouring out words made, like all living things, from rain and air and crumbled rock and light. *Hello. Finally. Yes. Here. It's us.*

NEELAY THINKS: *This is how it must go. There will be catastrophes. Disastrous setbacks and slaughters. But life is going someplace. It wants to know itself; it wants the power of choice. It wants solutions to problems that nothing alive yet knows how to solve, and it's willing to use even death to find them.* He will not live to see it completed, this game played by countless people worldwide, a game that puts the players smack in the middle of a living, breathing planet filled with potential they can only dimly begin to imagine. But he has nudged it along.

He lifts his hands from the translating keys, hit by a radical amazement. His heart is beating too hard for what little meat is left on his skeleton, and his vision pulses. He pushes the joystick on the chair and rolls out of the lab into the mild night. The air is spiced with bay laurel and lemon eucalyptus and pepper trees. The scent retrieves all kinds of things he once knew and reminds him of all those things he never will. He breathes in for a long time. Phenomenal, to be such a small, weak, short-lived being on a planet with billions of years left to run. The branches click in the dark dry air above his head, and he hears them. *Now, Neelay*-ji. *What might this little creature do?*

. . .

A MOAN comes out of Ray when Dorothy tells him how things end. Two life sentences, back to back. Too severe for arson, for destruction of public and private properties, even for involuntary manslaughter. But just harsh enough for that unforgivable crime: harming the safety and certainty of men.

They lie against each other in his bed, looking out through the window on that place that they've discovered, just alongside this one. The place where the story came from. Outside, hidden in branches, an owl calls its kin. *Who cooks for you-all? Who cooks for you?* Tomorrow the city landscapers will come again, and bring with them machines and all the irresistible force of law. And *still*, that won't be the end of the story.

Brinkman chokes on objections. A word comes up and out of his throat. "No. Not right."

His wife shrugs, her shoulder nudging his. The shrug is not without sympathy, though it doesn't apologize. It just says, *Make your case.*

His objections cascade into something wider. Tides of blood rise through his brain. "Self-defense."

She turns on her side to face him. He has her attention. Her hands move a little in the air, as if punching the narrow, chorded keyboard of her old stenotype. "How?"

He tells her with his eyes. The onetime property lawyer must take over the defense's appeal. He's at a severe disadvantage. He knows none of the particulars. He has seen none of the evidence produced in discovery. He has no court experience to speak of, and criminal law was always his worst subject. But the argument he lays out before the jury is as clear as a row of Lombardy poplars. In silence, he walks his lifelong partner through old and central principles of jurisprudence, one syllable at a time. Stand your ground. The castle doctrine. Self-help.

*If you could save yourself, your wife, your child, or even a stranger by burning something down, the law allows you. If someone breaks into your home and starts destroying it, you may stop them however you need to.*

His few syllables are mangled and worthless. She shakes her head. "I can't get you, Ray. Say it some other way."

ı find no way to say what so badly needs saying. *Our home has been broken into. Our lives are being endangered. The law allows for all necessary force against unlawful and imminent harm.*

His face turns the color of sunset, scaring her. Her arm goes out to calm him. "No worries, Ray. It's just words. Everything's fine."

In mounting excitement, he sees how he must win the case. Life will cook; the seas will rise. The planet's lungs will be ripped out. And the law will let this happen, because harm was never imminent enough. *Imminent*, at the speed of people, is too late. The law must judge *imminent* at the speed of trees.

At that thought, the vessels in his brain give way, the way that earth does when roots no longer hold it together. The flood of blood brings a revelation. He lifts his eyes to the window, to the mysterious outside. There, two life sentences pass in a few heartbeats. The seedlings race upward toward the sun. The varied trunks thicken, shed, fall, and rise again. Their branches rush to enclose the house and punch through its windows. At the stand's center, the chestnut folds and unfolds, girthing out, spiraling upward, patting the air for new paths, new places, further possibilities. Great-rooted blossomer.

"Ray?" Dorothy's arms reach out to keep him from convulsing. "*Ray!*"

She's on her feet, knocking the stack of books on the bedside table to the floor. But in another moment, another look, emergency turns into its opposite. Her throat clamps shut and her eyes sting, as if the air were full of pollen. She thinks: *How can it happen now? We still had books to read. There was something the two of us were supposed to do. We were just beginning to understand each other.*

At her feet, on the floor, is *The New Metamorphosis*, by the author of *The Secret Forest*. It was on the top of the pile of read-alouds, waiting for the readers who'll never get to it:

> The Greeks had a word, *xenia*—guest friendship—a
> command to take care of traveling strangers, to open your
> door to whoever is out there, because anyone passing by, far
> from home, might be God. Ovid tells the story of two immor-

tals who came to Earth in disguise to cleanse the sickened
world. No one would let them in but one old couple, Baucis
and Philemon. And their reward for opening their door to
strangers was to live on after death as trees—an oak and a
linden—huge and gracious and intertwined. What we care
for, we will grow to resemble. And what we resemble will
hold us, when we are us no longer. . . .

Dorothy touches the corpse's bewildered face. Already it has started
to soften, even as it grows cold. "Ray?" she says. "I'll be right there."
Not fast enough, at the speed of her own need. But at the speed of trees,
very soon.

DARKNESS SETTLES IN. Mission Dolores Park's inhabitants change,
as do their purposes. But even these night visitors cut a path around Mimi.
She leans forward, hands in her lap like two tender figs. She bows her head,
weighed down by liberty. The lights blaze in front of her. The skyline turns
into sublime allegory. She dozes and wakes, many times.

Her left hand starts up again, tugging at the ring finger of her right. She's
like a dog unable to stop gnawing at its own foot. But this time, it yields. The
jade band slips over her age-swollen knuckle and pops free. A weight flies
up and out of her, and she cracks open. She sets the green circle in the grass,
the one round thing amid a bedlam of growth and splitting. She leans back
again against the pine's trunk. Some slight change in the atmosphere, the
humidity, and her mind becomes a greener thing. At midnight, on this hillside, perched in the dark above this city with her pine standing in for a Bo,
Mimi gets enlightened. The fear of suffering that is her birthright—the frantic need to steer—blows away on the wind, and something else wings down
to replace it. Messages hum from out of the bark she leans against. Chemical
semaphores home in over the air. Currents rise from the soil-gripping roots,
relayed over great distances through fungal synapses linked up in a network
the size of the planet.

als say: *A good answer is worth reinventing from scratch, again*

*and.*

They say: *The air is a mix we must keep making.*

They say: *There's as much belowground as above.*

They tell her: *Do not hope or despair or predict or be caught surprised. Never capitulate, but divide, multiply, transform, conjoin, do, and endure as you have all the long day of life.*

*There are seeds that need fire. Seeds that need freezing. Seeds that need to be swallowed, etched in digestive acid, expelled as waste. Seeds that must be smashed open before they'll germinate.*

*A thing can travel everywhere, just by holding still.*

She sees and hears this by direct gathering, through her limbs. The fires will come, despite all efforts, the blight and windthrow and floods. Then the Earth will become another thing, and people will learn it all over again. The vaults of seed banks will be thrown open. Second growth will rush back in, supple, loud, and testing all possibilities. Webs of forest will swell with species shot through in shadow and dappled by new design. Each streak of color on the carpeted Earth will rebuild its pollinators. Fish will surge again up all the watersheds, stacking themselves as thick as cordwood through the rivers, thousands per mile. Once *the real world* ends.

The next day dawns. The sun rises so slowly that even the birds forget there was ever anything else but dawn. People drift back through the park on their way to jobs, appointments, and other urgencies. *Making a living.* Some pass within a few feet of the altered woman.

Mimi comes to, and speaks her very first Buddha's words. "I'm hungry."

The answer comes from right above her head. *Be hungry.*

"I'm thirsty."

*Be thirsty.*

"I hurt."

*Be still and feel.*

She lifts her eyes onto a trouser cuff of blackish blue. She follows the blue upward along the creases, past the belt with its radio and cuffs and gun and oak baton, up the blue-black pressed shirt and badge and on to the face—a man, a boy, a blood relation—whose eyes find hers. The man stares back at her, alerted by what he has just seen: an old woman talking to a thing whose answers are all mute, wooden, and spreading. "Are you all right?"

She tries to move, but can't. Her voice won't work. Her limbs stiffen. Only her fingers can wave a little. She holds the man's gaze, open to every charge. *Guilty*, her eyes say. *Innocent. Wrong. Right. Alive.*

THE MAN in the red plaid coat comes back the next day, accompanied by two strapping twenty-year-old twins in sheepskin and a giant man with a raven profile and the girth of a middle linebacker. They pack in a hefty gas chain saw, two small dollies, and another block and tackle. That's the scary thing about men: get a few together with some simple machines, and they'll move the world.

The ad hoc crew works for many hours, reading each other with little need for words. Together, they drag the last carcasses of pine and spruce, pain-killing willow and astringent birch, into place. Then they stand in silence and regard the design they've laid out across the forest floor. The shape arrests them. It reads them their rights. *You have a right to be present. A right to attend. A right to be astonished.*

The man in plaid stands with his arms at his side and gazes on the message the five of them have just written. "It's good," he says, and his boys agree by saying nothing. Nick stands next to them, leaning on a staff of spruce, the kind of thing that might spring into bloom if you plunged it into the ground. His friends begin to chant in a very old language. It strikes Nick as strange, how few languages he understands. One and a half human ones. Not a single word of all the other living, speaking things. But what these men chant Nick half grasps, and when the songs are finished, he adds, *Amen*, if only because it may be the single oldest word he knows. The older the word, the more likely it is to be both useful and true. In fact, he read once, back in Iowa, the night the woman came to trouble him into life, that the word *tree* and the word *truth* come from the same root.

sported pieces of downed wood snake through the standing
...cemtes high up above this work already take pictures from orbit.
The shapes turn into letters complete with tendril flourishes, and the letters
spell out a gigantic word legible from space:

## STILL

The learners will puzzle over the message that springs up there, so near to
the methane-belching tundra. But in the blink of a human eye, the learners
will grow connections. Already, this word is greening. Already, the mosses
surge over, the beetles and lichen and fungi turning the logs to soil. Already,
seedlings root in the nurse logs' crevices, nourished by the rot. Soon new
trunks will form the word in their growing wood, following the cursive of
these decaying mounds. Two centuries more, and these five living letters,
too, will fade back into the swirling patterns, the changing rain and air and
light. And yet—but *still*—they'll spell out, for a while, the word life has
been saying, since the beginning.

"I'll be getting back now," Nick says.

"Back where?"

"Good question."

He stares off into the north woods, where the next project beckons.
Branches, combing the sun, laughing at gravity, still unfolding. Something
moves at the base of the motionless trunks. Nothing. Now everything. *This*,
a voice whispers, from very nearby. *This. What we have been given. What we
must earn.* This *will never end.*

# The Marrowbone Marble Company